THE CHAOS CREW

THE COMPLETE SERIES

EVA CHANCE
& HARLOW KING

The Chaos Crew: The Complete Series

First Digital Edition, 2023

Cover design: The Pretty Little Design Co.

Ebook ISBN: 978-1-998752-51-5

Hardcover ISBN: 978-1-998752-52-2

KILLER BEAUTY

THE CHAOS CREW #1

EVA CHASE

ONE

Decima

THE WALLS of my rooms were so thick that the screams of the dying couldn't reach me.

At least, I assume there were screams—and shouts and cries and the rest of the noises people make when they're facing their end, especially if it's violent. In my experience, hardly anyone goes silently.

But like I said, I couldn't hear them.

I was finishing up a pretty typical evening in my part of the house with no idea what havoc was being wreaked beyond my door. I'd worked out in the gym for a couple of hours before dinner, running through the new exercises Noelle had given me. After a gazillion years of workouts and assignments under my primary trainer's watch, it took a lot to bring the burn into my muscles. I threw everything I had into the jabs, kicks, and flips until I'd broken a real sweat.

Slacking off wasn't an option. I had to keep pushing myself, keep stretching the time before fatigue started to set in. I never knew how long I might need to keep fighting or running to see a mission through, and a second's weakness could mean failure. A.k.a., curtains for me.

It was a dangerous world out there, and the only way to ensure survival was to be the most dangerous thing in it. I'd been doing a pretty good job of that so far.

Anna brought dinner at the usual hour looking totally normal, so the massacre mustn't have started until after that point. She'd set a novel on the tray beside my plate.

"I just finished that one," she said, tapping it with a smile. Anna gave out smiles easily—not like Noelle, who I only got a rare grin out of when I'd kicked ass particularly well. "I thought you might like it, Decima."

"Thanks," I said, practicing my smile in return.

I wasn't thrilled about the book, because I wasn't much of a reader. I got impatient with words strung together with so many details that hardly seemed important, characters meandering around with no idea what they wanted, so I'd start skimming and then lose track of the story. But Anna always tried her best to be kind to me, and she meant that kindness a hell of a lot more often than most people I'd encountered. I was grateful for that.

When I was little, once I'd figured out what a family was from books and movies, I'd wondered if Anna was my mother. She used to spend more time with me between my training sessions back then. She'd laughed when I'd asked her, looking a little sad at the same time, and said no, that my mother and father had been taken from me by the bad people out there right after I was born. But the household would stop those people from getting me too. The household would look after me. They'd make sure I was strong enough to handle the world outside our home when it was time.

And they'd definitely come through on that promise.

Hungry after the long workout, I wolfed down the lasagna and salad, and then I just couldn't settle down. My pulse kept thumping a little too fast as if the exertion of the workout hadn't worn off. Maybe some part of me sensed a shift in the air, a vibe of brutal chaos that seeped through the walls even if sound couldn't.

None of the movies or shows available on the TV—the nature documentaries, thrillers, and ridiculous comedies that Noelle had decided didn't have any lies distracting enough that they might interfere with my missions—caught my interest. I couldn't make it through two pages of Anna's book. I brought up a game on the new console she'd brought last year, which Noelle approved of for honing my reflexes and observational skills. Not even assassinating my way through an office building took the edge off the restless itch crawling under my skin.

Finally, I went into my bedroom, sprawled out on the bed, and dipped my hand between my thighs.

Getting off like this usually brought a rush of energy and then a mellow lull that helped me relax after an intense mission or get to sleep. I kept my eyes shut and my mind blank, focusing completely on the physical sensations I summoned with the pressure of my fingers. If I let my thoughts stray, the chilling memories that would rise up might kill any chance of release. All that mattered was the slowly building pleasure and the thumping of my heart alongside it—

The whir of a lock disengaging jolted me off the bed. Every tingle of bodily enjoyment vanished in an instant.

With all my senses on the alert, I darted into the main room, instinctively sticking close to the furniture. Unexpected visits after dinner time were unusual. It could be Noelle coming with an urgent mission or with some kind of test, in which case I'd better show I'd prepared myself quickly.

But it was the other door that was swinging open, away from me into the room beyond. The door that led to the rest of the household.

No one *ever* came through there after dinner.

As I froze, bracing for the unknown, Anna staggered into view. Even clutching the door's outer handle, she was crumpling toward the ground. She'd always been so separate from the harsher parts of my training that it took my brain a second to process that the red all over her dress was *blood.*

The blood pulsed from beneath her other hand where it was pressed to the side of her neck. It seeped from a bullet wound that'd seared through her dress and stomach, and another at her hip. Holy hell.

I dashed to her, my mind automatically taking stock of the arteries and veins that were most likely severed, the amount of fluid she'd already lost, the odds of survival.

She was bleeding out. She'd *already* lost more blood than most people could have endured.

For both my safety and the rest of the household's, I wasn't supposed to leave the boundaries of my rooms without approval. I'd *never* crossed this specific threshold, only leaving by the outer door into the yard. When I reached the doorway, tension locked around my muscles. I stopped with my feet on the threshold and caught Anna just before her head hit the hardwood floor.

"Anna!" I said, her name coming out like a protest. My throat had constricted. I felt like I was choking.

I'd seen a lot of people dying before, but mostly people I'd killed with the full intention of doing so, and the others I hadn't known anyway. This—this wasn't right—how could this be happening?

Anna's grip on my forearm was weak. She couldn't lift her chin enough for her eyes to meet mine. She seemed to be staring at my running shoes braced on that uncrossable line between my rooms and the rest of the house. Her blood dripped in a rhythmic patter against the floorboards.

"Garlic milkshake," she croaked, or at least something that sounded like that, since the words I thought I'd heard made no sense. She coughed and sputtered. Her normally cheerful voice came out thin and warbled. "Leave. Find… somewhere safe. I—I think they're gone… Played dead until—couldn't leave you locked away in here with no one—"

"Don't talk," I ordered. I meant to sound firm, but the words came out more frantic. "We have to—if I can stop the bleeding—"

But it was too late. I'd known that before I'd reached her, even if every cell in my body resisted the fact. As I moved to turn her so I could treat the wounds, her muscles went slack. Her body sagged, the last fragments of life slipping out of her.

I knew death well enough that I couldn't deny it when it was happening right in front of me. No amount of CPR was going to restart a heart that'd already lost twice as much blood as any living human being should. My hands itched to start the chest compressions anyway.

But what good would that do? It would only waste time, when—

The enemy had come here. To my own fucking home. What else had they done?

What was I going to do about it?

With my pulse thudding in my ears, I let Anna's limp body come to rest on the floor. My insides had tied into a string of knots from the base of my throat to my gut. I forced myself to stand, to take stock.

I had the door open in front of me, leading to a small room and a short hallway beyond it. It was the path to the rest of the house, a total unknown I'd never ventured into. Blood streaked the floorboards from around the corner, some of it in the shape of handprints. Anna had dragged herself here with her last bit of strength.

She'd let me out, given me permission to go, so I could—so I could do *something*.

The years of training kicked in with a wash of adrenaline, rolling back the haze of shock that had settled over me. My spine pulled straighter, my gaze flicking over my surroundings with an increasingly analytical sharpness. All my thoughts narrowed down to getting through the next however many minutes alive—and taking down the thugs who might still be lurking around, looking to add to their list of murders.

Unfortunately, Noelle always brought my mission kit to me before she sent me off on an assignment. I didn't have any firearms of my own in my rooms—no official weapons of any kind.

I walked to the trim wooden table where I'd eaten my dinner and snatched up the dinner knife. Blunt, but better than nothing. With a brisk motion, I smacked my water glass against the edge of the table just hard enough to crack it and pried out a long, deadly shard. My fingers clenched around it.

All right. Time to see what the hell was out there. Time to make whoever had invaded the safety of this house and riddled Anna with bullets very, very sorry.

I paused on the threshold, looking down at her lifeless body. The knots inside me tugged tighter. I had the urge to offer a gesture that would honor her in some way… but I had no idea how, and I didn't have much time to figure it out.

She'd thought the killers had left, but she could be wrong.

I stepped around her body with a silent, awkward apology and slunk through the room beyond. It was set up like a home office with a small desk and bookcases along the walls. One of those bookcases had swung out to reveal the door to my rooms. I hadn't realized they kept it quite that hidden.

With my ears perked, I stalked into the short hall, setting my feet down gingerly. No sounds reached me except a soft, distant rustling.

I peeked around the first bend and found a broader hall. Brass light fixtures gleamed, casting their bright glow over side tables and a geometric-patterned rug that ran the length of the hall. The furnishings had the same modern styling as in my rooms, but with a much more opulent feel to them that reminded me of the swanky hotels I'd run some of my missions out of.

The contrast was jarring enough that it took me a moment to notice the pair of feet protruding from a doorway at the other end of the hall.

I eyed the feet for a minute, but they didn't move. Keeping my back to the wall, I sidled toward the first doorway, much closer to me.

It opened to a dining room nearly as big as my entire main living space, with a gleaming ebony table that could have seated twenty people. It only held two at the moment: a man and a woman face-down on the wooden surface, blood pooling beneath their lolled heads. And not just beneath their heads—one of the bullets had caught the man at just the right angle to spray more blood all over the wall behind him.

I walked closer. I didn't recognize either of these people, as much of them as I could see. But then, I hadn't had much contact with the household other than Anna and Noelle and the occasional temporary trainers who'd taught me skills that weren't in Noelle's wheelhouse. I *might* have met one or both of these two a decade or longer ago and simply not recognized their faces with the gore in the mix.

I patted them down out of necessity, but neither turned up any weapons or phones or anything else I could use. Offering them a silent benediction, I crossed the hall to the next room.

This one was a huge living room filled with white leather sofas and chairs, a large ebony liquor cabinet, matching side tables… and a whole lot of corpses.

"Fuck," I muttered under my breath, taking in the spectacle. Eight bodies lay scattered across the furnishings, their blood staining the pale leather and walls in every direction like some kind of sick abstract art. A meaty, metallic smell soured the cool air. Nothing moved except the swaying of a curtain where a draft was coming through a shattered window. That was the rustling I'd heard.

I'd killed a lot of people in my life, but I'd never made this much of a mess doing it.

I picked my way between the bodies, bile rising to the back of my mouth, and realized the mess was purposeful. The style of certain wounds was distinctive—this man and that woman had clearly been shot to clip an artery for maximum spray while they were still moving around, before the killing strike. From the pattern of splatters around the guy over there, someone had neatly sliced his wrists and let him flail around before putting a bullet in his skull.

Whoever had done this had *wanted* it to look messy. Why?

I stopped by a woman sprawled in front of one of the sofas whose dark brown hair was streaked with gray. She'd taken not one but three shots to the face, which both struck me as excessive—a total waste of bullets—and had mangled her features into a fleshy pulp.

I swallowed hard. Was that Noelle? Had they managed to take even *her* by surprise? There wasn't enough left for me to tell for sure.

She wasn't the only body the killers had battered beyond recognition—and I was sure now that it was killers, plural. I could identify at least two different types of shot wounds reflecting different sizes of bullets from different guns. It'd have been nearly impossible for one to take down so many in the same space quickly enough anyway, especially with a knife in the mix.

A grim weight was forming inside me, pressing down on my stomach. Whoever had carried out this massacre was both very good at what they did and had reveled in the savagery. I didn't think I'd ever gone up against an opponent quite like that.

For all these years, the people of the household had looked after me and trained me so that I could hold the cruelty of this world at bay. But it hadn't been enough to protect them in the end. I hadn't even known this was happening.

I couldn't save them now, but I could ensure their killers were properly repaid. One last mission to set one small thing amid the awfulness out there right. To create some kind of justice for Anna and Noelle and everyone else who'd provided for me.

And then…

When I tried to think about it, my mind stalled, so I just didn't think that far.

The killers had left no trace of their identity that I could spot other than the unusual approach to their kills. Three more bodies lay in the space where I'd spotted the protruding feet, which was a music room with a sleek white piano and framed concert posters on the walls. Blood was splashed and smeared across all of it. Two of the bodies had been cut in an odd zigzag from their throat to the left side of their collarbone.

None of the bodies provided me with a gun or even so much as a pocket knife. Had the entire household really been unarmed, or had their killers removed their weapons afterward?

The latter seemed more likely. It was what I'd have done with a job anywhere near this big, to ensure anyone I hadn't taken down yet couldn't add to their options for striking back at me.

After making a circuit of the lower floor, I headed upstairs. The many bedrooms up there reminded me of the lavish penthouses where I'd carried out a few of my killings. There was one woman lying dead in her bed, her face smashed in with the impact of the bullets and the ivory duvet drenched red, but otherwise they were empty.

A quick search of the dressers and vanities turned up no weapons but a couple of wads of cash and several expensive-looking necklaces and bracelets, glittering with gold and gemstones. I stuffed what I could into the pockets of my track pants and dropped the rest into a tote bag I found hanging over the back of a chair. Missions took a lot of funding even when I knew who my target was. I wouldn't have the household's credit cards smoothing the way for me this time.

I wouldn't have the household at all. When I left here, it'd be for good.

The thought hit me hard enough to stop me in my tracks in the middle of the hall. A momentary chill flooded me.

I'd left the house plenty of times before, of course, but never for more than a week for a particularly complicated mission. Rarely for more than a couple of days. The rooms behind the bookcase had been mine for as long as I could remember. I'd barely talked to anyone other than Anna and Noelle except to get what I needed from bystanders in the middle of an assignment.

And in the blink of an eye, it'd all been destroyed.

My fingers curled around the makeshift blades I was holding until the pinch of the glass warned me to loosen my grip. None of this should have happened. I'd worked so hard—

I gritted my teeth. I'd keep working until the vicious assholes who'd done this were just as lifeless as the bodies they'd left behind.

When I was finished checking every inch of the house, I headed back to my rooms. I stuffed a box of energy bars and a couple of changes of clothes into the tote bag before pausing over the plush tiger toy perched on the headboard of my bed.

The stuffed animal's fur was worn from the many nights I'd gone to sleep hugging it when I'd been very young, and one of its glossy eyes was coming loose. But looking at it brought a sharp sense of possessiveness into my chest.

Damn it, it was *mine*. Somehow it felt like the only thing in this place that truly was, which didn't make any sense since it must have come from the household like everything else. Holding it had always given me a weird sense of comfort even though I couldn't remember who'd given it to me or when, I'd had it so long.

Without letting myself second-guess the impulse, I grabbed the toy and stuffed it into the bag with the rest of my belongings.

On my way out, I stopped by Anna's body with another twinge of regret. My practical instincts told me that I shouldn't let it be obvious she'd opened this hidden door.

My presence here was meant to be a secret. That might still matter to someone—it might matter to me. I'd have an easier time dealing with the pricks who'd done this if they didn't know I existed.

I eased Anna's body a couple of feet farther into the office room so I could push the bookcase and close the door. The bookcase swung back into place against the wall, concealing all trace of the entrance. I didn't know how to open it again—I couldn't have returned to my rooms even if I'd wanted to.

There was no way to go but onward.

I snuck out the back door I'd noted in my survey of the first floor and headed to the garage. Inside, a thick, oily scent laced the air that set off my inner alarm bells. I opened the hoods of each car in the row and found the engines' cables snapped, the compartments cracked by swift blows.

Of course. The killers had probably come through here before they'd entered the house so no one who managed to flee would have a vehicle to escape in. I couldn't repress a flicker of respect for their thoroughness, even if it made my jaw clench at the same time.

I'd just have to find transportation outside the property.

As I slunk across the expansive treed yard, the night's darkness cloaked my movements. Thick clouds blotted out the stars. A damp breeze licked over my face and my bare arms. It tasted like incoming rain.

The stone wall that surrounded the property stood a foot higher than me, but with a running leap, I clambered onto and over it. I dropped to the sidewalk outside with only the faintest rasp of my shoes on the pavement.

The whole rest of the city—the whole rest of the big, bad world—stretched out before me.

Clutching the tote bag close to my side, I touched the wall in silent farewell and set off through the shadows. Resolve hardened inside me.

The killers who'd descended on the household might be good, but they were going to pay the price anyway. They couldn't have counted on tangling with me.

TWO

Julius

BLAZE FLICKED between video feeds on his laptop's screen with the frenetic energy that rarely left his wiry frame. He'd mounted eight discreet cameras around the mansion's perimeter so we could monitor things after the job, and he zoomed in on one stream of video after another, each shrinking to join the row of smaller squares when he switched. He tapped his foot softly on the tiled floor of the deserted rooftop patio. The guy could never stay still.

Ages ago, his restlessness had irritated me, but now that he'd been part of the crew for years, I appreciated it. His mind was always in motion too, homing in on every important detail that could make the difference between a successful operation and a disaster.

The wrought-iron gate outside the mansion stayed closed and the sidewalks along the stone walls totally empty. This late at night, that wasn't surprising. We'd counted on a lack of foot traffic. Out here in the suburbs, it wasn't as if there was much nightlife. And with the damp pressure in the air hinting at a rain shower to come, who would want to be out anyway?

Talon watched the screen too, his hands resting on the top of the chair next to Blaze's. "We didn't miss anyone," he said in his low, implacable voice. He glanced from the screen to the streets around us, although the long-closed restaurant we were camped out on top of was a few blocks from the mansion, too far away to really see without the cameras. The glow from the screen gleamed off his smoothly shaved scalp and glinted in his icy-blue eyes. "No hitches."

"Obviously no one managed to put out a call for help either," Blaze said with a grin, running his hand through the pale red hair that fit his chosen name, which fell to the collar of his shirt. Another tiny window on the computer screen was monitoring the police frequencies. "No cops, no nothing."

Garrison propped himself against the edge of the table next to the laptop, his lips curving with his typical cocky grin. "The Chaos Crew doesn't botch missions. Especially not when I've laid the groundwork."

Of course, Blaze couldn't resist arching his eyebrows at the youngest and newest member of our crew. "You mean like that time in Cairo," he said teasingly.

Garrison glowered at him, the hazel eyes that seemed to shift in color depending on what he was wearing nearly black now in the dim light. "It was only my second time out, and *someone* forgot to fill me in on a key piece of intel."

Blaze smiled cheekily back at him. "I didn't forget. It was part of your training to see how you'd handle a gap. Good thing you recovered fast from that stumble."

"But I did," Garrison grumbled. "We got fucking paid. That's what matters."

"Enough," I said before they could take their scrap any further. That one word from me was enough for them both to fall silent. I nodded to the laptop. "We don't assume any mission is successful until afterward. We're going to wait a little longer, just to be sure."

I couldn't blame them for being keyed up. We all were after a job like that, exhilarated by the rush of the violence, the blood splattered in perfect disarray, the justice seen through. If sometimes I enjoyed the carnage itself just as much as the justice, there was no need to acknowledge that to anyone else. But after another half hour or so, we could pack up, go home, and leave this scene behind us.

Blaze sat up straighter, his shoulders stiffening. "Hey, guys."

As he clicked the trackpad to enlarge one video feed, the rest of us leaned toward the laptop screen. A woman had just stalked into view, walking alongside the stone wall, her arms tucked close to her sides and her head low. The waves of her long black hair veiled most of her face.

"A neighbor getting home late," Garrison said, flicking his shaggy blond hair away from his eyes. "No big deal."

"But she came out of nowhere." Blaze frowned at the screen. "She didn't show up on any of the other feeds, she was just suddenly there. I don't know where she came from."

"Look." Talon pointed at the figure just as she passed the camera, motioning to her T-shirt. In the darkness, the feed didn't show much in the way of color, but there was a dark smear on her chest that made my instincts ping in the same way my colleagues' must have. "Is that blood?"

Blaze zoomed in, but she'd passed by, now angled away from us and heading toward the edge of the camera's view. A tote bag bounced lightly against her back from where it was slung over her shoulder.

"She can't have come from the house, right?" our tech expert said. "We did two full sweeps—we caught everyone who was on the manifest."

We had, but I couldn't shake the sense that this woman wasn't just some random pedestrian either. It was too strange.

The Chaos Crew didn't leave loose ends. I couldn't *let* us leave them. That was how an operation could go to hell in an instant.

Talon lifted his gun. "We could kill her now."

I shook my head. "We don't have definite evidence she's connected to the job." Cutting her down would have been the easiest option, but it went against everything I stood for. We didn't have many rules, but those we had, we held to. And "Kill no innocent bystanders" was at the top of the list.

No one died because of us who didn't have it coming to them—not today, not ever.

But we couldn't let her just walk away either, not when she might not be remotely innocent after all.

I snapped my fingers, already moving toward the stairs. "Garrison, you're with me on foot. Talon, you and Blaze take the car. Keep me up to date on her movements. We'll see where she goes from here and then make an educated decision."

They sprang into action in an instant, taking my word as law. One of our other few rules was that no one challenged my leadership of the crew when I gave an order. It kept our team working as a unit. A highly sophisticated and efficient unit that didn't make mistakes.

Until, maybe, now.

That possibility sat uneasily in my gut as we hurried down to the street. Blaze's voice hummed through my headset. "She's crossed Blantyre Avenue, heading east."

"Acknowledged." I picked up my pace, Garrison following close behind. The woman had a substantial head start on us, but we could close the distance quickly. I set my feet carefully even as we hustled toward her location, making only the faintest patter.

Coming up on the next corner, we slowed and peered around the bend. "She's in our sights," Garrison whispered into his mic.

The woman we'd spotted had made it to the end of that block, but she'd stopped by a sedan parked by the curb, which had given us more of a chance to catch up. What was she—

She yanked at something by the top of the window and then tugged on the door, which opened. She immediately dove into the driver's seat.

I muttered a curse under my breath. She'd broken into the damn thing. I headed along the street as quickly as I dared, sticking close to the shadows outside the shops on the opposite side of the road, Garrison right behind me.

If she noticed us, she'd probably bolt, and we weren't close enough yet that I was sure of chasing her down. If Talon and Blaze could get in place…

"Just coming around Carling St.," Blaze reported, and in the same moment, the car's engine revved.

"Fuck," I snapped under my breath, and broke into a sprint. "She's broken into a car and she's already got it running. Get over here *now*."

The stolen car's engine sputtered into silence and then roared back to life. The woman who'd hotwired it in a matter of seconds peeled away from the sidewalk. I'd never seen anyone take over a vehicle that fast. Who the hell was she?

The chances of her being innocent were quickly dwindling.

"She's getting away," I hissed into the mic. "Where the hell are you?"

Our car whipped around the corner before Blaze needed to reply. It jerked to a halt beside us, and Garrison and I threw ourselves into the back seat.

The second Garrison had hauled the door shut, Talon hit the gas. The stolen car was just turning a corner up ahead.

"There," I said with a jab of my finger. "The dark gray sedan. Follow her."

Talon sped after her and swung around the same turn she'd taken. The sedan came into view a couple of blocks ahead of us, easy to spot in the gleaming streetlamps along this slightly broader road. Even here, traffic was sparse, only a few other pairs of headlights gleaming farther in the distance.

A heavy droplet of rain splashed on the windshield, briefly blurring the view. Another followed, and another, until Talon had to start the wipers going.

"You couldn't catch her on foot?" he asked over the rhythmic tapping of the drops.

I grimaced. "The bitch is fast. She must have set a record hotwiring that car. I don't even know how she broke into it to begin with."

"Not exactly your typical pedestrian out for a stroll," Garrison said in a wry drawl. "What are the odds that a woman who can hotwire cars in a split-second *isn't* involved in this?"

I didn't have an answer to that question. I narrowed my eyes at the car in front of us. Blaze licked his lips and clicked a few keys on his laptop, leaping from feed to feed. He was following along with the official traffic cams now. There wasn't a government resource in this city he couldn't find a way to infiltrate.

"Not very good," Talon replied for me.

Garrison sank back in his seat. His breath was still a bit ragged from the jog to catch up with the woman—I'd have to remind him to get in more physical training on our days off. It wasn't his main area, but we all needed to pull our weight in every way possible.

"We should just kill her and get it over with then," he said. "Whether she has something to do with the job or not, she just committed a crime. So she's not innocent, so the rule doesn't apply."

Blaze swiveled in his seat with another of his heckling looks. "And by 'we,' I assume you mean anyone other than you with your weak stomach."

Garrison kicked the back of Blaze's seat. "I just know what I'm good at. And I know that every move that woman's made since the moment we saw her has screamed that she's up to something."

He was right, but at the same time, something about the situation still felt off to me. Killing the woman without sorting it out wouldn't necessarily mean we'd fixed the problem, only that we had no way of telling what else might have gone wrong.

"We catch her and talk to her first," I said. "Find out who she is and what she knows. Make sure there's nothing else we missed. It's no good tying off one loose end if that stops us from following it to a dozen others we didn't know about."

Garrison opened his mouth as if to argue but shut it immediately when I caught his gaze. He set his expression in a mask of indifference. Our social chameleon could put on whatever front we needed to get the players in position at the start of a job or ferret out information Blaze couldn't hack his way to. Even I couldn't tell which of the emotions that crossed his face were real. Were any of them?

It didn't matter. Nothing mattered except the security of this crew, and we couldn't know how the woman might threaten that without confronting her.

The rain picked up to a heavier downpour. It washed over the windshield between the swift flicks of the wipers. The stolen car slowed, and so did Talon, drawing up less than a block from her brake lights.

"Stay as close as you can without spooking her," I said. "We don't want to lose her. As soon as she stops, we have to be on her ass."

Even as I spoke, the woman took a sudden left turn. Talon fell back a little before following her. Two blocks later, she took an abrupt right. She hadn't signaled either time.

Blaze spoke up cautiously. "Are we sure she hasn't already gotten spooked? Did she see you before she grabbed the car?"

"We were too far back," I said. "I made sure she didn't see us—I hadn't expected her to take off that quickly."

"She was going straight ahead until a minute ago," Talon pointed out.

The stolen car veered through a gas station's lot and out the other side. Talon gunned the engine to hurtle after her.

Garrison folded his arms over his chest. "This is ridiculous. We should force her to pull over now instead of chasing her all over town."

If we'd already been made, that was our best course of action. I exhaled roughly, and just then, one of the parked cars along the curb swerved into the street in front of our target.

Too fast, too close. The woman must have pulled hard on the steering wheel to avoid crashing into the other car, and the slick surface of the road sent her vehicle skidding. It careened across the road and rammed hood-first into a telephone pole. The screech of crumpling steel cut through the drumming of the rain on our roof.

THREE

Decima

THE HOUSEHOLD HAD BEEN thorough in my training, which meant I'd gotten a lot of driving practice in to prepare me for the occasional missions that required I get behind the wheel of various vehicles. I hadn't been on the road at night all that often, though. Or in the rain. The combination of the two, with the droplets slipping over the windshield with increasing frequency, made my hands tighten on the steering wheel.

Thank God the streets were pretty empty at this time of night. I could manage to navigate the periodic streetlights and the rows of parked cars along the side of the road just fine.

Which was good, because my mind kept wandering. The image of Anna's bloody body lingered in the back of my head.

Was there something more I should have done for her? For all of the people in the household? At the time, it'd seemed like leaving quickly was the best thing I could do, but now a pinch of guilt dug into my stomach. I hadn't felt guilt over a dead body in a long time, even all the ones I'd been responsible for.

I was totally alone now. I had nobody left. How could it be normal to leave behind the only home I'd ever known just like that?

But then, there was obviously nothing normal about the massacre I'd walked into.

I sucked my lower lip under my teeth and let my mind shift to the practicalities. I had too many questions that I needed to answer, and emotions would get me nowhere.

Who had done this? More importantly, how was I going to find them? And in what way would I end their lives? Would I make their deaths long and painful, allowing their arteries to spew blood for minute after minute before they died? That was how they'd killed everyone in the household, after all. It would be *fitting.*

I suspected I'd like that style of poetic justice very much.

Where would I start? I'd never been assigned a mission with so little preparation and such a vague objective. Noelle had always come with weapons, supplies, and a dossier of everything I needed to know to locate and take down my target. I'd never had to think about anything other than how to get into a specific building, evade bodyguards, or make a swift escape.

Right now, I had nothing but a stolen car, a bag of clothes and jewelry, and the knife and chunk of glass I'd tossed on the seat with the bag, which barely counted as weapons. I had no idea where I was going or who I needed to find. The possibilities spiraled away from me, so endless my mind froze up trying to process them.

It was probably shock. I couldn't be blamed for that, right? Discovering that everyone around you had been brutally murdered was pretty fucking shocking. I just needed time to think.

Headlights gleamed in my rearview mirror. I glanced at the mirror and realized the black car I'd noticed behind me earlier was still heading in the same direction. It'd pulled closer, only about a block away.

There wasn't anything so strange about that. I was on a fairly major street. I'd walked several blocks from the household before I'd found a car I could steal, and I hadn't seen anyone tracking me from there. I'd stuck to the speed limit and followed the traffic laws to a tee, so I shouldn't have raised any red flags for anyone who'd seen me drive by after.

But it was arrogance to assume I'd done everything perfectly. The car *could* be following me for one reason or another, and that meant I should act as if it was.

I slowed, monitoring the car behind me, and took an abrupt turn. They hadn't put on their signal, but they appeared behind me around the bend several seconds later. They left enough space for another car to pass, but… was this a coincidence?

The rain pelted my windshield. I frowned, squinting at the road ahead. There was a little side-street right there.

I swerved quickly but not violently, my heart jumping when the tires skidded on the wet pavement more than I'd expected. With a jerk of the steering wheel, I managed to straighten out the car. There. They'd drive on by, and I'd see I was just being paranoid and—

Headlights flashed behind me. The damn car had made the same turn again.

Apprehension gnawed at my stomach. This definitely didn't *feel* like a coincidence now. What were the chances that someone just happened to take this exact same route, when there was hardly anyone on the roads at all?

I had to lose them. That was all there was to it.

Spotting a gas station on a corner up ahead where the side street met another larger road, I pressed slowly on the gas to increase my speed. The moment I came up on the station, I whipped to the side, careered past the pumps with my pulse beating in my throat, and flew onto the road on the other side.

That might not be enough. I had to take the next turn that—

A parked car I hadn't been paying attention to pulled out into the road right in front of me. I was going too fast. I hit the brake, but the tires screeched and slid in the rain. Shit.

I hauled on the wheel before I slammed right into the asshole who'd cut me off. The car kept skidding, spinning to the side and then forward—and crashed into a telephone pole on the other side of the road.

The impact jolted me in my seat, the hood crumpling in toward me. In the same moment, the airbag burst out with a *bang*, smacking into my face, chest, and the arm I'd flung across the wheel to turn it. Pain radiated through my hand and the side of my torso, and my eyes stung. A chalky powder prickled down my throat.

I blinked hard, and the stinging sensation only deepened into a sharper burning. Even as the airbag deflated, the world around me looked blurred. Involuntary tears flushed the chemicals from my eyes, but I still couldn't see for shit.

Damn it. I had to get out of here—grab my things, run for it, find another car or a bus I could jump onto.

I groped for the tote bag, and another jab of pain shot through my wrist. I could hardly move it without gritting my teeth. Fucking hell. The crash had hurt that too.

I twisted at the waist to reach for my bag with my other hand and winced at the ache that spread through my side. My ribs had gotten in on the game as well. From the feel of them, they were only bruised, but I'd broken enough of them in the past that they were way too sensitive to getting bumped around.

Hazards of the job.

Clenching my jaw against the various pains, I snatched the handle of the tote bag and shoved open the driver's side door. The world outside swam before my still-blurry eyes, but I had to keep going. I took a deep breath and pushed my way out of the car, trying to do most of the work with my left arm.

It didn't work as well as I'd hoped, and I staggered out of the car, my legs wobbling and a fresh rush of pain penetrating my chest. The rain drenched me in an instant. It also flushed my eyes, alleviating a bit of the sting but not clearing my vision particularly well. I couldn't tell how much of the blurring was because of the water and how much from the airbag's chemicals now.

"Hey," a deep voice said from behind me. "Are you all right?"

I whirled, and my legs swayed again, still shaky from the crash. I stumbled right into the chest of a large, muscle-bound man. He caught my elbows, and I jerked away instinctively.

Who the hell was he? What did he want with me?

"Hold on," he said. My hazy vision made out a broad-shouldered form nearly a foot taller than me, the square-jawed face topped with dark hair. It was hard to make out what expression he was even making or anything else beyond that.

He held up his hands in a gesture of surrender. "I'm just trying to help you. That was a hell of a crash."

Oh. That did kind of make sense, didn't it? Good Samaritans or whatever. Probably just looking for the ego boost of saying he'd come to someone's rescue, but nothing necessarily nefarious.

It wasn't just him, though. Three more figures gathered around us, all male, all with at least half a foot and fifty pounds on my well-toned but trim frame. Where had they all come from?

Where was the car I'd thought was tailing me? Had these guys come out of it? If they had, what were they planning on doing to me?

I tugged the tote bag's strap over my shoulder instinctively so I'd have my hands free to fight, not that one of those hands felt up to engaging in combat at the moment. At the same time, a slimmer figure with a face framed by light red hair leaned toward me. "Is she okay?"

"I'm fine," I lied automatically, taking a step back and dodging another man who'd come up beside me. "Really, thank you for your concern, but—"

I turned, and banged my hip on a newspaper box I hadn't seen between the darkness and my blurred eyes. My right hand shot out automatically to help me catch my balance, and agony lanced through my wrist. I couldn't stop myself from hissing at the pain.

"You don't seem okay," the first guy said, swiping rain from his face. "That wrist might be broken. We should call an ambulance."

Another of the men who'd approached us jerked around as if to stare at the one who'd spoken. All I could make out of this one was a sharp chin and blond hair plastered to his skull. "Julius," he said in a voice that had an edge to it.

Julius. The name seemed to fit the imposing masculinity that radiated off of every inch of the first man's frame.

I didn't want to stay here with him and whoever these other guys were, and I didn't want to be taken to any hospital. If the people who'd slaughtered the household were looking for me, I couldn't afford to leave any kind of paper trail.

That was one of Noelle's first rules. Never, *ever* let anyone make a permanent record of your presence.

"I'm fine," I said again, taking another step back. My legs were getting steadier, at least. I blinked, unsuccessfully willing my vision to clear more, and restrained a shiver at the chill of my soaked clothes and hair. "No need for an ambulance. I was almost home anyway. I can make it there on my own."

No need to follow me. Just let me leave.

"I can't let you go walking around when you could be battered up more than you realize," the man named Julius said. "Here, if you don't want an ambulance, I've got some basic medical training. Let me look you over quickly, and if I don't see any reason to worry, then you can be on your way."

He made the suggestion sound perfectly reasonable. His firm baritone was the kind of voice used to making commands and having them followed. But that only made me balk even more.

I didn't take orders from him or any other random guy. I didn't want him or his friends getting any closer to me than they already had.

He'd accepted my refusal of proper medical attention awfully easily, hadn't he? Was that normal, or did it mean *he* hadn't really wanted to bring anyone else onto the scene either?

"You really don't need to go to that much trouble," I said. That sounded decently normal, right? "If I start feeling worse, I have my own doctor I can call. I'd be more comfortable with that than a stranger, obviously."

The men shifted on their feet around me. I had trouble keeping track of them all in the hazy darkness. I started to swivel to keep all of them in view, and the blond guy grabbed my elbow, more gently than I'd have expected given the tone of his voice earlier. "You've obviously hurt your wrist," he said with a new air of concern. "And it looks like you've got blood on your shirt. Did something happen before the accident?"

My gaze jerked down and made out a blotch of red on the blue T-shirt now plastered to my body. It had to be Anna's blood, from when I'd caught her in the doorway. My pulse stuttered. "I—I must have gotten scratched up a bit in the crash. It's nothing serious. Really, I'd rather just go home. On my own."

"We can't leave you alone in the rain when you're injured and defenseless," Julius said.

I had to hold in a laugh at the word "defenseless." He didn't have a clue. Even injured, I had little doubt I'd be able to hold my own against one of them, maybe even two. I could have broken the hand the blond guy still had on me if I'd really wanted to, if I wasn't trying to play normal in case they were ordinary bystanders after all.

Instead, I just tugged my arm away from him, and to my relief, he let me go.

"Look, I'd rather be on my own than surrounded by strangers," I said. "I'm just a little bruised up. I've got to deal with the car and the rest of this mess, but I can handle that. You can all go back to whatever you were doing."

The blond guy's head cocked. He stepped back with a shrug. "Fine, if that's what you really want."

"It is," I said, turning toward the sidewalk—and a sharp pinch bit into my lower spine.

The last thing I was aware of was the give of my knees as blackness swam up over my vision and completely blanked my mind.

FOUR

Talon

JULIUS CAUGHT the woman before she'd quite hit the ground. She lolled in his arms, obviously dead to the world. I pocketed the syringe I'd used to knock her unconscious and glanced at the crashed car, swiping the raindrops that were finally starting to let up off my smooth scalp. "Do we want to do anything about the vehicle?"

Julius considered it. "I don't think going to that kind of trouble is necessary. It wasn't hers to begin with, so there's nothing to tie it to her or us. Check inside for blood or anything she might have left behind, though."

She'd never gotten around to closing the driver's side door. As Julius carried her back to our car, I peered into the darkened interior. I couldn't see any bodily fluids on the seats, even after I flicked on my phone's flashlight to be sure. I plucked one dark hair off the leather surface.

There was a coffee cup that must have belonged to the car's owner, since this woman hadn't had a chance to stop for a drink. A shard of glass and a dinner knife lay on the passenger seat. None of the windows had shattered, so the glass hadn't come from there. Odd but not really useful. I tucked them into my pocket alongside the syringe anyway.

I made it to our car just as Julius lowered the woman into the trunk. My gaze lingered on the smooth planes of her face. She was young, no more than her early twenties, but she didn't look scruffy or like any kind of punk.

What had driven her to steal that car? What had she been doing by the mansion?

Garrison had grabbed the bag she'd been carrying. He tossed it into the trunk with her and stalked to the door to get out of the rain. Julius closed the lid of the trunk, and the rest of us piled into the car afterward. I took the driver's seat again, but I didn't start the engine, waiting for Julius's cue.

"What the fuck are we going to do with her now?" Garrison asked. He'd put on a softer front briefly with the woman when he'd been trying to cajole a little information out of her, but now he was back to his usual snarky self. "Not take her home like a stray puppy, I assume."

"If she's from the mansion, we should probably kill her," I said. I didn't relish the thought—killing in the middle of a job, where everything was orchestrated and certain, felt very different from murdering a random woman we'd picked off the street—but I wouldn't balk either. If that was what needed to happen, then so be it. She was nothing to us.

Julius had gotten in beside me. He rubbed the bridge of his nose, more pensive than decisive at the moment. That didn't seem like a good sign. Pensive was for planning a job. Once it was underway, Julius kept everything running with brutal efficiency. It was one of the reasons I trusted him with my life.

"We still don't know if she has anything to do with the job," he said. "We don't know anything about her."

Blaze spoke up from behind me. "She was pretty cagey. Most people wouldn't argue about getting help after a crash like that. But she might have been nervous about the whole stolen car thing or whatever made her steal the car."

He glanced at Garrison. The two might squabble in their bantering way a lot, but Blaze knew as well as the rest of us that the youngest member of our crew was the best at reading people. That was one of the reasons we'd brought him on.

"She definitely didn't want anything to do with us," Garrison said, slouching back in his seat and shaking some of the rain off his pale shaggy hair. "She was nervous, avoiding questions, and more worried about getting away from us than her injuries. But none of that tells us anything for sure." He paused. "Why don't we turn her over to the client and let *him* sort out this shit?"

"If it turns out we missed something important regarding her, dropping her in the client's lap isn't going to look good for our reputation," Julius pointed out. "We need to understand exactly how she fits into this situation before we can handle her properly. And she *wasn't* on the manifest. Whatever else she's gotten mixed up in, we wouldn't want to turn her over to the kind of people who'd hire us if she's got no connection to the mansion after all."

He frowned, lapsing into silence for another moment, and then said, "We'll take her to one of the safe houses and question her when she wakes up. She doesn't look like she'd pose much of a threat. Garrison, you can get just about anything out of anyone, and she'll be shaken up anyway. It shouldn't take long to drag the story out of her. Then we decide whether we need to end her or cut her loose."

Garrison opened his mouth and shut it again. I could tell he was both pleased with the praise, which Julius doled out sparingly, and annoyed at the diversion from our plan. "Fine," he said finally. "I'll get her talking, no problem."

Blaze had perked up. "When we've got proper lighting, I can take a picture of her face and send it through my app. Run any IDs she's got on her too." *He* never shied away from the opportunity to put his skills to use.

A prickle of uneasiness ran through my gut. This woman was an unknown variable—who knew how she might disrupt our carefully constructed operations? But that was the only emotion I felt about the situation—about as much emotion as I ever felt. I didn't react to things with the same energy other people seemed to, which meant I never totally trusted my own judgment when it came to dealing with other people, unless I was simply judging the most ideal way to kill those people.

Julius and I had been in this since the beginning, but there was a reason he was in charge and I was his right-hand man. Following his orders had never led me astray.

"Sounds like a plan," I said, starting the engine. "The nearest safe house is over on Grant St."

Julius shook his head. "That's not quite soundproofed. We don't want anyone hearing her if she starts making a racket. Let's go with the one on Carmichael Blvd."

I pulled away from the curb without another word. He was right about that too. The Carmichael safe house was a basement apartment beneath a house we periodically used for short-term rentals to make it look inhabited. There was no one in it now, and the basement was outfitted with plenty of insulation. Not even a scream would make its way outside.

When we reached the apartment, Julius carried the woman straight to the smallest of the three bedrooms. I understood immediately. As a basement, all of the windows were narrow, but our captive was pretty slim. None of us would have stood a hope in hell of squeezing through any of them except the main one in the living room, but she might have managed the slightly larger ones in the bigger bedrooms. This one was too small even for her.

The air in the place smelled stale, unused—which made sense, since we hadn't come by in a while. I was pretty sure I had a change of clothes stashed here somewhere, though. I could get out of the damp shirt and jeans when we were done with our initial inspection.

Julius flicked on the light and laid the woman on the twin bed, which was made up with sheets and a thin blanket on the off-chance that we needed to crash here some night. If we were sticking around until she woke up, I guessed one of us was taking the sofa.

Garrison patted down her wet clothes quickly, which was his usual role in the middle of a job, since he didn't generally get involved in the killing part. He let out a hum and pulled a few jewel-laden necklaces from one pocket, which looked expensive even to my inexperienced eyes. From her other pants pocket, he produced a wad of cash. He unfurled it and fanned it out. "There's at least three grand here. And those necklaces are worth maybe twice that much."

"Could be stolen like the car," Blaze suggested, shifting his weight eagerly on his feet. "No wallet or anything?"

Garrison grimaced. "This is it. Unless there's something in her bag."

Julius upended the tote bag onto the chair in the corner. Several more pieces of jewelry tumbled out, along with a small heap of clothing… and a worn stuffed tiger that looked as if it'd seen better days.

Garrison raised an eyebrow at that. "Cash, stuff that can be pawned for more cash, clothes, and a personal belonging. That paints a pretty clear picture. She was running away—from someone or something."

"Without any ID on her?" Blaze said, obviously frustrated that he couldn't work his computer magic on it.

"Could be whoever she was running from had it under lock and key," Julius said. "Take your photo of her face. You can still use that."

As Blaze got out his phone, Julius turned the woman so she faced the ceiling, her black hair fanning out across the thin pillow. Her face had come out of the crash relatively undamaged, only a faint bruise forming at one corner of her jaw.

Blaze tipped his head to the side with a skeptical look. "Not sure how much we'll get with this. People's faces take on a different shape when they're slack like that, and without her eyes open—but I'll see what I can turn up."

When he'd snapped his picture and started tapping away on his phone to set up whatever he needed to do in that app of his, Julius bent over the woman and started to ease aside her outer clothes with an analytical precision. "Let's see if anything else about her appearance can tell us a story."

As he uncovered her torso from waist to collarbone, baring

everything except her breasts in their modest sports bra, Garrison sucked in a breath. I went still, staring.

Her abdomen was lean and strong with an array of muscles I could tell came from regular, intense workouts. But more unusual were the scars marking it: dozens of them, long and short, some cuts and some burns, darker or fainter depending on how long it'd been since the wounds had been dealt.

The largest one covered a section of skin about as long and wide as my thumb next to her belly button. A thinner but longer line cut across her shoulder, disappearing beneath her bra and showing on the other side where it crossed her ribs. The others dappled her skin all across her torso, many no bigger than a tiny nick.

Garrison let out a low whistle. "I could come up with a few theories now about *why* she'd have needed to run away."

Blaze glanced over, and his eyes widened. "Someone was messing with her on a regular basis."

"Or maybe she was messing with other people," I said, raising my chin toward her sculpted abs. "That kind of musculature would have taken years of hard, rigorous exercise to build. She isn't any wimp."

It took my body two years to become a mold of pure power and strength, with a lot of effort every day to maintain it. The girl before us could have been my smaller, feminine twin.

"She doesn't have any fresh wounds," Julius observed. "The blood on her shirt didn't come from her."

"Turn her over," Garrison suggested.

Julius did, and we all noted the newly forming bruises that covered her right side where she'd taken the worst of the airbag impact. He was careful not to press on those and to move her injured wrist gently. Was he worried about her? It was hard to wrap my head around that kind of compassion when nothing like it stirred in me.

But then, you didn't need to feel sympathy to know avoiding further injury of someone who wasn't your enemy—yet—was the just thing to do. And if Julius followed any kind of code, it was for justice.

The woman's back was mottled with the same sorts of scars. I spotted at least one that looked as if it'd been from a wound so deep it must have taken weeks to recover from it.

What the hell had she been doing to take a blow like that? Or had she not been doing anything, just enduring abuse from some other party while she trained to get ready for her escape?

The form in front of me looked like both an opponent and a victim. I didn't know how to fit those clashing elements together in my understanding of her.

"Hey, look." Garrison leaned forward and swept her hair to the side of her neck, revealing a tattoo on the base of her skull just above her hairline.

We all bent over, examining the small shape. It was hard to make out much with it embedded under her hair. Garrison's attempt at uncovering it had still left it looking like little more than a blotch, vaguely circular with a couple of bumps protruding on either side at a diagonal. I didn't recognize the shape as anything meaningful.

"That's not any gang symbol I'm familiar with, as far as I can tell," Blaze said, "but I'll see if I can dig up anything on that too."

Julius tugged her shirt back down and rolled her onto her back again. We gazed at her in silence for a long moment.

Blaze lowered his phone, a sly smile crossing his lips. "If nobody else is going to say it, I will. She's fucking hot."

Julius rolled his eyes. "Not exactly a productive observation. Get on with your computer work."

Garrison stepped back too, but I thought I caught a glint of approval in his eyes when he looked her up and down one last time.

I hadn't let myself think about it while she'd been exposed, since we'd been focused on the business of unraveling the mystery she presented, but now, studying her leanly muscled form with Blaze's comment ringing in my ears, a twinge of arousal woke up in my groin. It would be something to fuck a woman that physically capable. To feel that strength moving against me in tandem with my own. Her face with its straight, sloping nose and high cheekbones was hardly difficult to look at either.

Not that I expected to have a chance to indulge that kind of urge with her. I only fucked women I didn't have to see again, who were completely separate from every other part of my life. This one had already gotten more entangled with my work and my crew than seemed safe.

Hell, we might still have to kill her. Anyway, I doubted she'd be in the mood to be thinking about getting it on with anyone when she woke up and found out she was a prisoner here.

Julius motioned us all out of the room. "Go get some sleep while she does. I'll check over her injuries more closely and then do the same. We'll see what she can tell us when she wakes up to fill in all the blanks."

FIVE

Decima

THE AIR around me was clammy and chilly. Without opening my eyes, I reached for the covers at my side—covers that I must have kicked off while I slept.

As I moved my arm, a painful ache in my side worked its way into my consciousness. Then a jab of pain shot through my wrist. Why was I hurt?

A flash of Anna's bloody, pain-marred face passed through my mind, and my eyes snapped open. They stung for a moment until I blinked the tinge of discomfort away and focused my vision on the ceiling.

The paneled ceiling. The ceiling above my head in the household had been smooth and white—not *paneled.*

The previous night floated up through my memory—the attack on the household, my hurried departure, that oh so wonderful drive through the rain… and the crash. The men who'd supposedly come to my aid.

And then I'd blacked out.

But where had I ended up after that? This wasn't a hospital. No tang of antiseptic cleaner and sterilized surfaces hung in the air. It smelled of dust and stale coffee with a hint of masculinity.

I turned my head slowly, taking in the small, cement-floored room that contained nothing but a bed, a wooden chair, and a large rug. At least I could see properly now, the chemicals finally wiped from my eyes. Still, fear trickled through my chest. I squared my shoulders against it.

Fear was weakness. Fear would be the reason I got killed. There were plenty of other emotions—powerful emotions—to choose from, so I needed to pick wisely. Rage and vengeance were my top two options, but I chose the third, the one that had served me well many times in the past.

A cool, focused calm.

I pressed my left arm into the mattress and pushed myself upright, trying to avoid clenching the muscles that I knew would bring a deeper ache into my ribs. Even so, a groan slipped from my lips. I examined my right arm, which had been placed in a firm plastic brace as I slept.

Otherwise I was dressed exactly the same as when I'd left the household. I didn't look or feel as if anyone had violated my body. A quiver ran down my spine at the thought, but I dismissed it. No point in worrying about what *might* happen, only what was actually happening right now.

I released a long breath, my bruised ribs throbbing with the deep exhale. My gaze lifted to the door. My instincts urged me to run for it, but the trained part of my mind knew I had to play this smarter. Whoever had brought me here would be waiting outside that door, and escaping that way might be impossible, especially with a sprained wrist and bruised ribs.

Instead, I allowed my eyes to flick toward the window. It was set high in the wall, which confirmed what I'd already suspected from the smell and the floor: I was in a basement. A stream of sunlight seeped through the glass, offering a thin yet cheery light, but my heart sank.

There was no way I was squeezing my shoulders or hips through that tiny rectangle. I'd had enough practice at wriggling through small openings to judge it at a glance.

Shit.

I needed another strategy, and I needed it quickly. Did I have anything like a weapon on me?

I patted my pockets, thinking of the dinner knife and the shard of glass. My stomach clenched for a different reason. My pockets were totally empty. Not just of weapons, but of the rolls of cash and the jewelry I'd grabbed to fund my self-assigned mission.

How the hell was I going to track down the murderers who'd killed Anna, Noelle, and the others if I didn't have anything to pay my way?

I glanced around the room, but the tote bag I'd stuffed the rest of my belongings and more jewelry into was nowhere in sight. My pulse hiccupped.

No, no, no. I had no money, no weapons, and injuries that'd slow me down in a fight. I had no one to turn to for help. I had nothing. Nobody.

Gritting my teeth, I took a deep breath to steel myself. I was Decima, protector of the household, and I'd get through this. I'd see my mission through.

But the first step in doing that was figuring out where I was and who'd brought me here. I wasn't tracking down any murderers while I was stuck in this room anyway.

Whoever had taken me, they'd stolen the loot *I'd* rightfully stolen. And it hadn't even really been stealing when I'd done it, since I was the sole remaining survivor of the household—everything left in the house might as well have been mine. Of course, what did I expect from the kind of person who'd haul an unconscious woman into a strange room somewhere?

I considered the window again, scooting to the edge of the bed. I should be able to reach it if I pulled the chair over—my ribs were going to just love that move. But even if I couldn't escape through that opening, I might be able to catch the attention of some passerby…

A click caught my attention. My head jerked toward the door. The previously locked door, judging by the rasp of a deadbolt shifting with the turn of a key. All my senses went on even higher alert. I tensed where I sat, preparing to fight for my life if I had to.

The door swung open to reveal a man.

A *massive* man. He stood several inches over six feet and ducked through the low doorway, a habit he'd likely developed after hitting his head a handful of times in the past. His dark brown hair, short and methodically cut, matched the scruff that covered his jaw and neck. Beneath the neckline of his tight-fit shirt, there were various places where tattoos peeked out from his brawny chest, though I couldn't tell what they were.

From the lines just starting to form at the corners of his eyes and mouth, I estimated he was in his late thirties. And he hadn't had the easiest of lives. The bottom of his left ear was ragged with missing flesh. I couldn't tell from this far away what'd done it, but it'd obviously been an unpleasant situation.

"How are you feeling?" he asked, his voice just as deep and gruff as I'd expected from his appearance. It was a familiar voice.

"You were at the crash," I said. The big guy who'd reached me first, who'd offered his medical training. I hadn't been able to make him out well enough between my blurred vision and the rain to recognize him on sight, but that commanding voice was unmistakable.

He nodded, taking a slow step forward. "That's why I'm asking how you're feeling. You collapsed on us, and we weren't sure what to do, since you were pretty insistent on not going to the hospital. I hope you can forgive me for not being willing to leave you lying in the road. We brought you back here, and I've patched you up." He nodded to my wrist. "It's just sprained, not broken."

"Fantastic," I said tersely. The sarcasm wasn't polite, but I didn't see any need to put on a friendly front with this guy. He was making it sound as if I'd fainted, but I hadn't *felt* dizzy beforehand. Had the crash caught up with me suddenly… or had he and his friends messed with me somehow?

But as long as he was playing the good guy, I could play along a little too. "To answer your question, I'm a bit sore but otherwise fine."

"That's good to hear. There wasn't much I could do for your ribs." His gaze traveled over my chest, but without any trace of a leer, and then back to my face. "I'm sorry—you must be pretty confused. If you didn't catch my name last night, I'm Julius."

The nickname I most often went by when dealing with anyone

outside the household fell from my mouth automatically. "Dess." Sometimes I had other aliases for a specific mission, but Dess was my all-purpose public name, just a shorter version of Decima. Noelle said it was always best to have one you could respond to easily, naturally.

Julius moved another step closer, and it took every ounce of my willpower not to shoot forward and knock him to his knees so I could dash past him. If I even could knock him over. He was bigger and probably stronger than me, all my training aside, and I was in pain. I still didn't know what exactly he was up to.

"Dess," he said, testing the name—weighing it for who knows what. As he said it, he cocked his head to the side, and a flicker of deeper recognition sparked inside me.

Maybe it was the tone of his voice or the way the light hit the chiseled planes of his handsome face at that angle, but I had the abrupt sense that I'd seen him before. And not in a bad way. The tug of emotion inside me felt almost reassured by his presence and his authoritative stance.

What the fuck? I must have been more shaken up by the crash than I realized. I mentally shook myself and studied him surreptitiously. The sense of familiarity remained, but I couldn't place him.

It didn't matter. What mattered was figuring out his motivations: had he and his friends really been playing hero, or had they knocked me out and dragged me here for some nefarious reason? And if the latter, did that reason have anything to do with the massacre in my home?

"What were you doing there last night?" I asked abruptly.

Julius blinked and gave me a quizzical look. "We were heading back here after a party at a friend's house, and we saw you hit that telephone pole. We're not the types to just keep driving when someone's obviously in trouble." He paused and reached behind him to pick up something he'd left by the door. My tote bag.

My gaze tracked it as he held it up, my fingers itching to grab it. It looked as full as it'd been when I'd left, but that didn't mean it had anything except my clothes and that stupid stuffed tiger in it.

"We were actually wondering if you were in more trouble than just the crash," Julius said, his voice dipping lower. Something about the assured baritone sent a whisper of heat over my skin that I almost… liked?

Focus, Decima.

Julius was still talking. "When we checked you over for ID to try to find out who to call to let them know where you were, we didn't find any, but we did notice this stuff." He pulled out one of the necklaces and then waggled a roll of cash. "And you've got blood on your shirt even though you don't have any cuts on you. What happened to you before you got into that car?"

"I don't really see how that's your business," I said, like a regular person who had nothing to hide but wanted their privacy would. Right? I didn't have enough practice at being a normal person to be sure, but the response felt reasonable. "Thank you for stopping and helping me, but I don't know you, and I'd really like to get out of here now."

Julius contemplated me, his gaze curious but penetrating. I met it, narrowing my eyes and daring him to question me further.

The way he effortlessly held my gaze drew up another unexpected feeling in my stomach that fluttered and multiplied. The strength that he exuded, both literally and with his mere presence, called to a part of me that had long remained dormant. This was a man who got things done.

But what was he going to do with me?

The question didn't unnerve me as much as it should. Julius folded his arms over his chest, and the movement brought up his sleeve to reveal a pointed shape that was part of one of his tattoos creeping over his bicep.

Were we playing some kind of game of cat-and-mouse where neither of us was showing all our cards? I still couldn't tell what his intentions were, and that made me hesitate to make any aggressive moves.

If this was a game, he probably figured *he* was the cat in it. Ha. I doubted he could possibly imagine how many men like him I'd taken down in the past several years.

Julius offered a casual shrug. "I just want to be sure we're not sending you out there into some kind of danger. It's hard not to worry, considering the state we found you in. Or maybe we should be worried about whoever you got this hoard from."

Oh, it wasn't me who was in danger. It was the people who'd massacred the household and made the grave mistake of leaving me alive, and when I figured out who they were, they wouldn't know what hit them. Every feeling I'd experienced as I held Julius's gaze faded, replaced with the same steady rage that would continue driving me until I completed this mission successfully.

If he wanted a story, I'd give him a story.

I blew out a breath as if I was frustrated with the situation. "Fine. If you insist on knowing—my boyfriend won that crap in some stupid poker game. He was so drunk he passed out, and I saw my chance to get away, and I just—I grabbed it and ran for it. Things haven't been so great between us for a while."

I swiped my hand across my face and looked down at my shirt. At the bloodstain the rain hadn't quite washed out where a spurt of Anna's blood had hit the fabric. My mind leapt to the next explanation. "I get nose bleeds when I'm stressed sometimes. It must have happened while I was leaving without me even noticing it, and some got on my shirt. I don't know what else I can tell you."

Julius nodded, but his wary expression didn't change. Something I'd said wasn't lining up with his assumptions, and I didn't know how to fix it. Had I shown the wrong emotions for the story I'd given? I'd never had a boyfriend before, let alone an awful one. I didn't know what it was like to be someone desperate enough to take off on that boyfriend in the middle of the night. Maybe I should have tried crying? But tears didn't come easily to me.

I hadn't even cried for Anna, not really.

Julius didn't argue with me, though. He set my tote bag down on the chair. "We didn't find a phone on you. I'm guessing you don't want to check in with this boyfriend, but is there a friend or relative you were heading to that you'd want us to get in touch with? If someone was expecting you, they must be panicking by now."

I shook my head quickly. "I don't have a phone—he broke my last one a few days ago. No one knew I was coming. I didn't even know where I was going yet."

That last part was true enough that a twinge of loss ran through my chest and into my voice. Something shifted in Julius's expression.

He motioned to the bag. "Well, you can take that with you when you leave. I don't want to get in the middle of some domestic dispute. And by the sounds of things, you'll need that stuff."

Seriously? I resisted the impulse to snatch the bag up right this moment and kept my voice carefully neutral. "So I can go, then? The question period is over?"

"This isn't a prison," Julius said. "I *do* have first aid training from my time in the military, and in my opinion, especially if you don't have anywhere specific to go, it'd be better if you stayed here another day or two to make sure there aren't any lingering effects from the crash. Unless you're more comfortable with the idea of going to the hospital now?"

Would he actually take me to one—out of this room, into a place where I could much more easily escape him and his friends? I wet my lips and decided to call his bluff.

"You know, I was panicking last night and obviously not thinking clearly. I probably should get a doctor to check me out."

Julius stepped back toward the doorway without any sign of apprehension. "I'll take you right over there, then." He motioned for me to join him.

That easy, huh? Still wary, I stood up and reached for the chair to take my bag.

The moment I took a few steps, a wave of dizziness crashed over me. My head spun. I stumbled and banged my knees on the edge of the chair, grasping it with my good hand just before I fell all the way to the ground.

"Whoa, there," Julius said. He gripped my other arm just above my elbow and guided me back to the bed. My vision swam, my thoughts still jumbling with dizziness. "I think you'd better get a little more rest before you try to go anywhere. I'll get you something to eat—maybe that'll help you get your strength back."

He sat me down on the bed and walked right out of the room, closing the door behind him.

I pressed the heel of my hand to my forehead, but now I just felt exhausted. Whatever had happened to me during or after the crash, it was definitely worse than it'd seemed before I started trying to move around.

Didn't that mean Julius really should get me to a hospital fast? Should I insist he call an ambulance?

I couldn't focus well enough to decide what the smartest course of action was. One clear thought pierced through the jumble alongside a sinking sensation in my gut.

No matter what Julius had said, this room was essentially a prison, and if he decided he didn't want me leaving, I was stuck in it with no clear way out.

I'd rest all right. I'd rest and heal, as quickly as I could, and then I'd show these assholes that no one kept me caged for long.

SIX

Decima

I TRIED a few times to stand and approach the door, but when I nearly crashed to the floor on my third attempt, I waited until the dizziness in my head had faded. The last thing I needed was to approach Julius weakened and unable to defend myself if it became necessary.

It wasn't until the daylight outside beamed with the full brightness of mid-day that I managed to take several experimental steps around the room without wobbling. I tested my newfound strength by changing from my blood smeared clothes which were stiff from drying on me after getting drenched by the rain, into a fresh pair of sweatpants and a T-shirt from my tote bag.

When I felt confident enough in my ability to stay steady, I walked to the door. I clutched the handle with more confidence. Sure, my ribs hurt, and my wrist ached, but all of that was manageable pain.

Whatever needed to be done so I could get out of here, I'd make it happen.

I twisted the knob. It turned easily, no longer locked. Every nerve on the alert, I eased the door open.

The walls in this place must have been thick, because I'd only caught faint murmurs through them before, nothing I'd been able to decipher as words. The moment I peered into the wider room outside, a rush of sound washed over me.

It was an open-concept space, nothing but a kitchen island separating any part of it into specific zones. To my right, in the kitchen area, Julius was standing by a slim man with pale red hair who was talking animatedly while spinning his fork in a plate of spaghetti.

"But the size of that thing! It's not just a snake, it's a fucking green anaconda. Seventeen feet long! It'd eat you and a hundred snakes for breakfast."

"You've got to stop watching those documentaries," muttered another man who was standing beyond them by the stove. "Or at least quit it with the random fact regurgitation." His pale, shaggy hair sparked a sense of recognition—he must be the one who'd talked to me last night at the crash scene after Julius.

At the same time, a dull thudding reverberated from the other side of the room, catching my attention next. A fourth man, his shaved head gleaming under the recessed lights and lean muscles flexing over every inch of his body, was slamming his fists into a dangling punching bag in rapid succession. He stepped back, bouncing on his toes, before going back in for the metaphorical kill. His technique impressed even me, and I'd been practicing all forms of combat my entire life.

His lean, sculpted physique spoke of years of training too. Not just strength but discipline. The sweat dampening his shirt emphasized those planes even more, and an errant thought slipped through my mind: What would it be like to run my fingers over those muscles?

A flicker of heat tingled over my skin, and I yanked myself back to reality. What was it about these guys that kept pulling my head in ridiculous directions? I had a job to do, and as far as I knew, all four of them stood in my way.

I stepped over the threshold, and the door I was still holding squeaked. The room fell silent in an instant. The three men in the kitchen turned toward me, even the redhead pausing with his spaghetti-laden fork halfway to his mouth. The man at the punching bag lowered his arms and turned my way with studied precision. For a second, I found myself pinned by his icy blue eyes, even from ten feet away.

"Dess," Julius said, and my attention snapped to him. I kept tabs on the guy with the shaved head from the corner of my eye. Turning my back on any of these men felt like a dangerous game.

Julius smiled, subdued but warm, as if we were all friends here. Yeah, right. "How are you feeling now?" he asked.

"Better," I admitted. That much would be obvious, considering I'd made it this far without tripping over my feet.

Should I ask to leave again? Apprehension held my tongue. They'd been careful about it, but it'd seemed pretty clear these guys didn't really want to take me anywhere. Were they just run-of-the-mill pricks, or did they know something about me and maybe even the massacre at the household after all? I had no idea how much of the story Julius had given me I should believe.

If I acted like I was in a hurry to get out of here, they'd go on the defensive. Better for me to study them a little and get a better sense of what I was up against before I made my escape, especially when I had injuries slowing me down.

"It's good to see you on your feet," the redhead said with a grin, recovering his previous exuberance. "Dess is an interesting name. I don't suppose you've got a last name too?"

I wasn't sure why that mattered, but I had my alias all lined up anyway. "Parker," I said briskly, and glanced around the room, the back of my neck prickling with the sense of having all four pairs of eyes still fixed on me. "You all know my name now, but I only know one of yours."

Julius raised his eyebrows at the others. The first to speak was the man by the stove. He flicked on the burner under a kettle and turned toward me. "Garrison," he said, raising a hand in greeting. Yes, that was definitely the voice I'd heard with the blond guy last night.

There was something unsettlingly perfect about his smile, as if he'd picked the exact right angle of his lips to convey friendly warmth. Maybe it was because the warmth he seemed to be conveying didn't match the irritated tone he'd spoken to the redhead with just a minute ago. He'd made a similar switch in attitude last night, hadn't he?

He looked to be the youngest of the bunch, early to mid-twenties if I had to guess, but there was something older in the steadiness of his gaze.

The redhead smiled too, but his grin was a little crooked and overwide, which made it feel more genuine. I figured he was in his twenties too, though closer to the other end. He glanced around at his companions. "I like her." Then he met my eyes, his own dark ones sparkling with curiosity. "I'm Blaze, and he's Talon," he said, gesturing to the man who had been pounding the punching bag moments ago, who let out a grunt of acknowledgment.

Blaze. That'd be easy to remember with that hair, which fell past his ears, nearly long enough that he could have pulled it into a ponytail. And Talon… I couldn't think of a name more fitting for a man who looked built for mowing people down.

Julius had mentioned time in the army. The younger guys didn't look military-fit, but Talon was. Had he and Julius served together, maybe? The shaved head made it harder to tell, but I thought they were about the same age.

I didn't have a whole lot of experience with the lives of regular people, but it was a little odd for all four of them to be here in this apartment together, wasn't it? I took another careful step forward, putting on a smile of my own as if I was relaxing into their company. If I seemed to let down my guard, they'd be more likely to let down theirs.

"Julius mentioned that you're all friends," I said. "And roommates too, I guess? Or are you family or something?"

I doubted the latter, considering how different they all were in coloring and build, but it was a way to frame the question without outright asking, *Who the fuck are you and is this an attempted kidnapping?*

Well, maybe not just attempted considering I was here in their apartment with no definite way out. My gaze flicked briefly over to the windows. The one near the punching bag and another in the kitchen area were as high as the one in my bedroom, but big enough that I thought I could leap through one pretty easily… if I got the chance.

"We're kind of both," Blaze said, still grinning. "And we work together too."

Huh. "What kind of work?" I asked in a getting-to-know-you sort of tone.

"Landscaping," Julius said smoothly, and Blaze snorted as if something about that answer was funny.

"We're very good at it too," Garrison said, giving Blaze's stool a teasing kick. "Every place we work on we leave looking much better than before we got there."

I took in the amusement now dancing in Blaze's eyes and the other men's impenetrable expressions and wondered what the joke was. But at the same time, I couldn't help noticing how easily they interacted, building off each other's responses, even Talon nodding at Julius's statement. I didn't see that kind of camaraderie often.

I wasn't sure I'd ever felt it with another person myself. Even with Noelle, who I'd spent way more time with than anyone else, I'd always been tense around her, driven by the need to meet her expectations and the wariness of what would happen if I didn't.

No, she and I had never been *friends*. I'd trusted her with my life, but I'd still had my guard up, presenting myself the way I knew she'd want.

Would I ever get a chance to work with a team like this now that everyone who'd had a hand in raising me was gone?

An unexpected twinge ran through my gut. I swallowed hard, willing the bloody memories of the carnage away.

"I hope that taking care of me hasn't interfered with your work," I said, putting out another feeler to test their reaction. "I wouldn't want my stupid accident getting in the way of your job."

Julius waved his hand dismissively with the same assurance he'd had from the first moment I'd smacked into him. "It's no problem. We're on our weekend right now."

He was obviously the leader. The others followed his cues.

I tapped my lips. "Right. That's why you were out last night when you saw me get that fender bender. Where were you going?" Julius had already told me there'd been a party, but I wanted to see if his story would stay straight.

Talon moved closer with controlled strides that were closer to a prowl. He frowned as he reached me, his shoulders squaring and his cool eyes flashing. It was obvious what *his* role in the group was: the intimidator.

"I'd like to know what *you* were doing in that part of town," he said.

If he thought I was going to cower in the face of his flex of power, he had the wrong woman. I raised my chin and stared straight back at him. "I'm pretty sure I asked you that question first."

His voice lowered into something closer to a growl. "A lot of shady shit happens in that neighborhood. You're in *our* apartment—I think we have a right to know what we've dragged in here, even if you needed the help."

I bit back a snappy retort about how I hadn't asked for their help, and in fact I'd told them to leave me the hell alone. If they didn't know why I'd been driving that way, did that mean they didn't know where I'd come from either? Was it the cash and the jewelry they'd spotted on me that'd made them bring me here, and nothing more than that?

Julius had seemed to indicate that he was accepting my story. Maybe he would let me walk out of here if I said I wanted to.

Before I could decide on my response, Garrison walked over almost close enough to touch me, bringing a whiff of cinnamon and musk with him. "Okay, enough badgering her, Talon. She's been through some shit. Cut her a break." He turned to me. "Don't mind him. He gets a little overprotective of our space. I'm making hot chocolate—would you like some?"

Hot chocolate? An eager jolt ran through me so abruptly that it took all my effort to suppress my outward reaction. My mouth was watering in an instant.

I'd actually never tasted the beverage before, but my favorite part of every birthday was the chocolate bar that Anna would bring alongside my dinner. That was the only time Noelle had approved of the treat, saying it was all empty calories. And these guys had it lying around their apartment, just casually downing a cup of it here and there like it was no big deal.

"I would," I said, schooling my voice into a neutral tone. Might as well get one benefit out of this crazy situation. "Thank you."

Garrison went back to the stove. He set out a second mug, sprinkled a packet of powder into it, and poured boiling water from the kettle to prepare my liquid gold. Blaze beckoned me over to the stool across from him, which wasn't especially close to any of them and should allow me to keep all of them in sight.

I hesitated for a second and then walked over to take it. Better there than staying beside Talon the guard dog.

Even if that guard dog came with the most impressive set of muscles I'd ever laid eyes on.

I told that part of my mind to shut up and perched on the stool. Garrison poured a dollop of cream into both mugs and then set them on the island, one a little closer to me. He raised his to his lips, watching me through the rising steam. "It's just instant stuff, nothing fancy, but I like this brand."

As if I cared about fancy. It was *chocolate*—I was already sold.

It took all of my self-control not to shoot forward and chug the scolding liquid. Instead, with purposeful control, I curled my fingers around the handle and raised the mug as slowly as Garrison had.

My first sip nipped my tongue with a burning sensation, but the rich, nutty sweetness smoothed out the pain in an instant. Fucking hell, it tasted like heaven.

"Is it good?" Garrison asked with a glint in his hazel eyes that suggested he could already tell just how much I was enjoying it.

"It's great," I said, restraining my enthusiasm, and allowed myself a larger swallow. Some small piece of me asked in a very tiny voice whether it would really be so bad to hang out with these guys a while longer, especially if I could talk them into sharing several more mugs like this with me, and I told it to shut up too.

Talon ambled over, his gaze shooting daggers at Garrison. "Now that you have some fucking hot chocolate, do you plan on answering some of our questions?"

I narrowed my eyes at him, watching for his reaction. "I never asked you to bring me here. I don't think I owe you anything."

He scowled. "I think you owe us a little more of an explanation after we saved your ass."

Garrison clucked his tongue chidingly and shot me a conspiratorial smile. My hackles automatically went up again. Did he think he'd won me over just because I was enjoying what he'd poured in this mug?

"What I think my friend here *meant* to say," he drawled in a teasing tone, "is that we want to make sure *you're* not in any danger right now. Julius says your stash of money and jewelry came from a boyfriend? Is he likely to be out there searching for you?"

My non-existent boyfriend would probably have run screaming at the sight of just Talon's glare, but I wasn't going to prop up the guy's ego by saying so. I sipped my hot chocolate, distracted by a momentary swoon. A weakness, maybe. Delicious? Absolutely.

"Nah," I said, putting on a shudder as if remembering something that bothered me. "He liked to push me around when I was there, but he's probably too high to get much past the front door." I cut my gaze to Talon. "Yes, it's a bad fucking neighborhood. I grew up there. Is that a crime now?"

Often with assholes the best way to get what you wanted was to put them on the defensive. They weren't used to it. And the truth was, I felt more at ease talking to Talon with his body carved out of muscle and snarling face than Garrison with his kindness I couldn't help being suspicious of. At least with the guard dog, I knew where I stood.

"It's pretty strange that you don't have anyone at all you need us to call," Talon said, seeming unfazed. "No family? No job? All you've got is this man of yours?"

I bit my lip. I might not have any experience with romantic relationships, but I had plenty of grief and horror to draw on thanks to last night's events. "That's all he let me have," I said in a small voice, as if ashamed.

"You really need to let up on her," Garrison said to Talon, swatting at him, and turned back to me with a gentler expression. "The guy sounds like a total prick. Is it because of him that you've got all those scars?"

All those scars. A shiver traveled down my spine. "How do you know I have scars?"

I already knew the answer. They must have looked me over—including under my clothes—while I was unconscious. Had they *touched* me?

But somehow Garrison managed to look even more horrified than I felt. "Oh, God, don't get the wrong idea! While we were carrying you in, your shirt rode up a little, that's all. It was hard not to notice them."

For real? I couldn't put my finger on anything, but something about his demeanor kept rubbing me just a smidge the wrong way.

"Just answer the question," Talon snapped.

"Why?" I asked with the sudden sense I was being interrogated. The questions were starting to go beyond what anyone would be concerned about with a stranger who'd theoretically be walking out of their lives any minute now. "I already told you that you don't have anything to worry about. It's not like anyone even knows I'm here."

Which was the point, wasn't it? Why were all of them so intent on questioning me in their own ways? Sure, they may have been concerned about who they brought into their home, but if they'd actually been worried, they could have kicked me out right now. They could have dropped me at the hospital despite my original protests.

Unless they thought I'd done something worse than steal some crap from an abusive boyfriend. The massacre at the household must be all over the news by now. Had they realized I'd been coming from that direction, wondered about the blood on my shirt and my loot because of that?

Did they think *I'd* committed the murders?

SEVEN

Garrison

I WATCHED Dess cradle her hot chocolate. She seemed totally unaffected by Talon's relentless front of hostility. I'd seen people crumble under one of Talon's mere stares. This woman was a mystery, that was for sure.

I cut in again, tired of participating in a game that she seemed all too good at playing. The only reason we continued this good cop, bad cop routine was her reaction to *me.* Talon's threatening accusations didn't seem to get under her skin, but my gentle questioning did. I could see the way I unsettled her.

It was easier to get a read on how honest a person was being if their emotions were off kilter. I still couldn't quite pick apart how much of her story was true. I thought I'd caught flickers of genuine distress and shame in her expression, but was it a fraction of a larger trauma she was trying to suppress or a sign that she wasn't really all that affected?

"Where do you live in that neighborhood?" I asked. "One of us could go to your house and gather some belongings for you. If your boyfriend is as useless as it sounds like, I'm sure Talon or Julius could handle him just fine."

Dess scoffed, revealing nothing but mild distrust behind her storm gray eyes. Right now, they resembled steel—sharp and clear.

I had to cut through that steel in whatever way I could—subtle but penetrating, the way I always worked a job.

"You think I'd give away my address to four total strangers?" she asked, looking around and meeting everyone's eyes before turning her gaze back on me. Cold. Detached. Unreadable. Blaze shifted in his seat across from us but kept his mouth shut. He knew not to interrupt a gambit once it was in progress.

Talon stepped forward with the air of menace he gave off so easily, but I put out my arm, stopping him in his path. "Enough." I stepped around the island closer to Dess, my body language poised to be open and inviting. "We just want to help you, really. Even that lout does. But if you're still not comfortable, I totally get it. I'm not going to push."

Reverse psychology was absolutely a thing. In my experience, most people who'd balk at a direct question found themselves spilling the beans as soon as you told them they didn't have to answer after all, as long as you framed it right. Especially women, who were so often programmed to please.

Not Dess.

She stayed silent, her muscles stiffening as she turned her mug of hot chocolate in her hands and then took another sip. I couldn't suppress the twitch of my cock as I watched her savor the liquid, her tongue darting out to swipe the last traces from her lips, her expression briefly relaxing with apparent delight. She looked so damn sexy relishing the offering I'd made for her.

I shut down that twinge of attraction, just as she flipped the script.

"How about you explain why you brought me to your apartment instead of the hospital," she said, arching an eyebrow.

I didn't allow anything to show on my face. "Were we not allowed to be concerned?"

"I'm pretty sure a normal concerned person would have taken me to the emergency room."

Talon smacked his hand down on the island. "Now you're complaining about being here? You made it pretty fucking clear that you wanted nothing to do with any hospital."

"I think I also made it clear I wanted to be left alone," Dess shot back.

I held up my hands. "You can't expect us to leave a woman who's fainted from her injuries lying at the edge of the road. We're not some kind of psychopaths. Whenever you need to leave, the door's open to you. Hell, we can take you to the hospital after all if you want."

Years of practice allowed me to smooth out the edge that wanted to creep into my voice. What kind of game was she playing with *us*? It was starting to feel like one, and I didn't like that at all. I was supposed to be the one who ran the games around here.

How the fuck would this look to Julius and the other guys if I fell on my face in the one job they'd given me today?

Dess adjusted her stance on her stool again, and I noted the drooping of her eyelids. I'd slipped a sleeping pill into her mug—she'd blame her growing exhaustion on the accident. The more physically helpless we could keep her, the easier it'd be to hold her here while we figured out what she was really up to without giving away that we wouldn't actually let her walk out the front door.

As soon as she figured out she'd essentially been kidnapped, most of my usual strategies would become useless. You needed to generate a certain amount of good will to con a person.

"I'm still thinking about it," Dess muttered. It'd clearly taken some effort for her to speak clearly. The pill was kicking in fast now.

I cocked my head with a sympathetic vibe. "You're looking a little wiped. You *are* still healing from that crash. If you need to—"

"I'm fine," she insisted.

I raised my arms in a gesture of surrender. "Again, what you say goes. You know yourself way better than the rest of us do."

The line of bullshit I spoon-fed her didn't seem to loosen her guard in the slightest. The good cop, bad cop routine had gotten us nowhere. The kindness that I tried to show her hadn't had any effect on her.

For the first time in nearly a decade, I had no idea how to get a true read on a mark. She admitted nothing with her words or glances, other than a few tiny details that would give us no advantage.

The question ran through my mind again. Who the hell was this chick?

And why wasn't she pushing harder to get away from us? I'd been prepared for that, and she obviously didn't trust us any more than we trusted her… but she hadn't come out of the room demanding to leave immediately. She hadn't even taken me up on my supposed offer that she could walk away right now, although maybe that was because she could tell she wasn't in any state to make it very far on her own.

She took another deep swig of her drink, likely in an attempt to jar her into alertness. If anything, it'd have the opposite effect.

Her body started to sway, and her spine went even more rigid. She was definitely noticing that she wasn't at her best. I could read that much in her posture.

After taking one last gulp from the mug, Dess pushed herself to her feet. She held her legs tensed, managing to keep her balance despite the toll the sleeping pill must have been taking on her senses. "You know, maybe I do need to get some more rest. Thank you again for the hot chocolate."

"Get as much sleep as you need," I said, and Julius nodded.

She strode stiffly but quickly back to the bedroom where we'd set her up, just barely keeping it together. I still caught her teeter just as she reached the doorway. She kicked the door shut behind her.

I'd bet she'd flopped right down on the bed the second we couldn't see her. She'd been trying to keep up a front of being in control, but she'd be out like a light in a matter of minutes. Those pills were potent stuff.

Blaze started tapping away on his phone. Talon sighed, shaking the tension out of his stance and looking more like the imposing but not outright murderous guy he normally was—when we weren't out murdering people, at least.

Julius waited a few minutes and then went to the bedroom door. He opened it a crack. "Dess?"

No answer. He stepped inside, and I heard the rustle as he must have given her a shake. He came back out, shutting the door again, and rejoined us. "She's dead to the world. What did you make of her?"

My stomach sank before I answered. "I got next to nothing," I had to admit. "She's intimidated by kindness more than hostility, which might make sense if the abusive boyfriend story is true, but I couldn't even tell for sure about that. She didn't respond in a typical way to just about anything, but it was all in different atypical ways." I raked my fingers through my hair in frustration.

"Fuck." Julius rubbed his hand over his face, looking equally annoyed. And there was no one to blame but me. "Do you think she was lying about everything?"

"I don't know. If she lied, she's a *great* liar, but she didn't say anything in a way that screams 'truth,' either. It could have all been a lie."

"Or it could have all been the truth," Blaze put in.

"Yeah, that too."

Talon didn't seem to react to the news, which was par for the course, but both Blaze and Julius looked uneasy.

"At least we know her full name now," Blaze said, turning back to his phone. "Here we go. Dess Parker. It's pretty uncommon, I think—yeah, there's her driver's license photo."

He showed us the image on his screen, which was unmistakably the woman currently sleeping in the other room, maybe a year or two younger. I was hit by a jolt of surprise. Somehow I'd assumed she'd given us a fake name.

"Twenty-two years old," Blaze said, flicking through the various files he'd brought up. "No criminal record. Brief stint working for a clothing store downtown. Has a credit card that's always been paid off on time. Went to elementary and high school in the city but no sign of a college education." He frowned. "This is… this is weird."

"What's so weird about any of that?" I demanded. "Lots of us aren't brainiacs who jizz at the idea of sitting through years of boring lectures."

Blaze rolled his eyes at me and waved his phone, his leg swinging in his usual fidgety way. "That's the thing. There's *nothing* remotely weird in here. It's all very basic, very typical… I don't know. It just feels too clean to me."

"Are you suggesting she's got an entire history of false documentation set up?" Julius asked with a tone of disbelief.

Blaze held up his hands in surrender. "I don't know. Nothing about any of this looks faked either. Usually I can spot a clue or two. I guess if she's been under a boyfriend's thumb for most of her adult years, she just might not have been interacting with the outside world much."

Was it really possible that we'd kidnapped an abused woman fleeing a monster, a victim who'd just happened to end up in the wrong place at the really wrong time?

Before that question could sink in, my phone buzzed. I pulled it out of my pocket and checked the ID. My back drew a little straighter. This might be a problem too, but it was a problem in my usual wheelhouse.

"It's the client," I said. "I'll take this outside."

Julius motioned me onward. He knew as well as I did that we didn't want to take any chance at all of Dess overhearing this conversation.

I went out the door and up the steps to the scruffy enclosed backyard. Julius and Talon had built an arching greenhouse-like roof over it which I appreciated year-round for the privacy it offered, though especially during the colder winter months. During the summer, we kept a couple of panels propped open and a fan going to circulate the air. The yard was still a bit sweltering.

As soon as I'd stepped outside, I cleared my throat, deciding on what persona I'd use for this call. I always dealt with the clients, and I never used the same voice or demeanor more than once. The less our clients knew about us, how many people we had working for us, and who those people might be, the safer we stayed. We couldn't work in the shadows if they knew much more about us than our group name.

I forced my voice up an octave. "You've reached the Chaos Crew."

"Put me on with the man I spoke to last time," the man on the other end demanded.

I suppressed a laugh at his stupidity. It had always been me. I could have transitioned back into the deeper, more masculine voice I'd used before, but he didn't have control over this conversation. I did. "I'm representing the Chaos Crew today."

"I don't give a fuck who's representing them. They didn't complete their job," he spat into the phone, and I stiffened. "Something is missing from the house that should have been there."

"The Crew killed every person inside that house, per the manifest, and they didn't take anything with them," I assured him. "It was a successful job with no hiccups."

"Did they find any hidden areas in the house that weren't mentioned in the manifest?"

"Are you implying that the brief you provided was faulty?" I asked. "I certainly hope you didn't put the Crew in danger by leaving out information."

The man remained quiet for a moment, giving me the answer that I needed. There *had* been information he hadn't included in the job details they'd passed on. It didn't matter what words he spewed to deny the claim after that telling pause.

After dealing with Dess, it was almost a relief to be able to spot the lie so easily.

"I gave you all the necessary information to ensure the job was completed successfully," he snapped. "But clearly you screwed up somewhere."

I wished I had chosen a more intimidating persona, maybe channeling Talon. Too late now. "Are you going to tell me *what* exactly was missing?" I asked. My thoughts darted to all that jewelry Dess had been carrying.

But what were the chances she was a thief who'd broken into a home, found a vicious massacre there, and decided to continue with her robbery like it was nothing? And why would the client be so worked up about some pieces of jewelry anyway? It'd been expensive stuff, sure, but he'd placed more money in escrow for the job than the whole lot would have come close to being worth.

"That isn't your business," the client said. "What matters is that it's gone, and you're the only people who've left the house in the timeframe."

Jackass. How did he expect us to help him if he wouldn't even explain what the problem was?

I let my voice get clipped. "*We deliver expertly orchestrated chaos.* Our motto doesn't lie. Your instructions were to kill everyone inside the place, and I guarantee that the inside of that house was a chaotic bloodbath when the crew was finished. Nobody escaped. Those were the terms, and they were met to anyone's satisfaction. And now you're accusing us of *stealing*?"

The man hesitated. "I'm not accusing your team of anything. But something *was* taken from that house, and we will be doing a close investigation to determine who was responsible. If we find that the Chaos Crew interfered in any way that was not outlined in the contract, there will be severe consequences. For the sake of your crew, I hope that you have nothing to do with this. We aren't playing Candy Land here."

I had a snarky remark at the tip of my tongue, but he ended the call before I had a chance to launch it.

I looked down at my phone, my forehead furrowing. We hadn't taken anything from the mansion. Hell, we hadn't even *touched* anything in the place other than our bullets and blades severing all those bodies—and me patting them down for weapons and phones after. As always, we'd followed each clause in the contract, and we'd completed the task with no hitches. Julius wouldn't tolerate anything less.

Well, there'd been almost no hitches. What could we call Dess?

EIGHT

Decima

IF THE FOUR men who'd taken me into their home were at all offended that I insisted on making my own plate at dinner—acting as if I didn't want to impose on them any more than I already was—none of them called me on it. I didn't intend to let any of them touch my food or drink again.

I didn't know what had made me so tired earlier today. It could have been an aftereffect from the crash. Or it could have been something funny about the hot chocolate Garrison had given me. He might have used its deliciousness to cover up something much more ominous.

I'd only woken up just before dinner, the smell of frying chicken and garlic making my mouth water. It seemed reasonable to eat when I could to get my energy up for my escape. I was increasingly sure that as soon as I pushed the issue, it'd come to a fight. I had to be totally ready for that fight, or I'd end up even worse off than I was now.

When I ducked into my bedroom after dinner, I tucked bills from the rolls of cash into my pants pockets, my bra, and even the waist of my panties—as much as I could carry without my cargo being noticeable through my clothes. I didn't want the men to have any clue I intended to make a break for it until the last second. The jewelry I'd have to leave behind, but it'd have been a hassle to pawn it anyway. Cash was simple and straightforward, like any good mission should be.

I lingered for a moment over my tote bag. Leaving behind my other change of clothes was no big deal—I could buy or steal more—but a strange sadness prodded my chest when I thought of abandoning the stuffed tiger.

Ridiculous. It wasn't as if I could stuff *that* in my bra and have no one notice. A fuzzy toy wasn't exactly necessary to any of my plans.

I pushed the unexpected ache deep down inside me like the other random emotions that rose up now and then and ambled back into the living area, acting as casual as I could.

Four pairs of eyes tracked my movements the moment I emerged. I wasn't getting away with much at this exact moment. I'd need to examine the door and the windows more closely and position myself when I asked about leaving so I could spring for my best escape route as soon as they showed their hand.

For the time being, I sat down on the sofa in front of the TV and groped around for the remote. There *had* to be information about the murders on the news, right? Maybe I'd hear something that would help my mission, like potential suspects or evidence police had uncovered.

I turned the TV on and flipped through the channels, watching for a newscast. I hadn't actually watched the news often. The broadcasts never showed up on my TV in the household, and whenever I'd been in the middle of an assignment and had access to a TV, channel surfing had felt like an unprofessional distraction.

Even now, as my finger tapped the button, Noelle's voice echoed in the back of my head. *When you're on a mission, nothing matters but that mission. Keep your eyes on the prize.*

The muscles in my hand twitched, and I almost put the remote down. But looking for news *was* part of my current mission, even if Noelle hadn't assigned it to me. I wasn't getting to the prize of destroying the people who'd slaughtered the household until I knew more about them.

Blaze plopped down on the sofa a couple of feet across from me. "Planning to watch anything in particular?"

"I feel like I've been out of touch for days," I said. "I figured I'd check the news and see if I missed anything important."

"Ah, you want channel 26, then. All news, all the time." He grinned.

I tapped in the numbers, and the screen immediately flashed to a view of some kind of political press release room. The newscaster's voice droned over the visual. "The surprising outcome of Bill 401 is sweeping through the nation. Damien Malik, with the tie-breaking vote, sent this historic bill into effect. Now, we as a nation must ask ourselves: What does this mean for us? We can expect—"

We could expect me not to give a shit. I leaned back, waiting for the story to switch.

Over the next half hour, the reporters covered a business merger, an overseas military operation, some storefront vandalism, and a rabid raccoon. Apparently all of those things were more pressing than a dozen people brutally slaughtered in their home. I frowned at the TV. They *were* going to get to the household eventually, weren't they?

"If you're looking for something specific, you could borrow my laptop," Blaze offered, gesturing to the computer on the coffee table.

I eyed the device and then glanced at the man beside me. I'd rarely had unrestricted access to a private computer, but I knew that one internet search could bring up thousands of results. But should I be suspicious of his motives?

"If you wouldn't mind," I said.

He snatched it up before I could reach for it myself and handed it over with one of his wide smiles. "Anything for a pretty lady."

A prickle ran down my spine at the flirty compliment, but he didn't move any closer, and his tone was more playful than… than the low, sweet tones in my memory that made my hackles come up. I smiled back mildly, containing my adverse reaction, and opened the laptop.

Sliding over on the sofa, I tucked myself into the corner and surreptitiously angled the screen so none of the men in the room should be able to see it. Then I quickly typed in the city name and the word "massacre."

Nothing came up except a couple of results about a short story competition years earlier where one of the winners included that word in the title. Was I being too poetic about it? I switched to the more basic "murders."

That got me a bunch more articles, but none of them were from the past couple of days. Knitting my brow, I found the option to sort by date, but that didn't help either.

What the hell? How could no one have reported on this yet? Had nobody noticed the carnage after a whole day?

I guessed it was possible. I had no idea how much the people in the household normally interacted with anyone outside, who might have come by in the past twenty-four hours and discovered the bodies. But still…

An apprehensive twang ran through my nerves. It didn't feel *right*. And my instincts were honed by years upon years of experience with dangerous situations.

"If you're having trouble finding something, I'm happy to lend a hand," Blaze said in the same light tone. "Not to brag, but I can track down just about anything on the internet. And it'd be a pleasure to be of service." He winked at me.

Another unwelcome shiver shot down my spine. Where was he trying to take this?

"That's all right," I said. "I can manage."

I'd braced for another overture, but he just shrugged, still smiling and got out his phone. He might have liked attempting to flirt, but he didn't seem to be all that committed. My pulse stopped thumping quite so fast.

It was fine. He wasn't like—like the one who'd—

I shoved that thought aside before my gut could completely clench up and studied the screen again. Maybe if I modified by region? Tried a different word like "killings" or "slaughter"? I even added "household" to the string, as if the people who'd trained me were likely to use that term with anyone outside our home.

Nothing relevant popped up for any of that. I sucked my lower lip under my teeth, just barely restraining myself from giving in to the urge to nibble at it—a bad habit Noelle had badgered me about for years. I hadn't hidden my reaction quite well enough, though.

Garrison sauntered over to the sofa, stopping behind Blaze but watching me. "You look awfully bothered by what you're seeing, Dess."

He had more snark in his tone than concern. I contemplated him as my fingers moved over the keys through the processes I'd learned to clear my search history. As perfect as his kindness earlier had been, it'd vanished in the time I'd been asleep, so I had to assume he'd been faking that reassuring persona. I couldn't tell if this was the real him or some other front he was putting on, though.

Well, if he liked to snark, let's see how he reacted to having it thrown right back at him.

"What, your face?" I retorted, looking him over. "I imagine you get that reaction a lot."

That couldn't be less of the truth, and he probably knew it. The sandy blond hair that fell in tousled waves gave him a beachboy vibe, and the rest of him—broad shoulders with an understated strength that wasn't as spectacular as Julius's brawn or Talon's sculpted form but more impressive than the average guy—wasn't exactly hard on the eyes either.

And when his lips curled with a hint of a smirk, a flicker of adrenaline shot through my system that wasn't entirely unpleasant.

"You'll be comforted knowing that my face has never been called bothersome before," he said.

I raised my eyebrows as if in disbelief. "I guess your company hasn't been very honest with you, then."

Blaze cut into our conversation, leaning forward and reaching for the laptop. "What *are* you looking up?"

"Nothing now." I tossed it back to him and got up, stretching my arms as if I was bored with the conversation but taking the opportunity to meander a little closer to the door.

The second Blaze flipped open the laptop, my gaze darted to him. He aimed one of those bright grins at me as if he was enjoying showing off. "Easy enough to find out for myself."

Wait. He couldn't—

But he was tapping away on the keys, his gaze sharpening into an intentness I'd only witnessed briefly before. Cold fingers clamped around my stomach. All at once, I was sure he could dig up my searches no matter how thoroughly I thought I'd erased them.

If he found them, he'd know where I'd really been last night. Or at least that I'd been involved in something much more horrifying than a spat with a cruel boyfriend.

Whether these men knew more about the massacre than they'd let on or not, I was screwed. If they *did* know about them, I was super screwed.

I backed up a step, my pulse racing twice as fast as before. This wasn't how I'd meant things to go.

"Here we are," Blaze said cheerfully, and then his eyebrows drew together. His gaze leapt to me with a look that was unmistakably startled—and far too knowing.

Shit.

Pure instinct, driven by panic and self-preservation, sent me bolting toward the front door. A shout went up behind me. Talon charged after me. He reached me before I made it there, snatching my arm and spinning me around.

Thankfully, he'd grabbed my injured side, leaving my fully functional arm free. My well-honed body leaned into the momentum and jabbed my opposite elbow into his face. He dodged that blow only to step straight into the path of my ramming knee.

I caught him in just the right spot that pain spasmed in his expression and his grip on my arm loosened. Not much, but enough that I could yank free.

Julius had already moved to block my way to the door. With a fresh burst of adrenaline thrumming through my veins, my gaze locked on the nearest window, in the kitchen area. I hurtled toward it, ignoring the throbbing that was already spreading through my bruised ribs at the exertion.

I leapt onto the counter without breaking stride and flipped over to slam both my heels into the glass. It didn't budge. *Come on.* I whipped my feet toward it even harder, and with a cracking sound, a line formed down the middle of the pane.

Before I could shatter the glass completely, two pairs of hands clamped on my body and dragged me off the counter.

I flailed out with my good hand, my elbows, my knees, and my feet, all seeking the most vulnerable spots I could strike. The throbbing in my side expanded into a piercing agony that made my breath catch, but I couldn't afford to stop. In my line of work, stopping usually meant dying.

My knuckles caught Talon in the throat. One of my knees clocked Julius across the cheek so hard he grunted, and his hands shifted. I tried to squirm free, intent on making it back to the window and the small hope of freedom it offered.

But the stomp of my foot into Talon's calf, hard enough to fracture bone on a good day, landed weaker because of the pain searing through my torso. I had an opening when I could have gotten a stranglehold on Julius and maybe even broken his neck—but on my bad side, where my wrist screamed the second I swung it into action.

I let out a grunt of my own, my focus wavering, and Talon slammed his taut arms around me from behind. He pinned both of my arms to my sides in an iron grip. I pushed and flailed against him, but he managed to hold me so my heels only clipped his legs without doing any real damage while my ribs felt as if they were stabbing right into my lungs.

"Nice try," he grumbled in my ear, "but you're not going anywhere."

He swiveled me to the side just as Garrison shoved a wooden chair with wide arms into place next to us. Talon shoved me into it, using his knee to hold my legs down, bracing my forearms against the arms of the chair. All I could move was my head, and his was too far away for me to butt it, as much as I'd have liked to right now.

He wasn't just strong. This asshole knew how to fight—*really* fight. But if I hadn't been injured...

I met his eyes with a glare, and he gazed back at me with no sign of anger or even irritation. Suddenly I was sure even his supposed frustration with me this morning had been as much an act as Garrison's kindness. His pale blue irises held nothing but cool indifference, like this was just a job to him rather than a matter of survival like it was for me.

I should have been chilled, but the sight woke up something else inside me. I was abruptly hyperaware of the flexing of his hands against the bare skin of my arms, of all the power emanating from his pose over me. Of how close he was leaning—not close enough for me to launch another attack, no, but enough that his breath grazed my face with each exhale.

He was breathing a little raggedly. As strong as he was, I'd given him a challenge even with my injuries. And he'd given me a hell of a challenge too.

An unexpected heat pooled between my legs, a sensation I'd never felt before except when I touched myself there. The image passed through my mind of him leaning even closer, pressing all of that sculpted power right against me, and I didn't shy away from it. If anything, my body welcomed the idea.

I'd never wanted a man before. Except maybe that one—for the short time before I'd realized the poison that lay behind his sweet words. Talon wasn't like that at all. He was pure, brutal strength, on display without excuses or any kind of veneer, and something about that called to the deepest part of me.

As Talon stared down at me, I thought something shifted in his gaze—a flash of what I almost imagined was his own arousal. Then Julius strode into view, holding several plastic ties in his hands, and I jolted back to my horrifying reality. I was a captive here, way more so than I'd been a few minutes ago.

The leader of the group wrapped the ties around my wrists and then my ankles, binding me to the chair. He tugged the plastic strands tight enough that they bit into my skin—or in the case of my wrist in the brace, enough to make the sprain ache. He wasn't going easy on me, that was for sure.

As soon as the restraints were in place, Talon stepped back—and pulled out a pistol. I hadn't even been able to tell he was wearing one. He pointed it at me, aimed straight at my forehead, his expression back to its impervious blankness.

No matter what other feelings I might have briefly stirred in him, I had no doubt that he'd put a bullet in my brain without a second's hesitation.

Garrison stood next to him, his arms folded over his chest. Blaze came up at Talon's other side, his laptop still open, clutched in his hands, carrying the evidence I'd inadvertently provided him with.

Julius stepped back from the chair, swiping his hand across his cheek. A bruise was already purpling the skin there. I held in a smile of satisfaction. If I was going to go down, at least I'd left a mark on these pricks.

When he spoke, Julius's voice was hard and unrelenting. "It's time that you tell us exactly what you were doing last night."

NINE

Decima

AS THE FOUR guys stood around me in the kitchen, their silence ate away at my confidence. Talon had a gun, Julius and Garrison both looked ready to kill me first and ask questions later, and Blaze… well, Blaze looked excited, bouncing his weight from foot to foot.

I should have strategized or, at the very least, taken a moment or two to *think* rather than making a kneejerk response. Noelle preached to always act, never react. Maybe I could have come up with some excuse to buy me more time to make a proper run for it. Maybe I should have known not to use the laptop at all, realizing Blaze would be savvy enough to crack the typical protections.

My jaw tightened as my frustration with myself and the situation I'd gotten myself into grew. I'd made too many poor decisions within the span of a few minutes, and those decisions could have deadly consequences.

"Are you going to say anything?" Julius asked, his voice taking on an even more commanding tone.

Would they torture me? I couldn't tell how far these men would go for the information they wanted. I cleared my throat and allowed my lower lip to tremble.

"Don't you fucking dare," Garrison said sharply, and my eyes shot up to meet his. "We're not going to fall for waterworks."

I couldn't suppress the feeling that my entire life—everything I'd ever been trained to do—had been for nothing. It didn't matter now. I was tied to a chair, a gun pointed at my head, and I might never get my chance to avenge the household.

Garrison might not be buying the innocent act, but that didn't mean the others wouldn't be swayed. In my experience, few men were totally unaffected by a woman in tears, one way or another.

"I don't know why you have me here," I said, willing a quaver into my voice. "Please."

"How did you know about the murders?" Blaze asked, pointing to the laptop's screen.

"I don't—"

"Don't fucking lie to us." Julius leaned over my chair, bracing his hands next to my elbows. His tone refused any argument, deadly serious. "There's no way in hell some regular woman off the street knows how to fight like you just did. So don't try to pretend that's what you are."

His aura of authority wafted over me, and a tingle ran across my skin. I had the ridiculous urge to rise up to meet him, to soak up all that commanding confidence. I couldn't remember ever being in the presence of a man who wielded more control than he could with just a few sentences.

But I couldn't let him control me, even if some stupid part of my brain was swooning.

His eyes, blue like Talon's but a much deeper shade, held mine unwaveringly. I had the unnerving sensation that he could read what was going on inside my skull. That he might even be able to sense the way my panties had just dampened, damn them.

I sure as hell hoped not.

"You don't have anything to say for yourself?" he asked.

Since silence wasn't working, I tried turning his cool confidence back on him. "I don't owe you answers any more than I did before," I replied, hardening my expression. "Even less now, really. Am I supposed to trust you after you tied me to a fucking chair? Dream on."

Blaze let out a low whistle, and Garrison shot a glare at him.

To my surprise, Julius straightened up. His expression shifted from menacing to contemplative.

"You make a fair point," he said. "We're asking a lot from you. So maybe it's only fair that we explain a little more about why we're asking these questions at all. But what I'm going to tell you could put our jobs and our lives at stake. Once I've told you, we can't let you leave until we're sure of *you*."

Interesting. I arched my eyebrows at him. "Since it doesn't look like you have any intention of letting me leave anyway, I'll take that deal."

The corner of his mouth twitched—with the start of a smile or a frown? I couldn't tell, he smoothed it out so quickly. The man had iron control over himself as well as everyone around him.

"All right then." He tipped his head toward the other men. "It's possible you've already guessed that we're not actually landscapers. We're cops, and right now we're investigating a horrific murder spree that took place in a house not that far from where you had your accident last night. Actually, we saw you while we were on the way to the scene of the crime after a neighbor called in a report of hearing gunshots fired."

A little of the tension in my chest loosened. "You're with the police?" That fit a lot of what I'd observed about them that hadn't made total sense before. And if it was true, it also meant that I was a little safer than if they'd been mass murderers or some other kinds of psychopaths themselves. Cops could still push people around, and from what I'd learned in my training, you couldn't trust any of them not to be dirty, but there were limits on how violent they were likely to get.

They might happily toss me in jail and throw away the key, of course. My situation was still pretty freaking shitty.

"Undercover detectives," Julius clarified. "We caught you speeding away from the scene of what turned out to be a major crime, with blood on your shirt and what looked like stolen goods on you. And when we ran the plates on that car and contacted the owner, it turned out it'd been stolen—from someone you've never mentioned in your stories. Understandably, we couldn't let you just wander off."

They'd known about the massacre and the stolen car the entire time I'd been here. Somehow I wasn't surprised. I did have to point out, "I'm pretty sure kidnapping is still illegal no matter how many badges you have."

Garrison didn't look quite so peeved anymore. His lips curved into a cocky smile. "When you're undercover, you don't have to follow the rules quite so closely."

I drew my gaze back to Julius, since he was the one in charge. "Why didn't you tell me all this to begin with? Why make up all those other stories?"

"A lot of people in trouble freeze up when they're around cops," Julius said. "We wanted to see if you'd let anything slip when you weren't on your guard. Obviously that hasn't worked out so well. So here we are." He paused. "We have reason to believe that the perpetrators of those murders are still on a rampage, looking for something they expected to find in the house but didn't. Seeing as you had all that fancy jewelry on you, you might be not just connected but another target as well."

I kept my expression impassive, but inside I itched with confusion. If the murderers had been looking for the jewelry I'd grabbed, why wouldn't they have taken the stuff before they'd left? They'd been gone by the time I did my search of the house. It wasn't as if the stuff I'd taken had been hard to find.

But then, just because these guys were cops didn't mean they had everything right. He might have completely made up that part in the hopes of intimidating me into spilling my guts.

"You obviously have *some* connection to the murders," Blaze piped up, his usual energy almost subdued as he studied me. "Your searches prove it. You were trying to find news on a massacre that happened in this city in the past twenty-four hours. There haven't been any other murders in the past three days, and this situation hasn't been publicized yet."

"Yeah," Garrison said, raising his chin. "There's no way you could know about it unless you had an inside scoop. So why don't you get on with explaining yourself, now that Julius has laid everything out for you?"

I wet my lips, absorbing all the new information *they'd* given me. I couldn't tell them the truth—that was out of the question. But I had to tell them something they'd believe. Something that wouldn't set me up for jail time.

I could easily retract some lies and replace them with new ones. Now that so much more was out in the open, I could concoct a ruse that better fit the circumstances—one that nobody would suspect.

And now that I knew who they were, maybe I shouldn't be trying to leave. They were cops with access to police resources—things like running plates, which I couldn't have done on my own. And they'd already made progress toward identifying the murderers. If I stayed with them, I'd get information that I wouldn't be able to find on my own.

It'd be awfully useful to have two strong fighters, a tech genius, and a skilled manipulator doing a bunch of my legwork for me. Noelle always taught me to utilize every available advantage. This could be a *huge* advantage. They might lead me right to the perps, and then I could deal out my own brand of justice.

"Will I go to jail for stealing?" I asked, letting myself nibble at my bottom lip so I'd appear anxious.

Julius shook his head, pulling a second chair in front of me and sitting with his legs spread wide. "We handle bigger matters. We don't give a shit about petty crimes."

"You won't report it?"

"We won't."

I didn't necessarily believe them, but if they tried to prosecute me later, I could deny this conversation had ever happened. I nodded slowly, compiling a story out of details I'd used on various jobs in the past, tweaking it to fit the unique situation.

"I did go to the house where the murders happened," I whispered.

"Looking back, I wish I hadn't, but I can't change it now. One of my friends lives—*lived*—there, and she said I could come and stay whenever I needed somewhere to go."

"Why did you want to stay?" Julius asked.

I forced a pained look into my eyes. "I know you saw some of my scars. I didn't lie about having a boyfriend with a temper."

Julius motioned for me to continue. "So you went to the house to escape him?"

I dipped my head, a piece of hair falling into my face. "Yes. I'd finally worked up the courage—I was going to hide out there until I figured out how to get my own place where he wouldn't find me—but I didn't know what had happened there until I got inside. My friend's parents didn't like me, so I always snuck in by going over the wall and through the back door. I slipped inside last night, and that's when I found… that's when—"

The sadness that filled my voice as I envisioned Anna gasping for air was no act. I cut myself off, my throat constricting. My mind flashed to the faceless woman who could have been Noelle, and the sense of loss deepened.

"Your friend's name?"

"Anna," I said, because it was easier to sell a lie when you mixed some truth into it. "She—she was dead with the rest of them."

Julius's brow furrowed, his gaze unrelenting. "Your friend offered you a place to stay, so you went to her house, found her dead, and decided to rob her and her family?"

When he put it like that…

I ducked my head as if I was ashamed of myself. "I had nowhere to go. No money, and nothing but a bag of clothes. I didn't have a *choice.* My friend would have wanted to help me in any way she could, but she died. What use would a few things have been to a dead person, anyway? I saw all that blood, all the bodies—and I just panicked. I hardly even realized what I was doing. I don't know what else to tell you."

"Then you stole a car," Garrison pushed.

"My boyfriend taught me how so I could help with some of the crap he was mixed up in," I said in a small voice. "I'm not saying I made great choices that night. I was in so much shock—but that's no excuse. I'm sorry I didn't explain all of this earlier, but I had no idea what you guys wanted with me. I wish I'd stuck around and called the police when I found them. If there's anything I can do now to help catch the psychos who did that, I'll do it. Anna and the rest of them—they deserve justice."

The men looked at one another, their expressions unreadable as they silently communicated amongst themselves. I could lie about my history and backstory all day long, but the truths I'd incorporated—the way I genuinely cared for Anna and Noelle, my determination to avenge their deaths—should have helped sell the story.

"It sounds like you've endured a lot," Blaze said before anyone else had the chance to speak, and a flicker of relief passed through my chest. He sounded convinced.

I only nodded weakly in response.

Julius was still frowning. "How did you fight us so well?"

Good point. Even held back by my injuries, it had to be clear that I was well-trained to men who'd done plenty of training themselves.

"Mixed martial arts starting when I was ten years old," I said with a shrug. "Competitive MMA when I turned twelve, added karate to the mix when I turned fifteen."

"Then how did your boyfriend manage to beat the shit out of you?" Garrison asked.

His insensitivity made my anger flare. "You're an insensitive prick, aren't you?" I snapped at him, the way I thought a woman in my circumstances might. "I got into training because I thought it'd help me—my father used to—" I shuddered. "But I guess it backfired on me. That's how I met my boyfriend—he was one of my instructors. He was always a little better, a little stronger than me."

The one benefit to my injuries was that I could hope these men hadn't been able to tell just how unlikely that'd be when I was at my full capacity.

"All right," Julius said. He didn't look particularly affected by my sob story, but he wasn't trying to pick it apart anymore either. I'd call that a win. He took a step closer, looming as he peered down at me. "We can't let you just wander off. Like I told you, we can't risk you compromising our covers. You could be a key component in our investigation—and it's possible the murderers are out for your blood too. You'll be safer with us anyway."

I glanced down at my wrists and tested my luck. "Are you going to keep me tied up the whole time?"

Julius did offer a hint of a smile then. "I think we can give you that much freedom. Just be aware that if you try to make a break for it again, we will intervene."

Something in his words cued Talon to put his gun back in his concealed holster. Julius reached for the ties, pulling a knife from his pocket. I held myself totally still as the gleaming blade sliced through the plastic.

When my first wrist released, I swiveled my hand, loosening the stiff muscles. How much could I convince them to loop me in on their progress with the case? I had to work this advantage in every way I could while I had the opportunity.

"I might be able to help your investigation," I suggested as the tie around my wrist brace fell away and Julius bent down to tackle my ankles.

He glanced up at me, no less commanding when he was lower down. "How do you expect to do that?"

I groped for a reasonable proposition. "It was dark when I got to the house, and obviously I didn't stick around to pay a lot of attention to the place. Maybe if I could look around the property in the daylight, I'll see something that you all missed. I've been there enough times to have a pretty good memory of how it should be."

Julius let out a thoughtful hum. "We'll see. We've definitely had enough excitement today. Talon, take her back to her room for the night."

Talon moved forward to escort me. I leapt up from the chair and to the side before he could outright grab me. "I can walk on my own." I turned to look at Julius again. "And I *could* help you. I want the bastards responsible to rot in hell."

Julius didn't respond as Talon motioned me toward my bedroom. He might not be aiming his gun at me, but we both knew he had it on him. The other three were probably armed similarly. Gritting my teeth, I strode back to the bedroom one step ahead of him.

The second I walked inside, Talon closed the door behind me. Then came the unmistakable sound of the lock clicking into place.

They didn't trust me all that much, not yet. I'd just have to find a way to change that.

TEN

Blaze

EVEN FIRST THING in the morning at this time of year, the roofed backyard was hot enough to send sweat trickling down my back. I wanted to pace to let out my restless energy, but walking around only made the heat more uncomfortable.

Nothing was as uncomfortable as the tension between the four of us, though. I couldn't remember the last time that the Chaos Crew had been so divided in our opinions, but a pretty girl and an angry client seemed to bring out our different moral compasses.

"Toss her to the client, and let him handle the little thief. Wiping our hands of her will be the best thing we could do," Garrison said, shaking his head. "What's she worth to us anyway?"

"It doesn't matter what she's *worth,*" Julius said evenly. "It's a question of what's justified. If we believe her story, then she barely had anything to do with the job. It might look worse for us to admit someone got past our surveillance to see the scene of the crime. And whoever hired us for the job, they're not likely to want witnesses walking around."

Despite what he was saying, I could hear the doubt in his words.

Dess could be a threat to us as much as to the client, depending on how much exactly she'd seen. Julius put the security of the crew above all else.

"*If* we believe her," Garrison said in a scoffing tone.

"She hasn't acted as if she knows we had anything to do with it," I had to point out. Dess hadn't exactly warmed up to us in the past day, but we hadn't given her much of a chance to. She hadn't seemed scared of any of us—the opposite, really. I'd rarely seen anyone *less* nervous when faced with Talon's physical prowess and icy gaze.

Garrison grimaced at me, which meant he couldn't argue against that specific statement. That fact didn't stop him from going on, though. "You heard her. She stole from her friend after finding her dead. Do we really want a chick like that sticking around?" He took a swig from his morning mug of hot cocoa.

I didn't know how he didn't end up as wired as I was with all the sugar and caffeine he put in his system. The guy downed the stuff like an insomniac chugs coffee.

Talon grunted. "It didn't sound like she had another option. Desperate people do desperate things. But that applies to how she might act with us too. She's unpredictable."

Talon would go along with whatever Julius decided in the end, but he'd want to come to that decision quickly. The guy always preferred to deal with potential threats as swiftly as possible.

"Exactly," Garrison said. "And the client is breathing down our necks. If it's those necklaces and the cash he's after for whatever reason and he finds out we kept them from him, it'll be our heads on a platter. We're just seeing the job through."

What he said made logical sense. I couldn't deny that. But something in me balked at his suggestion anyway. The same something clenched up when I saw how pensive Julius looked as he rubbed his jaw, as if he was seriously considering Garrison's suggestion.

Dess had a quality to her that I couldn't quite put my finger on, but it intrigued me—maybe *because* I couldn't identify it. She wasn't like any other woman I'd ever come across, and I'd made the acquaintance of quite a few in my time.

I wasn't thinking just with my dick, though. She might have been mysterious, but I didn't think she was an enemy. She'd done what any of us would have done when trapped: fought to escape. Her story was tragic but understandable.

If we threw her to the client, he'd almost definitely kill her. How would we be any better than the asshole boyfriend she'd finally escaped?

I cleared my throat. "We all know what'll happen to her if we hand her over. She's going to end up dead, and possibly tortured plenty before then. All because she ended up in the wrong place at the wrong time? I thought we only hurt people who deserve it."

"It wouldn't be *us* hurting her," Garrison said with a twitch of his jaw that indicated he wasn't as indifferent to Dess's fate as he was pretending. "Would you rather we handed ourselves over instead?"

The sneer in his voice would have raised most people's hackles. I knew it was just Garrison being his usual arrogant asshole self.

"Well, personally, I'm confident that I can defend myself if the client tries to pick a fight," I replied evenly, deliberately poking at him with the words. The implication was, of course, that *he* wasn't so sure of himself.

Garrison's eyes flashed, and his jaw tightened even more. "Why would we put ourselves in danger if we can avoid it?"

I shrugged. "What part of our code makes using an innocent girl as a shield an acceptable approach? Or are you in favor of throwing out the whole code now, just because she made you feel incompetent?"

"We *think* she's innocent," Garrison retorted. "Do we really know her?" At the edge that came into his voice, I knew I'd hit another solid blow.

It was way too easy heckling Garrison. He'd never drop his mask completely, but he couldn't put on a total front with us. We might not know all of each other's dirty secrets, but we knew the biggest one that mattered right now, the one we were all mixed up in. It was good for him to remember that.

Besides, Julius was listening. I was mostly talking for his benefit.

I shot Garrison a wide smile. "I think I know her better than I know you."

His mouth snapped shut. It only took him a few seconds to loosen up his posture, taking a deep breath and regaining his composure. "Then I'm doing the job Julius hired me for well."

"Enough," Julius ordered, raising his hands. We both fell silent, our attention turning to him. He frowned, and then tipped his head toward us. "We don't know how true her current story is. We also don't know if those necklaces are even what the client was worried about. Acting without information—or with the wrong information—is what screws people over. We'll take her to the mansion today and see how she reacts to the crime scene."

Talon frowned. "The client could have eyes on the place now."

"The client doesn't know who we are or what we look like," Julius said. "We can play it cool, just walking by. We won't stick our necks out too far, but we'll see what she gives us. If she puts one *toe* out of line, she's gone."

Garrison sighed but nodded. Talon rubbed his hands together as if he was ready to get going immediately. Relief coursed through me. I didn't know what'd happen to Dess after today, but I'd convinced Julius for now. Which meant I had a little more time to figure out that intriguing part of her.

"Do we have any leftover pasta from dinner last night?" I asked, springing to my feet. My stomach had been growling for the last half hour, and I couldn't wait any longer. Carbs were the fuel for the energy I couldn't help expending even when I was sitting still—well, relatively still.

Julius's mouth curved into an amused grin. He gestured me toward the door. "It's in the fridge. We all know better than to get between you and your noodles."

I snorted and trotted down the steps to the safe-house apartment. When I reached the fridge, I paused, the door to the bedroom we'd stuck Dess in drawing my gaze.

Our guest deserved some breakfast too, didn't she? Although somehow I suspected pasta first thing in the morning wouldn't be to her tastes.

I strolled to her door and knocked, turning the lock in sync.

"What?" she said, sounding alert enough to reassure me that I hadn't woken her up.

I peeked inside. She hadn't turned on the overhead light, so the only illumination came from the small window at the top of the wall. Dess sat on the bed at the edge of the stream of sunlight, one leg crossed and the other pulled up next to it, providing her chin a place to rest. She considered me with obvious wariness. Her long black waves cascaded down her arms and brushed her raised leg, where her toned muscles showed through the fitted sweats.

With legs that looked like that, I'd fight for her to stay here forever.

"Good morning," I said. "I thought you might like some breakfast. Come out whenever you're ready."

Leaving the door open, I ambled back to the kitchen, dumped the garlic chicken linguine onto a plate, and shoved it into the microwave. By the time I'd finished tapping on the controls, Dess had emerged into the main room of the apartment.

She glanced at the other guys, who'd just come back in, and then at me. "I wouldn't mind breakfast. What are you offering?"

I'd already looked through the cupboards. Steffie updated our safe-house stashes on a quarterly rotation, so while we didn't have much of anything fresh on hand, there were plenty of non-perishable options. "Since I'm assuming you're not a weirdo like me who would eat pasta ten times a day if I could, there's pancake mix, frozen waffles, and a couple different kinds of cereal." We'd thawed the freezer milk for the latter yesterday.

Dess cocked her head. "Cereal sounds fine. Point me to it, and I'll get it out."

She'd learned to be cautious. Did she realize that we'd drugged her before, or was it force of habit? She'd still been shaken up by the accident when she'd accepted that mug of cocoa from Garrison yesterday.

I appreciated her sense of self-preservation even if it worked counter to our goals. As the microwave beeped, I made a quick motion. "On top of the fridge. Bowls are in the cupboard beside it. Help yourself."

I grabbed my linguine, sat on a stool at the far end of the island, and started shoveling down my fuel, pausing to savor the first bite. I might eat it mainly for the energy boost, but I enjoyed a well-prepared plate all the same.

As Dess contemplated the two boxes of cereal and tentatively poured herself some of the nut-laced, not-so-sugary kind Julius favored, Julius and Talon drifted over. Julius took the cereal box after Dess finished with it, and Talon grabbed a smoothie he'd mixed earlier out of the fridge. Watching him chug it, I held back a grimace. I'd seen what he put in those things, and I'd sooner have licked the lawn out back.

Garrison sat on the sofa, watching us as he nursed the rest of his cocoa. Sometimes that was all he put in his stomach until lunch.

Dess perched on the stool a few feet over from me, braced toward the edge as if she thought she might have to spring off it at any second. I didn't need Garrison's skills with body language to pick up on the signs that she'd needed to be on guard a lot in her life before now.

She ate a couple of spoonfuls, chewing slowly and thoroughly. Her gaze dropped to my leg, which was doing its typical bounce against the rung of the stool.

"Do you ever sit still?" she asked, not with the snarky tone Garrison would have used but like she was genuinely trying to understand.

I'd spent my entire childhood being chastised for my restlessness, but I wasn't that kid anymore. I had better things to worry about.

I flashed her a smile. "Rarely. It helps me focus. All the energy I need to power this brain ends up filtering down into my body too, and I've got to let it out somehow."

She cocked her head again as she chewed. I liked the hint of playfulness that came into her face at that angle. "I guess that makes some kind of sense."

"About as much as Blaze ever does," Garrison had to remark. We both ignored him.

"I find many good ways to put it to use," I said, letting a teasing note come into my voice. I wasn't going to turn all my charm on a woman who'd just fled an abusive relationship, but a little light flirting couldn't hurt. Maybe it'd make her feel better knowing at least one man could appreciate her without beating up on her at the same time.

"Feeling better today?" I added. I took another bite of pasta and motioned to her wrist.

Dess let out a soft chuckle. "I feel kind of like I was hit by a small train."

Her tussle with Julius and Talon yesterday wouldn't have helped her healing, but she didn't sound upset about it.

"Not a large one?" I joked.

"A large one would have finished the job," she said dryly.

A laugh I didn't have to force tumbled out of me. Dess didn't strike me as a woman who put much stock in being funny. She seemed like she lived a serious life with serious problems, but she obviously didn't let it get her down too much. I liked that about her too.

"Well, I'm definitely glad you didn't meet one of those, then," I said.

"No? It seems like I've messed with your job quite a bit."

"Aw, totally worth it to have a pretty face like yours around instead of only having these lugs in sight." I winked at her and gulped the rest of my pasta. Even a heaping plate always seemed to vanish so quickly.

Dess's posture tensed. Maybe I'd said something that'd reminded her of her boyfriend's comments. I chucked my plate and fork in the dishwasher and came back to lean against the island a little closer but not *too* close to her. "But hey, having a new voice with new thoughts in the mix is an excellent addition to the crew too."

She relaxed enough for a sly glint to come into her eyes. "Does that mean you've considered my offer to check out the crime scene and see if I can help?"

"That's Julius's call. I'll let him talk to you about that. But I can promise you that *I* have no doubt I'd enjoy your company."

She gave me a bemused look as if she wasn't sure how seriously to take me. "You hardly know me."

The words echoed Garrison's point—made with much darker intentions—so well that I had to counter it. "Well, everything I know, I like."

Just then, a strand of her hair slipped from behind her ear to drift across her face. I reached automatically to tuck it back, my fingers just grazing her cheek—

Dess moved so suddenly I didn't have time to so much as catch my breath. One instant I was touching her face, the next she'd lunged forward to shove me against the edge of the island, one forearm smacking the center of my chest and the other hand at my throat. There was no humor at all in her eyes now, only fury and… and something behind it that looked more like panic. The faintest tremor ran through her limbs against my body.

"Keep your hands off me," she snarled, her voice somehow soft and yet full of the promise of death at the same time. My pulse stuttered. All at once I was sure she *could* kill me in the space of a second if she'd really wanted to.

"Get *your* hands off Blaze, or you won't be around to have any opinions on what he does with his," Julius said with just as clear a threat in his tone. He'd whipped up his gun from where he'd taken a seat at the corner of the island, and he aimed it at Dess. Talon had drawn his as well. I couldn't see Garrison in my current position, but the click of a safety from several feet behind me told me that for all his snark, he'd leapt to my defense as well.

Dess jerked her hands back to her sides, with a wince as her braced wrist brushed her side. I stared at her for a moment before yanking my gaze away. The other guys gradually lowered their guns.

"I don't want him touching me, or any of the rest of you either," Dess said tightly, her gray eyes smoldering like embers. Then she sat back down on her stool and picked up her spoon as if she hadn't just pinned me against the countertop like I was a fifty-pound child.

My throat didn't even hurt, but my pulse was still racing. Someone had definitely hurt Dess before—bad. But she had more capacity to deal out hurt than I'd given her credit for too. I swallowed hard and stepped away.

I'd spoken up for her. I really hoped that hadn't been the wrong call.

ELEVEN

Decima

IN THE MOVIES I'd watched that involved the police, they pulled up at crime scenes, flashed their badges, and strutted all over the place. But those were uniformed cops, not undercover detectives. It made sense that the men who'd essentially taken me prisoner would operate differently to avoid blowing their cover.

We circled the block in their car, with me wedged in the back between Talon, who didn't appear to care, and Garrison, who I caught flashes of irritation from, though he mostly kept quiet. They seemed to think it was better that I wasn't squashed too closely against Blaze after my demonstration of my feelings on personal space this morning.

It'd been an involuntary reaction. I was probably lucky none of them had shot me in the heat of the moment. I hadn't wanted to hurt him, not really; I'd only wanted to make sure he never touched me like that, with all those wheedling compliments and admiring glances, ever again. That he never stirred up the memories of a time when I *hadn't* been able to enforce those boundaries, and everything… everything had been horrible.

A ghost of that old pain trailed over my thighs, and I willed it away. It'd been years. It shouldn't have still affected me. Or maybe it made sense that it did, when it was the only real experience I had with getting close to a man when I hadn't been focused on how to kill him or someone around him.

Still, I could tell my reaction this morning had been an error from a strategic perspective. Blaze had been by far the friendliest out of the four men who were holding me captive. He was probably my best shot of getting the information I needed and getting away from them when the time came—if I hadn't just blown that shot.

He was sitting in the front passenger seat now, monitoring video footage of nearby streets on his laptop. From the little bit he'd said out loud to the others, I'd gathered he'd been able to hack into the city's street cams.

Whatever he saw on them, he seemed satisfied with it. "We're good to go," he announced without looking back. He hadn't met my eyes since breakfast, as if he thought I might get just as pissed off about his gaze being on me as his hands.

Julius parked a couple of blocks away. We all got out onto the sidewalk, Garrison scooting after Talon and me rather than going out the door on his side, I guessed to keep me consistently surrounded. Lovely.

The man in charge had already given us the drill before we'd arrived. We were going to walk past the mansion's front gate and around the corner to check out one of the side walls. Any more of a circuit around the place, and we'd look suspicious. We were all wearing sunglasses and baseball caps in a variety of styles to obscure our faces, not that anyone could see much of me while I had four men who were all several inches taller than me around me.

With the June sunlight searing down over us, the dark glasses only cut down the glare, helping my ability to make out details rather than hindering my vision. As we reached the edge of the household's property, I scanned the stone wall, the vines that clung to it here and there, and the street around us.

It looked like a totally different place from the shadowy estate I'd fled across two nights ago, but my stomach clenched as we came up beside it anyway. Images from the massacre flickered through my mind, and I closed my eyes. Julius turned to look at me when I slowed, and I almost shook myself out of it, but caught myself just in time. I was playing the part of a grieving friend. He'd be more suspicious if I *didn't* seem affected.

"Sorry," I said quietly. "It's just hard, being back here, remembering what happened..."

"If she's not up to the job—" Garrison started.

Julius cut him off with a sharp tone. "We're here now." He nodded to me. "If you see anything that sticks out to you, say the word. If not, we're no worse off than when we started."

I had a feeling he'd still be annoyed that they'd taken the risk of hanging out around a crime scene they were trying to keep on the down low if I didn't come up with anything. I *needed* to show them I was a valuable asset so they'd share enough with me that I could use them too.

I got my first break as we came up on the gate. My gaze caught on a small, dark shape on the pole just outside the entrance, tucked against the fixture for the electric wires.

"There's a camera there," I said, tipping my head as subtly as I could. "I never noticed that before. It's on city property, so it couldn't have been put there by Anna's family, but it wouldn't make any sense for the city to want a view of their front drive. Maybe the murderers put it there."

"Why would they do that?" Julius asked.

I braced myself for a snide expression, but his face showed genuine curiosity. Perfect. I shrugged. "I don't know. If it was important to them to kill everyone in the house, maybe they'd want to monitor the entrance to be sure no one got away?" I shot another surreptitious glance at the camera as we walked right past the pole. "It looks new, too. No bird crap on it like there is on the post around it."

Julius checked it out for as long as he could before we'd ambled by, equally careful with the angle of his head. "You have a point there. Good work. Keep going."

I couldn't tell whether they'd been aware of the cameras already or I'd pointed out something new, but the praise sounded as genuine as his earlier curiosity. Garrison was studying me from the corner of his eyes a little more assessingly, as if he was realizing he might have underestimated me. Yeah, I'd call that good work.

The perps had been good with their work too, but then, I'd already known that. After we rounded the corner, I almost missed the subtle telltale signs. When my attention snagged on them as I studied the wall, I peered closer for a few beats and then dropped down as if I needed to tighten the shoelace on my sneakers.

"What are you doing?" Garrison asked, but without quite as much snark as before. He couldn't help being curious too.

I suppressed a smile. "I just wanted to give you a chance to look too without it being too obvious why we're stopping. This works, right? I think this might be the spot where the murderers got onto the property. You can see a couple of places where the vine's pulled off just a little—that happens sometimes when I'm climbing over, but I was on the other side last night. And there's kind of a scrape mark on one of the stones near the top, just a small one."

"What makes you think that had anything to do with the murderers?" Blaze asked from behind me. I couldn't see his face, but he didn't sound as tense as I'd have expected speaking to me.

I straightened up, and we started walking again. "I could be wrong. It just seems pretty high up for it to have been someone simply bumping into it. And the vines would have grown back unless they were disturbed pretty recently. I don't think people were climbing into the property very often."

The scuff had also shown the faintest hint of the tread of a shoe, but showing *that* much perceptiveness might make these guys suspicious rather than impressed.

And they did seem to be impressed. A trace of a smile had touched Julius's lips. Talon let out a low chuckle. Garrison kept his mouth shut, which at this point I counted as a win. Blaze was tapping something into his phone behind me at a pace that sounded eager.

"You've got keen eyes," Julius said. "Where'd you pick up observational skills like that?"

Okay, so maybe he was impressed *and* suspicious. An answer leapt to my tongue. "I guess all the physical training I did taught me to think on my feet. It's a lot more than just strength and fitness, the instructors always liked to say. You have to anticipate your opponents' moves in advance as much as you can." That wasn't even a lie.

I hesitated as if embarrassed to admit the rest, which was totally made-up. "And, you know, living with my dad and then my boyfriend… I had to stay on my toes, keep alert to their moods and any clues about what they were getting up to so I knew how to avoid trouble as much as possible. Not that it helped me all that much in the long run." I ducked my head and rubbed my elbow.

The tapping behind me stopped momentarily. "You got away from them in the end," Blaze said softly, and it hit me that I'd been forgiven. At least by him. The knowledge sent a weird flutter through my chest.

Julius didn't argue with my story. I couldn't help pressing my advantage. I'd coughed up some intel for them—now they owed me.

"So," I said as we meandered on along the long stretch of the side wall, "do you have any idea *why* this happened? I mean, some of the people Anna lived with could be jerks, but—I can't imagine—for someone to kill them all like that… *She* never hurt anybody."

Garrison made a scoffing sound, his usual attitude returning. "I don't think you knew your 'friend' all that well."

"What do you mean?"

"All those people definitely weren't a family," he said in an almost gleeful tone, as if he enjoyed the possibility that he'd horrify me with his revelation. "And they were mixed up in all kinds of shady shit. Human trafficking would be at the top of the list."

"Garrison," Julius said with a warning in his voice, and the younger guy had the decency to look chagrinned.

I was too busy reeling from his comment to appreciate seeing him chided. Human trafficking? The household? In all the work I'd done for them and with my trainers, I'd never seen any hint of that kind of activity.

"That's ridiculous," I couldn't help saying. It must have been stories made up by our enemies, the ones we'd been working so hard to protect ourselves against. Maybe even the same pricks who'd ended up slaughtering everyone else in the house.

Garrison just grunted. I'd cut off the information supply instead of opening it up. I had to turn the momentum of the conversation around quick.

"If you think that, you must have found out a bunch about them and who they supposedly worked with or whatever, right?" I said. They'd said someone was sniffing around about missing items from the house. "You must have an idea already of who did it."

"Not something we can share with a bystander," Julius said, his tone firm. "That sort of information is classified."

They definitely had suspects. "I'm hardly just a bystander anymore," I pointed out. "I might not have known much about what went on around Anna, but I talked with her pretty often. Sometimes she mentioned people who'd come around. If you give me a description or a—"

"What part of 'it's not happening' do you not understand?" Garrison snapped.

I was pretty sure he was just sore about the fact that Julius had laid down the law. "I'm *trying* to help."

"And we'll let you know if you can offer more assistance than you already have," Julius insisted.

We were getting close to the corner of the property. "This is the spot," Talon remarked in his cool, deep voice, the first time he'd spoken since we'd left the car. Maybe even since we'd gotten into it. I was way too aware of his muscular frame just inches from my own body. His voice wasn't as commanding as Julius's, but it drew my attention all the same. My mind kept tripping back to the startling hunger he'd stirred low in my belly when he'd leaned over me in the chair.

"The spot for what?" I asked, refusing to let his presence distract me.

As we kept walking, our pace slowing just a little, Julius fished a plastic bag out of the leather messenger bag he was carrying. "I know you were in a tough spot, but you have plenty of cash. I don't think you need the jewelry you grabbed. My suggestion is that you leave it here so that there's no chance of the murderers tracking you down. If they are looking for those items, you're better off without them."

My hackles rose. "You went through my things again?"

"Only to give them back to you." He handed the plastic bag to me. "I don't see any cameras right here. No one but us would know how the jewelry ended up in the yard. It's your decision, but I recommend you take my advice. It'll also mean we have no evidence we could bring against you in court."

He'd promised they wouldn't arrest me for robbery—but of course I couldn't trust a promise from cops, especially ones who played as fast and loose with the law as this bunch did.

My fingers tightened around the plastic. But the necklaces inside meant nothing to me. I didn't even know who they all belonged to. I did still have the cash, currently tucked into my pockets.

And that point about no evidence against me was pretty compelling.

We'd almost reached the corner. I met Julius's eyes, and could see plainly in them that I had to do this if I ever hoped to get them on my side.

Let this gesture buy me a sliver of trust.

I lowered my hand and swung my arm upward at just the right angle to send the bag sailing over the wall without the gesture being too obvious. Because maybe there were cameras even *I* hadn't spotted. My loot thumped to the ground on the other side.

"There," I said, picking up my stride and forcing the men to walk a little faster around me. "Now let's catch the assholes who killed my friend."

TWELVE

Decima

AS I WALKED with the men back to the car, my mind spun through the possibilities. I couldn't tell whether I'd gained any real trust by abandoning my stash of stolen jewelry. Julius was stonewalling any attempt I made to find out more about their potential suspects, which to be fair was probably what his job required. I'd hoped he'd be more flexible on that policy like he had with certain others, but it'd hardly been a guarantee.

For now, I also had a little more freedom than when I was shut up in their basement apartment, which was where I had to assume we'd head right back to if I didn't come up with another idea quick.

What would I want to do with this freedom? Where would I want to go?

My thoughts drifted to the few contacts Noelle had introduced me to during various assignments—people she'd told me I could turn to for supplies or a little assistance, though she'd warned me never to reveal too much to them. The main ones weren't located anywhere near this suburb, and I couldn't see any easy excuses that might let me get to them without drawing too much attention from the cops around me. But there was one about a half hour's walk from here.

If I couldn't drag any information out of the guys, I might as well turn to my own sources. I might have gone to this one in the first place if it hadn't been the middle of the night. I only knew where to find him when he was at work.

It was mid-afternoon now. I could make this work. I'd *better* make it work, or what the fuck had all my training been for?

I rubbed my mouth as if I was thinking hard and then spoke up. "I don't know if what I saw around the house was helpful, but if it was at all, we could try retracing the route I took to get to the house the other night. Maybe something else will jump out at me that could be connected."

Garrison's head whipped toward me. "Awfully confident already, aren't you? We didn't sign up for a walking tour. What are you going to want next—your own badge?"

I narrowed my eyes at him. It was obvious that out of the four men, this one was going to be the *least* likely to ever warm up to me.

"A little less snark from you would be great," I replied.

Garrison let out a huff. "It comes with the package, sweetheart."

Julius had tipped his head to the side, considering. "We're already out here," he said. "I don't see how it could hurt. We wouldn't want to leave any stone unturned, would we, Garrison?" He shot the younger guy a pointed look over the top of his sunglasses.

Garrison grumbled under his breath, but Blaze piped up from behind me too. "It might also be good to know where Dess was coming from, in case the murderers figure out she was involved and try to track her down."

There was something odd about his tone even though he was technically supporting me, but I couldn't put my finger on it. And it didn't really matter, because Talon nodded, and Garrison shut up with a resigned sigh.

"You're at the wheel," Julius said to me.

"Okay, take the next right."

We wandered along the sidewalks, turning here and there, with me making a show of stopping to "remember" which way I'd come or to examine an occasional signpost or front yard. After several blocks, Julius deemed it safe enough for me to step right into the lead, relying only on my cap and my sunglasses to hide me. I hadn't spotted any more illicit cameras since we'd left the mansion behind, so I wasn't particularly worried.

If we ran into the murderers, I'd be happy to show them just how sorry they should be.

When the stretch of small shops I'd been watching for came into sight up ahead, I slowed down. I stopped a few doors down from my intended destination and looked around with my hands on my hips, blowing out a frustrated breath.

"No luck, huh?" Garrison just had to say.

"I'm sorry," I said, biting back the sharper words I'd have liked to aim at him. "I really thought there might be a chance… but then maybe the pricks responsible never came anywhere near here."

"This is where you live?" Blaze asked, coming up beside me. His thumb kept flicking over the screen of his phone even while he was gazing at the buildings around us.

"Not quite. I figured if I haven't seen anything yet, we're out of luck. I don't want to get *too* close in case my boyfriend—if he saw me —" I hugged myself, hating playing a wimp but knowing it'd work in my favor.

"We'd make short work of *that* prick," Talon muttered in an unexpected show of protectiveness.

"I'd still rather not have to deal with him." I winced and looked around, pretending to notice the bakery for the first time. "I could try to make it up to you for wasting your time. Moe's has the best cookies. I don't know about you, but I could really use a pick-me-up right now."

The guys exchanged a glance. "We don't need anything," Julius said, "but you can grab something for yourself. You're not going alone, of course, so if you were thinking about making a run for it—we're sticking with you until we know exactly what and who we're dealing with."

I rolled my eyes as if it didn't matter to me. "You made that clear already. Fine, come in and enjoy the heavenly sweetness. No skin off my back. You can protect me from any murderous psychos who might be lurking between the donut racks."

Blaze snorted and ignored Garrison's glare.

We ambled over to where we could see through the bakery's window. It was a popular spot, with several customers already squeezed into the small space.

Julius motioned to Talon. "Watch the back door. I'll go in with her. You two loiter outside like you do so well." He aimed a slightly wry look at the two younger men and then moved to open the bakery door for me.

When we were inside, he stationed himself next to the entrance. Perfect. He thought he had to worry about me taking off—it'd never occurred to him that I might be looking for something inside this place.

The smell really was heavenly, a mix of buttery pastry and dusted sugar. I licked my lips automatically. Weaving through the browsing shoppers, I scanned the area behind the counter and display cases for a familiar bearded face.

My heart sank. I'd just assumed he'd be here today, but of course he didn't work *every* shift. The only employee behind the counter was a heavy-set woman I'd never met.

Well, I still had to put on a show of going through with my story for being here. I got into the line of people who were ready to place their orders, tapping my pocket with its roll of cash. I didn't really want to waste any of my limited money on cookies if I *wasn't* getting a meeting with the contact out of it, but I might be able to spin this at least a little to my advantage. Noelle had let me get a cookie here the few times we'd stopped by—to keep up our appearance as customers—and I hadn't been lying about them being damn good. The only thing better was pure chocolate.

As the woman right in front of me paid for her order, another figure strode out of the back, carrying a large tray of fresh cookies. Relief washed over me at the sight of his round face with its scruffy beard. He was here after all.

I restrained a smile that would have given away that I was pleased about more than the baked goods and stepped to the side as if I wanted to check out the cookie offerings more closely.

The guy glanced up and froze at the sight of me. He looked as if he nearly dropped the cookie tray. Setting it down behind the display case quickly, he shook his head as if to clear it and met my eyes again.

The tag on his uniform said *Jay*, but I'd be willing to bet that was at least as much of an alias as *Dess* was, if not totally separate from his real identity. People who worked on the underground side of things had to be careful.

"Hey, Jay," I said quietly, leaning against the glass. "Those are some great looking cookies there."

"Let me know what you'd like, and I'll box them up for you," he said in a professional tone, and then dropped his voice so no one would hear it through the chatter of the store except me. "Are you okay? I heard—I wasn't sure if you—it's awful. I'm so sorry."

The condolences made my stomach wobble in a strange way. He was the first person I'd talked to in almost forty-eight hours who had some idea of who I was and what I'd really gone through. But I couldn't afford to get emotional with Julius watching over me.

For an instant, I wanted to blurt out everything—Anna dying in my arms, the crash, the cops. Maybe Jay could help me get away from Julius and the others. But as soon as the impulse rose up, I had to quash it.

What were the chances that this guy, who was barely out of his teens, could fend off four highly skilled cops? I'd only be getting him in deep shit. I had to stick to what I'd come for—and maybe I'd still get something more out of the undercover detectives if I had some patience. If I blew their cover right now, I could be screwing myself over too.

Jay's comments told me that even if the cops were keeping the murders quiet, news had already spread through underground channels. I dipped my head in acknowledgment and held up my arm with the wrist brace. "Thank you. I got out, but it was… Let's not talk about it." I pointed at the chocolate chip cookies with their blobs of cocoa-y goodness. "Five of those. Pack them slow. Have you heard anything about who was responsible? I didn't see them."

Jay grabbed a fresh pair of gloves and tugged one and then the other over his hands to buy time. "No idea. Sorry about that too. People are talking about how bad it was, but no one's mentioned anyone taking credit so far."

Damn it. I guessed that'd been a lot to hope for. "Does anyone seem particularly happy about all those people being gone, even if they're not claiming responsibility."

"Not that I've noticed." He paused as he folded the box he was going to put the cookies in. "I did hear through the grapevine that someone's looking for you."

My spine stiffened. "Me? Who's looking?"

"I mean, they didn't give your name. Or theirs." He cut a sly glance my way. *He* didn't know any of my names either. "But word went out through one of the more private channels that if anyone ran into you, they should pass on a message."

My heartbeat sped up. Now we were getting somewhere. "And what was that message?"

He made a face as he stacked the cookies in the box. "It didn't make a lot of sense to me. The whole thing was that 'the woman with the red polka dots wants Noelle's black-winged sparrow to visit her.' I knew that had to mean you." He nodded to my dark hair.

The woman with the red polka dots. My spirits lifted alongside my thumping pulse. I knew who that was—one of the other contacts Noelle had introduced me to. *She* must know something.

Now I'd just need to figure out a way to get to her that my current jailors would accept.

"Thank you," I said to Jay again, and moved to the cash register for him to check me out. The exhilaration of the progress I'd made took away any sting out of handing over the money.

I strode out of the shop without glancing at Julius, figuring he wouldn't necessarily want people knowing we were together anyway. Outside, I quickly ambled several feet from the bakery so Jay wouldn't be able to see my companions through the window. I didn't want *him* passing on strange stories about the new company I was keeping.

If I'd had any dreams about breaking for freedom, the cops would have banished them in a snap. Julius came up right behind me, Blaze and Garrison converging on me in the same second. Talon prowled out of the alley to round out the squad that was either my protective duty or my captors, depending on how you looked at it.

"There," I said breezily. "We all survived, didn't we? And I bought cookies for all of you anyway. You really do need to try them. I promise you'll thank me."

I popped open the box as if I wanted nothing more than to share my treat. My buoyant attitude came easily with the news I'd just gotten, even if I didn't know how I was going to take my next steps yet.

I wasn't surprised that Blaze grabbed his cookie first. He sank his teeth into it, and his eyes widened. "That's fucking fantastic! I think the walking tour was worth it."

Garrison picked up his and sniffed it before looking at it skeptically. "It smells like a goddamned waste of time to me."

"If you don't want it, I'm happy to have two," I said, holding out my hand, but he jerked it back and took a bite, if only just to spite me.

When I held out the box toward Talon, he hesitated, looking almost startled by the tiny gesture of kindness. He picked one up gingerly and looked from me to the cookie and back. Not the same as Garrison's skepticism, but a wariness nonetheless. Something about it made my gut twist despite my good mood.

Julius accepted his without any sign of how he felt about it, which I guessed was better than a refusal. I picked up the last cookie and pushed the edge into my mouth.

The buttery, chewy dough flooded my mouth alongside a punch of chocolate. A satisfied hum escaped me, maybe close to a moan. When I opened my eyes, Talon was still studying me, though the flash of heat I caught in his gaze stirred my emotions for a totally different reason.

"It's just a cookie," Garrison muttered, but I noticed he'd already polished his off and was trying to surreptitiously lick the crumbs off his fingers. Ha.

I didn't have many tools to work with here, but I'd milk what I had for as much as I could. Who knew? Maybe a little literal sweetness would soften these jaded cops enough to give me the opening I needed.

THIRTEEN

Decima

I SAT in the basement apartment with only Talon and his silent stare to keep me company.

Had it been the cookies that'd convinced the four men that I was now safe with just one guard, or maybe my willingness to throw the jewelry back to its rightful place? Whatever the case, they'd left right after dinner, and I felt three times less suffocated by masculinity as I leaned back on the well-worn sofa.

Unfortunately, their loosened security didn't get me closer to my goal. I needed to go and see the contact who'd sent out a message to me, and it wasn't like I could slip past Talon's penetrating gaze.

She must know something important, or she wouldn't have reached out like that. But I needed to go *alone.* No way were the cops letting up on my supposed protective detail completely.

Sitting for long periods had always made me irritable and impatient. Being watched by a brooding man with icy blue eyes—eyes that matched his cool demeanor and impervious personality—only amplified my restlessness. I couldn't find the people who'd murdered the household while I was stuck in here. All I could do was wait until I got an opportunity to escape that I was sure I could take advantage of in my injured state.

My eyes caught on the punching bag across the room that I'd seen Talon working over to impressive effect. If I couldn't go anywhere, I could at least put my body in motion. I shouldn't let my body go soft while I lounged around here.

I only gave myself a moment to contemplate my injuries before standing. After grabbing an elastic from my bag in the bedroom to tie back my hair, I walked over to the bag. I ran my fingers down the leather surface, finding it just as heavy and sturdy as the punching bag I'd used for years in the household.

All the pent-up feelings that I'd held inside myself for the last few days were close to erupting, and this was the only way I'd be able to lessen the strain. Working out had always been a way for me to focus, to feel in control. With my bruised ribs and a sprained wrist, my exercise would be limited, but I could still make the best of it.

I turned my back on Talon, refusing to let his unwavering gaze influence me as I worked out my frustrations. No doubt he watched me as I stretched in place, my ribs protesting. I pushed through the pain, knowing that it wasn't as important as my need to feel in control of *something* in this apartment. The ache centered me and reminded me of my strength.

I did three rounds of floor work, eyeing the bag with each crunch. I had to improvise on some routines, unable to do a full sit-up with the rib pain that stabbed through me when I tried. My pushups, usually flawlessly executed, had to be one-handed, so I could only do half my usual reps. Every move was a fight through discomfort, but once I'd completed the first stage of the workout, I gave myself a satisfied smile. I'd won the battle.

Standing, I faced the punching bag. I closed my left fist in the way I'd been trained for years to do. My other wrist throbbed when I tried to flex it beneath the brace.

No problem. Noelle had seen that I was well-trained on both sides.

I threw my first punch.

My ribs protested as I shifted my body into the strike, but it felt *good.* A sliver of tension fell from my neck and shoulders. I mocked a right punch, stopping before my fist collided with the bag, and twisted left, allowing my full force to fall behind the blow.

I lost myself to the flow of my punches, allowing my breath to flow in sync with them. As my breathing accelerated, so did my fists. I allowed the memories of the previous days to sweep through me and strengthen my blows. The anger. The denial. All of the emotions swelled within me until my strikes became the only thing keeping me grounded. The feeling of entrapment became a song for my fists to use as guidance.

I switched to a few kicks, and Anna's pain-stricken face drove my next strikes. When I returned to punching, a small part of me expected my fist to go all the way through the bag, destroying it with the frustration and grief tangled inside me.

A touch on the small of my back jarred me from my trance. I whirled with my fists up, one already flying out for a knockout blow.

Talon caught my left hand with his much larger fingers, guiding the momentum of it to the side of his face and forcing me to stumble to the side with the sheer force of the attempted blow.

I shook myself as I caught my balance, gritting my teeth in anticipation of a mocking criticism. To my surprise, I got the opposite.

"You've got good form," Talon said, without showing a hint of emotion.

I raised my eyebrows at him. "I thought you'd already figured that out."

He gave a subtle shrug. "You weren't exactly focused on technique the one time I've seen you fight."

Fair. I cocked my head. "Can I keep going?"

He nodded to my hands. "Your footwork is more suited for a dominant right hand."

That came as no surprise. I might have strengthened my left side for the sake of practicality, but my right side had always been my strongest.

"Yes," I said. "I imagine it is, considering I'm right-handed." A little impressive that he'd been able to tell just by watching me for a while, though.

He considered the brace holding my stronger wrist captive. If only he knew the things that I'd done with my left hand alone. The guns I'd used to take lives. The knives I'd wielded against my opponents.

I was *proficient* with my left hand. That was all I needed.

"I can show you a couple of adjustments that would help you switch over," he offered. "If you want."

He may not have been expressive, but I caught the undercurrent of interest in his voice now. He was impressed. Maybe only as if I were a toy he could play with to see what it could do, but I'd caught his attention enough for him to give some kind of a damn.

Was that a good thing or a bad thing?

Having seen *him* in action, I could tell he might have a few tips that would actually be useful. That was why I was still here, right? To use these men however I could?

I gave Talon a single nod. As he kneeled in front of me, I forced myself to hold still. He nudged one of my feet and then the other, adjusting their placement and angle just an inch here and there. His fingers brushed my calf before he straightened up, and even with the fabric of my sweatpants between his skin and mine, a quiver of heat shot up my leg.

When he stood, I lifted my fists and tested a punch. I felt the way my body moved in line, allowing just a little more power to fall behind the blow. I smiled and met his eyes. "Thanks."

"Can I join you?" he asked, and I froze in place, not prepared for that question. He went on into my startled silence. "I have some punching mitts for practice. We can use those."

I opened my mouth, closed it again, and shrugged. It'd be a welcome change from the punching bag—a new challenge. "Sure, why not?"

He grabbed the punching mitts out of a trunk against the wall near the punching bag and tugged them over his hands. Before he was fully prepared, I threw a punch, testing my form. The strike hit the padding over his hand with a loud thud.

Talon let out a grunt that might have been approving. "Good one," he said, holding both mitts up between us.

I gave him a satisfied smile. "It should be."

The breath that escaped his mouth could have almost been

mistaken for a laugh. Almost. "You're very sure of yourself when it comes to certain things, aren't you?"

Right, I couldn't forget that I was playing the role of Dess the abused daughter and girlfriend. But that Dess had still trained her ass off; she'd escaped the villains in her life.

I let my lips curve slyly. "This is the whole reason I'm still alive." He had no idea how true that was.

Then I struck.

Talon was ready. He met my left-handed strikes with the gloves, and when I lifted my knee in an attempt to get an advantage, he whipped his hand down to stop the blow before it made contact with his gut.

He did leave a small opening with the gesture, though. With my free right elbow, I twisted and caught him in the ribs. A woosh of air left him as he bowed at the waist slightly.

I tried to press my advantage by getting in a jab to his jaw, but Talon had already recovered. He fended off each of my strikes with a precision I'd only seen before from people with a military background. That only strengthened my suspicion that he and Julius might have that background in common. I guessed it wasn't so unusual for former soldiers to end up joining the police force. Similar lines of work, just different in scale.

Abruptly, Talon shook off the mitts and took a swing at me. My reflexes were well-honed enough that even in my surprise, I jerked out of the way. His fist narrowly avoided colliding with my face.

I sucked in a breath and took a step back, raising my arms defensively. Adrenaline thrummed through my veins, much more pleasant than the frustration that'd gripped me before.

"Oh, you think you can take me?" I taunted, wiping a bead of sweat from my brow and jumping from foot to foot.

"I know I can," Talon said.

He lashed out again, so fast I had to duck beneath his arm, my ribs groaning in protest at the maneuver. He might not have been quite as bulky with muscle as Julius was, but that allowed him more speed—and he was fucking fast.

While squatting, I jabbed him in the stomach with a fist and then stood, aiming for his face. Talon batted my hand aside. He came at me with his full body weight and flying punches, and the only option I had was to run away—which wasn't an option I was interested in taking—or to meet them head-on.

I blocked with my uninjured arm and kicked out at his thigh to create distance between us. It'd have been easier with two fully functional arms, but I'd make do with what I had.

I hadn't gotten to spar like this in years. Even Noelle hadn't been this much of a challenge recently. It was *amazing*. I could feel myself stretching, pushing harder to match my opponent, like I hadn't since I was a teenager.

When I aimed another kick, Talon grabbed my ankle, twisting so viciously that I nearly lost my balance. He yanked me toward him and whipped me around before I could recover. One of his arms wrapped across my waist, pinning both arms to my side like he'd done when he'd caught me trying to break the window, and the other rested against my collarbone, too close to my throat for comfort.

My breathing shallowed as I recognized the danger. What did I know about Talon, really? He was in law enforcement and insistent on keeping me "safe," but who knew how much of that was just a front? Maybe that was all Julius's idea, and he'd rather get me out of the way so they could focus on their real work.

I jerked my body to break his hold, but his grip tightened. "Dess," he said, my name a faint whisper of breath against my ear, "you might be more skilled than most, but you're not better than me."

It should have been fear that froze me to the spot, but I felt something else much more unexpected. The feel of his body pressed against mine sent a sudden flare of heat to my core.

With Blaze's touchy flirting and gentle advances, I'd felt nothing more than annoyance and a jolt of panic at the associations that came with that kind of come-on. Talon's dominating presence provoked a completely different sensation, something that made me want to grind against him in an embarrassing way.

I reined in that ridiculous urge and turned my head to the side, allowing my lips to hover a mere breath from his as I spoke. "What a testament to your skills: fighting and winning against an injured opponent. You must be *so* proud of yourself."

All at once I was aware of his pulse thumping through his body against me, picking up in tempo. He wet his lips. How *would* it feel if he pressed that mouth against mine? Would they be as strong and firm as the lean muscles that pressed into my body, or would they be cold and sharp like his icy eyes and terse responses? What would it be like to have a man like this work over my body as skillfully for pleasure as he did in combat?

Would it be so awful to find out, if it was what I wanted and not something being forced on me?

My pussy outright throbbed. Talon's gaze seared into mine, no longer so icy after all. In that instant, I thought I might actually *get* to find out.

Then his arms shifted around me, and his elbow tapped the most painful spot on my ribs. My head jerked down, a hiss of pain escaping me.

Talon let me go immediately. "Sorry." He stood tall, the artificial light gleaming off his shaved scalp and chiseled features. Another flicker of heat flashed in his eyes before fading away.

It seemed like whatever had happened between us in that brief moment hadn't only gotten to me.

I cleared my throat. "I'd like to try that again when I'm fully healed. I always appreciate a challenge." I knew I could take him when I wasn't held back by unwanted handicaps. He moved quickly and swiftly, but so did I.

"It won't make a difference," Talon replied.

"Who's confident now?" I said, grinning.

But he didn't reply, just picked the mitts off the floor and tossed them back into the trunk. Apparently sparring practice was over.

I eyed the punching bag, but I was bored with it now—and maybe I'd made some headway with Talon that would get me something else I wanted.

I set my hands on my hips. "So where did everyone else go while they left you to babysit?"

Talon didn't look at me. "It's official business."

"Yes, I realize that. They're still working on tracking down those pricks who murdered Anna and her family, right?"

He turned to face me then, his eyes narrowing. "Official. Business."

"Buzzkill," I said, rolling my eyes. "I might be able to help."

"Stop," he demanded.

"Are they looking at the crime scene again? I could check out the house itself, put on a more thorough disguise if you're so worried. Maybe I'd—"

"I'm not talking to you about an ongoing investigation or making any decisions about your involvement," he said, slowly and firmly. My heart sank. Every word felt like a new, sturdier wall he was erecting between us.

I thought I'd gotten somewhere with him, that he was starting to respect me.

"You can't really think I'm incapable of contributing after the things I spotted around the property today," I insisted.

He sighed and motioned toward the bedroom I'd been using. "I think it's time you went to bed."

I gaped at him and folded my arms over my chest. "Excuse me?"

"Go to bed," he repeated forcefully.

"That's what I thought you said." I took a step toward him, staring him down. "I don't care if you're a cop, a military man, or a damn alien. You will not order me around like that. I am *not* a child."

His gaze darted down over my body, lingering for just a second on the curves of my breasts and hips. When he met my eyes again, my skin tingled with more unsettling heat.

"I'm well aware of that fact," he said, in a tone that drew my eyes back to his mouth with the thought of the other uses it could be put to. Then it pressed flat before he said, "But I'm still telling you it's time to turn in for the night. Our apartment, our say goes."

I scoffed at him. "You and your whole damn team are insufferable." But I didn't really want to be out here with him if he was going to be such a prick about it. I spun on my heel and marched into the bedroom. The door closed with a kick and a thud.

I sank down on the bed. My gaze fell on the tote bag on the chair, and all at once my fingers itched to dig inside it for the stuffed tiger, to hug it to my chest as I curled up on the bed. As if I really *were* a kid again, trying to drift to sleep in my lonely rooms in the household.

But I wasn't that kid anymore. What was wrong with me?

I lay down on the firm mattress with my back to the chair, but a ghostly impression of the toy tickled my arms as I tucked them in front of me. Some small part of me, one I squashed deep inside but that I couldn't totally ignore, did feel like a little kid again. A confused, lonely kid far from home…

Even though this was the first time I'd been away from the household without knowing exactly where I was and what I was meant to be doing, something about that sensation was so familiar. How could that be?

FOURTEEN

Decima

"WE'RE TAKING YOU SOMEWHERE," Julius announced, and took a swig of his morning coffee.

I considered him from my perch at the kitchen island, where I'd just finished a bowl of cereal I'd again insisted on pouring myself. His expression gave nothing away, but then, it never did.

The fact that I might be getting another opportunity to see something beyond the confines of this apartment had to be a good thing. "Where?" I asked, picking the imaginary lint from my shirt as if his answer didn't matter to me all that much.

Garrison arched his eyebrows at me from where he was sitting on the other side of the island, savoring a typical mug of hot chocolate. It was just close enough for a trace of its creamy scent to reach my nose, and I started salivating even though my stomach was perfectly full.

"Do you really think you have a choice, sweetheart?" the younger guy asked. "This isn't a city tour, even if you tried to treat it like one yesterday."

I ignored him, fixing my attention back on the man in charge.

Julius gazed back at me evenly. "Do you want to help with the case or not?"

I made a face at him. "I'd kind of like to know where we're going first, that's all. Is that so much to ask after you've basically taken me prisoner?"

Julius frowned. "You're not a *prisoner*."

"Really? Then what would you call it?"

"You know you're here for your own protection. We're keeping you safe."

I shrugged and carried my bowl over to the sink. "And protecting *your* covers. I haven't seen any reason yet that proves I need this level of protection." *Tell me more about what you're up against, what kind of people you think I should be scared of. Give me some details.*

Julius looked at the ceiling as if he needed a moment to regain his composure. It wasn't my fault. I tried to ask the necessary questions to get right to the point, but he and the others repeatedly deflected. I didn't *want* to play a game of back and forth with the guys, but I didn't have another choice if I wanted to get anything out of them.

"You could just tell me where you want to take me," I suggested. "How hard is that?"

I could tell that he'd decided to appease me before he opened his mouth. He took a deep breath, but before the first word came out, the window above the kitchen counter burst inward with a crash of shattering glass.

As I spun around with a lurch of my heart, two smoke grenades careened inside and thumped on the floor. A dense fog billowed through the room, prickling into my eyes and obscuring everything around me from view. All I could rely on were my ears—which picked up the screech of the front door's hinges being slammed apart by some massive force and another crash of glass from the living room.

Footfalls thudded from all three directions. Gunshots boomed. I dropped to the ground, my pulse still racing but falling into a familiar rhythm that steadied me.

This was the kind of moment I was made for. Every instinct quivered on the alert. All my attention narrowed down to the simple goal of staying alive—and taking down anyone who wanted me to be otherwise.

More shots were ringing out. Was it enemy fire or the cops shooting back? There was no possible way to distinguish friend from foe with the suffocating smoke.

I pulled my shirt over my nose and mouth, gaining little relief, although my lungs were now prickling along with my eyes. At least the smoke didn't taste like it'd contained anything outright toxic. I'd experienced pretty much every awful hand weapon known to humankind over my years of training, and there were plenty worse than this.

Of course, most of those were only used in the middle of a warzone. What the fuck was going on here? Who would have wanted to attack a bunch of men most people shouldn't even know were cops?

Did it have anything to do with the massacre at the household?

The shots had fallen away into grunts and the fleshy smack of fists landing blows. They must have realized only a fool would fire into a room where they couldn't tell whether they'd hit an enemy or an ally. The sounds didn't tell me how many attackers we were facing, but from my initial impressions, two or three had come in through each access point, maybe a couple more than that through the front door. We were outnumbered as much as twice over.

We? What was I even thinking? I didn't owe the cops anything, and I wasn't in any position to take on as many as a dozen attackers whether they were related to the household's murders or not. It was the cops' job to handle these assholes. I'd seen how capable they were at that job. They didn't need me anyway.

This was the perfect opportunity to escape and never look back.

I army-crawled in the direction of the door, careful to make no noise as I went. Here and there I had to adjust my course to squeeze around a piece of furniture or dodge stomping feet. More punches and kicks thudded around me; a bone cracked. Someone groaned.

It sounded vaguely like Julius.

I hesitated next to the sofa. I had to keep going, didn't I? It was a tough world, and I wouldn't risk entering a fight that had nothing to do with me.

Or did it have *everything* to do with me?

Julius had claimed that they were protecting me, and while I'd assumed it was an unnecessary precaution, maybe I'd been overly skeptical. What if this attack wasn't an attempt to capture or kill them, but to do those things to *me*?

A sharp cry of pain split through the air. Was that Blaze?

Logic told me to continue forward, but my body balked. Even highly skilled fighters could be overwhelmed when they were greatly outnumbered and taken by surprise. I might be able to make a break for it, but the four men who'd brought me here wouldn't necessarily survive this attack.

They'd held me here, refused to let me leave… but they'd also helped me after the car crash. Patched me up. Made sure I was reasonably comfortable and well-fed. They'd even catered to my request to walk around the mansion and then go buy those damn cookies yesterday.

It might be because of me that whoever was attacking them had even identified this apartment as theirs.

I hadn't been able to save anyone in the household. I hadn't even known the massacre was happening until every single one of them was dead or as good as it. This time, it wasn't too late to step in.

I didn't have to let another group of people die around me. I could save someone.

My chest clenched around a sudden rush of determination. I didn't second-guess the emotion. *This* was what I'd trained for. This was the one way I knew I could make a difference in the world, and I wasn't going to fail again.

Springing to my feet, I took in the room. As I swiveled, I made out thinning patches in the smoke.

There—that guy with the ski mask was one of our enemies.

I dove at him, reaching for his head. He didn't even see me coming. My fingers dug into his jaw, and I wrenched his face around so sharply his neck snapped even as he made his first movement to buck me off.

As he crumpled to the ground, Garrison scrambled up from where he'd been knocked down at the attacker's feet. He stared at me, but I didn't have time to worry about what he thought of my kill. There were more sounds of fighting all around me.

Another masked man hurtled out of a thicker patch of smoke. I struck first, knowing that my advantage would come from the man's shock.

He swung at me with a knife. I ducked and snatched his wrist with my left hand to prevent him from using the blade. At the same time, I swung my brace around, pummeling his temple with its stiff surface. The throb of the impact ricocheted up my arm, and my ribs groaned with the effort, but the man stumbled to the side, slightly stunned.

He lashed out at me again, but I had already moved, yanking his body off balance. I squeezed his wrist, twirling it around his back in a maneuver that I knew would jerk his shoulder out of its socket. A pop sounded through the room, and a groan spilled from his mouth.

"The fuck," he screamed, the knife dropping from his twitching fingers. I kicked the back of his knees, and he collapsed forward, a strange sobbing gasp coming from his lips.

In an instant, the knife was in my hand. I plunged it straight into his back, angled perfectly to ram between his ribs and into his heart.

I knew I'd hit home when the body beneath me sagged.

The smoke was clearing more, drifting out the shattered windows and the open doorway. A hint of a fresh breeze tingled in my throat.

As I spun around, I noted the three other bodies already on the floor—all of them masked, to my unexpectedly intense relief. One of them was bleeding out from a deep slash across his throat. Another had a bullet wound in his chest. The third might have only been unconscious, but these cops clearly didn't hesitate to fight to the death when their lives were on the line.

Exactly as it should be. Hopefully that'd mean they wouldn't get too judgy about the bodies *I'd* added to the collection of corpses.

On the other side of the sofa, Julius and Talon were fighting side-by-side. For the first time, seeing them from the sidelines rather than as their opponent, I could observe the way they worked in sync. Talon moved with swift but powerful precision, and Julius was the direction to his storm, leading with pure strength and skill as he smashed his knee into one attacker's face and jabbed out his gun hand to put a bullet in another.

Together, they were a force of nature. Outnumbered two-to-one, they still maintained the upper hand in the fight. I'd never seen *anyone* fight quite like that. It was almost beautiful to watch.

But not so beautiful that I didn't notice the man charging at me from the direction of the kitchen, wielding a switchblade in one hand and a butcher knife in the other.

I turned to meet the guy head-on. As I swiveled, I glimpsed Blaze holding his own against another assailant with a skill that I hadn't anticipated from the tech expert, even though his movements were slowed by a wound bleeding on his side. To be a cop, of course he needed to be somewhat physically adept, but it still surprised me.

My attacker was coming too fast for me to completely dodge him. I caught a blow to my shoulder and stepped back from the force of it. Shaking off the impact, I deflected the next one with my bare forearm. Up close, catching sight of my face in a way none of the invaders before had gotten a chance to, he jerked backward with startled eyes. "Who the fuck are *you*?"

It wasn't me they were after, then. They hadn't expected some chick to be fighting alongside the cops, let alone kicking their ass. Too bad for them.

His hesitation was all I needed to swing back and execute a perfect roundhouse kick that rammed into his head. I landed with bent knees, and the man toppled to the ground, unconscious without an ounce of fight remaining in him.

I glanced around the room with a nearly clear view now. All the guys were fending off other assailants, even Garrison, though the motions of his right arm looked awkward, as if he'd been injured too.

When I looked at Julius and Talon, I found Julius's motions were slowing. In the time I'd confronted one man, he'd taken down two, and Talon had incapacitated another. But Julius was favoring one side. The bottom of the left leg of his jeans was dark with blood—his.

Shit. Another attacker stepped into view from the dispersing smoke, his gun aimed at Julius, and I leapt toward the masked man without a second thought.

This guy was taller and broader than the others I'd fought. With only one fully usable arm, I knew I had a challenge ahead of me. I didn't allow myself to glance at the bodies that littered the floor. I didn't bother acknowledging anything around me but my opponent.

He might be bigger than me, but I was *born* for this.

I fell into the rhythm of the fight, using my fists and legs brutally and efficiently enough that it didn't feel like I was impaired in any way. In fact, the brace over my wrist acted as a blocking tool rather than a burden. Using the footwork that Talon had adjusted yesterday, I found myself ducking, weaving, and punching with greater intensity—just as rapidly as I would have with my right arm fully functional.

The man's size didn't matter as he succumbed to my attack, careening to the floor with my assault.

The gun spun away from his hand, but he fell within reach of a discarded knife. He noticed it at the precise moment that I did. I stood no chance of reaching it before him.

So when the man jerked forward and snatched up the serrated blade, I did the only thing I could do. I veered right, clutched his wrist with my left hand, and slammed his forearm into my bent knee.

The first time, he didn't release it, though a groan of pain fled from his lips. I turned my back to his body's mass and used my right arm to add more force to the blow this time. The knife finally clattered to the floor. I pushed him away from the blade, and he held my leg like a lifeline, attempting to drag me alongside him.

I caught the cool leather grip of the knife and whipped it around as the man pulled me closer. With a jerk of my hand, I plunged it into his chest.

He slumped, his breathing sputtering and then halting completely, leaving the room just a little quieter.

I glanced toward Talon first, my eyes drawn to him automatically. He still moved like a storm—quick, brutal, and relentless. He left nobody unaffected in his path of skillful strikes. He looked to be enjoying his last opponent—taking his time with him. I saw the way the man tired, and I could tell that Talon was playing with him.

A yearning in the pit of my stomach arose as I watched him move. He was absolutely extraordinary.

But there were only two attackers left, that one and the one Julius was just heaving into the edge of the kitchen island. The cops could handle the situation from here. I'd done my bit, and now I needed to get going.

As I dashed toward the open doorway, Talon cracked his opponent's skull. I still could have made it, but just a few steps from the blasted-up doorframe, Garrison and Blaze stepped from opposite sides to block my way.

My fists jerked up, and in the same instant, Talon strode over to join them. He didn't seem to notice the blood trickling down the side of his face from a scratch on his forehead.

Garrison smirked at me, the effect only slightly weakened by the tensing of his jaw against the pain he was in. "Where do you think you're going, sweetheart?"

Fuck. I'd waited too long. I swiveled in the other direction, just in time to see Julius marching over.

He took in the room as he approached, limping just a little, and I got the sense he could pick out exactly which kills were mine, though that didn't make any sense when several of them had happened when it was too smoky to see where anyone else was. When he came to a stop a couple of paces away from me, he nodded approvingly.

"Thank you. We might have been in a tough spot if you hadn't stepped in." He gave the apartment another glance and sighed. "We can't stay here after this. Maybe it's time we take you home."

FIFTEEN

Julius

AFTER WE'D MARCHED out of hearing range of the car, parked at the other end of the alley with Dess locked inside, Garrison cleared his throat. His voice came out taut. "It was the Cutthroats."

"What?" I'd already been angry about the attack, but it was nothing compared to the surge of rage that hit me at those words. I'd assumed someone associated with one or another past hit must have been out for revenge and managed to locate us. For it to have been a fellow crew…

Garrison nodded, leaning back against the brick wall on one side of the alley and crossing his arms, moving the right one a little stiffly. His eyes flashed. Knowing how cynical he could be, he probably wasn't as surprised as I was, but I doubted he was any less pissed off.

"I managed to get one of the guys who came at me in a particularly painful position," he said, a mix of triumph and revulsion playing across his features. "He spilled the beans while begging me not to make the pain worse. The Cutthroats hired the bunch of them to take us out. A little less competition for the prime jobs, I guess?"

Blaze snorted, but he was scowling too. "Maybe if they got their acts together, they'd be able to *earn* those jobs instead of having to slaughter the competition."

"Then they'd actually have to put the work in," Talon muttered.

I dragged in a breath, glancing toward the car where Dess was perched in the back seat. I'd set the locks so they wouldn't open from the inside, but I half-expected her to burst through the glass. The woman was full of surprises.

For now, she was sitting there in the middle of the back seat, apparently calm. She'd have had a hard time smashing through those windows anyway. We had all our vehicles specially outfitted.

I turned back to my crew, shifting my weight and suppressing a wince at the lingering pain in my lower leg. One of those hired punks had lucked out and clipped my calf with a bullet in the initial turmoil of the attack. Blaze had taken a knife jab that'd come just shy of piercing his stomach. Our wounds were patched up now, but that didn't mean they were forgiven.

No one messed with my crew and lived to tell the tale.

We'd certainly left no one living in the safe house. That would make a powerful statement. It'd been easy enough to vacate, since we didn't keep anything there that could be traced back to us and the ownership of the place was through a shell company, but I didn't like that we were down a useable property on top of everything else.

"We'll wipe them out," I said firmly. "After we're done dealing with our current client and the loose ends he seems to think we left. Divided attention gets you killed. But we also have to make sure the Cutthroats can't get at us if they're stupid enough to try again." I turned to Blaze. "How do you figure they found the first place?"

"There's no way to connect us to it through the data trail," Blaze said. "There *is* no data trail that connects all the dots."

"We've been coming and going from that particular spot a lot in the past few days," Talon pointed out grimly. "The safe houses are set up for laying low, not regular activity. All it'd take is the wrong person spotting one of us in the area."

I nodded. "And that means we'd have the exact same problem if we tried to take Dess to one of our other safe houses. The only place that's totally secure is the penthouse."

Garrison bristled. "The only reason it's secure is because no one except us and Steffie has any idea it exists. We can't bring *her* there."

Garrison spat the word *her* as if it burned through his mouth. As if the idea of Dess was acidic and dangerous.

She was definitely dangerous. I'd only caught a few glimpses of her in the attack, the smoke hiding most of the fighting around me, but what I had seen—it'd been even more impressive than the way she'd tried to escape. She'd moved with ruthless efficiency, doing what needed to be done to take down the intruders and doing it fast and well.

And she hadn't needed to do it at all. The door had been slammed right off its hinges, the path to freedom wide open.

"I've said it before and I'm saying it again," Garrison said. "We've got to get rid of her, make her the client's problem. As long as she's with us, she's just going to be trouble."

I'd let myself assume that the whole crew would be unanimous on this question after what we'd just been through. I should have remembered never to take anything for granted.

"She fought with us," I said, hardening my voice. "She could have run for it, but instead she stayed and *defended* us. She took down at least a couple of the mercenaries. Early on, the fight was closer than I'd like. I don't know for sure that we'd all have even survived if she hadn't stepped in. She might have saved *your* life. We might not be clear on how she fits into this mess, but the one thing she's proven is that she isn't out to screw us over."

"Yeah," Blaze said. "I saw you get knocked on the ground, and then she jumped in. If she hadn't tackled that guy, you'd be lying there with the rest of the collection of corpses right now. And you really want to repay her by throwing her to the wolves?"

"The client goes by the name Viper, so technically it'd be throwing her to the snakes," Garrison muttered, as if that was what mattered.

"And that's much better?" Talon asked.

Garrison just glowered at him. I studied his expression and saw nothing but his usual dissociated prickliness. Now more than ever I'd have liked to know what lay behind those walls. Why did he have such a problem with this woman?

"Just because she knocked the knives from our enemies' hands doesn't mean she won't plunge one into our backs given the opportunity," Garrison said finally.

"Nobody said that we're going to trust her fully," I reminded him. "But it couldn't be more obvious that if she wanted us dead, she wouldn't have helped us. She risked her own life to fight with us, even though we've been holding her against her will."

"And I don't know why the fuck she did that, but the penthouse is our space. Crew only. She doesn't belong there."

"Steffie comes all the time," Talon pointed out.

Garrison rolled his eyes. "Steffie's practically crew too. You guys took her on before you even brought me in."

There was more to his defiance, though, wasn't there? I didn't think he only objected to Dess over Steffie because Steffie had been with us longer.

Garrison might never admit it, but I doubted he hated Dess as much as he pretended. I saw the way they bickered, and I'd noticed the light that had danced in his eyes—a genuine enthusiasm that I so rarely saw in him.

Dess wasn't a danger to our lives, but she *was* a danger to the steel walls he'd built to ensure nobody could get past them.

But then, I wasn't being totally honest with the others about my reasons for wanting to keep her with us either.

There'd been a moment toward the end of the fighting when I'd glanced over and caught a glimpse of her face in the middle of grappling with the last man she'd killed. Something about the cool stillness of her expression and the intense focus in her gray eyes had triggered a jolt of recognition. One that had made me want to run over and tear the guy trying to hurt her limb from limb.

It didn't make much sense. I couldn't place her, couldn't say where or when I might have encountered her before. There was no point in putting much stock in the impression. But even now, when I checked on her stance in the car again, that protective urge flickered up in my chest.

I planned my life and our careers according to hard data and strategic thinking, but I'd learned to trust my instincts too. And my instincts insisted that this woman was someone we should defend just as vehemently as she'd defended us.

I turned back to Garrison. "We already have an extra room, so no one's getting put out on the sofa this time. We can set up a cot in the weight room. With Steffie coming by regularly, she'll have an added layer of supervision. We'll have all our equipment right there, everything we need to take care of our work in one place. You can't get simpler than that."

"We can't hand her over to that Viper prick," Blaze added. "And we can't let her go when we still don't know what her real story is. Julius's approach is the only way that covers all the bases."

Garrison turned his glower on the techie. "You just want another chance to put the moves on her. Nearly having your windpipe crushed once wasn't enough?"

Blaze rubbed his throat. "She didn't hit me *that* hard. And I provoked her. She hasn't been remotely aggressive with any of us except in self-defense, has she?"

Talon hesitated as if he still had a few doubts, but then he dipped his head. "She hasn't. There's something more to her than she's said, but I don't think it makes her a threat to us."

Garrison's eyes became narrower. Then a switch flipped inside of him. He stood straighter, loosened his posture, and placed a cold expression on his face. "Fine, but if she kills us all in our sleep, I hope you die knowing that I was right."

"If we die, you will too, so you won't get much satisfaction out of it," Blaze retorted.

Garrison ignored him and stalked back to the car. He whipped the door open and dropped into the front passenger seat without so much as a glance at Dess. She looked at him and then the rest of us approaching, her expression coolly quizzical.

"We're taking you somewhere," I said as I got in on the driver's side.

She cocked her head, a glint of amusement coming into her pretty eyes. You wouldn't have known looking at her that just an hour ago she'd stabbed at least one man to death. But then, who knew how much shit she'd seen before she fell in with us. We weren't exactly broken up about the violence we'd dealt out either.

"Let me guess," she said dryly. "You're not going to tell me where."

"You're catching on," Garrison muttered.

I gestured to Talon and gave Dess a mildly apologetic smile. "For this trip, you're going to be blindfolded. I don't want you even *seeing* where we're going."

Her body stiffened just slightly, the light in her eyes vanishing as if storm clouds had rolled in. "Blindfolded? What the hell—"

"You'll be able to take it off as soon as we get inside," I said, cutting her off. "It's a precaution for both our security and yours."

I watched as an array of emotions flashed through her gaze, each pushed away until cool indifference was the last thing that remained. "I feel like it should be illegal for cops to blindfold people and take them places."

Blaze's laugh filled the car, and I went on before he could say something stupid. "It's also illegal to kill people, but on some occasions, it's necessary."

"You're not going to arrest me for that, right? Isn't self-defense allowed?"

"It is," I said. "You were our responsibility, and we're responsible for what happened in the safe house too."

She nodded slowly and leaned into her seat. "Fine, but you're going to take the blindfold off as soon as we get there."

As Talon placed a strip of thick cloth over her eyes, a sense of appreciation rose up inside me. For the trust she'd just shown us that I wasn't sure we'd earned, considering I was still lying through my teeth about who we were. For the way she'd fearlessly fought on behalf of four men she barely knew. Maybe she was some kind of kindred spirit, a piece we hadn't known the crew was missing. She wasn't an enemy—of that, I was completely sure.

But at the same time, I had no doubt that if she became a liability, I would kill her. The crew always came first.

I just couldn't help hoping it wouldn't come to that.

SIXTEEN

Decima

THE COPS HADN'T SAID as much, but I could tell as soon as my blindfold came off that the apartment they'd brought me to this time wasn't any kind of safe house. To them, this was *home*.

Julius insisted on replacing my wrist brace with a new one, considering the old one had cracked in the fighting. Then they backed off, giving me space to explore the place and take in all of the intriguing details.

I hadn't been able to track the route we'd taken, which had mostly been by car but also involved a descent down stairs into cooler air with a metallic scent, the squeak of a couple pairs of hinges, and a distant rumble that'd made me wonder if we were near a subway line. The last part of the trip had been by elevator, though, and the bright light that assaulted my eyes confirmed that this place was no basement.

The open concept of the room resembled the basement safe house, but it was larger and much more welcoming. A plump leather sofa and matching chairs stood in a cluster around a widescreen TV. The island by the kitchen was longer, and the countertops marble. There were three normal looking doors at either end, which I'd gathered led to the men's bedrooms, the bathroom, and a workout room were Talon was currently unfolding a cot for me.

It would have looked normal—just like an everyday if somewhat posh home—if it weren't for a few details.

The windows all along the wall opposite the front door allowed in plenty of light, but they were overlaid with a film that blurred all view of the outside—and presumably any chance of anyone else seeing in. From the time we'd spent in the elevator, I suspected it was a long drop to the ground.

The front door had a lock that took a keycode, and I could tell the deadbolt it activated was very solid from the sound of it thudding into place after they'd let me in. Another door in the far wall was similarly secured. Where did *that* lead? Weapons? Case files?

I'd just have to find out as soon as I had the chance.

One corner of the apartment had a desk with a massive computer and four monitors. I recognized that as Blaze's domain, so I assumed that the dartboard a few feet away was also his. Whenever he'd last been playing, he'd gotten two in the bullseye.

I had no idea who the knitting bag sitting beneath the small coffee table belonged to. The bag was black and as masculine as a bag could get with screen-printed skulls and knives printed on the surface, but there was no mistaking the needles and skeins of wool poking from the top. Interesting.

Beside the TV sat a movie stand, and plenty of familiar titles greeted me. Many were dramas, a few were horror movies, and the vast majority were action. No surprises there.

I glanced over my shoulder when Talon came out of the exercise room. He walked over to join Julius by a small wooden table next to a whiteboard set up like an easel. Julius had taken out a few plastic army figures which must have represented whatever he started talking to Talon about. He moved them on the board with careful precision and pointed something out, but I couldn't tell what he was getting at.

I wandered closer, hoping to catch a snippet of the conversation, but unfortunately that brought me closer to Garrison. He'd gone right to the stove and put on the kettle, and now he was pouring instant cocoa into a mug.

I resisted the urge to lick my lips—and the more insistent urge to ask him for some. I'd lived with chocolate only once a year for my whole life. Better I went without than trust anything he mixed for me.

Julius and Talon fell silent when I came closer, Julius running his hand over the short brown strands of his close-cropped hair. I put on my best show of not even noticing they were nearby, studying the frame around the nearest window instead.

It was actually worthy of examination. Hand-painted thorns and roses wove around the glass pane in an intricate pattern it was hard to imagine had been done by hand. If it weren't for the slight smear in the corner, I would have assumed it was some kind of wallpaper.

I leaned closer, taking a closer look. The thorns in the painting appeared to wind around and trap the vibrant roses, encompassing them and cutting them off from the rest of their brothers and sisters. Some of the petals looked cut and scratched by the same thorns.

For such a beautiful painting, it was vicious. Had one of the men around me done this? It was hard to picture any of them with a paintbrush in his hand, but then I'd say the same about the knitting needles.

I turned back toward the kitchen just as Garrison put away the box he'd taken the cocoa packet from. My eyebrows leapt up. There was an entire shelf stuffed with similar boxes, with different brand names and logos.

"That's quite the collection," I said.

"Some might even call it an addiction," Blaze piped up. He'd plunked down on the sofa with his laptop, which apparently he preferred to his more elaborate workstation.

I should have known better than to try to make any conversation with Garrison. He frowned at me and shut the cupboard with a thunk. "It's a collection I don't want you messing with."

I quirked my lips up into a cocky smile and lifted my hands in feigned defeat. I wasn't going to admit how much the thought of all that chocolate—so many different kinds!—made me drool. After all, the last time I indulged my own addiction, I could hardly walk back to my room before passing out.

I took in the whole room again, and another thought occurred to me. I hadn't spent much time questioning the men's living situation in the old apartment, which had felt distinctly temporary. This home was well-lived-in. They'd been here for a while.

I knit my brow and asked the room at large, "Is it normal for cops to live together like this? Can't any of you afford your own place?"

"We're married to our work, and that means practically married to each other," Blaze said, shooting me a grin.

"It's easier when we're undercover," Julius clarified.

I guessed that made sense. I didn't know much about the inner workings of law enforcement, other than it was best to steer clear of its agents altogether. You never knew when a pesky law might get in the way of seeing a job through.

I turned my attention back to the window frame. "Who painted the roses?"

The question had barely left my lips when the front door clicked open behind me. I spun around, my pulse skipping, every nerve going on the alert. Were we being attacked again? Did I need to dive for cover—or a weapon?

But the men around me looked totally unconcerned. And the woman who stepped through the doorway alone didn't exactly give off a threatening vibe. The tension trickled out of me.

"She painted them," Talon said in answer to my question, jerking his thumb toward the woman, which instantly made me focus even more attention on her.

She could have been cut out of a Hallmark card for grandmothers: short, plump, and with hair that was a messy mix of wheat-blond, gray, and white pinned into a bun on the top of her head. Her eyes met mine, soft but thoughtful. Beneath her loose floral dress, she wore white tennis shoes. Another mix: prettiness and practicality.

"What do we have here?" she said, looking me up and down. Her lightly accented voice—Eastern European, I couldn't place the exact country just yet—was brisker and firmer than I'd have expected from her grandmotherly appearance. There was clearly more to her than met the eye.

While we'd been examining each other, Julius had walked up between us. He rested a hand on the woman's shoulder, and she beamed at him—with all the air of a grandmother doting on her favorite grandson, although given that Julius looked to be in his late thirties and I'd have put her around sixty, she was hardly old enough for that to be true. Then she returned her gaze to me with a much more assessing expression.

"Dess," Julius said to me, "this is Steffie, our housekeeper. She comes by regularly to take care of laundry, dishes, and whatever else needs doing around the apartment. She'll be treated with nothing but respect. Understood?"

It surprised me that he felt he needed to say it and that he spoke with such cool but clear forcefulness about a woman who was essentially their servant. That added to my impression that there was something more to this situation. What kind of housekeeper painted the window frames after she was done cleaning, anyway?

Especially with such brutal yet beautiful imagery.

"Understood," I said, reining in my curiosity. I didn't think Julius would consider a barrage of intrusive questions to be very respectful. "It's nice to meet you, Steffie."

"Dess is going to be staying with us for a little while," Julius said to the older woman. "We have some business to sort out with her, and it's important that she stay safe."

It was a very vague explanation, but either Steffie could read more into it than I'd have expected or she wasn't in the habit of questioning her employers, because she nodded without complaint. "You'll barely notice me around," she told me with a twinkle in her eyes, and glanced back at Julius. "The trees are vibrant today. A few leaves fell on the sidewalk by the bank, but the breeze tossed them away. Otherwise, not so much as a rustle in the branches."

Huh? I studied her and then Julius, who nodded as if her comments had sounded totally normal to him. Something clicked in my head.

It was a code. She'd been passing on information she didn't think he'd want her saying explicitly while I could hear it.

What kind of housekeeper had a secret *code* set up with her clients?

Steffie bustled off without another word and grabbed a broom from the bathroom. As she swept the floor, the men went back to their previous activities. No one seemed all that interested in what I was going to do here.

Well, Julius might not want me badgering Steffie, but I didn't see why I couldn't badger him. He'd dragged me here along with them, after all.

I marched over to the table where he'd just set out another army figure and motioned to the array. "Does this have something to do with the massacre at Anna's house?"

"We work on a lot more cases than that one," Talon said gruffly, which didn't even answer my question.

I set my hands on my hips. "Of course you do. But that one is the most pressing right now, wouldn't you say? Or are mass murders a regular occurrence around here? For all we know, *we* just got almost murdered by the same people."

"They weren't the same people," Julius said in exasperation, and then snapped his mouth shut.

He hadn't meant to reveal that tidbit. They didn't really want to explain anything to me. I caught hold of the stray fact and tucked it away in the back of my mind. I'd already gathered that the intruders hadn't been after me, but if it wasn't related to the massacre at all…

I frowned. "Why would a bunch of guys come at you with guns blazing if—"

"That," Julius said firmly, "is for us to figure out and you not to worry about. There's no chance of anything like that happening in this building. That's why we came here."

I let out my breath in a huff. "I just want to do what I can to help with the investigation—you know, the one that made you think I'm *not* safe, at least anywhere other than with you—so I can get on with some kind of life that involves more things than sitting around watching you whisper to yourselves. Are we going to get a move on solving this case, or are you all just going to sit around knitting sweaters?" I gestured to the bag beneath the coffee table.

Blaze snickered. None of the men around me appeared fazed by my accusation. Steffie outright laughed, the unexpectedly full sound rolling through the room. "You're going to have fun with this one," she said, and went back to her sweeping.

"Look," Julius said, "you're not a cop, and you're not entitled to being part of the investigation. You don't know how this works. So why don't you treat this as a vacation and relax. There are worse spots you could be stuck, aren't there?"

I supposed he was right. But if I couldn't leave this apartment, I couldn't find a chance to slip away and talk to my other contact. How long was this confinement going to go on for?

"It's a very nice place," I said, making a show of looking around again. "Sorry if I get a little stir-crazy being stuck in the same small space for days on end."

Julius sighed. "Then you'll be happy to know that we're going out tomorrow. All of us, you included."

The clunk of Garrison's mug and his sudden intake of breath suggested *he* hadn't been in on that plan.

I smiled at Julius brightly. "Wonderful. Maybe you'll even tell me where we're going before we get there this time."

Steffie muffled another laugh. Garrison muttered something under his breath, but he didn't overtly protest. I stepped away from the table with a vague sense of triumph.

This would be my last-ditch effort to learn from the cops. If they led me astray one more time, I wouldn't stay with them. I had to find the savages who'd murdered the people in the household, and I would do it with or without their help.

SEVENTEEN

Decima

THE COPS INSISTED on blindfolding me again before we left the apartment. After the elevator stopped at the bottom, I tried to track the path we took, but they led me around half a dozen turns and along the same slightly musty-smelling passage where a rumbling sound passed us by.

The only thing I was reasonably sure of was that we were near a subway station.

We'd been in the car about ten minutes when Talon finally judged it safe to take the blindfold off, or maybe Julius had given him some signal. I blinked at the sudden brightness streaming through the car windows. We were cruising along a busy street, cars all around us and pedestrians bustling along the sidewalks, tall storefronts looming on either side. A cluster of skyscrapers towered over us just a couple of blocks ahead.

We'd come downtown. I was closer to my contact "with the red polka dots" than I'd been before, at least.

I leaned back in the seat where I was wedged between Talon and Blaze today and studied the back of Julius's head. Talon sat as still as always, and Blaze was jiggling his leg like he so often did when the rest of him couldn't be moving, so absorbed in his phone he probably didn't even notice. It was an odd contrast between the two of them, but I found I didn't mind. It beat having Garrison glowering at me for the whole trip.

But it was the leader of this bunch I focused my attention on now.

"Do I get any clues about where we're headed or why?" I asked, giving the back of Julius's seat a playful kick. "Did you want to make it a game of twenty questions?"

"I don't think that'll be necessary," Julius said dryly. "We're taking a look around one of the victim's workplaces. Since you were somewhat familiar with the family and maybe some of the others who were there at the time of the massacre, I figured it couldn't hurt to have your eyes on the scene too. But *no* touching anything. You see something that feels important, you call one of us over."

"Think you can handle that?" Garrison asked, taking a glance back at me. I hadn't completely escaped the dreaded glower.

I returned it with one of my own. "I promise not to touch anything unless it's a weapon someone's trying to kill us with." My gaze darted back to Julius. "Which victim? What was the job?"

"I'd rather not skew your judgment by giving you any additional information. If you go in cold, you're more likely to be receptive to all possible evidence."

That sounded reasonable enough, if annoying. I frowned at the buildings outside the window. It hadn't occurred to me that the people who worked for the household had careers outside whatever they did *in* the household, but maybe it wasn't even a job for most of them like it was for me. Maybe they'd all gone out to work elsewhere at least some of the time. What kinds of jobs would they have held?

I guessed I was about to find out.

The parking spots along the sidewalk were packed. Julius took the car past a stretch of office buildings and then pulled over in the first empty spot. He nodded back the way we'd come. "It's about two blocks that way."

We all put on our hats and sunglasses and stepped out of the car. The men fell into step around me like before. Still surrounded. Great.

It was a little tricky weaving through the crowded sidewalk in a clump like that, though. People brushed past us on both sides, whiffs of perfume and car exhaust mingling in my nose. The road provided a constant rumble of engines.

Then Blaze jerked to a stop. He motioned to Julius, who stepped over to join him, and pointed across the street. "Is that him?" he asked under his breath.

Garrison moved away from me to join them too. Talon, in front of me, simply turned his head, but a sense of opportunity washed over me.

This was my opening. Who knew if I was going to get another one? For these few seconds, I was free to step away and bolt, and the hordes of people surrounding us would make it impossible for the cops to find me once I'd melded with the crowd the way I'd been trained to.

I took a slow step back, careful not to appear tense. Any unusual motions would draw their attention back toward me, so I took three more easy paces backward before turning and slipping around a cluster of women in business suits. With a quick swipe, I removed my cap. I let my posture drop, my knees bending slightly and my back rounding so that my head dipped lower, more difficult to see.

The cluster of women headed into a fancy café, and I let them carry me along with them. The second I passed the door, I darted past the tables and the washroom, dashed along the hall past the kitchen so quickly and quietly no one even called out after me, and was out the back door in an instant.

A map of the city unfurled in my mind. I sprinted down an alleyway, loped across roads, turned several corners, and then hailed a taxi that happened to be passing by. There was no sign of the cops anywhere around me, and now I was going to vanish completely.

As I dropped onto the worn leather of the cab's back seat, a twinge of regret ran through my gut. I hadn't managed to find out anything all that useful from their investigation, and they'd obviously known more than I'd been able to drag out of them. But who knew if I'd *ever* have gotten anywhere with them?

My contact had specifically reached out to me. The information she'd offer could trump everything the cops had in their case file.

The address I gave the cabbie was on the other side of downtown from the household. The edges of the city there were pretty much the opposite of the suburban street where I'd lived. Trampled cardboard rested on the sidewalks, and homeless people sat begging on several of the corners we passed, their eyes tracking the movement of everyone who passed by. Trash blew along the curbs. The buildings could use a fresh paint job at best and gutting at worst.

I got out outside the sagging canopy over the entrance to the local mall. Inside, the florescent lights flickered with dying bulbs, and the smell of grease hung in the air as if that was the main ingredient in the food court—which maybe it was. At least the air conditioning was on full blast.

I walked on, leaving the heat of the summer day behind me. My heart started to thump in anticipation.

The storefront for the electronics store was one of the neatest in the place, phone models and the latest cheap gadgets displayed in rows in the display window. A fake potted plant stood next to the doorway to give the space a homier feel. I'd always thought it was kind of ridiculous, but what did I know about retail strategy?

The woman who'd reached out to me was leaning against the counter next to the cash register. She straightened up the second I walked in, a smile flashing across her face but her stance tensing. She was relieved and yet nervous to see me.

I filed away those observations as I came to a stop a couple of feet from the counter, as if I wanted to check out the hard drives and cables tucked away behind the glass underneath. My gaze stayed on her face.

This contact had picked her temporary code name to go with her message well. The first time Noelle had introduced me to her, I hadn't met anyone with so many or such prominent freckles before. I'd asked why she had polka dots on her face. And the red part—well, her fiery curls must have inspired the usual code name she went by too: Scarlett.

"You got my message, then," she said, sounding oddly breathless. "I was a little worried—I thought they might be wrong—well, it doesn't matter."

My body went on the alert. I stepped closer. "Who's 'they,' and what do they have to do with me?"

Scarlett pursed her lips, her eyes darting around the store and then coming back to rest on me. "Someone reached out—I don't know much about it—I don't really ask questions, you know? They passed something on to me that they wanted me to get to you if I could. They seemed sure you were alive, but after everything I heard about what happened..." She shuddered. "Just a second."

I shifted on my feet impatiently as she turned to rifle through a cabinet behind her. "*Who* passed this thing on?"

"I'm sorry, I really don't know," she said. "There wasn't any face-to-face communication. They left the package on the counter while I was in the back. I guess they must have known I had some connection to you, so I'd have a decent chance of getting in touch."

And whoever had gone to her hadn't hoped to find me directly. Hmm.

"Did they say anything else about me or the murders?" I asked.

She shook her head, her curls jiggling around her face, and tugged a padded envelope about the size of a paperback novel out of the cabinet. "Just that if I could get this to you, I should. They were very emphatic about that."

I peered into her pale eyes as she handed the envelope over. Had she been threatened with some kind of violence if she didn't manage to complete the task? Offered a reward if she did? There seemed to be more at stake here than just handing over a package as a favor.

"And you really don't have any idea who brought it?" I pressed. "Don't you have security cameras in this place?"

Her mouth twitched. Fear. I knew that emotion—I'd watched it cross the face of enough of my victims. But I didn't think it was me she was afraid of.

"Whoever it was, they were too careful to get caught that way," she said, but I wondered if she'd even dared to check.

"If you'd let me have a look—" I started, and she shook her head more vigorously than before.

"It's already been erased," she said without further explanation, only confirming my suspicion that she was terrified of pissing off whoever she thought she was dealing with.

A wave of frustration rushed through me, but I couldn't change what she'd already done or what she'd refused to find out. At least I'd gotten something here.

My fingers tightened around the envelope. "Thank you. I appreciate this."

She dipped her head in acknowledgment. Her jaw worked as if she was debating what to say next. "You'd better go now. After what those people did to your colleagues—who knows if they're looking for you too."

She had a point. I nodded to her and slipped out of the shop as quickly as I'd entered.

I stopped outside a discount clothing store, facing an inflated image of a model in a dress that was much more sophisticated than anything being sold in the dank interior, and tore into the envelope. A small, cheap plastic flip phone slid out into my waiting hand.

What the hell? I looked it over, tapped the power button, and the screen lit up. But there was nothing on it, just a few basic apps like the address book, which was totally empty.

No answers. No information. It felt like another dead end.

Gritting my teeth, I slipped my hand quickly beneath the collar of my shirt, shoving the phone into one place almost guaranteed to avoid detection: in my bra, under the swell of my breasts. It wasn't exactly comfortable, but it shouldn't catch the eye of roving pickpockets or anyone else who might be concerned there. I tossed the envelope in a trash can next to the shop.

I was just turning toward the entrance when I spotted them from the corner of my eye. Three unfamiliar men were sauntering toward me from the direction of the electronics store, just a little too quickly for a casual stroll. Even without looking at them directly, I felt their gazes on me.

My instincts clanged with alarm.

I swiveled and strode into the store, approaching one of the clothes racks farther inside. As I skimmed my fingers over the outfits without really noticing them, I monitored the entrance at the edge of my vision.

The three men came into the store, which was full of dresses and blouses, nothing they looked likely to wear. And they fanned out with casual precision, moving so that they nearly surrounded me.

Oh, they thought they were getting away with that, did they? I didn't know what their problem was, but I wasn't letting myself be cornered.

Grabbing a dress from the rack at random, I walked over to a clerk near the back of the store. She gave me a stiff customer service smile.

"You want to try it on, hun?" she asked, waving her manicured hand toward the dressing rooms. "You'll look stunning in that dress. Let me know if you need any help with sizes."

She deposited me in the corner dressing room, hidden by a wall from the rest of the store. I closed the door behind me and shoved the latch over.

It was a tight space. I examined the surfaces for any potential advantage before jumping and bracing my feet in the two corners of the room, holding myself well above the floor.

I waited.

When I heard someone's feet scuff the floor on the other side of the door, I held my breath.

"She was just here," a man's low voice growled, just outside. "She couldn't have gotten out."

"Is there another entrance?"

I heard rustling, and then the door handle beside mine jiggled. "They're all locked. Look underneath."

I waited until I heard the telltale sounds of a man crouching down before I struck. I whipped the door open and dove at him in a smooth motion. The man on the ground didn't have time to do more than jerk up his head before I'd tied the dress around his neck and kicked him in the nose.

He groaned and fell forward, and I hooked the other end of the dress on the doorknob, allowing his full weight to fall into the stranglehold of the fabric. As he choked and sputtered, the second man sprang at me.

I caught him in the side of the head with a roundhouse kick and rammed my elbow into the back of his skull for good measure. He collapsed with a groan next to his companion, and I sprinted out of the dressing room alcove.

Now only one man stood between me and the door. "You might want to check on your buddies!" I called to him cheerfully as I hurried toward the mall courtyard.

The guy lunged at me, and I sidestepped just in time to knock his feet out from under him. Then I sprinted to the mall entrance.

If my pursuers were any good, they'd regroup in a matter of minutes. I'd be even more ready for them then. I couldn't have staged an interrogation in the middle of the mall, but one of the grubby alleys in this end of town? No problem.

I loped a block and a half away and stationed myself behind a tree to wait for my chance.

EIGHTEEN

Garrison

"SHE HASN'T LEFT THE MALL," Blaze said from the front passenger seat, eyeing the computer that was never far from his fingertips. "There are street cams that cover any way she'd leave, and my app hasn't pinged."

He'd developed the software a few years ago—a facial recognition program he claimed was more advanced than the ones even the FBI used to catch criminals. Combined with the city-operated security cameras, Blaze could find anyone from anywhere.

I leaned back in my seat, tipping my head against the headrest. "And does anyone find it interesting that the first place she went after ditching us is a hotbed of criminal activity?"

Blaze grunted in reluctant acknowledgment. "At least three of the stores in that place are money-laundering fronts."

"And the neighborhood's got more robberies per capita than anywhere else in the city," Julius said from his spot behind the steering wheel. "We know. We still don't know what she's doing in there."

Talon stirred on the other side of the back seat from me. "It's a good thing we gave her some rope so we can find out."

I had to admit Julius wasn't being as soft on the woman as I'd been worried about. He'd come up with this idea to get a better sense of her motives and connections. Allowing her to escape had been the most practical way to discover exactly where she aimed to go and what she wanted to do when we were no longer on her tail.

But we'd never really been far away. She'd taken the bait the first second she could, and we'd been tracking her using Blaze's software ever since.

"There." Blaze tapped his laptop's screen. "She just came out the main entrance."

Julius put the car into drive and cruised around the corner toward the shabby mall. "We'll let her get a little more distance so she doesn't know we were following her the whole time, and then we'll pick her up and see what she has to say for herself."

I couldn't stop my gaze from lingering on the lithe figure on Blaze's screen. The way Dess carried herself was unlike anything I'd seen from her yet. As she strode along the sidewalk and across the street, she looked as if she'd just conquered the world. When she joined a small cluster of pedestrians, I narrowed my eyes, impressed by how well her entire demeanor changed. She *became* her surroundings, mimicking the mannerisms of the bodies around her.

It'd taken me *years* to cultivate the subtle art of merging with a crowd like that. You didn't develop it out of the blue. You had to learn it—either because you wanted to, or because it was the only way you could survive.

And we'd let this puzzle of a woman whose fighting skills could rival Talon's and who wore a façade as impenetrable as mine into our home.

"We're not going to bring her back to the penthouse, are we?" I asked.

"It depends on what she says," Julius said smoothly.

Why wasn't he more concerned about what'd just gone down? "You really think she'll tell us anything remotely true?"

"I think we'll learn *something*—and a lot of that is your job, isn't it? If she's part of something larger to do with the job that we weren't aware of, we need to know that. If this is about something totally unrelated, we need to know *that* so we can finally drop her and get on with our lives."

I snorted. As if there was much chance of that. Julius ignored me.

"She stopped," Blaze announced. "Not too far from the mall. She's just standing there by a tree… Is she waiting for someone?"

Julius parked, still a few blocks away, and frowned at the computer. "You can't tell?"

Blaze shook his head.

My skin crawled with apprehension. I hadn't liked how much uncertainty Dess had brought into our lives and our work from the first moment we'd spotted her outside the mansion.

I leaned forward and gripped Julius's shoulder from behind. "We should cut her loose now. Pretend we never saw her. It'd be easier—"

Julius's head snapped around, giving me a clear view of his right ear with its ravaged earlobe—a gift from a bullet or a piece of shrapnel sometime during his military career. He'd never given the details.

"No," he said, low and firm with a hint of menace that dared me to challenge him.

I pulled back, my mouth twisting. Julius was the boss for a reason, and questioning him was something that few people dared to do. And when he said no… well, that was final.

I nodded, though all of my distrust for Dess whirled through my mind in a frenzy. This was my crew. My brothers in arms, even if we weren't exactly fighting in any war. I'd kill or die for any of them, and no woman would change that. Dess shouldn't have me second-guessing myself and the leadership roles long-established within the Chaos Crew. She wasn't worth it.

We waited a few minutes, and Dess didn't budge. Blaze glanced at Julius. Our leader sighed and then stepped on the gas again. "Let's go get her."

He cruised down the street, and we all made a show of peering through the windows as if we were on the lookout rather than knowing exactly where our target was. When Dess came into view, Julius sped up. He veered up to the sidewalk right in front of her and fixed her with his best "you've got some explaining to do" expression.

Dess leapt backwards, her eyes flashing, but Talon and I had already hopped out and come up on either side of her. Julius got out too, letting his hand rest on the concealed holster at his hip in a subtle threat.

Dess halted in her tracks. "How…" she started, shaking her head. Her gaze darted toward the mall beyond me, and I wondered again about what she'd been waiting for.

"We've looked through half the city for you," Julius said, putting on an impressive show of frustration. He gestured to the street around us. "Do you know the kinds of things that happen on this side of town? It's even less safe than the last place we found you."

I didn't dare to glance away from her face as he spoke, but I found nothing of importance there. She looked calm, though the tightness in her shoulders suggested a hint of anger that she was caught.

If it weren't for Blaze and his software, she wouldn't have been, but we didn't need to reveal all our tools to her.

"You don't need to protect me anymore," Dess said, backing up another step, but the Chinese restaurant behind her with a foreclosure sign in the dusty window didn't offer any avenue for escape. "I survived the last couple of hours just fine on my own, didn't I?" She placed her hands on her hips, as if she'd proved something with her little escape attempt.

I saw the flicker of mischief in her eyes that nobody else caught. I noticed the way she shifted her weight from her left foot to her right one as Julius spoke to her, and I knew that she was hiding something. I knew better than to believe anything she said.

"You have no idea what you're dealing with," Julius said. "Whoever blasted their way through that mansion would make most of the criminals around here piss their pants. You may think you don't need us—you may even be right. But you're connected to this case, and until we figure out exactly how you're connected, you're not going anywhere. Get in the car."

Dess frowned at him. Then her eyes flicked to the side again, and an unexpected emotion touched her face—disappointment? Regret?

I risked glancing over my shoulder, but I couldn't tell what she'd seen that'd provoked the strange response. When I looked at her again, it was gone anyway. Her shoulders came down a smidge with what I'd have said was resignation, except she still didn't budge.

Julius moved forward with the full heft of his massive frame and grasped her upper arm. Dess tried to jerk away. "I'm not your property."

"That depends on your definition of property," I muttered.

The look she shot me should have killed me on the spot. "I'm pretty sure cops aren't allowed to take people into custody without—what—a warrant or something? Especially if you've got nothing to charge me with."

I let my lip curl into a sneer. "Did you forget so soon? We're not like other cops, sweetheart."

Julius tugged, and finally Dess came without more of a fight. Maybe she could tell that'd only end up worse for her.

Talon slid into the back seat, and Julius propelled Dess after him. I got in by her other side, more amused than I probably should have been by her irritated huff.

Some part of me kind of wanted to know what would happen if she *really* stepped out of line with Julius. He was ruthless and organized, and if something didn't go his way, his temper would ensure that it got back on track *quickly.* How would Dess react to that military-honed authority?

It'd be something to see, that was for sure.

"Let me guess," Dess muttered as Julius started the engine. "When you got your jobs, they added an extra line to your swearing-in." She raised a hand as if pledging allegiance to the police academy that I'd never attended. "I swear to serve, protect, and only illegally hold a civilian if I think it's absolutely necessary."

"Now you're getting the picture." I glanced over at her, doing my best not to pay attention to her lean frame tucked next to mine or how gorgeous her face was amid its frame of dark waves. Trouble shouldn't look that hot.

But as Julius had pointed out, my main job was figuring out the people we encountered on the job. Time to get that over with.

I folded my arms over my chest. "So, what were you up to out here? Just checking in with some friends? Or, wait, your boyfriend never let you have friends, did he?"

Blaze twitched with what might have been a wince, but he couldn't tell me to play nice. Nice hadn't gotten me anywhere with Dess before, and she wouldn't have bought that act now. I needed a reaction, whether because I hit her in the right emotional tender spot or because she got her story tangled trying to keep up with me. Either would work fine.

Dess simply rolled her eyes. "Maybe I was just trying to get as far as I could from the bunch of you. I used to live in this neighborhood. I know it pretty well—including how to avoid the wrong kinds of people." She gave me a pointed look as if to indicate I was one of the wrong kind.

"I guess that didn't work out so well for you, since here you are back with us. And nothing to show for it either."

I'd hoped for some indication that I was wrong, that she *had* accomplished something in her trek across the city, but I didn't get so much as a twitch of a muscle. "Yep," she said. "Right back where I started. Who should be more upset about that, you or me?"

I would have been annoyed, but some perverse part of me enjoyed how easily she could give back the snark I threw at her. There wasn't anything wrong with enjoying it, was there, as long as I cut to the meat of the matter before too long?

I shot her a smirk. "What makes you think I don't enjoy your luminous company?"

Dess guffawed. "Oh, only the fact that you've been pointing out how little you want me around for about two days now. Too bad your colleagues don't listen to you more."

Her jab cut *me* a little deeper than I liked. Well, if she wanted to play hardball, I could match her hit for hit. "At least I have a job. You've been scrounging off Daddy and then the boyfriend for years. Is that why you came out here—looking for someone new to leach off of?"

"How do you know I didn't already have someone lined up?"

Was she serious about that? I eyed her face and found the same analytical expression I knew that I'd find on my own.

As I opened my mouth with a retort, the car skidded to a halt so sudden it jolted all of us forward. My chest slammed into the seatbelt—

—the image of a shadowy highway flashed behind my eyes, the screech of tires and a shrill scream echoing in my ears—

—and I blinked, my hand clammy where I'd snatched at the seat in front of me, my pulse thudding at double speed. I stared through the windshield, absorbing the view of the guy who'd swerved into our lane, the daylight streaming over his truck and the street around us.

"…the drivers who don't know how to fucking drive," Julius was grumbling, pressing the horn.

I pushed myself back into my seat, willing myself to breathe steadily, to even out the thump of my heart.

It was nothing. Some jackass was in too much of a hurry to notice he'd almost caused a pile-up. No one had died. No one was going to die.

This time.

My involuntary panic reaction couldn't have lasted more than five seconds. I sealed the holes that had cracked in my walls, setting everything back to normal. But when I looked at Dess, she was watching me, and something had softened in her expression.

She'd seen it. She'd caught a glimpse of me that I'd never have wanted *anyone* to see, not even the men I'd worked alongside through life-and-death jobs for five years now. And in her reaction to seeing it, she was revealing something gentle behind the hardened, jaded front she put on too.

I wanted to destroy that softness. It wasn't what I needed from her. I needed to prove that she was a monster who didn't deserve our trust, not an empathetic girl who'd earned it.

"What?" I spat at her with more venom in my tone than I'd intended. Good. Let her hear the venom. Let her hate me. It would make my job a hell of a lot easier.

"You were in a car accident before, weren't you?" she said, not judging or prodding, just stating it as a fact. As if it was so obvious anyone could have seen it.

Anger flooded me. I'd worked for years so that nothing like this would happen, so that no one would ever dig down into the parts of my life I kept locked away even from myself, and I'd slipped up in front of the worst possible person.

I narrowed my eyes at her. "Maybe you should be worrying about your own troubles, not imaginary ones. You're in a car with four men who you hardly know, and we could do whatever the fuck we want with you. So keep your nose in your own damn business if you don't want to end up like all of your friends."

A flash of surprise crossed her expression, but there was no fear there. If she felt any, she hid it well enough that I couldn't detect even a hint of it. How the fuck could she be so good at seeing through masks and holding up her own?

And why the fuck did I find that talent so intriguing even as it infuriated me?

NINETEEN

Decima

WHEN WE GOT BACK to the apartment, I didn't exactly *sulk*, but I wasn't going to hang out with the guys like we were best buds and everything was cool either. Why the hell did the four of them have to be so determined to keep my ass around? Why'd they have to stumble on me right when I was about to beat some answers out of those losers who'd come after me in the mall?

And what was up with Garrison? I shouldn't have cared, but I knew genuine pain when I saw it. Somewhere deep behind his snarky front, he was hiding a hell of a lot of it.

It resonated inside me more than I liked. Even the anger he'd displayed when defending his weakness had been familiar. He didn't want me to see that side of him—the part of him that grieved for something he kept even more hidden.

Yeah, I knew a lot about hiding.

But I couldn't spend all my time here hiding away. If the cops were going to insist on having me around, then I'd just have to continue working that to my advantage in any way I could. I had to get somewhere with them eventually.

I'd been on the verge of taking my chances and making a break for it when I'd seen the men from the mall hustling out from the entrance. If I'd made a commotion then, they'd have noticed me right away and I'd have lost any chance of surprising them; if I'd waited until they were out of sight, I'd have lost them completely. And as soon as the cops had screwed up my shot at getting answers there, I'd been left with no further leads.

I had nowhere to go and limited cash. Coming back here with them had been the best of my bad options.

Weirdly, when I'd stepped through the front door with them, I'd been hit by a waft of relief. Like it was good to be "home." This place wasn't *my* home, and I'd sure as hell better not start thinking of it that way. Maybe Stockholm Syndrome was starting to take hold.

Shut away from the rest of them and the comfort of the rest of the apartment, I dug the flip phone out of my bra. It was a good thing I'd tucked it in there, because Julius had done a quick pat down of my pockets and waistline in the elevator.

The screen still offered me nothing. I made sure it was set to vibrate, no chance of a ringtone giving it away, and wiggled it behind a small equipment trunk in the corner which didn't look as if it'd been moved in years. There was less chance of the men finding it there than in my tote bag, which they'd already searched twice. I couldn't keep it on me without risking one of them noticing the odd shape beneath my breasts if I raised my arms at the wrong angle.

With that taken care of, a little more of the tension in my chest eased. I took off my brace to test the soreness in my wrist and run through some mild stretching exercises designed to speed along recovery. In a few more days, I might be able to take on all four of the men out there, police and military training or not. Smiling to myself and feeling ready to face them again, I tugged the brace back on and stepped out into the main room.

The only ones around were Julius and Talon. Julius was sitting at the small wooden table, currently cleared of army figures, his brow furrowed. A few sketchy lines that I couldn't decipher marked the whiteboard next to him. He had a notebook propped against the edge of the table, and even from across the room, I could see it held a neatly written list. I couldn't read it from so far away, and I knew better now than to try to get him to show it to me willingly. I might be able to take a peek later.

Talon was poised at one end of the leather sofa… with a pair of knitting needles bobbing and weaving between his muscular hands.

I blinked, making sure I wasn't seeing things. But no, the brutal, skin-headed undercover cop with combat skills that rivaled my own was definitely sitting there, knitting away. From the looks of things, he'd been at his current project for a while. About three feet of mottled red-and-orange scarf dangled beneath the needles and fell across his knees.

He caught my startled gaze and raised his eyebrows at me as if daring me to say something. "Is there a problem?" he asked in his usual cool tone.

I laughed and walked over to the other side of the sofa. "I thought that maybe it was Steffie who left the knitting bag here. If not her, possibly Blaze. Garrison would have been my third guess. You'd have been last."

I expected Talon to brush off the comment or outright ignore it, but the vibe between us had shifted since we'd sparred the other day. I'd earned a little respect somewhere in there… or else he'd decided I was more harmless than he'd thought, so he didn't have to be quite as defensive. I wasn't sure which worked in my favor better, but I'd definitely prefer the former.

"Any particular reason you'd assume that?" he asked, looping the yarn around the right needle before tipping it and sliding a stitch from the left needle. He continued the repetitive motions so smoothly and quickly I could tell this was far from his first project.

I sat down on the arm of the sofa, feeling safer there than on the cushion a foot or more closer to him. "Somehow I don't think it's going to shock you if I point out that you don't look like a knitter."

He chuckled under his breath as he finished a row. Stopping, he plucked a spare needle out of the bag and held it out to me. I eyed it warily before gripping the hard, thin rod.

"Tell me what you feel," he said.

Would we break out the tambourines after and sing "Kumbaya"? I gave him a skeptical look. "It's a knitting needle."

The corner of his mouth twitched slightly upward. I thought that was a smile. What exactly he was amused by was harder to tell.

He nodded toward me. "*Describe* the knitting needle."

I rolled my eyes. "Metal, smooth, pointy." I waggled it in the air.

"And what other things are metal, smooth, and pointy?"

Oh, all right, I saw where he was going with this. "Knives," I said, leaning back on the sofa and spinning the needle between my fingers. "Razors. Swords. But you're not stabbing anyone with these. You're literally knitting a scarf. Or a very skinny sweater."

"True," he said, taking up his stitches again. "But I *could* stab someone with them if I wanted to. If there's me and a knitting needle standing between you and someone who wants to kill you, you'd be a lot more likely to live than if I were holding a paintbrush or a lump of clay. So I'd say it's a very macho craft."

I could think of about a dozen ways to kill someone with both a paintbrush and some clay, but it seemed wisest not to mention that. Besides, he had a point.

"All right, grandma," I teased. "In that scenario, I'd still feel better if you had a gun."

He shrugged, eyeing the stretch of woven yarn before him wordlessly. I wasn't oblivious to the fact that each of the men did actually have a gun at their hip at all times. I'd bet Talon could do a good amount of damage with that needle too, though.

Curiosity itched at me. I swiveled so that I was facing him, planting my feet on the sofa cushion. "How'd you pick up the hobby? Were you drawn in by the pointy stabbiness and just decided to stick around for the wool accessories?"

I hadn't known if Julius was listening to our conversation, he'd seemed so deep in thought, but he snorted at that remark. Talon shot him a narrow glance over the top of the sofa and then returned his gaze to me. "Why do you want to know?"

"Because it's a mystery and I have a thing for unraveling them."

He tipped his head to the side in consideration and appeared to decide that my answer was acceptable. "It helps me decompress. When we're on the job, we spend a lot of time on edge, ready to act in an instant, needing to be ready for unexpected developments that could put us all in danger. The patterns I work through with the needles are predictable and straightforward. I want to make a scarf, and I get a scarf. It's a welcome change."

That made a fair bit of sense. Hearing him explain it kind of made *me* want to take up knitting. I watched him for another minute, unable to stop myself from admiring how those powerful muscles could move in such small but still incredibly skillful ways to create a product that had nothing to do with broken bones or blood.

Then he added, in case he thought I might forget what he was capable of, "It doesn't hurt to have a few additional weapons around the place either."

I had to grin. "Of course not."

Talon was the complete opposite of Garrison, wasn't he? Garrison held all kinds of fire in tight while putting on a blasé, disaffected front. Talon appeared unaffected... because he really was that way. I didn't sense that he was holding anything back in his answer. When he didn't want to tell you something, he simply didn't say anything rather than making something up.

I could appreciate that kind of straightforwardness too.

But that didn't mean the guy didn't have *any* emotions. He obviously got comfort out of this hobby. He liked to feel prepared, liked the reassurance of knowing the outcome in advance.

And I'd definitely seen sparks of something more heated in him when we'd gotten close during our sparring session.

It wouldn't do me any good to dwell on that. Watching his hands work was already making my skin tingle in odd ways. I latched onto an appropriate change of subject, what a normal person who hadn't focused their whole life on learning to kill might have said. At least, I thought so.

"What do you do with the things you knit?" I glanced around the room, not seeing any vast quantities of hats or mittens or blankets on display—not even one.

"I knit a new scarf for the guys every winter, because Blaze especially is always misplacing them, and the rest I donate to a clothing drive around Christmastime. What else am I going to do with twenty scarves a year?"

Just like that, my perception of him shifted yet again. There was something so… kindhearted about making clothes to keep his partners warm that didn't fit his icy demeanor at all. And donating the rest to charity? I guessed it'd have been a hassle to sell them or something, but still.

Maybe I should throw out the entire idea of categorizing Talon. It didn't matter how big the box was—he would never fit.

Annoyingly, that made him even more appealing.

Before I could figure out how to extricate myself from the conversation that had drawn me in more than I'd intended, the front door banged open. As Garrison and Blaze strode inside, I sat a little straighter.

Garrison smiled with a cool confidence that gnawed at my nerves, his gaze skimming right over me. Apparently I didn't even exist to him now. Fine.

Julius spoke before anyone else had the chance. "We need to talk," he said in that low commanding voice that his colleagues responded to immediately. Talon put away his knitting and got up. Julius walked over to the kitchen area, even farther from me than he already was, and the other three met him there.

I watched as they gathered on the other side of the island. Their conference began with voices too quiet for me to make out. I got up and ambled over as if I thought Julius's order might have applied to me too, even though I was sure it hadn't.

Julius noticed me before I was even halfway there. "This doesn't involve you," he said firmly, which made me even more certain their conversation had something to do with the household murders. If it had nothing to do with me, why would it matter if I heard a stray word or two?

I had the urge to demand they let me in on the discussion, but I'd seen how well that'd gone in the past—or rather, how badly. So I meandered across the room, not getting closer to them but not veering too far away, watching for alternative sources of information from the corners of my eyes as they fell back into their hushed exchange.

Ah ha. Garrison had left the kettle sitting on the dining table after his last mug of cocoa, and its stainless-steel surface reflected the kitchen interior like a slightly warped mirror. I sank down into one of the chairs at the table with my back to the men and reached for an apple out of the fruit bowl, just to give me a reason to be sitting there. As I ran my fingers over the smooth skin, I let my gaze linger on the kettle's shiny surface.

I couldn't see a whole lot more from here than from the sofa, but I could see it without them knowing I was watching. Their voices stayed low, but their body language relaxed incrementally.

Julius held his notebook up for the others to see. His small, delicate scrawl was indecipherable from here, but the gesture confirmed that he'd written down something important if I could ever get my hands on it. Blaze moved around the group in his usual energetic way, blocking my view of the others every few seconds. I gritted my teeth. If he would stay fucking still for five seconds…

He began murmuring to Garrison, likely heckling him in the way they *always* did with one another. When he stepped to the side, Talon said something with a wave toward Blaze and then his computers. Blaze grinned—and jerked his flattened fingers past his throat in a vicious gesture I only knew to mean one thing.

Death.

It was *Blaze* making the gesture, though, so maybe it was his over-dramatic way of indicating something less bloody that he was going to do with his computer system? Seeing it unsettled me all the same. Should a cop really look that eager about the idea of killing, even metaphorically?

Of course, as Garrison had gleefully pointed out earlier today, these men weren't typical cops.

Julius said a few more things with brisk motions of his hands. Then Garrison jerked out his phone. He was standing at an angle where the screen, which he was holding away from the other guys, showed up almost perfectly on the kettle's reflection. I restrained a satisfied smile as I noted the four-digit passcode he quickly typed in.

Jackpot. I filed the number away in my mind, tying each digit to an image to make sure it'd stick and I'd recall it when necessary later.

There'd been some development in the case that they didn't want me to know about, but that didn't matter. I crossed my feet beneath the table and brought the apple to my mouth. When I sank my teeth in the crisp flesh, its tart juice seeped down my throat, and then I let myself smile.

I didn't need their permission to learn whatever they knew about the case. I only needed to not get caught.

TWENTY

Blaze

I STRODE to the locked door that led to the stairs, typed in the code, and let it swing open, already feeling rejuvenated by the mere idea of meditation. I was just stepping out into the first waft of fresh air when Dess's voice followed me.

"Where are you going?"

When I glanced back, she was leaning over the side of the sofa where she sat beside Talon. She'd been watching the way Talon knitted so attentively that I hadn't thought she would notice me leaving.

The casual way she spoke to me gave me a weird sense of relief despite the way she'd reacted to me the one time I'd gotten particularly close to her. She hadn't shown a single particle of violence toward any of us since then, and obviously I hadn't damaged her trust in me irreparably. She seemed to have brushed that moment aside as if it'd never happened, and I was happy to let her do that.

I tipped my head toward the stairs. "I'm going up to the rooftop deck. You haven't seen that yet, have you?" I paused and then decided it was safe to ask as long as I remembered to keep my hands to myself, which I didn't think was going to be a problem after the lesson she'd taught me the first time. "Want to come?"

She sprang to her feet with the effortless yet practiced grace I couldn't help admiring. "Get out of this place for a bit? Hell, yes."

I opened the door wider for Dess as she approached, and she gave me a quick smile as she passed me before studying the stairwell on the other side. "These stairs lead to the roof?"

I pointed upward with a nod. "You've got to have some kind of outdoor space, or it's not much of a home, as far as I'm concerned. I try to get up there every day, at least for my ten minutes of meditation."

Dess had already started up the steps. She glanced back at me over her shoulder with an arch of her eyebrows. "You don't strike me as the meditation type. But then, I wouldn't have pegged Talon as a knitter either."

"I aim to surprise," I said in an automatically teasing tone, and caught myself just before I flashed her a flirty smile. I was too much in the habit of turning on the charm, and she made way too appealing a target for it. But she'd made her interest—or lack thereof—*very* clear.

"Julius taught me," I added in a more subdued tone as we tramped up the stairs, Dess in front of me. "He has a whole yoga routine he does, actually. He showed me all the moves, but the meditation part was the only thing that stuck. It helps me keep my focus for the rest of the day."

Dess hummed to herself but didn't ask anything else. *Her* focus was fixed on the door at the top of the stairs.

That one wasn't locked. There was no point, since no one could get up here anyway—we'd made sure of that.

As we stepped out into the warm summer sunlight, I made a quick scan of our security measures. The entire space was as big as the common room downstairs. The seamless wooden wall that surrounded it stood ten feet tall, and no structure nearby rose high enough to give a view inside. The outer walls of the apartment building itself were sheer and designed to avoid offering enough ledges or footholds for a person to climb up. The only way anyone was getting a peek or a toe onto our deck was by helicopter.

That was also the only way anyone was going to get off it, other than by going back down the stairs. Dess might have had amazing skills, but she couldn't scramble down a fifteen-story building that offered nothing to hold on to. And I didn't think she was going to be summoning any helicopters.

The space was safe both from intruders and from her making another escape attempt.

I rolled my shoulders back, relaxing with the mental confirmation of what I'd already known, and dragged in a deep breath of the warm air. Being up here was *way* better than the stuffy greenhouse-style yard at the safe house we'd left behind.

Dess took in the space with the same calm alertness she seemed to approach almost every situation. She ambled across the patio tiles and sank onto the wicker sofa near the door. After a moment, she tipped her head to the sky with a small smile.

The look suited her. In the full sunlight, she glowed with artless beauty. The light shone across her silky black hair, the faint breeze stirring the waves against her shoulders. Her smooth skin seemed to soak up every ounce of the sun's rays. Had any of the other guys seen her in this light, or was I the only one privileged enough?

It *was* a privilege.

I forced myself to look away, moving toward the center of the sun-warmed deck where I most enjoyed sitting. I settled there with my legs crossed and got started on my meditation.

With each deep breath, I let go of more and more of the thoughts in their constant whirl in my head. Vaguely, I sensed Dess stand up and move around the roof, but I didn't let her draw too much of my attention. A certainty filled me that even if she did pull off an impossible escape, I'd find her. I had before, and I would again.

Even knowing this, she had too much presence for me to completely ignore her, so I allowed my awareness of her to take a fundamental role in my meditation. Stillness had always been my enemy—something I couldn't quite capture—but the movement of the world around me gave my mind an outlet for its frenetic energy. A car honking below, the occasional shouts from the street, Dess's slow circuit of the deck. All of it centered me in a way I couldn't anywhere else.

Keeping myself still yet in tune with the motion around me despite the chaos in my life gave me a sense of calming reassurance. I could process and release all the input, and it grew sharper with each moment I breathed through the meditative exercise. When my mind latched onto a thought, I released it and allowed it to flow back out of me.

I'd missed my sessions here while we were staked out at the safe house, and now that I was back, I already felt more capable of tackling the world. I felt *invincible.*

I concluded with a few final deep breaths, adjusting to the shift in my thoughts and my sense of my body, no longer quite so restless—for now. Then I opened my eyes.

Dess was leaning against the wall near Garrison's telescope, watching me with her brow knit. I didn't acknowledge her expression as I stood and stretched, releasing the last dregs of tension that remained in my body. With a great sigh, I finally met her gaze fully. "That's better."

She gave me a smile that looked a little puzzled, and her gaze shifted to the telescope. She stepped closer, cocking her head. Garrison would have thrown a fit seeing her running a finger down the sleek black surface of his prized possession.

"Are you a stargazer too?" she asked.

I shook my head. "That's Garrison's department."

"Really?" She studied the telescope a little longer and then dropped onto one of the nearby deck chairs.

I followed suit, picking up a Rubix cube I'd left up here one day or another. My fingers fell into place around its surface, twisting one row and then another. It drove Garrison crazy that I didn't care that I never actually "solved" one of these. I just liked seeing the different arrays of colors that ended up appearing.

"Have you ever used one?" I asked, indicating the telescope.

Dess shook her head and looked up at the sky, exposing the sleek line of her throat. "I've never spent much time outside," she admitted.

"And I've never even seen one of these in person. You can really make out that many more stars than just with your eyes?"

"Yep," I said. "And planets and moons and that sort of thing too. I've got to admit, I don't really know what Garrison gets out of it. I can find prettier pictures of space on the internet in two seconds flat."

Dess let out a soft laugh. "Of course you can." She turned back to me, watching the swift but aimless flicks of my fingers over the Rubix cube. "So, what is it *you* like about meditation? It looks pretty boring from the outside."

I had to let out a laugh of my own. Her bluntness was as refreshing as the air up here. I could tell she wasn't trying to be insulting, only making an honest observation.

"I'd bet it does," I said. "Have you ever tried meditating?"

"No to that as well. Apparently I've missed out on a lot of things."

I thought about how to best explain it. I could have given her the response that Julius would have used—the one that claimed that yoga and meditation relaxed the body and improved potential. It allowed for cleaner fighting and a clearer mind.

But I didn't use meditation for those reasons.

I set the cube down on my lap. "Well, the *idea* is that it's supposed to ground you. It stills the world around you, and it allows you to simply exist without being affected by thoughts of the past or the future."

She made a sound of acknowledgment, picking up on my framing. "But for you it's different?"

"Yeah. I can't be still, not really. I've never been able to completely slow down. When I meditate, I can focus on the moving world around me, and it feels like it brings a sort of balance inside me. Recognizing that I'm surrounded by as much energy outside as I have inside me helps to still me in a way, I guess."

Dess nodded, giving me a thoughtful look. "You do seem to move around an awful lot."

I glanced down at my foot, which had begun to tap against the tiles, and grinned. "My mom always said I was full of beans. The doctor said I probably had ADHD, but my parents never really pursued that. They figured I should get it under control through self-discipline or whatever. Which is a lot easier to say than do. I pissed off a lot of the other kids at school, always running around, talking their ears off. We won't get into how many times they kicked my ass."

And worse things that I didn't want to think about. I'd moved on from all that.

"That's awful," Dess said, sounding offended enough on my behalf to gratify me.

I shrugged. "Kids being kids. Grown-ups refusing to do their jobs and rein them in. I figured out some things, made use of the skills I developed to put a few people in their places, and now I've put all that behind me. People can judge me as much as they want, but I am who I am. Take it or leave it."

"So, you just…don't care what people think about you?"

"Well, I care about the people who matter, like the guys I work with, in whatever areas are relevant. But otherwise, no. It doesn't matter what anyone thinks. I lived too long trying to be who people wanted me to be and beating myself up for not fitting their preferences. It was miserable—I won't go back to that. Now, I'm happy with myself. I live my life to the fullest and enjoy every twist and turn along the way."

Dess's gray eyes darkened. "But you're a cop—you've got to be chasing down criminals and figuring out murders and the rest all the time. How can you enjoy life like that?"

The question sounded genuine, and it tugged at my heart. "There's more to life than work. I'm sitting here chatting with you right now, aren't I? And I chose this career because I get a thrill out of a lot of it too—tracking people down, figuring out what they're up to." We'd just avoid the subject of what the crew *really* did with that information.

Dess nodded, but her expression stayed bemused. The idea seemed foreign to her, almost like a fantasy novel full of fictional characters that could never exist in reality.

Did she really have no concept of how to enjoy herself? God, what a number that prick of an ex-boyfriend had done on her.

"I'm sure you can enjoy your life too, Dess," I had to say. "I don't know the details of what you went through before you ended up with us, but after this case is over, you can go do whatever you want. It'll be your choice now."

Assuming the client didn't decide she was a loose end we had to deal with.

Dess smiled, but a trace of sadness lingered in it. What had she endured that made her believe that life wasn't worth taking pleasure in?

I knew so little about her. She'd mentioned a bad relationship, and we'd killed her friend during Viper's job, but that was it. I knew nothing about her past, and I had no idea what could make things better for her.

I examined her stormy eyes and found a restlessness and… something else I couldn't identify.

"I guess I've always been focused on satisfying other people's expectations," she said slowly. "Doing what they asked me to do as well as I could. And sometimes I liked that. But I've never really had a chance to make all that many decisions on my own."

I could hear the honesty in her voice, and it brought an ache into my chest, bittersweet. No one should have a life like that, but she'd trusted me enough to open up to me.

I leaned toward her, intending to grab her hand but stopping myself. She didn't like being touched, so I wouldn't touch her. But I could still help.

"Well, what's something that makes you happy?" I asked. "Just for you, not because you know someone else will be happy about it too."

"Just for me…" She trailed off, and I could see the wheels turning in her mind. Again, unwavering sadness washed through me as she struggled to come up with a single thing that made her happy for its own sake.

"I like chocolate," she declared, a smile springing to her face that looked almost triumphant, as if it was a victory for her to land on that one thing. Maybe it was.

I remembered the hot chocolate that Garrison had made and shared with her. She *had* looked shocked and utterly delighted when he'd given her some. That was an easy thing for me to offer, whether Garrison liked me dipping into his collection or not, and I had every intention of making sure she had plenty for as long as she stayed with us.

"What else?" I prodded.

She answered a little more quickly this time. "Exercising makes me happy. The adrenaline rush and feeling how much I can do with my body. Sparring and coming out on top."

Which I'd bet she did most of the time. I wished she'd pummeled that boyfriend of hers good before she'd taken off on him.

"What about entertainment?" I asked. "Like—movies, music, TV, books?"

She brightened up so fast my pulse skipped a beat. "Oh! There was this TV show I saw once… Years ago, and I think it was already kind of old. I just happened across it one day when I didn't have anything else to do at that moment, and then I got sucked in and couldn't help watching the whole thing. It was about a spy and her husband solving crimes." A crease formed in her forehead. "I missed the title sequence, though, and I never could find it again."

But it'd stuck with her all this time. I stood up, abruptly energized. This was something I could do for her, something no one else in the penthouse could, at least nowhere near as easily. And it'd be so worth it to give her a little more of the happiness she'd obviously been sorely lacking.

I beckoned for her to follow me. "Come on. We're going to find your spy show."

Dess leapt to her feet, her eyes widening. "Just like that? How—"

I grinned at her. "You'll see."

I marched back to the penthouse with Dess at my heels. Talon had moved to the kitchen where he was making himself a cup of coffee. He didn't comment when I grabbed my laptop and stole his spot on the sofa.

Dess sank down next to me. "Do you really think you can find it?"

There was something almost childlike about her hesitant excitement, something that contrasted sharply with the lethal fighter I'd witnessed in the safe-house attack. Yet again, I found myself wondering just how this woman had become who she was… whoever that was exactly.

"I know I can," I told her with total confidence, flexing my fingers over the keys. "All I need are a few details about the show—the plotline in the episode you saw, the characters, the setting—as specific as possible. We already know it had a woman who was a spy and her husband… was he a spy too?"

Dess frowned, tapping her lips. Somehow she got even more gorgeous when her expression went distant with thought, still lit with hope, the black waves of her hair tumbling around her face.

"I think he might have been a doctor?" she said hesitantly. "There was one part where she got shot and her arm was bleeding, and he had to give her stitches. He had some kind of medical experience, anyway." An amused gleam came into her eyes. "Maybe he picked it up in the army like Julius."

"Could be." I added that note to my first search string. "Did you recognize any of the actors? That would help narrow it down too."

She shook her head with a sheepish grimace. "I'm not very up on celebrities and that sort of thing. I remember she was blond, and he had dark hair. Both slim and fit. I think…" Her eyebrows drew together with concentration. "His name was Ron—Ronald. He hated it when she called him by his full name, so she did it to tease him sometimes. I can't remember what her name was… It might have started with H?"

Now we were getting somewhere. My fingers flew over the keyboard, typing in all that information, tweaking a word here and there as the search results spilled out across the screen, narrowing by date because she'd said the show had looked older—ah ha!

I clicked on an image of the DVD cover to enlarge it and turned the laptop toward Dess. It was a campy '60s show that'd only run two seasons, with a blond spy named Helen and her husband, a dark-haired paramedic named Ronald. They were posed in the image back-to-back beneath the title, *Spy Time*, her with her fingers held up in front of her in the shape of a gun and him looking shocked.

It wouldn't have struck me as the kind of show I'd expect Dess to be into, but her mouth dropped open immediately. "Wow. That's it. You just—it only took you a couple of minutes."

I waggled my fingers, flushing with pleasure. "The magic of the internet and a healthy respect for search algorithms. Now that we've found it, how'd you like to watch an episode?"

A small laugh tumbled out of her. "Can we really?"

"Of course. Your wish is my command. Just give me another minute or so…"

I sent my computer scanning through the hordes of legit and—being honest—mostly illegitimate media sites out there and found one that was streaming *Spy Time.* It was so simple I grabbed the TV remote and clicked it on at the same time. Dess scooted forward on the sofa, glancing between me and the TV. A couple more clicks, and…

The first episode started playing in front of us. Peppy '60s music spilled out of the speakers as the characters romped from one crazy scenario to another in the opening sequence.

Dess's lips parted. She gazed at the screen with an expression that could only be described as rapturous. Then she shot me a quick glance, her eyes shining. "Thank you. I really do appreciate it."

Her obvious delight sent a flutter through my chest. I'd done something good today.

"I was happy to," I said honestly. "Now watch!"

She smiled again, with a softness I wouldn't have expected to ever see from her either, and relaxed back into the corner of the sofa. She pulled up her knees in her usual closed-off way, but this time, she didn't seem like she was guarding herself, only getting comfortable. As she watched the show play out, the saddened expression that came from a life of hardships—I had to assume—transformed into perfect contentment.

What a sight.

One of the main characters cracked a joke on-screen, and Dess laughed loudly, covering her mouth as if even she was startled by the sound. The smile didn't quite fade from her eyes.

She could watch her show all she liked. I couldn't stop watching *her*. I didn't know when I'd see that joy again, and while it lasted, I couldn't look away.

I'd embrace every last second of it, and I already knew I'd do whatever I could to make it happen again.

TWENTY-ONE

Decima

EVEN AS I lay on my cot perfectly still, my mind wouldn't stop shifting back and forth between thoughts. Maybe I needed to try some of that meditation stuff. Although Blaze had said it didn't actually help him to settle down but just to feel more in harmony with the rest of the world or something, so who knew if it'd work for me either?

He'd said a lot of things today. Things that had set my mind into this whirling of uncertainty. I'd felt so… so *good* watching that episode of *Spy Time*, everything else in my life falling away, laughs tumbling out of me like I couldn't remembering happening since I was a kid.

But then, as the credits had rolled, he'd turned to me and asked if I wanted to watch another, and reality had come crashing in. There *were* a hell of a lot of other things in my life, things I couldn't—shouldn't—forget. How could I sit there laughing at some silly TV show when Anna and everyone else in the household were dead, when I'd barely made any progress into figuring out who'd killed them, let alone bringing them justice?

Blaze could treat life as a game all he wanted, but he didn't know what mine was made up of. He didn't understand how important it'd been for me to stay focused and train as hard as I had. Every time I'd left the household, I'd been risking my life to take down a threat, with the whole household depending on me. Happiness was a distraction, not something I should have been chasing.

And yet… some part of me wanted so badly to go out there and beg him to put on that second episode. What was wrong with me?

I couldn't stand keeping my body motionless any longer. Pushing myself upright, I eyed the exercise equipment that filled the rest of the room the cops had given me. Working out had always been my surest method to blow off steam and regain my focus.

I needed to get my priorities straight, and all of the emotion boiling inside of me was accomplishing the opposite. It had to go.

A half-hour sprint on the treadmill would start the job well, and an extended arm workout after that—weights and maybe some bodyweight work—would finish the job. The prospect of exhausting myself thoroughly brought me a much more comfortable sense of relief.

I pulled my hair back from my face and went through several opening stretches. Getting on the treadmill, I allowed myself to ease into its grip and resistance before jogging on it. I'd used them before, but every machine was a little different. You could roll an ankle if you started at top speed on equipment you weren't familiar with.

Once I'd set my ideal pace, I flew. Remembering Noelle's coaching, I willed my breathing to remain steady until the entire process became a constant thrum of instinct and will. The running drove me forward, my legs and lungs started to burn, and the long days of emotion-filled events peeled away from me one layer at a time.

I turned the treadmill up another notch, adjusting my form and easily keeping pace. My heartbeat increased in tempo with it. My ribs thrummed with each hard pound of my feet, but they were nearly healed. The pain was mild enough that I could breathe right through it in a matter of minutes.

Just how I liked it.

When the burn started to prick at my muscles, switching from exhilaration to exhaustion, I slowed my sprint to a fast lope and continued, closing my eyes. I'd seen normal women jogging along the city streets before, passing by me while I was immersed in a mission. Did they get the same release out of it that I did, or did they run for some other reason?

The door to the workout room opened with a squeak of the hinges, and I spared a glance behind me. Talon stood in the doorway, a towel slung over his shoulder and a jug of water dangling from his hand. I tilted my head up in greeting but didn't give him more of an acknowledgment than that.

"I heard you going at it and figured I'd join you," he said. "The others have all headed out, and I could use something to keep me occupied." He paused as if waiting for my approval.

I wondered if he'd turn around and leave if I told him to. Had it been anyone else, I might have tested that question, but I knew Talon wouldn't attempt to make small talk while he worked out. Anyway, it was his exercise room. I was just an interloper here.

I gave him a sharp nod, and he didn't say another word as he walked over to the rack of dumbbells. The weights clinked as he lifted a couple. I waited until his sounds of effort filled the room before I slowed to a fast walk and caught my breath.

My legs ached beautifully, and a thin layer of sweat covered my entire body. I raised the hem of my shirt and wiped the sweat from my face as my heart regained a normal, steady tempo. As I came down from the high of the exertion, my gaze traveled over to Talon, just as he lifted the weights he'd picked up.

Oh, fuck. I'd already known he was an immaculate specimen of manhood, but watching the muscles all through his shoulders, arms, and back flex to perfect effect made my sex clench. As he raised and lowered the weights with absolute control, the image rose up in my mind of what it would feel like to be held against that body, handled with the same muscular precision.

If watching a TV show could bring some kind of bliss, imagine how good indulging in *that* kind of "enjoyment" could be.

My lips tightened as I registered the thought that had just crossed my mind. I'd come in here to burn away my unwanted emotions, not stir up more of them. Apparently, I hadn't run myself ragged enough on the treadmill.

With a groan, Talon placed his weights back on the rack and met my eyes, the blue of his as intense as ever. Sweat glistened atop his shaved scalp, enticing me to run my hands over the smooth skin.

"Are you done?" he asked. "I thought maybe we could spar."

I raised my eyebrows. "Eager to show off your skills at dominating an injured opponent again?"

He gave me an even look, unfazed by my jab. "I find it's the best kind of workout. Keeps the mind sharp as well as the body in shape. And you're a good challenge even when injured. But I wasn't planning on dominating."

He strode to the chest at the side of the room and opened it, pulling out a pair of boxing gloves and sparring pads, creased with use but still shinier than the ones at the safe house.

He passed the boxing gloves to me, and I tapped his arm with one after I took them. "You should wear gloves too. You're not my teacher, and I don't need you to go easy on me. If we're going to spar, let's actually spar."

He eyed me, still holding the pads that he'd planned on using to direct and deflect my hits. "You don't want to box with me."

"Don't I?"

Whatever Talon found in my glance must have convinced him, because he dropped the pads and lifted his own pair of boxing gloves. "You don't want me to go easy on you, huh?" he asked, falling into a fighting stance.

The pose came to him so naturally that I almost questioned my decision. Not because I didn't think I could take him, but because something low in my belly liquified at the sight of his confident power.

No. I wasn't going to stand here and drool over him like some kind of nitwit. I tugged both boxing gloves onto my hands, one over the damned brace that I often contemplated chucking out the window. "Do your worst."

He shook his head. "I'm not doing my worst with you. An easy warm-up first, then we can get into light boxing." I *swore* I detected a hint of humor in his tone.

I didn't want to warm up more. I wanted to get rid of all those pesky feelings that continued to multiply in his presence. Didn't he understand that?

Of course, he didn't. He barely ever showed so much as a flicker of emotion. In a way that was good. I wasn't the slightest bit worried that he'd put on a cajoling front and turn on the sweet talk that would bring up horrible memories rather than desire. He wasn't *trying* to seduce me. But I still had the urge to provoke him in other ways.

If I pushed hard enough, I could get something from him. He was a man, after all, and even the most stoic ones could be pushed to their breaking points.

I should know.

Rather than starting easy, I swung my left fist with all the intensity I could, and Talon quickly deflected it.

"What kind of cops are you, anyway?" I asked, throwing another punch. I'd either get some information out of him or rile him up. I'd be fine with either outcome. "Living together undercover, breaking all kinds of rules—you've got to be some special type. FBI? CIA? Some other string of three letters?"

Talon shook his head. "Just the usual kind."

"Do you deal with a lot of cases like what happened at my friend's house? How often do total massacres happen around here anyway?"

He went quiet, and I ducked one of his slower punches, elbowing him hard in the gut when he left a small opening. A burst of air shot out of him, and he clenched his jaw as he jerked back.

"Take it easy," he said firmly, leaving no room for argument. He clearly didn't know me as well as he hoped.

I moved in with a swift one-two, ignoring the twinge in my bad hand when he batted it aside—because that gave me a chance to shove my other fist into his stomach.

The glove's padding muted the impact, but Talon still groaned from the force of the blow. The frustration that blazed in his eyes for just an instant left me a little giddy. One point to me.

"That's it? You're just going to ignore my questions?" I said.

His blows remained easy, practically mocking, as if he still didn't believe I could keep up. "There's nothing to say. You know that we can't discuss our other cases."

"Fine, what about *this* case?" I insisted, bouncing from foot to foot and awaiting another opening. He had his face guarded with ironclad defenses, but his abdomen—the same spot I continued assaulting—couldn't be defended properly with our height difference. I hit him there again and deflected his returning blow.

Cool. Calm. Collected. I needed to break him out of his careful control.

"No," he said, and his tone left little room for argument. "It's classified."

"Yes, so you all keep saying," I shot back. "I think you just don't want to admit how stumped you are. I told you more in that one little trip by the house than the bunch of you had figured out on your own, didn't I?"

I threw a combination of punches to Talon's abdomen, looping one around and hitting him in the side. His mouth twitched toward a frown.

"Enough talking," he demanded, and I knew I was getting somewhere. "This is sparring, not an interrogation."

"Why can't it be both?" I taunted, bobbing and weaving around him. "Prove that you've figured out *anything at all* about the people who murdered my friend. Give me some hope that you're going to find the pricks who did that to her. Do you have any idea what it's like, seeing someone you care about slaughtered like that? Haven't you ever given a shit about a single person in your life?"

His eyes flashed again, searing hotter as he glared at me. I'd hit a nerve, a good one, but I wasn't done. "What, is it because nobody ever loved you? Is that your excuse for being cold as an ice cube—why you can't be bothered to give me even one ounce of closure? Why the fuck should you care about anyone other than yourself?"

His defenses dropped just a fraction, and I struck. I smacked him hard across the face, and his head seemed to whip to the side in slow motion.

Then everything sped up to a blur. In a single moment, he shook off his gloves and snatched both my wrists in his hands. He shoved me, and I could do nothing but backstep with him until my back was pressed flush against the cool wall. His body caged me there as he pinned my arms above my head.

The musky scent of his sweat and a feral tang that was all him washed over me. He leaned so close his breath grazed my face. "Give it up," he snarled, his voice deeper and more threatening. "You're not getting anything out of me."

The pure masculinity that oozed from him—the fierceness in his stance, the power in his hold even though I knew I could break it if I tried hard enough—sparked an uncontrollable, insatiable flare of desire that couldn't be suppressed. His mouth had come so close to mine, and all at once I could think of nothing but closing that distance.

My brain short-circuited—that's the only way I can explain it. I lunged, not to break free but to steal a kiss.

My mouth met Talon's roughly. He froze, his grip loosening in shock, his lips surprisingly soft but unmoving beneath mine. Panic flashed through the flood of my desire. Had I wrongly assumed there'd been interest on his side?

Just as I started to pull back, embarrassment flushing my cheeks, Talon shoved his body more solidly against mine and kissed me back hard.

His grip on my pinned wrists tightened, but somehow that only made the kiss more delicious. I groaned against his lips, and he all but devoured me. His tongue swept into my mouth, his teeth grazing my lips, all the muscular planes of his body pressing up against me. The power radiating from him brought me to my metaphorical knees.

As he kissed me again, our mouths crashing together even more violently, I brought my own tongue out to play. I'd never known how thrilling it would be to spar like this instead. His hips rocked into me, a hard bulge brushing my lower belly, and every nerve in my body clanged with need.

His lips moved to my neck, nipping and licking and claiming every inch of skin. Abruptly, he released my wrists, grasping my thighs instead. He pushed me up the wall just high enough so that the hard length of him could settle against my sex.

Oh my fucking God. The friction of it drove me wild, making me want to claw at him until I'd torn off all the layers of clothes between me and him, until he could be plunging right inside me.

What had gotten into me?

The thought had only just flitted through my head when the ravaging of my neck transformed into kisses that were almost tender. An image flashed through my mind—teasing words in a sweet voice, gentle caresses, never letting up, never stopping no matter how much I tried to wrench myself away—

I stiffened, transported out of the moment and back to that other time and place I wished I could forget.

I closed my eyes tightly, trying to ground myself back in the present. It'd felt so *good* a second ago. But I couldn't get back to that place where this intimacy felt like a gift rather than an assault, not when Talon had gone soft on me.

Maybe that was crazy, but I already knew I wasn't a normal woman. My body needed what it needed.

I flung both boxing gloves to the ground alongside his and gripped his shirt with a clenched fist, yanking on it until he raised his head to meet my eyes. The lust hazing the icy blue irises had me soaking my panties. But I had to make this clear, or we couldn't go any farther. And holy fuck did I want to find out how far this could go.

"I'm not a porcelain doll," I said, low and determined. "So don't treat me like I'm one. Give me everything you've fucking got. Make it war, not love."

Something flickered in his gaze. Then he reached a hand behind me and wrapped it around my ponytail, pulling my head back and exposing my throat to him. He bit hard on the side of my throat, and I gasped, a slight moan escaping my lips.

Yes, that was what worked. I felt my entire body melt at the gesture. This was nothing like the asshole who'd violated me with false sweetness before. This was something totally different—different and fucking amazing.

Talon shoved his free hand down my pants, palming my pussy, and a jolt of blissful heat rushed through me. My breaths fractured into panting.

"How rough do you want it?" he said into my ear, tugging back on my ponytail with more force.

I let out a strangled sound as his finger flicked over the sensitive spot between my thighs. One touch set off a quiver of pleasure that took my breath away completely. Was this what sex was supposed to feel like? What it normally felt like for most people? If so, how the hell did they manage to do anything else?

"I want you to make me scream," I whispered, and slammed my mouth into his once more.

Talon's next move nearly accomplished my request in one go. He plunged two fingers into me, still stroking the place right at the core of me that made me squirm and whimper with need. The place that had been too long deprived of a touch other than my own. The way he touched me there—the roughly oscillating motions he made combined with the crush of his lips against mine—flooded me with so much giddy heat I could barely think.

I broke away from his lips long enough to rip my shirt off over my head, leaving only my sports bra. Talon dove in to leave tingling bites up and down my neck, finally dipping his head to the exposed hollow of my cleavage as his fingers kept pumping in and out of me. I writhed against the wall, desperate to reach some point I couldn't even explain. One of my hands dropped to that tempting bulge behind the fabric of his pants.

Talon jerked back with a muttered curse. He withdrew his hand from my own pants and lifted his fingers slick with the proof of my hunger. Holding my gaze, he licked my arousal off him, and I just about went up in flames.

The smile that pulled to his face was pure, unadulterated masculine assurance. A heady tremor rippled through me even with him barely touching me.

He took a step back. "Don't move," he ordered.

I had absolutely no desire to be anywhere but here. Where the hell was *he* going, though?

He all but hurtled out of the room and barreled back in mere seconds later with a foil wrapper in his hand. Understanding clicked in my head. Of course. I hadn't even thought—

But why would I? I'd never gotten this close to any man except the one who'd taken what I hadn't wanted to give. And besides, Noelle had brought me to get a birth control implant inserted into my arm years ago, after that incident—one of the most effective ones, if she was to be believed. Just in case.

It didn't protect against everything, though. Who knew how many women Talon had been with before me? I didn't bother to mention my own version of protection as he prowled toward me. Every thought but the act we were about to commit fled my mind.

Talon hooked his fingers around my bra and yanked it off me. Before he could close his hands over my bare breasts, I wrenched at his T-shirt. He tossed it aside, and I took in the expanse of black and gray lines. Intricately woven tattoos covered his chest and his broad shoulders. It was an utter masterpiece of guns, bones, and military tags, shaded to a terrifying perfection, mesmerizing and beautiful.

No, *beautiful* wasn't the right word for the grandeur of Talon's naked torso.

He was a mountain of sculpted scars and tattoos, muscles bulging through all of them and tanned skin weaving it all together. His body was a fine piece of art. From the ragged scar poking up from his hip to the small, thin lines that ran across his biceps, he stood as a living, mesmerizing sculpture.

That masterpiece lifted me onto a clear section of the weight rack and peeled off my pants and panties with one swift gesture that left me even wetter than before. As he dropped his own pants, I couldn't take my eyes off the thick, corded length of his cock.

He smoothed the condom over the hard shaft and then pinned my arms over my head again. I arched my back instinctively, and he looked over my entire exposed body—every small scar and curve.

He lowered his head to suck one and then the other nipple into his mouth, tugging with his teeth on the release. A gasp tumbled out of me at the shock of combined pain and pleasure. Then he lined himself up and thrust into me, balls deep.

With that motion, he fulfilled my request. He made me scream. The sound reverberated through me alongside the electric burst of bliss. No sensation I'd ever been able to produce with my hand had come close to this.

Talon hesitated, examining my features, and a prickle of panic rose up again. I hissed through my teeth. "Fuck me hard."

Something flared in his eyes. He pulled back and thrust into me again, dipping his head to reclaim the peak of one of my breasts in tandem. Each roll of his hips brought a delicious burn between my thighs that spread all through my torso.

He was big, but I'd been so wet and ready I could take him. The stretch was nothing short of paradise.

Talon could still have hurt me if he'd been too rough about it. I could tell he restrained himself just slightly, adding a little twist here, shifting his angle there, in ways that made me moan. But through it all the force of his thrusts and the scrape of his teeth against my skin kept all sensation except enjoyment at bay.

As he found his rhythm and saw what I could handle, he picked up his pace to a brutal speed. I bucked into him, riding the surge of sensations, gasping at the pleasure that shot through me every time he buried himself inside me. It washed through every inch of my body, every part of my soul. And then, with one final plunge, he shattered me.

Ecstasy tore through my body, leaving me shaking and clenching around him. A cry burst from my throat. Talon continued his relentless rhythm, drawing every ounce of writhing lust from me.

He didn't take long to follow, tipping his head back when the orgasm swept through his body. He let go of my wrists and gripped both of my hips, his thrusts growing sporadic as he finished his release. Then he bowed over me.

We stared at each other, damp with not just our own sweat but each other's now. Talon's face remained as impenetrable as ever. I couldn't even tell whether he was happy we'd crashed into each other like this or upset. Or whether he really didn't care at all.

"Well, that was one way to keep ourselves occupied," I said in a rough attempt at a joke, playing off his earlier comment.

Talon didn't even acknowledge my words. He withdrew and

touched me only enough to help me down from the rack. "I'd better shower," was all he said. Then he picked up his clothes and walked out.

Okay, then. I sat down on my cot, hugging myself. Had I made a mistake?

It hadn't felt like a mistake at the time. Remembering the way he'd hammered into me, the feel of his hands and his teeth, I bit my bottom lip. My sex was already throbbing at the idea of having another go.

If it'd been a mistake, then it was one I wasn't sure I could avoid repeating. I'd had no idea—I mean, obviously sex had to feel pretty good if people bothered at all, but for it to be *that* amazing…

I shook off those thoughts and grabbed my own clothes. As fantastic as it'd been, it obviously wasn't happening again today. Possibly not *ever* again with Talon, depending on what was going on in his head right now.

As I pulled on my shirt, a faint rattling sound reached my ears. What was that?

Then it hit me. The phone. I'd left it on vibrate.

I dashed over to the trunk where I'd stashed it and tugged it out from behind. Thank God it hadn't gone off while Talon was here. I flipped it open in my hand—and then just stared at the text message that had popped up on the screen.

This is Noelle. When you see this, respond immediately.

That was it. No expression of concern or acknowledgment of the horror I'd witnessed in the mansion, no curiosity about where I might be. Just a simple demand.

Something about it made my hackles rise. *Was* it even Noelle? Scarlett hadn't known who'd left the phone for her, or at least that's what she'd claimed. She hadn't acted as if it was someone she trusted.

And—Noelle was *dead*, wasn't she? I'd seen that woman with the right sort of hair and build in the middle of the massacre…

But of course, the corpse's face had been too mutilated to identify. I wasn't sure it'd been my trainer.

Where would she have been if not at the household, though?

Too many questions cluttered my head. If I even confirmed that I'd gotten the phone, would I be alerting someone I didn't actually want to tangle with, at least not yet? Maybe this was some kind of trap arranged by the same people who'd rampaged through the mansion.

Whether it was them or it really was Noelle, I'd find out. I could use this connection. I just needed a day or two to think to be sure I made the right decision. I was running this mission on my own, making the calls. When I'd acted hastily before, I'd nearly screwed myself over.

Taking a deep breath and ignoring the tension clamped around my stomach, I turned off the phone and shoved it back into its hiding place.

TWENTY-TWO

Decima

I ENDED up throwing myself into another workout, pushing the muscles in my arms and legs to the limit, until the tension inside me faded again. Every now and then, my mind flashed to the other release I'd gotten not long ago, to the way Talon's hands had held my body and his hips had thrust into me, and my panties dampened all over again. I pushed myself harder.

I'd learned something from him, something about myself and what my body was capable of that I hadn't known. That was the important part. It wasn't as if I could pursue any kind of *relationship* with him, not that he seemed likely to want that. He was a cop, and I killed people on a regular basis. Also, he and his friends had essentially kidnapped me, even if I'd sort of allowed them to the last time.

But I couldn't say I had any regrets about the interlude we'd shared. If nothing else, it'd give me plenty of fodder when I took matters into my own hands in the future.

When I was done, feeling looser than I had in ages, I ducked into the bathroom, because I could definitely use a shower too. I lingered there for longer than usual, scrubbing all the sweat from my skin and working a lather through my hair. The soap I grabbed had a bit of Talon's tang to its scent—it must have been his. There was a weird intimacy to having it wrapped around me alongside the water streaming over my body.

When I'd dried off and dressed in a fresh pair of clothes—Steffie had run my discarded outfits through the laundry like she did for the guys, which I couldn't complain about—I stepped into the main room to find that all four of the men were now home.

They'd gathered around Julius's small table next to the whiteboard, and the man in charge was pointing out a few details in a sketch he'd made that looked roughly like the layout of a building. He had several army figures set out on the table. He motioned to them, moving a few, knocking one over, and the other men nodded. Blaze tapped away on the laptop he had balanced against his lean chest, his expression unusually serious.

They were up to something, making plans—I could taste it in the energy in the atmosphere as well as their body language. But other than a quick glance Garrison and then Julius shot my way, they didn't acknowledge me. They didn't intend to loop me in on this particular plan.

I could pretend I hadn't realized that, though. I ambled over with an air of casual curiosity. "What are you all up to, tucked away in the corner like this?"

"Discussing business," Julius said in that commanding tone of his. "Why don't you relax in your room until it's dinner time?"

I folded my arms over my chest. "If it's about the massacre at Anna's house, it involves me too. I want to know what's going on."

"It's got nothing to do with your friend," he said, but his expression was so impervious I couldn't tell whether I should believe him.

They'd all fallen silent, waiting for me to leave. Talon looked at me briefly with no sign he even remembered how tightly we'd been entwined a couple of hours ago. What would his colleagues have thought of him if they'd known?

I didn't have any interest in throwing him under the bus, though. That'd just destroy any chance there was of getting a second opportunity to enjoy the intense pleasures he could offer. Still, the thought of going back into the exercise room where the smell of sweat and him still hung in the air made my skin itch.

"I'll just go hang out on the sofa," I said, turning away, thinking I might get a chance to spy on them like I had before, but Julius cleared his throat.

"No, I think it's better if we have the room completely to ourselves."

Damn it. I held back a frown, not wanting him to realize how much I'd been counting on learning more about their mysterious mission.

Glancing around, I realized that I might be able to turn this into a different sort of opportunity. "Fine. Can I go up to the roof instead? I'd rather get some fresh air if you're going to insist on me being out of your way."

Julius's gaze followed mine in a moment of contemplation. I braced myself for a refusal, but he nodded. "I don't see how that could hurt anything."

He didn't think I had a hope in hell of escaping the apartment that way, he meant. We'd see about that. It'd be far from the first time someone had underestimated me.

I followed Julius as he strode to the locked door. He typed the code into the numeric lock quickly, angling his body to prevent me from seeing the numbers, and I made a show of not caring anyway. If they were going to let me go up on my own, I didn't need to sneak up there. I just needed to figure out what I'd do once I had the whole outdoor space at my disposal.

The door opened with a click. Julius pushed it wide and gestured to the stairwell. "I'll leave it unlocked so you can get back in when you're ready."

A small act of generosity. I gave him a similarly small smile. As I marched up the stairs, I felt his eyes on my back until the door thumped shut behind me.

Emerging onto the rooftop deck, I simply stood there for a few moments, looking at the bright blue sky and sucking in the fresh afternoon air. I hadn't been lying when I'd said I enjoyed it. Another thing to add to my list for Blaze. *Air* made me happy.

How pathetic was that?

But then, I hadn't gotten to savor the outside air very often. I'd stayed in my rooms in the household for days at a time in between missions or the occasional outdoor training session. My section of the mansion hadn't even had windows. The household had wanted to ensure no one could possibly find out I was living there, their secret weapon. The secrecy protected both them and me.

It made sense. But that didn't mean I couldn't enjoy this sort-of freedom while I had it, right?

The solitude was nice too. Other than when I'd been in one bedroom or another, this was the first time I'd been totally, blissfully *alone* since the moment the men had surrounded me after I'd crashed the car.

It probably wouldn't last. How long did I have before one of them came to check on me or tell me to get back downstairs?

That thought brought my mind back into full alertness. I had a small mission of my own here, and I needed to see it through before I was interrupted. I wasn't sure I'd want to take off on the men right now, still with no real sense of direction, but it'd be good to be prepared in case I decided I needed to make a quick escape later.

I started by walking the entire length of the wooden wall, feeling for imperfections or rot. No surprise, the wall was as secure as it was tall. When I returned to the spot beside the door, I stepped back, analyzing the barrier from more of a distance.

It was taller than the wall around the household by a few feet, so jumping it would be impossible without help, but with a chair stacked on top of the patio table, I knew I could make it to the top. But from there… I didn't know exactly how high up we were, but the length of the elevator ride and the absence of any taller buildings in view suggested it was at least ten stories. I'd bet more.

With a grappling hook and a good length of rope, I'd have been just fine regardless of what the outer walls looked like. Somehow I didn't think I could ask the cops to pick up those items for me at the store. Tying sheets and other items together was always an option, but

I didn't think there were enough in the apartment to guarantee I'd make it close enough to the ground to jump the rest of the way.

Maybe there was another building nearby, or a tree or cables or some other object I could make use of. I wouldn't know until I got up to the top, though, and if they caught me clambering along the wall, they'd never let me up here alone again. I had to be sure I was ready.

Lost in thought, I ran my tongue over my teeth and found myself meandering over to the telescope I'd examined earlier with Blaze. I drummed my fingers on the smooth metal. Too bad it wasn't an X-ray machine like one of the gadgets in *Spy Time*, built to let me see right through the wall.

Who said it might not show me something in the sky that would be useful, though? A more distant building or some other landmark? That would help me orient myself and the apartment in the city.

I bent down, leaning toward the place where I assumed I needed to put my eye.

A snarky voice carried from behind me. "Most people know not to touch other people's belongings without asking. Hands off the telescope."

I jerked back and whirled around to find Garrison stepping out onto the deck. I'd let myself get so lost in thought I hadn't heard the door open. *Sloppy*, Noelle said in my head with a tsk of her tongue.

Blaze had mentioned that the telescope was Garrison's. Garrison stood watching me with his hands slung in his pockets in a careless pose, but his expression was chilly. Why did he have to be such an ass all the time?

Well, there was nothing stopping me from poking the bear and seeing what came out.

With a taunting smile, I lowered my fingers to the telescope and stroked it. "Get my hands off of this?"

Garrison tilted his head and looked between me and the telescope, his hands not leaving his pockets. "Do you know how to use it?"

"Not particularly."

"Then I'm sticking to my demand. Hands. Off."

I rolled my eyes and folded my arms over my chest, stepping toward him. "Buzzkill."

Not dropping eye contact, he sank onto one of the lawn chairs surrounding a small coffee-style table. He stretched out his legs and leaned his head back as if making a statement about how little he was intimidated by me.

He just didn't know better.

"Let's not pretend you're actually up here to stargaze," he said.

I made a sweeping gesture toward him. "Feel free to enlighten me about my own motivations, then."

He glowered at me. "You're looking for escape routes. Hopefully you're smart enough to have figured out by now that it's hopeless."

I let the corner of my lips quirk upward. "You think I'm smart, huh?"

Garrison let out a huff of annoyance. "That wasn't what I was getting at."

"But you said it anyway." I plopped down onto the chair kitty-corner to him, matching his careless demeanor. I didn't think I'd given away anything about my intentions. He was just guessing, and when I'd tried to run off on them a few times already, guessing that I might be thinking about doing it again didn't exactly require major brain power. "What makes you so sure I'm in a hurry to get out of here?"

"You've been trying to take off since the first day. What makes today any different?"

I could think of a few things that made today different, but I wasn't going to mention them to him. Instead, I scooted to the edge of the chair and leaned forward. If I'd slid my foot out, I could have brushed it against his ankle.

"What's wrong?" I teased. "Are you worried you'd miss me if I got away?"

I could see his hackles rise—the way he sat up straighter and the cunning smirk on his face tightened, remaining only because of his iron will to remain cool and collected.

"If you got away," he said, "it would solve every single problem I've had over the past week."

I smiled and pushed him further. "You've been worried about me *that* much? I'm flattered."

Garrison scoffed and gripped the armrest. "You'd like to think so, wouldn't you? Having someone worry about you instead of giving you reasons to worry would be a nice change of events."

Wow, if I really had been fleeing an abusive boyfriend, that would have been a low blow. I feigned a wince. "Ouch. Well, maybe it takes one to know one."

His eyes flashed, and I restrained an outright grin. Another item to add to my happiness list—I enjoyed this back and forth with Garrison. Rolling with his verbal punches, finding the best way to throw the jabs back at him. It was like a different kind of sparring. Not quite as thrilling as the way I'd tangled with Talon but exhilarating in its own right.

Garrison considered me with a scowl. "Why *did* you come up here then, Dess?"

"Like I told Julius, I wanted some fresh air." What else could I say to shut down that subject? I tipped back my head. "And maybe I wanted to sunbathe too. Got to look pretty when I have four manly men studying me all day."

I flicked at my hair in what I hoped looked like a flirtatious gesture. Unfortunately, flirting was *not* my thing, and only half the hair I flicked went over my shoulder, the other half catching in the breeze and flying back into my face. I swiped it aside as if I'd meant to do that.

"Something tells me that you don't particularly care about looking pretty for us," Garrison said, looking me over.

With anyone else, I'd have worried it was an insult, but with Garrison, I couldn't totally tell. He wasn't wrong, after all.

I raised my eyebrows. "Are you saying that I haven't been meeting your exacting standards? Feel free to tell me where I've fallen short."

His mouth twisted, and I knew that I'd made it difficult to respond. He could purposely offend me, and I had no doubt that he was considering doing just that. But if I knew Garrison at all, and I had a feeling that I was quickly learning his preferred method of snark, he wouldn't go for the obvious insult.

He liked the challenge of our conversations too, even if he pretended they irritated him. Why would he have kept up the snark with me if he didn't? He could have just ignored me.

My mind flashed to Talon and the aggressive, dominating way he'd taken me in the exercise room. What would it be like to "spar" with Garrison *that* way? An image darted through my mind of us continuing our battle in the bedroom, fighting to claim our pleasure.

Maybe it was the thrill that came with the thought that propelled me onward, a spark of inspiration lighting in my mind. I didn't give him a chance to spit out the response he was brewing. Instead, I took charge.

I sighed dramatically. "It's okay if you don't find me pretty. There's more to me than looks. I wonder if the same can be said about you?" I cocked my head to one side. "I'm starting to think not so much."

Garrison's eyes blazed, and I knew part of him was seeping through the mask he wore so well. "I'll have you know—"

"That your sharp tongue is only to deflect attention from your many flaws? That's what I thought."

He uncrossed his legs and brought himself slowly to his feet, standing over me in a way that would have intimidated a lesser woman. I'd expected it. I could see the way his frustration with me and his fascination roared inside him, battling for dominance.

He didn't hate me. Not really.

"I think we're done here," he said. "Time to go downstairs."

Oh, no, he wasn't getting out of this that easily. I pushed myself off the chair, planting myself just inches away from him.

"Don't be silly," I said with a sly smile. "We're just getting started."

Then I grabbed the front of his shirt and tugged him toward me so I could capture his lips.

I hadn't been sure if he'd kiss me back. I'd only been counting on a startled moment or two before he pushed me away. But the next thing I knew, Garrison was gripping the back of my head, molding his mouth to mine. A torrent of hidden emotion flowed into me with the fervor of his kiss.

Oh, he didn't hate me at all.

As if he'd realized what he'd given away in the same instant I had, Garrison jerked back. His cheeks had flushed, but his eyes glinted with annoyance.

"Don't fucking do that again," he spat, running a hand through his shaggy blond hair.

I gazed back at him innocently. "Really? You didn't exactly seem to mind in the—"

"I said don't." He took another step away, as if he needed the distance between us to control himself. Which maybe was true. Then he jabbed his hand toward the stairs. "Get back inside where you'll make less trouble."

He ushered me down the stairs, staying a few feet behind the whole time, and then stalked off toward his bedroom the second we'd come into the apartment. Blaze and Julius were still discussing something by the whiteboard. Talon had gone into the kitchen to heat up the dinner Steffie had left for us.

Perfect.

I turned toward Blaze's workstation as if eyeing it curiously—and pulled out the phone I'd snatched from Garrison's pocket while he was distracted by the press of my lips. A satisfied smile tugged at those lips now. He'd had no idea I'd made off with it.

But now I had to search it for what I needed before he or any of the others noticed.

I tapped in the passcode I'd observed through the kettle's reflection. A part of me expected it not to work, but when the entire phone opened to me, I couldn't help outright grinning. Jackpot.

I went immediately to the recent text messages, scanning them for anything important, though I had little context for most of them. The only message that really caught my eye was from Julius, sent this morning, and it was basic—*102 Freeton Ave*, which was an address I didn't recognize, and the words, *Blaze says this is the one.*

Was this the address that they'd be visiting later? For their plans that supposedly had nothing to do with the household case?

The address was easy enough to commit to memory. Then I opened the browser history and knew my mistake the moment the page loaded.

A porn site was the last opened page, a woman and her pussy exposed wide to the camera. I rolled my eyes. Typical.

I opened the other tabs, finding only unimportant questions he'd typed into the browser. Nothing substantial.

Every second I had the phone on me was a risk. I closed all the apps I'd opened and turned it off, then ambled over to the sofa. When I sat down there, I let the phone slide between the cushions.

He'd assume it'd fallen out of his pocket sometime earlier. Nothing at all to do with me.

Now I just had to figure out why Blaze said that address was "the one" and what exactly the guys meant to do there.

TWENTY-THREE

Decima

I LAY awake on my cot long after I'd supposedly turned in for the night. The men had made a show of turning off all but the dim security light that shone over the front door and heading toward their own bedrooms, but I hadn't believed their act for a second. They were just dodging any more questions I might have asked.

It might have been two hours or maybe three when my perked ears caught the faintest rustle of movement in the main room. I retrieved my new phone from where I'd stashed it under my pillow tonight and slunk to the door. There, I eased it open the slightest crack.

The four cops had already gathered near the entrance. They weren't talking, just equipping themselves with a few last weapons—Talon tucked a pistol out of sight by his waist; Blaze checked a holster strapped to his calf and then tugged his pantleg over it. Julius stood closest to the door.

The flip phone was an old model, but it still had basic camera functions. I pressed the button to zoom the screen in as much as it'd allow me, just as Julius reached to tap in the lock code. He didn't bother to hide it now, since he had no idea I was watching. Most people wouldn't have been able to pick out the numbers he'd pressed at that angle in the dim light, but my well-honed eyes translated the movements into a sequence I immediately memorized.

It was far from the first code I'd had to stealthily obtain, and I doubted it'd be the last.

As soon as I'd seen that, I let my door ease all the way shut again. No point in risking them noticing the tiny gap when I didn't need to.

I sat on the floor next to the door with my ear tipped close. There were a few more rustling sounds, and then the soft click of the door shutting behind them. I waited several more minutes to be sure they didn't unexpectedly come right back. Then I nudged my bedroom door carefully open and slipped out into the main room.

There was no sign of any of them. I checked each of their bedrooms to be sure, getting whiffs of their varying scents that brought a tendril of heat into my belly alongside my eager anticipation.

Tonight, I was going to get some real answers.

I ducked back into my room to stuff my remaining cash and the phone into my pockets. I'd need both out there in the big bad world sooner or later, depending on what I ran into on the way.

My reaching hands hesitated over my tote bag. The stuffed tiger's worn head poked out the top.

Part of me wanted to snatch it up, but that was ridiculous. I couldn't bring it along on a mission. Even if I'd had a bag that wouldn't get in the way, there'd still be a small chance of it throwing me off balance or snagging in a tight space.

We go into every mission with just the bare bones, Noelle used to say. *That way we can stay focused on what we really need and what's really important.*

What the hell did I want a toy for anyway? I might be back. And if I wasn't, oh well.

But for some silly reason, a weird pang shot through my chest as I stood up and walked away from it.

I didn't like going out unarmed, but the sharpest thing I could find in the kitchen was a dinner knife. Did the guys just never use anything sharper with their food or had they hidden them all after I'd arrived? I frowned at it, and then my gaze slid toward the sofa.

There was a different kind of weapon here.

With a wry smile, I marched over to Talon's knitting bag and dug out a spare needle. I could wield that more effective than the blunt knife. He could get a little satisfaction from knowing I'd taken his comments to heart even if the theft annoyed him.

Tucking the needle into my pocket, where a few inches of it still protruded, I strode over to the front door and typed in the code. The bolt thudded over in an instant. Another smile sprang to my face, my triumph washing away any lingering uneasiness about what I was leaving behind.

The short hall outside held only an elevator, no entrance to a stairway that I could see. That seemed like one hell of a fire hazard, but I wasn't here to complain about how up to code the building was. I pressed the button to summon the elevator.

It whirred to a halt, and the doors parted. When I stepped in, my first time riding it without a blindfold, I noted the rows of buttons on the righthand side. Fourteen floors. I'd estimated well.

But none of them were lit up, and the little screen over the door that usually would have shown the current floor was blank. Interesting. Another mystery I didn't have time to investigate now.

There were a couple of underground levels for a parking garage, but I didn't know how to find the guys' secret passage that most likely involved a subway tunnel. The main entrance should work just fine. I hit the button for the lobby.

As the elevator descended, the carpeted floor under my feet thrummed. I shifted my weight, staying limber and on guard.

There were an awful lot of things I didn't know in my current situation, but that was okay. I'd get through it. I had an address, and I knew at least a few of the people I expected to see there. I'd completed plenty of assignments with no more information than that.

There was nothing all that impressive about the lobby the elevator let me out into. The paisley-print carpet looked clean, the glass doors that led out past the mailboxes to the street unsmudged, but it didn't hold the same sense of wealth that the household's mansion did. It actually reminded me more of my own rooms in that house: simple and practical but well-made and maintained. Somehow that brought back the pang in my gut.

I was going to avenge all those lives lost. Tonight might be my first step to really achieving that vengeance.

As I pushed past the outer door, the night air washed over me, refreshingly cool but tinged with the familiar reek of gasoline and tar you couldn't escape down here on the street. No wonder the guys liked their rooftop deck.

I hurried away from the apartment building, scanning the darkened road. It was past midnight now, only a few cars rumbling by on the street. I'd have looked for a quiet side-street where I could have stolen one, but I wasn't familiar with the street I was heading to or what part of the city it was in. I wasn't sure where I was going.

I headed toward a busier street up ahead. Just as I came around the corner, I caught sight of a cab with its available light on. At my wave, it pulled up by the curb, and I hopped in, calculating what would be a safe distance from my actual location.

"55 Freeton Avenue," I said, figuring that'd drop me a couple of blocks from 102. The cabbie nodded and gunned the engine. I settled into my seat, glad to see he didn't appear to be much for small talk.

Even with barely any traffic, it took about thirty minutes to reach my destination: a grim street of dingy office buildings and warehouses not all that far from the mall where I'd met Scarlett. When the driver stopped outside number 55, a medical supply outlet store that was obviously closed, he gave me a skeptical glance over his shoulder. "Are you sure this is the right place?"

I smiled brightly at him. "This is it." Then I handed him enough cash to cover twice the amount on the meter. He didn't complain after that.

I watched him drive off and then set off toward 102, crossing the street and sticking close to the fronts of the buildings. Half of the streetlamps were broken or burned out, which made keeping to the shadows easier. When I reached the right address, I slowed, studying the building.

It was a little smaller than the others, squat and windowless other than a small pane of glass next to the door. The grout between the bricks was crumbling. No sign hung over the door to suggest what purpose the place served.

I slunk over and tested the front door handle tentatively, careful to stay silent. It resisted my hand, locked. That was fine. The men hadn't looked as if they were going somewhere they expected to be met with open arms.

Had they even gotten here already, or had I managed to beat them to it? Maybe they'd made another stop on the way.

For all I knew, they weren't coming here tonight at all and this was a target for later. It might be even better if I could poke around uninterrupted.

Slipping around to the back of the building, I found another regular door as well as a garage-style one, which suggested this was some kind of shipping warehouse. Both were closed, a tiny window in between them pasted over with faded newspaper. Whatever the place was used for, it didn't look as if it was used very much.

What could it have to do with the household? Or was it really part of some other case?

I worried my lower lip under my teeth for a moment and then tried the back door. To my surprise, that handle turned in my grasp.

Just as I nudged the door open, the muffled bangs of a pistol with a silencer reached my ears.

My pulse jumped. Someone was here, all right, and they weren't happy. Were the cops in there shooting at someone or having criminals shoot at them?

The murderers I'd been searching for might be right here in front of me.

Along with my body's innate apprehension about walking into danger, a thrill of adrenaline coursed through my veins. I stepped into the short, dark hall on the other side of the door, my gaze fixing on the streaks of light showing around a corner just up ahead. Grunts, moans, and more gunfire reached my ears from the room beyond my view.

I'd recognize those noises anywhere. Men were dying over there.

I darted toward the sounds with a growing sense of protectiveness. If the bastards who'd mowed down everyone in the household were trying to slaughter my men now too, I'd make them doubly regret everything they'd done. Hopefully I could get my hands on a better weapon than Talon's knitting needle first.

When I peeked around the bend, all I could make out were a couple of shipping crates at this end of what appeared to be a much larger room, illuminated by thin yellow light. The lids of the crates had been popped off haphazardly, them and a few crumpled beer cans lay on the floor near the wall. Holding my breath, I dashed behind the nearest crate, dodging the debris, and peered around it to get my first real look at the scene.

It was nothing like I'd anticipated.

Blood splattered every wall—every possible surface in the main warehouse room. Bodies slumped on the floor and against a table heaped with bulging baggies—some kind of drug operation, from the looks of it. Figures moved through the darker areas around the edges of the room.

One of the bodies wasn't a corpse quite yet. The fallen man groped for a gun that'd fallen a few feet from his hand, and another bullet slammed into his skull, making him crumple. Blood was already flowing from a wound across his wrist, staining the cement floor red.

Why would you shoot someone in the *wrist* first and not the head to begin with?

My gaze caught on one of the figures circling the room, and a jolt of recognition shot through me. I'd have known the graceful, deadly way Talon moved anywhere. His honed brutality had drawn my attention from the first moment I'd met him, and I'd only become more familiar with it in our various sorts of sparring.

Before my eyes, he lunged behind a delivery truck parked at the side of the room and hauled out a guy who'd been crouched there. A curved knife gleamed in his other hand. Without hesitation, Talon plunged the blade into the man's chest, jerking it upward in a zigzag motion that sent even more blood spraying across the side of the truck.

My eyes stayed glued to the slash as he tossed the guy aside to crumple on the floor. That jagged line across the throat and upper chest… I'd never seen anyone make a kill like that. But I had seen a matching wound.

My stomach lurched. I yanked my gaze away to scan the other bodies with sharper attention.

It wasn't just that corpse, or the one who'd taken a shot to his wrist that'd opened his artery. I spotted two other men who'd gotten Talon's knife treatment, and another who'd been shot across the forearm in just the right way. Others were sprawled in positions that hid their wounds, but from the amount of blood all over this place, letting off a meaty stench into the stuffy air, every kill had been carried out by a meticulous plan to maximize the gore.

It was brutal.

It was utter *chaos*, perfectly constructed to achieve that effect.

And I'd stumbled on a scene so very much like it just days ago.

One last guy made a dash toward the other end of the room, and Blaze stepped into view, the jaundiced light turning his pale red hair orange. He raised his gun and shot the wannabe escapee in the face.

A satisfied smile crossed his lips. He'd pulled off the kill as if he did it every day before breakfast, just for fun.

Who the hell *were* these men who'd dragged me into their lives? What kind of cops would take down a drug operation like this? Shouldn't they… shouldn't they only shoot people in self-defense? Where were the handcuffs and the announcements of people's rights? Didn't they want to, like, question any of them or something?

No. This was all very, very wrong.

The groans and the gunshots faded from my ears. I'd arrived at the tail end of the massacre, and it appeared to be finished. The silence that descended over the room turned the thump of my heartbeat in my ears almost deafening.

Garrison ambled out of the shadows, bending to check the bodies and pull wallets, phones, and weapons from their pockets. I'd seen the results of his meticulousness in the past too. He glanced over his shoulder, and Julius strode out to where the lights were brighter, just tucking his gun into its holster under his arm.

"I thought they'd put up more of a fight," Garrison remarked, tossing another phone into the plastic sack he was carrying.

"Drug dealers are sitting ducks most of the time," Julius said, just as casually. He swiped at his forehead with the sleeve of his shirt.

Despite all the blood around me, the four men had managed to stay impressively clean. I noted only a few flecks on Julius's shirt and one splash on Talon's, which he was already peeling off.

He tossed it into Garrison's bag. "Are we done here?"

"Just got to take a few more pictures," Blaze announced. He was patrolling the room in his usual energetic way, now snapping photos with his phone.

A sickening certainty coiled around my stomach. These men weren't any kind of cops. They were outright killers.

And this wasn't the first kill scene of theirs I'd witnessed.

At the household—those zigzag cuts, the clipped arteries, the spectacle of blood… I'd never seen it before, and I hadn't again until right now.

There was no way it could be a coincidence. Julius and his gang had slaughtered everyone in the household and then tracked me down and taken me… as some kind of prize? To toy with me for fun while they decided what to do with me next?

That part didn't make sense to me. I couldn't wrap my head around why they'd have brought me into their lives the way they had. They would have just shot or stabbed me at the scene of my car accident.

But who the hell knew what went through their heads? I'd had no idea who these guys were, so I couldn't go by my original impressions.

I'd come here hoping I'd get a clue about who'd destroyed the household, and I'd gotten a hell of a lot more than that, so much that I didn't have any idea what to think. My head was spinning.

I drew back behind the crate. It was all right. I couldn't take them on here, with no real weapons and no preparation—but I knew where they lived. I knew how they worked. I could sneak back there and lie in wait for when they returned…

But the unexpected revelation had set me more off-balance than I'd realized. As I backed toward the hall, preparing to make my escape, my heel smacked one of the beer cans I'd forgotten to watch out for.

It rattled across the floor into the wall, and footsteps pounded toward me in an instant. I bolted for the hallway, bracing for a shot—

The footsteps stopped. "Dess?"

I should have kept running. But the sound of Julius's commanding voice was so familiar, so *normal*, that I couldn't help spinning around as I reached the hall. Tucking myself around the corner so my body was shielded, I stared at him, wondering what he could possibly plan on saying to me.

He was holding his gun, but he'd lowered it to his side. Talon, coming up beside him, had dropped his weapon too. They both looked utterly shocked—even... horrified? A lot more upset than they'd been about the actual horror they'd just carried out.

I wanted to vomit. My lips clamped shut against the urge.

"How did you—" Julius cut himself off with a shake of his head. He glanced behind him and winced as he turned back to me. "Let me explain. I know it looks bad, but—"

Looks *bad*? An incredulous guffaw tumbled out of me. "*You* killed them," I snapped. "You killed Anna."

And then, because my brain had finally started working again, I whipped around and pelted toward the back door.

Julius hollered my name. Shoes scraped against the concrete floor behind me. But I rammed the back door open and sprinted down the alley, rounding the corner onto the sidewalk before I even heard the squeak of the door opening again behind me.

I kept running on and on, spikes of adrenaline propelling me forward. Nausea twisted my gut.

I'd quite literally slept with the enemy. I'd been *living* with them. I'd sworn to avenge the household, and instead, I'd shared my body with one of the men who killed the people there. I'd befriended another.

I ran harder, and all those roaring emotions built to an apex, flooding over in a trickle of tears. Noelle's voice rose up from long ago in my childhood training sessions. *Crying is a weakness. Crying is a weakness.*

The chiding statement echoed in my mind over and over, but it didn't stop the tears from spilling fast and violently down my cheeks.

I knew I was far enough away that the men shouldn't be able to track me now, but I couldn't bring myself to stop running—not until I found myself nearing a residential section of town where porchlights beamed through the night.

The last thing I needed was a suburban mother calling the real cops on me, so I slowed to a brisk walk, still breathing heavily. I dropped my arms, and my left wrist brushed against my pocket. I stopped and looked down at the bulge.

The phone.

Noelle had always been the voice of reason in my life. If the men I'd thought were on the side of the law were actually my enemies… then maybe the person who'd reached out to me was my friend after all.

I forced myself to place one foot in front of the other as I strode onward and pulled the phone from my pocket. Bringing up the message from last time, I examined it for several minutes.

What did I have to lose? Julius and the others knew that I'd seen them. No way was I getting back into their apartment undetected. All I had was a shrinking ball of cash, the clothes on my back, and this phone some mysterious benefactor had left for me.

I spotted a small shed to the side of one of the houses, and I veered in that direction, walking as if I belonged on the property. I shook the shed's handle, and when it didn't open, I slammed my brace down on it.

It snapped with a crack. One glance over my shoulder was all I allowed before I ducked inside and closed the shed door behind me.

A lawnmower and some gardening tools sat inside, but it was mostly empty. Plenty of room to hunker down and gather myself. It felt safer than walking the empty streets.

I dragged in a breath and typed out a short reply on the phone—an adequate one. The question I should have asked to begin with, knowing anything offered through Noelle's contacts was more trustworthy than a bunch of strangers who'd all but kidnapped me.

How do I know it's you?

I hit send before I could second-guess my decision, and then I waited. My mind ran rampant, the events of the past several days flickering past me. How had I been stupid enough to trust the very people I'd meant to hunt down?

The incoming text arrived with a vibration of the phone. My gaze jerked to the screen.

Meet me at the Volcano Aquarium tomorrow morning at 7am.

I stared at the words, and they clicked in my mind. Anyone from around here would know that there were no volcanos or aquariums nearby. It shouldn't have made sense, but to me and Noelle, it did.

A sewer tunnel—hot as the inside of a volcano, I'd grumbled more than once—ran parallel to the duck pond in the center of the town. It was an emergency meetup point, one set aside only to be used in the direst circumstances.

Only Noelle and I knew about it. Only the two of us knew the quirky name I'd given it as a preteen—The Volcano Aquarium, named after the heat, the location, and the smell of dead, rotting fish.

It was Noelle. I knew it was. We'd never had to use it before. But if there'd ever been dire circumstances, it was now.

TWENTY-FOUR

Talon

"WHAT GOOD IS your fucking facial recognition if it can't find who we're looking for?" Garrison groused at Blaze, who was typing on his laptop frantically in the back seat next to me.

"I'm working on it."

Julius turned in the driver's seat, his eyes smoldering with tension in the darkness. Only a faint glow reached the inside of the car from distant streetlamps at the edge of the vacant lot we'd parked in.

"Work *faster*," he demanded. "That's your job, isn't it?"

Our leader always kept a controlled front, but I knew Julius well enough to tell he was struggling as much as any of us, maybe more. He expected perfection. He took pride in our missions, worked out every minute detail of the operation, and they *always* went according to plan. We made sure of it.

Then Dess had come into the picture, and nothing had gone completely according to plan since.

Blaze stopped and looked at Julius with a cold expression that rarely came over his face. "If you can get the job done better, do it yourself."

I'd never seen Blaze talk to anyone—let alone Julius—that way. Maybe we were all unhinged by Dess's intrusion tonight. She must have been distressed by the bloodbath that she'd seen, but when she'd spoken her final words to us, she hadn't been staring at the corpses that littered the floor. She'd stared right into Julius's eyes, and we'd all seen the fury there.

She knew it'd been us who killed her friend and everyone else in the mansion. She knew that we'd been lying to her from the start.

It wasn't a total surprise that Blaze's nerves were frayed. He'd seemed to be forming some kind of friendship with her—and he'd spoken up for her from the beginning. I'd almost have said his eyes had been brighter and his steps a little lighter after they'd spent time together yesterday morning.

What did surprise me were the shifting tides inside *me*. I hadn't said a word since Dess had run off, and I wasn't sure I could even if I wanted to. The strange pang inside me wasn't anywhere near crippling, but… I couldn't remember the last time I'd felt even that much about anything.

Julius inhaled slowly as if gathering his cool. He spoke more evenly than before. "Why isn't it working?"

Blaze didn't bother looking up. "The same reason it wasn't working an hour ago and three hours before that. I can't scan faces in the dark, so unless she walks right below a streetlamp and looks toward the camera at the same time, we're not going to find her until dawn. Which is… about a half hour off still."

"We'll find her," Julius said. "We have to. We don't leave loose ends."

"Assuming she's even still in the city, let alone the state," Garrison muttered.

There it came again—the slight discomfort in my chest that grew each time I thought about Dess hating us. Leaving us. As if I'd *lost* something.

But that didn't make sense. As close as we'd gotten during our heated encounter in the exercise room, as much as I'd enjoyed it, it'd been purely physical. We'd barely talked, and she hadn't seemed to mind that.

Blaze jerked his head toward Garrison. "If she isn't, then I'll find her wherever she went. But there's no reason to assume she's gone that far."

Garrison raised his hands. "I'm just saying, no one would stick around here knowing that we're going to come after them, having seen what we can do. Even I can admit she's smarter than that."

"She's obviously smarter than any of us gave her credit for," Julius said, raking his hand through his hair. "How the hell did she even manage to follow us? Did you see anything out of the ordinary during the drive?"

Blaze shook his head. "I saw you lock the penthouse behind us. She couldn't get into the passages without us noticing, let alone the garage. I've already checked the cameras down there—no sign of her."

"Then she went out the main entrance. But how the hell did she get there, and how did she know where to go afterward?"

"What does it matter?" Garrison asked. "She *did* find us, she's seen what we can do, and now we're screwed."

"She only knows our aliases," I pointed out. "Not our real names or anything that would identify us to the actual cops." Talking eased the discomfort inside me just a little, as if it helped that I was contributing. But a small ache remained. Exactly as if a hole had been carved out of my chest, one only she could fill.

No, it didn't make sense at all. It would probably fade in a matter of hours anyway.

"If she got out of the building, then she knows where the penthouse is," Blaze pointed out. "So much for that being our secure base."

"And she can pass on physical descriptions to the police." Julius scowled. "Or whoever else she might want to tell about this. I'm even more sure now that we never got the full story about who *she* is and how she's involved. Which is why we need to track her down, fast."

"I'm trying," Blaze grumbled.

Watching them debate our situation and Dess's part in it brought the pang back into sharper clarity. I couldn't decide if it bothered me or if it was kind of a relief to know I was capable of that kind of emotion.

I didn't *need* to feel things. I got by just fine in my usual unaffected state. A lot of guys would have scoffed at the idea of feelings and acted as if they were a weakness anyway.

The ache for Dess didn't seem like a weakness, though. It felt like a sense of direction, propelling me forward.

Despite Julius's determined words, Garrison's snark, and Blaze's frustration, I got the sense that this wasn't just about loose ends for them either. No, we didn't want to deal with the fallout if we couldn't contain what she knew… but she'd intrigued all of us in different ways.

"We never should have brought her to the penthouse to begin with," Garrison said, tipping his head back with a groan.

A growl came into Julius's voice. "Don't you dare say 'I told you so.'"

Garrison glowered at him. "Fine, I won't say it. I'll just think it very loudly. We have a loose cannon running around—one who knows our address, our occupation, and the fact that we killed her friend. If she tells even one person, any person, our job just got a hundred times harder." He paused, and his mouth twisted. "Also, I liked that apartment."

"We might still get to keep it," Blaze said, always the most optimistic of us.

A haze of pre-dawn sunlight was beginning to glaze the horizon beyond the windshield. Blaze stayed ready for his facial recognition program to kick in, not daring to look away from his laptop. "It didn't seem like she had anyone *to* tell. Maybe we can…"

He trailed off, obviously knowing there weren't many solutions that involved us finding her and ensuring she didn't talk that wouldn't involve her as dead as the drug dealers we'd just mowed down.

"I don't think she'll go to the police," I said slowly. Julius and Garrison looked at me, seeming surprised that I'd jumped in. I continued, expanding on my reasoning so they knew I wasn't just shooting my mouth off. "She stole a car when we first met her. She was running from something, and she was trying to avoid leaving a paper trail at a hospital. When she thought we were cops, she held herself back from telling us anything."

Garrison grimaced. "Considering the stuff her boyfriend was mixed up in, if any of that was even true, she might tip off some other criminal crew instead. That'd be a whole different kind of headache. I think I'd rather deal with cops. At least they're a little more predictable."

"None of that matters until we find her and—and see what she has to say," Blaze said, as if she was likely to say anything at all and not fight us tooth and nail.

We all fell silent, the others possibly thinking the exact same thing I just had. Julius sighed. "We can't know for sure how it'll play out until we get to that point. The one thing I'm sure of is that we definitely don't know everything there is to know about Dess. I don't think we've even scraped the surface."

Nobody could argue that claim.

He looked down at his hands, the knuckles marked by a few small scars, and flexed his fingers before going on. "If she has ties to a criminal syndicate, we'll use her as a message. She can't be left alive if she's with one of our enemies. If we decide she's a risk in other ways, we'll deal with it appropriately. I think we can all agree on that. But we have to wait and see."

The ache inside me dug a little deeper at the thought of ending Dess's life. An image flashed through my mind from one of the movies I'd watched—secretly in my room on the small TV I had in there, studying the actors' faces and body language as they played out some heartbreak. Trying to understand the pain they were going through that was unconnected to any actual wound. My hand rose to my chest, putting the slightest pressure there, like I'd seen the characters do sometimes.

I couldn't tell if it helped.

I thought back to sex with Dess—to how hungry she'd seemed for the physical connection once we'd collided. There'd been nothing artful or scheming about our coming together, just pure bodily lust, so much it'd seemed to unnerve her in brief moments when I'd caught a flicker of uneasiness in her eyes. And yet she'd kept going. She'd clung to me, urged me on. And when she'd come apart, it'd been like she'd ascended to the heavens.

She'd lost something too—and not just her friend. There'd been an emptiness inside her she'd been longing to heal. And for just a little while, I'd been able to fulfill that need.

I'd fucked bad people. I'd talked to them and worked with them my entire life. Dess was wounded in a way I couldn't explain, but she wasn't like those people at all.

"I don't think she'd be out to hurt us vindictively," I said. "She's scared, and who wouldn't be after what she saw?"

Julius looked at me, studying my expression. Maybe picking up on the fact that I had experiences with her I hadn't shared. But he didn't prod me about them.

"We can't know that for sure," he said, "but I hope you're right."

Blaze's demeanor changed like the flick of a switch. He sat up straighter and pointed to his screen. "I've got her. She's on the move."

We all peered at the grainy image of a figure striding into what looked like a city park. There was no denying it. That was Dess, and she walked with purpose.

"Let's go round her up," Julius said, and slammed the car into drive.

TWENTY-FIVE

Decima

I EASED down into the sewer tunnel on the far side of the pond, using an entrance behind a small maintenance building. The stench hit me fast. I started breathing strictly from my mouth as I eased my way down the ladder and into the humid corridors.

Thank God it hadn't rained in the past week, or this excursion could have been a lot messier.

The heat sent sweat trickling down my back. My shoes squelched onto the ledge alongside the channel of sludge, but I didn't allow myself to glance at whatever nasty things I'd stepped on.

It didn't matter. All that mattered was confirming that Noelle was alive—and then working with her to carry out the mission I'd first set out on: destroying the people who'd slaughtered the closest thing we had to a family.

Those people being the four men I'd spent most of the past week with.

My stomach tied itself into knots. I wasn't usually all that anxious when I got down to work, not after all my years of practice, but this situation was like nothing I'd dealt with before.

Noelle would straighten it all out. Noelle would see the way through. She'd always been there to point me in the right direction and make sure I was prepared. Why would now be any different?

Assuming it really was Noelle, and this wasn't some horrible trick.

I approached the meeting spot quietly, avoiding piles of waste that'd collected along the edges of the rounded tunnel. I wanted to get a good look at whoever was waiting for me before I showed myself. My footfalls were silent, so as a slender, muscular woman's figure came into sight in the wide alcove up ahead where a few different tunnels joined, I had time to analyze her.

While I remained cloaked in darkness, hazy light seeped over the woman from a grate high overhead. From the back, her shoulder-length salt-and-pepper hair looked just as familiar as it always had. She stood with a typically rigid posture, both hands clasped behind her back. Then she turned her head, revealing her profile, and my shoulders sagged with pure relief.

There was no doubt that the woman before me was Noelle. I wasn't alone in this mess. Everything could go back to—well, not normal, but closer to normal than the craziness of recent days.

"Noelle," I called out, stepping closer.

She whipped around, and her cool, hardened eyes—so ready to take down any threat—soothed me. Finally, I had someone on my side.

My steps sped up as she looked me up and down.

"Where have you been all this time?" she asked in her usual demanding tone, as if this were a regular meeting and I'd shown up late for a training session. "It took *days* for you to get your hands on that phone, and practically another day to answer me."

Her voice echoed through the tunnel, and I nearly flinched at the accusation I heard in it. I stopped in my tracks, still several feet away from her. "I didn't have the opportunity right away," I said. "There's a lot I need to tell—"

Noelle didn't let me continue. "Why did you leave the household at all? Your orders are always to remain in your rooms unless otherwise instructed."

The knots in my stomach came back, tighter than before. This wasn't the reunion I'd pictured. I hadn't expected hugs and fawning praise, of course, because that'd never been Noelle's approach, but I'd thought she'd be relieved to see me too. Concerned about what I'd been through. Upset about the deaths we hadn't been able to prevent. Angry, yes, but at the people who'd carried out the massacre.

Instead, she only appeared to be annoyed with *me*, as if I'd veered off track on an assignment I'd already had a playbook for. As if nothing had been lost but my obedience to instructions she'd never actually given me.

It felt… wrong.

My legs stayed locked in place. "I didn't have a choice. Everyone was dead. I couldn't save any of them. I thought you were dead too. The only thing I could think to do was track down the people responsible."

Isn't that what you'd have wanted? something in me said, but I didn't ask the question out loud. The answer was obviously no.

Anger crackled through Noelle's words now, but it was directed at me. "One of the first lessons you learned was to keep to your part of the house. You weren't given permission."

Given *permission*? Did she really think I should have stayed put after I'd seen what had happened in the rest of the mansion—that any sane person would have pretended all was well? How could I have known there was anything or anyone to wait for?

My uneasiness prickled deeper into my skin. I shifted my weight from one foot to the other, instinctively testing the surface beneath me. "I didn't think I needed permission in a situation like that," I said. "And—and I had it anyway. Anna opened my door. She *told* me to leave."

Leave. Find somewhere safe. I hadn't followed the second part of those orders all that well, but I wasn't sure that was my fault.

Noelle's lips curled into what I could only describe as a sneer. "Anna wasn't responsible for your security. Anna was your cook and your housekeeper. She was useless. I'm the one who makes the real calls about where you go and what you do."

I knew that Noelle was a cold woman, but I'd always thought that if my life were in danger—if I were in a perilous situation—she'd be there to help me. Judging by the way she looked at me now, that wasn't the case after all. She didn't seem to care about *anyone*.

"Anna was my friend," I said. "Your colleague. And she died making sure that I lived."

Noelle must have picked up on the horror in my tone. She placed a hand on each of her hips and offered a small gesture toward sympathy. "Her loss was unfortunate. As were the losses of all the faithful people who worked for the household. However, they're not important now. They're dead. You're alive, and your deviation from protocol could have gotten you killed."

I didn't bother reminding her again that I hadn't disobeyed anybody. In fact, I'd been nothing but obedient by leaving the household at Anna's command.

Why the hell would I have stayed there when leaving and finding the killers was an option? I'd been trained for years to hunt down targets, and now, when I'd put those skills to use against the people who'd not only threatened but destroyed the household, Noelle was chastising me for it?

I stayed silent and gritted my teeth. How had I been so wrong? I'd looked at her as a guide—as someone I could trust and whom I'd protect with my life. She was talking like… like I was a misbehaved pet, or a possession that'd purposefully been misplaced. Not a person at all.

The respect I'd felt for her didn't seem to go both ways.

But she still had to know more than I did. It wasn't as if I could walk away.

"Why did it happen?" I asked. "Why did someone kill the whole household and leave them like that?" There was no point in mentioning right now that I knew who'd done it. I still didn't understand why the men I'd spent the last few days with would have. Had they been long-time enemies of the household? Had it been some kind of *game* to them? They'd acted so casual about the shootout in the drug den, even taking pictures…

The pieces didn't fit together.

Noelle released a hoarse laugh. "Why? Decima, dear, I'm not the one who killed them. You would need to ask the assholes who did that question."

I frowned. What had *she* been doing for the past week, then? "Haven't you been investigating to figure out who did this and why?"

"No, I've been busy trying to track *you* down and confirm you weren't actually caught in the crossfire. Nothing else was as important as that."

Nothing else was as important as finding me, but she'd spent the entire time since I'd turned up berating me? My head was starting to ache.

Abruptly, I found myself thinking of the men—the fake cops. The way I'd seen them work together, a perfectly cohesive unit when they needed to be even if they bantered and snarked at other times.

I had no doubt at all that if one of them were killed, the other three would go to the ends of the earth to get justice for that death. I'd always given the same loyalty to the household, and I assumed that everyone who was part of it held the same sentiment.

Noelle had brushed it off like an afterthought.

How could the people who were obviously the bad guys make me feel safer than the woman who'd made me who I was? And yet, ridiculously, I couldn't help craving the men's presence around me: Julius's impervious authority, Talon's cool strength, Blaze's hyperactive cheer, and, hell, even Garrison's defensive snark.

"You really have no idea why an attack like that would have happened?" I tried again. "Did we have so many enemies that there's no way of knowing who would have had the resources?"

Noelle sighed. "We can get into all of that later, Decima. It's time to leave. We can regroup, and then I'll tell you everything you need to know."

Everything she decided I needed to know, not everything I wanted to. The same frustration I'd felt when the guys had stonewalled me surged up again, twice as strong when it was coming from her. "I want to know now."

She scoffed. "You would be smart to listen to me if you want to live. The dangers of the real world are worse than I could ever explain to you, and some of those dangers are after both of us for being part of the household. The longer you sit here and argue with me, the more likely it is that they'll find us and kill us both."

Would they? Julius and the others had obviously known something about how I was connected to the household all along. But they'd given me a bed and good meals and space to move around in. If they'd wanted me dead, I had to admit they could have killed me a dozen times, at least in the first day when I'd been disoriented and hadn't realized how formidable a force they were.

How well did Noelle really know what she was talking about?

I squared my shoulders. "If you would just tell me—"

"You know what? I'm done with you disobeying me." Noelle snapped her fingers. "Garlic milkshake," she said, emphasizing both words in that odd combination.

Something inside me clicked, my mind going just a little dull and hazy, detached from the rest of my body.

"Garlic milkshake," Noelle repeated. Despite my resistance, my posture snapped to attention, my limbs tensing with readiness. She smiled. "Good. No more questions."

I tried to open my mouth anyway, but my jaw refused to budge. What the fuck? I stared at Noelle, backing up one step and then another.

Her eyes narrowed. "Stay where you are."

My feet seemed to meld with the ground. My heart thumped faster. How was she doing that?

Noelle ran a hand through her hair and took a deep breath. "You used to try my patience like this when you were much younger, you know. You had a phase where you had to ask 'why' about everything, and it was *infuriating*. Good little killers don't ask questions." She chuckled darkly, striding toward me and walking around my stiff body. "But with the right words, we can be sure you don't get too caught up in your own initiative."

I didn't remember hearing the phrase she'd used before—except I did. It hit me with a sudden chill. Those nonsensical words had fallen from Anna's lips as she attempted to suck in her last breaths, to save me.

An even more chilling thought hit me. If Noelle could control me like this, would I even have been able to step outside my rooms without Anna saying that special code?

Noelle smirked, taking in my stillness. "Now, take a step forward."

I willed myself not to do it. With every single ounce of restraint I had left, I rallied against the order and told myself not to obey. But my left foot—of its own accord—swung forward to plant itself farther forward before my right foot came to meet it.

"Good. Now follow me. We're leaving."

Noelle turned, and without any control over my own limbs, I trailed behind her. One foot after the other. On into the dim light of the alcove toward a metal ladder against the far wall that Noelle was approaching.

Panic rose in my chest. I was locked inside my own mind, unable to send any signal to the rest of me. I pounded on the internal wall that stood between me and my bodily functions, but it didn't break. It didn't *move.*

I didn't recall a specific memory, but a sensation from a long, long time ago flooded me—one of helplessness. I could remember another time when I'd been out of control of my movements. I was young, and my limbs were restrained as my body was taken… taken somewhere I didn't want to go.

As quickly as the memory came, it flashed out of focus, back into the depths of my mind. The reminder sent a jolt of fear and iron will through me, and I stumbled over my next step.

I couldn't remember the last time I'd been able to make a choice for myself in the household, but right now, I had to resist. Noelle couldn't do this to me. I *wasn't* her pet or her possession.

I was my own person—a person who loved chocolate and the TV show *Spy Time*, who could take happiness from the simple pleasure of a breath of fresh air, who craved the brutal intimacy a man like Talon could offer. I was *me*, and no random combination of words could give her ownership over me.

With the force of that defiant thought, I came to a halt. I looked down at myself with a thrill racing through me.

I'd done it. I'd broken her control. I'd made my own decision.

I'd been directed by Noelle my entire life, but for the last week, even with the men deciding where we went and what they'd tell me, I'd been freer than I'd ever been before. I *wouldn't* go back to being a puppet. I owed the household their justice.

I'd give them that. But I'd give it to them on my terms.

"No," I whispered, my voice still difficult to use.

Noelle spun around and narrowed her eyes at me.

"Garlic. Milkshake."

My body stiffened, but I forced it to relax. I was free. I would stay that way. I'd thought I could trust Noelle—I'd put all my faith in that fact—but I'd been wrong.

Trusting Noelle was worse than trusting the men. At least they were loyal to their own. After what she'd just done, I'd count on them to give me the real story about why they'd attacked the household before I believed any story she spun for me.

"*No,*" I said again, louder. "I have a say in what happens here too. I don't belong to you."

Noelle let out a sharp guffaw that made me want to punch her. As my hand clenched, she shook her head.

"We could have done this the easy way, but you've given me no choice."

I widened my stance automatically, preparing for a fight. Noelle wouldn't be easy to take down. I'd been able to for a few years now, but it'd often been tricky. And those times I hadn't been working around a still partly sprained wrist. She might have weapons on her too.

I hadn't considered that it might not be her fighting me at all.

Noelle made a brisk gesture with her hand, and ten menacing figures sprang out of the tunnels on either side of her, charging straight at me.

TWENTY-SIX

Decima

NOELLE STAYED EXACTLY where she was, totally unfazed by the new arrivals. Of course. They were running toward me, obviously on her command.

As I backed up, looking to put myself in a better defensive position, my thoughts whirled. Why would Noelle have come with trained fighters ready to attack me—to capture me—when I'd shown up with every intention of following her out of this tunnel? If she'd approached me with an ounce of concern, I would have followed her demands to the ends of the earth. I'd done that for so long that breaking the trend tugged at something inside of me.

But I refused to be a slave.

Two of the men, one on either side, drew ahead of the others to reach me first. I didn't see guns or knives in any of their hands—no, they didn't want to kill me. Only to force me to obey where Noelle's special phrase had failed.

Then I couldn't think at all, my body switching over into the grips of my well-honed combat instincts. I squatted and veered, raising my brace to deflect a blow aimed at the side of my head, ducking away from grasping hands.

The men were obviously well-trained, but nowhere near as practiced as me. Too bad they had the numbers to make up for it.

My arm didn't ache in the way it had on the day I'd sprained it, and the pain in my ribs was barely detectable, but there was enough of the injury left to slow my motions. I caught a glancing blow to my cheekbone—avoiding the full brunt of it by pure luck. The other men were pressing in on me, ducking and weaving around each other to snatch at me in an attempt to gain the upper hand. I was outnumbered severely, and I couldn't dream of winning this fight if I fought fair.

It was a good thing that I knew how to fight dirty.

My fingers closed around the knitting needle I'd wedged into my pocket. I slashed out with it, slicing the tip through one man's palm, jabbing it at another's gut. It stabbed into his flesh, and he grunted in pain, but then he jerked it out and tossed it aside, out of my reach.

Fuck. I dropped down again and scanned the ground for any debris that could be used as a weapon. It was hard to make out much in the hazy light with attackers coming at me from left, right, and in front. I spun and kicked one way while aiming an uppercut in the opposite direction, moving my body at the fastest possible speed, scrambling to find an advantage.

In another scenario, I'd have been looking for my best chance to make a break for it. There was no point in fighting a battle where the odds were stacked against you if you could get out of it. But fleeing would mean losing track of Noelle. I hadn't wanted to go with her like a puppy on a leash, but she knew *something* about the murders at the household. She was the only connection to my old life that I still had.

If I left here with just as few answers as I'd turned up with, I'd be even more stuck than before.

As I whirled, wincing when a blow I couldn't completely deflect caught me in my ribs, my gaze caught on a chunk of broken concrete about the size of a fist. I dove for it, snatched it up, and swung it at the nearest head. It slammed into the man's skull with a crack of breaking bone. He dropped, and I knew he wouldn't be getting back up again.

That left… way too many more fighters.

My other hand groped and collided with a rusted pipe protruding from the wall. I yanked at it, only intending to use it for leverage, but it snapped off in my hand. Water gushed from the wall in a powerful burst.

The spray hit two of my attackers. I darted under the arc of water and swiveled to come at them from behind, but my left foot landed on a blob of slick sewage material—okay, being totally accurate, I stepped on shit—and slid. I barely caught my balance, and then the nine remaining men were closing in on me again.

I tried to dodge around them or dash between them to get at Noelle. Maybe if I could take her hostage—if I even could overpower her—her attack dogs would back off. It wasn't a strategy I'd used often, but I was running out of options.

I dipped and wove, jabbed out with an elbow and snatched a handful of hair to ram one head into another. Tripping one guy, I used his back as a springboard to launch me free of their tightening ring.

The move would have worked perfectly if I hadn't hit my landing right on another gross glob.

My feet skidded, my torso jerked around in an attempt to catch my balance, and pain flared through my freshly banged ribs. A solid body rammed into me, tossing me onto the ground where even more putrid liquid soaked into my shirt. My groan was both pain and disgust.

"Got her!" my attacker shouted.

Oh, he thought so, did he?

In a motion that Noelle had drilled into my mind years ago, I hooked my foot over his leg and pivoted my hips. The man lost his balance, falling off me and allowing me to switch our positions. I sat atop him, and he reached for me, but I pushed his hands under my knees, grabbed his head, and snapped his neck in one swift motion.

I was tempted to slam it into the muck for good measure, just for being such a prick, but the other men were hurtling toward me.

Snatching up the nearest of my makeshift weapons, I sprang to my feet, wobbled, and heaved off the wall to add power to my heel kick. I lashed out with the broken pipe end at the same time. It carved a gash in one guy's cheek, but all he did was wince and keep coming.

I'd ended up out in the open with no wall to protect my back. My breath was coming in short spurts now, burning in my throat, and not just with the stench. I flung another punch, ducked, and slipped right onto my ass.

In an instant, four hands gripped my arms. I thrashed between the two men who'd grabbed me, but another wrapped his arms around my torso. They dragged me toward Noelle, one clamping his hand around my wrist brace so tight the tendons pinched with a lancing agony.

The same feeling from before—the utter helplessness I'd felt when Noelle had given her hypnotic command—seeped back into me. "No," I whispered, not able to prevent the word from leaving my lips. I *never* begged. Never. I'd sooner die than let someone hear me plead for my life.

But Noelle had no plans to kill me. It wasn't my life I was begging for; it was my freedom. That was… new. I'd never experienced the sweetness of freedom before, and losing it—losing the small taste of making my own choices—wrenched me to the core.

I slammed my foot back, and it made contact with someone's shin, but his hold on me didn't release. The iron grip on my arms didn't slacken no matter how I twisted and heaved. There were too many of them.

"Good," Noelle said. "Bring her to the truck."

My captors dragged me one more step—and the *bang* of a gunshot reverberated from the nearest tunnel.

The man at my left jerked, blood blooming in the middle of his forehead. As he toppled, I dropped as low as I could go, lifting my legs so my weight would put more strain on the men who held me. I didn't know what the hell was going on now, but I didn't plan on being caught in any crossfire.

"Seven more," an oddly familiar voice hollered. "No, eight. Take them all down—just be careful of Dess."

My gaze shot up to see Julius emerging from the shadows of the tunnel, pistol in hand. Garrison came into view just behind him, clutching his own gun, his nose wrinkled but his eyes as intense as his boss's. Talon marched out of one of the other tunnels, his muscles taut, a knife in one hand and a pistol in the other, with Blaze at his heels. The hacker let out a low laugh and raised his gun.

Someone swore. The two men who held me kept their grip tight, their hands digging into my flesh. The others hurled themselves at the newcomers.

My attackers had been unarmed—it would have been too risky trying to subdue me with any kind of weapons on them that I could have grabbed and used against them—and now that meant they were screwed unless they could take control of the battle at close contact.

Having seen Julius and his crew in action, I could have told them they were screwed either way. But I kept my mouth shut.

Shots blasted through the alcove. Noelle's voice broke through the thundering sounds: "Get her out of here, now, *now*!"

My captors tried to haul me the way she was beckoning them, but with only two of them, I found a weak spot as soon as they were in motion. I swung my legs up again but this time rammed them into two kneecaps.

One of the men took the blow hard enough to stagger, and the second he was off-balance, I bounded off his body into a backflip. The hold on my arms and waist snapped. As I landed, I rammed the other man into the wall of the tunnel where another pipe protruded. It neatly cracked his spine.

As he crumpled, I rotated toward the man who was clutching his knee. "You're next," I murmured.

He had the good sense to look afraid. I *wasn't* helpless, and no one around here was going to control me.

When the man tried to lunge at me, I dodged and then came at him with a hail of punches. One, two, three, clocking him across the head, smacking him in the jaw, swinging out with my leg next and knocking him right off his feet. As he sprawled, I leapt over him and stomped on his throat with all my might. He gagged for a second before I crushed his windpipe completely.

My ears were ringing with the gunshots that had careened through the space around me. It was silent now. The other five of Noelle's men lay in pools of blood mingling with the puddles of sewer water.

Julius and his men stepped toward me—and toward Noelle herself, who was standing there by the narrowest tunnel, staring at the guys with her lips pressed flat.

She looked… afraid. She took a step backward, glancing behind her. I knew there was nobody else—only her and the ten men she'd brought who'd all been disposed of.

She'd brought that huge force just to take me down, to compel me to come with her. I needed to know why. What was really going on here?

I saw the second Noelle made her decision in the flick of her eyes. She whipped around and sprinted into the nearest tunnel. I swiveled to chase after her, and Julius's voice rang out at the same time.

"Talon. No one leaves."

The other man was a few steps closer. He reached the entrance of the tunnel before I did.

"No!" I shouted, just as Julius grabbed my arms. Before I could break free, Talon had already fired the shot.

There was a thump from down the tunnel that must have been Noelle's falling body. My gut clenched.

"You asshole," I yelled as Talon stalked down the tunnel to check. "I needed her alive! She's the only one who knows—who knows anything…"

But maybe that didn't matter, not when the four men who'd already slaughtered everyone else I'd ever depended on had me surrounded.

I yanked myself out of Julius's hold and spun around, my back prickling with the awareness of Talon somewhere behind me. When I shifted to the side, that put Garrison behind me, still with a gun in his hand, but I liked my odds slightly better that way.

Julius watched me with a thoughtful expression. "Are you okay?" he asked. As if that mattered to him. As if they'd come—

Why *had* they come? They'd killed everyone… except me.

Talon emerged from the tunnel and gave Julius a brisk nod. "No one left who can say Dess was with us."

"*With* you?" I demanded. "Who says I'm going anywhere with you? What the hell is going on?"

"We just saved your life, sweetheart," Garrison said. "What does it look like?"

But *why*? I met Julius's steady gaze, confused and ready to do battle all over again, even if I didn't stand a chance against four fully armed, highly skilled killers. But it was Blaze who spoke.

"You don't need that woman," he said softly. "She'd only have lied to you anyway. I'm pretty sure that's what she's been doing your whole life. If you'll give us a chance to explain, I think I've found something that'll give you the answers you need."

TWENTY-SEVEN

Decima

I STUDIED BLAZE'S FACE, but I didn't know if I could trust my instincts when it came to him. He looked as genuine as he always had. And he'd been lying to me the whole time, just like the others.

My gaze slid between the other three men. They watched me warily, but they were holstering their guns. I didn't appear to be next on their list of targets.

But that didn't change the crimes they'd already committed.

"Why should I listen to or believe anything you say?" I asked, annoyed at how rough my voice sounded. "You killed everyone in the household—you killed them *horribly*..."

"Hey," Garrison said, "I think we actually did a very nice job with that one."

"Shut up, kid," Julius said, sounding weary. He turned back to me. "We had nothing against the people in your house, whoever they really were to you. It was a job. We work for hire. Someone paid us to go in and deal out our specific brand of chaos, so we did."

A job. They hadn't even known Anna or the rest of them?

I glared at him. "So you slaughtered them for money? Is that supposed to make me feel better about it?"

"They weren't good people," Blaze piped up. "What Garrison said before about human trafficking was true. They were a branch of some secretive criminal syndicate—secretive enough that it was hard for me to dig up much about them, but I found enough. I always confirm that we're only taking on targets society is probably better off without."

I guessed to someone else's eyes *I* might be a criminal. My kills had all been for the protection of the household, but their enemies wouldn't have seen it that way. And somehow I had trouble summoning my usual conviction about the people I'd been protecting after the way Noelle had just tried to haul me away.

"What about me?" I said. "You didn't kill me."

"You weren't there when we were carrying out the job," Julius said, and I realized they honestly didn't know I'd lived there. I'd lied plenty to them too. "You weren't on the manifest. I don't know why or how you ended up in the building or what your relation is to those people, but our client didn't want you dead. It's possible you're the missing thing he expected to find, but he hasn't specified, so we can't be sure."

He paused, as if waiting for me to fill in a few of the blanks for them. I crossed my arms over my chest. "I don't need to tell you anything."

They were my enemies… weren't they? I'd sworn to kill the people who'd slaughtered the household.

But this wasn't quite the situation I'd pictured. If the men before me had been hired, if they hadn't held any grudge or had personal reasons for taking all those people down… then the real villain was whoever had hired them. *That* was who I should take my revenge on.

In a way, Julius and his crew had simply been a weapon wielded by someone else to wreak their intended havoc. What good would destroying the weapon do when the person behind it could just pick up another one?

Maybe they were my enemies, maybe they weren't, but they were definitely my only tie to the person responsible.

"Who hired you?" I demanded.

"We don't know," Garrison said, setting aside the snark for once. "Everyone goes by code names. All communication is highly secure. They don't know who we are, and we don't know who they are, not really."

They obviously had some means of communicating with them, though. I wet my lips.

"We don't have anything against you, Dess," Julius said. "We don't want to hurt you. But we need to understand how you fit in so we can make that call. What we've found... It's raised a hell of a lot of questions."

I swallowed hard, thinking of Noelle's betrayal. Of the way she'd talked to me, of the secret phrase I hadn't known was programmed into my brain to make me obey.

"After what happened here today, I'm not totally sure how it all comes together either," I admitted. I wasn't ready to tell them more than that.

"Can I show you something on my phone?" Blaze asked. "I was able to pick up a signal from a laptop in that woman's vehicle, and I scraped a bunch of the files. A lot of them relate to you. It might give you a starting point."

I stared at him. What could he possibly have found?

What could I lose by letting him show me? I nodded tentatively, still braced to defend myself.

Blaze slid his phone from his pocket and began typing. "There were a bunch of videos. I only had a chance to glance at one of them before we came down here—I wouldn't even have stopped to do that if we'd known how much trouble you were in. But that one reveals a lot all on its own. I can play it for you."

He was talking to me as if I were fragile. He *knew* I wasn't. The unease that roiled in my stomach begged for me to turn down the offer, but the part of my mind that yearned for information took control of my voice. "Show me."

He nodded and turned the phone to face me, the video already playing. He stretched out his arm, and I allowed myself to walk a couple of steps closer, drawn in by the images moving on the screen.

A little girl, no more than a toddler, stood in a blank white room.

Her wavy black hair was strewn around her face, and her eyes were red-rimmed. Tears streaked down her cheeks.

She didn't look much like the face I saw in the mirror these days, but I recognized her immediately. It was me. In my training room in the household. What the—

A man stepped into view, dressed in sweats, his hands wrapped. "Fists up," he said. "We'll go through it again. You need to focus, and then you'll get to have your playtime."

Child-me sobbed and shook her head. "I want Mommy and Daddy. I want to go home. Please, I want to see them. Please, please, please."

My heart wrenched. Mommy and Daddy? I didn't remember this at all. I didn't remember ever thinking I had parents I could have seen if I asked. And the household had always been my home.

Hadn't it?

A woman came into the frame with brisk strides I recognized immediately. She was younger, no gray in her hair and her face unlined, but there was no mistaking Noelle.

She looked down at child-me with a cold expression so much like the one she'd aimed at me just minutes ago. "You can't see them. They're gone. This is your home from here on. You belong to us now, and we're shaping you up so that the bad things that happened to them *never* happen to you. Now listen!"

The little girl's sniffling intensified, but the loud sobs stopped as she hung her head. With obvious reluctance, she raised her tiny fists.

My throat constricted. What the hell was going on there? It didn't fit with anything I knew.

"I don't remember this," I admitted. "I don't remember anything before being part of the household."

"Kids don't typically keep their memories from that young," Julius said. "It's not surprising. But from the looks of it, you didn't have much choice about the company you were keeping."

My voice came out in a whisper. "I had no idea."

"You didn't know they took you from your family?" Blaze said, sympathy filling his eyes.

"No, I thought—I thought my parents were gone, like Noelle said there. But that they'd been part of the household before. That I'd always been part of it."

But that wasn't true. The child me hadn't acted as if I'd already known Noelle or the man. I'd asked for some other home where I thought my parents would be. And Noelle had talked as if they'd only recently taken me in. *You belong to us now.*

My legs wobbled under me as I grappled with the questions spinning in my head. Was Blaze right? Had I been stolen away from some family who had nothing to do with Noelle and the others?

Who was I really? And why would the people in the household have kidnapped a terrified little girl… and shaped her into the killer I was today?

I looked at Blaze and then Julius, and they gazed steadily back at me. I didn't know where we'd go from here, but for at least the next little while, I had no interest in fighting them.

I nodded toward Blaze's phone. "I need to see more."

KILLER LIES

THE CHAOS CREW #2

EVA CHANCE

ONE

Decima

I WASN'T sure I'd ever seen anything quite as horrifying as the videos Blaze had loaded onto his phone.

They weren't disturbing in a gory, blood spewing everywhere kind of way. That, I could have stomached no problem. Instead, I watched a child—no more than four years old—learn to fight like a professional killer. I could see the way she put all of her efforts into training for the sake of appeasing her tutors. She wielded a knife with her right hand and repeated the motions that she'd been taught only once.

She moved unlike any other four-year-old I'd ever seen. Which made sense, considering that this video was two years into her training. She would have given an experienced soldier a hard time despite the little hands and the angelic face that was occasionally whipped by the long braid of dark hair that ran down her back.

She was deadly. Fast. Strong.

She was *me*.

In the past two hours, I'd watched dozens of these videos. They'd started when I was around two years old, crying for a mother I didn't remember. By four years old, it looked like I'd completely forgotten her, which I guessed also made sense. Most people couldn't remember their earliest years. I'd been *so* young when they must have taken me.

It hadn't taken long before Noelle was both my family and trainer in one.

Now and then, I still struggled to wrap my head around the fact that the little girl in the videos was me, especially when I didn't remember that entire chunk of my life. But she was. Even the video files were named "Decima" with a date and series of numbers attached. If they hadn't been, I still would have recognized myself in that childish face. As I got farther into the videos, I started to come across training sequences that had stuck in my memory from way back then.

As the video I was currently watching came to an end, I decided I'd had enough. What more could I learn from them? The household had stolen me from my parents when I'd been a toddler. They'd instructed me in fighting arts and stealth for reasons I didn't understand. No explanations were given in the video records. Noelle must have carried them on her for some kind of reference if she'd needed to push on a specific part of my training.

It wasn't just physical training in there, after all. A few of the videos had shown the psychological conditioning I hadn't even realized I'd gone through. The conditioning that had embedded the awful phrase that had let them take over my free will: *Garlic milkshake*. And programmed me with other innate responses through hypnosis and punishment too.

Suddenly I understood why I'd always felt uncomfortable about the idea of turning on the TV in any of my hotel rooms while on assignment unless I had to in order to gather information. Why I'd never been the slightest bit tempted to step outside my rooms in the household without explicit permission. Why I'd barely asked any questions about my role in the household until I'd finally escaped it.

They'd honed my body and shaped my mind into the exact tool they'd wanted me to be. A shudder ran through me at the thought.

I shifted on the picnic bench and reached across the space between that table and the one where the guys were sitting, handing the phone back to Blaze. We'd come to this secluded corner of a park in the wan early morning light so that he could show me more of what he'd discovered. We hadn't wanted to linger at the scene where Noelle had attacked me—and where she and her men had met their deaths.

I was still wary of the four hitmen eyeing me from across the distance between the tables, but I couldn't resist flopping back on my own and closing my eyes, trying to put a cap on the emotions that were roaring through me.

Who was I really? Were my parents still out there? Why had Noelle and the others treated me like this?

The strongest emotion by far was confusion. That and queasiness at the awareness that I had no idea who I'd been before I'd been kidnapped or who I'd have grown to be.

But that part didn't matter, really. I was Decima now, and nothing would change that.

The yawning sense of loneliness I'd never understood before opened up inside me. I'd been missing my real family this whole time without knowing it. My fingers itched for my stuffed tiger toy—the one I'd seen myself clutching in the earliest videos before I'd become more compliant. I must have brought it from home.

No wonder I'd had such a hard time leaving it behind. It'd been my one connection to the home I'd lost.

Blaze's foot tapped against the pine boards of his picnic bench. He'd been stirring restlessly since I'd started watching the videos, but so far he'd managed to keep his energy contained enough to avoid peppering me with questions. Apparently the hyperactive hacker's patience had run out.

"How much of all that do you remember?"

I pushed myself into a straighter sitting position, eyeing the guy. The breeze tossed through his floppy, pale red hair until he pawed it behind his ear.

What could it hurt to be honest? I cleared the lump from my throat. "I know that I was trained all through my childhood and teenage years. I remember a few of the sessions I saw in the videos, as I got a little older, but none of the really early stuff. And I have no idea about anything before the household. But there has to be a before, right? I wouldn't have been crying for my mom if there wasn't. I was so young..."

Blaze gave a sympathetic shake of his head. "You couldn't have been older than one and a half or two in the first videos," he said with a flash in his eyes that was unexpectedly protective. Then he paused. "What were they training you for?"

They still didn't know that part. Well, they could probably guess, given the training *they* must have received for their own line of work. No one learned to wield a knife like child-me had just to carve up a turkey. And the guns...

I drew in a breath and hesitated. Four pairs of eyes remained locked on me. I still barely knew these men, even though I'd been living with them for several days. I hadn't been aware that they were contract killers rather than cops until last night. That was a pretty major deception.

But then, I'd lied through my teeth to them when it came to so much about myself. They were brutal killers... and so was I. If anyone could understand the life I'd been living, maybe it was them.

There was still so much I didn't know about who I was, and they might be the only people who had a real chance of helping me figure it out. They'd come to back me up when I was in trouble. And I had to admit that even with *their* initial kidnapping taken into consideration, they'd treated me with more respect than anyone in the household truly had.

"What do you think it was for?" I said. "You've seen how I can fight. I was learning how to kill. Once I was older—starting when I would have been around eight or nine, I think—they started sending me on missions. Small local ones at first, then farther out." I wrapped my arms around myself instinctively. "They told me I was taking down bad people—that the world was an awful place and almost everyone in it was awful, and getting rid of the men and women they pointed me at would make things a little better. Make the household a little safer. I never saw any reason to believe anything different..."

Because the people who'd taught me hadn't allowed me to. Until now. Until their carefully constructed façade had crumbled when *these* men had blasted into the household and blown them all away.

I still didn't totally understand that either, even if I believed the guys that they'd been hired by a client to do it, that it hadn't been personal for them.

I sealed my lips as I looked over the four imposing men at the picnic table parallel to mine. Blaze was still jiggling his knee. Garrison sat on the bench, his ankles crossed as he watched me intently with his piercing hazel eyes. In the sun, they appeared lighter than usual—a pretty, almost green color.

Julius leaned against the side of the table with one foot propped on the seat, his massive, muscular frame giving off a typically commanding air. With his military short hair, he looked every inch the ex-soldier. Talon was poised on the far bench with his elbows braced against the tabletop, his icy blue gaze fixed on me beneath the sheen of his pale, shaved scalp. The coldest killer of the bunch had the look of a lion ready to strike, but I didn't think any of his animosity was directed at me.

"It makes sense that they could have convinced you," Garrison said, somewhat grudgingly. The lanky blond man had tried to rankle me with his snark nearly every time we'd spoken to each other in the past couple of weeks. I didn't think he liked offering any sympathy. "You had them brainwashing you from when you were so young. Even older kids are pretty impressionable." Then he shut his mouth tight as if he'd said more than he thought he should.

Blaze frowned. "They started sending you off to *kill* people when you were still just a kid? That's—"

His voice halted abruptly at a sudden movement from Julius. The crew's leader straightened up. He took a step closer to me, peering at me with his deep blue eyes. Something in them sent a weird but not totally unpleasant shiver over my skin.

"I knew we'd met before," he said with a startled expression that looked odd on his normally assured face. "I helped you once."

I blinked at him, and a twinge of the unexpected sense of familiarity I'd felt here and there before rose up inside me again. "If we'd actually interacted, I would have thought I'd remember that."

"Maybe not, given the circumstances." His surprise faded away, replaced by his usual confidence—and a warmth I wasn't totally used to. "It was more than a decade ago, not long after Talon and I had started the crew. Blaze and Garrison weren't in the picture yet. The two of us were working a job in Miami one night. I had a bike back then—a Triumph. I was just getting on it in the alley where I'd parked when this girl who wouldn't have been more than eleven or twelve came running down the alley toward me. It was dark—you were frantic—but it must have been you."

Talon lifted his head to look at his boss. "*That's* what really happened to the Triumph? You told me you totaled it."

Julius shook his head. "She was bleeding from a cut on her side, and I could hear people running after her. The alley was a dead end. I wasn't going to leave some kid for a bunch of creeps to find. So I told her to wait there and marched out, told the people who were charging over that I'd seen her running off in a different direction. And right when I went back to check on her, the bike came roaring out of the alley with her perched on it. She left me in the lurch." He chuckled, seemingly unoffended in hindsight. "I figured I could always get another one. She obviously really needed it."

My mouth fell open. I *did* remember him now that he'd pieced the details together. I'd partly bungled a mission, caught a trip wire on my way out of the house where I'd made the kill and gotten several guards on my tail. One of them had shot at me and nicked the side of my chest. It was the first time I'd had a mission go haywire, and I'd been freaking out underneath. In the darkness and the haze of my panic, I'd barely registered the facial features of the stranger who'd protected me.

Then cool logic had kicked in thanks to my training, and I'd made use of the resources available to me. A.k.a., his bike.

"I did," I said. "Need it. Thank you. I probably would have figured out how to get out of that mess one way or another, but… you made it a lot easier."

Once I'd left the city well behind, I'd ditched the bike at a junkyard and called the household to orchestrate my pickup. I'd never mentioned that anyone other than me had been responsible for getting me out alive. Julius couldn't have known that story unless he'd really been there. And studying him now, I could easily superimpose his authoritative presence over the shadowy impression in my memory.

And now we'd somehow stumbled back into each other's lives when it turned out I might need him again—in a much bigger way. The realization brought a strange mix of relief and unease.

Garrison let out a light snort. "What kind of mission did they have you on at eleven years old? Did you kill your mean science teacher?"

My gaze darted to him, and the uneasy sensation within me expanded, twisting around my gut. "The household never told me any details about the people they sent me to kill other than what I needed to know to get the job done. That one… That one was a rich man who had a big house guarded by men with semi-automatic rifles. He kept a pet bearded dragon in his bedroom. I slipped in through a back window, dodged all the guards, and cut his throat in his sleep. I just… ran into a little trouble on the way out. I didn't have as much practice then."

Garrison blinked at me, his smug smile vanishing. "Okay, I stand corrected."

Blaze's eyebrows leapt up. "Twelve years ago in Miami? Was he an older man, in his 60s, with a house in North Beach? Big stucco number with bizarro gargoyle mounted over the door?"

I stared at him. He hadn't even been in the crew yet then—how did *he* have any idea about this? He couldn't have been out of his teens back then himself. "Yeah… How did you know?"

The hacker let out a disbelieving guffaw. "That hit still gets talked about in the circles we run in. That was Milo Evangelez—the gemstone baron of the southeast."

Something shifted in Julius's expression. He cocked his head. "What are some of the other missions you carried out? The particularly memorable ones?"

My skin started to itch with a deeper discomfort. Noelle had drilled it into me that I wasn't supposed to talk about anything I did outside the household. And… a gemstone baron… Why would they have wanted to kill him?

Suddenly I wasn't so sure I wanted to hear what else the guys might tell me.

But I couldn't be a chicken about this, and Noelle didn't dictate my life anymore. I wracked my brain for missions that stood out more than the others and forced my mouth to move.

"Like I said, I wasn't told things like names. Even if I overheard information like that, I put it out of my mind." Probably thanks to all Noelle's hypnotic suggestions, I realized now with a grimace. "There were three businessmen in Italy who always went everywhere together. That made them difficult to take out. They acted all jovial and friendly in public, but in their hotel room, they were assholes to each other. I half-expected them to kill each other themselves before I poisoned them. Managed to sneak some special ice cubes into the drinks in a room service order they placed."

I paused for just a second, pulling my lower lip under my teeth before I continued. "Another of the harder ones was this man in Osaka. I had to kill the guy in a bathhouse, and he was as big as a sumo wrestler. Do you know how hard it is to strangle someone who outweighs you by five hundred pounds with nothing but the towel they walked in with?"

The guys were staring at me in silence. It was kind of unnerving. Even Garrison the Indifferent was gaping at me.

Unsurprisingly, Blaze lost the ability to contain himself first. "Are you hearing this?" he said, glancing around at the others with an awe I wouldn't have expected from my sparse descriptions. He met my gaze again. "The man in the bathhouse—the sumo wrestler type—that would have been Akio Nakamura, the founder of Nakamura Tech. The Italian brothers must have been the co-founders of the aerospace center in Rome—a big source of political debate."

Those… didn't sound like the horrible criminals Noelle had made them out to be either. My stomach started to knot. "How can you be so sure?"

"It all makes so much more sense now. Holy crap." Blaze clapped his hand against his knee. "*You're* the Ghost."

I stared at him. "The what? What are you talking about?"

Julius cuffed his younger associate lightly on the shoulder. "What Blaze is doing a very bad job of explaining is that the mercenary underworld has been tracking certain high profile and highly skilled kills for years, trying to figure out who's pulling them off. People started referring to the mysterious assassin they assumed was responsible for most—if not all—of them as the Ghost, since the assassin never left a trace. The three hits you mentioned were all attributed to the Ghost."

"Somehow I don't think anyone would have predicted it was a teenage girl," Talon remarked in his deep baritone. I couldn't tell from his tone whether he was impressed or merely stating a fact.

"Everyone's been incredibly impressed by your work—and curious as hell about who you are," Blaze said, *his* eyes shining with unrestrained excitement. "Holy shit, we've had the Ghost staying in our apartment for days and we didn't even know it."

Garrison recovered from his shock enough to look me up and down with a skeptical expression. "From what I've seen during that time, I wouldn't say you quite live up to the expectations we all built up."

I rolled my eyes at him. "I'm sorry if I couldn't immediately overpower four highly trained hitmen while on my own with no preparation and multiple injuries. Also, FYI, I probably *could* have killed you at least five times if that was what I really wanted to do, but I was waiting you all out to see what you knew about the murders at the household."

"So, your excuse is that supposedly you were going easy on us?"

I shrugged, leaning forward on the bench. "You could try me right now. I think I'm ready to take off this brace." I tapped the plastic structure around my arm that'd been shielding my previously sprained wrist. "One-on-one, let's see who comes out on top."

I didn't really mean the challenge, but even Garrison of the many masks couldn't stop uncertainty from flickering in his eyes as he looked me over again. Facing me—a woman with an immaculately deadly reputation—scared him in a way that he wouldn't admit.

The entire crew was *impressed* by my kills and the reputation I'd built up with them—a reputation I'd had no idea about. The idea that mercenaries all around the world might have been discussing each of my hits and comparing notes and theories made me want to squirm. All I'd been doing was following orders.

With that thought, the knots in my stomach turned into a dull ache. "The people I mentioned," I said tentatively. "And whoever else it seems like I killed, that you attributed to the 'Ghost'… Were they involved in illegal activities as well as the legit businesses? Were they some kind of criminals?"

Julius sobered in an instant. "Some of them definitely had questionable ties," he said quietly. "But many of them, as far as any of us knew, were sticking to at least the letter of the law. We assumed they were being taken down by competitors or people with a personal beef, not for any real crimes."

I dragged my gaze away from him to stare off through the trees. Why had Noelle really ordered me to kill each of my targets, then?

I'd been surrounded by lies my entire life, so was it really a surprise if the people I'd killed weren't as deserving of their horrible fates as I'd been told?

I'd been nothing but a tool for the household, a tool for their own selfish ends. *They* were the bad guys in this scenario, not the heroic underdogs they'd painted themselves as.

Nausea trickled through me, and I had the sudden urge to march right back to the mansion and kill them all over again.

Within a few seconds, the flare of rage faded into more queasiness. I rubbed my face. I'd learned so much, and all of it only made my life and the mission I'd given myself more complicated. Where the hell did I go from here?

And how was this crew of hitmen going to factor into it?

"What now?" I asked, focusing on Julius, since ultimately it'd be his decision. "You know who I am, I know who you are…"

He contemplated me for a moment. "That's up to you. What do *you* want to do with everything you've discovered?"

I'd never heard those first four words before—never been given the freedom to do whatever I wanted. What *did* I want to do?

I felt my answer out slowly. "I want to know who I really am—or who I was before I was taken. I want to find out why the household took me and trained me, and why you were ordered to kill them. I need to understand where I fit in and why they want me back."

Blaze was the first to speak. "We can help you with all of that." He glanced at Julius for confirmation.

Julius nodded. "Whether you like it or not, we're all tangled up in this mess together. After everything we put you through getting to this point, maybe we owe it to you to find you some answers. And frankly, I'd like to know what those answers are too."

With his dark eyes on me, I couldn't help wondering how much he was seeing me, the fully grown woman with fifteen years of kills under her belt, and how much the scared eleven-year-old girl who'd been briefly in over her head all that time ago. But I wasn't going to argue against his decision, not when it benefitted me so much.

I couldn't help checking Garrison's expression. He didn't exactly look thrilled, but he only scowled without a word in protest. Talon gave a brief dip of his head as if it didn't matter much to him either way. I studied him next, searching for a sign of the man who'd turned so intense when we'd collided in the exercise room days ago.

As far as I could tell, he wanted to pretend we'd never had scorching-hot sex up against a wall. I guessed if he preferred to avoid the subject, I would too, even though I wasn't sure I'd mind a repeat of our encounter.

At least he didn't seem to feel he needed to avoid *me*.

I leaned back on the bench, taking the crew in as a whole. Julius may have agreed to help me, but I still had a choice. I would never sacrifice my free will again—not for these men or anyone else. I could still go off on my own to find answers if that suited me better.

What good would sticking to my own devices do me, though? I had little money and fewer resources. The contacts I'd known were all tied to Noelle, so I couldn't trust any of them.

This crew was the best resource I'd found by far. Was I really going to throw that away just because I still cringed a little at the thought that they'd been the ones who'd torn the household apart?

I had no loyalty to the people who'd lived there. Noelle and her colleagues had kidnapped a toddler, brainwashed me, and controlled me for years. They'd sent me off to kill people for no reason but their selfish gain.

The men in front of me had connections and skills… and they'd also offered me something nobody else ever had: freedom. They were *more* than just a resource.

Resolve unfurled through my chest, steadying me. My mouth curved into a small smile. "What are we waiting for then? Let's get started."

TWO

Julius

WE SAT around the dining table, Blaze's usual spot filled by Dess as he squeezed in at the corner, too close to Garrison for either of their liking. If I had to hear another second of bickering from them…

"You eat so much pasta that you smell like it," Garrison chided, taking a bite of his chicken.

My mouth became a thin line as I awaited Blaze's comeback.

"You eat so much chocolate that… you know what? You don't smell like chocolate." Blaze smirked. "You smell like a heaping pile of dog—"

"You both fucking stink," Dess cut in, her mouth full as she spoke. My spine straightened as she said it, and I couldn't help but chuckle a bit. Having someone else break up the constant heckling between them was a blessed relief.

She looked at me with a glint in her dark eyes. "Don't think that you smell any better."

Everyone looked at Dess for a moment, and she smiled at us. "Talon's the only decent one here, isn't that right?" she added, giving him a wink.

Talon, for all it was worth, looked pleased with her announcement. He continued eating with a hint of what might even have been amusement on his face, but he didn't reply.

I looked around the table again, noting the homey feel that had settled over our group even with a relative stranger in our midst. Of course, the truth was that Dess barely felt like a stranger now. We knew who she was on a level she'd shared with almost no one before, and the same for her with us. I didn't need to watch her from the corner of my eye every few seconds, checking for hostile moves.

It was so much better this way, having everything straightforward and clear. It would make our jobs easier, and we'd be able to help her more when we weren't blinded by lies.

Dess stood up from the table and took her plate to the sink. Now that I knew what she was—what she'd been trained to do—I could pick up on the strength and agility that marked even the simplest movement, every motion she made deliberate and coordinated. Everything about her screamed "dangerous" if you knew how to look right.

But there was still so much about her that none of us knew, her included. So many things about her past that could prove more dangerous than she was.

Who was she? Who was after her? We could obviously expect further threats to arise, but where and when and to what extent?

Not knowing how to prepare left me on edge. I dealt in certainties and absolutes, planning our missions and our overall security down to the smallest detail. Anything left to chance could pop up and bite us in the ass at the most inopportune moment.

I didn't have much choice, though. The only other option was turning her loose, which she didn't want… and neither did I. Every particle in my body said both she and we were better off with her among us.

I *wanted* to help her.

The thought of those people wrenching her from her family and forcing her to become their murderous tool brought a bitter taste to my mouth. Fury flared to the surface at the memory of the fight in the sewers this morning, when her former trainer had sicced all those men on the woman she'd raised since early childhood. I'd like nothing more than to rip through every person responsible for Dess's imprisonment, and I'd be counting the days until we found them.

My hand dropped to the military-issue Beretta M9A1 at my hip. The feel of the cool, smooth metal settled my nerves, even though there was no one in front of me to shoot just yet.

"I think we need dessert," Blaze said, cutting off my train of thought.

Dess laughed lightly as she rinsed her plate at the sink. "Do we? Let me guess, you have a sweet version of pasta for that."

Blaze snorted. "If only. How's this for an idea? We have ice cream, and I know that Garrison keeps a tub of chocolate syrup in here somewhere. To celebrate your newfound freedom, why don't I whip you up a chocolate milkshake?"

I doubt any of us had failed to notice Dess's enthusiasm for all things cocoa-related. Her face lit up the second Blaze mentioned the syrup. But as he finished his suggestion, an uneasy twitch ran through her slim frame. The eagerness in her expression dimmed.

"That's all right," she said, her voice oddly stiff. "I'm actually pretty full."

I studied her for a second, my brow furrowing with confusion, before it hit me.

In the videos, her bitch of a trainer had used the phrase "garlic milkshake" to completely control Dess as a child. She must have unpleasant associations with that combination of words—and maybe with each of them on their own as well. *Very* unpleasant, if it'd shaken her adoration for chocolate.

"Thanks anyway," Dess added quickly, and headed to the exercise room that'd become her honorary bedroom in the apartment. Blaze started after her, puzzled and apologetic. "But... she *loves* chocolate," he murmured to himself after the door shut behind her.

Garrison scoffed and cuffed the back of his head lightly enough for the gesture and the words that followed to come across more teasing than hostile. "For someone supposedly so smart, you can be one dim motherfucker."

Blaze scowled, and I stepped in before they got going again. "You remember what her control word was at the household?"

Blaze's eyes flickered the way they always did when his brain was moving at a million miles a second putting the pieces together, and then he smacked himself in the forehead. "I think we need a codeword for milkshakes."

"Maybe we should simply avoid them for the time being," I remarked dryly, but afterward, my gaze slid to Dess's door. There might be other ways to start solving that problem—ways that got right at the source. If she wanted that.

There was only one way to find out.

As the others finished clearing the table, I walked over to Dess's room. After a second's hesitation, I knocked.

"What?" Dess asked from the other side.

"It's me," I said. "Can I come in? There's something I'd like to talk to you about."

"Sure, come in," she said, sounding normal enough. But when I opened the door and saw her sitting on her cot, I couldn't help noticing the slight slump to her shoulders and the pensive crease on her forehead that she managed to smooth away a moment later.

I considered asking the most obvious question: *Are you okay?* But I knew how quickly *I'd* deflect an expression of concern like that. And I was coming to see that Dess and I had a lot in common.

I sat across from her on the workout bench, spreading my legs as I leaned my elbows into my knees. "Do you want to talk about it?"

She sighed and made a face. "Not really."

I nodded. "I get that, but I might be able to help if I know what's going on. We heard the phrase your trainer used in the videos. I'm guessing it still bothers you?"

Her mouth twisted tighter, a little of the pain I didn't think she wanted to admit showing through. "It doesn't just bother me. It can *control* me." She swore under her breath and pressed her palms to her forehead. "What if I can't fix what they broke? Not completely."

My heart ached for both her and the girl I'd encountered all those years ago. What if I'd taken her under my wing then? Not that I could imagine she'd have let me, but her life… it could have been different. Better.

All we had to work with was where she'd ended up in reality, though.

I shook my head. "You're not broken. You just have some interesting features."

She raised her eyebrows at me, and a small smile curved her lips. "That's one way to look at it, I guess."

"Maybe all those features will come in handy one day."

Her eyes sharpened. "If this situation doesn't get me killed first." She sucked a sharp breath in through her teeth and held it for a few seconds before releasing it. "During the fight, Noelle used the code word, and it almost worked. I followed her halfway to the exit before I could stop myself."

I winced inwardly. No wonder that wound was raw for her. "Noelle's dead now," I reminded her.

"Yeah, but she didn't work alone. Anyone else who knows or gets ahold of that phrase could use it to give them enough time to take me down. Even one second of distraction in a fight could cost me my freedom. You don't know how it feels to have someone else in control of your body, screaming at yourself to stop and getting nowhere."

Her breathing quickened as she spoke, and she was right. I had no idea how that felt, and I didn't even want to imagine it. But that didn't mean I couldn't offer her anything.

I clasped my hands together in front of me, holding her gaze. "In my special ops training, we learned a variety of techniques for avoiding mental conditioning. It's easier to put up those barriers before the conditioning happens, but the exercises can help to fight off the compulsions too. Mental conditioning is dangerous, and it's a testament to your strength that you broke through it so quickly. Most people could never hope to do that, especially when they've been programmed since early childhood."

Dess tilted her head with a curious expression. "Did anyone ever try to condition you in that way?"

"No," I admitted. "Nobody ever caught me for long enough. But I practiced the techniques all the same, and I talked to guys who were held prisoner who managed to resist."

"I guess it can't hurt to try." She straightened up, the new resolve in her stance already reassuring me that she wasn't shaken too badly. "Can you teach me those techniques?"

"That's what I was thinking. I can give you the grounding, but what's most important is that you make sure to practice them regularly on your own once you've got the hang of them."

"Oh, if there's one thing I've got in spades, it's self-discipline." Dess's mouth quirked into a more genuine smile, one that brought the beauty in her face into clearer focus. Damn, this woman was gorgeous when I let myself notice.

But now wasn't the time for thinking about her looks. She needed guidance, not ogling.

I motioned to the floor. "We need to sit for the first exercise. It's a meditative experience, and it's best to get centered on a flat surface with nothing to distract you."

She lowered herself to the ground and crossed her legs, pulling them in tightly as I followed her. "Is this how you learned that you like to meditate?"

I blinked at her. "How did you know I meditate?"

She shrugged. "Blaze mentioned it. He said he learned how from you."

"I practice yoga," I said. "Meditating is the only part Blaze enjoys, so that's what he does. I do it all. There's a lot more to it."

A sly glint sparked in Dess's eyes. "I bet that makes you flexible."

Damn it if my dick didn't start to harden just with that brief remark, as if she meant anything like *that* by it. I gritted my teeth against the pang of arousal and evened out my breathing.

"Yes, but that's not what you want to be focused on right now. There are two main strategies that we can use, but before we attempt either of them, you need to be relaxed. I suspect that's going to take some work. I can feel your tension from here."

"I'm not sure I know how to relax," Dess admitted.

"You've got to learn, or none of this will help you," I said, and she huffed. I watched as she willed her shoulders down. "Good. We'll work on relaxing you more, but first I want to tell you the two things we're going to try. Visualization and disassociation."

"Those sound like fancy words for sitting on my ass. Is this really all that meditation is?"

I took a deep breath. "Do you want to learn or not?"

She winced. "Sorry. Continue."

I took in the way her black hair tumbled across her shoulders. Her spine remained straight, her slim figure on lovely display within her fitted tee and sweats, but her pert chin dipped in concentration.

Then I mentally swatted myself across the head for leering at her. Maybe I shouldn't be lecturing *her* about staying on topic.

I reined in my other impulses and thought back to some of my earliest lessons. "The conditioning is in your head, so you're going to need mental tricks to deal with it. That's why it's best to clear your thoughts as much as possible first. With visualization, you can imagine that the conditioned commands are a wave that simply washes over you without catching hold. Picture yourself holding firm while the words roll over you and slip away. Can you try that?"

Dess nodded, her movements already slowing as she sank into the sort of mental zone I was familiar with. She did pick up training fast, didn't she? She stayed still for a while, her chest rising and falling within her cotton shirt, and I definitely wasn't noticing how well her toned curves moved beneath that fabric.

"You said the other way is disassociation?" she prompted after a few minutes. "What does that involve?"

And so eager to learn. Another thought that shouldn't have sent a twinge of desire to my cock but did.

I pushed those emotions aside yet again. "That's right. You can disassociate yourself from the girl who went through the conditioning—convince yourself that it happened to a different woman, separate from who you are now. If you aren't the one who was conditioned, then the effect can't work on you."

Dess hummed to herself. "That makes sense. I like that one. I *feel* different already."

"That's a good place to start, then."

She inhaled and exhaled even more deeply than before. I could see the loosening effect spreading through her entire body. Gradually, more of the tension fell from her posture and her face. A softness crept over her features, totally at odds with her usually tough exterior.

Not many people would have gotten to see the vulnerable side of this woman. I was honored to witness it.

What was passing through her head right now as she sat there, a goddess of death incarnate? She looked so breakable, but I saw the illusion for what it was. I knew how *un*breakable she truly was.

The two factors in combination made her all the more appealing. When had I ever known a woman like this in my entire life? A woman who could hold her own against me in so many ways…

But as lust flickered up from my belly, a memory snuffed it out. The memory of the eleven-year-old girl with desperate eyes, dashing into an alley.

Dess needed help now just like she had back then, not to be treated like a conquest. I wasn't going to take advantage of her while she worked through her tangled past. Maybe when she'd healed more—

No, I wasn't even going to let myself think about that.

Other questions about the future lingered in the back of my mind. She could be here with us for quite a while. With her deadly precision and strength, she'd be an incredible asset in our line of work. Having the Ghost as part of the Chaos Crew? We'd be even more unstoppable than we already were.

Would she even want to join us? I couldn't see broaching the subject just yet. But while she was with us, I'd get the chance to see just how well this cunning assassin could fit within our ranks.

The rest we'd have to take from there.

THREE

Decima

AFTER A RESTLESS SLEEP that stretched into the afternoon, the first thing I saw when I opened my eyes was that damned stuffed tiger.

The thing that used to bring me so much relief and comfort now felt like another lie that I would never be able to fully trust. I scowled at the plush creature even as my fingers itched to wrap around its soft, well-worn fur and pull it close.

Was it something that Noelle had gotten to soothe me as a child? No, she'd never cared about my emotional wellbeing, and I'd hidden the toy from her over the years. I'd always had the sneaking suspicion that she'd throw it away if she knew how much I treasured it.

Anna, the only emotional comfort I'd ever had at the household, had never said anything about the tiger that I could remember either. I'd caught a glimpse of it in a couple of the earliest childhood videos…

Did that mean it'd come from the life I'd had before the household? It could be a clue—or simply a tool my kidnappers had used to placate a distressed toddler in the moment.

I didn't allow myself to dwell on the thought as I got up from my bed and quickly changed, but I couldn't help brushing two fingers across the striped fabric of the tiger before I strode out of the room.

I found Blaze sitting at the dining table, a half-devoured plate of fettuccini alfredo poised at his left and his laptop propped open at his right. He rapidly typed with one hand as he forked pasta into his mouth with the other.

I suppressed a laugh. "You take multitasking to a new extreme."

Blaze's head whipped toward me. Rather than turning the computer from me or closing it, he gestured to the seat at his side. "Come and sit down. Maybe you can help me."

Something in my chest tightened at the welcome with a startled pang. He trusted me enough to share whatever he was working on.

Of course, what he was working on was *me*. As I dropped into the chair, the window open on the laptop's screen jittered with an occasional flicker of an image. As I watched, one of those flickers flashed into a folder at the bottom of the display.

"What's all this?" I asked as Talon emerged from his bedroom and headed to the refrigerator behind us. "Who are you looking for?"

Blaze shot a smile at me, his knee bouncing with his usual frenetic energy. "Technically, I'm looking for you. Or anything that could lead us to your birth family."

Talon grunted. "Why bother with your fancy software? Wouldn't one of those DNA sites do the trick faster?"

I sat up straighter in my chair. "Is there a website that'd connect me to my relatives by my genetics?" I had a vague sense that I'd heard about something like that before.

Blaze studied me. "I keep forgetting how much you've been out of the loop the last twenty-or-so years." He turned to include Talon in his answer. "Any of the public companies that run DNA matches come with too many problems. To start with, it'll only help us if one of Dess's relatives has already gotten a test with them too, so it won't even necessarily turn up anything. And they *are* totally public. If the people hunting for her have set up flags in any company's systems, we could inadvertently lead them right to us."

"So do it privately then," Talon said.

Blaze rolled his eyes. "I don't happen to have the skills to sequence her DNA, so unless you took a secret course in microbiology, that's not happening. There aren't any significant private databases that I'm aware of that would give us a decent chance of finding a match anyway."

I peered at the laptop screen. "What *are* you doing, then?" He'd clearly come up with some kind of solution. The tech genius seemed to have an answer for everything. Compared to my minimal computer skills, the stuff he could pull off might as well have been DNA sequencing.

Blaze gulped down another mouthful of pasta before answering. "I took a bunch of stills from the videos of you right after you were taken and now I'm having my facial recognition app run them against all the missing child reports it can dredge up from around the right time period for kids around the right age. Since we don't know how much global reach this organization had, I'm taking them from all around the world. There are a lot—it's going to be a slow process."

My heart sank. "You haven't found any matches yet."

"Nothing definite. I'm having it pick out ones that are somewhat close in case they did something to your appearance before any of those videos were taken. And if this doesn't pan out, there are plenty of other strategies I can try."

His optimism took the edge off my disappointment. But after I'd plowed through a bowl of cereal, I found myself wandering through the apartment, desperate to hear a *ping* of an alert that might mean a match. When it didn't come, I finally planted my hands on the other side of the table.

"I can't just sit around and wait for something to happen. There's got to be a way I can investigate too."

Talon let out a doubtful sound from where he'd moved to the couch and dragged out his knitting bag. I was never going to get totally used to the sight of that musclebound killer weaving the needles back and forth with their yarn, as close as the movements might come to the jerk of a knife.

"Whatever bad idea you're about to suggest, the answer is no," he grumbled.

I made a face in his direction. "Who says it's a bad idea?" Even as I said that, an actual idea occurred to me. One that had the potential to be dangerous, sure, but leaving the crew's apartment would always be a risk. I wasn't going to find the answers that'd reduce the danger if I stayed cooped up in here.

"I don't know," Talon replied in his typical impassive voice. "The last time you took off, you nearly got kidnapped again. Whether it's bad or not, I'm pretty sure it'll be hazardous to your health."

"Hey," Blaze piped up. "We should at least hear what she's got to say. It is *her* life we're trying to piece together."

"Thank you." I folded my arms over my chest. "I could go talk to the contacts I know in this city. They were connected to the household. Maybe they know more than I do about where else this organization operated or who they really were."

Despite his earlier support, Blaze frowned. "Because they're connected to the household, they could be under surveillance. You might be walking into a trap."

"I'd be careful about it. This isn't my first rodeo, remember."

"I don't think you want them knowing you're even still in town," Talon put in.

I threw my hands in the air. "Fine. Then I'd just spy on them from a distance and see if they lead me anywhere useful. Happy?"

His mouth still slanted in at a skeptical angle. But thankfully, at the same moment Julius strode into the room. "Since you're arguing loud enough for me to hear you through my door, I'm going to weigh in." He nodded to me. "You obviously understand the risk."

Relief started to trickle through me at his confident tone. "Yes. I *am* the one who almost just got kidnapped and then found out that my whole life has been a lie. Believe me, I'm not going to be giving anyone out there the benefit of the doubt."

"Good." He gave Talon and Blaze a look as if to remind them that he was in charge here and then returned his attention to me. "I trust that you'll be discreet, and you should be able to take an active role in this investigation. Like Blaze said, it's your life. And we're not your jailors anymore."

My shoulders relaxed. "Good. So you're not going to make a fuss about me leaving?"

The corner of his lips twitched upward in a subtle smile that shouldn't have been so sexy. "I hope you'll come back of your own accord this time, but no, I won't. I don't want you going in and out of this building alone like you did two nights ago, though. It's too visible. If the people searching for you haven't connected you to this place, I'd like to keep it that way. I can escort you out through our private route and meet you when you get back, if you'll agree to those terms."

"Sure," I said, my spirits rising. I didn't know if I'd totally believed until this moment that the men really were going to treat me like an equal among them rather than a prisoner. "That's fair." I didn't want anyone involved with the household tracing me here either.

"Excellent." He dug into his pocket and handed me a wad of cash for good measure, with a glint of amusement in his eyes. "And I can't let you go out there without proper resources. I'm guessing you'll find a way to spend this wisely."

I leaned against a light fixture a few shops down from the bakery, a light brown wig covering my tightly concealed locks of black hair. The hat that I wore atop it hid any irregularities to the wig, and sunglasses masked the rest of my face. I knew from my observations of Blaze's software that revealing my full face even for a second put me at risk of being captured by a street camera and IDed.

So far, I hadn't been able to find any sign of the guy I was looking for. I'd strolled past the bakery a couple hours ago and again a few minutes ago, and Jay's curly hair hadn't been anywhere to be seen through the front window.

It wasn't a big shop. If he'd shown up for his usual late afternoon shift, I should have spotted him.

A waft of the sweet, doughy scent carried on the breeze and set my mouth watering. It was too risky to go right inside and ask after him, but man, what I wouldn't have given for one of those chocolate chip cookies to hop its way out here.

Maybe Jay had taken today off? Maybe he'd changed his schedule? Leaving the apartment had been enough of a hassle that I didn't want to give up on my quest without getting some idea of when he'd actually be here. Julius might have been willing to escort me out, but he'd insisted on keeping part of the route secret, leading me blind. As a precautionary measure in case I was captured, which I couldn't blame him for when it'd already nearly happened yesterday.

I got a break when one of the women I *had* seen working behind the counter emerged from the alley. She must have left through the side door. She was just running her fingers through her billowy hair, which was creased from being trapped in its net for however many hours.

As soon as I clocked which direction she was headed in, I ducked through a nearby shop, darted around to the end of the block, and ambled toward the bakery as if I'd only just arrived in the area. When I came up on Jay's coworker, I made a show of stopping in my tracks.

"Hey!" I said brightly. "You look familiar. You work at Moe's, don't you?"

The woman halted abruptly and then laughed. "Now I feel like a celebrity. I do."

"I was just heading over there. Best cookies ever." I didn't have to fake the enthusiasm in my voice with that comment. I groped for the right impression to give to sell my next question and settled on slightly coy, as if I had a crush. That was a normal reason for asking about a guy, right?

I dipped my head and twisted my hands in front of me with feigned nerves. "Say… is that guy with the curly hair and the goatee working today? I was hoping I'd get to say hello."

The woman started to grin, but then the smile faded. "You mean Jay. He *was* supposed to be in today…" She bit her lip.

My pulse hiccupped. "What? Did something happen to him?"

Enough real distress must have come into my voice to convince her to reveal a little more. "Oh, I'm sure he's fine. Just being flaky. I heard he's missed his last couple of shifts. The manager couldn't reach him today. He's probably just not answering because he knows she'll chew him out."

"Oh! Well, at least I'll get to have those cookies," I said, and gave her a little wave to let her carry on her way.

I didn't go into the bakery, of course, but walked right by it, my forehead furrowing. Sure, Jay hadn't seemed like the most dedicated worker ever, but I didn't like that he'd suddenly "flaked" on his job within days of me reaching out to him.

It was probably a coincidence. I hoped it was a coincidence.

Shrugging off my uneasiness as well as I could, I flagged down a cab and gave the driver the address of the old mall on the other side of town.

Jay had just been a grunt worker. He'd had no stake in the bakery. Scarlett had *owned* the electronics store where I'd talked to her last time, as far as I knew. Noelle had said she'd worked there for years, usually on her own. She couldn't just flake out and not bother to show up.

She'd know more about the household than Jay would have too.

I had the cabbie stop a couple of blocks away from the mall, handed him a good chunk of my remaining cash, and meandered along the street toward the low building while giving the area a careful scan.

No one I passed looked like anything other than a regular pedestrian who didn't give a crap about me. I didn't notice any new cameras mounted nearby or other signs of surveillance. Even if I'd missed them, nothing about my appearance right now should tip anyone off to my identity.

I ambled through the dingy mall haphazardly, as if I didn't have any particular destination. Just window shopping, whatever the hell that really meant. But when I came into view of the electronics shop, my stomach knotted.

All the other stores were still open. The mall didn't close up until well into the evening. But Scarlett's shop was fully shuttered—not like she'd just stepped out for a moment. Like she'd closed up for the day.

Swinging past it as close as I dared, I noted the faint dusting of grit along the bottom of the shutters where it'd been sprayed by last night's cleaning crew working over the floors. She hadn't opened up at all today, at least. Possibly the shop had been closed for longer.

The memory wavered up of the way she'd talked when I'd come to her store last week, the edge of nervousness in her voice and body language. I'd wondered who she was worried about.

Maybe she'd been right to worry. Jay *and* Scarlett—that couldn't be a coincidence, could it?

I kept my pace casual as I headed back toward the mall entrance, careful not to draw any attention, but my heart was thudding. When I'd made it several blocks from the building, I stopped and dragged in a deep breath. My pulse kept racing on.

The last two people I'd had contact with outside of the crew were missing. What had happened to them—and had it happened because of me?

FOUR

Decima

BLAZE STILL SEEMED cheerful when I returned to the apartment, led by Julius, but he mustn't have had any exciting news, because he nudged his laptop aside and asked, "Find out anything interesting?"

I scratched my hairline, which was still a bit itchy from the wig, and frowned. "They were gone."

Garrison's head snapped up from where he'd been flicking through his phone in the kitchen area while waiting for the kettle to boil, and Talon set down his knitting. "Gone?" the bigger man repeated with a frown.

"Vanished from the face of the Earth. The guy at the bakery hadn't shown up for his shift in at least a couple of days, and the other woman's shop was all closed up." A frown of my own tugged at my lips. "I don't like it."

A laugh tumbled out of Blaze. When I narrowed my eyes at him, not understanding how the situation was funny in any way, he waved his hand. "The bakery, huh? One of your sources works there?"

"Yeah, so what?"

The words had barely left my mouth when I realized the tidbit of information I'd revealed. It hadn't been that long ago when I'd been hiding as much as I possibly could from them.

Garrison had arched his eyebrows, his tone more sardonic than Blaze's. "It wasn't the chocolate chip cookies you wanted out of that place after all."

I rolled my eyes. They knew I'd lied about a hell of a lot of other things. This one wasn't a big deal.

"It was at least as much for the cookies," I retorted. "I know you thought they were amazing too. Anyway, it doesn't matter. My contact there is gone, and anything he could have told me is gone with him. And I have no idea what happened to him or my other contact."

Julius ran his hand along his chin. "It could be that once you'd made contact with them, the household called them in to find out what they knew about *you*."

"Maybe." But how long would that have taken? Why wouldn't they be back sooner?

I shoved those uncomfortable questions aside and focused on Blaze. "I've got nothing. Did you come up with anything here?"

"You mean did his fancy app come up with anything," Garrison remarked.

Both Blaze and I ignored him. Blaze looked back at the computer and made a face. "We might need to move on to plan B."

My heart sank. "The program's gone through all the missing kid reports and didn't get a single match?"

"Well…" He pulled the laptop back to him and started clicking on files. Talon came over and Julius drew closer as I did for a better look. Garrison, being his typical nonchalant self, stayed where he was like he didn't give a shit, but his gaze lingered on us anyway.

"These are the sorts of things I got in the loose matches," Blaze said, motioning to the screen.

I snorted at the first one. "The household didn't change my ethnicity."

One girl in the image—young, no more than two years old—did have gray eyes and black hair like mine, but the shape of her features marked her as clearly East Asian in heritage. I guessed mine weren't *that* different, but they were different enough to set our ancestors continents apart.

"Yeah, I know." Blaze clicked open another, which showed a girl whose eyes, nose, and chin mimicked my toddler self so closely I could see how the software might have picked up on the similarity… but her wavy hair was bright red, and freckles dappled her cheeks. "And this obviously isn't you either, unless they managed to inject permanent dye receptacles right into your hair follicles."

I stared at him for a second. "That's not actually possible, right?"

He chuckled. "No, thank God, or my job would be a lot harder. Anyway, the others are all like this—specific details that make it clear they're not you—and there were no exact matches. I *did* end up connecting one missing toddler to her adult self living out in Des Moines… I'm not sure she has any idea her dad stole her away from her mom after they separated… I sent a tip with the information to the police department who handled the original case so hopefully they can finally set things straight."

He grinned with satisfaction at the victory that had nothing to do with our original mission. It was hard to feel too frustrated about it in the face of his delight at solving some problem, even if it hadn't been ours. He hadn't needed to go to the trouble—he could have shuffled aside that case and moved on—but it'd mattered to him to give the woman and her mother some peace.

There was a lot more to Blaze than the incisive hacker and gleeful backup shooter, wasn't there? As he tapped away at his keyboard to bring up whatever he wanted to show me next, I couldn't help noticing the way his head tilted to the side and his bright brown eyes sharpened with concentration. The late-afternoon sunlight streaming through the apartment's tall windows highlighted the planes of his smoothly handsome face and the light red hair that fell nearly to his shoulders.

Before, his regular flirting and gestures of affection had put me so on guard that I hadn't really appreciated how attractive he was. But when he was caught up in a puzzle, eagerly putting the pieces together, there was no denying he had a certain appeal.

Maybe I should give kindness another chance.

The thought provoked a memory of honeyed words and a vicious smile that sent a shiver through me. Thankfully, Blaze redirected my thoughts.

"My best guess is that your kidnapping wasn't reported," he said. "Possibly you were taken in a country with an incompetent police force."

"Or she wasn't kidnapped at all," Talon said.

Blaze cocked his head at the other man, and I knit my brow. "What do you mean? The household obviously—"

"They were connected to human trafficking operations," the former military man interrupted, firmly but more gently than I'd usually expect from him. "We found that out during our initial research. Kids who get trafficked aren't always taken from unaware families. It's possible you were sold."

A chill washed over my skin and condensed in my chest. I'd had a vision in my mind since seeing the videos of me as a child—a vision of a happy family who'd loved me and tucked me into bed every night. I'd assumed that it was the only explanation. People didn't just *sell* their children to random criminals, right? My parents wouldn't have looked at me and decided that loving me wasn't worth it.

But they could have done just that. Now that the possibility had been presented, I had to admit it was plausible, especially with the lack of a missing child report. I was coming to recognize that Noelle had been correct about one thing: the world was a dark, brutal place for anyone who didn't have the means to defend themselves.

"It's possible," Blaze admitted, looking between me and Talon. I could tell that he didn't want to admit it—not with me here. My heart dropped into my stomach, and he drummed his fingers on the table in front of him. "It's more than possible. There's no way to trace the connections if that's the case, though. Even within the organization, any trail of records would be long-destroyed by now."

I swallowed hard. What was the point in searching for my birth parents if they hadn't cared enough to hold on to me to begin with? We didn't know for sure, but did I really want to know if it was? I tried to push down the painful emotions rising through me, but a tendril of hopelessness twined around my gut.

Before I could dwell any longer on the thought of a family who'd purposefully given me over to be trained as a murdering machine, Blaze switched gears, clicking through to a different set of photos—these ones of Noelle. I recognized her emerging from an alley near the entrances to the sewer system where we'd met, and another of her through the windshield of a vehicle stopped at a red light, dressed in the same sleek clothes. A flash of anger burned through my momentary despair.

Whether my family had wanted me or not, the household still had to account for the way they'd treated me. The lies and the training I'd been forced into. The freedom they'd stolen from me. *That* mattered.

"I managed to get these screenshots from traffic and security camera footage from yesterday morning," Blaze said. "They should be clear enough to run the facial recognition on. Since we can't trace your origins, we can see what we can find out about the people who took you, and she's our best lead." He tapped on the touchpad, and the screen started flickering with its search.

I folded my arms over my chest. The idea of spying on Noelle brought out a kneejerk refusal that I tamped down on. The household didn't get to decide what lines I shouldn't cross now. But all the same—

"She's dead. How much are we really going to learn this way?"

Blaze smiled at me and the men flanking me. "I'm hoping that we'll turn up some other associates who are less dead. She's probably had meetups in public places for various reasons. When you don't trust anyone outside your own organization, that's the way to go. And who knows what other connections she might have?" His smile widened. "Silly question. In a few hours, *we'll* know."

"How much can you even search?" I asked, watching the screen. Images streaked into new folders every few seconds, much faster than when he'd been running the search for my childhood face. Of course, most of them were probably loose matches that wouldn't turn out to be Noelle at all.

"My software can crawl through all the still images and video footage that's ever been uploaded onto the internet, from social media sites to news outlets," Blaze announced, his voice warm with pride. "And it'll peek into more private avenues too where I've opened up access. She might be dead, but she'll still give us some answers. And this kind of interrogation is a lot less hassle than the bloody type."

He paused and glanced up at me. "Is this bothering you? I know she was… important to you."

That was probably the best way of putting it. I wasn't sure Noelle had ever cared about me, at least not for anything other than how well I could carry out her assignments. And after finding out that and how thoroughly she'd programmed me to be her tool, I wasn't sure I cared about her either. But her death and my discovery of her betrayal were still so fresh, maybe it made sense that my emotions were a little muddled.

An assassin couldn't afford to focus on emotions. I needed a clear head and a steady hand. Noelle had been right about that too, no matter how many other ways she'd been wrong.

"It's okay," I said. "I want the answers too, as fast as we can get them."

"It looks like we've already got a few exact matches. Let's see what we've dug up…"

He opened a folder and clicked on the first file. A slightly grainy image filled the screen.

It was a selfie, a blond girl posing in front of an old stone statue with her mouth pursed into duck lips. She didn't look remotely like Noelle. I was about to ask Blaze if his software needed a tune-up when my gaze caught on the figures in the background.

Just beyond the girl's shoulder, a woman with dark brown hair was walking along a park path. I could only see her face in profile, but every nerve in my body jangled with recognition. It was Noelle.

And she wasn't alone. She was talking next to a skinny man with graying hair whose mouth was open in animated conversation. I narrowed my eyes at him, straining my mind.

"Do you know him?" Julius asked.

I shook my head as I committed the details of his face to my memory. I *would* know him if I saw him again. "I didn't usually interact with anyone other than Noelle and Anna within the household. There are probably all kinds of people they worked with who I'd have no idea about."

"It doesn't matter," Blaze said, chipper as ever. "I'll save him and send him through the scans later. Leave no stone unturned."

The next one was a video clip. We had to watch it three times, me leaning closer to the screen with each iteration, before we picked out Noelle in the bottom of the frame at the left side. From the length of her hair, I could tell this footage was from at least a couple of years ago.

She'd briefly turned to glance at something behind her, but around her a mass of other people were gazing toward something up ahead. Several of them were waving signs and banners. I studied them all, not sure what to make of this. "What's going on there?"

Talon pointed to a podium that showed at the upper corner of the shot. "Looks like a political rally. Damien Malik."

Julius made a thoughtful sound. "This must be from when he was running for re-election a few years back."

"Damien Malik?" I said. "Should I know who that is?" I was aware of the current president of the country and various other major figures, but that name sounded familiar only in the vaguest of ways.

"He's a congressman," Garrison spoke up from his spot on the other side of the room, where he wasn't even doing a show anymore of not following our search. "Current majority whip in the House of Representatives. Kind of a big deal for anyone who hasn't been living under a rock."

I glowered at him, half-heartedly wishing I had a rock to toss at his head, and turned back to the screen. Unfortunately, I had to ask, "What exactly does a majority whip do?"

"He's supposed to rile up the rest of the representatives in his party to pass the legislation the president wants," Julius said. "Although there've been murmurs about Malik pushing his own ideas a little harder than people would prefer."

That didn't sound too ominous. When the household wanted to "push an idea," they obviously knocked off whoever was standing in their way rather than just talking about it. I'd presumably helped them do so more times than I wanted to think about.

"Should we read anything into her being there?" I asked.

Blaze shrugged. "I wouldn't think so. A rally would be a good place to blend into the crowd and carry out some kind of surreptitious transaction that has nothing to do with the purpose of the gathering. Can you see if she's reaching out to anyone there?"

We squinted at the recording again, but the part that'd caught Noelle only showed her making that brief turn. We couldn't even see what or who she'd been looking at. I blew out an irritated breath.

"Hey," Blaze said reassuringly, "we've got lots more to get through. Those answers are in here somewhere."

We checked out a few more photos, none of them very enlightening. Here was Noelle walking down a sidewalk alone. Here was Noelle exiting an organic grocery store with a shopping bag over her arm. Here was Noelle sitting at a patio table with a different man from the first picture, but one who was equally unfamiliar to me.

Blaze set that one aside for further investigation and opened the next file, which was another video. The three of us behind him leaned in automatically to take a closer look. But I immediately recognized the scene, so definitively that my heart skipped a beat.

It was a different day. Noelle wore different clothes, and the cast of the light was different, as if the sky had been overcast rather than cloudless. But there was no mistaking the signs and the banner by the podium.

She was at another Damien Malik rally.

Blaze hummed. "Well, that's starting to look like a pattern."

Julius's forehead furrowed. "I'd say."

I stared at the screen—at Noelle, who turned her head to stare straight toward the stage with her usual implacable air.

Was Damien Malik tangled up with the household somehow? And if so, what kind of part did he play in this mess?

FIVE

Garrison

I HAD to admit that it was impressive how quickly Blaze could dig up information, not that I'd ever tell him as much. The last thing he needed was me swelling his head even bigger.

So when I finally let myself come over to join the group discussion after he'd dug up Dess's former trainer at a third Malik rally, I watched him replay the clips without any overt reaction. My gaze slid to Dess instinctively. She was good at hiding her emotions, nearly as good as I was if not better, but even she couldn't stop the tension from showing through right now. Didn't the other guys see it?

Maybe they did and they were just giving her the space to work through her emotions on her own. Why did her response have to itch at *me* so strongly?

As I refocused on the laptop's screen, Dess shifted on her feet. "How could this Malik guy be connected to the household? Does he have some kind of stance that's friendly to criminals?"

I couldn't help snorting at that suggestion. When she gave me a baleful look, I shook my head. "Couldn't be more obvious how out of touch you've been, sweetheart. Anyone who knows anything has heard about how strict Malik is on crime."

Blaze nodded. "He's constantly pushing for harsher sentencing, as well as increased funding and authority for law enforcement."

Dess frowned. "Yeah, that doesn't sound like a guy who'd support kidnapping toddlers and murder for hire. Maybe he was a potential target."

I shrugged, still studying the video recording. It was hard to make out much of this Noelle woman's body language in the mass of the crowd, but she wasn't giving anything away with what I could see. Other than her brief glance backward, she was simply watching the stage where Malik must have been speaking. Was she preparing for some kind of gambit? Standing guard?

I couldn't tell with so little to work with.

"You don't know much about how politics work," I reminded Dess. "People can be total hypocrites, and I'd say that's twice as likely when it comes to our dutiful representatives."

"He's kept a pretty consistent façade if it is one," Julius remarked.

Blaze tapped at the keyboard of his own initiative and brought up a recent news clip of Malik answering questions at a press conference. A twinge of apprehension ran through me. Whenever I saw the guy with his implacable face and his gray hair slicked back impeccably straight, he set off warning bells in my head. That face was a mask—I'd have bet all the money I had in the bank on it.

Of course, every politician wore a mask, just as much as I did. But I couldn't remember ever seeing Malik's so much as waver. It was as complete and unshakeable as those silvery strands smoothed over his skull. Either he didn't have much to hide anyway… or he was so used to hiding that he could do it effortlessly by now.

In my experience, the second possibility was way more likely.

"There's got to be *some* connection, right?" Dess said. "We've found Noelle at three different rallies now, all in different states. And we haven't found her image at any *other* rallies. Just his."

I arched an eyebrow at her. "Maybe she was just a big fan."

Dess glowered at me again. "Of a guy who'd want nothing more than to shove her behind bars for the rest of her life?"

I couldn't hold back a smirk. "Hey, some weirdos get off on that kind of thing."

Dess let out a huff, but the upward twitch of the corners of her mouth suggested she wasn't completely impervious to the joke. "I guess it takes one to know one," she shot back, and it was my turn to restrain a laugh.

As irritating as I sometimes found her ability to snark back at me, I had to admit I kind of enjoyed it as well. She knew how to give as good as she got, and she never got her back up too much about it the way Blaze sometimes did. I wouldn't have dared to say some of the jabs I'd aimed her way at Julius or Talon for fear of my life.

Maybe she did bring something a little bit refreshing into the honed dynamic the four of us had formed.

That thought brought a flash of memory to the front of my mind: her mouth colliding with mine, our brief crash of passion on the rooftop deck. I wet my lips instinctively, lust unfurling in my groin imagining *her* tongue flicking over the same terrain.

She could bring as much heat to her touch as to her banter. Even looking at her gorgeous face and the curves of her slim but powerful frame stirred my dick. Fuck.

I clamped down on those sensations as hard as I could and shoved them away. The fact that I couldn't completely erase the flare of attraction set my teeth on edge. She shouldn't have been able to get under my skin like this. Any emotional pull I couldn't shut off was a weakness.

While I'd been grappling with my dick's desires, the gears had obviously been turning in Blaze's head. "I'll start searching for the other people we've found with Noelle in the photos. That'll help us get a fuller sense of the big picture."

Julius nodded and gave him a brisk pat on the shoulder. "Get to it. And let us know as soon as you find any leads that the rest of us can follow up on."

I inhaled deeply and found my nerves were still jangling too much for comfort. I needed to gather myself and get my head on straight again before I could get back in my element. There were a couple of things that could help with that.

I moved to the kitchen, flicked the kettle on, and grabbed one of my favorite instant cocoas from the cupboard. Just looking at the spread of boxes and tins sent a twinge of nostalgia through my chest that was reassuring despite the pang of homesickness mixed in.

Mixing up a mug of hot cocoa had always been my mom's favorite way of unwinding after a stressful day, and she'd never minded sharing. I liked thinking that every flavor and brand I sampled was in her honor, as if she wasn't missing out on them after all.

"I'll be on the rooftop thinking deep thoughts if anyone needs me," I informed the others, shaking off those remnants of the past.

Dess's gaze had followed my movements. At the sight of the mug, her eyes lit up. She glanced toward the stairs that led to the deck with unusual hesitance and asked, "Do you mind if I join you?"

Did I ask *for company?* I thought automatically, but I caught the acidic reply before it fell off my tongue. She was grappling with a hell of a lot more than I was. It was a big deck. I could still get my space—and maybe a little more banter with her would bring me back to myself better than solitude. I just had to keep my mind on what mattered.

"As long as you keep your paws off my telescope this time," I said, and grabbed another mug.

By necessity, I'd gotten a very efficient kettle. It was singing in less than a minute, and I filled both of the mugs with a practiced stir to dissolve all the powder and a dollop of cream in mine. I'd noticed Dess preferred hers as unadulterated in its chocolatey-ness as possible. Not that I'd been taking notes or anything.

When I nudged the mug across the island toward her, she scooped it up with an expression of childlike delight. The gleeful glow in her face contrasted with the hardened killer I knew her to be so completely that it tugged at something in my chest. I couldn't tell whether I was relieved or regretting that I'd agreed to include her.

I opened the door and let her climb the stairs to the deck ahead of me, definitely not ogling her pert ass in those well-fitted jeans. When we came out into the cool evening air, Dess stepped off to the side. She gazed up at the moon as she took another sip, and then closed her eyes with a smile of absolute bliss that made me want to lick the cocoa right off her mouth.

"I never thought I'd find someone who enjoys this stuff as much as I do," I said, to stop myself from simply standing there drooling over her. "Somehow you've got me beat."

"I've been chocolate-deprived," Dess replied. "Got to make up for lost time." She took a gulp followed by a pleased hum that went straight to my groin and then fixed her dark gray eyes on me with a glimmer of mischief. "I assume this cup isn't going to knock me out?"

I winced inwardly. I'd never admitted to drugging her first drink with us, but it wasn't surprising that she'd clued in. "You were hiding a lot from us back then," I reminded her. "We were taking necessary precautions."

"Well, at least those precautions came with a whole lot of chocolate-y goodness, so I guess I'll forgive you that one transgression."

"Thank you so very much," I muttered. "If I'd known we were dealing with the Ghost, I might have spiked it with something stronger."

She laughed. "I'm an assassin, not an elephant."

The humor in her voice set me at ease again. "Are you sure?" I asked. "We do know you a lot better now, but I'm not assuming there aren't a few things you're still hiding."

"If I decide to take off my human suit, you'll be the first to know." She paused, breathing in the steam from the mug and returning her gaze to the sky. The amusement faded from her face. "*I* didn't even know how much I was hiding from you back then. I had no idea how complicated my situation was."

The trace of anguish in her voice made my chest constrict. "We'll figure out the truth," I assured her. "There's nothing Blaze can't ferret out. Just don't tell him I gave him that vote of confidence."

This time, the joke didn't budge her pensiveness. She swiped her hand across her mouth. "I know. It's just...weird. I feel like I've been playing a role all this time without even realizing it—and I have no idea who I really am beyond that role. I want to be someone real, not just what Noelle and her associates sculpted me into. But I don't know where to start finding that person."

Most people would never understand the desire to stop pretending and start being herself. *Most.* Her words struck a chord deep inside me, somewhere that I hadn't been affected in far too long.

I'd built my life around playing roles and being the person my crew and my clients expected me to be. Being real—yeah, that was the tricky part.

But I could tell she was talking genuinely with me right now, offering more honesty than I was sure I'd earned.

"You're getting there," I said, with the urge to match her openness with my own. "The real you is clearly a chocolate addict."

Her smile came back, a minor victory. "Okay, I'll give you that."

"And simply recognizing that you feel a little lost—that's something real too."

Her attention settled on me, and I had the impression she was evaluating my own motives. "Do *you* really think so?" she asked. "Or are you just trying to get me to open up about my secret elephant nature?"

A chuckle tumbled out of me. "I guess you'll never know."

She grimaced. "I'm not sure I can even tell with myself. Putting on a front has become so automatic."

I knew what she meant there too. Her candor loosened my tongue more than before. The question fell out before I could second-guess the impulse. "Were you being real when you kissed me up here before?"

Dess considered me intently enough that heat washed over my skin without her even moving. "It was strategic," she said finally. "I was using the kiss to get something I wanted. But if it makes you feel better about it, I did like it too." The corner of her mouth quirked upward. "Didn't you?"

From that coy smile, I had to assume she'd been able to tell how much I had. But I hadn't expected her to answer so honestly on that subject either. For a second, I lost my voice.

"I don't know," I heard myself saying, with the same automatic defensiveness she'd admitted to in herself. "It was over awfully fast."

The sly gleam came back into Dess's eyes. She set her mug down on the nearest table and stepped toward me. "Well, I guess there's one easy way to confirm."

Then she grasped my shirt by the collar and bobbed up to capture my mouth with hers.

I'd been lying when I'd said I didn't remember whether I liked the last kiss, and this one brought that lie into sharp relief in an instant. I liked this—hell yes, I did.

I ran my fingers along her jaw and tugged her just a little closer to deepen the kiss, savoring the tart sweetness of her mouth the way she'd reveled in her drink. Her arms wound around the back of my neck, and I couldn't resist bringing my other hand to her hips and pulling her flush against me.

She let out a little growl that electrified me from head to toe. When she ground her groin against mine, I just about spontaneously combusted.

Holy hell, this was some woman. Why had I wanted to avoid getting tangled up in her again?

My cock had hardened in an instant, straining against the fly of my jeans. I kissed Dess harder, flicking my tongue between her lips to duel with hers. Her fingers curled against my scalp with a flurry of sparks, and I nudged her backward so she was pinned between me and the wall. The way her body molded against mine, somehow soft and tough all at once, had my nerves clanging with need.

Just how long could I wait before I buried myself right inside her?

No sooner had that question crossed my mind than footsteps thumped on the steps leading to the deck. With a mumbled curse, I tore myself away from Dess. I jerked my shirt straight and willed the flush on my skin to cool just as Talon appeared at the top of the stairs.

He looked from me to Dess, who'd propped herself against the wooden wall with her arms folded over her chest as if nothing at all unusual had been going on. The moonlight shone off his shaved head. His icy blue eyes gave no sign of suspicion, but Talon might not have cared even if he could guess what we'd been up to.

"Dinner's here," he said. "Steffie brought takeout from that Greek place down the street."

Dess straightened up. "Great. I'm starving."

Talon nodded and headed back down. Dess started after him, but as she passed me, she brushed her hand across mine.

"So," she murmured. "Do we have a verdict?"

It took a second for my brain to catch up. My cocky attitude snapped back into place over the walls I'd dropped for just a moment.

"I liked it just as much as you did," I replied dryly, and ignored the pang of longing that resonated through me at the flash of her smile before I watched her graceful form move down the stairs ahead of me.

Maybe even more. And that right there still felt like a problem.

SIX

Decima

I KNEW something was up the next morning the moment I entered the kitchen and saw all the guys talking around Julius's card table of army figures. They spoke quietly, not even glancing over as I grabbed a glass of water. I lingered for a moment, trying to catch a snippet of conversation.

Then it clicked.

This scene looked familiar. It was exactly what I'd seen when they'd been planning their last mission. I watched as Julius moved a few figures across the board, and Talon readjusted one, saying something in his usual low tone. Blaze shifted from foot to foot as he added a few lines to a sketch on the whiteboard, and Garrison monitored the expressions of his friends rather than the board itself.

I itched to go over and find out what they were up to now, but… this was their work. If they'd wanted me involved, they'd have asked me, right?

They were doing so much to help me without my even asking them to, without my having any hope of repaying them in any material way. I didn't want to overstep and sour the budding peace we'd made.

The restless itch didn't leave with those thoughts, though. I turned and headed back to my room, which held both my cot and the guys' exercise equipment. Working out was always my go-to method of burning off tension.

As I stepped onto the treadmill, I paused. How much was this habit my own, and how much was it simply something Noelle had drilled into me?

My hesitation only lasted a few seconds. My trainers had pushed me to stay strong and lean, but when I'd decided that I needed a release in the middle of the night, it hadn't been Noelle who'd compelled me to do sets of cardio exercises. I'd turned to that outlet of my own accord.

I set the pace slow to start, a brisk walk that transformed quickly into a jog. When my legs felt warm and supple, I turned the jog into a sprint and finished the last quarter of a mile. As the second mile rolled around, I sprinted half of it and slowed to a jog. By the time I finally slowed to a walk again, my breath was coming a little rough. Good.

I took myself through some stretches, and then I jumped into a weight training rotation that had me sprawling on the floor, breathless and satiated. The rush of exhausted exhilaration after a good workout was something that I'd never be able to top any other way.

Well, maybe I'd found at least one other way recently. My attention settled on the weight rack for a moment, remembering Talon's firm hands hefting me up there, his body scorching against mine, his cock filling me. A giddy flush rose over my body.

I stood and strode toward the cabinet against the wall, pulling out a scratchy towel and wiping away my sweat. When I brushed the towel over my face, I caught a hint of laundry detergent, but it had been overpowered by the reek of male perspiration. Despite being clean, the towel still smelled of musk from overuse.

I couldn't stop myself from running it over my face again and breathing in the scent deeply. It reminded me of Talon—of how sweaty we'd gotten during the collision of our bodies in that very atypical workout the other day.

The exercise hadn't totally burned away my restlessness, though. My nerves still twitched with uncertainty. I needed something more.

I stalked out into the common room to find the guys had vanished while I'd been working out. Steffie had arrived and was wiping down the kitchen sink. Giving her a wide berth, I paced from one end of the apartment to the other. That didn't help. I clearly wasn't going anywhere.

"Full of bees," Steffie said in her dry voice.

I turned toward her. "What?"

She swiped her cloth across the kitchen island. "Full of bees. It's what my mother always used to say when I couldn't sit still. Like I had a hive riled up inside me. A frequent problem of Blaze's, you might have noticed. Seems like you've got the same difficulty at the moment." She shot me a crooked smile that didn't totally fit with the grandmotherly vibe of her gray-and-white streaked bun of hair and softly plump figure.

"Yeah…" I wasn't sure how much to say to her. The guys had introduced me briefly to the woman who took care of their cleaning and errands, but I'd barely spoken to her before. Did she even know what they'd found out about who I was and why I was here?

I ambled over and started unloading the dishwasher, which was both something to occupy myself and a show of solidarity. Joining someone in their work was one way of forming a connection. I'd mostly used that trick with targets I was planning to kill, but there was no reason it couldn't work with a potential ally.

Steffie raised her eyebrows but didn't shoo me away. When I was halfway through sticking the dishes back in the cupboards, I judged it safe to venture, "How long have you been working for the crew anyway?"

"Oh, years and years," she said. "I watched them train Garrison in. But obviously I have seniority over all of them." She winked at me.

"So, what, they put up a job application online or something?"

She burst out laughing: a rich, vibrant sound that spoke of a big personality within her subdued exterior. "That wouldn't do for work like this. No, I was… part of a job, and they decided it was a good idea to keep me on to do jobs for them."

It was hard to keep my jaw from dropping. I had a sudden image of Steffie stalking through dark corridors alongside the guys with a gun in her hand, which would have seemed totally ridiculous if not for the glint in her eyes. "A job? I mean—I know what kind of jobs they do."

"Yes, they mentioned that the air had been cleared." She moved to start wiping down the front of the fridge, scrubbing hard at a few stray splatters of food. For a minute, I thought she might have decided she didn't trust me enough to say anything else. Then she sucked in her breath.

"They're good boys—you should know that. I'd been sold to the people they were hired to go after. People who used me as a slave. I'd been with them for years too. I hardly remembered… I didn't have anything but my name when Julius set me free. But he saw something in me and he knew I'd been cleaning for the men who'd 'owned' me, so he suggested that I could look after this apartment for them. And then when that worked out, other properties they wanted kept up. And other responsibilities on top of that." She shot a glance at me over her shoulder with a quirk of her lips. "I know a good situation when I've got one. I made myself as useful as possible."

The thought of Julius extending that offer of kindness to her wasn't too hard to believe after he'd opened his home to me too, but hearing her explanation sent a waft of warmth through me. These men were killers, but they weren't *just* that, any more than I was.

"You have your own place now and everything?" I asked.

"Oh, yes." Steffie beamed with obvious pride. "Blaze found the perfect apartment for me nearby. I pay for it all myself with my earnings—a woman needs some independence. Now I have a space just for me."

I could tell how much that mattered to her. Maybe I understood that emotion more than she realized. I'd had a space of my own in the household, but even those rooms hadn't really been *mine*. Everything that'd belonged to me in the household had been constructed around their needs and what they wanted from me.

"I'm glad you got out of that awful situation," I said honestly.

Steffie nodded and went back to her cleaning. "They didn't have to offer their hands to help me up, but they did without hesitation. I'd do anything for them. I'd kill for those boys."

Her faint accent that I couldn't quite place thickened her words, and I could hear the slight warning behind them. *Hurt them, and you'll regret it.* But after the rest of her story, I respected her more for her vehement devotion.

"They've earned it," I said, and she smiled again.

With the dishwasher empty and Steffie reabsorbed in her tasks around the apartment, I meandered over to the television. I hadn't had much chance to make use of it in my past life. Maybe it could provide the stimulation my body insisted I still needed.

I picked up the remote and flipped through the channels, wishing I knew how to bring up that show Blaze had tracked down for me with the spy lady and her husband. None of the scenes that flashed by me grabbed my attention. I started hitting the button so hard that I'd already switched channels when my gaze caught an image that made my heart stutter.

I flipped back as quickly as I could. The newscast was just cutting away from Damien Malik's face. "With Representative Malik's proposal shut down by one swing vote, it remains to be seen what steps he'll take next to forward the party's agenda," the reporter said in that droning monotone they all seemed to use.

Then she started talking about a heatwave in Alabama, as if I cared about that. I glared at the TV, but the force of my will couldn't make the show switch back to talking about Malik again.

Oh, well. It wasn't as if it'd sounded like what they were talking about connected to the household anyway. It'd just be easier for me to understand Noelle's interest in the man if I knew more about him.

What had his recent proposal been? Something to crack down on criminals, like the guys had said he liked to do?

I shut off the TV and leaned back on the couch with a deep sigh.

A familiar baritone voice carried from one of the bedroom doorways. "You look like you're contemplating the meaning of life."

I jerked straighter on the sofa and turned to meet Julius's assessing gaze. Something about the boss of the crew always made me want to impress him, to show how together and capable I was—as if I hadn't already proven that in both my dealings with his crew and the history of assignments they'd only just realized belonged to me.

"Not exactly," I said. "Just the meaning of the household."

"Come up with anything?" he asked, ambling over.

I couldn't stop my gaze from lingering on the ample brawn of his massive body flexing beneath his fitted T-shirt and dark jeans. Anyone with eyes could have recognized that he was one prime specimen of manhood. The kindness Steffie had told me about somehow brought that appeal into even sharper relief.

I shook myself mentally. Less than a week ago, I'd hooked up with Talon. Yesterday I'd been admiring Blaze's looks and kissing Garrison. And now some part of me was wondering what it'd be like to have the man in charge pinning me down on this sofa?

Was there really anything wrong with that? If I was interested in all of them, and they were interested in me…

Maybe there wasn't a problem with that, but I didn't actually know that Julius was interested in anything other than maintaining the order in his home now that I'd crashed into it.

"No," I said, remembering his question. "I guess that's the problem." I turned back around and frowned at my hands in my lap. "Every part of my body is clamoring to do *something*. To take action. But I don't have anything *to* do."

Julius leaned against the back of the sofa at the other side, a few feet away but close enough that my skin tingled with my awareness of his presence. "What did you do at the household when you were between missions? It doesn't sound like they had you constantly on the go."

"No," I admitted. "I guess it's just… I'm *not* really between missions, am I? I'm on one right now—the one to figure out where I came from, who exactly took me, and why—but I have no idea how to carry it out. So far Blaze has been doing all the work. I don't have any innovative computer programs I can put to use."

Julius hummed, the warm sound washing right through my nerves. "Well, I'm not sure I can help you with that mission, considering I don't have any action *I* can take toward it either while

Blaze is still working his technological magic. But how would you feel about putting your skills to use in other ways in the meantime?"

My gaze shot back to him, a jolt of adrenaline racing through me at the implication of his words. "What did you have in mind?"

Julius smiled, his deep blue eyes brightening at my enthusiasm. "How would you like to work with the Chaos Crew on a job?"

I blinked. It was hard for me to imagine being part of their work. The two jobs I'd witnessed—after or nearly at completion—had been a totally different style from my type of job. The way the crew worked was purposefully messy and, well, chaotic. And they obviously had their roles down in perfect cohesion and cooperation.

He continued before I could reply. "If you're not comfortable with it or you want to recover more from your injuries before pushing yourself, you're under no obligation, but I'd love to see the infamous Ghost at work."

I bent my wrist, not feeling even a tinge of pain from it anymore. The car accident that had bruised my ribs and sprained my wrist could have been so much worse, but even a wrecked car couldn't get the drop on me for long. I no longer needed the brace, and aside from an occasional twinge of pain in my ribs, I was good as new. No weaknesses to hold me back.

"What *is* the job?" I asked.

"It's a fairly straightforward one. Go in, kill the assholes we've been hired to kill, get out. We're taking care of it tonight." He cocked his head. "Having watched you fight while injured, I expect it'll be quite a show seeing you fully in action."

Was that a flicker of another kind of interest in his eyes? I'd swear I caught a hint of the same heat that was trickling through me at his nearness, but it was there and gone so quickly I couldn't quite tell. Julius didn't hold up walls of defensiveness the same way Garrison did, and he wasn't as impassive as Talon seemed to be naturally, but he kept his emotions close.

"I usually work pretty differently from you and the crew," I had to point out.

Julius shrugged. "It'd be a trial run. Maybe it'll turn out to be a bad idea… or maybe it'll be a brilliant one." He shot me a rare smile that showed his teeth—and nearly melted the panties right off me.

I still wasn't sure about the whole chaos thing, but the prospect of getting to do any kind of work sent a thrill through me. And this was an awfully immense show of trust. Julius had enough faith in me to invite me along and let me take part in the kind of job he staked the crew's reputation on.

That alone felt like more than enough reason to jump at the chance.

I only had one more hesitation. I'd been forced to kill people for years—people I now knew might not have done anything all that wrong. Going forward, I could make those decisions for myself.

I studied Julius's expression. "Are we sure that the people you're taking down deserve it?"

Julius analyzed me right back, scanning my face as if evaluating my motives for asking the question. It really was very simple. The killing itself didn't bother me, but I wanted to know who I killed and why I killed them. The idea of murdering someone innocent—someone who didn't deserve the brutal wrath reaped by the Chaos Crew—made my skin crawl.

Maybe Julius could read some of that with his gaze. "It's important to you that we don't kill innocents."

"Yes," I said firmly. "It is."

He smiled again, slower and softer, but somehow this one sent an even deeper surge of attraction racing through me. "Good. We feel the same way. I believe in dealing out justice alongside the chaos. We require that our clients provide information on the targets' background, and Blaze confirms it independently. We only accept jobs that involve marks who've been doing plenty of destruction of their own."

A sense of certainty clicked into place inside me, as if this was exactly what I'd been waiting for. "All right," I said. "I'm in."

SEVEN

Decima

THIS TIME, the crew didn't hide their final job preparations from me. So I got a clear view of the tactical vests, weapons cases, and other mission paraphernalia they were assembling near the door.

"Did you rob an army surplus store?" I couldn't help asking.

Garrison released a harsh laugh, and Julius shot him a pointed look. I wondered if there had been an argument that I'd missed while they'd been gearing up for the mission.

Garrison cast his gaze over me next. "Better to be overly prepared than not at all," he said, eyeing the exercise clothes I still wore from earlier.

"Where do you expect me to get an appropriate outfit for a job like this—out of my ass? I don't even know what the job is."

Julius spoke up before the younger man could get another word in edgewise. "We've got a few more pieces to see to. We'll pick you up some tactical clothes on our way back. Garrison, you can stay and fill Dess in on the details of the mission."

The blond man's eyebrows shot up. "You're leaving me behind now? What am I, the babysitter?"

His boss looked like he was restraining himself from rolling his eyes. Or strangling Garrison. I could relate to both impulses, as much as I'd enjoyed kissing him last night.

"You're supposed to be the smooth talker in the crew," Julius reminded him. "I think you can handle a little conversation. Your skills aren't required for this last bit of prep."

Garrison grumbled wordlessly under his breath, but he didn't raise another overt protest as the other guys tramped out of the apartment. I studied him, my nerves prickling.

Was he really that annoyed about having to spend time with me? I'd thought we'd made a sort of peace on the rooftop, but maybe I'd been wrong. There was still so much I didn't really get about relating to other human beings, at least ones I wasn't supposed to be either training with or murdering.

It shouldn't have mattered anyway. Caring about things like whether people *liked* me only complicated my life.

But that way of thinking, that forming social bonds wasn't important—that was definitely Noelle's teaching. How could it be anything else when I'd never had the chance to live any other way? Part of me was starting to think I'd appreciate a few complications of that sort.

"Why don't we go up to the deck?" I suggested. Garrison usually seemed more at ease there, and I liked the atmosphere too. "I could use some fresh air."

Garrison marched ahead of me without a word and led the way up. He didn't wait for me, striding right out onto the deck while leaving the door open, and stood with his back to me as I emerged.

"I'm sure that Julius explained that this is one of our easier missions," he said abruptly. "You shouldn't have much to worry about."

I grimaced at his back. "I wasn't worried. It would be nice to know what we're actually doing, though. I can handle whatever it is, but I prefer to go in *prepared*, like you mentioned earlier."

Garrison finally turned to look at me. It wasn't a sidelong glance or a hostile glower. He considered me analytically. "I know you can handle it."

That ounce of approval settled my nerves. I didn't need reassurance when my track record spoke for itself, but it was good to know that Garrison was still capable of moods other than intense snark.

He flopped into a lounge chair near his precious telescope, and I ambled closer. I propped myself against the wall nearby. "So, the job..."

"All right already. We're going to L.A. Via private jet, obviously, since regular airlines won't accept all of our equipment."

I blinked. "You guys own a whole *jet*?"

Garrison smirked. "Well, half wouldn't get us very far." Then he sobered up enough to add, "It's not ours. The client is paying for it. Our skills are in high demand, so we get requests all over the country, sometimes overseas, and for those we require travel in style as part of the payment. They're happy to supply the vehicle in exchange for having us doing their dirty work."

"Wow." I'd never thought about just how much the crew might be getting paid for their work. I'd never seen any money from my missions—and when would I have had a chance to spend it anyway?

Had the household profited from my kills? I'd assumed all my targets were people they personally wanted taken down, but it was possible they'd hired me out to other parties too, wasn't it? The thought made me want to scrub my skin raw.

Just how many ways had they exploited me?

I shook off those unsettling questions and focused on Garrison again. "And who are the targets of this job?"

Garrison lifted his eyes skyward. "We're supposed to shoot up some people on an indie studio movie set. The production's being run by a bunch of gangsters who cast themselves and all their buddies into the roles. From what I gathered in our conversation, not that he admitted this outright, the client is pissed that he wasn't invited to join in. So he's hiring us for revenge."

"Wait, this man is having you kill people because he's jealous? You guys get involved in that kind of drama?"

Garrison laughed darkly. "Half of our jobs are based on this kind of drama. All that matters to Julius is that the people we're taking down are scummy too; the reasons we're getting paid to do it don't really matter."

"You have to admit that this setup sounds a little bizarre."

"It's ridiculous, but it should be a cut and dry job. They're all doofuses, so it won't take long to get in, make a bloody mess of killing them, and get out. Blaze said that there isn't much security from the digital standpoint, as far as he can tell from a distance."

"We're going to go in based on what he can tell from across the country?"

Garrison narrowed his eyes at me. "Of course not. He always takes a survey of the situation on location once we arrive. We're not idiots."

I held up my hands. "I was just asking. I've never worked with anyone before."

"Right, the lone wolf. You should give us a little credit."

His tone had turned cutting again. I frowned. "Do you have a problem with me coming along?"

He propped his arms behind his head. "Why would I have a problem with the famous Ghost coming along for a joyride?"

I narrowed my eyes at him. "I don't know. Why don't you tell me?"

"How about this?" Garrison said. "You don't know who you are or where you belong, so you sure as hell can't know how you'll fit in with us. That kind of uncertainty gets people killed."

"The only people who are going to get killed tonight are the ones we were hired to kill. I'm absolutely certain about that. I don't let my personal life get in the way of a mission."

"So you say. I'm just not all that keen on giving that theory a test run with real guns and real bad guys."

I pushed off the wall and stepped closer to him. If he was going to try to push my buttons, I'd push his right back. "Is that really it, or are you worried about your *own* performance? You do seem to have a habit of getting a little… distracted when I'm around."

Garrison scoffed. "Now you're just making shit up."

I let a knowing smile play with my lips. "I don't think so. Although if you've forgotten what happened the last time we were up here, maybe you should get that head of yours checked out."

He shoved himself out of the lounger to face me eye to eye. The heat in his gaze scorched through me all the way to my pussy. "I remember that *you* couldn't keep your hands off me. I'd say that makes you the problem more than me."

I snorted. "Oh, yeah, and you were *such* an unwilling participant."

Garrison's tongue flicked across his lips, and the sight sent another wash of heat through me. If he was a complication, then yeah, some part of me wanted to dive right in. Especially if that would mean releasing the tension that'd been building between us since the first time I'd planted my lips on his days ago.

"Why shouldn't I take what's freely offered?" he said. "It doesn't mean I'm going to be dreaming about happily ever afters while we're getting down to work."

I cocked my head. "Who said anything about happily ever after? Ecstatic right now sounds good to me."

He waggled his eyebrows, taking a step closer. "I'm glad you have so much confidence in my ability to make you scream."

"I don't know. So far you seem to be all hot air and no follow-through."

I gave him a light nudge to the chest, both to provoke him and as an excuse to feel the taut, lean muscles beneath his button-up. Oh boy, did he respond. The next second, I found myself shoved against the wooden wall with Garrison's hands on my waist and his hips pressed tight against mine.

"I'll show you follow-through," he muttered, his breath searing over my lips, and slammed his mouth into mine.

The times before, there'd been a hint of hesitation to his kiss. Even when our mouths had collided and he'd kissed me back with a surge of passion, part of him had been holding back, not quite letting go.

This was different. He was taking what he wanted with every particle of his body where it aligned with mine, and the need radiating through him turned me into a puddle.

His tongue swept into my mouth, clearing away all tastes that weren't *him.* I wound my arms around his waist, pulling him closer as I rose to my toes to deepen the kiss. One of his hands rose to twine his fingers in my hair, hanging loose down my back. He tugged, pulling my head back to expose my neck to him.

Garrison kissed his way down to the hollow of my throat with a force that left me breathless. When he nipped my collarbone, I gasped. His grip on me tightened. I'd known he had a fire in him that could burn us up together, and now that he was releasing it, I wanted nothing more than to go to all the way up in flames.

Garrison nibbled his way over to my shoulder, yanking my shirt to the side to get better access to the crook of my neck. Then he paused, pulling back just enough to speak with his lips grazing my skin. "You're not going to suddenly go all assassin on my ass like you did with Blaze if I get any more handsy, are you?"

A flush that was more embarrassment than desire this time tickled over my skin, remembering the incident all the guys had witnessed—when I'd slammed Blaze into a kitchen counter after he'd flirted with me. I dug my fingers into Garrison's shirt.

"There are certain overtures that I have… bad associations with," I said. "And so they set off a defensive reaction. As long as you don't get too sweet on me, we should be able to manage this without you getting your ass kicked."

Garrison chuckled with a wash of hot breath, but when he lifted his head to meet my eyes, I thought I saw a glimmer of understanding there. Of course the master at reading people would be able to piece together enough from my brief explanation to guess.

To my relief, he didn't pry any further. The corners of his lips curled wickedly. "You want it rough and hard then, huh?"

A thrill raced through my veins at the promise in his voice. I grinned back at him. "Do your worst."

The words had barely left my mouth when he was slamming me back into the wall. His hand dipped down and shoved inside my sweatpants.

"Do you want to know what I'm going to do to you, Dess?" he asked as the pants tumbled down my legs and only his hand remained against my panties, caressing the spot at the apex of my thighs teasingly. I bucked into his hand, and he laughed. When I looked down at the way he worked me, he gripped my chin and forced me to meet his eyes. The grip wasn't quite bruising, but it showed he understood exactly what I needed. "I asked you a question."

Anticipation unfurled through my belly. "What—what are you going to do?" I whispered eagerly.

He released my chin and tore the panties right off me. Then he plunged one of his long fingers inside of me as he continued working my clit.

"Sweetheart, I'm going to fuck you so hard that you're going to beg for me to slow down." He bent closer to my ear, growling the next part. "But I'm not going to. Not until you fucking *explode.*"

A giddy shiver passed through me, watching him take on an even more asshole-ish persona than the one he usually wore—one determined to get me off by any means necessary. Oh, yes, please. Garrison must have noticed, because he straightened his shoulders and licked his bottom lip. He was so fucking hot when he wasn't being a prick. Or at least, when he was being a prick for my benefit instead of to heckle me.

Speaking of pricks…

I reached forward and curled my fingers around his erect cock through his pants. At the first stroke, he jerked against me with an involuntary thrust. "As long as you explode with me," I murmured. The dark smile that spread across his face fueled my hunger, sending jolts of excitement through my veins.

Without warning, Garrison spun me around. I had to whip my hands out to catch myself against the wall. His fingers didn't miss a beat, one now circling my clit, another delving deep inside me for that even more sensitive place far within. He didn't stop until I jerked and cried out, the sweet spot inside getting more sensitive with every blissful stroke.

"Down you go, sweetheart," he said, slapping my back like a light spank. "You'll take this whether you like it or not."

I'd seen him in action—I knew he could have struck hard enough to hurt me if he'd wanted to. He was finding the balance between giving me what I needed and keeping me safe, and somehow that turned me on even more. My mouth watered as I bent at the waist, my forearms sliding down the wall.

The sound of torn foil told me he'd had protection on hand, thank God—I was so tangled up with need I might have told him to keep going without it. I had a birth control implant, but I had no idea how cautious these men usually were when it came to other possible consequences of casual sex.

Garrison's pants dropped, and there was a soft hiss as he must have slicked the condom over his erection. Arousal flooded my sex. My pussy felt as if it were dripping.

He gripped both of my hips forcefully, tugging my ass back to meet him, and then he thrust into my cunt without a moment of preamble.

I saw stars.

He hadn't lied when he'd said that he'd fuck me hard. His thighs pistoned back and forth, his cock ramming into me as deep as it could go. Pleasure rushed through me with every thrust, and I cried out for him, loud enough that the people way down on the street below might have heard. I didn't give a fuck.

Garrison reached around and grabbed hold of my chin again, grasping it as he pounded into my cunt. I arched toward him as my climax swelled within me. My noises of pure pleasure multiplied until everything came crashing down—rupturing and leaving me shattered beneath him, barely able to hold up my own body with legs that had become jelly.

As my channel clamped around him, he gave a pleased grunt. Instead of continuing to his own release right then, he withdrew with a jerk and tugged me around so fast I swayed. He lay me down on the lounger, prowling over me, his hazel eyes darker than I'd ever seen them.

"I could fuck this pussy all day," he murmured. Then he plunged into me again.

As he fucked me the second time, his gaze held mine, searing with his own desire. His ragged breathing matched mine, carrying through the air around us. With each buck of his hips, I spiraled toward a second release. I barely felt the thick cushions beneath me.

I wrapped my arms around Garrison, digging my fingernails into his back. His chest hitched, and he pushed even deeper inside me, raising my hips to meet him at a better angle. The rush of sensation nearly had me sobbing.

He wasn't being half as rough now as he'd been before, but I was so lost in the moment it didn't matter. I'd have killed anyone who tore us apart before I reached my peak.

Thankfully, it didn't come to that. Garrison plowed into me, and a renewed wave of ecstasy flooded my nerves. My eyes rolled back to take in the light speckling of stars across the evening sky. My moan reverberated off the walls.

Garrison bowed his head over me with a deep groan of his own. He gripped the sides of the lounger as his movements grew choppy. With one final thrust, he sagged over me, barely holding himself up with his elbows.

Before he suffocated me under his weight, he rolled to the side, tipping me with him so we both fit on the lounger together. The cool air licked over my naked legs. Neither of us had bothered stripping off our shirts, but the half-nakedness felt weirdly more intimate than if we'd been totally nude. It was a testament to how desperately we'd needed this moment.

I didn't know what to say, but there didn't seem to be any need for words. I lay there in the cocoon of warmth we'd formed, savoring the afterglow.

Garrison stroked his hand over my hair and along my jaw. He tipped my chin up just enough to press a kiss on my lips that felt almost tender, especially after the brutality with which we'd initially come together.

If he'd led with that move, my body would have flinched with panic. After what we'd just done, I was relaxed enough with him that it didn't bother me. He'd been nothing like the man who'd violated me so horribly. He *was* nothing like that man.

When Garrison lay his head against the cushions again, I peeked over at him. Curiosity stirred inside me. He hadn't shied away from the role-play I'd asked for—and he'd more than delivered. He must be fairly experienced. More than I was, but then, who wasn't? All the amazing sensations of sex were one more freedom the household had stolen from me for too long.

"Do you get a chance to do this sort of thing—with other women —very often?" I asked, tilting my head to the side to watch his expression. "I mean, I'm guessing it's hard to keep up a relationship in your line of work."

Garrison's lips twitched, whether with amusement or discomfort, I couldn't tell. "Yeah, but it doesn't matter to me. I haven't been looking for a relationship anyway."

I let out a teasing huff. "Who's the real lone wolf then?"

"At least I know how to *work* with other people on a regular basis," Garrison retorted. He kept his tone light, but a trace of tension wound through it.

"I'm sure there are a few emotional—and other—needs that the rest of the crew can't quite fulfill for you. Nothing so strange about that." I paused. "I guess that's a trade-off to this kind of life."

Garrison shifted, easing a little apart from me. "It's not a trade-off. Some people aren't interested in grand romance or becoming a family man. I'm perfectly happy with the life I'm already leading."

I squinted at him in the growing darkness, having trouble believing him. Garrison was a master not just of reading people but of presenting himself to others the way he wanted. I wasn't sure I'd ever seen him without some kind of mask on. How much was he hiding even from himself?

"Is that really true?" I asked without thinking. "Or is it just easier to tell yourself and everyone else that because you don't think you can have everything you'd really want anyway?"

Garrison heaved upright and grabbed his pants. "I'll thank you to save the psychoanalysis for someone who needs it," he snapped, any lingering tenderness wiped away. Before I could figure out what I'd done wrong or how to fix it, he stalked across the rooftop and down the stairs.

EIGHT

Decima

THE FLIGHT to L.A. was far shorter than I'd expected, and once the wheels hit the ground, the guys sprang into motion. By the time the sun had fully set, they had the plan solidified.

The studio was a squat brick building on the outskirts of the city, about as far from actual Hollywood as you could get while still being within the L.A. city limits. I approached the two security guards on the outside of the side door, peering around the street as if I were lost or looking for something. The warehouses nearby were either abandoned or shut down for the night. There was no one around but us and the shadows.

This was my first act on the job, so I intended to prove just how much of an asset I was. I meandered past the guards without a glance at them, pretending to be too distracted to take notice.

"Hey, sweet cheeks," one called out just after I'd passed him.

I was already whipping into action. I swung around and disarmed the guy who'd spoken with a brisk snap of my hands. A second later, I gave him a kick to the gut that sent him staggering toward a darkened alleyway—where Julius yanked him aside and put a bullet across the back of his head with a splatter of blood and brains.

The remaining guard was mine to handle, and I made it quick, dodging his fist and snapping the gun from his grasp. When he threw another punch, I allowed his momentum to drive him forward while I slipped behind him, wrapping an arm around his throat. The crack of his neck took only a sharp jerk of my body, and he fell to the pavement dead.

I turned and looked at Julius—his tactical uniform already speckled in blood. The black material masked it well, but in the hazy glow of the security lights, the liquid glints shone. He'd made a mess of his kill while I'd done mine clean, like I'd been taught. Suddenly my meticulousness wasn't a benefit. A prickle of uncertainty ran through my body.

If I wanted to fit in with the crew, I needed to do things their way. *Expertly orchestrated chaos*, Blaze had recited for me gleefully. The gore made an impact that their clients wanted.

Well, I could learn. How better to learn than on my feet, watching them in action as an immediate model?

Julius didn't remark on the difference between our kills, and neither did the other three men as they converged on us, though I thought Garrison raised his eyebrow with a hint of disdain at my corpse. He'd barely spoken to me since our evening hookup, and he didn't break that pattern now.

We slipped into the studio, where large swaths of fabric hung from the industrial-height ceiling to section off the filming set. Julius, Talon, and Garrison headed to the left, while Blaze and I headed to the right, setting our feet so we didn't make any noise. It didn't sound as if the actors and crew were likely to hear us over the melodramatic shouts carrying from the soundstage.

"All is lost! How can we ever regain our former glory?"

I reached a gap between the curtains and peered through. For a second, I just stared.

The actors were dressed in… aluminum foil? Or at least suits that appeared to be made out of it, with motorcycle helmets coated in silver paint over their heads. One of them swung an elongated gun that wobbled in his grasp, clearly made out of foam rather than metal. Another poked at a small cardboard box covered in blinking lights that didn't appear to do anything in response to his jabbing fingers.

Julius had said this was a low budget production, but this was really scraping the bottom of the barrel. I'd witnessed high school theater productions with better costumes and props than this.

It seemed to be a sci-fi flick. At least, I guessed that the mottled teal and purple surface under their feet and the mauve crepe bushes in the background were meant to be alien terrain rather than a sign that their set designer was colorblind. And the jumble of cracked metallic objects off to the side, which included a couple of cans I could still see torn scraps of soup labels on—that must be their crashed ship, I was guessing?

Confirming my suspicion, the actor with the box started talking. "There is still hope! The conditions on this planet can support our life. Perhaps there are other beings we will encounter, a grand new society we can become a part of."

At his pompous tone, Blaze clapped his hand over his mouth to muffle a laugh. His amusement sparkled in his eyes despite his best efforts. I bit my own tongue, a giggle bubbling in my throat.

"How can you say such things, Robin?" the actor with the foam gun asked, swishing his weapon again for dramatic effect. "Earth is destroyed. *Destroyed.* We shall never set eyes on it again. All we have left are these tools… and our memories."

I caught sight of Julius peeking through a gap at the other end of the sound stage, his mouth twitching at the ridiculousness in front of us.

"We still have each other!" the other actor declared.

"I suppose that is true." The man with the gun swiveled toward the camera. "And if the world is on fire, then I can burn other things too."

I had no idea what that sentence had to do with the story, but I could tell it was meant to be a tagline, one they imagined would be printed on the movie posters and quoted all around the world. Dear lord. We were really doing society a service here by putting them out of their—or everyone else's—misery.

"Cut," the director shouted. "That was the best take yet, guys.

Really, you outdid yourselves. Take five and see if you can loosen up for the fight."

Loosening up apparently involved shaking their heads and arms while making baboon noises. I clamped my mouth shut against another giggle. Then a conversation reached my ears from the crew on the other side of the curtain.

"This new camera setup is *sweet*, isn't it?"

"Hell, yeah. And that stuck up jerk at the depot will never miss it."

The first guy cackled. "Not from his grave, that's for sure. Remember how he squealed like a pig going down?"

The other guy snickered without any hint of remorse. "I wish we could use it as a sound effect in the film."

My jaw clenched. They weren't just making a shitty film—they were shitty people. We really *were* doing the world a favor by taking them out of it.

The phone in my pocket quivered with a faint vibration. Julius had given his signal. It was time to get to work.

The others didn't waste any time. Bullets sprayed across the set from where Julius was still concealed in the folds of the sheets. I couldn't help marveling at his precision: every shot, even fired so rapidly, clipped an artery in a neck or wrist or thigh, maximizing the blood that spurted across the soundstage.

But I didn't pause in my admiration. I whipped up my own gun, already calculating how I'd use my skills to create a similar effect. The challenge sparked a jolt of excitement in my chest.

I didn't have time to revel in the thrill. The plan was for Julius to handle the north side of the set and me the south. *Avoid the kill shot until they've had a little time to stagger around,* he'd told me. *The longer they live, the more they bleed.*

My first few shots slammed into legs and shoulders, hindering my targets without killing them—but not making much chaos either. Although the cast and crew brought plenty of their own chaos to the scene, running and stumbling around with panicked shouts. I caught another guy in the gut and the jerk who'd described his victim's squeal across the forehead, carving a gouge that made *him* squeal.

The men I hadn't shot immediately scrambled for their guns. I blasted their hands and forearms, sending the weapons spinning. One fled toward the exit, and I sent a bullet into the back of his skull. Well, this was my first time out. Julius had also emphasized that the security of *our* crew trumped every other consideration.

My gaze caught on Julius, who'd stepped partly into view among the shadows cast by the sheets. He aimed his gun with an intent expression, and every shot was perfection. Blood sprayed and hissed from every artery he severed. It was painting the teal-and-purple set a brutal shade of red. Damn, the man was good at what he did.

The wounds he inflicted were vicious enough to send his targets crumpling to the floor in agony, clutching at their broken flesh. Some never moved any farther, still sprawled there when he put the final bullet in their brain or heart a little later. Others crawled toward the doorway and were either blasted in their tracks by him or stopped by Blaze, who I knew was lurking around the fringes with his pistol, ready to pick off those who tried to flee.

Talon wove his way through the flailing mass of figures, his serrated knife flashing under the set lights. He dug the blade into the necks of his victims, wrenching it downward across their chest in a zigzag pattern I'd seen before that seemed to maximize the flow of blood, even though it was instantly fatal. He mowed through the bodies with all the predatory grace of a panther. I had to drag my gaze away.

I'd just shot a few more of the men on my side of the room when a big boar of a guy charged at me in a full suit of foil, as if that was going to protect him any. He probably figured he had a chance of knocking me down compared to the guys because I was smaller and, well, female. But he'd learn the error of that assumption just like all the other people who'd fatally underestimated me in the past had.

I pulled the trigger when he was only a few feet away—and managed to hit him just to the left of the most vital part of his throat. Blood sprayed, and the guy staggered and gurgled, but he stayed alive enough to lurch this way and that for another several seconds before he crumpled.

There. I could be messy too. I'd just needed a little practice.

None of these idiots could stop us. We held all the cards here, and we were dealing out their fate for the equally violent lives they'd lived. All of us, working together in unison. The exhilaration of the collaboration brought an unexpected smile to my lips.

I'd never felt like this on a mission before. I'd gotten satisfaction out of a difficult job well done, sure, but it'd never been a joint effort. Something I was creating *with* other people, something bigger than I could have managed on my own.

I'd thought I preferred working alone, but there was something special about this kind of team effort that it'd never occurred to me I was missing.

Another shot exploded near the front of the room, despite the bodies that already littered the floor. I looked up to where the sound had originated and smiled as Blaze took down another gangster who'd hurtled toward the exit despite the blood pouring from his wounds. True to his assigned role, he was keeping our chaos contained.

Garrison played an active role too, even though he wasn't involved in the killing tonight. I knew he'd gotten information about the filming schedule and personnel ahead of time using his manipulative charms. Now that the bodies all lay motionless or sagging, nearly dead, he stalked between them. He scanned the bodies, checked for pulses, and motioned the rest of us to those that hadn't quite given up the ghost yet. He also emptied their pockets of anything that could be useful or a threat. Like in the job I'd crashed days ago, he tossed all of those items into a sack.

As I delivered one last kill shot, the adrenaline in me softened from a rush to a pleasant buzz. Blaze pulled out his tablet. "No security has been alerted. I'm not seeing any sign that the police have flagged concerning activity in the area either." He turned. "I'll collect the hard drive that the security cameras are feeding into."

"I'm going to make one final circuit of the building," Garrison said, his hand drifting to the holster he kept at his hip just in case.

If I'd been working alone, all the work of double-checking and securing the scene would have fallen on me. Another benefit of teamwork.

Because my efforts hadn't been quite as bloody as the other main killers on the crew, my clothes had survived relatively unscathed. I simply pulled a hoodie over the fitted shirt with its protective padding. Julius and Talon chucked off their tactical gear in exchange for tees and jeans that'd look more natural moving through the city, wiping off stray streaks of blood with rags. Somehow their well-muscled forms, Talon's more compact and Julius's bulkier, had gotten even more mouth-watering after seeing them fully in action.

Garrison brought the car around, and we all piled in, leaving the chaos behind. The strip where we'd landed the jet was only a twenty-minute drive away. By the time we reached it, the guys had already fallen into the sort of casual conversation I'd gotten used to around the apartment, as if we'd done nothing more than crash a party in the normal people way.

"Could you believe those props?" Blaze crowed, shaking his head. "Those were a crime all by themselves."

"Don't get me started on the dialogue," Garrison muttered. "It couldn't have sounded more wooden if it'd been delivered by a couple of two-by-fours."

Julius gave one of his quietly confident smiles. "I'd say we made a much more interesting picture with what they gave us to work with." He nodded to me. "And Dess more than held her own. You did good out there."

With him, it was hard to tell how much of a compliment that was—mild or ecstatic or somewhere in between. But I'd take it. I scrambled onto the jet with a bounce in my step, still a little hyped up from my earlier rush.

As I sank into one of the posh leather seats and the engine started to rumble, Garrison pulled a bottle of wine out from a cooler between two of the seats. "To a job well done!" he said, raising it and popping the cork.

He took a swig and passed the bottle on to Talon. The older man downed a gulp of his own and clapped Blaze on the shoulder in a rare show of physical comradery, however brief. The hacker let out a whoop when he grabbed the bottle for his turn. Julius watched over them all with his usual penetrating gaze, foregoing a drink himself, but his smile lingered on his lips.

When the bottle finally made its way to me, I let myself have a tentative sip. I didn't usually bother with alcohol unless I needed to put on a show for a job, and then I actually swallowed as little as possible. I wasn't totally sure how the effects might blur my mind. I couldn't help noticing that when Garrison made a grabby motion to get it back, he directed it at Blaze, who passed it over from me, instead of looking me straight in the eyes.

As the plane soared through the sky, the men fell into a discussion about the most ridiculous moments in past missions, pausing to correct themselves or each other and to exaggerate the situations even more. Soon, even Julius was chuckling. I laughed along from my seat, but I couldn't help feeling a little off to the side.

I hadn't been part of any of those missions. I wasn't really a part of the crew, even now. I'd only been a guest star for this job. Who knew if Julius would *want* to have me along again? I'd held my own, but I knew I hadn't been as much in my element as the rest of them.

They knew each other better than I knew… anyone. Maybe they weren't related by blood, but they were a family in every other way that counted. A pang ran through my heart with the longing to be in their midst, just as much a part of it as the rest of them.

I didn't know who my birth family was or how they'd lost me—or given me up. Maybe I never would. But this family right here was something I knew with a sudden certainty I wanted in on. Noelle had made me a lone wolf, but every nerve in my body clanged with the sense that I was meant to be part of something bigger.

As long as I was with the Chaos Crew, I had a chance to form those bonds, didn't I? I'd just have to make sure I proved myself worthy in every possible way they could want.

NINE

Decima

WHEN I WALKED out of my room the next morning, everything seemed completely normal, like we hadn't just blasted away a dozen or so gangsters the night before. Garrison stood in the kitchen over the stove, sipping hot cocoa from a mug and flipping bacon in a frying pan, both sending delicious smells into the air in a mix of sweet and salty. Julius and Talon were sitting at the table polishing off the last bits of what looked like pancakes, and Blaze was cross-legged on the sofa with a typical plate of pasta on one knee and his laptop on the other in an impressive balancing act.

But in a weird way, the fact that it felt normal was the most abnormal thing. I walked over to the kitchen without a single quiver of apprehension running through my nerves. Blaze gave me a little wave of welcome, Julius nodded to me, and Garrison—well, Garrison flicked a brief glance my way and tensed his jaw, which was par for the course. No one made a big deal of my presence.

It was like I belonged here. Like I'd always lived here with them, as much a part of the crew as they were. Was the change in them or in me—or both?

As I grabbed my usual box of cereal out of the cupboard, wondering if I could get Garrison to spare any of that bacon for me and suspecting the chances were nil, Julius motioned to Talon. "They've just gotten a new model of dagger in at our favorite shop. I think you'd like it. The balance is impressive. You should take a look."

Talon grunted. "I'm pretty happy with the one I have."

"You can never have too many weapons," Blaze piped up from the sofa. "Always carry at least two backups, I always say."

"You always say since when—this morning?" Garrison teased.

"I'm sure I've said it at least once before. I've definitely *thought* it." Blaze glanced at me. "Did you sleep okay after the flight?"

"Yeah," I said automatically. "It was good to be ho—"

I cut myself off in mid-word with a sudden, startling realization. I'd been going to say *home*, and... the crew's apartment did feel like home now. I knew where everything important was. I knew what to expect from the guys, at least well enough to relax around them. They were treating me like a standard inhabitant and not an interloper.

It was hard to imagine that the apartment I'd lived in for not much more than a week had so quickly replaced the house where I'd spent more than twenty years of my life, but maybe that said more about how homey the household *hadn't* been than it did about this place.

While my thoughts drifted back to that past period of my life, Blaze checked his laptop and let out an uncharacteristically disheartened sigh. It wasn't hard to figure out why.

"Still no useful results from all those searches?" I asked. The other men looked over as well in anticipation of the hacker's answer.

Blaze frowned. "Nothing that sends us down a longer trail. I keep finding more people to check out but none of them turn up anything suspicious or concerning. I have no idea whether the people I'm looking at now are even remotely connected to your household." He shook himself and shot me a rejuvenated smile. "But don't worry. I'll keep at it. There's got to be a solid lead in here somewhere."

"And if there isn't, we have other avenues we can pursue," Julius put in.

Did we, or was he just saying that to reassure me? I popped a spoonful of cereal into my mouth and chewed pensively.

There'd been so much I hadn't known about my old home and the people living there. But that home could tell stories of its own, couldn't it?

My heart leapt, and my head jerked toward Garrison. "You collect all the wallets and phones and similar things from the scenes of the jobs. Do you still have all that from the household?"

Garrison might not have wanted to make super friendly, but he did meet my eyes and offer an apologetic grimace in response. "We dispose of them within twenty-four hours of finishing the job. It's too risky carrying evidence like that around when it doesn't seem needed. And that early on, we had no idea it would be relevant."

I let out a huff of breath. "Understandable."

But there'd been a lot they'd left behind. Maybe no obvious identifying information, but there could have been mail in a drawer, notebooks on shelves, even a reminder scrawled on a post-it note might point us in a useful direction to finding the larger organization the household had been a part of. The people Noelle had obviously still been working with, since she hadn't come for me alone.

The thought of walking back into the space that I'd last—and only—seen splattered with blood made my gut knot, but with every passing second, my certainty grew that it was my best course of action, if I was going to take any action at all. And damn, did I want to.

"I need to go back to the mansion," I said. "They were working out of that building for decades. There's got to be some kind of evidence left behind."

Talon's attention shifted to me. He didn't speak, but his somber gaze emanated concern.

Julius expressed what all the others might have been thinking. "That'd be pretty dangerous. Our client has been hassling Garrison about the missing 'item' from that job, which we have to assume means you. He probably has eyes on the place."

I shrugged. "You should know by now that I'm aware of how to stay under the radar. I can avoid whatever and whoever I need to."

"We don't know exactly who we're dealing with here or what kind of resources they have," the crew's leader reminded me. "And you might not find anything to make it worth the risk. His people have clearly been through the house since we left for them to have figured out that you're gone. There's a strong possibility they'll have grabbed anything tied to the household's criminal operations already."

I shifted restlessly on my feet. "I know that too. But I need to try. Even a small possibility that I'll turn up the start of a trail makes it worth it."

Julius sighed, but he inclined his head at the same time. "I can understand. This is your life and your family we're talking about, and I've already made it clear that we're not your keepers. You've proven yourself more than capable by any measure."

"Thank you."

When he lifted his gaze to meet mine again, a tingle of heat raced through me. I'd earned his trust, but suddenly I wanted more than that. I wanted to peel back the layers of who *he* was and get at the beating heart beneath that fueled his commanding presence.

I reined in the impulse, but not before I thought I saw a matching spark of interest flash in his eyes—and vanish.

He sucked the last of the syrup off his fork in a gesture that made my panties dampen in an instant and stood up. "Finish your breakfast, and I'll take you through the tunnels again. But once you're out there, you'll be on your own."

"Until I get back," I said, the corner of my lips quirking upward.

The slow smile I was appreciating more every time I saw it curved his own mouth. "Yes, until you get back."

I did three circuits as I approached the mansion, first a few blocks away and then getting increasingly closer as I confirmed there were no watching eyes—living or digital—pointed my way. I'd put on a thin hoodie with the hood raised over the wig I'd bought earlier, sunglasses hiding my eyes.

But it seemed that precaution wasn't totally necessary. The mansion was in a sprawling residential neighborhood, and there wasn't a whole lot of activity in the middle of the day. It'd have been easy to spot any suspicious signs.

There were a few cameras mounted around the property's walls, but I simply steered clear of them and scrambled over the same way I'd scrambled out a few weeks ago. On the ground in the yard, I stalked across the lawn even more cautiously. There was a new camera mounted over the front door, one that the average person wouldn't have been able to pick out it was so well-disguised, and another at the back.

That was fine. Noelle wouldn't have done her job right if I hadn't learned how to get in by plenty of means that didn't require doors.

I jimmied a ground floor window open, eased aside the curtain, and peered through the room to check for surveillance or human presence on the inside. The sitting room was totally empty other than the posh furniture. Looking at it gave me an unsettling feeling of déjà vu.

Hadn't I walked through this room on my first prowl through the mansion after I'd left my section of it on the night of the massacre? Hadn't there been a bloody body sprawled across that armchair?

If so, all trace of both the body and the blood had been washed away. You'd never have imagined anything even as violent as a papercut had happened in this room.

I slipped inside and took a quick inventory of the space. It held nothing but the furniture, the drawer on the side table and the surface of the coffee table totally bare. At the doorway, I peeked into the hall.

Ah ha. Someone had mounted another discreet camera at the far end, pointed down the length of the hallway. I pulled back, leapt out through the window, and moved to another farther down.

The dining room I climbed into next I'd definitely seen before—complete with bloody bodies slumped across the table. As with the first room, all evidence of them had been wiped clean. Could that even be the exact same table? I had to think the blood would have stained the pale wood beyond repair.

Who the hell had done this—and why had they bothered with this careful reconstruction? It was obvious the police had never been through. There was no caution tape or chalk markings of bodies. It was as if the household's inhabitants had been utterly wiped from existence… except for me, of course.

My stomach knotted. I didn't know whether to feel relieved that the crew's job here had allowed my escape and freedom or horrified by the callous aftermath. I had no idea who any of these people had been. Sure, they'd all been criminals, but Anna hadn't been all bad. There'd been at least a little real kindness in her treatment of me.

Of course, while treating me that way she'd also enabled me to kill who knew how many innocents. Their blood was on her hands too.

The thing was, whoever had ordered their deaths clearly hadn't had good intentions either. They wanted me for their own purposes, which I hardly thought were good, especially with how cagey they were being with the crew about what they were "missing." They sure as hell hadn't ordered the massacre for my benefit but for some gain of their own.

My jaw working with suppressed tension, I stalked around that room and then the next and the next. With the last, I was able to cross the hall on my belly, below the view of the camera, to reach the staircase and investigate the second floor.

I found no books on the shelves, no papers on any desk, no paraphernalia of any kind in the drawers and closets. The clothes still dangling from their hangers told only the story of people who'd had a lot of money. They were designer label but nothing particularly distinctive.

Once I'd returned downstairs, I crawled beneath the level of the camera into the first room on the opposite side of the ground floor. After determining that it held nothing useful and ducking out its window, I hit my first real problem.

The grand living room, the place where I'd encountered by far the most bodies, had windows that appeared to be jammed shut. No matter what I did or what tools I put to use from the kit Julius had lent me, I couldn't get either of them to budge. Had someone gone out of their way to more tightly secure them?

Did that mean there was something worth finding on the other side?

I clambered back into a room I'd already investigated and studied the camera from a doorway. I couldn't get to the living room without coming into view of it. I also wasn't going to be able to make it to the side hall that led to my old rooms as long as I was avoiding it either—there were no windows into that part of the mansion.

I'd just have to take a gamble and bust my butt finishing my inspection.

Blaze had offered me a slim paintball gun specifically in case I needed it for this purpose. I aimed it at the camera's lens and fired.

A blue blotch hit the lens, obscuring all view of me. If anyone was currently monitoring the feed, they'd know right away that an intruder was in the house, just not who it was. I had to hoof it.

I dashed into the living room. My pulse stuttered at the contrast between the sleek leather surfaces and polished floors now and the carnage that'd been strewn across the space before, but I didn't let that uneasiness slow me down. I sprinted from table to cabinet, pawing through every nook. All I turned up were a few blank pieces of notepaper. For fuck's sake!

As I whirled around, my gaze slid across the ceiling instinctively, even though I'd already checked for cameras. My eyes paused on an odd mark I hadn't noticed carved into the old-fashioned trim in one corner of the room. Between the white paint and the position, it was almost invisible unless you happened to look straight at it from the right angle.

I stepped closer, squinting at it. It looked vaguely spherical, though narrower at the top than the bottom... almost pointed, like a teardrop. A straight line sliced through it on a diagonal. I couldn't remember ever seeing that symbol before.

It wasn't much, but it was something. I whipped out my phone and snapped a picture of it, zoomed in as far as I could go.

Then I whirled around and rushed across the hall to the passageway that led to the small study with the secret bookcase entrance to my old rooms.

Somehow, even after seeing the whole house in its current state, coming up on the spot where I'd left Anna's crumpled body sent a fresh wave of queasiness through me. Even here in this remote corner of the house, whoever had swept the mansion clean had removed all indication that she'd existed too. There was only the desk, the filing cabinet—empty—and the bookshelves, which contained a scattering of not particularly impressive looking volumes.

I glanced over the titles on the spines, flipped open a few to check for inscriptions, and swept several aside to check the back of the bookcase for a way to access the door behind it. There, I came across the symbol from the living room for a second time. A tiny version of it was carved into the topmost portion of the bookcase that covered the secret entrance to my quarters. The etching was no larger than the pad of my thumb, just above the line of the shelf.

I knit my brow at it and took another photo. My heart was thumping faster. I was running out of time. I jabbed my fingers at the carving and then all across the rest of the bookcase, but nothing made it budge.

Right now, who knew how many enemy forces could be racing this way?

Cursing under my breath, I backed up and glared at the bookcase. But then, maybe it was silly to put myself in any more danger to try to get into the rooms where I'd spent years upon years already. The household people had never left anything in there that'd tipped me off to their true agenda before, so why would there be anything useful in that section of the building now?

My desire to see that space one more time was more nostalgia than anything else, and I didn't have time for foolish emotions in the middle of a mission.

I spun on my feet and hustled to the nearest window. With a leap over the sill and a lope across the lawn, I put the mansion that'd been my home and my prison for far too long—and the ghostly emptiness inside it—far behind.

TEN

Blaze

ONCE DESS LEFT THE APARTMENT, we were all on edge.

I tracked her from the city's security cameras, though with her disguise and her skill at stealth, I could only find her in brief glimpses because I knew exactly where she'd been going.

Julius lingered by his board of army figures, moving them around sporadically as if he had a full mission to plan. He did so with vicious swipes of his hand and a lethal intensity in his expression. I knew he was preparing for the possibility that Dess would be caught.

Garrison strode past me a few times as he paced around the house. He didn't say anything to indicate he was worried, but the fact that he was so quiet at all instead of snarking away at us showed his uneasiness.

Talon shut himself inside the workout room. Every once in a while, we heard a particularly thunderous sound of his fist hitting the punching bag or the clank of metal weights returning to their racks.

Only when I told everyone that Dess was approaching the covert entrance to the building did they seem to calm down enough to get back to their normal lives. Garrison strode out of the kitchen and toward the roof, almost as if he'd been waiting for this confirmation before leaving the main room. Julius slid his figures back in place and left through the front door, heading down to retrieve her. Talon gave the punching bag a few more swings and then headed into the bathroom to shower.

I couldn't peel my eyes away from the laptop screen until I saw Dess vanish near the entrance, approaching the spot where Julius would be waiting for her. It didn't take long before she came striding through the door. She had a pensive air to her that made it hard to tell whether she'd found what she'd been seeking.

She looked at me the moment she entered the room, and the gray in her eyes seemed to lighten. She veered toward me immediately. Julius, coming in right behind her, looked her up and down as if double-checking that she'd returned in one piece before heading to the fridge to grab one of Steffie's premade sandwiches.

Did he know what Dess had found already, or was she telling me first?

She sat down at the dining table kitty-corner to where I was sitting with my laptop. The guys—well, mostly Garrison—often hassled me about how little I used the workstation actually devoted to my work, but I focused better with the ability to move around as a whim took me.

"I didn't turn up much, but there was one small thing that might lead us somewhere," Dess said. "At least the trip wasn't a total bust."

"You can show me everything you saw there," I told her. "There might be more significance to some item than is obvious at a glance."

She shook her head. "It's not that. There was *nothing*. Everything had been cleaned up and cleared out—I mean, the furniture was there, but the drawers and shelves were pretty much empty. There was no sign of the murders either. But someone was monitoring the place—there were new cameras outside and one inside." She sucked her lower lip under her teeth in a gesture that sent a little flare of desire through me. "All I got was this."

She brought up a photo on her phone and set it on the table for me to see. It was a symbol carved into a molding somewhere in the house—a teardrop shape with a line bisecting it at a diagonal. And maybe a tiny notch at the lower part of the line? It was hard to make out. But something about the design gave me a vague twinge of recognition.

Where had I seen that before?

"It was in the living room, and also on the bookcase that hid the secret doorway into my quarters in the house," Dess said. "Maybe other places, but that's all I found in the time I had. Do you have any idea what it could mean?"

She flipped to the photo of the bookcase with the symbol carved into the dark wood. Seeing it on that surface made something click in my head. I stared at it for a moment longer and then turned to her.

"It's the same as your tattoo."

Dess blinked at me. "Tattoo? What tattoo?"

I guessed it wasn't surprising that she wouldn't know. She hadn't known about an awful lot of things her "household" had done to her, and the tattoo had been placed somewhere it'd be almost impossible for her to discover on her own.

"Come here," I said, beckoning for her to stand. I walked her over to the full-length mirror near the front door and switched my own phone to selfie mode so it would act as a second reflection. "Lift your hair up from the back of your neck."

Dess looked puzzled, but she did it. And there was the little black tattoo I'd remembered, marked into her skin at the base of her skull where her hair mostly concealed it. Carefully, I parted the strands to reveal the shape a little better, not even touching her skin, and held my phone so she could see the image that was reflected in the mirror.

Dess drew in a startled breath with a hiss. "What the hell?"

"We saw it when we were checking you for injuries after your crash," I told her. "It's hard to make out the details through your hair, but it looks incredibly similar to that carved symbol to me. I don't think that's a coincidence."

Dess let her hair fall. Her eyes flashed. "They did this to me. The people from the household—whoever took me. They fucking *marked* me like I'm their property."

My chest clenched at her anger—not because it bothered me, but because she was so justified in it. "You're nobody's property," I reassured her firmly. "And you can get it removed. I'm sure there are services that could manage it, just shaving the hair there first."

But in typical Dess fashion, she'd already moved on to the next part of the problem. She spun toward the table with my laptop. "The symbol has something to do with the people who ran the household. It could lead us to more of them."

"Absolutely," I said, glad to have something concrete to focus on that might help. "Send the photos to me, and I'll get some image recognition searches running."

Dess did as I asked and sank back into her chair, watching me type with open curiosity. "This'll work like your facial recognition searches?"

"Exactly. Although it'll probably take a lot longer for the app to complete the search since it has to check *every* kind of image it can dig up, not just ones it recognizes as containing faces. But I can leave it running in the background for however long it takes." I finished the last commands and sat back. No trouble at all.

We sat there for several minutes, both of us braced in case an immediate result came up. When nothing happened, I glanced at Dess with an apologetic twist of my mouth. "Like I said, it could take a while. It's obviously not a very common symbol if we haven't found anything right away, but I guess we already could have guessed that."

She let out a discontented hum, her forehead furrowed. Watching her, the constricting sensation came back into my chest.

I couldn't imagine what she was going through with so many unanswered questions and so few leads left. I couldn't think of a single way to ensure we got the answers she longed for or to fix the trust the people in her past had damaged so thoroughly.

But maybe that wasn't up to me. Maybe she could just use a chance to let some of those emotions out.

"How are you doing?" I asked, nudging the computer aside. It'd notify me if anything popped up, and watching wouldn't make the search run any faster.

Dess's gaze jerked up to meet mine. "Me?"

A gentle smile stretched across my face. "Yes, you. You've had your whole world upended in the last week. How are you hanging in there? I can't even imagine how tough it is, even for someone as tough as you."

The corner of her mouth twitched at the compliment. Then she sighed. "I don't know. How I am feels like such a complicated question now. I hardly know *who* I am."

She paused, and I didn't rush her. When she spoke again, the words came out in a rush. "I do know that I'm grateful for everything that you and the rest of the crew have done for me. Nobody has ever been here for me the way that you guys have. You've welcomed me into your home and done everything you can to help me find answers. It's just even with all that, the sense of how much of my life is still a mystery won't stop gnawing at me. I don't like having all these questions hanging over me with no way to answer them."

"That makes sense," I said. I didn't have any way to hold the gnawing at bay either, though. I made a face at my laptop as if that would encourage it to spew out some results.

But there was one thing I'd been able to offer Dess before that might help now—if not in a concrete way, then at least to allow the time to pass more comfortably.

I stood up again. "It's hard to focus and come up with ideas when you're all tense about the situation. There's nothing else we can do to dig into the problem right now. Why don't you unwind a little?"

She raised an eyebrow at me. "Like how?"

I grinned. "I happen to know a TV show you're very fond of."

Dess couldn't suppress the eager spark that glinted in her eyes, even though she made a show of muttering, "Oh, all right," as she got up. I ushered her over to the sofa and motioned for her to sit down. Then I hustled over to my main computer setup to start the next episode streaming to the TV. I'd already downloaded the entire three seasons that'd aired, as well as a long-lost Christmas special I'd managed to dig up.

There wasn't much that made Dess really happy, and she deserved all the joy I could provide.

By the time I'd returned to the sofa to the theme song of *Spy Times*, Dess had relaxed right into the cushions. She stared at the TV avidly, a little smile playing with her lips.

I'd meant to watch the show with her, but the truth was, I wanted to watch her more. My gaze kept sliding back to her no matter how hard I tried to concentrate on the goofy storyline.

It wasn't really her looks. Yes, she was beautiful, from the dark locks of hair that tumbled down her back to the toned muscles and curves of her body honed by years of training. Even her slender but strong hands, capable of ending a life in an instant, fascinated me. But none of those things were what drew me in the most.

There was a stillness to her that I'd never been able to reach myself, a sense of inner certainty and confidence even in the middle of the storm her life had become that called to me like a beacon. I admired the same qualities in Julius, but somehow Dess exuded them even more than our commander.

Just sitting next to her, I absorbed a little of that calm. Her presence grounded me more than anyone I'd ever known. My knee didn't bounce and my foot didn't jiggle with the urge to stay in motion as I studied her. I could slow down and sink into the moment in a way that so often eluded me.

And here in this space, it was hard to imagine that anything but the woman sitting across from me mattered at all.

That last thought hit me squarely in the heart. I hesitated, feeling it out.

I didn't just admire her. I was falling for her.

But what difference did it make if I was? I'd made a few flirty gestures in the past, and she'd demonstrated *very* emphatically that she wasn't open to those kind of overtures… from me, anyway. I could still vividly remember the clamp of her hand around my throat. I didn't want to push her into feeling she had to defend herself from me ever again.

A laugh burst out of Dess at a particularly comical scene, and she glanced over at me to share the amusement. I chuckled too, though I wasn't totally sure what the joke had been because my attention had been so much on her. But she didn't appear to notice my distraction. Still smiling, she turned back to the TV.

A swell of resolve rose up inside me. Being her friend might be the closest I'd ever get to her, and that meant it'd just have to be enough.

ELEVEN

Decima

JULIUS REACHED FORWARD and tightened the strap of my bulletproof vest. I sucked in a breath. "This isn't supposed to be a high-risk mission," I reminded him, rolling my shoulders to give myself some more breathing room.

"Anything that involves a high-profile target comes with a greater risk," Julius said.

"But Malik isn't a target."

"Malik *is* the target. We might not be killing him, but we are collecting information from him. With any luck, this operation will go smoothly, but we have to be prepared if it doesn't."

I nodded, glancing around the posh hotel room three hours from our usual stomping grounds. Julius had been the crew's leader for years, and his strategies had never led the guys astray. I could trust him on this.

He was the one who'd found out about our current opportunity. Damien Malik had been invited to speak at a political convention being held in the convention center next door to the hotel. Malik and all the other participants were staying here, which gave us the perfect opportunity to dig for information more directly than we'd had the chance to before.

Garrison had sweet-talked the front desk staff until he'd wrangled us the room right over Malik's. Now it was just a matter of making a quick trip down.

"Stay alert, and I'm sure it'll all go fine," Julius said, giving me one last onceover. "Talon and I will be keeping an eye on the convention—we'll let you know if there's anything to be concerned about."

"Right," I said. We'd determined that Malik and his team should be busy until well into the evening, no time to stop back at his room unless there was a sudden deviation from schedule.

I turned toward Blaze, who was already strapped into his harness beyond the open doors to the balcony. "Let's do this."

He grinned at me, the breeze ruffling his hair. "Ready when you are."

As I walked over to fit my own harness around me, Julius and Talon headed out. Garrison watched them go with a subtle frown and poked at something on his phone. He tipped his head toward us, focusing on Blaze rather than me. "Everything still looks good from my vantage point."

The cool air raised goosebumps on my arms, but the adrenaline starting to thrum through my veins drowned out any discomfort. I grasped the rappelling line, gave it a testing tug, and motioned to Blaze.

We lowered ourselves toward the balcony below in tandem. I knew from experience that my stomach would accept the trip a lot better if I avoided looking at the fifteen-story drop below my feet. I could have made the drop in a few seconds, but I restrained myself to Blaze's less swift pace in case he ran into any trouble. He handled the descent with the obvious skill of someone who'd done it before, but clearly he hadn't made as much a habit of it in past jobs as I had.

"That's better," he said with a rush of an exhalation when his feet touched the balcony railing.

I laughed softly under my breath and sank down in front of the balcony doors. It only took a little prodding and a few twists of my picks to deal with the simple lock. No one expected intruders to be coming from this direction, especially not fourteen floors up.

Leaving our gear attached so we were prepared for a hasty getaway, we slipped into the dark hotel room, our ropes trailing behind us like massive tails. Blaze immediately spotted the laptop on the desk. He opened it, his eyes darting across the screen as it blinked to life.

I took my position by the front door of the hotel room, listening for any sounds of unexpected arrivals while watching Blaze work his magic. He was the one handling most of this mission. I was just here to keep the hacker safe.

Even though technically all he was doing was typing, he was something to look at. He maneuvered that keyboard like I might have a knife or a gun, his gloved fingers flying with brutal efficiency, his gaze fixed on the screen with total intentness. When he broke past the security, he let out a muted cheer of victory before diving farther in with a sharp grin.

He rarely came across as vicious in his everyday life—not like Julius and Talon, who exuded physical menace with every move they made, or Garrison, who could take a weaker person's head off with a verbal barb. But Blaze clearly had the same killer instinct. How could he not, as part of the Chaos Crew?

He knew what he did well, and he accomplished it with feral intensity.

As I watched him in the partial darkness, the stream of sunlight from the displaced curtains catching on his pale red hair and determined expression, a tendril of wanting unfurled low in my belly. When he wasn't being flirty—when he didn't remind me of that time that I longed more than anything to forget—I couldn't help wondering what it'd be like to have his attention focused on *me* with the same intensity. To have those fingers moving over my body with all that energy and passion…

I shook myself mentally. This wasn't a good moment to be dreaming about hooking up with another member of the crew. If that was something he ended up wanting too, we'd figure it out some other time.

Maybe it was understandable that my sexual urges were going into overdrive when I'd gone so long without the opportunity to fully satisfy them, but I hadn't lost my sense of self-control.

I was being careful not to break Blaze's concentration, but when he leaned back for a moment with a cock of his head, I let myself speak. "Have you found anything?"

"Nothing that would connect him to you so far." He clicked open a few more documents and scanned them. "Malik has his fingers in a lot of pies, but I'm not seeing what would have drawn your trainer's interest to him or anything that ties him to the household."

"And no hints of anything criminal either?"

"There've been occasional murmurs about misconduct in the past, but either they weren't true or he's very good at hushing people up. I haven't come across anything on here that'd point to wrongdoing right now." He glanced over at me. "Honestly, it wouldn't be surprising for the guy to have had a few unstable moments where he got in a bit of political trouble earlier in his career, but I wouldn't read much into that."

I raised an eyebrow. "Why not?"

"Back when he was first making a name for himself, one of his kids died, very young—a car accident that killed her and the nanny. That could throw anyone off kilter. And besides, a lot of people feel he's a little *too* harsh on crime, so for him to be involved in a criminal organization at the same time..." He rubbed his mouth, frowning.

A vague flicker of memory returned to me. "He's got some new bill he's been pushing, doesn't he?"

Blaze nodded. "He's advocating for more severe sentencing across the board as well as increasing the usage of convicted criminals in forced labor."

"Maybe Noelle and whoever else she's worked with saw him as an enemy, then." I suggested. "They could have simply been keeping an eye on him."

"Possibly. I'm not sure why she'd have felt the need to travel around going to his rallies in person for that. His activities are pretty well-publicized. She'd have found out more reading articles on the internet. So, maybe his supposed political stance is a really thorough cover-up for his real interests. Stranger things have happened." He let out a huff of breath. "Well, I'll download everything on here so I can do a more intensive search when we've got the time."

He plugged a hard drive a little bigger than his hand into the side of the laptop and clicked a few more times. A progress bar appeared on the screen.

The bar was nearly full when footsteps reached my ears on the other side of the door, shuffling along the carpeted hallway. I would have assumed it was another hotel patron heading to a different room if not for the voices I heard a moment later.

"Did he say where in the room we'd find it?"

"Of course. You know Damien—everything in its place. He left the notepad on the table at the left side of the bed."

Damien. My nerves jittered, and I leapt away from the door. "We have to go *now*," I hissed under my breath.

Blaze's eyes widened, but he didn't let panic throw him off. The progress bar had just topped out. He tugged the hard drive free without a sound, closed the laptop, and sprinted across the room toward the balcony.

I ran after him, jerking the doors shut behind us. The curtain would hide us—but who knew if Malik's staff would find some reason to come out here?

I yanked my rope taut in an instant. Blaze fumbled with his. Acting on instinct, I whipped myself into his arms.

"Hold me," I whispered as the door at the other end of the room squeaked open. Blaze hesitated for a split-second but wrapped his arms around me before I had to repeat my command. I grasped the rope and hauled both of us up there with the strength of my arms.

A burn spread through my muscles—and through my torso where I was pressed tightly against Blaze's lean body. It wasn't exactly an unpleasant sensation. When we reached the level of our own balcony, Blaze immediately rolled over the railing so he could release me, and some part of me regretted the loss of contact.

I leapt over the railing after him and hauled any remaining rope up out of view. I couldn't hear anything from the balcony below. It didn't sound like we'd been spotted.

Exhaling in relief, I glanced at Blaze. He gave no sign of having noticed how our closeness had affected me, though his own cheeks looked a bit flushed from the hasty escape.

"A tight one, but we made it," he said, offering a fist for me to bump.

I couldn't help smiling as I returned the gesture. "We make a good team."

When we hurried into our own room, Garrison was pacing by the front door. "Nothing from Julius or Talon yet?" I asked him.

He shook his head, only catching my eyes briefly before diverting his attention. I braced for some of his usual snark, but nothing came. The exhilaration that'd rushed through me with our escape dulled.

I *wished* he'd start snarking at me like he used to. At least then I'd know things were normal between us. Something about our passionate interlude on the deck had thrown off the dynamic between us, and I didn't know what to say to fix it. Especially when he seemed determined to interact with me as little as he could get away with while fulfilling our missions.

I might have tried to rile him up, but just then, Talon strode into the room. The urgency of his entrance hummed through the air.

"Malik's talk got bumped to an earlier slot," he said. "He's going on in fifteen minutes. Dess, Julius wants you to come and see if you can spot anyone in the crowd or his staff you recognize."

"Of course." My pulse hitched. That'd always been part of the plan, but we hadn't thought Malik would be giving his main speech until later today.

I hustled out of the room at Talon's heels. He walked on swiftly and silently like the predator he was, but his lack of conversation didn't niggle at me the way Garrison's did. Talon was quiet most of the time—it was just how he was, nothing to do with me. He didn't hesitate to meet my eyes, and once we were inside the convention center, he guided me through a staff-only doorway with a brief touch to my waist that showed no signs of discomfort.

I wasn't sure if *he* was going to want any more passionate interludes, but his steady demeanor put me at ease.

He led me to a maintenance area and then a ladder that brought us high over the auditorium, near the lights. I peered down from the metal catwalk, letting my eyes adjust. We were far enough up that I didn't think anyone would notice us through the thin slats in the walkway floor. Of course, it was hard for me to make out the faces below in much detail either.

Talon was prepared for that. He handed me a pair of binoculars. I shot him a smile in thanks and sprawled out on my stomach for the most comfortable viewing position from this angle.

"Where's Julius?" I murmured.

"He's keeping watch from below, just in case we're made. Do you have a good enough view?"

"With the binoculars, no problem."

I swept my amplified gaze over the audience, from the back to the stage and then in reverse, pausing just long enough here and there to fully absorb each group of figures. People sat in their seats, chatting amongst themselves and waiting for Malik, who I knew would be out soon.

I squirmed forward on my belly to lean my elbows over the edge, and Talon set a hand on my back as if to confirm my balance. There was nothing provocative about the touch, but it sent a pulse of warmth over my skin all the same. I glanced back at him. "Thanks. I'm okay."

He nodded at me with the briefest hint of a smile, which was practically a manic grin where Talon was concerned. "Of course you are." And all at once I was sure that even if he wasn't the type to want to hash out his intimate encounters after the fact, he didn't feel any regrets about what we'd shared either.

I couldn't dwell on that enjoyable realization. From the growing enthusiasm in the voices traveling up to us, Malik should be arriving at any moment. He might simply be waiting for whatever notes he'd asked his aides to go back to his room to grab for him. When he showed up, the lights would probably dim over everything but the stage, and I'd hardly be able to make out anyone.

I continued my scan as quickly as I reasonably could. The seconds ticked by. Then, just before I tilted the binoculars onward, my attention snagged on a face that'd turned to the side, on the far side of the auditorium near the back. I zoomed in with the binoculars as far as I could go, and certainty reverberated through my chest.

"Talon," I whispered. "There's a man here who was talking with Noelle in one of the other photographs Blaze found with his search."

At the same moment, the lights near us blinked out. Only a spotlight on the stage remained. The spot where the man had sat was swallowed in darkness.

Talon grunted and motioned to me. "We'd better get out of here. You'll be able to point the guy you saw out in that picture?"

"Definitely." I could already see the image in my mind's eye, with the man walking just ahead of Noelle in a city park.

A cheer rose up, drowning out any other answer I might have given. Damien Malik had just walked on stage, his arm raised and his face beaming with a smile that could have lit the room all over again. My heart skipped a beat.

Was I looking at another of the household's targets… or the very man who'd orchestrated my kidnapping for a secret dark agenda of his own?

To be more discreet, we left the convention in two cars, me with Julius and Talon, and Garrison and Blaze on their own. I hoped they wouldn't end up biting each other's heads off before they made it home, but at least Blaze had the search for the new mystery man to keep him busy. He was already analyzing the convention records when we left.

Julius turned on a classic rock station at a low volume, and those tunes filled the car as he drove. I leaned my head against the window and tried not to wonder too much about the politician I'd just watched greet his audience. Speculation wasn't going to lead me anywhere. If there was evidence to tie Malik to the household or to me, Blaze would find it.

We'd been on the road only half an hour or so when Talon's phone rang. He answered it on speaker. "What's up, Garrison?"

"We have a problem," he replied in a flat, terse tone that had my spine jerking straight. Whatever the issue was, it was serious.

"Are you and Blaze okay?" Julius asked.

"For now. But I just got a call from our client from the household job. I think it's best if I just play it for you."

"We're ready."

I wasn't sure if I was, but I braced myself in my seat. It took a moment and a few clicks before a rough voice spilled through the phone, taut with anger.

"You might think you can play us for fools, but this isn't a fucking game of Candyland, no matter what you seem to think. We know you have a young woman from the job site in your possession, and you need to turn her in before you're in even worse violation of your contract. Otherwise, expect that she'll be retrieved by whatever means necessary."

TWELVE

Decima

THE LAST WORDS in the voicemail message rang in my ears long after the call had ended. *In your possession. Retrieved by whatever means necessary.* Like I was a fucking *bauble* the crew had stolen that should be returned to its rightful owners. I had the urge to claw the tattoo with their awful mark right off the back of my neck.

Then the image filled my mind of the shadowy figures from the other end of the phone call storming in on the crew and slaughtering them to get to me. For them to have run the kind of assignments they'd sent me on, the people behind the household must have enormous resources. Now that they knew where I was, how the hell could we escape them?

I wouldn't be a prisoner again. I simply *wouldn't.*

My ribs felt as if they'd closed in around my lungs. Dragging air into my chest was a struggle. I squeezed my hands into fists against the back seat of the car and willed myself to calm down, but it didn't work. A faint wheeze crept into my breath.

I needed more oxygen. Somehow I couldn't get enough.

"Dess?" Julius said. I couldn't answer when it was taking all my concentration holding in the panic bubbling inside me.

He didn't say my name again, only jerked the wheel to pull us over onto the shoulder. The car slammed to a halt. He and Talon burst out, both coming around to the door next to me.

"Come out," Julius said firmly. "Get some air. Walk it off."

I fumbled with the seatbelt and pushed myself into the open terrain. We'd stopped in a desolate strip of countryside, only patchy fields around us and forest up ahead, no buildings or other vehicles in sight. For some reason, that reassured me just a smidge.

I started walking, pacing away from the car into the tufts of grass and back again. Frantic thoughts kept whirling through my mind.

The crew went to great lengths to keep the location of their home base secret, but they weren't completely infallible. And we couldn't live shut away in there for the rest of our lives anyway.

What would I do if the client found us and managed to capture me again? There was no reason for Julius to risk his whole crew for a woman he'd just met. But I couldn't let the people who'd run the household take me back. I'd *die* before I let those bastards touch me again.

I closed my eyes, retracing the steps my feet had already found without needing sight. *Get a grip on yourself, Dess.*

"He was bluffing," Julius said with deadly certainty. "Empty threats. No one would risk coming at us head-on, if they even knew how to find us. And if they tried, we'd destroy them. We fulfilled our obligations. You were never part of the deal."

"And now you're part of our crew," Talon said, simply but steadily.

Julius didn't argue with him.

Was I? Was I really one of them now, just like that? It was hard to wrap my head around the idea. But they'd both spoken with so much confidence that the quivers of panic inside me started to subside. I dragged a deeper breath into my lungs.

"That's right," Julius said, somehow commanding and gentle at once. "Let yourself come through it. You're still every bit as powerful as you were before. *You* won't let those fuckers take you down. I know that."

His words settled my nerves even more. He was right. I didn't have to let anyone control me ever again. I decided how I lived now—or how I died, if it came to that.

I stopped a couple of feet away from the car and the two men, a shamed flush creeping over my cheeks as I met Talon's and then Julius's gaze. "Sorry. I don't— I usually have more control over my emotions than that."

"You've got a good reason to be particularly emotional on this subject," Julius said. "But what I said stands. Anyone who thinks they're going to come at you will have to get through us first, and they'll find that a losing game."

Could he really be so sure? He had no more idea exactly who we were up against than I did. My throat tightened, thinking of how much the crew had helped me—and what a horrible way of repaying them it would be if I got them slaughtered for their trouble.

"I wouldn't expect you to stand up for me," I said, keeping my own voice even so they'd know I meant it. "This is my battle, and you don't owe me your support. If anything, I owe it to you to keep you out of it. You'd be risking your careers, even your lives."

Julius stepped forward and gripped my hands, his gaze holding mine with a fiery fierceness searing through his deep blue eyes. "No one will ever get their hands on you again. You won't be torn from us as easily as they seem to think. You're a part of the crew now, and we protect our own. We *kill* for our own. And I say that without the slightest hesitation."

Those words held more loyalty and devotion than anyone had ever offered me before. The heat in Julius's eyes sent a different sort of flush over me. A connection hummed between us, electric enough to send a tingle over my skin. I wanted to sink right into it, to wrap myself in his strength and assurance.

If I leaned in and kissed him right now, how would he react?

He'd never given any clear sign that he was interested in me that way. I didn't want to ruin the moment by asking for too much.

My gaze slid to the other man, the man who I knew could match my hunger even if he'd kept his own under wraps lately. Talon gazed back at me without retreating.

"How about you?" I asked. "Are you ready to put your life on the line so I can keep my freedom?"

Talon inclined his head as if he didn't even need to think about it. Which maybe he didn't. "You're one of us now," he said. "And no one threatens the crew and gets away with it."

If there was one thing I was sure about when it came to Talon, he didn't lie—not when he didn't need to. He was being totally honest in his dedication to me. But in that moment, with the remnants of my fears still racing through my veins, I needed to absorb his commitment with every part of my being. Words didn't feel like enough.

Without letting myself rethink the impulse, I moved toward him and gripped his shirt to tug him into a kiss. The moment I pressed my lips to his, his body reacted, his arms coming around me, his chest molding against mine. He loomed over me and surrounded me all at once. The confirmation in that kiss resonated through me.

It was brief, though, and then Talon shifted, starting to draw back. As he released my mouth, his gaze slid to Julius where I knew the other man was standing behind me. Talon's hands came to rest on my waist.

I glanced over my shoulder, weighing my options. Desire wound through me, chasing away the last of my panic. Julius was watching us, his shoulders pushed back and his stance commanding in his usual way, his expression unreadable. I could only imagine the ways he could make me feel if he touched me with all his power and authority brought to bear. The way that huge, brawny build would move against me if he fucked me as hard as I'd like.

A small, wicked smile crossed my lips. "You could join in too." I reached toward him, trailing my fingers down his chest over his shirt.

Julius caught my hand before it'd made it halfway to his groin. Heat flashed in his eyes. "No," he said, his voice rougher than usual. "You were upset—maybe you're not thinking straight. I'm not going to take advantage."

The hunger in his expression told me he was holding himself back for *my* sake, not his. It seared through my skin and stirred a deeper longing inside me.

"I'm thinking perfectly straight," I said. "I've wanted this—I've wanted *you*—since long before today."

"That doesn't mean it's the best thing for you right now."

I met his gaze firmly. "I decide what's best for me. I'm not the little girl you saved all those years ago, Julius, and I wasn't all that innocent even then. You know how many people I've killed. You know how much I've survived. I don't need to be coddled. When I say I want something, I expect you to believe me."

The muscles in his arms flexed with the effort of keeping himself still. "This is a far cry from killing, Dess."

I flicked my fingers against his chest again, as much as I could reach while he still gripped my hand. "They do call it the 'little death' sometimes, don't they? Anyway, I can't think of a better way to say 'Screw you' to the assholes who want to lock me away than by screwing both of you instead of freaking out."

With those last words, I pulled away from Talon's grasp to brush my lips against Julius's. A groan reverberated from his chest, but his mouth crushed against mine, his resistance shattering. His hand leapt up to tease into my hair.

He was just as fantastic a kisser as I'd imagined he'd be. His lips and tongue moved together to caress my mouth, until every sensitive part of me throbbed with lust. I moaned against his lips, and he tightened his hold, one arm across the small of my back and one around the back of my neck, bringing me to him until my body was flush against his.

I heard rather than saw Talon approaching. He returned his hands to my waist and stroked them down my thighs and around to my ass. I ground back into him instinctively and then against Julius's hips to show him just how ready I was.

This time, both men groaned. Julius nudged me against the side of the car and kissed me harder. Talon leaned in beside us to slide his hands up under my shirt. As Julius worked over my mouth, his friend yanked my bra off with the same force that'd gotten me so wet for him in the workout room before.

These weren't tender, gentle men, but tenderness wasn't what I was after. I wanted them to fuck the living daylights out of me.

I swiveled my head from Julius to seek out Talon's mouth. The other man kissed me with the brutal force I craved, his hand slipping farther down to cup my pussy. As I whimpered, Julius tugged up my shirt and closed his lips over my bared breast.

The rush of sensations was nothing short of heaven. I was starting to get the impression this might not be the first time they'd shared a woman. They seemed to have the whole coordination thing down pat.

I was definitely not complaining.

The searing heat between my thighs was becoming torturous. I rocked into Talon's hand and groped down his chest to the fly of his jeans. When my fingers closed around his bulging cock through the coarse material, his breath stuttered against my lips. I grinned.

It was such a thrill knowing that I had some kind of power over these powerful men. That I could conjure just as much desire in them as they did in me.

Talon stopped fondling me and tugged at my sweatpants so they pooled at my feet. When he teased his fingers over me with just the thin fabric of my now-soaked panties between us, a very undignified sound escaped me. I nipped his lip and hauled Julius up from my breasts for another kiss.

The two men ravished every part of my body with an unshakeable assurance that didn't trigger any of my horrible memories. They knew what *they* wanted, and now they were taking it, much to my delight.

I popped the button on Julius's jeans and delved my hand inside his boxers. He thrust his cock into my eager hand. "Fuck," he muttered, his lips scorching against the crook of my jaw. "You've got me close to bursting already. But I'm not coming until I hear you scream."

A giddy shiver passed through me. "Yes, please."

He cut his eyes toward Talon. "The emergency blanket from the back."

Talon didn't need any further instructions. He flung open the trunk and grabbed the blanket. In a matter of seconds, he'd spread it out on the ground next to the car.

Julius spun me around so my back was to him, tucking his hand beneath my panties between my legs. As he plunged his thick, skillful fingers right inside me, he lowered me onto my knees on the blanket. Talon sank down in front of me, tugging up my chin to claim another kiss. His mouth was pure fire. Every part of me was awash with flames of pleasure now.

With a jerk of his hand, Julius snapped the panties right off me. There was a crinkling of foil and the hiss of his jeans dropping, and then he gripped my hips. The head of his rigid cock rubbed against my opening.

As I moaned for it, he thrust into me. He was even bigger than Talon, stretching me with a blissful burn that radiated through my whole body. Seeking out even more of that incredible sensation, I pressed into him as he eased back and plunged even deeper.

But I couldn't leave the other man neglected. I made short work of Talon's fly and freed his cock with one hand as my body swayed to match Julius's rhythm. Another gasp tumbled out of me, and then I was closing my mouth around Talon's jutting dick, taking both men at the same time.

I'd witnessed this act, the sucking of a cock, in the middle of missions before, but this was my first chance to try it out. It hadn't always looked that enjoyable for the woman, but I found the feel of Talon's silky, pulsing shaft against my lips and tongue was an entirely new kind of thrill. Especially when he groaned and wound his fingers into my hair with the perfect sharp tug to make me hum with pleasure around him.

My hands dug into the blanket as I swiveled my tongue around his cock and bucked into Julius's thrusts. I had the two strongest men I'd ever met on their knees around me, and I could handle them both without missing a beat. A heady jolt of exhilaration raced through me.

As I swallowed Talon's shaft deeper into my mouth, Julius hit the spot that could send me screaming into release, just like he'd asked for. I could only moan around the other man's dick. He hit that spot again and again, clutching my hips tighter as he must have felt the shudders starting to race through my limbs.

Then all at once the pleasure of it completely burst inside me. I cried out, gasping against Talon's cock before sucking it back down, my body shaking with the force of my orgasm.

Julius finished next, thrusting deeply and erratically before he bowed over me with a grunt. As he tipped back, ragged breaths spilling out of him, Talon withdrew from my lips and pumped himself twice more before spilling his seed across the blanket before me.

I flopped down on the coarse fabric between the two men and grinned dazedly up at the blue sky that now seemed to beam back at me. Julius rubbed his hand over my thigh, and Talon brushed my sweat-damp hair back from my face. Sprawled there with them poised on either side of me, a realization struck me harder than ever before.

"No one owns me," I said with total conviction. "Nobody except myself."

Julius's lips curved with an approving smile. "And that's how it's going to stay as long as we have anything to say about it."

THIRTEEN

Talon

JULIUS AND DESS took the lead as we approached the old factory that Blaze had pulled up the address to. The symbol that marked the wall and bookcase in the mansion where Dess had lived—and the back of her scalp—had turned up in a photo on what Blaze called an "urban explorer blog." From the looks of the worn brick building, no one other than particularly bold and determined explorers had been inside here in a while.

Possibly they'd entered through the same loose window we found. The main door was locked.

As Julius shoved the pane high enough for us to squeeze inside, the stench nearly made me stop in my tracks. Garrison made a gagging sound.

"I *told* you it used to be a meat factory," Blaze said, but he pulled a face too as he slipped inside. Dess waved her hand in front of her nose.

Inside, hooks hung from the ceiling where carcasses must have once dangled. It was hard to tell how much of the ruddy marks on them and their chains were rust and how much old blood. The coppery tang to the stink suggested there was plenty of the latter still around. The owners hadn't done much of a cleanup when they'd cleared out.

I'd smelled blood, and I'd seen houses that had been covered in it, but in the middle of our jobs, it was fresh. The factory smelled of old, rotten blood.

"Whoever left this place like this should be drowned in raw sewage," Garrison grumbled, pinching his nose as he looked around.

I had to agree. And maybe we could burn the building down for good measure too. No one should be subjected to this ever again.

"Why are we here instead of tracking down that guy from the rally again?" Garrison added, shooting Blaze a baleful glance that the hacker returned.

"Because this is a way better lead than anything my searches for him have turned up."

A cockroach the size of my thumb scampered across the floor in front of Dess's feet. She stomped on it faster than I could blink, but the crunch of its shell made me grimace. "Let's search the place and then get out of here," she said.

"No argument here," Blaze piped up.

"Which part of the building was the photo taken in?" Julius asked him.

The hacker spread his hands. "I'm not totally sure. This particular blogger went for flowery descriptions of his exploits over concrete details. The geotags indicate it should be in the back end of the building on the western side. We should check the whole place over to be sure we catch all the evidence that might be useful, though."

"We'll find it." Dess marched ahead with her chin held high, and an unexpected flare of admiration and desire washed through me. My mind flickered briefly back to the amazing fuck the two of us and Julius had shared by the side of the road, of all places.

I generally preferred to have four walls around me if I was going to get down and dirty, but Dess had an effect on me that I couldn't explain. She was some woman, that was for sure, striding through the wide room all cool and collected like she owned the place.

She skirted the thickest patches of reddish-brown on the floor beneath the hooks. "I wonder what exactly they killed in here."

"At this rate, it'll be me next," Garrison muttered. "Suffocated by the stink."

"Pigs," Blaze said. "The blog did mention that. Apparently there are rumors of hauntings in here. According to the guy—if he didn't just make this up for views—when the factory was operational, an occasional human body was tortured alongside the hanging pigs. I guess that's one way to cover up murder."

"Sounds like a myth to me," Julius remarked, but he eyed the hooks pensively.

Dess marched onward to the door at the far end of the room. "I don't know why this place would be connected to the household. Let's grab what we came for and get out of here. I don't have a great feeling about this."

Neither did I. Apprehension prickled over me as I moved through the room. I headed to the front hall and unlocked the heavy deadbolt from the inside. "So we can make a quick getaway if we need to," I told Julius when I saw him watching me.

He nodded in acceptance.

When I returned to the others, they'd split up between the side rooms. Dess was searching a smaller area with a few long metal tables and shelves built into the walls. The shelves were empty.

"It looks like a... filleting room—is that what it's called?" she asked. "You know, the place where the pigs were skinned and cut up."

I shrugged. "The butchering room, maybe? I don't know."

She peered under the table and nudged the shelves to see if they'd move. "At least they cleaned up a little better in here. The smell isn't quite so bad."

I checked a cupboard at the far end of the room and found only a couple of old butcher knives. Dess came up beside me and reached past me to snatch one up with a low whistle. Her arm brushed mine, sparking another rush of heat where our bodies touched.

"I bet you could make good use of these," she said, and spun the one she'd grabbed in her hand without moving away from me. "Do you think the ghosts would mind if I pilfered one just for our explorations here?"

A tickle of amusement rose in my chest. "I'm sure they'd forgive you."

Even twirling it casually, I could see the skill in the way she handled the blade. "Guns are more direct, but knives let you stay connected to the act, don't you think?" she remarked.

I couldn't restrain a chuckle. "I think I wouldn't want to go hand-to-hand with you with any kind of weapon, but especially not that."

She peeked through her eyelashes at me with an abruptly flirty expression. "Oh, I'd go easy on *you*. It'd be more fun that way."

She flipped the knife in her hand again and drifted toward the doorway, not even waiting or pushing for a response. No demands. No expectations.

That might be the most miraculous thing about her. Despite the physical intimacy we'd shared twice now and the fact that we were still around each other regularly, Dess didn't seem to need or even want me to fawn over her, to treat her like more than a colleague. I knew she appreciated our physical connection, but she wasn't insisting on it becoming anything fraught and romantic.

I knew how unusual her attitude was. Because of that problem, I'd stopped sleeping with women except an occasional one night stands when the itch got strong enough. If I'd hooked up with the same woman more than once, it would inevitably turn into long text chains, hopeful phone calls, and teasing pet names fishing for one in return. No matter how clear I tried to be about only looking for something casual, that never stuck.

Until Dess. She knew how to take the good and not worry about the depth of emotion I couldn't offer her. Strangely, that fact stirred more actual affection in me than I could remember feeling for anyone… in a very long time.

I wasn't totally sure what to make of it, but since she wasn't nudging me for passionate declarations, I didn't have to make anything of it at all.

I trailed after Dess into the next room. Just as I made it through the doorway, she called out, "Hey, I got something. Is this the wall from the photo?"

I hustled the rest of the way inside, the other guys converging around us. Dess was standing by a sagging metal desk in what appeared to be the factory's office room. On the wall across from her, up near the ceiling, a spiderweb of cracks stretched through the plaster. They crossed through the deeper groves of a carved symbol that matched the one in the mansion.

"That's it," Blaze confirmed, snapping his own picture of it.

"It's obviously been there for a long time," Julius said. "We need to figure out why. Spread out—maybe there's been some kind of record left behind. Even a scrap of torn paper on the floor might give us the link we need."

Garrison moved to a creaky filing cabinet in the corner. The drawers appeared to be mostly empty, but he fished out the few papers he found inside, glanced at them, and stuffed them into the satchel he'd brought. Dess started paging through the few decrepit binders left on a shelving unit next to it. Julius checked the desk drawers, and Blaze and I knelt down to paw through the stray documents that had fallen to the floor.

They were grimy with the grit that scattered the linoleum, a coating of dust—and an occasional footprint. Those were probably from the "urban explorers" who'd passed through, but they could be more relevant than that. I passed them to Garrison to add to his stash.

"Hold up," Blaze said suddenly, freezing in his hunched stance next to the desk.

The rest of us stiffened automatically, even Dess. She'd been around us long enough to recognize that if any of us sounded a warning, it should be heeded.

"What's the matter?" Julius asked.

"There's a fixture on the ceiling in the corner," Blaze said without looking directly at it. "I didn't notice it before because the shelving unit blocked it from my line of sight near the doorway. I don't know *for sure* what's inside it, or if there's anything at all, and if it's what I think it is, there's a strong possibility it isn't even active—"

"*What* do you think it is?" Garrison demanded through gritted teeth.

Blaze shot a glower at him. "A camera. If I were going to bet on it, I'd say there at least *used* to be a security camera in there."

Dess frowned, but her stance stayed tensed. "Why would anyone still be monitoring security feeds in this place? It's obviously been abandoned for years."

"Exactly," Blaze said. "That's why I said it probably isn't even active. If it even is a camera. But still… if it *is* active and monitored, it's too late now. We've already been caught on it." He paused. "And if I missed that one at first, it's possible there are others I missed too." He muttered a curse at himself.

A deeper chill prickled down my spine. Was *that* why I hadn't liked the feeling of this place—some part of me had sensed that we could be being watched? Of course, the stink explained my uneasiness perfectly well on its own.

"They apparently didn't mind the urban explorers before us," Garrison pointed out. "No reason to think they'll have a problem with us. If someone is watching."

Julius's expression had turned even more stern than usual. "We shouldn't take the chance, especially since we don't know how long we might already have been under surveillance. Grab all the loose material in here that you can quickly, and let's move out."

Dess swept the binders into a bag of her own and opened it wider for Julius to shove handfuls of crumpled papers into. Blaze and I scooped everything we could off the floor into a heap that we crammed into Garrison's satchel. We might have missed a few bits and pieces, but I agreed with Julius that it was best not to tempt fate by thumbing our noses at the risks any longer.

Tramping back into the thicker stink of the front room with the hooks, my stomach lurched despite myself. I hesitated, wondering whether we should squeeze back through the window or walk out the front door.

And then that question didn't matter anymore.

The front door burst open, and at least a dozen men charged in through it. More leapt through the window we'd opened and smashed others besides. In an instant, we were all but surrounded.

My hand shot to my ever-present weapons, a gun at one hip and my knife at the other. Garrison dropped his satchel and brandished his own pistol. Blaze and Julius whipped out their weapons. Dess waggled the butcher knife she was still carrying, her free hand dipping toward the gun strapped to her calf.

We might have retreated into the rooms we'd just left, but the incoming attackers charged at us without giving us a second to prepare. As they opened fire on us, I leapt toward the cabinets along one wall for some kind of shelter, dragging Dess with me and shooting as I went. Weirdly, the second I had my arm around her, the bullets flying my way seemed to falter. But bangs were still echoing all around me.

My comrades had all dived for whatever other cover they could find. Our attackers kept shooting in their general directions, but they all marched toward the spot where I'd ducked down with Dess next to me.

An icy sense of understanding snapped into place in my head.

They were here for her. They'd kill us to get to her, but they didn't want *her* dead. They were aiming to take her back, just like Garrison's contact had threatened.

Fury unfurled in my chest, searing hot. They'd only capture her over my dead body, and I didn't intend to give them that.

I fired off a few more shots, and the advancing men fell back to the side where I couldn't reach them without leaning out of the minor shelter I'd found. My gaze caught Julius's, and then Blaze's, and then Garrison's around the room. A matching rage shone in all their gazes.

All of us were ready to fight to the death to protect this woman. I had no doubt about that. She was one of us now, and we protected our own.

Bullets started rattling the side of the cabinet, some puncturing one or two layers of metal. It wouldn't be long before they passed right through the side where we were crouched. Dess sucked a breath through her teeth with a hiss, and I knew what I needed to do.

Yanking the cabinet door in front of me like a shield, I lunged out and squeezed the trigger.

FOURTEEN

Decima

AT THE SAME moment as Talon sprang forward, blasting shots at our attackers from behind the cabinet door, I leapt past him toward a small cluster of men who'd been closing in on us from the other direction. I yanked my pistol from my calf holster as I rolled across the floor, shot three of them in the head in quick succession, and had my butcher knife ready to plunge into the chest of the fourth the second I reached him.

More bodies swarmed around me. I kept low to give the crew clear aim at our attackers and dashed for the shelter of a meat processing machine. From that vantage point, I surveyed the room.

Two things became clear very quickly. The first was that this room offered lots of advantages I could put to use. All those hanging chains would allow for swift movement over the heads of our attackers, and the hooks on their ends could serve as makeshift weapons.

The other was that the horde of fighters appeared to be mostly focused on me. They spewed bullets at the men in the crew as they charged forward, but they were barreling toward me again, even though Talon was still by the cabinet where I'd left him.

A chill trickled through me. I didn't need to see any more than that to understand. This building belonged to the people associated with that teardrop symbol, and those were the same people who thought they owned me. They'd come to collect.

The crew were doing their best to defend me, as Julius had sworn they would. Talon kept firing on the incoming attackers, and Julius sprayed bullets from the other side of the room. Blaze and Garrison were getting in as many shots as they could too, but we were vastly overwhelmed. There had to be at least twenty men still rushing through the room. They shot at the guys the second any of them tried to take even a step from cover, and the vests they wore absorbed any shots that caught them in the torso.

"Aim for their heads!" I hollered out, although I suspected the crew had already figured that out for themselves, and scrambled onto the top of the sprawling machine. With a swift jump, I grasped one of the chains and swung out over the men who'd nearly reached me.

I had to keep one hand around the rust-speckled chain, but with the other, I hailed bullets on the men below. They scattered in an instant, but I caught two in the skull, splattering brains and blood across the already gruesome floor in a mess the crew might have appreciated if we hadn't all been fighting for our lives.

Unfortunately, the chain chose that moment to give out. It unraveled abruptly from the fixtures on the ceiling, and I thumped to the ground, managing to brace my feet beneath me just in time to save me from landing on my ass.

I whirled around, finding myself in the midst of the attackers I'd just been harassing from overhead. As they converged on me again, the crew burst from the shelter they'd taken, Talon and Julius whipping out knives to take on our opponents in ways that wouldn't risk me taking one of their bullets. I shot one man who loomed over me in the throat, wishing I hadn't needed to leave behind my own knife.

When I ducked and swiveled, arms wrapped around my waist from behind. I slammed my foot down on my attacker's and heaved him over my back. With a well-timed shove, I rammed him into one of the dangling hooks with a sickening crunch as it penetrated his spine at the base of his skull. His body jerked and went still.

More of the men were grabbing at my limbs. I kicked, punched, and aimed careful bullets to avoid my allies, opening a path through the menacing swarm. I hurtled out of the worst of the crowd in time to see Garrison dueling another attacker who'd lost his gun. As he aimed a punch at the guy's face, another man lunged at him from behind, right near me.

I didn't think, only moved. Flinging myself at the man, I knocked him to the ground just inches from where Garrison stood. I snapped the attacker's wrist, yanked the knife he'd been wielding from his loosening fingers, and plunged it into his back right through the vest. Bulletproof didn't mean blade-proof.

Garrison had just managed to get a clear enough opening to shoot his opponent in the forehead. He spun around and saw me on the floor behind him, wrenching the knife free from the dead man who'd meant to do the same to him. I glanced up, and his hazel eyes locked with mine.

His jaw twitched. "Thanks," he muttered, not sounding particularly grateful despite the word.

I didn't have time to lecture him on his tone, because another bunch of men launched themselves at us—mostly at me—in the same moment. I hurled myself away behind another machine, but they pounded after me.

My breath was coming ragged from the intense pace I'd been keeping up. More gunshots reverberated through the large room.

I had to give the crew more of an opening. Get our attackers into a tighter space where they'd have less room to maneuver, and then we could surround *them* despite having smaller numbers.

The pricks were after me, obviously. So I'd just have to lead the way.

I dodged the closest attackers and sprinted toward the hall. The slaughtering room where I'd found the knife seemed like my best bet. I could grab another blade there if I needed to. I veered toward it—and realized I'd failed to take one factor into account.

A few more men had broken into the factory through other windows at that end of the building—maybe backup that'd just arrived. I dashed into the room I'd been aiming for, several other attackers right on my heels, and nearly ran straight into three others. Suddenly, I was the one surrounded.

I fired off two quick shots, managing to take down one man and wound another in the leg before someone behind me closed in enough to wrench my wrist and disarm me. When I swung around, snatching up the abandoned butcher knife in my other hand, the men behind me leapt at me. I caught one in the gut with a backward kick, slicing at the ones coming at me through the doorway, but there were too many. If the crew were following, they hadn't reached me yet.

A bulging arm slammed around my throat. I went still, knowing that thrashing could force him to crush my windpipe, willing my body to relax so I could move swiftly as soon as I saw my opening.

"The boss wants us to take you in alive," my captor snarled by my ear. "But we're authorized to kill you if we can't accomplish that. It's up to you whether you walk out of this shithole with your life."

A sudden chill washed over my mind as I stared at the mass of attackers closing in around me. The crew might not make it to me in time. I could take down another three, maybe four of these assholes… more if I was lucky, but I didn't like relying on luck.

The odds were against me. If I kept fighting, I might very well die here at these pricks' hands.

A flicker of panic shot through me—and then faded away. In its place, my nerves went totally still with a weird sense of calm.

I didn't care. If I died, I died. I'd rather become a corpse than end up locked away and essentially a slave all over again. This was *my* choice.

"When you bring back my dead body, I hope they kill you out of spite," I said. In the same instant, I jerked my body to snap his hold.

My knife caught another guy who leapt at me in the neck. I kicked the one behind me into the edge of one of the tables and dropped to the floor both to avoid the groping hands and to snatch up the gun I'd lost.

I flipped onto my back and fired at the faces looming over me. Someone dove in with a knife that raked across my shoulder when I deflected it from my throat at the last second. Hissing at the sting of pain, I clamped my free hand around his wrist and wrenched to plunge the blade into his own chest.

I tripped another attacker with a slam of my heel, rolled under the table and shot a few legs before someone slammed a steel-toed boot into my ribs from the other side. With another wince, I whirled around and shot the kneecap on the offending leg. The man toppled over, and I added another bullet to his head.

More attackers swarmed on me, but other shouts joined the fray—voices I was much happier to hear.

"Take this, fuckers!" Blaze called out with fierce exuberance.

Julius's growl followed. "This is what happens to anyone who messes with the Chaos Crew."

What followed was a blur of adrenaline, movement, and gunfire. I snatched my last cartridge from my pocket and shoved it into my gun as the guys did their work and then added more of my own bullets to the deluge from beneath the table. Bodies swayed and crumpled around me.

One final attacker sprang at me with a knife in both hands, but my kick to his belly sent him sprawling—right beneath the swing of Talon's knife.

In the sudden quiet, I scrambled out from under the table. Our dead opponents littered the room around me, and I could see others sprawled in the hallway outside. Julius looked the scene over with a grim smile.

Blaze's gaze snagged on me—and the cut carved into my shoulder. "You're hurt."

I pressed my hand to the wound. "I'll be fine. It's not that deep." The stinging had already dulled to a faint ache.

Garrison looked up from where he was crouched in the corner, checking the attackers' pockets. "I'm not finding any ID, but this prick is still alive," he said, motioning to a man who was bleeding from his thigh and stomach. "Maybe he can cough up some details for us?"

A hard glint came into Julius's eyes. "I'll bet he can. But we shouldn't wait around here for more of these assholes to come at us. Bring him. With a little convincing, I'm sure we can find out everything he knows."

Talon went over to haul the guy into his hold. The injured man flailed ineffectually as we strode back through the factory.

Blaze glanced at me, managing a wry smile. "Not such a bad lead after all, in the end."

I nodded to the man. "Let's see if he gives anything up before we make a final judgment on that."

FIFTEEN

Garrison

I KNEW my time to interrogate was coming when the screaming had faded into an occasional dull whimper of pain. A few minutes later, Talon came striding out of the basement room in the old warehouse we'd stopped by, wiping his hands across a tan towel that had been stained red.

This was how we did interrogations. Talon broke the fuckers apart, and I pieced them back together just enough and in just the right way to get the answers we needed. If they hadn't already spilled their guts to get Talon to stop. The odds were about fifty-fifty.

This guy was one of the more resilient ones.

Talon nodded to me. "He's ready for you."

I glanced behind me to where Dess sat beside Julius, leaning back in her chair and appearing unfazed by the entire situation as he finished bandaging her shoulder. Blaze eyed his laptop, trying and failing to find out exactly who had access to the camera within the factory. He swore at the computer under his breath.

"Gave you a tough time, did he?" I asked Talon with purposeful bravado. The man was fucking good at what he did, but that gave me an extra ego boost when it turned out my skills were the ones that'd get us what we needed.

"He's stubborn, but he's weak and out of it now," the other man replied. "Threatening him only made him clam up more."

That was useful to know. Some people coughed up the information we needed in the face of someone physically intimidating. Some responded better to psychological threats. Others needed a more nuanced approach. It sounded like this guy belonged to the last group.

As I stepped into the room, I was already formulating a strategy in my mind. I walked in with a slight slouch and a hesitant expression on my face, watching our captive's reaction from the corner of my eyes. Sometimes after a battering, what an opponent responded best to was the chance to exert some kind of power over another person. That meant looking meek and nervous, but not so much that he couldn't get any satisfaction out of lording it over me.

The man was slumped in the chair we'd tied him to. We'd bandaged the wound on his stomach, because we didn't want him bleeding out before we were done with him, but little rivulets oozed from the shallower wound on his leg and other minor cuts that Talon had added to his collection, in between the mottling of bruises. A few fingers dangled limply, broken, and the guy's lip was split.

He raised his head slowly, swaying, at the sight of me. When I let myself make eye contact, it was only for an instant before jerking my gaze away. At that show of uncertainty, he managed to draw his posture up a little straighter.

Ah ha. He thought I was someone he might be able to gain an advantage over, and he liked that idea. I'd just keep playing to that tune.

I wandered over to the torture table laid out with Talon's instruments—mostly various types of blades, his favorite tools. "Always on clean-up duty," I muttered to myself. "As if I want to be around all this blood and crap."

I sighed and turned to look at the man again, as if I were sizing him up. At the same time, I shrank in on myself a little. But I spoke, making it sound like I was forcing out the offer despite my nerves. "It doesn't have to be that way, you know. We could both get something out of this."

The man studied me warily. "What do you mean?" he asked, his voice rasping.

I twisted my mouth at an uncertain angle. "This doesn't have to end with them killing you. If I could show I got something out of you—something they want to know—then they'd see that I can be more of a part of their stupid crew. And I'd make sure you get the chance to escape."

The man scoffed weakly, but a glimmer of hope lit in his face at the same time. I'd presented him with a picture of a man who didn't like killing and hungered for more recognition, and he'd lapped it up. "I'm supposed to believe that?" he asked anyway.

I shrugged, walking around him but careful to move closer to the weapons than to him—to show that I didn't want to be near him and risk myself. I didn't want him to think I was outright afraid, but I certainly didn't want him to believe I was fully comfortable, either.

"I don't have any interest in cleaning up another corpse," I said, with a shudder I didn't have to fake. The gore of our killings did actually make me a little queasy, even if I stomached it for the sake of the job. "So really, it's all a favor to me. But I can't let you go if you don't give me anything. Then they'll kill *me.*"

The man blinked at me, his eyes going momentarily bleary. Talon had left him in quite a state. He couldn't focus or think clearly, and I knew that if I pushed the right buttons, he'd slip up and give something away.

He shifted against his restraints. "I can't tell you anything, man. I'm at the bottom of the information chain. No one even told me why we were going after you and the girl."

"I guess you could start by telling me who this 'we' is? What group are you with? Who sent you on the job?"

When he hesitated, I grabbed one of the short, serrated blades off the table and walked toward him. His mouth flattened and his nose flared, and I could tell Talon was right. He wouldn't say a word if I was threatening him with a weapon.

That was fine. I hadn't picked it up to do that.

"I can show you I mean what I'm offering," I said, coaxing just a hint of a quaver into my voice. Bending down, I sawed through the rope that bound his left wrist. With a few quick jerks, the cord fell away. I jumped back, out of range of his reach.

The man turned his hand over, staring at it in disbelief. He swayed again and sucked in a ragged breath.

"I told you I don't want you dead," I said in a pleading tone. "Just tell me what you know."

I set the knife back on the table, but at the edge as if I anticipated needing it soon to finish releasing him. The man considered it and then me. His jaw worked.

"This won't do you any good, you know," he said. "No matter what you hear from me, you're all going down. We were just the first, because we've got the direct connection. A call went out, wide, with quite the bounty on your heads. Every mercenary group in the country will be eager to bring in your heads."

A gleam had sparked in his eyes. He was relishing the idea of intimidating me.

I let him have a minor victory, wincing and hunching my shoulders a little more. "Why would they care so much about us?"

He shook his head, a hint of a grin crossing his lips, weary though it was. "Like I said, I don't know. I just know you're dead meat."

Big talk for a man who didn't currently look like much more than meat himself. I kept that observation silent and prodded in a different direction, letting a hint of panic color my words. "Fuck, I knew we were screwed. *Who* put out the call? Who's got it in for us?"

"A man you're going to regret you ever crossed," our captive said darkly, and then sputtered several wet-sounding coughs. I suspected there was some internal bleeding going on.

I switched tactics just a tad to prompt him to spill more. "The guys I work for are the most powerful crew out there. That isn't possible."

The man managed a feeble-sounding snort. "They might like to think so, but they're nothing compared to the real kings of the criminal world."

I honestly had no idea what he was talking about. Maybe the Chaos Crew wasn't anywhere near as big as various mafia-style organizations, and we didn't have as wide a reach as those, but we weren't aiming to be some kind of syndicate. We could have taken down any of those trumped-up pricks any time we wanted. But I guessed they liked to think that wasn't true.

"Some kind of mafioso, huh?" I said doubtfully. "We've tangled with the Russian mob and the Italians, even the Chinese. Sounds like you're just bluffing."

The man just sneered at me with so much confidence that I found my own was shaken. Was there someone higher up than the mafias who had it out for us? Just how well connected were the people who'd run Dess's household?

They *had* managed to nearly get the better of us at the old meat factory. That didn't bode well.

"Please," I said, going back into meek mode. "If we can't get out of this shit situation, at least give me something so I can protect myself. I'll make a run for it after I cut you loose and let the others deal with this fucking problem."

He shook his head again. "*I* don't even know his name. Just that when he says jump, you'd better jump. And a whole lot of mercs are doing that right now."

I sensed that I'd gotten everything I could out of that line of questioning, as much as it frustrated me. But now that I had him feeling superior to me, it was the perfect time to throw a spanner into the works and see what came out of him when I took him by surprise.

I sucked in a breath and frowned at him. "How does this all connect to Damien Malik?"

The guy stiffened too quickly for him to hide his reaction. He forced his body to relax a moment later, but I'd already marked his response. He knew *something* about Malik—something that related to this powerful criminal figure he'd been taunting me with.

Was Malik on this master criminal's payroll too? Had the guy been lying and he happened to know that Malik *was* the master criminal?

I stepped toward him. "We know he's mixed up in this somehow. You obviously do too. Do we have to watch out for him?"

The guy's eyes narrowed. His walls were going up again. "I'd say we all have to watch out for that fucker."

"What do you mean? What's he been doing?"

The anxiety I showed didn't get me anywhere this time. The man had turned even cagier. He simply shot me a tight smirk and sat in silence.

This information could be the key to everything—to the attack on us, to Dess's kidnapping and training—all the mysteries we'd been working so hard to unravel. I released my cautious demeanor just a little, framing my eagerness as desperation. "Come on, man. Just give me this one thing, and I'll cut you loose right now."

The man just kept giving me a crooked but mocking smile even as his head started to droop again, and a prickle of real frustration shot through my chest. I was *so* close, and this asshole decided to balk now?

"Look at you," I said, moving close enough to give his chair a little shove. "You're halfway free already. Help *yourself*, you idiot!"

He chuckled, but it was a hopeless sound that knotted my stomach. If a person started feeling they had nothing left to lose, you had no more leverage.

"Your boys will kill me anyway," he said in an even raspier voice than before. His eyelids quivered as a swell of pain must have washed over him. "And if somehow you got me out of here, *he'd* kill me because he'd assume I'd talked. There's no fucking way out. Just give it up."

No. I didn't give in that easily, and neither should this halfwit. I shoved his chair again, distantly aware that my cringing front was falling away and not particularly caring. I had to shock something out of this asshole before he slipped from my grasp completely. Julius was counting on me—Dess was counting on me—

The chair skidded a few inches to the side, its legs grating against the concrete floor. I recognized my mistake a split-second too late.

I'd jostled the guy toward the torture table. His free arm whipped out, and his fingers closed around the handle of the knife I'd left on the edge.

If he'd slashed it at me, it wouldn't have been so bad. I'd have dodged with maybe some split skin for Julius to stitch up. But instead the captive let out one last, hollow laugh and plunged the blade into his own throat.

Blood gushed forth, soaking him and spraying me in an instant. I jerked back with a noise of strangled horror—both at the sudden, stinking mess and the fact that I'd allowed it to happen.

Our victim had found an escape route after all, and it was one where I couldn't chase after him. His body was already crumpling in the chair, the life draining out of it. I knew without feeling for a pulse that he was a goner. He sure as hell wasn't talking any more with a knife in his throat.

Shit. *Shit.*

I paced from one end of the room to the other as the blood formed a thick puddle beneath the chair. My hands balled into fists at my sides. I had to go up and tell Julius about my fuck-up. I'd found out a few things, but it was all too vague to be really useful—and I'd screwed up when I could have gotten so much more.

How could I have let myself get so impatient? For fuck's sake, I knew better.

I dragged a breath through my clenched teeth, and the door eased open. The most likely source of my frayed control peered inside. My jaw tightened even more.

"What happened?" Dess asked, staring at the scene.

"What does it look like?" I snapped. "I pushed him too far, and he found a way to jump right over the edge."

Her gaze slid to me, and something softened in her expression. Somehow that made me even more pissed off. How dare she *sympathize* when half the reason I'd screwed up was that I hadn't felt totally like myself since she'd come barging into our lives?

"I'm sure you were doing your best," she said. "It's not like torture is an exact science."

"I still should have done better than letting him off himself. Why don't you get out of here and let me clean up my own mess?"

Dess knit her brow. Her voice came out terser. "I'm trying to help. It's not like there's anyone in the world who doesn't make mistakes."

I sputtered a laugh. "This is more than just a mistake. I don't need you sugar-coating it. I can face my fuckups like a man."

She folded her arms over her chest. "Then maybe you should act like a man now and stop bitching about this. Stop acting like *I'm* the enemy. I don't know what the hell your problem with me is, but I'm getting sick of you treating me like I either don't exist or like I'm garbage."

I winced inwardly but contained my reaction. I couldn't afford to let her see how much she affected me. No fucking way.

"I'm not going to cater to your every whim just because—" I started, and just then, Julius stormed into view behind her.

"What the hell is this all about?" he demanded.

Part of me wanted to shrink back like I'd been pretending to do around our captive. I forced my chin up and my shoulders back. "I screwed up. He got too close to a knife and offed himself."

Julius swept his hand through the air. "I'm not talking about the interrogation. We were going to kill him anyway. I'm asking why the hell you two are fighting after all the shit we've just been through?"

Dess stiffened. "I was just telling Garrison to stop acting like such an ass all the time."

Julius gave her a stern look. "Garrison is how he is. But he can learn to watch his mouth when the situation calls for it." He glowered at me next. "We've got enough people attacking us without going at each other."

Annoyance started to flare in me again, but Dess lowered her head. The slant of her mouth and the slight deflating of her posture gave more of an answer than any words could have.

She wasn't *angry* with me. She was hurt. I'd been pushing her away ever since we'd hooked up, and… and it genuinely bothered her.

She wanted more of a connection with me, more comradery and warmth, and I'd been shutting her out. Even though if I let myself think about it instead of giving in to my kneejerk reaction to push her away, I knew I wanted the same thing.

Julius kept studying both of us. "I was hoping the two of you could collaborate on the next steps we need to take from here. Is that going to be a problem?"

I shook my head quickly. "No. We can work together. It wasn't Dess's fault. I was frustrated with the interrogation, and I shouldn't have taken it out on her."

Julius nodded and turned to Dess. She tipped her head in

acknowledgment of what I'd said, but her expression was a little more skeptical than his was.

I guessed I couldn't blame her. Whatever connection had already formed between us, I must have hammered a lot of cracks into it over the past few days.

This wasn't how I wanted things to go, not really. I'd better figure out my bullshit before it got in my way again.

SIXTEEN

Decima

GARRISON CLEANED UP *NICE.*

Seeing him in his new tailored tuxedo, I couldn't seem to peel my eyes away from him. He strutted up the sidewalk toward the hotel that was the site of our current mission with a confidence that shouted, "I'm rich, and you're below me." A mask, I had no doubt, but one that would fit the fundraiser we were crashing perfectly.

His hair had been arranged elegantly atop his head—all the shaggy dirty blond strands falling in a way that looked both styled and messy simultaneously. His well-built frame might not have been quite as massively brawny as Julius's or as dangerously toned as Talon's, but it filled out the suit to impressive effect, one I suspected the other men around us had to envy. He moved with a sense of power that practically radiated through the air.

Which was good, because our fellow attendees were among the most powerful figures in business and politics in this part of the country. I only hoped that I could give off half as convincing a vibe.

I was more used to slinking through the shadows than being on display. Noelle had taught me how to handle myself among the wealthy and pompous, of course, but it'd always taken more energy than the stealthier parts of my missions.

After he flashed the fake IDs at the door and we'd been ushered in thanks to Blaze's prep work, Garrison tsked his tongue at me teasingly. "You're staring… again."

"Just making sure you're not giving off any red flags," I said, which was a total lie, but he didn't need to know that. His ego was big enough as it was.

Anyway, I should be focused on the job, not my co-conspirator. I tugged my gaze away to take in the mass of people circulating the room.

Champagne was flowing, its crisp scent tickling into my nose, and rich patrons in designer clothes tittered in that way that passes for laughter when you need to keep up appearances. I resisted the urge to tug at my own sleek silk evening gown.

This was a fundraising event for Damien Malik, and we intended to use it to find out exactly what intel the guests had on him and his activities. Rich people *always* had information that didn't belong to them. I'd learned that through my years of infiltrating similar parties.

It only took a bit of manipulation to get people like this talking, but that was Garrison's specialty. I was going to practice my pickpocketing skills.

I caught Garrison's eye with a subtle nod to indicate I was going to get started, and he returned it with a flash of a smile that was warmer than anything he'd aimed at me recently. I couldn't tell whether it was part of his act or whether he'd actually gotten his head on straighter since Julius had chided us for our argument the other day. For now, either was fine.

Leaving him behind to work his verbal magic, I roamed through the crowd. Some thieves relied on distraction to get the job done, but that meant drawing the target's attention to you first. I didn't want anyone even thinking about me when they noticed their phones were missing.

I dipped my hand into one woman's sparkly purse and tugged another phone from a posh gentleman's back pocket. Discreetly tucking them into my own purse, which was the largest I could get away with wearing this outfit and doctored with special lining to block the signal, I stalked onward. I'd take as many as I could get, as many devices as offered themselves in easy reach. There was no telling who might have passed on a stray observation or bit of gossip about the man we were most interested in.

A couple of guys I recognized from Blaze's research into Malik's security detail stepped into view. I handily dodged them, weaving my way toward the other end of the room. Spotting a man who looked particularly well-connected based on the numbers of hangers-on gathered around him, I managed to trip one of the women next to him without her even realizing what'd knocked her off balance, brushed past the man as he leaned in to steady her, and scored his phone from the inside pocket of his jacket quick as lightning. No one suspected a thing.

My purse was starting to feel pretty full. It weighed on my elbow, where I'd left it dangling. I grabbed a glass of champagne to give myself the extra cover of alcohol if anyone noticed any odd movements and circulated through the crowd some more, keeping my ears pricked for interesting conversation rather than my fingers slippery.

I was right in the middle of the vast ballroom when my gaze caught on Damien Malik himself. At the sight of his neatly slicked silvery hair and polished smile, my stomach dipped. I sidled out of his line of sight, monitoring him from the edge of my vision. My pulse thumped harder.

The man the crew had interrogated had all but confirmed that Malik was involved in the organization that ran the household. I had no idea whether he knew anything about my kidnapping and training or if his connection was in some other area, but a thread of tension ran through my chest all the same.

How big a menace was this man who pretended to be trying to make the country a more peaceful place?

My fingers itched, and I couldn't help wondering whether it'd be better just to kill him now. I could wait until he strayed away from the crowd and accomplish it so quickly no one would realize what'd happened until I was well away. Or slip into the kitchen and quickly concoct one of the basic poisons I'd learned and slip that into a drink or hors d'oeuvres.

I reined that impulse in. All of my missions before I'd met the crew had been with the intention to kill, but that wouldn't actually help me now. Malik was our main lead to the rest of the surviving organization, now that Noelle and everyone else from the household was dead. He'd lead us to the people responsible for my imprisonment one way or another.

Besides, we didn't know for sure that his association with those people was as an ally and not a victim of some sort. It was possible that the man we'd interrogated had refused to talk because he didn't want to reveal other plans his employer had in the works that would target the politician.

I might have gone for one last phone—Malik's—but I doubted there was anything on there that Blaze hadn't already found on his computer, which didn't amount to much. No, right now we wanted to know what people who didn't necessarily have his best interests at heart were saying to or about him.

After a few more minutes, I spotted Garrison, and then I stopped in my tracks. I couldn't approach him, because he was obviously still doing his own work—which at the moment involved leaning close to a middle-aged woman with a sculpted updo as she giggled at something he'd said. She tapped the lapel of his suit, and he responded with a reserved grin I suspected was designed to give her hope while not promising his continued attention. He let his fingers trail over her wrist.

My teeth set on edge. A different urge gripped me, one to march right over there and tear them apart. Which was ridiculous, because he was only doing his job getting her to open up, and besides, we weren't really anything to each other than colleagues. He'd made it very clear that one hookup on the rooftop hadn't changed that.

Still, seeing her fingers caress his sleeve provoked another flare of jealousy. I distracted myself by turning away and searching out one of the attendants carrying their trays of little treats. I ate the bit of toast and caviar I selected slowly, trying to make even my bites look elegant. Then I meandered over to a table in the corner.

To my surprise, Garrison sauntered over not long after. He stopped beside me, taking a sip from his glass of champagne, and tipped his head casually toward my purse. "Good haul?" he asked quietly.

"Nothing to scoff at," I replied. "How about you?"

"A couple of interesting tidbits that will lead Blaze down a rabbit hole, I'm sure, but nothing definitely useful. I'm just taking a breather before I hit up a few more of these idiots."

He didn't look or sound tired, but I studied him more carefully. A question I probably shouldn't have been asking tumbled out. "Is it hard? Not just talking with people but, like, getting flirty with them and all that?"

Garrison raised an eyebrow at me. "Still having trouble keeping your eyes off me, huh?" He gazed out at the horde again, and his voice sobered. "It's totally easy when I don't mean it. Everything's easy when I don't mean it."

Suddenly I felt as if he'd just said something more honest than even he had realized in the moment. A brief glimpse of the man behind the many masks. Maybe that was why I found the courage to venture, even as my throat constricted a little at getting this personal, "Is that why it seems to be so hard for you to even stay friendly with me? Because you would mean it?"

Garrison's eyes jerked back to me, startled and wary. I found myself wishing I could take the question back. But I still wanted to know the answer.

I thought he'd meant at least some of the friendly overtures he'd made, as seldom as they were. I didn't think I'd imagined the momentary tenderness after we'd had sex. I'd assumed his hot-and-cold routine had something to do with my own behavior, but maybe it was only about him. About not wanting to let those masks down once he realized he'd started to.

The personas I put on for my jobs had always felt just like that—like a job. I couldn't wait to strip off the posh demeanor I'd put on for this mission the second we were out of here. For Garrison, though, I was getting the impression that his masks were a way of life.

His mouth tensed, and he let his attention drift away again. I thought he was going to pretend I hadn't spoken. But then he said, with his eyes on the crowd, "Maybe that's some of it. I don't hate you, that's for sure."

"Well, that's reassuring," I grumbled.

"If you were looking for reassurance, I'm not the guy to come to."

"Yes, that's been abundantly clear." I paused and shook my head. "I'm sorry. I didn't mean to make things awkward. I'm just trying to understand. I realize I haven't always been completely upfront with you, but when I was playing those roles before, it was a matter of survival. I didn't know if I could trust any of you at all. Since you found out the truth, I've been trying to be the most *myself* I can, even if I'm still figuring out who exactly that is."

Garrison was silent for a moment. Then the corner of his mouth curled upward. "I have a pretty good idea of who Dess is. And I—I appreciate that you're honest, even if I haven't been the best at showing it."

At that admission, I couldn't resist prying a little more. "Then why is it hard to act like you do?"

Garrison swiveled the champagne flute between his fingers. He stared down at it, and his shoulders squared as if he'd gathered some sort of resolve.

"It's really just been me for a long time," he said in a low voice I could barely hear over the chatter of the crowd. "When I was a kid, my family was in a car accident—my parents and my brother were killed. It was *my* fault. I started a stupid argument with my brother, distracted my dad at the wheel… Since then, I've always had this idea in my head that I deserve to be on my own. That it's fair punishment for what I did."

The tightness in my throat became an ache. The memory came back to me of the pain and grief I'd thought I'd glimpsed in him briefly weeks ago. No wonder he'd buried it down deep.

"Of course it isn't," I had to say. "It sounds like it was just an accident. Don't kids squabble all the time?"

He shrugged. "Not to the point it gets their whole family killed. Anyway, I've never been worth anything as myself. When I become someone else, I can offer something of value—I can con things out of people, open doors that need opening… So that's all I've been doing for ages now. That's all I'm used to."

"I bet there's a lot you could offer as yourself," I said stubbornly.

A dry chuckle fell from his lips. "I'm not sure how you can say that when I don't even know what it'd be. But that's *your* talent, huh? You always see right through my bullshit. I guess I don't really know how to deal with that, so I deal with it badly." He lifted his gaze to meet my eyes again. "I'm sorry about that. I got my head up my ass and was too chickenshit to pull it out again and admit I'd screwed up with you. But I'm trying to get my act together now. Or my not-an-act."

A smile tugged at my own lips. A giddy sense of light spread through my chest. "Well, good. I'm looking forward to getting to know the real Garrison more."

He eased a little closer, his arm coming to rest against mine. "The real Garrison can also admit that I haven't been able to take my eyes off *you* all evening. I usually go for the red dresses, but damn, do you make purple look sexy as hell."

I looked down at myself, having some trouble wrapping my head around the idea of me as "sexy." But I could see the heat in his eyes when I glanced back up at him. He meant it.

"I wanted to kill the woman I saw you flirting with," I offered up as my own truth.

Garrison grinned—a broad, open grin, not the studied ones he'd flashed at the people in the crowd. "And I'm sure you could have in two seconds flat. But let's not slaughter these obnoxious people while they still might be at least a little useful to us."

I had to laugh. "Deal."

He slipped his arm right around me, his hand coming to rest on my waist with a stroke of his thumb that lit up every inch of my skin. "Also, for the record, I wouldn't mind a repeat of our time on the deck. Maybe even several."

A flush washed over my face, but I kept smiling. So nothing about our hookup had messed things up at all. And I couldn't say I didn't share the sentiment.

I let myself lean into his solid frame just slightly. "Same here."

I was just wondering if there was some alcove we could duck into and celebrate our new honesty in passionate fashion when Garrison's watch vibrated on the small of my back. He let me go so he could check the message that'd appeared on its digital face. His forehead furrowed, and he tilted it toward me.

It was a text from Blaze. *Pull out of there ASAP. I'm seeing activity I don't like. I think we could be in for some more trouble.*

SEVENTEEN

Julius

DESS AND GARRISON were the last to arrive, and I had to do a double take. I'd seen Garrison in his finery while he was getting ready, but I hadn't been here when Dess had come out of her room, dressed in that resplendent purple gown. Striding through the room in that get-up, she looked like something out of a dream.

She nodded greetings to the rest of us and ducked into her bedroom to change. Garrison stayed behind, shrugging off his tuxedo jacket and loosening his tie. He took off the vest of his tuxedo and hung it on the back of Blaze's chair before pulling both of his white undershirt sleeves to his elbows. Then he leaned across the counter of the kitchen island where Blaze was tilted toward the screen of the laptop. "What was so important that you pulled us out of the mission?"

Blaze frowned, his gaze still flicking back and forth as he took in the data streaming by him. "There's a lot of activity in the criminal underbelly of the city, and throughout the night, it's been spreading."

Garrison shook his head. "And? Forgive me, but that's not exactly a new pattern."

Blaze nodded and opened his mouth, but then he closed it again. "I'm going to wait for Dess to get into the details. In the meantime, did you get any information at the fundraiser?"

"Would have gotten more if we hadn't been pulled out," Garrison muttered, and tipped his head toward Dess's room. "You'll have to go through all the phones she pilfered. I have a couple of notes for you to follow up on, but nothing that seems all that promising."

I held myself back from clenching my jaw in frustration. I'd hoped the fundraiser would get us more of the answers we needed—and it might have if we hadn't needed to end the mission halfway through. But the activity Blaze had picked up on had felt too ominous to risk leaving our people in the field. Their safety came before anything else.

"Here you go." Dess strode into the room in her usual T-shirt and sweats and tossed her purse onto the counter. It landed with a heavy metallic thump.

Blaze's eyes lit up as he unzipped the purse. He started pawing out phones onto the countertop until Garrison cleared his throat. "Are you going to get to the point now?"

"Tell them," I said. Dess moved to stand between Talon and Garrison, a shadow of worry crossing her expression as she watched Blaze.

The hacker motioned to his laptop. "I'm seeing activity that specifically suggests that several other groups of mercenaries have arrived in this area and are trying to track down our location with the intention of attacking us. A few of them stopped by the meat factory, looking like they were attempting to pick up our trail there. Another two groups found the safe house that was compromised by that idiotic attack by the Cutthroats."

"We still have to pay *them* back," Talon muttered.

"This is what the guy we interrogated warned us about," Dess said, rubbing her hand along her jaw.

"Exactly." Blaze exhaled in a rush. "These are crews from all across this part of the country. I wouldn't be surprised if we start seeing some from farther abroad once word gets out that there's a huge bounty and no one has cashed in yet."

Dess's arms went rigid where she'd braced them against the counter. "It's because of me," she said.

My head jerked toward her. "What?"

She met my gaze steadily but with unmistakable horror in hers. "They're all trying to track you down because they know I'm with you. That's why the men at the factory attacked us too. If I wasn't here, they wouldn't bother you at all."

A growl formed in my throat so swiftly I had to swallow it down before I spoke. "It isn't your fault. You can't blame yourself."

She tilted her chin a little defiantly. "Why not? I'm just pointing out the facts. You wouldn't be in this situation if it wasn't for me."

Damn, did that woman have an effect, even when she was just standing there in plain clothes. She gave off such an assured air even now that I had no doubt she was capable of meeting this threat on her own if she had to. Just as capably as she'd moved those skilled hands over my body days ago. A flicker of heat coursed through me at the memory of her leaning back into me, taking my cock with abandon as she sucked off Talon at the same time.

But she didn't need to be alone to face the threat, any more than she'd needed to satisfy her physical desires alone. As strong as I knew she was, I *wanted* to protect her. She sure as hell didn't deserve to go through even more shit than she already had in the past two decades. I wanted to defend her from the pricks who were determined to stick her back in a cage… and I wanted to defend her from her own self-recriminations.

Blaze piped up first. "Technically, *we* kidnapped you, so even as far as you being in our company goes, that's our fault."

I could already see Dess gearing up to argue his point. I stepped in firmly. "And ignoring all that, it's not your fault that a lunatic has decided he owns you and pulled out all the stops to get you back. You *don't* belong to him, and nothing's going to stop us from helping you drive that fact home to him, no matter what he throws at you."

She stared back at me, but then she nodded just slightly in acknowledgment. Accepting the help while not compromising her pride. I had to admire her even more for her grit.

"We also need to give you more freedom even from us," I

admitted. "When we're done talking here, I'll take you through the tunnels and show you the exact route to and from the street and this building. No blindfolds, no tricky turns. I should have done that earlier. You've earned your spot with us, and you should be able to come and go if you need to by that secure route without having one of us escort you."

A more eager light came into Dess's cool gray eyes, one that warmed me to the core. "Thank you," she said quietly, but I could tell she understood what a show of trust the gesture was. She was going to be the first person who knew the hidden route to our main apartment outside of the four of us and Steffie.

I braced myself for Garrison to bicker the point like he seemed to so often when it came to Dess, but he actually relaxed at my offer. "About time," I thought he muttered under his breath.

A twinge of surprise shot through me. Had something happened to make him suddenly willing to support Dess without complaint? Maybe even *he* had finally gotten tired of all his grousing, however much it'd always been an act.

Talon folded his arms over his chest, his expression grim. "How are we going to deal with all these opportunists? Assuming we aren't going to try to simply mow them all down."

"I think that might be a tad beyond even our ample abilities," Blaze said. "At least with so many all at once. They're only following the money like we do most of the time anyway. Hard to blame them for that."

Well, I certainly could. There were lines I wouldn't have crossed when it came to those who were our closest colleagues. But then, I know our standards weren't necessarily typical.

"How secure are we as long as we stay in the apartment?" I asked. We had enough food stockpiled for at least a week in case of emergency, and Steffie could potentially get more to us without being detected.

Blaze's mouth twisted. "Well, we definitely run a significant risk any time we step outside it, now that so many people are searching for us. I don't think anyone has software on the level of my facial recognition app, but even if we rely on disguises, I wouldn't want to be taking many casual strolls." He paused. "The apartment itself is definitely our most secure location, but I can't say that it's impossible that one of these mercenaries could eventually connect us to it. Especially if they start cooperating and putting their minds together."

"And if we just hide away in here, then we have no chance of finding the prick responsible and putting an end to the whole bounty," Garrison pointed out.

Yes, that was the problem. I didn't love the idea of holing up in hiding regardless, but it was a losing game any way you sliced it. We had to cut to the heart of the problem.

We couldn't track down this criminal kingpin while we had dozens of mercenary groups on the hunt for us, and we couldn't get them off our tails without ending the bounty. Unless…

Unless we made it clear what the consequences of coming at us would be, in a way so emphatic that no one would think it was worth the risk of tangling with us. We might not be able to take down *every* crew out there, but if we made it obvious how easily we could take down at least a few of them before we fell ourselves, no one was going to want to be first in line.

I glanced around at my crew. "We have one other option, and I think it's our best one. We're going to take a trip to the Funhouse and make a statement."

Talon took the news in stride as I'd known he would. The trust we shared went back nearly twenty years and across continents. I wasn't surprised, though, that Blaze blinked, his eyebrows leaping up, and Garrison stared at me as if I'd announced we were going to take the crew to the moon.

They knew exactly what I meant by a *statement*. It wouldn't be pretty, and it would certainly be bloody, in expected Chaos Crew style.

Dess took in the guys' expressions with her penetrating gaze. She turned back to me. "What's the Funhouse?"

Blaze's mouth formed a smile that was tight with nerves. "The Funhouse is a sort-of nightclub in Pittsburgh. Very exclusive. Only the best-connected criminal outfits in the northeast know about it and can arrange to get in. People go there to hang out and make deals with each other."

Garrison was still eyeing me. "And it's understood that getting into any conflicts there is risky for a whole lot of reasons. But I'm assuming our fearless leader is about to explain how he's figured out ways around all that."

"Do you think the hit placed on us came from the Funhouse?" Dess asked.

I shook my head. "Someone this secretive and high up probably doesn't bother even with venues like that. But most of the crews who'd dare to come after us are part of it. The people there will know about the bounty, and they'll spread the word about any message we end up sending."

"Still going to be fucking crazy," Garrison said.

I gave him an even smile. "Sometimes setting expectations requires a little risk. We lay down the law, show what we're capable of, and then we'll be able to continue our investigations without interruption."

Frankly, I was tired of being on edge and reacting instinctively. The Chaos Crew orchestrated jobs, and we *never* tackled a problem without my diligent planning. It was why we'd always been so successful and why we'd remained on top for so long. Nothing good came from flailing around without a concrete strategy.

It was time that we took back control and showed our dominance to the underworld. I needed to protect my people, and this was how I could do it.

"If this is what needs to be done, I'm in," Dess said angling herself to fully face me. "Let's get started."

I felt my smile soften as I aimed it at her instead. Funny to think that a couple of weeks ago, she'd kept us at arm's length, and now she trusted me so fully that she'd stride into any kind of danger as long as I was leading the way.

This was how I liked seeing her most: rising to a challenge, fearless and confident in her abilities—and mine. The longer she was with us, the more certain I became in my assessment: She would make an irreplaceable addition to the crew if we could convince her to stay once all the trouble and mystery around her past was resolved.

My mind darted back to our encounter on the side of the road again, with a deeper wash of heat. Maybe if I could convince her to stay, she could be more than just a colleague.

I'd never expected to find someone I thought it'd be worth trying to navigate an ongoing relationship with, not in my line of work. Not with the bloodlust and yearning for justice that ran through my veins. But Dess understood all of that.

I also hadn't thought that if I did find a woman who could match me, I might have to share her with Talon. We'd had threesomes with the same partner in the past, but only as one-offs.

Somehow, looking at the woman in front of me, none of that seemed to matter. I was starting to feel like I'd be an idiot *not* to work her into my plans for my own life.

She was *my* woman now. She had been since she'd shuddered against me with my cock impaled inside her, and I wasn't going to let anyone tear her down or rip her away from me.

Which meant it was time to take care of business.

I let a slow grin unfurl across my face. "First, we're going to need some better guns."

EIGHTEEN

Decima

AS THE ELEVATOR careened up through what had looked like a bland office building from the outside, I was overly aware of the weight across my shoulders, belt, and abdomen. Two incredibly precise guns were strapped to my body, one now visible at my hip and the other hidden in my boot. My hoodie and jeans concealed various blades and a set of compact rappelling gear. Each of the guys in formation around me was carrying at least as much if not more.

I threw my hood back, revealing my face in the way Julius had planned. The guys did the same, pulling back the fabric that had been used to conceal our identities as we made our way here—as we waited for what we'd spent two days meticulously planning.

Anticipation hummed through the air. Nothing about the space around me told me this was anything other than an office building, but I had to assume that the men knew what they were doing. It wasn't the kind of mistake they were likely to make.

And where better to hide a top-secret criminal nightclub than in a spot so innocuous-looking?

"We're clear on the plan?" Julius asked, really a formality at this point.

We all nodded. My fingers tingled with excitement, ready to try out those immaculately sighted pistols. I held my hands still, keeping my calm with careful focus. I wasn't about to forget all my training and experience over a trip to Pittsburgh.

The elevator reached the third floor from the top and dinged. The crew had said that the Funhouse encompassed all three of the uppermost floors in the building. I straightened my back and threw back my shoulders, standing behind Julius and Garrison who did the same. I imagined that Blaze and Talon—sandwiching me between them—prepared themselves, too.

The elevator door swung open, and it took every effort for me not to drop my jaw at what lay ahead in the wide-open room before us. The men had described it to me, but somehow I still hadn't been prepared.

Julius strode out onto the entrance platform outside and paused there as we gathered around him. It was both a power move, showing he wasn't in any hurry, and an opportunity for me to adjust to my surroundings. I couldn't be more grateful for the kindness, because this place was unlike any nightclub I'd ever seen. Despite what the guys told me, I couldn't have ever imagined… *this.*

I understood where the place got its name now.

The Funhouse had windowless outer walls, but every surface between here and the roof—walls, floors, and ceilings—was made of glass. Some of it was transparent and the rest of it mirrors that bounced the artificial light back and forth and reflected it at unnerving angles. Even the elevator shaft this far up was glass. I suspected that from any point within the club, you could see every other corner of the place. You'd also see at least a few different views of yourself in those eerie mirrors.

In other words, there was no hiding up here.

Only sparse furniture scattered the glass rooms, but the pieces looked opulent—all silks and velvets, fine leather and mahogany. It was mostly placed around the far ends of the private booths so as not to interrupt the flow of light. I could see right into all those booths, of course, and about half of them were occupied right now. Some of the inhabitants had posh suits and carefully trimmed hair, others more urban clothes like us, but they all gave off a potent vibe of menace and power.

I had no doubt that these were among the upper echelon of criminals. And now an awful lot of them were watching our arrival with gazes I couldn't read.

"Our usual booth is free," Blaze remarked. As one, the crew began marching toward the place that they claimed with only their glances.

As I walked with them, my gaze flitted through the space like the light bouncing off the mirrors, taking in even more details. A handful of aerial artists dangled from knotted silks hung in various hollow columns of glass, twisting, posing, and swaying in a weird sort of dance to match the bass-heavy music that pulsed through the club. They all wore skimpy clothing that bared most of their bodies. Not just women, though—I spotted a couple of men wearing only thongs as well.

I traced the ropes up toward the ceiling high above us on the uppermost floor, and my jaw went slack a second time. There on the top floor, in an enclosure made of—what else?—solid glass, a fully grown *tiger* was prowling from side to side. Not just a nightclub but a zoo too, apparently.

We strode toward the mirrored staircase, and as I turned my head, I noticed the elevator descending, leaving a completely translucent glass case where it had been.

"It goes back to the bottom for appearances," Garrison explained with a smirk. "Can't have anything blocking the view."

My lips twitched with amusement, but I wasn't sure I wanted to show anything other than a solemn front with all these hardened criminals watching. I was an unknown quantity here, and I didn't want them pegging me for a silly girl. Other than the female dancers and some of the servers prancing through the levels from the bar at the very center of the club, I might have been the only woman in the place.

Oh, no, maybe there was one lady down there in the far corner with a couple of men, her hair cut short but her lips a stark ruby red. Still, we were clearly a rare breed.

We passed one of the female servers on our way to our booth, and she trailed her hand over Blaze's bicep and leaned in to whisper something quick in his ear. Huh. From the look on her face, she was aiming to hook up—with full knowledge of what to expect from him.

Had he slept with her before? From the playful wave one of the other servers aimed his way, he was pretty popular around here.

I'd known he was a flirt, but I hadn't realized he followed up on it with much action. Now, he tugged on a lock of the first woman's blond hair but said in a warm tone, "Not tonight. Tonight's all business."

But other nights? A spike of jealousy I hadn't been prepared for lanced through me and soured my mouth. I swallowed thickly and yanked my gaze back to our path through the club. It wasn't *my* business who he'd slept with before, especially when our relationship had never progressed to anything like that.

Julius marched first into the booth that was apparently the crew's regular one, the rest of us flanking him. A tan leather sofa stretched the length of one wall, impossibly buttery when I sank down onto it. Two matching armchairs sat at either end of it, and a glass coffee table with mahogany legs gleamed between them all.

Julius and Talon seated themselves on either side of me. Blaze flopped into one of the chairs, and Garrison stayed standing with a typically cocky air.

"Order me an Old Fashioned," he said. "I'm going to make the rounds." He arched an eyebrow at me. "Try not to get into trouble while I'm gone."

I had the urge to stick my tongue out at him, which really wouldn't have given the right impression at all. Instead, I wrinkled my nose, and he laughed.

He sauntered out of our booth and wandered to our nearest neighbors, and then the next occupied booth, and the next. From the nods and words exchanged, it looked like everyone was aware of who he was. His demeanor shifted slightly as he approached each group, subtly reflecting their pre-existing energy. I watched his chameleon-like skills with a flicker of admiration.

I'd never seen him so fully at work before. He was masterful.

Not all of his friendly overtures seemed to be met with equal enthusiasm. I noticed a couple of the men whose groups he approached tense up slightly as the others spoke to him, and made a mental note to remember them later.

A different server sashayed into our booth and asked for our drink orders. "A whiskey highball," I said, picking the low-alcohol cocktail I usually turned to on missions so I could sip it without being worried that it'd go too much to my head. "Extra ginger ale."

"Just club soda and lime for me," Julius said.

The server giggled. "Right, you're the teetotaler."

Talon asked for a beer and Blaze a marguerita, putting in Garrison's order as well. As the server headed out, I glanced at Julius. "You don't drink."

He lifted his shoulders slightly. "I have on occasion in the past, but only very rarely since I started the crew. You never know when you're going to need a totally clear head."

"And Julius is the one who makes sure we all keep *our* heads attached," Blaze said with a chuckle.

"Exactly," Julius said without any humor of his own. "I won't risk the crew's lives by being in any way mentally compromised."

It made sense, I supposed. Because he was the one who led most of the missions, he felt responsible for seeing them through entirely. And maybe even in between missions, he wanted to be on guard for unexpected problems. I didn't think drinking was an irresponsible decision, especially when we needed beverages in front of us to hold our cover, but I understood why Julius wouldn't do it.

The server came back in just a few minutes and set out our glasses in front of us. Remembering Julius's words, I only took the smallest sip from mine, rolling the tangy liquid around in my mouth.

As the woman left, Garrison strolled back in and plucked his Old Fashioned off the table before sinking into the free chair. I watched him take a small swallow. Was that really his drink of choice, or was it part of a persona he was putting on even now? I guessed any face you wanted to show to the criminal underworld, you had to keep it up every second you were in this place.

We relaxed back into our seats as if we were only there to enjoy the atmosphere. "Observations?" Julius asked Garrison.

Garrison cradled his drink against his chest and cocked his head. "I'd say there are four teams currently here who are aware of the bounty and seriously considering pursuing it, if not already working on finding our usual base of operations. The Chicago Turks, the Burning Whips, the Jackhammers, and the Angel's Fiends." He surreptitiously pointed out the groups as he spoke—one on the top floor near the tiger's enclosure, two on the second floor with us, and one down by the elevator platform. Among them were the groups I'd noticed getting edgy at his arrival.

"I thought we had pretty good relations with at least the Turks and the Fiends," he added. "It must be an awfully big pot for them to be jeopardizing that."

Talon hummed darkly. "They aren't friends if they're willing to betray us."

"How can you be sure?" I asked.

Garrison made a vague gesture and took another gulp of his drink. "I read it in the way they looked at me and talked to me. The tension was obvious, as much as they tried to hide it. They were startled to see us here, so between that lack of preparation and the nature of the Funhouse, I doubt they'll make any move on us."

I glanced at the glass floor beneath my feet and realized how impossible an attack would be in this place, at least one that hadn't been meticulously planned. One misplaced shot and you could easily damage the entire structure of this part of the building, shattering the floor beneath you or the ceiling over your head as well as destroying your target. Peace was enforced through a sense of mutually assured destruction.

But we were going to rise above that mutual assurance. Julius was the most meticulous man I'd ever met, and I knew he'd considered every possibility. The statement he meant to make would be a powerful one as long as we survived it.

"Just those four groups?" Julius asked.

Garrison shrugged. "As far as I can tell. The others might have hid it better, but that'd mean they've developed much better poker faces since the last time I met them."

"Four is plenty." The crew's commander scanned the club. I could practically see the final pieces lining up in his head. "Talon, you deal with the Turks up top. Dess, you take the Jackhammers down below. I'll handle the two on our level, although feel free to jump in if either of you finishes with your targets before I do. We need them all down ASAP, before they have a moment to *think* about striking back."

I nodded, enjoying the deeper thrum of authority that'd come into his voice. It was only the three of us doing the shooting for this operation—the three of us who were the most skilled. Blaze and Garrison were proficient enough to handle backup during a regular mission, but this one required too careful a touch.

They were contributing in their own ways, of course—Garrison with his rounds and Blaze now, glancing at his phone and watching the movements of the employees around the club. "Ready on your signal," Julius said to him.

"Just a few minutes," Blaze murmured.

We needed to time our attack perfectly. No servers or dancers could be in the way, but Blaze had said they followed obvious patterns. If we worked around their circuits of the room, we'd get a small opening to make our move without hurting any innocent bystanders.

I casually adjusted my visible gun, refamiliarizing myself with its exact position. We drank from our glasses and exchanged a few random remarks that passed through my mind without sticking. I was too focused on the task ahead, braced for the moment when Blaze would say—

"Now," the hacker murmured, standing.

Julius, Talon, and I leapt to our feet and sprang forward. Without looking back, I knew Blaze and Garrison would make their way to the elevator shaft while we did the dirty work.

Talon charged up the staircase, and I flew down it, dropping to grab my second gun from my boot as I went. My momentum whipped back my hair.

All my attention narrowed down to the squad of five men

lounging in the booth Garrison had indicated. I noted the carefully sculpted scruff on their jaws, the leather jackets that hung off their bulky forms, the bottle of brandy someone had bought now empty on the table between their glasses. The twitch of their heads toward me as they registered the sudden action around them—

But all that was in fleeting seconds, the space of a heartbeat or two. Then I was diving into their midst, pulling the triggers with my two guns aiming in separate directions.

We'd picked the guns and ammunition for both accuracy and more moderate power. Bullets that tore straight through bodies with enough force to crack the glass behind them would have screwed us over too. These would embed themselves in our targets' flesh and lodge there as the blood flowed out around them.

But I still had to aim well. Hit the fleshy parts that offered plenty of blood flow while also proving instantly fatal. We still wanted impact, but we couldn't afford any flailing around as the life drained out of them. Not when these targets were such skilled criminals themselves, equally armed and dangerous.

I shot one man three times in the chest in quick succession—above and below his heart to puncture the aortas and then right into the heart itself. As his body keeled over, blood gushed over the table and across the floor. At the same time, I shot one of his colleagues in the throat. More blood spouted out of his mouth and neck as he tumbled over.

Their three companions were leaping up with noises of shock. Those noises died as I buried bullets in two of their throats too. The fifth guy, the one who'd be our survivor to return to his larger organization and everyone they knew to spread the word, I simply shot in both arms, rendering them temporarily useless. He wasn't going to be tossing back any more drinks—or aiming his own weapons at us.

I whirled and dashed back up the stairs without a second's hesitation. Julius had already taken down three of the four men in his first group. He was just shooting the second guy in the other booth. I blasted the third and fourth in the skull, one in the front and one in the back thanks to the way they were standing. The fifth cringed and spluttered on the floor as Julius kicked his gun out of his hand.

Exhilaration rushed through me. I'd never had a job quite like this, and it felt *good* to stretch my skills again, to test the limits of what I was capable of. Especially next to men who were equally capable.

We were a pretty fucking fantastic team.

Speaking of capable men—

My gaze leapt to Talon on the floor above us. He was just plunging his knife into the chest of one of the men among his targets, two already lying dead from gunshot wounds, another's throat slit.

Talon launched himself at the fifth, who was groping for a weapon, and sliced that hand neatly off through the forearm. He whipped the severed limb into the tiger's enclosure, where the predator pounced on it with a pleased growl. Then he hurtled down the stairs to join us.

As Talon and I moved to the elevator shaft where Blaze and Garrison were already waiting, Julius held up his hands.

"We're done here," he shouted, his voice ringing through the entire club. Some of the other patrons had frozen, flattening themselves against the furniture defensively; others were groping for their own weapons.

Julius continued quickly, wanting to get his message out before we faced any backlash—if anyone dared. "We don't want to kill anyone who doesn't deserve to die. Remember what'll happen if you fire a shot and it goes badly. Well, we won't be the only ones who fall." He gestured to the glass surfaces around us. "This was just a reminder of the consequences if you mess with the Chaos Crew. Leave us be, and we'll leave you be too."

That sentence was the signal to depart. I hooked my rappelling line onto the elevator cable in sync with the men. With a collective breath, we dove into the abyss below, soaring down the shaft out of the Funhouse.

Not a single shot rang out after us.

NINETEEN

Decima

EVERYONE'S SPIRITS lifted the next morning when Blaze said the magic words that made our entire risky gambit worth it. "Most of the concerning activity that I noticed in the city has stopped. It seems like the groups who were after the bounty have backed off. We're in the clear to keep up our search."

I knew that we needed to accept the wins where we found them, so I didn't bother dwelling on the lack of information that search had brought us so far. We'd found a few puzzle pieces, and they would lead us to more clues. They had to. With the crew at my side, I already had one major advantage.

I strode to the side of the kitchen where Garrison was cooking bacon and Talon pouring one of his bottles of… something into a frosted mug. I looked down at it, and the immediate revulsion that rose in my chest was unprecedented. "What even *is* that?" I asked, leaning closer to him.

"Kombucha," he said, swirling it around and taking a long gulp before pushing it toward me. "Do you want to try it?"

The offer came genuinely, and I reached for the mug that he

extended, my fingers brushing across his as I took the mug. The contact of our hands sent a jolt of heat through my chest, and I ran my tongue over my teeth to keep the feelings at bay. His strong fingers brought back *plenty* of memories.

I lifted the glass mug to my lips and took a small sip, coughing and wrinkling my nose the moment the sour flavor registered.

"You like this?" I asked, scanning the counter for a less repulsive drink to wipe away the horrendous taste that plagued my tongue.

Talon shrugged, taking another gulp. "It's an acquired taste."

Garrison chipped in. "Don't let him fool you. Only he likes that battery acid."

"Thanks for the warning," I said, rolling my eyes and looking over Garrison's shoulder at the crispy bacon that he was now pulling from the pan. When he'd placed the last piece on his plate, I reached around him and grabbed one, plopping it in my mouth with a small smile before he could stop me.

Garrison didn't seem bothered as he looked over and met my eyes, his filled with just as much amusement as mine had been. I had the sense that reaction was genuine too. No masks or barriers, just Garrison and his genuine self. The realization sent an appreciative tingle over my skin.

I didn't think he could ever fathom how much that single look meant to me.

I poured my usual bowl of cereal and ambled over to the dining table. Talon had just sat down, and Julius was standing by one of the other chairs with his mug of coffee. As I slipped past him, I allowed my arm to brush his chest. His back straightened at my touch, and his hand came to rest on my hip just for a second to guide me past him.

Such a gentle gesture, but it sparked a flame of its own. I didn't look back at him as I took my seat, still chewing on my stolen piece of bacon.

"Do you want hot chocolate, Dess?" Garrison hollered across the kitchen.

I laughed. "Of course, I do."

A small, almost imperceptible smile pulled to Julius's face as he nodded at something in his own mind. I wondered what was on the agenda for the day, but before I could ask, Talon looked at Julius. "Are we still planning on haggling with that weapons supplier today?"

Julius exhaled slowly. "Well, it sounds as though sudden assassination should no longer be a major concern. And our stash does need a top-up after last night. I think it's better if it's just the two of us, though. Dess's former captor will still have his own people looking for her, and there's no reason for her to leave the apartment and risk being seen for this."

"*I* should come," Garrison pointed out. "You two can't haggle properly to save your lives. I'll have this guy wrapped around my finger in no time."

"I can stay here with Dess," Blaze piped up from where he was perched on the sofa with his laptop. "Happy to stand guard and protect her… even though it'll probably be the other way around if someone does come crashing in here." He grinned at me, and I had to smile back.

"That's fine with me," I said. After last night, my nerves could use a little break from the action anyway.

Garrison gulped down his bacon at a speed that could have rivaled Blaze with a plate of pasta, and the three of them headed out. I polished off the last of my cereal and went over to join the hacker on the sofa. He seemed intent on his computer even though he'd said the threat was mostly gone.

Still carrying out his own search for information to unravel my mysteries, presumably. I admired the way his intense concentration honed the lines of his handsome face, but didn't he deserve a break too?

"I'm sorry," he said before I could speak. "I still haven't turned up anything else that seems like a solid lead. The image searches will keep running, though. It could take a few more days before they've combed the entire internet."

"The app doesn't need you watching it to run those, right?" I said, nudging his laptop away from him.

He set it down on the coffee table in front of us, playful curiosity lighting in his eyes. "Do you have something else in mind that you need me for?"

"Yep. I need you to queue up another one of those *Spy Times* episodes, if you don't mind."

He laughed, exactly the response I'd been looking for, and leaned over to tap on his laptop some more. "I'd be more than happy to. Maybe I'll even let you watch two."

I raised my eyebrows. "So generous of you."

I couldn't have said exactly what it was about this show that hooked me so much. I could tell that a lot of parts of it were pretty silly, and most of the missions would have been total failures if the spy and her husband had handled them like that in real life, speaking from experience. But maybe that was why right there. It had the same kinds of scenarios and problems I was facing right now—and had faced throughout my life—but through a breezy, fun-loving sort of lens as if none of it could be that horrible.

Wouldn't it be nice if the challenges I ran into from here on could be laughed off and conquered with a few clever tools?

When the credits for the episode rolled across the screen, I stretched my arms over my head, sinking deeper into the cozy sofa and feeling more relaxed than I had in at least a couple of days. I looked over at Blaze to check whether he'd enjoyed the break too.

He wasn't looking at the TV but at me, but he did look happy. A soft smile played on his lips, and there was a light in his bright brown eyes that wasn't quite like any I'd noticed before. It brought a flutter into my chest.

He was a striking man, after all.

"What are you so pleased about?" I asked, aiming for a teasing tone but really wanting to know underneath.

Blaze's smile widened slightly, the corners of his eyes crinkling to match it. "I like seeing you really relax. I know you haven't gotten to very often. And I'm glad that I can help you do that."

The previous flutter turned into a swell of affection. He'd spoken simply but honestly, and I wasn't used to having people care about my contentment that much. I knew the other men in the crew would fight for me, but Blaze was the one who'd gone out of his way to bring joy into my life.

"I appreciate it," I said, a husky note creeping into my voice without my meaning it to. I had the urge to reach over and stroke my fingers over the light red stubble that gave his otherwise boyish face a more rugged look that was undeniably appealing.

Before I could decide whether to follow that urge, Blaze's smile slanted. He glanced at his hands and then at me again. "I don't want you to take that the wrong way. I really am glad to help you just as a friend. I know when I came on too strong before, it made you really uncomfortable—I definitely wouldn't push for anything you're not into."

My pulse stuttered, remembering the moment when I'd rammed him against the safe house apartment's kitchen counter in what'd felt like self-defense. The memory made my throat constrict now, but mostly because I knew he hadn't deserved that level of aggression. "Blaze…"

He held up his hands. "Really, it's okay. I can see that you've got more of that kind of connection with the other guys, and maybe something's even happened with them already, and that's okay. It's great that you're getting what you need with someone. I'd never assume it has to be me. I just want you to know that I'm here for you too, in whatever ways you need me."

My throat closed up completely. I couldn't imagine ever voicing all of my feelings the way he had just laid them bare before me. It was hard to picture any of the other men expressing themselves so plainly either. He didn't hide like Garrison or avoid feeling like Talon.

Blaze knew himself, and he didn't hesitate to share who he was. But at the same time, he wasn't forceful, and he didn't blame me for anything. He took responsibility for how he felt without pressuring me for even an ounce more than I wanted to offer. As his words sank in, they dissolved any lingering hesitation I might have felt about his interest in me.

Did he really think I wasn't attracted to him at all? I guessed my reaction in the safe house had driven the idea home too forcefully for him to notice any indications I might have given off since.

I couldn't stand the thought of him going on thinking that I was somehow *repulsed* by him when it was so far from the truth.

I grappled with my words for a few seconds before I managed to speak. “You should know—it was never *you* I had a problem with. Not really. There’s just… I have kind of an instinctive response to people getting flirty or acting sweet in a specific way. I had… a really bad experience with a seduction that started like that.”

Even as I said the words, a realization clicked together in my head as it never had before. I didn’t like that my reactions were so off-kilter to what was normal, but it was useful at the same time. I’d never had to worry that I’d be led astray by a man putting the moves on me in the middle of an assignment.

Which was very convenient for my handlers too, wasn’t it? And it was a pretty big coincidence that the man who’d warped his sweet words and caresses into something horrifying had just happened to approach me the very first time Noelle had given me a few hours of freedom to enjoy myself at that dance club. I’d been a clueless fourteen-year-old, and he’d homed right in on me… And Noelle hadn’t even seemed *that* surprised when I’d told her afterward what had happened.

Had she set the whole thing up? Maybe even *paid* that man to treat me that way, to force himself on me—

Inwardly, I cringed away from the memory. But it made a sick kind of sense. I’d just been noticing my physical urges, starting to daydream about the romances and sexual encounters that managed to seep into the sidelines of the movies I was allowed to watch. Scarring me like that had been a surefire way to prevent those sorts of feelings from compromising me in the field.

My anger toward the household and whoever had brought me into it flared with an even sharper edge than before.

The insinuation of my words clearly hadn’t been lost on Blaze. His own eyes flashed with fury. “Someone hurt you.”

“It doesn’t matter now,” I said. “It was almost ten years ago.”

“Ten years is nothing.” He reached for his laptop. “Tell me everything you remember about him. I’ll find him, and I’ll burn his whole fucking life down.”

The vehemence in his voice told me he meant it. He might be the kindest of the men in the crew, but that didn’t mean he couldn’t be fierce when he needed to be. That brutal protectiveness only increased the draw I felt toward him.

"You can't," I said. "I got free after it was over, and I killed him. He's gone." And the woman who might or might not have orchestrated the whole thing was dead too. It was all behind me except in the marks left on my soul. "I don't even really want to talk about it. I'd rather leave the past in the past."

Blaze let out a growl that electrified me, as if he wished he could raise the predator from the dead just to murder him all over again. But he took a deep breath and nodded. "Understood. I'm sorry."

"You don't have to apologize," I said quickly. "I like that you'd want to defend me. I—" I hesitated and then barreled onward. "I *am* attracted to you. I'm just not sure…"

I had the feeling if I asked him to turn on his charms again, my body would react instinctively no matter what my mind wanted. But it was hard to picture him putting on the same domineering front the other men either came by naturally or could pretend so easily, like Garrison. I didn't know if that was how I'd want Blaze anyway.

Resolve gripped me. I gave Blaze a gentle push into the back of the sofa and straddled him in one swift movement. He stared up at me, his pupils dilating with obvious hunger. "Dess?"

A sly smile curved my lips. "Maybe it'll work out if *I'm* the one doing the seducing. We could at least see how it goes."

He kept his hands carefully at his sides, but a grin of his own took his face from handsome to stunning. "I've always been a fan of experimentation."

Those words sent a heady quiver right down to my sex. Licking my lips, I leaned over him and looped my arms loosely around his neck. He smelled tantalizing too, with a crisply fresh cologne that reminded me of the ocean.

He was letting me take the lead, waiting to see what I'd take from him. I figured I'd start by stealing a kiss.

I dipped my head so my lips brushed his. Blaze kissed me back, but gently, cautiously, still giving me room to decide how far I wanted to go. Only when I melded my mouth to his more emphatically did he let out a rough noise and let his tongue flick out to play with mine.

I wanted more—I wanted his hands all over me. The thought of directing him to my exact desires sent a thrill racing through my veins.

Tipping back just enough to speak, I murmured against his lips. "Take my shirt off."

He complied without hesitation, a hotter spark dancing in his eyes now. His hands weren't the only thing I wanted on me.

"Kiss my neck," I added, tilting my head to the side to give him easier access. "Until I moan."

"My pleasure," Blaze murmured, and adjusted me against him so that he could bring his mouth to that sensitive slope of skin. His hands slid up and down my bare sides as he worked over my neck with lips and tongue and nips of his teeth.

I was gasping in less than a minute. It wasn't much longer before another skillful swipe of his tongue sent such a giddy surge of need through me that a moan spilled from my lips.

Blaze eased back and winked at me. "Mission accomplished. What next, my lady?"

I grasped the base of his shirt and tugged it upward. "This definitely needs to come off too."

He raised his arms so I could peel the garment off him. I sat there for a moment on his lap, running my eyes and my hands over the toned planes of his torso. He was the leanest of the Chaos Crew's men, but strength emanated from every one of those wiry muscles. I could tell he'd worked hard to build that trimly sculpted physique.

"Like what you see?" he teased playfully, desire burning in his gaze.

"Oh, yes. Very much." I bent forward to claim another kiss, drawing this one out until we were both breathless. My nipples grazed his chest through the fabric of my bra and immediately pebbled.

"My breasts would appreciate your attention," I instructed.

Blaze chuckled eagerly and trailed his fingers up my back to unhook my bra. Then he cupped both my breasts with his slender fingers, his nimble thumbs stroking along the curve and rolling my nipples in tandem. The second time, he pressed a little harder with the perfect flick at the end, jolting another gasp out of me. He clearly knew *exactly* what he was doing.

I arched into him, sucking in a breath as my pussy ground against his groin where his cock pressed rigidly behind the fly of his slacks. A faint groan reverberated out of Blaze in turn, but he kept to his orders, massaging my breasts and alternating between pinching and stroking the nipples until I was rocking against him with fraying control.

I traced a finger down his abs to the waist of his pants. "I need more."

"Fuck, yes." He teased his lips along my jaw. "Tell me exactly what you want, Dess."

"Pants off," I mumbled. "Both of us. *Now*."

With a rough chuckle, he squirmed out of his own slacks with a little help from my grasping fingers and then lifted me over him to yank down my sweats. As I stood there with my feet braced on the sofa and his face level with my pussy, a deeper, hotter urge came over me.

"Kiss me," I demanded. "Right—right here."

I brushed my fingers over my panties, and a grin of pure delight sprang to Blaze's face. "It would be an honor," he said, wetting his lips, and pulled my panties down too.

He gripped my thighs and swept his tongue over all of me, from my clit down to my channel. A whimper tumbled out of me at the rush of bliss. But it was only just getting started.

Blaze devoured me, suckling my clit and then plunging his tongue right inside me. His hands squeezed my thighs and slid to my ass. He spread me a little wider, but I barely wobbled in his firm grasp.

"That's right," he whispered against me. "So fucking delicious. I could do this for weeks."

I tipped back my head, my fingers curling into the fine strands of his hair. His tongue was both hard and soft where it needed to be, flicking small circles around me teasingly before dipping inside again, conjuring thrilling quivers through my entire being. My hips swayed toward him, still steadied by his hold. With a pleased hum that reverberated into my pussy, he brought me to the trembling edge of release, eased back just slightly, then repeated the torture all over again.

An ache spread between my thighs, the hunger to be filled more than his tongue could manage. I grasped his hair tighter, whimpering and gasping before I managed to speak.

"Blaze, I want you inside of me."

I didn't have to ask twice. He drew back, licking my slickness off his mouth with a satisfied glance at me, and grabbed a condom packet out of the pocket of his discarded slacks beside me. "Never hurts to be prepared," he said with a quirk of his eyebrows, but his tone was all heat.

The second he'd rolled it over his cock, I sank down and pulled at him so he sprawled over me on the sofa. I wanted him on top of me now, driving us toward our climaxes.

The soft kiss he offered me and the tender way he slid inside me didn't set off any alarm bells now. He was giving me exactly what I'd asked for. I was still in control.

Maybe someday I'd be able to enjoy sex like this without having to call all the shots. Eventually my body had to catch on to the fact that not every man who was gentle with me wanted to hurt me, right?

Blaze dappled kisses across my cheeks, jaw, and neck, bracing himself with one hand and stroking my breasts with the other. His hips pumped his cock in and out of me, deeper and deeper with every thrust. I raised my knees on either side of him automatically and cried out when he hit an even more sensitive spot inside me. My hand came up to clutch his shoulder as if I needed to hold him here with me to make sure he'd stay.

Our gazes locked for a second, nothing but passion and awe in his eyes. They started to haze as his thrusts sped up, and I knew his release was near. I rocked my hips up to meet him, chasing my own. So close—so fucking close—

He slammed into me, and his lips parted with a stuttered groan. We tumbled over the edge together, me quaking against him, his cock pulsing inside me. I clung to him, holding him close to me as the afterglow rolled over my body.

After a minute, Blaze tipped himself into a sitting position, pulling me onto his lap with him. He beamed at me, and my chest filled with the joy of the moment—both the physical release and the fact that I'd found a way to connect with this amazing man too.

I was just about to reach for my clothes when the door to the apartment swung open, and the rest of the crew strode in, stopping with a jerk when they saw us in our naked embrace.

TWENTY

Decima

ALL THREE OF the men now staring at me and Blaze had seen me in some state of undress before. I probably would only have felt a little awkward at them walking in not expecting the provocative sight if those gazes hadn't looked not just startled but also, on at least two of them, angry.

"What the fuck is this?" Garrison snapped, taking a couple of steps closer and then stopping with a grimace. His face had flushed red.

I grabbed my shirt and pulled it on, not bothering with my bra for the moment. Blaze scrambled for his boxers and slacks.

"I'd think it's pretty obvious," I said to Garrison, a little irritation creeping into my tone at the tone he'd taken with *me*. "We didn't know you'd be back so soon, or we'd have taken this somewhere more private." I wriggled into my sweatpants as quickly as I could, feeling more composed once all my own private bits were no longer on display.

Garrison's furious gaze whipped from me to Blaze and back again. "And that would have made it better—if you'd hidden it and pretended nothing was going on?"

I opened my mouth and closed it again, not just irritated but confused now. Why the hell was he so angry anyway? It definitely didn't seem to be just about getting unexpectedly flashed.

And Julius looked pissed too, in his own way. His stance was as cool and commanding as always, but his jaw had clenched and something in his deep blue eyes had hardened in a way I wasn't used to, at least not when they were aimed at me.

"What were you trying to accomplish with this?" he demanded, looming over me.

I stared at him, now utterly bewildered. "The usual things someone wants to accomplish when they hook up with someone? Was there a rule no one told me about that Blaze is off-limits or something?"

If so, *he* definitely didn't seem to know about it. He was standing there a few feet away from me, just in his slacks, looking tense but uncertain. I didn't think he was totally sure what was going on here either.

"I think you know that's not the point," Julius said, his voice unshakably firm, and I started to get pissed off too.

"I obviously don't," I shot back, folding my arms over my chest. "You didn't seem to have any problem with me sleeping with you and Talon, so I have no idea why getting it on with someone else in the crew would be such a big deal."

Somehow his jaw clenched even tighter, but he held himself with his typical restraint. I couldn't say the same for Garrison.

The younger man's eyes flickered from furious to absolutely enraged. "You fucked the two of *them* too?" he snarled. "And you don't think you have any explaining to do here?"

Blaze made a sweeping motion with his hands. "Let's all chill out for a second and have a reasonable conversation. There's obviously been some miscommunication somewhere."

"No fucking kidding," Garrison retorted.

Julius appeared to simmer down just slightly, but his voice was still taut. "I realize you haven't had a whole lot of experience outside of your missions, Decima, but I would have thought you had some concept of the fact that people generally inform their partners if they're seeing other people."

I blinked at the bunch of them, the pieces slowly connecting in my head. Was that all they were pissed off about? I frowned.

"I mean… I thought we were all already partners. Isn't that what you've been saying, about me being part of the crew? I'm attracted to all of you. You seem to be attracted to me. I didn't think hooking up would be that big a deal. It's not like we made any epic commitments —it's not like we were even going on dates or whatever. It was just sex."

"Just sex," Garrison repeated, rolling his eyes skyward.

"Yes," I shot back. "Just sex. Simple physical gratification. If any of you wanted more than that from me, none of you bothered to mention it. I'm not sure why I'm the only one at fault here when it seems like I'm the only one who actually was clear about what I wanted instead of keeping it a secret that I expected more."

I searched all their faces, even Talon's, who'd stayed silent through the conversation so far. I couldn't read his impassive expression at all, but that was pretty normal. He simply watched the conversation with a slightly stiffened stance as if he'd rather not have been there at all. Wonderful.

Blaze glanced at me. "I didn't realize—I figured if anything had happened with the other guys, you'd have talked about the fact that it wasn't just them. I'm not blaming you, but lack of exclusivity *is* usually the kind of thing people assume will come up."

"We're not usual people, are we?" I demanded.

Julius cleared his throat. "Are you really trying to say that you had no idea this would be an issue?"

"Yes! You're all so close with each other—you share so many things —I didn't think you'd suddenly get all possessive and decide you owned me just because we got off together." I scowled, my frustration growing. "It's not like I've been going around picking up random guys off the street."

Garrison snorted. "Thank God for that."

I glowered at him. "I wouldn't *want* to do that. For fuck's sake. Did you go around announcing that we'd slept together to the rest of the guys?" My gaze jerked to Julius. "Did you?" And then Talon. "Or you? Seems like no. Apparently it wasn't important enough for you to bring it up, so it doesn't make any sense to me that I should have known I had to."

Blaze reached over to give my arm a quick reassuring squeeze. "She does have a point. She didn't hide this from any of us. It just… never came up."

A rush of renewed affection for him washed through me. I'd have kissed him if I hadn't suspected that'd cause even more explosions around here.

Julius rubbed his forehead as if he had a headache. "We didn't know we needed to bring it up."

"And you did hide it," Garrison added. "Lying by omission is still lying."

"I never once lied," I spat, poking a finger at his chest. "You never asked if I was with anyone else, and if you had—if any of you had—I would have told you. By that same logic, you lied to your friends by not telling them that we had sex. I don't know what you're all so offended about. Is it so horrible that I was with other people you supposedly like and respect?"

For a second, none of them spoke. It appeared they couldn't fully put into words what *their* problem with the situation was.

I wanted to feel bad for whatever hurt I'd caused them, and in a way, I did. But I hadn't done anything in which they hadn't actively participated. I'd never broken my word with any of them, and I didn't understand why they were blowing up about this. I wasn't going to stand here and let myself be lambasted for doing nothing wrong.

"If we knew—if I knew—that this wasn't exclusive, I may have handled the situation differently," Garrison said finally.

I looked at Julius. "What about you?" Then I moved my eyes to Talon. "Or you?"

Neither answered outwardly, and I knew it was a different story for them. They'd taken me together, and it had never been exclusive for Julius. I'd never given the impression that it was. He should have been the least surprised out of all of them, but he still reacted as if I'd done something completely shocking.

"I don't know," Julius replied. "But that's why it'd have been good to have the information."

Talon only shook his head, refusing to verbally respond. Maybe he needed to gather his thoughts first, or maybe it simply wouldn't have mattered to him at all.

I sighed. "Fine. Whatever. You all know now. I find you all appealing, and I'd happily hook up with any of you again, and I don't see what's wrong with that. I'm sure as hell not going to let you force me into a box where someone else is telling me what I'm allowed to think and feel like my whole life before. I don't belong to any of you. I don't belong to *anyone*. I choose who I'm with and when. If you're up for it or not, that's the only part that's up to you. Period."

That was all I had left to say. I grabbed my bra off the couch and pulled it on without totally removing my shirt in a few hasty movements. Meanwhile, the men all eyed each other.

"I think we should discuss this amongst ourselves," Julius said in a definitive tone. "Just the four of us."

He motioned to the others, and they fell in line with him as he stalked to the stairs that led to the rooftop deck. I watched the door shut behind them with a horrible sinking sensation in my gut.

I still didn't see what crime I'd supposedly committed, but if they decided I'd misled them anyway… What if I'd screwed up the good thing I'd found here? The *only* good thing I'd had in my entire life? The way Julius had talked, it was like I wasn't even a member of the crew, only a bystander who'd thrown them off course.

I sucked my lower lip under my teeth and worried at it for a moment before I caught myself and stopped. Instead, I flopped down on the couch and pushed my hands back over my hair.

What were they talking about up there? What were they saying about *me*?

Would they even want me around after this, let alone want to keep helping me?

I hadn't done this out of spite or any intention to hurt them. I'd wanted to be *closer* to them. Because I trusted them. Because I enjoyed their company. Why couldn't they see it that way?

A loud ping filled the room, and I sat up straighter. It'd come from

Blaze's laptop, still standing open on the coffee table from when he'd gotten it to stream *Spy Times*. The screen had woken up, now showing a red alert box.

I leaned closer and saw it'd brought up a photograph. The alert contained the words *EXACT MATCH*.

And it was. The photograph showed a dimpled white wall with the bisected teardrop symbol etched into it, exactly as it'd looked when we'd encountered it before. My hand rose to scratch at the back of my neck instinctively.

Where was this picture from? I tapped on the window it'd appeared in and spotted a geolocation at the bottom. My mind absorbed the coordinates in an instant. That was nearby—right here in this city.

A cab could take me there in less than an hour. Julius had shown me how to surreptitiously leave the apartment building a couple of days ago, so I could handle that on my own. I could check out this lead and maybe even get back before the men even finished their conversation.

Or should I interrupt that conversation and fill them in?

I wavered for several seconds, my stomach twisting, and then strode to the door. I didn't even know if they'd want to continue this quest that was really for my benefit. I could handle this one part of the investigation on my own. It was probably better if they had more time to simmer down anyway.

I slipped out the door and hurried down the hall, my heart starting to thump harder. In less than an hour, I might have more answers about who I actually was—or at least who had stolen me from the life I'd been meant to have.

TWENTY-ONE

Talon

"SHE FUCKED ALL OF US, and you don't have a problem with it?" Garrison was griping at Blaze. "Because in all the years I've known you, I never thought you'd be into swinging like that."

He'd been going off on Blaze since the moment we'd reached the rooftop deck, but Julius and I needed a moment to process. I stood back, leaning against the wall and thinking about the signs that I'd noticed and written off as something insignificant. Was Julius thinking the same?

"She's allowed to make her own decisions. If it bothers you that much, don't sleep with her again," Blaze said, stating it as if it was the most obvious solution to the problem. And I supposed it was, even if the thought of not sleeping with her again sent a twinge of loss through me that clashed with the flare of jealousy when I remembered seeing her tangled up in the other man's embrace.

Julius stepped forward, and the two of them fell silent. "How long has this been going on?" he asked in a no-nonsense tone.

Blaze gazed steadily back at him. "Today was the first time we ever hooked up—or did anything remotely close to hooking up. You saw how she reacted to me the first time I got flirty with her." He paused, and a hint of a smile curled his lips despite the situation, one so pleased it provoked a renewed jab of possessiveness in my chest. "We got that all sorted out."

"Wonderful," Garrison groused, and turned to Julius. "It was only once for me too—that we slept together. The evening before the L.A. job. We fucked up here while the rest of you were out doing prep work."

He spoke callously, but I couldn't help noticing that he didn't clarify the way Blaze had about interactions that fell short of "fucking." He'd been the most obviously upset out of the four of us. Just how entangled had the two of them gotten?

At the same time, my mind was doing its own simple calculations. Unless Julius had welcomed Dess into his bed sometime before our threesome, which it certainly hadn't seemed like in the moment, I was the only one who'd been with her *before* we'd known who she actually was. I'd been the first.

Should I feel triumphant about that fact? I didn't really. The brief flickers of jealousy had faded, and now I only felt a dull discomfort when I thought about Dess waiting downstairs, shut out of our discussion despite how much it involved her.

She hadn't committed a cardinal sin. She hadn't betrayed any of us, not really. Our feelings were our own to deal with, weren't they?

Maybe I only thought that because I rarely had much of any feelings to do anything about, but I didn't like remembering the frustration and pain that'd shown so clearly on her face when Julius and Garrison had chided her in their own ways—and when we'd left her behind.

"What about you and Talon?" Garrison asked, his narrowed eyes flicking between us.

"Also once, on the way back from the convention center," Julius said. "It sounds like this hasn't been an ongoing situation then. She's just… given each of us a try."

I couldn't tell how he felt about that idea, but the need to correct his mistaken assumption prickled at me, alongside Garrison's earlier remark about lies of omission. I wasn't sure it'd make a difference, but I wasn't going to leave our boss with the wrong information.

"Actually," I said brusquely, "she and I also ended up getting together once before we found out about her real identity."

Blaze's eyebrows shot up in a surprised reaction that might have offended me if he didn't have way more of a reputation as a ladies' man than I'd ever possessed.

Garrison's eyes only narrowed further. "You got it on with her when we weren't even sure if she was the enemy?"

I frowned at him. "She wasn't, and I didn't compromise the crew in any way."

"Why didn't you say anything?" he demanded.

I gave him an even stare. "Why should I have? I didn't see how it was anyone else's business. It didn't affect the crew."

"Yes, of course you'd see it that way."

"Hey," Blaze broke in. "I didn't hear *you* announcing your involvement with her from the rooftops—even though that's apparently where it happened."

"Because I thought it was just me," Garrison retorted, and sighed. "Which obviously we all did. Well, except you two, it seems." He studied me and Julius in an evaluating way I didn't totally like.

"How we conduct our own private business isn't any of your concern either," Julius replied.

Garrison threw his hands toward the sky. "It isn't just private business anymore, is it? Look at us! We were thinking of bringing her into the crew permanently, and she has us at each other's throats. How can we trust someone who'd create this much turmoil?"

I didn't think Garrison trusted much of anyone anyway. But Julius stirred on his feet with unusual restlessness. "That is a point that's weighing on my mind."

Even Blaze was silent for a moment. The discomfort inside me congealed into a heavier ache.

Dess hadn't done any of this intentionally. From her reaction, she hadn't understood that what she'd done might bother us at all. She hadn't liked that she'd upset us—I'd been able to see that much in her face—but she simply hadn't viewed the situation the same way we had.

Some core part of me resonated with understanding and sympathy. How many times throughout my life had people gotten pissed off at me for not feeling the "right" way or as much as they thought I should? Teachers prodding me with concerned questions, my fellow soldiers joking that I should be sent to a shrink, friends and lovers from all the way back to my early teens shouting at me or turning their backs on me because I didn't perform to expectations. I'd always wished they could just accept that I simply didn't feel much of anything.

The crew had been the one group where that didn't matter. But they didn't seem to be able to extend that same recognition of our differences to Dess. After the brainwashing she'd been through, she had even more of an excuse to look at the world differently than I did, so why the hell were they demanding she fit their idea of a "correct" intimate relationship?

The strange thing was, I *did* feel something now. That ache, and a heat that pulsed from it with the determination to defend her. She'd woken up more emotion in me than I'd known I was capable of. Even if that still wasn't much, it showed she was something special. She deserved some kind of recognition. Or at least respect.

My brothers-in-arms had started sniping at each other again while I'd been lost in thought. "She's fucked up everything," Garrison muttered. "And we *all* let that happen." He shot an accusing glance at Blaze.

"Including you," Julius said darkly.

My fingers curled into my palms. This was my crew. They had my absolute loyalty, and I'd have killed a hundred men for any of them. But in this moment, I had the intense urge to knock their heads together until I could snap them out of this fit of jealousy they seemed unable to shake off.

Garrison shook his head. "We shouldn't be fighting with each other anyway when it was Dess who did this."

My voice erupted out of me. "Dess didn't do anything wrong.

Actually, she's totally right. She *doesn't* belong to any one of us, and we're lucky she wants all of us in whatever ways she does. She's an impressive woman who makes her own decisions, so who the hell are we to try to tell her what to do?"

The other men gaped at me, even Julius in a more subtle way than the others. I guessed I didn't often speak this much or so emphatically.

Blaze let out a low whistle that could have been teasing or approving. I shot him a quick glower before continuing.

"Frankly, after the way she's been controlled and manipulated for her whole life, it's wrong of *us* to even suggest that we have some claim on deciding how she's supposed to feel about us—or sex—or anything. I know she matters to all of us, and you know it too. What's the point in denying it? Do any of you really want to give her up just because you're not going to be the only man she turns to? We're a team in every other way. Why can't we be a team when it comes to taking care of Dess?"

I hadn't known I had quite that much frustration built up in me. Maybe it was flowing over from all the irritations I'd suppressed over the years. After the last words had burst from my mouth, a wave of exhaustion rolled over me, as if I'd scaled a skyscraper rather than making a relatively short declaration. Although for me, I supposed the latter was the more difficult act.

My colleagues seemed to be absorbing my words, each of them studying me in their own way. The animosity in the air simmered down. Blaze was the first to speak up.

"Yes. Everything Talon just said. That's exactly how I feel about it." He gave me a grateful nod.

Julius dragged in a breath. The fresh outside air swept over us with a gust of breeze, and he rubbed his close-cropped hair after the wind ruffled it. "I can see you have a point," he said finally.

Garrison's mouth had twisted. He dipped his head for a second, and I realized he looked almost… embarrassed. I wasn't sure I'd ever seen him show any kind of reaction so humble before.

"Okay," he said, still with a bit of an edge in his voice. "Maybe I went a bit overboard. I mean, it took us all by surprise, right? And *because* she's started to become... important to me, I didn't like the fact that she'd been with all of you too." He hesitated, and then his tone steadied more. "But this crew also means a hell of a lot to me, and I wouldn't be part of it if you weren't people I'd trust to treat her right."

I folded my arms over my chest and frowned at him. "We're going to be lucky if she wants anything to do with any of us after the way we just came down on her."

Blaze motioned toward the door to the stairwell. "I'd say we owe her a pretty huge apology."

Garrison followed his gesture, and his posture briefly stiffened. But then something softened in his expression. He nodded. "Right."

Julius echoed his nod. The tension seemed to be seeping out of his stance. He drew his back straighter, his usual authoritative presence filling the space. "We obviously need to keep lines of communication more open than they have been, but yes. We can start that process by going down and talking with her to clear the air. Hopefully she'll at least be willing to listen."

I followed the others down the stairs with relief coursing through me. It would all be okay in the end. We could straighten out this mess and get back to the things that mattered.

But when we emerged into the main room of the apartment, Dess had vanished. We glanced around, Julius heading over to the workout room that'd become her bedroom, Garrison poking his head past the door to the bathroom which stood ajar. As they both turned away with expressions that told me they hadn't found her, Blaze leapt toward the sofa.

He snatched up his laptop. "Oh, shit."

We all spun toward him. "What?" Julius asked.

"My image search turned up a match for that teardrop symbol," he said. "It's near here... I'll have to check exactly where... She must have gone out to take a look while we had our heads up our asses."

My gut dropped. "The pricks who want her back are still hunting for her, aren't they?"

Blaze nodded, looking miserable. "And there might be a few mercenary groups who haven't stopped looking to collect the bounty. I know she can handle herself… but she's completely on her own out there right now."

"Then we need to get to her *now*," Julius commanded, flinging open the cupboard near the front door to grab his bulletproof vest. "Gear up and move out. We're not letting her face any kind of trouble alone."

TWENTY-TWO

Decima

I ASKED the cab to drop me at an address several blocks from the geocoordinates. It wasn't the greatest part of town, a lot of the shops around me were closed up with FOR RENT or old CLOSING SALE signs hanging in the grimy front windows.

As I strode along the sidewalk, careful to keep my head down, I watched for other activity on the street, but no one much seemed to come out this way. Even in the few stores that remained open, I didn't spot any customers.

None of that detracted from my mission necessarily. The factory where we'd found the first match for the symbol had been rundown and abandoned too. But the quiet felt a little eerie. I wasn't sure I'd been in any part of the city before where there hadn't been at least a little more traffic just passing through.

The coordinates led me to a massive storage facility surrounded by a chain-link fence. I studied it from off to the side, not spotting any guards standing watch near the gate and only a few dingy looking cameras mounted on obvious posts. Several of the garage-style doors I could see had padlocks on them. Shouldn't there have been more security here if this facility was still active?

Maybe the owners were too lazy and their customers not concerned enough to hassle them about it, but I didn't like that either.

I obviously wasn't going to break open the gate and waltz in within full view of the main camera. Instead, I scaled the fence where it veered closest to one of the rows of storage lockers. In a matter of moments, I'd scrambled over the edge and was crouched on the building's flat, corrugated-metal rooftop.

I scanned the area again, taking in the aisles of matching buildings with their rows of doors and the utter stillness of the scene. In the middle of the day, no one was monitoring the gate in person, and no one was bringing stuff to or from their unit. I had no idea how normal that was, though.

Checking my phone, I determined that the exact geolocation from the image must be one of the units a few rows over at the dead end of the aisle. If I dropped down to the pavement below and walked over, I'd be boxed in once I reached it, with no easy avenue to climb to a better vantage point. Thankfully, I should be able to make my way over there across the rooftops. Most of them were connected, and those that weren't had only a narrow walkway separating them, which would make for an easy leap.

I started over, walking around one aisle and making my way along the far end of the facility toward the one I needed. The whole time, I kept searching my surroundings for other security measures.

As I came up on the one camera at the back of the facility, I slowed, preparing to figure out a way to avoid it. It was hard to tell from this distance, but it might have captured an angle that would show the unit I needed to get to.

I eased closer, careful to stay out of range for now. If I blocked the view, there was always the chance that would alert an off-site security force that something was wrong—not that it looked as if the storage company cared enough to have hired someone for constant surveillance. I might be able to duck under the camera's view with a quick roll and stay out of its sights the rest of the time…

As I drew closer, my forehead furrowed. I paused, studying the camera—and in particular its lens—more intently. There was something odd about the glass. It looked… smudged, or wet?

I edged even closer, and my pulse kicked up a notch with a surge of apprehension. Someone had sprayed a liquid on the camera's lens that'd left behind a thick film. It would be blurring the view and making any recording taken useless for identifying the figures it captured.

Normally, that would have worked in my favor. I could sashay right by and no one would be the wiser. But the film had clearly been purposefully added. And…

I knelt down and touched a droplet I'd noticed on the roof beneath it. My finger smudged the damp spot. Still wet. The substance had been sprayed on the camera *recently*.

Why would someone else have been here, in this desolate area of town, wanting to obscure the cameras on this exact afternoon? Where were they now?

None of this felt right to me. Every aspect of it was starting to scream *setup*. Someone had ensured there'd be no staff on site and obscured the camera lenses so they could get away with something awful.

After the way we'd been attacked at the meat factory, I couldn't help suspecting it was something awful they wanted to do to *me*.

This was a trap. I didn't know why the teardrop symbol was here, but the people responsible must have known about it too and realized we'd come here soon. Maybe I'd slipped up somewhere along my journey and they'd figured out I was headed this way right now.

It didn't matter which was true. The only important thing was getting out of here before that trap was sprung on me.

I turned, intent on marching to the closest spot where I could easily leap to the fence and vanish without a trace, but at the same moment, the thump of several footfalls reached my ears from the direction of the front gate. With a hitch of my heart, I ducked as close to the roof as I could get.

There was a rattling sound by the gate and a murmur of low voices. I flattened myself, braced to make a run for it as soon as I was sure I had a good opening. Then the gate swung open, and it wasn't enemies but the men I'd left back at the apartment who strode into the storage facility.

They didn't throw caution to the wind. I saw Blaze make a gesture toward the nearest camera and them all adjust their course to avoid it, and their heads swiveled to watch for any threat around them. But they marched quickly toward the aisle with the unit I'd already determined the geocoordinates pointed to with less stealth and wariness than I wished they'd used. They didn't notice me where I was crouched on the roof a few aisles away.

I straightened up and waved my arms, but they didn't glance my way again, already finished with their scan of the rooftops. They were focused on the environment at their eye level now. My chest itched with the urge to yell, but if this was a trap, that would only alert whoever was waiting to spring it that I was on to them. Shit.

Continuing to gesture in the hopes of getting the crew's attention, I darted along the roof with feet set as silently as I could manage. If I could just get in front of them instead of off to the side, they'd have to notice me. My pulse thudded through my veins.

Maybe I was wrong about the trap. Maybe there was a normal explanation for everything that'd unnerved me. I desperately hoped that was true—but I couldn't stake their lives and mine on that hope.

Why weren't they picking up on the same clues? I guessed I couldn't blame them for missing the cameras, since I hadn't spotted the oddity with them until I was up here. But coming through the front gate had been a bold move. It was as if they were in so much of a hurry that they'd set aside caution for haste. What was so urgent about this investigation?

Me, I realized with a jolt of shock. That was the only conceivable explanation. They'd obviously realized I'd come here following the alert on Blaze's computer, and they'd rushed after me. The bigger question was why exactly it'd mattered so much to them, but I could ask them that after we were all out of here safely.

They veered down the aisle they needed. I dashed faster. I was just coming up on that same aisle, preparing to start flinging pebbles at them if need be to shake them out of their intense focus on the unit ahead and judging the distance to where they were now halfway down the aisle, when a horrible screeching sound shattered my own attention.

Locker doors were flying open at the opening to the aisle—and at the far end, where we'd expected to find the symbol. At least two dozen men charged out, all of them with guns in their hands, surrounding the Chaos Crew in an instant.

In the same instant, my mind blanked with panic. I couldn't do anything but muffle a rising scream as the attackers fired. The guys threw themselves toward the nearest locked doors, ducking to the ground and rolling into the small indents of the entrances to avoid being hit. Then my instincts kicked in and launched me into action.

No one had noticed me still—my friends or their attackers. I snatched up the gun I'd brought in a concealed holster under my arm and took aim at the larger group closing in on the crew from the only direction they could make their escape.

As I fired my first shots, dropping one and then another man in quick succession with bullets to the head, someone in the crew tossed a small round object into the middle of the aisle. I braced for an explosion, but instead, smoke billowed out of it with a quavering hiss. In a matter of seconds, most of the aisle was clouded with a thick gray fog. Even from above, I could only make out the slightest impressions of the figures within it.

The men were flattening themselves into the alcoves of the locker doorways, which provided only a tiny bit more cover on top of the smoke. I couldn't tell whether they'd noticed my shooting amid what was coming from their attackers.

The attackers had halted on either edge of the expanding cloud. Several of them glanced my way and took aim, and I leapt behind a low protrusion on the roof. Bullets battered its metal surface.

More shots rang out below. Some must have been from the crew and some from their attackers aiming at them, but any sense of their direction was lost in the general blare of sound.

I scooted out from behind the protrusion with my own pistol at the ready. From that awkward angle, it was hard to aim well, but I managed to pick off a few more of the enemy before they disappeared into the edges of the fog. Apparently they'd decided it was better to tackle the crew in the midst of that than risk losing them altogether, although where they thought the men might escape to, I had no clue.

Since I could barely see them, I knew they couldn't make me out either. I eased out and scuttled over to the edge of the roof, still keeping low just in case. I had a vague sense of where the crew had been holding their ground before, but I wasn't totally sure they hadn't moved. The smoke had thickened around the spot where the bomb had burst to the point that I couldn't make them out at all.

I did catch glimpses of other forms at the edges of the fray. Whenever I got a clear enough view to be confident it wasn't one of *my* men, I took the shots I could. When I ran out of bullets, I swapped cartridges with a flick of my wrist. Gunfire continued to blare on the ground below me.

A gust of wind washed over me and cast some of the smoke even farther, thinning it on the ground. The smoke bomb must have finished spewing out the stuff, because no more rose up to thicken the cover in its place.

Now I could just make out the crew near their original positions. Garrison and Talon stood on one side, shooting relentlessly at the crowd pressing in on them. Julius crouched nearby, still pressed against the wall as he shot into the other side of the fray, and Blaze aimed his own bullets over the other man's shoulder.

They couldn't keep up their fire constantly. As I watched, Julius paused to reload, and Blaze increased his fire to stop any attackers who'd drawn too close. But then they both had to dodge back against the locker door when a hail of bullets careened toward them.

Squinting through the fog, I pointed my pistol at each attacker who got close enough to the crew to target them. I took shot after shot, counting down my bullets as I made the rest of that clip count, only taking the shots when the men got close enough to the guys. We'd only held them off this long because of the smoke, and I only had one clip left. We were still way too outnumbered.

I reloaded once more and then lost a few bullets when someone aimed their shots at me again. My own went wild as I flung myself down on the roof. I picked off that bastard, but I only managed to take down a couple more and partly injure one or two others before I was totally out. Gritting my teeth, I shoved the temporarily useless gun back into its holster.

A few of the attackers had pushed close enough to the crew to tackle them hand to hand. Talon engaged first, swinging his knife, as Garrison continued firing at the more distant people to keep them at bay. Talon wove between the two attackers unlike anyone else, but they were good, and they managed to land a few minor blows through his defenses.

It said a lot about their training, but Talon didn't even flinch. He dispatched one and then the other with well-placed stabs, taking a third man on when he charged in.

Julius gave a shout as several more attackers converged on him and Blaze. He shot one and punched another. Talon and Garrison swung around, both preparing to defend their comrades, and I spotted one last man from the group who'd come from the far end of the aisle slinking toward Talon's back through the lingering smoke.

He was already raising his knife. The boom of several more gunshots drowned out any noise his footfalls might have made.

"Talon!" I hollered, but my voice was lost in the cacophony too. The man sprinted forward with a final burst of speed, and I did the only thing I could: I lunged off the roof straight at the prick.

No one was going to get away with hurting my men.

I soared through the hazy air and smacked right into the guy, my momentum and my well-positioned tackle knocking him to the ground. I moved on instinct, relying on my years of training to guide my hands as I deflected his defensive blows and yanked the blade from his grasp.

He caught my wrists, holding the blade at bay for a long moment with shaking limbs. The flex of his arms, twice as broad as mine, nearly forced the knife into my own chest. But I put my body weight into my thrust, forcing the blade down inch-by-inch until it plunged into his throat.

He gasped and gurgled, his body going slack beneath me. I hunched down, scanning the smoke-laced air around me for more attackers. In the midst of my own struggle, the gunfire had faded away.

A few more shots rang out as the crew took on the final attackers. Those men collapsed, and for a second, relief rushed through me.

It was over. We'd taken them all down.

Then I noticed that Blaze had dropped down onto his belly. He still had his gun braced in his hands, his eyes intent on the men he'd just helped stop, but a crimson pool was spreading from beneath his stomach.

A cry of dismay broke from my mouth. As I dashed over, his head lolled to the side, and he sagged against the pavement.

TWENTY-THREE

Decima

NONE of us seemed to know what to do as Julius and Steffie patched up Blaze the best they knew how. The bullet he'd taken to his abdomen had passed through his body rather than lodging inside, and Julius had confirmed that it hadn't punctured any major organs, but the hacker was still clearly in a lot of pain. He alternated between groaning, hissing, and mumbling incoherently in a choked voice. Julius hadn't thought it was a good idea to give him any painkillers until they'd determined the extent of the damage.

"So damn lucky," Steffie murmured, a refrain she'd repeated more than once already, alongside phrases in what must have been her native language. She was stitching up the entry wound now with brisk but careful tugs of the thread. She and Julius worked well together, coordinating their actions with minimal speaking as if they'd done this a dozen times before.

Maybe they had.

Still, I couldn't stop myself from turning to Talon where we were watching from the far end of the room and asking, "Are you sure we shouldn't get an official doctor or something?"

Blaze cried out, as if punctuating my question. Then he grumbled something about "fucking needles, I'll pierce their goddamn eyeballs" which didn't make a ton of sense but was at least more understandable than the babbling before.

"Julius got some medical training through the military," Talon said. "And Steffie… The men who had her made her do first aid when they needed it, so she had some experience already. After she came to us, Julius saw that she got a more in-depth education so she'd be able to help in situations like this."

"She's practically a qualified nurse," Garrison put in from where he was standing beyond Talon.

I eyed the younger man warily. I hadn't asked him even though he generally had more to say than Talon because I wasn't sure where we stood after the way he'd laid into me this morning. So far, no one had mentioned anything about that argument, which was understandable given that we had much bigger things on our minds. I had no idea where I really stood with any of the guys, but Garrison had been by far the most furious.

Their comments reassured me a little when it came to Blaze's survival, as did Julius's a moment later. "We would get him to a hospital if I felt it was necessary. But he just needed some patching up." He pressed a sterile pad over the stitched wound and taped it in place. "As soon as we're finished getting on the bandages, you can have the good pain meds," he told Blaze.

The other man nodded rapidly, his mouth pressing flat. I wouldn't have thought he was capable of that much patience.

"Someone could go get that stuff now," Steffie suggested, and Talon moved before she'd even finished speaking. The woman shook her head as she looked Blaze over. "An inch farther, and the bullet would have torn through a handful of organs. I'd love to have the luck that sticks with you boys."

"You're with us," Blaze said with a rasp. "Very lucky. Wanna trade places?"

She snorted and finished her work on the exit wound. As they let Blaze roll fully onto his back on his bed, Talon reentered with a small case. Julius opened it, took out a syringe, and applied the contents directly to one of Blaze's veins.

The effect was almost immediate. A sigh rushed out of the hacker, and he settled a little more loosely into the bed. A crooked smile crossed his face. "Now we're talking." Then he cracked his eyes open a slit, glancing from me to the other guys. "There should be more talking. You all need to tell Dess what idiots you were being."

Steffie raised her eyebrows. "I don't think I'm needed for this conversation." She nodded to Julius. "I'll stay at the apartment until you're sure you don't need me to monitor him further."

"Thank you." Julius watched her go, closing the door behind her, and then shifted his gaze to me. Under his authoritative stare, my mouth went dry.

Was this really a conversation we should be having right now, while Blaze was half-dead from his injury? But then, it was Blaze who'd prompted it. He let out an impatient grunt when Julius didn't speak right away.

"I apologize," Julius said, with a shamed twisting of his mouth. "I made unnecessary assumptions and acted out of possessiveness when I didn't have any right to. I shouldn't have spoken to you the way I did. None of us should have." His eyes flicked from me toward the other men, focusing longer on Garrison.

I kept my attention on the crew's commander, my arms coming up to fold over my chest. I held them back from hugging myself the way I wanted to. "No, you shouldn't have."

He exhaled slowly. "It isn't an excuse, but I wasn't prepared. I do understand that you shouldn't have to rein yourself in from what you want—even if that's more than one of us. I have no interest in taking away your freedom. Hell, I'm dedicated to making sure you get more of it. I trust my crew, and I know you'll be in good hands with them." One side of his mouth curled up. "And I'll continue to be happy to contribute my own hands if you'd like to have them in the mix too."

My own lips pulled into a small smile. "I'll keep that in mind."

Talon cleared his throat. "I agree with everything Julius said. I should have spoken up sooner and not let them badger you the way they did. Thankfully I didn't have to go as far as cracking skulls to get them to see sense."

Had he been the one to force them to understand my perspective when they'd all been talking on the deck? Given how little the taciturn man normally spoke, I wouldn't have expected that, but his words and his solid presence steadied me as they usually did.

Maybe I shouldn't have been surprised. Talon didn't talk much, but he'd always been a sort of calm in the storm of chaos the crew thrived on.

My gaze slid to Garrison. He met my eyes for a second before his own jerked away, his mouth slanting at an awkward angle. His expression tensed and released as if he was grappling with himself. I braced for more snark or another accusation.

"You don't have to make yourself apologize if you're not really sorry," I couldn't help saying. "If it's just to get the other guys off your case, it won't mean much."

His gaze flicked back up to hold mine again. He swiped his hand across his mouth.

"I *am* sorry," he said. "Just not very good at saying it, obviously. Because I mean it."

The words echoed back to our conversation at the fundraiser in a way that sent a pang of understanding and relief through me.

Garrison tipped his head toward me and went on. "You never lied to me or broke any promises, and I shouldn't have accused you of anything like that. I only—I only got so angry because I thought *I'd* screwed up by trusting you. But you haven't done anything wrong, and I'm sorry I went off on you like that." He paused, and a hint of his usual smirk touched his lips. "I guess I should have known you're too much woman for any one of us to satisfy on our own."

Blaze chuckled lightly from the bed. "It's a good thing there's four of us."

A laugh tumbled out of me. "I don't know if that's a compliment or an insult."

"A compliment. Definitely a compliment," Blaze insisted.

Garrison's smirk grew. "Absolutely. Hell, if being with *all* of us makes you happy, who am I to argue with that?"

"Here, here," Blaze said with a wobbly nod.

Julius shot him a sharp look. "I know this is a difficult ask, but if you could manage to stay still for another twelve or so hours at least, I'd really appreciate it."

Blaze let out a huff, but he rested his head back into the pillow.

With that, the tension that had been wound through me since this morning started to dissipate. It didn't vanish completely, but at least the crew felt like a consolidated unit again and not one fracturing under strain. I wasn't sure whether things would actually play out so smoothly going forward, once they had to put that newfound generosity into practice, but it wasn't as if I was planning on hooking up with anyone in the middle of this mess. We had more important things to focus on.

"Now that we've determined that you're not all pissed off at me still," I said, "should we talk about what happened at the storage facility? It was obviously a trap."

Julius grimaced. "Yes. One you spotted well before we did. We rushed when we shouldn't have."

"We were worried about you," Garrison said quietly.

I shot him a baleful look. "And because of that, you made me way more worried about all of *you*."

"I should have known," Blaze muttered. "For the search to come up with a result this close to home after it's already been running for days… It should have popped up much earlier if it'd been there all along."

"Do you think someone planted the image specifically for us to find?" I asked.

Talon hummed. "It wasn't in the storage units where we thought it would be."

"Right," Blaze said. "No symbol there at all. They faked it as bait to get us to come while they prepared their ambush."

Julius sighed. "After our standoff at the meat factory, the organization behind Dess's capture must have realized we were looking for their symbol, that we were using it to track them down. They turned the main lead we have against us."

A gloom settled over me, seeping into my gut. A similar shadow had crossed Garrison's face.

"If *that* was faked..." he said. "If they've figured out that much about the way we're working... can we trust *any* of the leads we've gotten? Almost everything we've found has been through the image recognition app. All of it could have been manipulated to leave a false trail—the images and videos of Dess's trainer, the ones of the people we saw her with, the symbol..."

"The symbol is definitely real," I jumped in, even though a deeper sense of hopelessness was swelling inside me. "It's on my neck—it was in the mansion."

"But we don't know much other than that for sure," Julius said, frowning. "We can't trust any information that came to us from outside sources, no matter how innocuous it seemed at the time."

My heart sank. "Then what *do* we have, really?"

Garrison made a face. "We're basically back to square one."

Silence fell over all of us, even Blaze the chatterbox. I swallowed hard. After all the effort we'd gone to and the danger these men had put themselves in for me, we might not be any closer to answers than when we'd started this mission.

And I had no idea where to go from here.

TWENTY-FOUR

Blaze

PAIN PULSED through my belly from the bullet wound that'd hit just shy of my intestines. Every time I shifted my position in the bed or, well, breathed, it turned into a sharper jab. The painkillers had numbed the worst of it, but this was hardly the most comfortable I'd been in my life.

I hadn't let Julius dope me up too much. I could handle a little aching, and we had even more work to do than before now that all our previous leads had been called into question. Focusing on the data I could chase down and sort through on my laptop helped distract me from my physical discomforts anyway.

First I prodded at the image that had led us into the trap at the storage facility. It'd been well-positioned, but after several minutes of intensive prying, I dug up the evidence that it'd been posted to the internet only a couple of hours before the search had picked it up, not the many months the post that had held it had been designed to suggest. If we hadn't been in such a hurry to make sure Dess was safe, I probably would have investigated further and noticed that before we'd left.

Of course, if we hadn't rushed in there and Dess hadn't been so cautious herself, those men would have taken her out easily while she was on her own. I might have saved myself from this stupid injury if I'd trusted her instincts more, but… it was hard to feel that racing to protect her had been a mistake. I liked the idea of standing back and expecting her to figure out all the threats on her own even less.

We couldn't afford to step into any other traps, though. There weren't any new image results so far anyway. Our best bet was something totally unrelated to the investigations our enemies were already aware of. Something that would never have occurred to them to use as a trap, since they didn't know it'd appeal to us as bait.

There *had* been one line of inquiry I'd just started following up on the other day. I hadn't mentioned anything about it to the others yet since I'd been half convinced it'd lead nowhere.

I dove back into tracing that thread, uncovering one bit of information and then another, examining each of the pieces from every angle to make sure it was legit before moving on. As the picture started to form in my head of what exactly I'd uncovered, a slow smile spread across my face.

This could be it. This could be the answer—an answer the pricks who kept attacking us couldn't interfere with. Of course, there'd be a whole lot of other challenges to overcome, but the Chaos Crew had never shied away from danger. Still…

A knock sounded on my door. "Hey," Dess's voice carried through. "Steffie brought some fresh lemonade by. Do you want a glass?"

"Sure," I said, though I was more interested in setting my eyes on Dess's face than getting a drink. I'd been way too isolated in here thanks to my invalid status.

Dess slipped inside and set the glass of pale yellow liquid on the end table next to where I was propped up on multiple pillows. She took in my expression, and hers relaxed a little. "How are you doing? Can I get you anything else?"

"This is great," I said to reassure her, and took a gulp of the lemonade—which was the perfect combination of sweet and sour; excellent job as always, Steffie. Dess had come in to check on me more than any of my other comrades, worry always darkening her eyes when she looked me over.

Now, she stepped closer and tugged the fleece blanket draped across my legs a little higher on my body. "Julius and Steffie said you wouldn't want to let your muscles stiffen up with a chill."

"I'm warm enough," I said gently.

She backed up a step, her hands clasping in front of her with an awkwardness I hadn't generally seen from her. Dess was usually so focused and self-possessed. I liked her that way… but I had to admit there was a certain appeal to her new role as concerned caregiver. I could see how hard she was trying to make things better for me even though she wasn't sure how. Watching her like this set off a warm glow in my chest that told me I was falling for her even harder than before.

There was definitely no chance of me giving her up now, so it was a good thing the other guys had gotten their heads straight.

"How's the pain?" she asked. "Do you need any more medication?"

I shook my head. "Less, I think. I can handle it. And I want my head as clear as possible. I think I've found a lead we can actually use —one that can't be faked."

Her face brightened, and she eased right to the side of the bed to peer at my laptop screen. "What is it? Did you find out something about the symbol or Malik?"

I shook my head. "Something totally different, which is why it should be safe from traps. Not that I didn't examine it in minute detail to make sure it was legit on top of that. It's not at all connected to anything else we've been doing, so there's no way the people after you could know we're looking into it now."

Dess cocked her head. "If it isn't connected to anything else, how useful can it be?"

I chuckled, glad to have the chance to surprise her. But I felt the need to clarify first, "It'll be dangerous. Probably incredibly dangerous. But I think it'll be worth it, because if we can pull it off, there's a decent chance of us finding out *exactly* who you are."

She sucked in a startled breath, her eyebrows rising. "Okay, now you really have to tell me. I don't think dangerous is going to be a problem. It seems to be all of our middle names."

"True. That's why I bothered to track this down anyway."

I swiveled the laptop toward her and motioned to the screen. It showed a blueprint for a four-story building in the shape of a segmented cube. Dess studied it, knitting her brow. "Where is this, and what's so special about it?"

"From what I've been able to determine," I said, "this is a secret, high security government facility that holds *all* the genetic information collected by various governments, law enforcement agencies, and companies around the world. Every record our government could get their hands on, by both legal and not-so-legal means."

"Genetic information," Dess repeated. "Like DNA. I thought you said running a test on that would be too risky."

I nodded. "With any commercial company it would be. Your former captors could easily get access to those and put up alerts to notify them if anyone ran your DNA. But they may not even know this facility exists. I didn't for sure until a few minutes ago. And even if they did, they wouldn't have been able to plant code like that in its systems without the intrusion being detected quickly and destroyed."

An eager gleam lit in Dess's eyes, much better than the shadow of worry that'd lingered there before. "Then we could test my DNA after all."

"Exactly." I grinned at her. "Now, it isn't a guarantee that someone related to you will also have their sequence in this database, but there's a better chance of it than any other database in the world, since this is by far the most extensive. And it doesn't put us or you in view of anyone who has it out for you."

"That all sounds great. I'm guessing there are a few 'but's you haven't mentioned yet."

I waggled my eyebrows at her, my rising spirits making even the pain of the gunshot wound feel distant. "I'll talk about your butt all day if you'd like."

Dess snorted. "You know what I mean. What are the catches?"

I'd have pointed out that she was quite a catch, but then she might have smacked me even in my invalid state. I turned the laptop back toward me. "Well, for starters, I don't know how to sequence your DNA myself, and the other guys sure as hell haven't got a clue. So we'll have to outsource that. To a private individual who's capable of it, someone we can be sure isn't compromised."

"And?" Dess prompted, obviously picking up on the fact that the element I'd just mentioned couldn't be the highly dangerous part.

"And in order to compare that sequence against the database, we'd have to actually get into the building and run the processes ourselves," I said with a wince. "And it is a top secret, high security facility, as I might have mentioned before. There'll be guards out the wazoo. Not to mention locks and other technical safeguards."

Dess exhaled in a rush. "Okay. So we'd just have to get past all of that."

"Yes," I said dryly. "That's all. Well, okay, that's not totally all."

She glowered at me. "What else?"

"I don't think I'd be able to go in with you," I admitted, as much as it pained me to say it. "Even at the best of times, I'm not the most physically coordinated guy around. With my injury on top of that… I'm not sure how well I can walk, let alone dodge a pack of elite security guards."

"But wouldn't we need you to get past the tech stuff and tell the computers to do what we want to search for the DNA match?" Dess said.

"Yeah. I can program some things ahead of time, but quite a bit I'd have to be talking you through remotely. Which does make it a more difficult proposition. More chance of human error. I'd try to cover every eventuality, of course, but it's harder when I'm not right there."

"Understandable." Dess's expression turned pensive. She gazed into space for a long moment as if gathering her thoughts.

I knew that figuring out who she was had always been the largest driving force behind her quest. She wanted to take the people who'd kidnapped her to task, sure, but mostly she wanted to know where she'd come from. What family she'd once belonged to. Even if it turned out they were jerks, I could only imagine the release that knowledge would give her. I had no idea what it'd be like to feel so adrift with no human connections to the most primal part of your past.

"I'm sure we could manage it," she said finally. "You've had to instruct the rest of the crew from a distance for other jobs before, haven't you?"

"Yeah, now and then. It's not my ideal approach, but sometimes it's necessary. Never in a situation quite this complex, though."

She shrugged, a smile coming back to her face. "So it'll be a challenge. We haven't backed down from any of those yet. Unless *you* think we're not up to the task?"

I shook my head. "It's not that. I just—I hate the idea of all of you going in there and taking all the risks for a plan that's totally my idea, while I get to hang out somewhere safe and sound."

She patted my side, carefully avoiding the bandages there. "I think you've already proven very clearly in the past couple of days just how much danger you're willing to put yourself in for me and the crew. No one's going to criticize you for not being up to a high-stakes breaking-and-entering mission. I trust you to get us past anything we need your help with, and I know the rest of the crew will have no problem counting on you to look out for us too. If you believe we can pull this off, then I'm all in."

Her words sent a strange sensation unfurling through my chest, a little giddy but also so unfamiliar I wasn't sure what to make of it. I'd always been someone the guys could turn to for technical support and information, of course, and I'd helped in my own ways on the ground when I could, but the idea that people would trust me to protect their very lives made my pulse wobble.

I wanted to be someone my crew could count on that much, though. And this time—this time I'd do a good job of protecting everyone under my care.

Resolve rose up through me, and I shot Dess another grin. "All right, then. I'll talk it over with the guys, and then we're going to need to call in a favor. That DNA won't sequence itself."

TWENTY-FIVE

Decima

"IS THIS... a kind of job that you guys normally take on?" I asked, holding the leash of a small corgi that walked in front of me as if he was the one leading *me* down the sidewalk. I'd never thought much about how I felt about dogs, but this one had stolen my heart the moment we'd picked him up from the breeder.

I wished I could take him home with us, but I imagined the guys would have something to say about that. And he was kind of essential to our plan.

Julius shook his head where he was walking by my side. "Not on a regular basis. It's definitely not within our typical range of services. Only for special circumstances like these."

Like a genetic scientist who didn't happen to have anyone she wanted chaotically murdered as payment for her services. I couldn't suppress a laugh, and the corgi looked over his shoulder at me without slowing his pace. He ran into the back of Garrison's heel and stumbled over his sausage legs before correcting himself and walking a few paces behind Garrison.

Garrison shot the dog a look, but from the twinkle in his eye, I didn't think I was the only one taken with this bundle of brown fur.

"It seems pretty simple for the complex work she's going to be doing for us," I had to point out.

Garrison snorted. "For her, sequencing DNA is a piece of cake. We had to locate a dog that's a near-perfect match for hers, and now we've got to sneak it into her ex-boyfriend's house and retrieve the real one without him having a clue. It's a stealth mission that takes a lot of skill and prep-work, so I'd say she's getting one hell of a discount for our services."

At his tone, I couldn't resist gazing down at the dog and sticking out my bottom lip in an exaggerated pout. "And you're sure that we can't keep him?"

Julius looked over at me, and a chuckle escaped him. "He's already been assigned to a home, Dess."

I sighed. "Fine. But don't blame me if I find I'm unable to stop myself from bringing a different one back to the apartment one of these days."

Garrison shook his head, but his lips twitched with amusement. I glanced around at the quiet suburban neighborhood through my sunglasses, still alert within my disguise even though traffic cams were in shorter supply here. We had no idea how close our enemies might be to finding us, so we'd pulled together this job as fast as we could.

But at the same time, a sense of calm had settled over me, taking the edge off my nerves. We'd all worked together, making a convincing case for dog ownership when we'd picked up the pup, driving out to the edge of the suburbs while keeping our charge in a good mood, and now approaching our target's home like a group of friends out for a stroll. It was like nothing had changed, despite our argument a couple of days ago. No matter what our enemies might have in store, that knowledge filled me with relief.

"That's the house," Julius said without looking at it as we crossed the street. "Three down from the corner."

I took it in from the edge of my vision as we ambled by. It was one of the larger buildings on the residential street, white with beige shingles and a big porch. "Got it," I said.

We made a longer circuit, coming around to where Talon was waiting in our getaway car. Julius nodded to him, and the other man started the engine to drive over to the house on the opposite side of the block from our target's. Garrison headed back around to the front of the house, while Julius and I followed Talon on foot.

"You're sure you want to do the inside work?" Julius asked me.

I nodded. "I'm the smallest out of all of you—it'll be easiest for me to stay unnoticed. And he seems to like me." I bent down to scratch the dog behind the ears. "Hopefully his counterpart will too."

"All right. I'll be waiting by the fence for the handoff. Get in there as soon as you hear Garrison at the door."

We walked up the driveway of the house that backed onto our target's backyard as if we belonged there. We'd already confirmed that the owners and their neighbors would be at work. Too bad we couldn't say the same for our target, but apparently one of the reasons our client had broken up with him was that he'd decided to laze around at home all day playing video games while living off an unexpected inheritance.

Unfortunately, that'd also made it impossible for her to get the dog herself. He'd paid for one of its vet bills once and had found some lawyer who'd insisted he could make a case to sue if our client tried to take the dog with her, even though the dog had been hers for years before they'd ever met. I knew all about vindictive pricks, even if I'd never been in a relationship with one, and this guy was clearly a massive one.

I scrambled over the wooden fence with the help of a lawn chair, and Julius handed the corgi over the top to me. The dog squirmed a little when I tucked him under my arm, and I made a soft clucking sound that had seemed to soothe him in the car. When he went still, I gave him a quick pet. "Good boy." Then I stole across the overgrown lawn to the back door.

At least it looked as if this dude didn't treat the current doggie resident too badly. There were a few toys scattered in the yard, and when I peeked through the window in the back door, I made out a full water dish and a food bowl that looked recently cleaned of its contents.

No sign of the actual dog, though…

I couldn't see the supposed owner, but chances were he was camped out in the living room in front of his widescreen TV jabbing at a controller. Stroking the dog's fur comfortingly, I used my other hand to quickly pick the lock so I'd be ready to move as soon as I got the signal.

All good, I texted Garrison.

A minute later, the doorbell pealed out. The floor creaked as the occupant must have walked over to answer it. I eased open the back door at the same moment.

It let out a faint squeak, and I froze. But the guy was already swinging open the front door and didn't appear to notice. I slipped into the mudroom and set down the new corgi.

"You stay right there," I murmured to him, setting a few treats in the food dish. As he started gobbling them up, I stalked farther into the house.

"Here, Terry, Terry, Terry," I whispered, careful to keep my voice much lower than those carrying from the front of the house. I wasn't sure what story Garrison had come up with to keep the guy distracted, but it obviously involved a lot of talking. I clucked my tongue under my breath for good measure and waggled the toy that the client had told us was his favorite with the faint jingle.

To my relief, the click of little claws reached my ears a few seconds later. Another corgi, which did look remarkably like the one we'd picked up, came trundling over to meet me. I'd have thought our original one had left the mudroom if it wasn't for the collar around this one's neck.

"Good boy," I told him, and jingled the toy for him to follow me back to the mudroom.

There was an abrupt silence from the front. I halted in my tracks again, my nerves prickling, prepared to simply snatch up the dog and run for it. But then Garrison's laugh pealed out, the other guy's echoing it, and my breath rushed out of me.

We were okay, for now.

It took some wrangling and a couple more treats to get the original corgi to allow me to unbuckle his collar, and the new one huffed as I fixed it around his neck. Then I was darting out the back with a different but equally cute doggo under my arm.

The dog gave a small woof just as I closed the door, which Garrison must have heard because all of a sudden he gave a loud exclamation to draw the guy's attention. I dashed across the yard, narrowly avoiding tripping over a rubber bone, and lifted my cargo so Julius could take him over the fence. I clambered after him, and we both loped down the drive to jump into the waiting car.

I rubbed under the corgi's chin as we swung around to pick up Garrison farther down the street and shot a teasing glance at Julius. "Are you sure I can't keep *this* one?"

He gave me a mock-glower. "I think our client might have a few complaints about that."

No doubt Julius had been right, because the client was absolutely ecstatic from the moment she opened the door and saw the corgi in my arms. She took him from me, whirling around with him like he was her soul mate, and peppered kisses all over his furry head for the better part of a minute.

"That's right, Terry," she murmured. "You're back with Mommy now. No more meanie Kevin. You're all right."

The dog's tail was wagging so hard I was surprised it didn't fall off his body. Clearly he was happy to be back with her too.

Finally, the woman sat down at the desk in her living room and looked up at us. "There's no chance my ex will realize Terry is gone?"

We shook our heads. "We found a suitable replacement," Garrison said with a smirk. "From the sounds of things, he won't notice the difference."

She let out her breath. "Perfect. He was being such a scumbag about it." Then her face settled into a more professional mask. "I guess it's time for my side of the bargain. Whose DNA am I sequencing?"

I stepped forward and then stopped, not sure what she needed from me. "Mine."

She nodded and set the dog down at her feet with a fond pat. He stuck close to her legs as she retrieved some equipment from a case under the desk.

"I'll just need a small sample of your blood for the most accurate sequencing. I'll have to wait until I have the lab to myself for a long enough time, but I should be able to manage it in the next couple of days. After that, you want me to send it to the man who set up the exchange, if I understand correctly?"

"That's right," Julius said. "We appreciate your assistance."

"I appreciate having my dog back."

She motioned for me to hold out my arm. I tensed a little as she swabbed disinfectant over the vein she meant to use, my body automatically rejecting the idea of being handled by a stranger. I'd been pushed around so much during my time in the household that any touch I hadn't sought out felt like an imposition.

But I needed this. This was my ticket to finding my family. At least, it'd better be after the lengths the crew was going to on my behalf.

The woman knew what she was doing. The needle gave only the smallest pinch as she inserted it. The tube attached to it quickly filled with the dark red blood she was drawing. The whole process was over in an instant.

"There you go," she said, smoothing a bandaid over the spot. "I hope you find what you're looking for with this."

"So do I," I replied, and I'd never meant anything more.

TWENTY-SIX

Decima

"I AM *NOT* SHARING a bed with Blaze," Garrison said, pointing to the bed where Blaze lay sprawled, laptop on his chest and three pillows propping up his head. He tipped his head to the side, a sly glint coming into his eyes. "I'll share with Dess."

Julius shot him an unamused look. "This is not the topic we need to be discussing right now, but I'll remind you that if all goes well, *none* of us will be spending the night here."

"I just figured I should make my position clear now, just in case," the younger man muttered, and reached toward the array of weapons we'd all been assembling our arsenals from.

I fixed a few more tactical items to my belt and added another holster under my arm. We were loading ourselves down with even more equipment than when we'd taken on the Funhouse, but for good reason. We had to navigate the entire four-story building and eliminate any guards who got in our way… without actually *eliminating* them. Julius didn't feel right about mowing down random people who were simply doing their jobs working for the government, and I was inclined to agree.

The computers that would allow us to run the analysis on the DNA sequence now stored on a flash drive stood in the very center of the building's top floor, because of course they did. Each stage of our entry would have different difficulties. Some of them we'd need to handle on our own, and others Blaze would be talking us through from the hotel a mile from the facility, over the headsets we'd all put on.

"Remember," Blaze said for the dozenth or so time as he tapped at his keyboard, "*don't* split up. I don't have access to the cameras inside that place, and it'll be almost impossible for me to help two of you with two different problems at once."

"We promise if we split up, we won't get into any trouble," Garrison shot back.

Blaze glowered at him. I knew how nervous he was about having us go in alone while he was blind to what was happening, relying on only the bits of data he'd been able to dig up on the facility's layout, GPS trackers clipped to our belts, and our reports through our headsets. He'd told us everything he could to prepare us until Julius had finally—gruffly but gently—informed him that at the rate he was going, we'd mess up because we had too much information stuffed into our heads.

"We're in good hands with you here guiding us," I said, adjusting my bulletproof vest to make sure it was perfectly positioned and then going over to the side of the bed. I tucked the stuffed tiger I'd brought along—"For luck," I'd told the guys—closer to his side. If it'd come from my former family, maybe in some weird way, it'd help us take the final steps to getting me back to that family.

"And we've been through a hell of a lot of other difficult missions," I added. "You don't really think the Ghost would fail even at a challenge like this, do you?"

Blaze opened his mouth and paused, probably torn between protesting and not wanting to diminish my past accomplishments. Before he could decide which to go with, I bent down and pressed my lips to his. He settled on a pleased hum as he leaned into the kiss.

"We'll be fine," I repeated, pressing a finger to his mouth as I pulled away. "Trust me."

He kissed my finger gently, grabbing my hand and flipping until the palm faced upright. He kissed the palm too before exhaling a long breath. "Just be careful," he insisted as I pulled away.

"I don't think any of us wants to be in more danger than we have to be. And I know how prepared *you* are. We've got this."

I wished I felt as confident as I managed to sound, but at least my words seemed to reassure Blaze. He nodded and gave us a little wave as we headed out the door.

We marched to the elevator in a formation that'd come instinctively: Garrison and Julius in the lead with me in the middle and Talon bringing up the rear. Blaze should have been walking next to the cool-headed killer, but I didn't let myself dwell on that.

His injuries were healing. He'd managed to walk a few steps to grab a glass of water and a snack today. Soon he'd be back to his former energetic self.

As the elevator door stood closed, Garrison raised his eyebrows at me. "Why does *Blaze* get a kiss? He's the one lounging around on a bed while the rest of us do the hard work."

His tone was grumbly but with a playful note underneath. I rolled my eyes at him. "If you want something, there are nicer ways to ask."

Heat flared in his eyes. "Oh, I could come up with something *very* nice if we had a little more time."

"I'm sure you could." I stepped closer to him and gave him a quick kiss, one he turned hot and firm with a hand on my waist. Not wanting to leave anyone out, I turned to Julius and reached up to touch the massive man's cheek. He smiled, his dark eyes smoldering, and met my kiss for him with equal enthusiasm.

Talon touched my back before I'd even turned to him. He pulled me around and kissed me so soundly my panties were damp by the time he let me go.

"There," I said, folding my arms around my chest. "That evens things out." The desire now tingling through me wanted more, but my nerves were too keyed up by the mission ahead to give in. We had a lot of work to do, and any distraction could get us killed.

The easiest part of the job was getting *to* the facility. Beyond that, there was nothing easy about it. It was late enough that not even the hardest working lab technicians would remain, but security was tight and difficult to infiltrate at any time. From rotations on the perimeter to interior security, we'd detected no gaps in coverage. On top of that, Blaze had determined that the building held alarm systems that were sensitive to noise and probably the wrong sorts of pressure as well, although he couldn't figure out the specifics without going in.

"I see you're just outside," he said through our headsets as we crouched in the shadow of a nearby art installation, his normally easygoing voice terse with the tension. I could imagine him watching us as little blips on his laptop screen.

"Ready to move," Julius confirmed. In the glow of the security lamps that cut through the night, the building before us looked like a plain block of concrete, nothing high tech about it. I'd bet no one passing by gave it a second glance. But apparently the windows dotting the cement exterior were only for show. There wasn't any real way to look inside from out here.

Blaze spoke with total efficiency. "There are four guards on constant rotation around the entrance, as I expected. You have about a minute between them, and the fourth one is checking in with the supervisor every twelve minutes like clockwork."

"He's the one we need to avoid," Julius said, his whisper coming through my headset clearly.

"Exactly. You can't be seen by the fourth security guard, and he can't suspect that anything's wrong, or a ton of backup will come down on you. Don't make a noise knocking out the other three and get them out of sight, and he won't have any idea something's wrong until the guard rotation in an hour."

I eyed the entrance, which a man was striding by right now. "Which one is off-limits?"

"He's the lead, so he should have a golden patch on his left sleeve," Blaze instructed.

Thirty seconds later, another man rounded the corner, a rifle in his hands. I spotted the gold patch immediately. He surveyed the entire area with a keen eye. We'd definitely need to be extra careful with leaving evidence, as this man would spot any discrepancies.

"When he passes, you have four minutes max to deal with the other guards and get inside the door." Blaze's voice became even harder as he gave careful instructions. "Dess, I showed you how to use the keypad cracker. The rest of you, work to disable the guards and hide the bodies. Hide them *well.*"

Four minutes. I could do this in four minutes. When I'd practiced with the cracker on various doors around the city for practice, it'd never taken more than a minute to find the right combination. But Blaze had warned me that this one would likely take longer, and we didn't want to cut it too close. I only had one shot. If I pulled it off before it was done decrypting, it could set off the alarms in the building.

The second the lead guard turned the corner out of view, the next guard had come into sight. Julius leapt forward silently, capturing the weapon first, then muffling the man's gasp and knocking him out with a jab of a syringe. Maybe the same stuff the crew had used on me when they'd first taken me home. He pulled the man toward the sculpture where he'd restrain and more carefully hide him, and Talon moved forward to deal with the next guard.

The second the guard was unconscious, I bolted toward the metal front door, yanking the keypad cracker from its spot on my belt. With a glance at the lock, I stuck the device to the base of it and pressed the necessary buttons. It flashed, and the orange light began blinking, showing that it was scanning for possible combinations.

I looked toward where the rest of the crew stood by the modern sculpture, waiting for the next man on duty to come into sight. The seconds slipped by, and the steady rhythm of guard's footsteps reached my ears.

The lock cracker was still blinking. I tried to tune out the anxious twisting of my stomach. "What are we doing the second we get inside?" I whispered into my mic as I heard the faint scuffling of Talon effectively incapacitating the other guard.

"Go directly to the right, staying as close to the wall as you can and then keep going in that direction until you reach the stairwell door," Blaze replied in my ear. "The automatic lights will alert security if you go forward. You'll need to get to the employee's stairwell at the side of the building."

"Got it," I whispered. One more guard left. Well, that and the damned tracker. I stared at it, willing it to switch to green, but it just kept blinking that orange dot at me.

Julius had gotten into place to take down the third guard. Talon was still concealing the second. Garrison slunk over to stand at my shoulder like a guard dog, ready to bolt inside with the rest of us the second we could.

"We have time," he murmured into my ear, taking in my stance.

But we *didn't*. If this stupid box of circuitry didn't perform fast enough, the entire mission would be a bust before it'd even started.

The third guard's footfalls sounded. Julius was on him in an instant. Talon joined us at the door, Julius following seconds later. The fucking light was still orange.

"Blaze," I hissed. "It's almost time for the lead guard, and the cracker hasn't—"

The light blinked green, and the lock clicked open. At the same moment, I heard the lead guard approaching. He hadn't turned the corner yet, but we had the space of a few heartbeats to get out of sight.

I yanked the device from the door, shoved it open, and flung myself inside and to the right, just as Blaze had said. The others had heard his instructions too. We all flattened ourselves against the wall in the sudden, thicker darkness that had no streetlamp glow tempering it.

The door shut with a faint tap. I held my breath, braced for thudding footsteps and an angry shout.

Nothing came. More seconds ticked by with the pounding of my heart. The lead guard must have walked right by with no inkling that anything was wrong.

Next to me, Garrison gave me a gentle nudge. I nodded even though he couldn't see me and started sidling on down the righthand hall.

I couldn't make out any of the technology that made this place so special in the pitch black we'd found ourselves in, but I could hear it. An electronic hum droned through the air as if from all around us. It sent a shiver down my spine.

The seemingly endless corridor finally brought us to a push-style door. A dim light on the other side showed a narrow stairwell.

"We've reached the stairs," Julius murmured to Blaze under his breath.

I could almost hear Blaze nod. "Go up. There aren't many other guards until you get to the top floor, and the ones who are on the lower floors aren't likely to be on the stairs. If you do run into anyone… you know how to handle them."

Julius had another syringe ready in his hand. Garrison brandished a stun gun. I flexed my fingers, mentally rehearsing the move Noelle had taught me that could briefly knock out a man if you applied the right amount of pressure on just the right spot by his neck.

We slipped up the stairs one after the other, giving the doors we passed on the second and third floor a cautious glance before hurrying by. Several steps down from the fourth landing, we paused again.

"We're just about at the top," Julius reported quietly. "What are we facing up here?"

"I couldn't find out all that much specific detail, unfortunately," Blaze said. "But since the control room is up there, it's where the most security presence is concentrated. Avoid any loud sounds and try not to touch anything I don't tell you to. The control center is in the middle of that floor, with data banks all around it. Make your way to it as quickly as you can, and any guards you need to deal with, do your best to keep them out of sight afterward."

That sounded a whole lot easier said than done. I dragged in a breath and glanced at the others. They all nodded.

"I'll stay in the lead," I murmured, and darted to the door.

I edged it open just a smidge, enough to spot a row of machines on the other side that stretched to the high ceiling and flickered with a multitude of tiny lights—and two guards waiting in the hall just a foot from where I was standing. I held up two fingers to the men and then leapt forward.

I threw myself at the man farther away so the guys could tackle the closer one. One hand clamped around his mouth. The other dug into his flesh where I would find just the right nerve.

I squeezed hard, flinging a leg around his to bring him to the ground so he couldn't buck me off him. A second later, he slumped over.

Talon was already on the second guard with a needle, and Julius gave mine the same treatment, since the effect I'd produced would be short-lived on its own. After a moment's silent debate, we dragged them into the corner of the stairwell, figuring that was the safest place for them.

"There's a pattern marked on the floor farther down the hall," Garrison murmured, and eased a little closer to describe it to Blaze in more detail.

The hacker hummed. "That'll be one of those touch-sensitive alarms. That's got to be the way to the control center. But you'll have to disable it to get past it."

"And how do we do *that*?" I asked.

"Look around. There should be a small utility room to your left. The wiring will probably run through there."

I spotted a discreet doorway past another row of humming, flickering computer units and hustled over. "I found it."

"Good, go inside, and I'll direct you. We have to be careful not to cut the wires for the wrong devices, or it'll trigger an alarm. We can't afford that."

No kidding. I reached the utility room, unlocked it with some jabs and twists of my lock picks, and slipped inside. The others crammed into the small space after me to avoid being seen. Garrison glanced around.

"We could chuck a few bodies in here too," he remarked.

"Not right now," I muttered, and stared at the mess of cables that covered the wall in front of me. "Blaze, I'm going to need some serious guidance."

"Okay. You want to find a cable labeled 4J. A place on this level, they've got to be up to code. Do you see it?"

I scanned the cables in the thin light and caught sight of it partway down the wall. "Here. I cut that one?"

"Not so fast! There'll be a dual trigger. If either of them shuts down without the other, we're screwed."

My heart started thumping faster again. "What's the other one?"

"Usually it'd be a switch… They like to use blue ones for this type of system. Do you see any blue switches?"

I did, but there was a slight problem. "Five of them."

Blaze muttered a curse under his breath. "Okay… They would have it lower than the cable's entry point, and to the left—no, no, to the right. Lower and to the right."

There was only one blue switch that met that description. I rested my fingers on it. "Are you sure?"

"Yes. Cut the wire and flick the switch at the exact same time."

I pulled a knife from my belt and braced it against the cable. My fingers curled around the switch. Then, in unison, I jerked both hands into action.

The cable split. The switch dropped. My jaw clenched, but no blare of alarms filled the building.

"Did it work?" Blaze asked in my ear.

I exhaled shakily. "I don't like that you're asking me that. It seems like it. Let's check the hall."

I'd just said that when Julius and Talon leapt out ahead of us. I understood why a few seconds later when they dragged two more unconscious guards past me into the stairwell. We were certainly leaving a trail of bodies behind us, if not in the typical way.

"The pattern on the floor has vanished," Garrison reported.

Blaze let out a little cheer. "You're good to go then. Well, as far as that's concerned anyway. Still proceed with extreme caution, watching for a set of glass double doors to your right that'll lead into the control room. If you're quick, maybe you can make it there before any more patrols reach that part of their circuit."

We weren't quite that lucky. I'd just spotted the double doors between two stretches of looming data storage units when another two guards rounded a corner up ahead. Apparently on this floor they worked in pairs.

Julius dashed forward with a speed I wouldn't have expected from such a massive man if I hadn't seen him in action before. He mashed their faces together, muffling their shouts of alarm against each other's flesh as Talon and Garrison dove in with syringes.

We dragged the limp bodies into the control room with us and then paused to stare at the array around us. It looked like something Blaze would have wet dreams about. Screens and computer towers filled every inch of the walls. Beneath one cluster of monitors sprawled a vast black keyboard with five times as many keys as usual. Or, well, when I got closer I saw that many of them were actually round buttons or rectangular switches.

"We're in," I said. "Here goes nothing."

Blaze had already gone over this final part of the plan in detail, because he'd mostly been able to predict what to expect ahead of time. He'd also warned us that the control room was probably checked by guards at least every ten minutes. We had to work fast.

I pulled the flash drive that Blaze had given me from the secure pocket where I'd kept it. Garrison motioned to a port that would accept it on the base of the keyboard. I jabbed it in and tapped the power button. A few of the screens blinked on immediately.

"The drive is in," I whispered.

"Good. Is it already working on the password?"

"Looks like it." Blaze had set up the drive to run its sequence of operations automatically on contact. A window had appeared on the main screen, letters and numbers whipping by too quickly for me to make out more than a blur. Abruptly, that screen vanished, and a spread of icons appeared. A program opened as if of its own accord.

"I think it's starting the search now," I said.

"Good." Blaze's relief rang through his voice. "It'll take a couple of minutes to get through all that data, but it's got to be one of the most advanced systems in the world. This laptop of mine would take a hundred times that long." He chuckled.

I leaned against the nearest console and inhaled deeply. "I think we did it."

Julius shot me a crooked smile. "Let's not get cocky. We've still got to get out of here."

The computer next to me whirred faintly, and a spiral of DNA showed on the screen. My pulse hitched. "I think it found a match."

"Perfect. It'll be downloading onto the drive now. Wait until the screen stops showing any activity, then grab the drive and get moving."

Abruptly, a beep emanated from the console where I'd inserted the drive. I frowned. "Is it supposed to beep when it's done?"

"What? I wouldn't think so, but—"

I missed whatever else Blaze said when the screen flared all at once with blinking red letters. *UNAUTHORIZED ACCESS.* I jerked back, just as the blare of a siren screeched through the room.

TWENTY-SEVEN

Decima

"SHIT, SHIT," I muttered to myself over the alarm's siren wail. Around me, the men's hands flew to their weapons.

Blaze could obviously hear the alarm on his end without us needing to tell him that something had gone wrong. He mumbled a curse of his own. "Get the drive, and get out. *Now.*"

I yanked out the flash drive and shoved it into my secure pocket. We whirled toward the doors—just in time to see another metal door slowly sliding out over them to seal us in. It'd already covered a quarter of the second door's surface, including the handle.

"There's a secondary door, steel, closing over the first," Julius said into his mic. "There's got to be a failsafe to shut it off somewhere."

Blaze swore again. "I don't know what it'd be without more information than you have time to give. There'll be at least a dozen guards coming at you. Can you get past it by force?"

I threw myself at the glass pane on the door, but it only jarred in its frame. The thunder of racing footsteps carried through it. Talon motioned me aside and hurtled past me, taking a few shots at the glass to crack the thick layer before slamming his elbow into it with the full impact of his body weight behind it.

The pane shattered. Talon burst through, and the rest of us charged after him, Julius dragging Garrison the last few inches before the automatic security door pinned him to the frame.

We didn't have any time to appreciate that narrow escape. Squads of guards burst into view at both ends of the hallway.

We ducked low instinctively. My fingers closed around my gun. We didn't want to kill anyone just doing their job, but if it was us or them, we wouldn't have much choice. We'd agreed that we'd shoot to injure rather than kill if that would be enough, but it was going to be hard with this many opponents.

"Stay close to the data storage equipment!" Blaze shouted through my headset. "They won't want to risk damaging the machines."

We all flung ourselves upright and pressed tight against the towering machines with their blinking lights. The guards slowed as they approached, their guns drawn but silent. Blaze had been right.

"Hands up!" one in the lead barked at us. "Drop your weapons. You're surrounded and outnumbered."

That might be true, but I'd be willing to bet that these men hadn't been in quite as many tricky situations as I had. I'd never let the hopelessness of a fight stop me from giving it my all before, and I wasn't going to start rolling over now.

As my pulse thudded behind my ears, my vision narrowed down to the most important details of the figures around me—how they were spaced around each other, which hands each had on their guns, what sort of protective gear they wore that could deflect a bullet. Then I sprang into action.

Keeping my back against the computer equipment, I fired into the squad of guards closest to me, hitting a wrist, a hand, a bicep, a thigh. Weapons clattered from fingers that could no longer hold them; arms sagged, and legs staggered. Julius started shooting at the bunch in the opposite direction, and Talon squeezed his trigger too, adding to the injuries on both sides.

A couple of the guards farther back that we hadn't been able to hit immediately took a few shots at us, but they were so careful about the machines and their colleagues across from them that we managed to dodge. Then they barreled straight toward us, barging past their wounded comrades—but that gave us time to deal out a few more shots precise enough to crumple them to the ground without outright killing them.

"Come on!" Garrison yelled, motioning for us to leap over the slightly smaller squad and get out of there.

I thought a silent mental apology at the men I'd had to shoot—and who I now kicked and stomped on to fend off their snatching hands and waved batons as they tried to stop us even in their blood-soaked state. Someone was hollering into a radio that Julius shot out of his hand to a yelp of pain, but we had to assume that more backup was on the way.

We dashed down the hall the way we'd come—only to discover that another steel security door had already snapped into place over the entrance to the stairwell. There was no escaping that way. But the alarm's wail had faded away, maybe so the security officers could track us easier, and more footsteps were pounding toward us. The guards must have had another route through the building.

"Blaze," I hissed. "The main stairwell is sealed. How do we get out of here?"

"I'm trying to find—the blueprints must have been altered after the version I have—shit." He was typing frantically enough that the clatter of the keyboard sounded over the headset.

"Get out of sight," Julius ordered the rest of us, jerking his hand toward the utility room we'd used to disable the floor alarm.

We dashed into the room and tugged the door shut. Only seconds later, guards stomped by outside. I had a brief moment of hoping that they'd forget about this room, but the government didn't hire any slouches for their top-secret facility. Someone grasped the handle and turned. There was no way to lock it from the inside.

Talon grabbed the inside handle and hauled backward, holding the door shut with his considerable strength. Unfortunately, the men on the other side had clearly figured out that someone was in here. There were more shouts, and a couple of shots rattled the handle. They were less concerned about sending bullets in here. There must have been backup elsewhere in the building for the vital electrical systems. Maybe we'd have been safer staying in the hall.

And now we were trapped in a box of a room, hardly bigger than a coat closet, with a horde of furious armed men on the other side.

As my gaze darted around the dark room searching for some kind of answer, an uncomfortable knot formed in my stomach. We'd ended up here because I'd wanted so badly to know who I really was—to figure out what family I'd been stolen from and why. But had it really mattered so much that it'd been worth putting not just myself but the men who'd supported me in this much danger?

I could have decided I was simply Decima and walked away. Focused on taking down anyone who tried to capture me again until they gave up. Instead, I'd gone chasing danger with the only men I'd really cared about—the only people who'd ever really cared about *me*—by my side, and now we could all be screwed. I was good, but even I knew that maximum security prisons weren't a piece of cake to break out of.

Julius had braced himself with his gun ready. I supposed we had a small advantage from the fact that we had a wall at our back and only a narrow doorway that our enemies could come at us through. Our enemies who were now managing to jostle Talon in his rigid position despite the strained bulging of his arm muscles.

Then my eyes caught on the edge of a rectangle on the ceiling, mostly hidden by the shadows and the top of the cabinet beneath it. My breath caught.

"Blaze, are there air vents that reach the utility room?"

On the other end of our connection, he sucked in a breath. "That isn't shown on the blueprint I have either, but it'd make sense for them to add one. Every room with a door should have adequate ventilation. It'd be a tight fit for Julius, though."

"I'll make it work," Julius said grimly. "I've squeezed through tight spaces before. It's all a matter of angles. But we have to get up there without getting shot on the way."

"Move the cabinet," Garrison said quickly.

We heaved at it together and managed to shift it toward the door. Julius gave me a boost toward the ceiling, and I unscrewed the grate covering the vent in less than a minute. Talon let out a grunt where he was still pulling back the door with all his might.

"You and Garrison get up there," Julius ordered. "I'll knock the cabinet over, and it'll block the doorway long enough for me and Talon to jump off it to follow you. Just keep moving."

"I think once you're in there, you just need to head left and you should find a connecting vent that'll take you down to the first floor," Blaze said helpfully in my ear. "One good thing about it being narrow is that you should be able to brace yourself against the sides and scramble down without falling. Just don't get stuck."

"No fucking kidding," Talon muttered.

I grasped the edge of the vent and dragged myself up into it on the left-hand side. Immediately, I crawled forward on my hands and knees. I didn't think Julius would be able to manage more than an army crawl in this tight space. Good thing he'd have gotten professional training at that.

There was a thump as Garrison clambered up after me. Then a clang resonated from below as Julius must have shoved the cabinet in front of the doorway. With a grunt, the other two men hauled themselves into the vent in quick succession.

Gunfire rang out below as I scuttled forward as fast as I could go. But the cabinet must have blocked the entrance long enough to shield Julius and Talon, because I heard three sets of breaths in the passage behind me, terse but not pained.

"Everyone okay?" I murmured, just to be sure.

"I've had more enjoyable nights," Julius retorted. Talon simply snorted. I decided to take both of those responses as a yes.

"Stop joking around and get the hell out of there," Blaze chided us. "I've just picked up on transmissions in the neighborhood—there's going to be a whole army on the doorstep if you don't get out in the next five minutes."

My heart hiccupped. I pushed myself forward even faster and nearly toppled right into the downward vent before I realized I'd found it. In the total darkness, the only warning was a slight ripple of the metal lip around the opening.

There was no time for negotiating who'd go first. I wedged myself around the corner so I could drop my legs in and then slid the rest of the way, balancing myself between my back and my feet with my knees brushing my chest.

With little hitches of jumps, I careened several feet at a time, catching myself and then doing it all over again. The rasping and thudding above told me the men were following me using the same strategy, although the bigger guys wouldn't be able to move as swiftly.

Blaze was already planning our next steps. "It bottoms out over the first-floor ceiling. You'll want to go back in the same direction you reached the vertical vent from. About twenty feet along, you should find a grate that's just a short dash from the main entrance."

"Perfect," I said around a gasp for breath.

With a few more jumps, my feet smacked into a metal surface below me. A metallic *clunk* rang out, making me wince. I couldn't hear any voices filtering through the ceiling of the hall below me, but it was only a matter of time before the guards who'd swarmed us upstairs figured out our strategy and caught up with us.

Contorting my body, I squirmed around until I could crawl through the horizontal vent passage and hurried onward. Garrison, Talon, and Julius followed me with a soft grunt for each landing.

"I could hear the guards rushing down through the wall," Julius reported. "They've got to be at least to the third floor by now."

Crap. I shoved myself farther and spotted a glimmer of light just up ahead. There was the grate.

I caught hold of the metal rectangle and brought my tools to bear on the screws. My fingers flew, and in a matter of seconds, I was tossing it aside. I poked my head into the hall below to look around, and my heart all but stopped.

"We can't get out," I said, jumping down into the open, currently empty hall so I wasn't blocking the men's way. I stared at the door we'd come through—which was now completely sealed off by another one of those steel security doors. No handle, no clear controls. And we only had a minute or two before a mass of guards would be surrounding us from both sides.

Garrison dropped to the ground and came over to stand beside me. "There's got to be a way to get it to retract."

"Do you see any panels in the walls nearby that you could open up?" Blaze asked.

I stared at the walls around us. "There's nothing."

Talon and Julius leapt down and studied the door in turn. A distant thunder reached my ears—the thudding feet of the multitude of guards who'd be on us in mere seconds now.

We'd run out of options. In less than a minute, they'd be shooting us down. Even if we could manage to take on all the guards in here, despite the fact that we couldn't rely on any nearby equipment to prevent them from shooting us, by the time we'd accomplished that, the army Blaze had warned us about would be gathered outside.

We were all going to die.

I didn't say the words out loud. They felt like a betrayal of everything the Chaos Crew had done to get me here. The risks they'd taken for a mystery that only really mattered to me. I swallowed hard.

"I think there's another exit," Blaze said, but his excitement vanished an instant later. "Only it's on the other side of where the secure staircase has to be. All those guards are between you and it now."

The answer came to me like a signal flare in the dark. This was my quest. I should be the one to make the ultimate sacrifice. I could dash over and draw the guards' attention, get them to chase after me, and buy the men enough time to escape.

They'd done so much for me. Given me so much. They shouldn't have to give their lives too, especially not when it was my fault we were here at all.

Who I was didn't matter if I was dead, especially not if the men around me died too.

I gathered myself, preparing to race toward the sound of the stomping feet with an explanation shouted over my shoulder, and my gaze inadvertently caught on Garrison's.

I should have known better than to look at him, the man who made a living out of reading people's deepest secrets.

The moment my eyes met his, he narrowed them, detecting something in my expression that I hadn't thought to keep hidden. In the time it took for me to push all my thoughts down, I was afraid he'd already seen what I was planning.

Garrison took a discreet step closer to the door and shook his head lightly—too lightly for the others to notice. I countered by shaking mine.

"You can't—" he started, and then his attention jerked to something over my head. I might have made a break for it then if a hopeful light hadn't brightened his expression.

"Paper!" he said abruptly. "Who's got a piece of fucking paper?" He snapped his fingers, fishing something out of a pouch on his belt at the same time.

I had no idea what he was talking about, but the other men responded automatically, trusting that their comrade had a good reason for his request. Talon's hand jerked to his own belt, but Julius was already thrusting a piece of folded notepaper from his pocket toward the younger man. Garrison scraped a match against its book, brought the flame to the paper, and held the now-flaming sheet up… to a sensor next to a sprinkler system fixture I hadn't noticed mounted on the ceiling.

The first floor must be all regular offices, no high-tech equipment the government workers would be too worried about getting wet. And they'd wanted to protect the ground floor from any sort of fire that might spread upward to all those precious hard drives.

A different sort of alarm careened through the air, and a burst of water sprayed down over us. In an instant, I was drenched.

In the same instant, the steel security door began to whir open.

A bellow reverberated through the hall behind us. We leapt toward the front door as one being.

"Thirty seconds until the first cars reach the building," Blaze called through the headset.

It took ten for the door to open all the way. Julius and Talon fired a few shots down the hall, and then we dove out into the night.

Our feet pelted across the pavement. We hurtled down the sidewalk and around the block, dove into the waiting car, and didn't properly breathe until Talon was gunning the engine to tear down the road away from there.

I sagged into the back seat, drenched and chilled but giddy with relief. “Oh my God.” I glanced at Garrison next to me. “How did you know that would work?”

He shrugged, a pleased gleam in his eyes. “I didn’t know. I just guessed. It wouldn’t make much sense to allow the employees to be locked up in there if the place caught fire. Like Julius said, there’s always a failsafe.”

“Thank fuck for that,” Julius rumbled, a sentiment we all echoed with a round of exhausted laughter.

TWENTY-EIGHT

Decima

BLAZE GREETED us at the door to the hotel room, his eyes wild with manic energy. "What took you so long? I had about five panic attacks thinking they'd surrounded you and gunned you down on the way back."

Julius gave him a baleful look as we all tramped inside and nodded to Talon, who swiftly but gingerly picked up Blaze and hefted him back to his bed.

"There's this thing called traffic," the leader of the crew said dryly. "And I didn't figure it'd be a good look to speed the entire way back here once we'd gotten away from the scene. Trying not to draw undue attention to ourselves and all that."

Blaze huffed but sank back into the pillows, tucking my tiger under his arm. "You did practically die about ten times in the past hour. I think a little concern is understandable."

"You shouldn't be on your feet," I told him. "You didn't pull your stitches, did you?"

He threw his hands up in the air and then winced, which made me worry that he'd done it right then if he hadn't already. "Pull my stitches, when you were facing off against a thousand highly trained government security officers—"

"I don't think it was *quite* that many," Garrison put in.

Blaze glowered at him. "It would have been if you'd gotten out of there even ten seconds later."

I sighed and sat down on the edge of the bed next to Blaze. "But we didn't. We're okay. We're back now. And a lot of that is thanks to you, you know."

The worry fell from his face enough for him to smile back at me.

Garrison cleared his throat. "That last brilliant brainstorm was all *me*, I'd just like to point out."

I rolled my eyes at him. "And you get full credit for it. But right now…" I pulled the flash drive out of my pocket. "We went through an awful lot of trouble to get this loaded up. Let's see if it actually finished processing and made all that trouble worthwhile."

I spoke casually, but as Blaze grinned and snatched the drive from my grasp, my pulse started to stutter almost as badly as when we'd had a horde of armed guards on our tails. We *had* gotten out, and not even with any serious injuries, but I was still going to feel massive guilt if we'd gone through all that craziness for nothing.

And it wasn't as if we'd be able to break in *again* for a second try. This had been my one chance.

Blaze tossed his computer onto his lap and jabbed in the drive. His fingers raced over the keyboard so quickly they were almost a blur. Julius came up behind me, setting a firm hand on my waist as if to steady me while we both watched the screen. Garrison and Talon gathered on the other side of the bed.

The hacker let out a whoop of excitement. "There was a match!" A record sprang onto the screen. "A close one too. Parental—paternal." He skimmed down past several paragraphs of data that apparently weren't relevant to him. "Your dad's name is…"

I was so keyed up with anticipation that when he trailed off into sudden silence, I couldn't keep quiet. "*What?*"

Then my eyes settled on the name in bold partway down the screen. I blinked at it, read it again, leaned closer, and read it a third time. It didn't change.

Damien Malik.

My lungs seized up. It was a few seconds before I could breathe again. I kept gaping at it, my thoughts whirling in my head.

"That's why Noelle and the people she worked with were interested in him," I said as the pieces slowly came together. "Because… because he was related to me. But how can he be related to me? Did he have some secret kid that somehow the media didn't find out about in the two years or whatever before I got kidnapped? What the hell is going on?"

My voice got louder with each question. Julius lifted his hand to squeeze my shoulder instead. He and the other men were staring at the screen too.

"I don't know," Blaze said. "This doesn't make any sense. Unless—" His eyes widened. His fingers darted over the keyboard again.

He brought up an article with the headline *State Rep Malik Loses Daughter to Car Crash*. Nodding, he tapped the date. "I never checked the exact details because it didn't occur to me that they'd be relevant. That's just a week before that first video we found of you being trained, Dess. She was the right age—twenty-one months, just shy of two years old."

"What are you talking about?" I demanded. "I'm not some zombie who got raised from the dead."

Blaze turned to look at me, his eyes shining with a mix of excitement and sympathy that made my gut twist up. "No, you're not," he said. "I'm saying that Damien Malik's daughter never died at all. Your household people must have staged the accident, left remains that were a convincing enough match that anyone would believe you'd died. But instead, they kidnapped you. It's a near-perfect crime. If the parents think a kid is dead, then they're not going to search for them, right?"

"But I… Could it be some kind of mistake?" I was still having trouble accepting this new version of events. I'd been wondering if Malik was the one who'd *stolen* me, for fuck's sake, and now he was my dad? "If there was a family resemblance, wouldn't we have noticed?"

Blaze brought up some photographs, flicking through them until he found one he was satisfied with that showed Damien Malik and his wife just a few months ago. "There aren't any of the daughter. Usually the press is a little sensitive about showing photos with young children." He cocked his head and zoomed closer. "His eyes are kind of like yours. The same color. I never noticed before because I wouldn't have thought to compare. And she has black hair with a similar wavy texture to yours."

"So do lots of people," Garrison pointed out. "Otherwise, there aren't many similarities." He squinted at the photograph, and his eyebrows rose slightly. "Although… see if you can find any pictures of the wife when she was a lot younger. I think she must have had work done to her face a while back."

"You mean plastic surgery?" I asked as Blaze dove back into his searching.

Garrison nodded. "The signs are only subtle—it was well done—but it's hard to hide the evidence completely if you know what to look for."

After a few minutes while we waited in tense silence, Blaze crowed in victory and brought up a slightly grainy photo of a dark-haired woman in a robe. "Her high school yearbook photo, senior year. Holy shit."

My jaw went slack. The woman in the picture wasn't a perfect match for me, but I felt as if I could have been looking at a younger sister. She had not just the same wavy black hair, but a long nose and thin lips that made her face echo mine.

"That's her?" I murmured.

Blaze nodded.

"Looks like she had her nose done to give it more of a cute ski-jump thing," Garrison observed, and glanced at me. "I personally think the version you've got is more elegant." His gaze darted back to the photograph. "And a little plumping to her lips. Enough that the resemblance was obscured. But there's no denying it seeing that picture."

My mouth had gone dry. There really wasn't any denying that this woman was related to me. I had no idea what to say or do about it. My whole body had frozen in place.

Blaze looked over at me. "Are you okay, Dess?" he asked in a gentle tone.

"I—I guess." I rubbed my temple. "This all still seems so bizarre." I paused. "Even if the household did kidnap me, why would they still be keeping tabs on Malik *now*? It's been over twenty years. It must be obvious he doesn't realize I'm alive."

Julius frowned. "Maybe there's more to their plan beyond simply kidnapping you. Let's take a look at his recent activities again with the new perspective we've just gotten."

Blaze typed away without any further prompting. A list of search results popped onto the screen—and the first one made my heart lurch to the base of my throat.

Damien Malik, Majority Whip, Victim in Brutal Attack. And the time stamp next to the headline was just this evening.

KILLER HEART

THE CHAOS CREW #3

EVA CHANCE

ONE

Decima

FROM A DISTANCE, I stalked Damien Malik.

Over the past week, I'd learned a lot about the majority whip, partly with the help of my crew—in particular, Blaze's hacking and surveillance skills and Garrison's ease at charming information out of people. When Malik wasn't in Washington D.C. working with the House of Representatives, he spent most of his time in the smaller nearby city where the Malik family home was located. Unless he had a particularly early meeting, every morning he went for a jog through a local park along a tree-lined pond. Then he stopped at one specific coffee shop to grab a hazelnut cappuccino.

At least two bodyguards stayed with him at all times. I trailed far behind all of the men as I took a little jog of my own. Then I followed them up the stairs into the coffee shop.

When I got up there, Malik was already sitting at his favorite table with his fingers curled around the handle of his mug. The sunlight beaming through the broad windows gleamed off his silver hair, slicked neatly back as always, and brought the hard angles of his polished face into sharper relief.

Now, still-healing scrapes marred the otherwise only faintly lined skin at his temples and jaw. A week ago, just hours before a DNA comparison had revealed that this man was a parental match for me, a lunatic had broken into a late-night planning session at his Washington office and shot two of Malik's staff before blowing himself to smithereens. It seemed clear that the guy the news reports were calling a domestic terrorist had been hoping to take Malik with him.

He'd almost succeeded.

I yanked my eyes away and walked over to the counter to order a small latte. Anything bigger wouldn't be wise. Even a little caffeine got me hopped up with energy until I could have done a fair imitation of Blaze's restless fidgeting.

As I waited for the barista to assemble the drink, my hands clenched at my sides. No matter what the news said, I couldn't help suspecting that the attack had been connected to the household where I'd been held for over twenty years after they'd stolen me from my birth family. My trainer had been keeping an eye on Malik. Their intentions toward him couldn't be anything but malicious.

Had they decided to go after him more overtly now that they'd lost their grasp on me so completely?

I hadn't been here to stop them. I hadn't had any clue that I should be. But now that I knew what Malik was to me—that he was my *father*—maybe I'd be able to protect him if they came at him again.

I'd damn well better be able to.

Sipping the latte and wincing at the bitter flavor, I sat down at a table where I had a view of both Malik and his bodyguards, who gave him a little space by sitting several feet away while surveying everyone who entered the shop. I didn't want to barge right over, but I couldn't wait too long either. I'd promised myself today would be the day I actually approached him. There wasn't anything left I could figure out without speaking to the man himself.

But how would he take the news? Would he even believe me? The story sounded so crazy… and there were parts I couldn't exactly admit upfront. Maybe ever. "By the way, I'm a highly trained assassin with hundreds of murders under my belt," didn't seem like the kind of thing *any* parent wanted to hear.

I'd just have to dive in and see how the first part went.

When I'd made it halfway through my latte and become convinced that I really should have ordered a hot chocolate instead, I noticed the signs that Malik was nearing the end of his own coffee. He closed the newspaper he'd been browsing and sat a little straighter in his chair.

My pulse lurched. I inhaled deeply to steady myself, abandoned my mug, and walked over to his table.

As I put myself in his view, Malik glanced up at me. His expression was mild, not particularly curious but not hostile either. Probably warier than it'd been before last week's attack.

He had a faint bruise on his cheek that I hadn't noticed before from a distance, nearly healed but giving that patch of skin a slightly greenish hue.

I yanked my attention back to my purpose. "You're Damien Malik, aren't you?" I said, as though I hadn't been watching him in person and through screens for nearly every waking moment for seven days straight. I could have recognized him from behind at a distance of a hundred yards at this point.

He put on his practiced politician smile and extended a hand to shake mine. "It's always nice to meet a supporter."

I hesitated and then accepted his hand, giving it a quick shake. I couldn't believe I was actually touching him—my father. The first member of my real family I'd spoken to within my memory. My throat tightened abruptly.

Something must have shifted in my expression that troubled Malik, because he pulled back in his chair as he dropped his hand.

"I—I was hoping I could talk to you about something important," I said, blurting out the appeal faster and more clumsily than I'd intended.

"What would that be?" Malik asked cautiously, his other hand rising just slightly.

I knew what that meant. I'd seen him gesture to his bodyguards before when he felt he was getting too crowded. He was seconds away from summoning them, and then I'd never get through everything I needed to say.

I'd wanted to ease into this, but there was no easy way to manage it.

"Please, don't call them over," I said, sinking gingerly into the chair across from him. "I'm not here to hurt anyone. This is about—you had a daughter. Rachel." My birth name still felt foreign rolling off my tongue. "You think she died in a car crash, but it was a set-up. It was arranged so you wouldn't know she'd actually been kidnapped."

Possibly it was a good thing that I'd blurted it all out like that, because I startled Malik enough that he just gaped at me for a second, his whole body motionless. Which meant he wasn't summoning his bodyguards. But it was only a moment before anger jolted him out of his shock.

"I don't know why you'd come to me with a story like this," he said with an edge in his voice, starting to stand up, "but you should get some help and—"

"No!" I protested, leaping up. "I know it's true. I know—because I recently found out that *I'm* her. I'm Rachel. I'm your daughter."

Malik paused and stared at me again. I knew some of the evidence was right there before his eyes. We'd found pictures of his wife—my mother—back in her college days when he'd first met her, before she'd had the plastic surgery that'd upturned the elegantly straight nose I'd inherited from her and plumped up the thin lips we'd once shared. Our hair was still the same, black and wavy.

He *had* to see the truth. I didn't know how else to convince him. I couldn't exactly tell him I'd broken into a high-security genetics facility with a crew of hitmen to test my DNA.

A glimmer of recognition lit in Malik's eyes. Then he closed them and shook his head. "It's not possible."

"I had a stuffed tiger," I said quickly. I was pretty sure the toy had come from my former life, since it'd already looked worn in the earliest videos of my training sessions, before Noelle had stopped letting me bring it along at all. "Orangey-yellow fur with brown stripes and button eyes. My kidnappers—they let me keep it."

Malik pressed the heel of his hand to the bridge of his nose. As he lowered his arm, he peered at me through his fingers. I thought I saw the doubt in his expression fading.

The tiger hadn't been mentioned in any of the news reports about the car crash. I shouldn't be able to know about it unless it'd belonged to me.

I barreled onward, figuring the more I said while he was listening, the better. The Chaos Crew had helped me construct a story that would fit the timeline and sound plausible without getting into the, well, bloodier parts of my role in the household.

"I had no idea I was kidnapped for a long time," I said. "They told me my parents were dead. I finally figured out that something was wrong a couple of years ago and managed to escape them, but it took me the rest of that time to figure out who my real family was. Where I came from."

Malik cleared his throat, likely trying to gather his thoughts. Was he going to tell me that he'd finished grieving his long-lost daughter, that I couldn't be her no matter what I said? Would he send me away in disbelief? Anxiety roared through my veins as I waited for a response.

He hadn't called the bodyguards yet. That was a small sign in my favor.

Malik took a few slow breaths. Then he fixed a more piercing look on me than he'd given me before in his initial surprise.

"If you are who you say you are, do you remember what you were wearing the day you were taken?" he asked, his gray eyes that were nearly identical to my own intent on mine.

I couldn't tell whether he really wanted me to answer that question. It'd be easier for him if it turned out I was lying, wouldn't it? He could go back to his normal life where he'd set aside his tragic loss decades ago.

I sucked my lower lip under my teeth. "I was so young. I don't remember my life before the kidnapping at all."

He sighed and leaned back in his seat. I groped for a better answer I could give him, and my mind latched on to my memories of the old videos Blaze had lifted from Noelle's laptop.

I *had* been young in them. In the very first one, I'd been just a crying toddler begging for her mommy and daddy. That image was ingrained in my mind now. The clothes I'd been wearing had been dirty and wrinkled, not like the trim tees and sweats I'd been dressed in later.

Was it possible they'd left me in my original clothes for the first few days while they tried to ease me into my new situation? It was worth checking.

"I did have one old set of clothes—an outfit I don't remember my kidnappers giving me," I added, improvising. "They were different from the others. A little yellow romper with frilly sleeves and a sunflower embroidered over the chest. Was that it?"

Malik's stance went rigid again, but this time there was nothing but amazement on his face.

"And a little bow on the collar," he said, barely more than a whisper.

A smile touched my lips, a wave of exhilaration rushing through me. "Yes."

He brought his hand to his mouth now and then lowered it again. He couldn't seem to peel his eyes away from me. "Rachel?"

The name meant nothing to me now, but I nodded. I could hardly tell him I'd rather go by Dess or Decima, the names the household—my kidnappers—had given me. Regardless of its source, it felt like me far more than "Rachel" did. But he'd hardly understand that.

Malik opened his mouth and closed it again. I'd never seen him lost for words in all the videos I'd watched of his political activities.

His bodyguards must have noticed his agitation, because they strode over to our table, glowering at me. "Is everything all right, sir?" one asked.

"Yes," Malik said, motioning for them to go back to their seats. "Yes, I think it is." He kept staring at me. "You look exactly like your mother did when I met her."

"I've seen pictures of her in college," I said, glad I could be honest about that. "That's part of how I figured it out."

"You—She'll be so—" He caught himself and composed his expression. His voice came out more measured, falling into professional mode. "I need outside confirmation. I'm sure you can understand. Can I take a strand of your hair—or you could spit in a cup for me—I'm not sure what would work best."

"Well, there's lots of cups here," I said. I'd expected something like this, and it'd work in my favor when he got independent confirmation of our connection. "I guess I'd better use a disposable one."

"Yes." Malik leapt up and hustled to the counter to ask for one of the takeaway paper mugs with a lid. He returned to the table and handed it to me. Feeling a little awkward, I summoned a dollop of saliva onto my tongue and spat it into the cup.

Malik took it from me, holding the cup like it was made out of precious crystal. "I need to go," he said. "But as soon as I've checked—what's the easiest way I can contact you?" He pulled his phone out of his pocket to make a note.

I recited the number from the burner phone Julius had given me, and my father entered it with swift taps on the screen. He tucked his phone away and gazed down at me one last time. Relief was trickling through me that I'd managed to mostly convince him, but my gut twisted at the same time.

It was a lot of pressure, living up to someone's vision of their dead child come back to life, wasn't it? I hadn't totally been prepared for that.

"You're okay for now?" he asked.

"Absolutely," I said. "I've got a job and a place to live, friends who've been helping me out. I just hope we can get to know each other better once you get the results back."

"Of course." He ran his fingers back over his hair and dipped his head to me, a shadow crossing his eyes. "I'll be in touch soon. In the meantime, be careful out there."

I thought about telling him that I could take down a man like his domestic terrorist in three seconds flat if I had to, but that would be revealing a little too much information for comfort. Instead, I smiled at him. "Thank you. I will."

But if any of the people associated with the household came at me or my father again, I was going to make sure they regretted it.

TWO

Decima

AFTER I'D FINISHED TELLING the crew about my first conversation with my birth father, I couldn't stop pacing the room. Which wasn't for the best, because the hotel we were staying in was a converted factory that'd kept many industrial-style features for atmosphere. The ceiling of the large suite held bare heating ducts, two of the walls were old brick… and the lighting fixtures dangled on steel cables at random intervals, just low enough that I could bonk my head on them if I wasn't careful.

I wasn't so sure about that particular design choice.

"It sounds like the meeting went well," Julius said as I dodged one of the dangling lamps.

I peeked at the leader of the Chaos Crew from the corner of my eye, not bothering to say anything. He should have looked intimidating with his substantial height and brawn and the spiky tattoo that showed around the collar and sleeves of his tight-fitting shirt, but I could tell he was hesitant to make a more definitive statement. Julius rarely showed uncertainty, but he cared about us more than he would have openly admitted. The last thing he would have wanted was to hurt me by saying the wrong thing, especially when the stakes were so high.

Garrison, on the other hand, rarely set aside his casually disaffected mask. He shrugged, his hazel eyes cool. "I don't think you could have expected it to go much better, honestly."

I shifted my gaze to the lightbulb that hung alone above my bed, squinting as the brightness seared into my eyes. They didn't understand. With a sigh, I flopped onto the admittedly luxurious mattress. The Chaos Crew always picked high class, if sometimes unusual, accommodations.

"It doesn't matter how well that first chat went," I said. "He knows nothing about me. I could barely tell him anything. He'd never be able to accept who I really am—what I've been doing all this time… He'd probably want me shipped off to a maximum-security prison."

Blaze, in his usual upbeat manner, shook his head with a swish of his pale red hair and moved to sit at the other end of my bed. "I don't think you're giving him enough credit. He *is* your dad. He's finally got you back in his life after thinking you were dead for so long. How could he give that up?"

I turned my head and raised my eyebrows at the hacker. "You know more about his anti-crime policies than I do. He'd like to see small-time drug dealers serving 20 years in federal prison, so how do you think he'd react to an assassin who's murdered her way around the globe?"

Garrison snorted. "Obviously you wouldn't tell him about that part."

"So I'll be lying to him the whole time. And it might come out anyway. Even if I keep it hidden, how could he possibly relate to me?"

Talon, normally a solemnly quiet presence among the others, stepped forward with a flex of his square jaw. "We don't kill innocent people. We take down the same criminals that he wants to put away for life. It's not so different."

I grimaced. "*You* don't kill innocent people. I've been doing it my entire life without knowing it."

"Which is exactly why it isn't your fault," Julius pointed out. "And you've taken up our approach since then. By killing criminals, you're helping his agenda, exactly as Talon said. Maybe you can't tell him that, but you can remember that in a way, you're on the same page."

They were trying to reassure me, but even from the short time I'd been studying Damien Malik, I felt sure he'd never see my situation that way. He'd think I was an even worse criminal than the ones I'd eliminated. If he ever realized what I was and what I'd done, any familial warmth would vanish in an instant.

I'd lose the only real family I'd ever had before I'd really gotten a chance to experience what it was like having one.

And that was if he called me back at all. What if the test he ran on my saliva got messed up and gave him a negative? What if he decided having me back in his life would be a complication his career couldn't afford?

I groaned and flung my arm over my eyes in a way even I knew was overdramatic.

Garrison tsked his tongue at me and headed to the suite's kitchenette with a swipe of his hand through his shaggy blond hair. "It'll be fine. And any part of it that's not fine, we'll *make* fine. I brought a couple of tins of hot cocoa mix with me—including one of your favorites. I'll make you a cup, and you can focus on that instead of this guy who should have jumped at the chance to have you as a daughter."

My lips twitched with a hint of a smile at the understated compliment in his words. Garrison didn't often give out anything resembling praise—and I didn't think he liked sharing his treasured hot chocolate all that much either. Beneath his typical snark, I knew he cared about me too.

The thought of hot chocolate filling my mouth sent a spark of excitement through me despite the uncertainty and stress that had taken over my senses. I shook my head anyway. "I'm still a little jittery from the caffeine I drank earlier," I admitted. "I'll stick with water for now. Why don't you tell me what you and Blaze found earlier? That'll take my mind off things."

I hadn't been the only one at work when I'd confronted Malik. Blaze and Garrison had been continuing their own mission investigating the bombing at his office. If it'd been connected to the same people who'd run the household, we needed to know ASAP—and then we needed to deal with them before they attacked my father again.

Garrison leaned back against the counter, his mouth twisting. "I talked to a *lot* of people. No one saw much other than presumably those who were killed by the initial shots or the blast following it. Everyone seems to honestly believe that Malik was targeted by an extremist who disagrees with his politics, someone acting independently. But none of them had any real proof of that."

Julius rubbed his jaw. "What are they making of Malik's reaction to the attack?"

"If anything, it's bolstered people's good opinions of him," Garrison said. "He's been the perfect boss, accommodating and kind in all the ways that matter. He's visited the families of those who were killed, and he's given a substantial number of extra paid days off for the close friends of those who were lost."

"That seems like a good sign in general," Blaze said. "He cares about the people he works with."

The people he worked with weren't mass murderers, but I didn't say that out loud. "So, you weren't able to figure out much about the bomber from the people you talked to."

Garrison sighed and made an apologetic expression at me. "They didn't have much to cough up. If they'd tried to dodge my questions, I'd have gotten it out of them."

Blaze shot him a self-deprecating smile. "I'd question your supreme confidence, but the truth is, I couldn't find much on my end either. I'd rather believe there simply *isn't* much there to find than that we're both incompetent."

As Garrison glowered at him, Blaze scooped my socked foot into his hands and started massaging the arch absently. I welcomed the gesture, but it wasn't enough to take my mind off the issue at hand. "You couldn't track down any leads at all?" I asked.

"Unfortunately, no," the hacker admitted. "Nothing substantial enough that I'd want to put ourselves at risk pursuing it. I'm still looking at everything I uploaded from his computer. There was a lot to scan through, but so far no indications that he had any idea an attack was coming or records of previous hostility. I tapped into the security cameras in the building where the bombing happened, but with the angle the guy was standing at, the hood of his jacket hides his face. All I could tell you for sure is that it was a man, he was pretty average in height and weight, and no one in the office appeared to recognize him. He was a total stranger."

"That's the same impression I got from the footage," Garrison said in grudging agreement.

I let out a huff of frustration. "Why does this have to be so *hard*?"

"Well, either it was a random lunatic, in which case there's nothing else to find," Julius said with his usual strategic precision. "Or if it was connected to your 'household,' we're dealing with people who have a lot of power and resources. They couldn't have pulled off all this without a hell of an advantage."

"Great," Garrison muttered. "Someone with power and influence right outside of Washington D.C. That sure lowers the suspect pool."

The pressure of Blaze's massaging fingers started to make me tense up more than relax me. I eased my foot away and sat up, my hands curling into the blanket on the bed. There was too much I didn't know, even more questions hanging over me than ever before, and who knew how many lives hung in the balance while we searched for answers?

Talon walked over and rested a hand on my shoulder. "We're not going to get any farther into this right now. Do you want to spar and let out some of that tension?"

I looked up into his steady ice-blue gaze. He was trying to help me the best way he knew how. We'd blown off plenty of tension in the past with our fists, sometimes leading into… other activities that could provide an excellent release. Not that I was feeling at all turned on while I had this ball of stress in my gut.

But it was a good suggestion. Maybe a workout was exactly what I needed—to burn away all of my energy and emotions before revisiting the situation. I needed to think about it with a clear mind, and right now my thoughts were muddled with uncertainty and self-doubt.

I was just standing up when my phone rang. My pulse hiccupped. The number on the display wasn't one I recognized.

My hand shook as I raised the phone to my ear. "Hello?"

"Is this Rachel?"

My immediate reaction was to say no, but I caught myself just in time, recognizing the voice and understanding why he'd used it. "Y—yes. That's me."

The sound of Malik's joy carried through the connection. "It didn't take long for my people to run the DNA test, and the results couldn't be clearer. I'm sorry for keeping you waiting while I verified it. You really are my daughter."

There was so much awe in his words that my chest constricted. I struggled to find the right way to answer. This was exactly what I'd wanted to hear, but now I had no idea what happened next.

"I'm so glad to hear from you," I managed after a moment. "Where do we go from here?"

"We have so much to discuss, and I'd prefer not to do it over the phone. Now that you've come back to us, I want to really be there with you as much as possible. If it wouldn't be too much all at once, I'd love for you to meet the rest of the family. I'll be home for the day tomorrow. Maybe we can spend some time getting to know you and the young lady you've become."

If I'd had any doubts about that plan, the eagerness in his tone—eagerness to get to know *me*—would have dissolved it.

"Yes," I said, a smile crossing my face. "I think I'd like that a lot."

He gave me the address and the time I should arrive. I could barely keep up with his enthusiastic voice when my entire world and everything I knew seemed to be heading in a direction I'd never have expected it to go.

I had a family—one who couldn't wait to meet me. I wanted to believe it would go well, but there were so many factors that could make everything fall apart.

What if I was too awkward after all my time shut away from the regular world? What if they realized that I was nothing like them and hated me?

I dragged in a deep breath as I said my goodbyes and hung up. I had to go and face this new challenge no matter how nervous I was.

But I couldn't shake the looming sense that if I screwed things up tomorrow, I'd lose my family all over again, and *that* would be all my fault.

THREE

Decima

JUST OUTSIDE THE Malik family home, I hesitated.

I knew that I had the right place—a large, two-story home with cedar porch furniture and decorations that looked… cozy. I'd imagined a mansion like the household's or a large, sleekly designed home from a magazine, but this was a more modest building, and one that looked lived-in. Around the side of the wrap-around porch, I spotted a splash of brighter color from beach towels and a pair of swimming trunks hanging over the railing to dry. I couldn't see the pool from the front of the house, but I imagined the porch would lead me there if I continued around.

Instead, I eyed the beige front door, a wreath hanging there with the word "welcome" written in a calligraphic style across the center. All I had to do was knock, and I had no doubt these people would welcome me into their home as if I truly was one of them. But once they met me… would everything change?

I was nothing like the Maliks. I'd never lived in a cozy house with a pool. I'd never had people who loved me the way that a normal family loved one another. I wasn't even sure what love *was*.

I raised my hand to knock on the door, but it opened before I had the chance. Damien Malik greeted me with a wide smile, wearing khaki shorts and a collared shirt with a vibrant Hawaiian print.

Was this how he dressed when he was home with his family? I couldn't remember ever seeing him in anything that wasn't on the grayscale, but all my images of him were from his work life. Apparently the guy knew how to relax a little.

A plethora of emotions flashed through his eyes as he looked me over, likely taking in the dress shirt and slacks I'd worn in a misguided attempt to fit in. I'd assumed that meeting a politician in his home would be similar to doing it in his office, but this was nowhere near as formal as I'd anticipated judging by my father's clothing.

After a second, Malik shook his head. "Sorry, I didn't mean to leave you standing outside. My wife would fillet me for my manners. It's just… it's hard to comprehend that you're really *here*—the daughter I'd spent over twenty years thinking that we lost." He sucked in a deep breath. "Enough of my sappy rambling. I can tell it's making you uncomfortable. Come in, please."

This was the defining moment, so I plastered on my best ingratiating smile and stepped through the doorway.

The inside of the house gave off the same welcoming energy as the outside of it. I walked inside through the entranceway, and despite what appeared to be a coat closet, a few pairs of shoes scattered the entrance rug, and coats hung from makeshift hooks on the walls—over a dozen at least.

How many people had gathered for this get-together?

Malik's hand hovered over my shoulder and then dropped to his side as he thought better of attempting physical contact just yet. "The rest of the family is in the living room waiting to meet you. I hope you won't find it too much. Your mother and I couldn't help sharing the news, and everyone wanted to see you with their own eyes." He chuckled awkwardly. "I promise that none of us bite."

That was such a dad joke—so much of a dad joke that I recognized it as one from my limited knowledge of pop culture without ever having had a dad before—that it put me more at ease.

"I can't wait to meet them," I said, which was kind of true. I did want to get to know my whole family, but I'd expected this first visit to be just Damien and his wife… my mother. I was still having trouble wrapping my own head around that idea.

Maybe it was better to get all the introductions over at once and to get a sense of the overall family vibe. They must be close-knit if they'd all jumped to visit this quickly.

Malik—Damien—my mind balked at thinking of him as *Dad*—motioned me to a doorway to the left of a broad wooden staircase. "We'll have a little private get-together with the immediate family first. The others can wait. I don't want to drop too much on you all at once."

I dragged in a breath with a little relief. "Okay."

Damien led me into a small sitting room. A woman I recognized as his wife from the photos and an unfamiliar young man who looked to be in his late teens stood up from the sofa at our entrance.

Mrs. Malik froze in place, staring at me with wide eyes. Damien went over to her, and she clutched his shoulder, never tearing her eyes from me.

"My Rachel," she whispered, and pressed her hand to her mouth. She took a step closer, searching my face, and I found myself searching hers too, looking for the college girl who'd looked like me.

I could catch traces of that younger woman in her eyes and the line of her jaw, though the shape of her nose and lips had been altered by her plastic surgery. Fine lines were starting to creep from the corners of her eyes and mouth like they did on Damien. But even with the subtle signs of age, she was beautiful with her naturalistic makeup and striped sundress.

Damien beckoned me over, and I stepped hesitantly toward the two of them. "Mom?"

The word sounded alien falling from my lips, but a beaming smile spread across the woman's face. She wrapped her arms around me in a hug that I had to stop myself from tensing against.

My instinctive resistance only lasted a second. Then I started to relax into her embrace. It felt… warm. Motherly, even. I laughed inwardly at my little joke and let my arms rise to return the hug.

I had a mother. A mother who'd been missing me all this time.

"Rachel," she murmured, and eased back to gaze into my eyes again, her own shining with joy. "My sweet girl has come back to us. It's a miracle."

A strange sensation swelled in my chest. I'd never felt anything like it before. In all my years at the household—all the years of Ana taking a semi-maternal role—nobody had ever hugged me like this. Nobody had ever shown I *mattered* like this.

I tore my gaze away to glance at the boy who'd stayed by the sofa, where he was eying me skeptically. He had the same storm gray eyes as both Damien and me, but his were lighter than mine, diluted with a touch of green like my mother's. *Our* mother's? He also had the tawny brown hair I'd seen in pictures of Damien when he was younger and a height that matched the older man's, though he hadn't quite filled out that height yet. His limbs were still a bit gangly.

My mother stepped back and took a deep breath, dabbing beneath her eyes with her finger. "Goodness, I'm going to make a mess of myself," she said with a laugh. She reached toward the boy and tugged him over. "You can keep calling me Mom, of course, but if you're more comfortable with first names while you get to know us, I'm Iris. This is our son—your brother—Carter."

Carter gave an awkward wave, and I did the same thing back. Neither of us knew what to say about that. From the looks of him, he'd been born a few years after I was kidnapped. We'd never existed in the same space until now.

Then the door to the other part of the house flew open, and a short woman with frizzy gray hair burst into the entranceway. She spoke before anyone could get a word out. "Now I know my son told us to stay in there, but I was beginning to think that he was blowing smoke up my ass with the story of his daughter coming back from the dead."

Her presence made the room feel cramped. I took a step back, and more people flooded in behind her. But the plump old lady took all my attention from the others. She was small and wizened, but she bulldozed over Damien's brief protests, and I knew immediately that I *didn't* want to be in her path.

She looked me up and down as she approached, and I wondered

what she saw when she looked at me. Her sharp eyes didn't look as if they missed much. A prickle ran down my back

"Grandma Ruby, you're scaring her," Carter said, giving her a playful poke in the arm.

She shot an affectionate glower at Carter, and I could finally breathe. "Now Carter, let me have my fun. She's as much my grandbaby as you are." The woman looked at me and smiled. "Rachel," she said with undiluted affection in her tone, and pulled me into a hug just as my mother had.

I didn't know how to react surrounded by this much affection. It felt like they were excited to see a woman who wasn't here. Who even was Rachel? I knew that'd been my name years ago, but I'd never used it within my memory. Each time they called me by her name, I felt like an imposter. I was Decima, and I didn't know how to be anyone else.

I knew better than to ask to go by the name my kidnappers had given me, though. I could only imagine their looks of horror.

So, I stood there, allowing the crowd to come and devour me with tight hugs. Aunts, uncles, and cousins looked me over, commenting on how much I looked like my mother or father—comments that I knew were more for politeness than anything.

My eyes caught on a few of them more than the others—people who were easier to read, maybe? Maybe their personalities complimented mine, making it easier to meet their gazes. One family in particular—my first cousin, aunt, and uncle on my father's side—drew my attention.

The man and wife each had fiery red hair. Their daughter, who looked around my age or a tad older, had the complexion of a redhead, complete with freckles her foundation couldn't quite hide, but she'd dyed her wavy locks black. My aunt and uncle clasped each other's hands as they took me in, but my cousin seemed almost as interested in her phone as my arrival.

Maybe I should have been insulted, but something about her disinterest reassured me. I wasn't a big deal to everyone. To her, this was just another day. Maybe it didn't have to be such a momentous occasion.

Damien began tossing out names, and I tried to commit each one to memory. The woman with the dyed black hair was Margaret. Despite her apparent boredom, my father clapped her on the shoulder. "Margaret's twenty-five, so she's the closest in age to you. I'm sure you two will get along great. She and your Aunt Mabel and Uncle Henry come around a lot, so you'll see plenty of them."

He was talking as if I was going to be living here from now on. A prickle of apprehension ran over my skin, even though I knew he wouldn't be taking that step so quickly.

Margaret lifted her gaze from her phone. Her voice came out low and monotonous. "Did they torture you? Like kidnappers in crime shows or whatever?"

"Margaret!" Aunt Mabel said with a gasp.

I wasn't actually offended by the question, but I wasn't sure how to answer it either. I guessed Noelle and the others had kind of tortured me by forcing me to train, but I couldn't say that without getting into the whole "I was raised to be an assassin" thing it seemed better to keep on the down low.

"No," I said, forcing a small laugh. Every pair of eyes focused even more intently on me, curious as to how I would answer her. "No, of course not. I didn't even know that I was kidnapped until recently. They acted like I was a part of their family." A brutally disciplined and distant family, but close enough.

Grandma Ruby was the next to speak. "They kidnapped you. How did you not realize something was wrong? They took you from us, and they never even mentioned that you came from somewhere else?"

I gave an apologetic grimace. Did she really blame me?

"I guess I was so young that after a while the old memories didn't stick with me," I said. "I grew up with them, and they acted like their way of life was normal and that they were the only ones who could protect me from the dangerous world."

And the whole time they'd been the most dangerous people in it. People who'd already torn apart my real family.

"Well, something has to be done about them," my grandmother spat out. My grandfather—Bo, one of the others had called him—came over and slung his arm around her shoulders, but she barely seemed to notice his presence in her fury. "It's disgusting what they did to you and to us."

Her husband looked down at her. "Don't be getting upset. She's here now, and that's what matters the most. Isn't that right, Rachel?"

I nodded, and the smile that had felt forced before seemed to stick in place without much effort now. How lucky was I that I'd found a family who cared so much about someone who was essentially a stranger to them? Even if their questions made me edgy, they only asked because I mattered to them.

If I'd died during a mission for the household, Noelle would have replaced me, and she and her colleagues would all have moved on with their lives. Nobody there would have mourned me.

I was finally a part of something bigger in a good way, not just a pawn to be maneuvered and manipulated for the sake of someone's selfish ends.

With that thought, the secrets I was keeping to protect myself left a bitter aftertaste in my mouth. Julius's face flashed through my mind. Then Talon's and Blaze's. Garrison's.

They were a family in a way, but they weren't like this one. I was tied to them through loyalty and mutual respect, not blood. But they knew my story and what I'd done with my life. They knew everything about me, and they accepted it all without restraint.

I was going to spend this entire encounter acting like a woman who I didn't know—one who was so far from the woman I had become. I'd created a story to explain the time I'd been away from this family, and if I ever told them the truth…

Well, I didn't know if I could ever tell them the truth about myself. It was hard not to imagine that if I tried, I'd lose them all.

I looked around at all the cousins, aunts, and uncles, then toward Grandma Ruby and Grandpa Bo who stood tall and held her. Then, I turned my attention to my parents, standing side-by-side with Carter in front of them.

Damien's face had become a rigid mask of determination. "We're going to bring the people who kidnapped you to justice," he swore.

My heart skipped a beat as I absorbed that promise. Maybe he knew more about my kidnappers than I'd expected. If it'd been personal—and how could it not be to some extent, with the lengths they'd gone to in order to steal me away—he must know who at least some of his enemies were.

"I don't know how much help I'm going to be in accomplishing that," I said, sucking my lower lip under my teeth. I knew more than I was going to admit, but I couldn't lay everything on the table. Not yet. I needed to know what information would be the most useful in finding the people responsible without jeopardizing my own secrets. "I was isolated from everyone except for the few people who were looking after me, and when I realized what was going on, the situation had turned so dangerous I couldn't stay to find out anything that'd help track them down."

My father frowned. "What about those people who looked after you?" he asked, tightening his jaw, but he loosened it with a deep breath and shook his head. "You were around them a lot. I'm sure there are some things that you discovered, even if you don't realize it."

"Well," I said with a wince, "the woman who spent the most time caring for me was killed by some other group of criminals, so she's out of the picture. That's when I ran. It must have been some kind of gang war or something."

I shuddered, completely for effect. That was how a normal person would react when thinking of a murder, right?

Damien stared off at a place on the wall for a moment, his expression pensive. Was he angry because I couldn't provide him with a lead, or was it more than that? Did he have ideas about who might have been involved that he didn't want to share with me out of fear of re-traumatizing me?

I had to show I was at least a little more resilient than that. "If you have any leads or ideas about the investigation, I'd really like to be a part of it," I said, struggling to hit the right level of enthusiasm. "I want to know the reason I was taken as much as you do."

My father rested his hand on my back with a reassuring pat, though his face was still serious. "There's no need for that. I'm sorry for badgering you about it at all. You've been through enough already. The investigators will want to talk to you, of course, and get any details you can offer, but I'll make sure it ends there."

How did I convince him that I wanted to be a part of this investigation? "I'm honestly happy to help however I can. I want to see these people brought to justice too." Preferably by my own hand, I added silently. "Please don't worry about it being an imposition."

Damien's jaw flexed, but the smile held in place. "Enough on this awful subject," he said, squeezing my shoulder lightly. "Let's focus on everything good that's come out of today. We have you back with us—nothing could be more worth celebrating than that. Why don't we go sit down to lunch and we can talk more there, about lighter subjects."

I couldn't continue pushing without sounding suspicious, so I simply nodded and let my gaze slip over the gathered family members again. "I'm looking forward to getting to know you all better."

As everyone streamed into the hall, heading for the dining room, I caught a glimpse of another shadow crossing Damien's face, there just for a moment before he caught my eyes and aimed another smile at me.

Something was bothering him. Was it just that I hadn't offered a clear path to finding the criminals he must want to bring to justice more than any before?

Or was there something more going on here that I was missing?

FOUR

Julius

I SWUNG my putter and nailed the golf ball, sending it up the small hill. As I watched, the neon green sphere raced straight toward the hole, ricocheted off the back border, and rolled back toward us, invalidating my entire swing. "Fucking hell," I grumbled, stepping back for Talon to take his turn.

I didn't bother watching him, knowing that if he didn't get an immediate hole-in-one, he'd come close to it. I should have never suggested we join in this mini golfing expedition to keep an eye on Dess and her family, but once they made it deep enough in the course, we would have struggled to keep an eye out without being spotted if we weren't players ourselves.

Dressing like golf-course employees had been the second option, but the margin for error was too high. This place didn't employ that many people. It would have taken only one genuine employee to catch us and kick us off the course.

So here I stood, groaning as Talon sent his ball toward the hole. With a single bank, it clattered in effortlessly. He tugged at the lapels of his polo shirt with a satisfied air.

I glowered at him. "You could at least *act* humble."

A sliver of a smile crossed my long-time partner's lips, and I'd worked with him *so* long that I could recognize it as a taunt when most wouldn't have. "You could act like you know what you're doing," he retorted.

He was the only member of the crew who'd have dared to make a comment like that, and he'd only have made it when the younger men weren't around. I let out a disgruntled huff and lined up my shot before hitting it haphazardly. I knew how to aim guns, not golf clubs.

My ball didn't go anywhere near the hole, but it stayed atop the hill, so we strode up there together, looking over at the next part of the course as we walked.

Dess stood before her ball. She swung the putter with about as much skill as I had, which soothed my wounded ego a little. The ball lifted and soared into the rocks outside the range. Her mother let out a soft giggle and patted Dess on the shoulder with a few words of encouragement. Dess shook herself, and I could see her reining in her natural competitive instincts to plaster an easy-going smile on her face.

I had to restrain a grimace at the sight of that artificial friendliness. She didn't *fit* with this family: her mother perfectly outfitted in white capris and visor, her brother slouching along the side of the course as he leaned on his club nonchalantly, her father completely at ease with his putter as he tapped it on the greenery.

"Must be a rich person thing," I muttered as I eyed them and then my ball. "I'd have thought they'd stick to the real thing, but I guess this is just a mini version of the country club."

Blaze had surveyed this place after Dess had gotten the invitation. I'd wanted to see how her birth family interacted with her for myself, for reasons I didn't feel I needed to spell out. The Maliks did head off to a country club where they had a membership every weekend that Damien was home, but the owner of this miniature course was a donor to their campaign, and sometimes the family came by here to play.

"They're easing Dess up to the full challenge," Talon remarked in his usual unemotional way.

"She doesn't need that kind of challenge. She's got plenty of other things on her plate."

"They don't know that."

"If they had any brains, they'd figure it out." I managed to hit my ball into the hole, finally, and straightened up. Damien was just taking his own turn, easily hitting a hole-in-two. My hackles rose for no reason I could put my finger on. "He's just keeping up appearances by coming here, buttering up the donors."

Talon shrugged. "That's part of his job, isn't it?"

"I don't trust anyone who mostly thinks about what they can get out of the people they're supposedly working on behalf of," I replied.

As we moved to the next part of the course, Talon spun his ball in his hand and studied me. "He's her father, and he planned a simple activity to keep them entertained."

"His being her father doesn't mean anything. Family doesn't automatically make someone a good person." As Talon should know, although my own sense of personal consideration stopped me from saying that out loud. He didn't need salt rubbed in the wound openly.

From the way my friend's eyes flashed, the remark had hit home anyway. "Playing the role of parents in public doesn't mean much, but he's been good with her so far. She seems happy."

I had to admit, if only in brooding silence, that he was right. I'd thought that seeing her happy would be the only thing I'd want, but as I watched her exchange small talk and the occasional grin with these people, I couldn't shake the feeling that I wished she *wasn't* so relieved to be with them.

I wanted her to have *sustainable* happiness, but the Maliks—and their political lifestyle—didn't seem like a life I'd ever have envisioned for her. Maybe it was the right fit for her and she'd just never had the chance to grow into it, but I had trouble believing that after seeing her in real action.

But I couldn't pretend away the victorious bounce in her step after she knocked her ball into the hole. Or the way she leaned into her mother's hand when the woman touched her hair as if confirming her daughter was really still there. Or her chuckle as she gave her brother a light punch to the shoulder and laughed harder at his playful complaints in response.

God, that laugh could have sent me into an early grave. The sight of her tipping back her head to the sun, delight shining in her pale face and dark eyes, tugged at my heart.

Had she ever laughed with the crew like that? I wasn't sure I'd seen that much joy fill her face when she talked to us. Sometimes she looked mischievous or content. She'd smiled in amusement, but never unadulterated happiness like this.

Would she decide to stay with us when her birth family could give her something I doubted we ever could?

Damien came over and motioned to Dess like he was giving her advice on her swing. My jaw started to clench until I forced it to relax.

"Look at the way he hovers over her," I couldn't help saying to Talon. "He needs to give her some space."

Talon didn't comment, simply getting into position on the next mini green. I watched him line up his shot before I switched to studying the Maliks some more. "It also seems pretty careless to take his family out in public when his life is under threat. Do his bodyguards have any idea how to do their job? We've been behind him the entire time, keeping watch, and nobody has looked twice at us. Shouldn't he be more concerned about protecting his family? Especially the daughter who he just got back."

I narrowed my eyes at Damien. He didn't even bother to position himself to block his family's backs.

Talon raised his eyebrows at me. "Do you actually think he's being sketchy or are you just bothered seeing Dess that happy with them?"

"Why would that bother me?" I shot back automatically, and then my gut twisted. It had been bothering me. I wasn't going to lie to myself.

"The reporters are keeping their distance because Malik insisted that they give Dess some room without having cameras in her face," Talon said into my silence, pointing to where I remembered seeing them outside the mini-golf place. "That shows that he cares at least a little bit about her healing from her kidnapping."

"It's the least he could do," I muttered.

"He could have been milking the publicity." Talon rubbed his jaw. "And this place isn't *that* public. We walked through a metal detector to get in. The course has a pretty good wall around it. I wouldn't be surprised if it's easier to get into the country club grounds."

"All right, all right." I glowered at him, and he gazed evenly back at me. "*I'm* looking out for her here too," I reminded him.

"And so am I," Talon said. "But the more people who are doing it, the safer she'll be. So far, he hasn't appeared to be a threat to anything except how much time and attention she has left to give us."

He took his swing. The damned ball soared across the green and thumped to the ground right next to the hole, which it promptly rolled into.

I should have brought Blaze. He wouldn't have golfed me under the table.

But Talon had a point. I had to acknowledge that Malik could have taken the opportunity to advance his political capital and instead had focused on his family's needs. Having a kidnapped child would go a long way to prop up his anti-criminal agenda, and not using the story to his advantage showed a level of commitment to Dess that I couldn't deny.

I wondered if the reason I was so hesitant to trust Malik—the reason I struggled to trust Dess alone with him—wasn't because of Malik at all. I'd witnessed powerful people making decisions that hurt everyone around them plenty of times, and I'd rarely stepped in unless I was getting paid to. The only difference was that Dess was involved, and the thought of something happening to her… Even imagining it for a second sent a jab of pain through the center of my chest.

I didn't have a strategy or any sort of plan to fix this situation if it went sour.

I watched Dess bite her bottom lip as she looked between her ball and the hole. She was so gorgeous she literally took my breath away. She clutched the putter and took a shot that wasn't half bad this time. With a grin I could tell wasn't forced, she bobbed on her feet and glanced at her parents, soaking in their approving exclamations.

Normally I was in total control of my reactions. Why was I letting Dess's association with her birth family get to me so much?

Because every time she stepped out of arm's reach, some part of me screamed that I had to protect her. I'd always treated her as an equal within the crew… but she was more than that. I sure as hell didn't have the same urges and impulses with the other men as I did with her. I wanted her—and I'd also have done anything to know she was safe and happy.

Shit. Was I *falling* for her?

I'd never cared this much about another woman—that much I knew. But as I watched her with her family, I wasn't sure it mattered anyway. She'd eventually have to make a choice. Her father was a criminal hunter, and I was a criminal. Telling her how I felt would only make it harder if she decided to pursue a life with her family. I couldn't do that to her.

I *wouldn't* do that to her. I'd keep my mouth shut until she decided where she wanted to take her life from here.

My phone vibrated in my pocket. I tore my eyes away from Dess as I pulled it out. A text from Blaze had popped up on the screen. I scanned it and then turned to Talon reluctantly.

"Blaze has found a concerning post online that he thinks we should see. It looks like Dess is safe enough here. We'd better check this out."

We found Blaze in the hotel room with his gaze skimming back and forth between his laptop and his propped-up tablet. At the pace with which he flicked through the content on both, I wondered how he could read anything they said.

I closed the door firmly behind me, jarring him from his state of concentration. He swiveled in his seat and then pressed his hand against the spot in his side that still gave him a twinge of pain when he moved too quickly. "I wasn't expecting you back this fast."

"More like you lose all sense of time when you get in that state," Garrison snarked, coming over as we gathered around Blaze at the table. "Are you going to spill the beans now?"

I nodded. "Yes, what did you find that was so important?"

Blaze dragged in a breath. "It could be nothing. But the details, and the way it's written… Well, I'll let you have a look first so you can draw your own conclusions."

He spun toward the devices and clicked on his keyboard. Several windows fell away, leaving one that he maximized on the laptop's screen.

"I have a constant search on the web with several keywords related to our work, and I added some for Dess once we knew her situation. This result popped up today. It's from a DC newspaper."

It was a column of missed connections postings, people searching for someone whose eye they'd caught on a busy bus or across a grocery store. One of the longer posts was highlighted. I leaned closer, squinting at the screen to read it.

Rachel – You got coffee and talked about your accident. You think you've finally come home. There's so much more I need to tell you. Not all the answers are in our saliva. If you care about the truth and not just making a family, please get in touch.

Then there was a phone number.

A chill rippled down my spine. "Could it be someone jerking her around?" I demanded. "How many of those details—the coffee shop, the faked accident, her giving Malik her spit—have been reported in the media?"

Blaze exhaled in a rush. "Good. You don't think it's a coincidence either. The specifics are so on the nose—and most of it *hasn't* been reported. Malik had a blood test done to confirm the result he got from the spit test before they went to the media, and the public stories have only talked about that. And he's never given any details about their first meeting in the coffee shop." The hacker paused, his leg jiggling with nervous energy under the table. "Whoever this is, they were watching Dess when she confronted him. Closely enough to hear at least a little of what she said too."

"And he—or she—thinks they have some important 'truth' to tell her?" Garrison said, scowling. "Why the fuck should we trust this shady creep?"

I folded my arms over my chest. Resolve wound around my chest, stilling the shiver of anxiety inside it. "We shouldn't. But we have to show this to Dess. It's addressing her—it should be her call what she does about it."

"It could be someone who knows something about her kidnapping," Talon pointed out. "Creep or not, we'll want that information."

I wished we could charge in there and demand it ourselves, but as much as I wanted to protect Dess, lying to her wasn't going to accomplish that in the long run. She deserved her freedom after having it denied for so long.

"I'm sure Dess will agree," I said. "We'll fill her in as soon as she gets back, and she'll make the call about what we do next."

FIVE

Decima

I TOOK a deep breath and glanced across the car at Julius, who was poised behind the wheel. A van rumbled by in the parking lot we'd chosen for its central location in D.C. The leather seat felt stiff under my ass.

"Your honest opinion," I said, holding my phone in my right hand and fidgeting with the hem of my shirt with my left. "Is this going to be worth it?"

The leader of the Chaos Crew didn't respond immediately. His hands flexed against the wheel. Then he looked back at me steadily. "That's impossible to judge when we don't know who this person is or what they want."

"It could have something to do with the people who kidnapped me." The organization with the logo like a droplet with a line slicing diagonally through it. The people who'd stolen me from my family and tried to kill the men who'd helped me more than once. "Or the people who hired the crew to kill *them*."

"Even if that's the case, what this means depends on what answers are still important to you. Now that you have your family, how much does it matter to you to understand the rest of your past?"

Maybe it would have been better if I could have simply moved on and forgotten all that. But the urge to find out who'd controlled me so thoroughly for so much of my life nagged at me no matter how many visits I had with the Maliks.

I needed to know why. I needed to understand the reason my life had been rewritten. I needed to be sure the people involved wouldn't hurt anyone close to me ever again.

I wasn't sure I'd ever said anything truer than the words that tumbled from my mouth next. "It's the most important thing to me."

Julius gave me a quiet smile. "Then it'll be worth it no matter what happens, just to know you tried."

Blaze's voice resonated through the headset I was wearing, identical to Julius's. "My equipment is ready. As soon as this person picks up, I can start to triangulate their signal. Be sure to keep whoever it is talking as long as possible. That'll give me the best chance of narrowing down his location."

I nodded. "Got it."

I tapped the number we'd gotten from the strange missed connections ad into my phone and brought it to my ear, easing off that side of the headset. The phone on the other end rang in what felt like slow motion. After the fourth ring, I wondered if anyone would pick up at all. Maybe it'd had nothing to do with me. Just a huge coincidence.

Then there was a click and a momentary silence. My heart jumped. "Hello?"

"Who am I speaking to?" a man's voice asked. It was hoarse. Confident. I got the impression of a fair bit of age in the gravity of his tone.

I almost said "Dess" but caught myself just in time. "Rachel," I said, giving the name he'd used in his ad. "I think you were expecting to hear from me."

There was a faint rustling on the other end as if he'd shifted his position. Blaze's voice carried into my other ear. "He's in the south end of the city." Julius, who was hearing the same report, started the ignition and drove out of the parking lot.

"I'm glad you found my message," the man on the phone said. "You're obviously a sharp one, Rachel Malik."

He knew exactly who I was then, but that wasn't a surprise.

"A friend who knew some of the details of recent events in my life noticed the post and pointed it out to me," I said. I wanted to demand to know what it was about, what he wanted, but Blaze needed this conversation to be drawn out as long as possible. So I stopped there and waited.

The man gave a brief hum. "A friend, not family?"

"I *said* a friend, didn't I?"

"What people say and what they mean aren't always the same thing, as I'm sure you'll become aware of soon if you haven't already."

"What's that supposed to mean?" I asked, a prickle of apprehension running down my spine.

"I saw you on the news with Damien Malik," the man said, ignoring my question. "Back from the dead. I knew you deserved better than to go in blind. I had to reach out to you."

"And you chose this way?"

He barked a laugh. "We have to be subtle in my line of business."

I frowned. "And what exactly is that? Who are you?" I clamped down on all the other questions that wanted to fly from my mouth.

"I've been investigating the Malik family for some time," he said, again not offering the specific information I'd asked for. "I've turned up some unsettling information. You shouldn't trust them wholeheartedly."

"They're my family," I retorted automatically.

"Not all families mean well. Every villain is part of a family."

I guessed that was true. I squirmed in my seat again, wondering how much longer it'd be before Blaze could home in on this guy even more. I wanted to talk to him face to face, to force him to give me some straight answers.

As if sensing my thoughts, Blaze's voice came again. "I'm closing in on him. Northeast."

Julius nodded and took a turn at the next intersection. I focused on the phone again. "Who are you to be investigating anyone anyway?"

"I'm a special government agent. All politicians have people keeping oversight on them, as I'm sure you can understand. Damien Malik is my assignment."

"And what makes you think there's anything to be worried about with him?"

"I haven't been able to gather enough evidence to prove anything in court," the man said. "You wouldn't believe me if I told you the details. But I know what I've seen. I know you should watch your step."

"This all sounds like a bunch of vague fearmongering to me," I shot back. "Why should I trust *you*? I don't even know your name."

"My colleagues call me the Hunter. And I can hardly jeopardize my mandate by giving away too much to someone who's become so close to the target of my investigation. I simply wanted to deliver the clearest warning I could."

He sounded like he was about to wind up the conversation. Blaze was muttering on his end, obviously still working at tracing the signal. My heart thumped faster. I had to keep this weirdo talking.

"If you're really a government agent, shouldn't you have been able to track down my phone number?" I said. "Why did you contact me in such a roundabout way?"

"I wanted to make sure you were interested in knowing the truth. And that your father wouldn't be hovering over you when we connected."

"Well, you managed that. He's not here now. So why don't you tell me more about whatever it is you think he's done."

Blaze spoke up again with a ripple of excitement in his voice. "I've narrowed it down to a ten block radius. Sending the coordinates for the area to your phone, Julius."

The phone mounted on the dashboard pinged with the incoming transmission. The map we'd already had ready zoomed in on a particular section of the city.

The Hunter, if I really had to think of him by that name, shifted his position with another rustle. "There are a lot of things you don't know."

I gritted my teeth. "Then tell me. Tell me what's so wrong with my family. What have you seen? It isn't much of a warning if I don't even know what to watch out *for*."

"I told you, you wouldn't believe me—not when you're so close to the situation. You'll have to see it for yourself."

"Are you going to show me then?"

"I don't believe it's safe for me to get that involved," the Hunter said. "But now that you know to be cautious, you'll be going in with your eyes open. If I find more evidence—better evidence—I'll share that with you."

His words sounded like a promise of help, but it was only more vagueness when you really looked at it. I was becoming increasingly certain that he had no intention of telling me anything at all. Which probably meant this was all bullshit. But I couldn't stop now.

When I got my hands on him, I'd find out the reason for the bullshit.

Julius took another turn, accelerating as he went. The car swayed lightly under me. I peered out the window at the buildings we were rushing by as he swerved around the sparse traffic.

"Five blocks," Blaze muttered, and the map zoomed in even more. Then he let out a huff of frustration. "Something's interfering with the signal."

I spat out the first question that came to mind that might keep the Hunter talking. "Can't you at least tell me if there's anything specific I should be watching out for? The general type of thing that's made you uneasy?"

"I think you should draw your own conclusions, Rachel," he said. "You're smart enough for that. You'll recognize the rot when you come across it."

Now he was talking in ominous poetry. I groped for something else to say to stop him from hanging up, and Blaze's voice pealed into my other ear.

"There! It was passing through an electric field meant to scatter the transmission, but I modified the search and found it. I've got an exact building now. Probably the top floor."

Julius revved the engine faster. Relief rushed through me. "Well, if you feel like enlightening me more at some point," I said to the Hunter, "you have my number now."

"Indeed I do," he said.

I didn't want to let him go just yet. He'd be more likely to stay in place if I kept him talking. There was no way he could know that we were descending on him right now.

"If I call you again, will you pick up?" I asked. "Or will you be busy with your government business?"

"I suppose that depends on when you call. I'm afraid there's nothing else I can tell you right now."

We'd almost reached the marker on the map. "Wait!" I said. "I need to know—is it just my father you're worried about, or the rest of the family too?"

Julius pulled over to the curb outside what looked like a normal two-story house, a little shabby with pale yellow paint that was flaking off the bricks, but nothing horribly rundown. He jerked his head toward it.

I slipped out of the car, not even shutting the door so I wouldn't make much noise, and darted around to the back door. There were no signs of occupation, no vehicles in the driveway, no lights gleaming through the windows under the overcast sky.

"It's difficult to say without delving in more," the Hunter said. "But for now I'd be wary of all of them."

He was just a bucket of joy, this guy, wasn't he? I whipped out my lockpicks and had the back door open in a matter of seconds. After I'd eased it open, I padded silently through the first-floor hallway, confirming there was no one in those rooms before heading up the stairs.

"Even my brother?" I prodded, letting skepticism color my voice. "The kid's only eighteen."

"I've met killers who were twelve," the Hunter said. "Don't put much stock in age as an indicator of innocence."

The idea of my grumbly teenage brother being on the same level as a killer—a killer like *I* was—nearly made me snort. I swallowed the sound and darted along the upper hall to the room at the front of the house. The door was ajar.

I didn't bother to say anything else into the phone. I sprang into the room—

And found nothing but a vacant chair with a folded paper sitting on it.

A low chuckle reverberated from the phone as I picked up the note. *Nice try,* it said in neat letters.

Amusement colored the Hunter's voice. "It seems you're good at this, Miss Malik, but you need to be ready in case someone turns out to be even better."

Then the line went dead.

My fingers dug into the paper, creasing it, as I lowered the phone. "What happened?" Blaze asked through the headset, but I didn't know what to tell him. The Hunter's last words were still whirling through my mind.

He'd been here. Obviously he had—who else would have left this note? But somehow he'd either faked his signal or managed to get out of here just before I'd arrived without any of us noticing.

And now he knew that Damien Malik's recently rediscovered daughter was more than just a restaurant hostess with a fraught past—that I had the skills to track a man like him down.

A chill tickled over my skin. Just how much about myself had I inadvertently revealed to this man with his tricks and his warnings? About the *real* me, not Rachel Malik?

SIX

Decima

THE SPREAD of food across the Maliks' outdoor dining table looked more like a Thanksgiving feast than a basic luncheon with close family, although the options were more suited for a summery meal than a fall one. Chunks of watermelon and pineapple lay in large ceramic bowls next to sweetly creamy dips. Sandwiches cut into bite-sized pieces stood heaped on platters. Each placemat had a glass on the top filled to the brim with what looked like a frozen red juice.

It was all so… extravagant. But then maybe my frame of reference was off considering that I'd only ever eaten alone for all the meals I could remember until just a few weeks ago.

"Did you bring a bathing suit, Rachel?" my mother asked, following behind me and Carter as we approached the patio table.

I eyed the large pool and the stone patio surrounding it. Lounge chairs and pool inflatables littered the patio. From the new assortment of towels draped over the porch railing, it looked like the family had made use of the pool earlier this morning in the late summer warmth.

"I don't really swim," I admitted.

I *could* swim, of course. It'd been a part of my training with

Noelle. But if I wore a bathing suit, way too many of my scars would be exposed. I wondered how my mother would react to them, no matter what excuses I came up with to explain them away. I'd told the Maliks that the people who'd kidnapped me had treated me like one of their own, and it would be suspicious to change up the story now.

I was wondering a whole lot of things, really. After my phone call with the man who called himself the Hunter, it was hard to take this cheery family get-together at face value. *Had* he discovered something about the Maliks that should make me concerned? What could they possibly be up to?

Or had he just been trying to create tensions for his own bizarre agenda? I had no idea who that man was.

Of course, the truth was I barely knew who any of these people were either.

I glanced at Grandma Ruby and Grandpa Bo, the only other Maliks in attendance today, who'd followed us over to the table. Grandma Ruby had her nose turned up at the feast waiting for us as if she found it wanting. I couldn't imagine what it was missing, but then, Damien's mother seemed to enjoy criticizing whatever she could. And she got worse on days like today when her son had been called into work. I wasn't sure whether I felt more or less at ease without my father among us.

"Well, everyone take a seat." My mother pointed to one of the trays of small sandwiches. "I made sure to have some pepperoni and cheese sandwiches made special for you, Carter. Rachel, do you have a sandwich preference?"

I wanted to laugh. I'd never been offered options. At the household, they'd given me whatever they pleased, and I was expected to eat it or starve. With the guys, I'd grabbed whatever I found in the refrigerator or what Steffie, their housekeeper and general assistant, made for us.

"I'm not picky," I said with a small shrug. "I'll eat pretty much anything."

Did Carter make a bit of a face as he sat down? I hoped he didn't think I was implying anything negative about him having his own favorites. His shoulders rounded into their typical slouch in his chair, and I hesitated before taking the seat next to him. Sometimes he joked around with me a little, but sometimes he seemed like he'd rather I wasn't around.

It had to be pretty weird having a big sister drop out of the sky without any warning. I couldn't blame him for being a bit awkward.

"Maybe I'll try the pepperoni and cheese if you can spare some," I said to him, shooting him a smile. "I do like pizza."

The corner of his mouth twitched into half a smile. "These are the closest things I can get to it at one of these dos."

Our grandparents sat across from us, and my mother sank down at my other side. She looked around the table, and a smile stretched across her face. "Wow. I could have never imagined this in my wildest dreams. Sitting at lunch with my family, my daughter at my side. My son a seat down. Damien's parents across from us. I'm so grateful."

She sounded a bit choked up by the end of that speech. Even if the Hunter had sown some doubts in my mind about the Maliks in general, I was completely sure that my parents were grateful to have me back in their lives. Iris got close to tears at least once during every visit, and I could never tell what the best response would be.

Today, I ventured a touch of my hand on top of hers. She flipped her hand and squeezed my fingers, and I knew I'd judged the situation correctly. The physical contact put me a little on edge, but it seemed to soothe her as she took a deep breath.

"I don't think any of us could have predicted how happy we'd be, Iris," Grandma Ruby said, piling watermelon on her plate and sprinkling a generous amount of salt on top. Her gaze veered to the garden. It was full of blooms with narrow yellow petals around a dark center. I didn't know much about flowers, but they appeared to be in excellent health to me. Vibrant in a wild sort of way.

"You need to get out there and pull those weeds," my grandmother remarked. "They're taking away the effect of the black-eyed susans."

"I think it looks really nice with a little wildness in there," I said, trying to offset the criticism of her statement.

My mother waved my protest off. "No, she's right. I haven't been out to pull weeds in the flower beds for a couple of weeks. It's about time."

"You don't have a gardener?" I asked.

I never would have imagined my mother pulling the weeds from the garden on her own. I glanced over at her perfectly manicured nails —not a chip in sight.

She laughed. "Oh, we do have a groundskeeper who sees to all the yard work, but that garden is an important symbol to the family. I like to handle it myself. Black-eyed susans symbolize justice, you know, and so much of our work—especially your father's—goes toward bringing more of that into the world."

"Look at how well they grow for our family," Grandma Ruby said, gesturing to the lush garden. "We're clearly doing a good job of it. They couldn't be in better bloom." She paused. "Well, maybe a little better without the weeds."

"I'll get on that this evening, Ruby," mom said with a genuine smile. She must be used to the nagging after nearly three decades of marriage into the family.

Other than the nagging, all of these people seemed so… nice. Even Carter's awkwardness came across as more shy than hostile. Maybe it was *because* the idea of them having some nefarious side seemed so absurd that I couldn't get the Hunter's warnings out of my mind.

If he'd been lying, why? Why would he have it in for the Maliks? He hadn't appeared to know anything about my past, so I had no reason to think he was connected to the household, but a man as high up in politics as Damien Malik could definitely have made more than one enemy.

As I chewed on one of the pepperoni and cheese sandwiches, which actually were pretty good, I considered how I could get at whether the family might be aware of this man's vigilance.

"I heard some people talking about hunting when I was at a corner store in town yesterday," I said, making up the story as an excuse to broach the subject. It seemed like something Garrison would do to get people talking. If the gambit worked, I'd have to let him know his influence had rubbed off well on me. "Is that a common hobby around here?"

"Oh, sure." Grandpa Bo nodded, speaking up for the first time. He mostly seemed to let his wife do the talking between the two of them.

Given her personality, maybe that wasn't surprising. "Every couple of years I go out with a few of my buddies, and we bring back a buck or two."

Carter grimaced and gave a little shudder, and my mother shook her head. "Let's not discuss that at the table while we're eating." She glanced at me. "Carter saw him bring back one of those deer when he was younger and just thinking about it makes him queasy."

"I'm fine," Carter mumbled, but he did look a bit green. "I just prefer my animals either alive or already in a form where you can't tell what they were before they made it to the grocery store." He waggled his sandwich in the air to indicate the pepperoni.

I raised my eyebrows slightly. "I guess you all don't spend a whole lot of time with avid hunters then." I motioned to Grandpa Bo. "What are your buddies like? The hunters who go with you? I've never known anyone who was into that kind of pastime."

Grandpa Bo chuckled. "Between you and me, they're all old men who like to shoot their mouths off more than they like to hunt. One is nearly deaf, and one can't walk through the woods for more than ten minutes without needing a breather. The two of them live in Ohio, so they only come around when we plan a trip."

I resisted the urge to clench my jaw in frustration. The man on the phone had shown no sign of hearing problems, and he'd seemed very familiar with the city. He also hadn't sounded as old as my grandfather.

"Does Damien—my dad—ever go with you?" I had to ask.

Grandpa Bo laughed again and patted Ruby's hand. "My son has never been interested in hunting, and he certainly has never asked to go with me."

Well, it was totally possible that the Hunter's moniker had nothing to do with any interest in hunting animals, only his penchant for hunting down information. I switched tactics. "I guess Dad has to stay pretty conscious of the image he presents even on his down time. Maybe all of you do. Do you find you're under a lot of scrutiny because of his political career?"

"Oh, it's nothing we can't handle," Iris said quickly. "We're proud to see how much he's accomplished." Then she paused. "But you've been thrown into the mix out of the blue. If you find anyone's bothering you, you only have to let us know. We can help you navigate those waters. And I know your father has already been working to ensure no one intrudes too much on our privacy despite the investigation into your kidnapping."

"He has," I acknowledged. "I've actually been okay."

Members of the FBI had questioned me, and I'd given them an expanded version of the story I'd told Damien, saying that I had no idea where I'd been held and that I'd escaped when my usual caretaker had taken me on a trip and our van was attacked. It was an easy way to avoid having to point to any locations where I'd supposedly lived. I didn't want them digging too closely into the real details of my life, or they might uncover more about me than I was ready to share.

My mother had seemed awfully eager to respond to that question, though. And Grandpa Bo had been quick to dismiss my inquiries about hunting. Was it possible they didn't want me digging too deeply into the inner workings of the family?

I shook myself mentally. That was ridiculous. The Hunter's words had gotten under my skin and made me overly suspicious.

"If you feel it'd be easier living closer to home…" my mother ventured. "I realize you might not be comfortable moving in here, although of course you'd be welcome. But we could see about setting you up with accommodation closer by. I'm not sure how nice a place you've been able to arrange on your own."

"Oh, you don't need to worry about that," I said. "I'm happy where I am."

"I just know that hotels can be so expensive around here, and not always all that comfortable. And we've gone years without being able to support you the way we should have been."

"Most of the hotels around here are shitholes," Grandma Ruby announced. "Your mother's just too polite to say it outright. You really should be with family."

Iris winced. "Ruby, language."

I wanted to laugh at the way she looked offended. The curse word had flown right by me, especially after spending so long with the Crew. The foul language that came from *their* mouths would have sent my mother into an early grave. I made a mental note to make sure nothing similar fell out of my mouth around her.

"I'm only saying the truth," Grandma Ruby said with a huff.

"I promise, I'm fine," I said before the conversation could become a full-out argument between my mother and her mother-in-law. "I enjoy where I'm staying. And I… I'm proud of how I pulled myself back onto my feet when I escaped the people who took me, and I prefer to have some independence for now. I went too long without having any."

It was immediately obvious that I'd played the right card—so obvious a jab of guilt hit me in the gut. My mother's eyes clouded with grief before she nodded. "I understand that. If you need anything, though, please don't hesitate to ask."

I gave her a grateful smile. "I appreciate that." The emotional direction our talk had taken left my skin itching. And I still hadn't found out anything that could convince me one way or another about the Hunter's intentions.

I had one more strategy I'd meant to employ, one that didn't involve any talking at all. "Would you mind if I went inside and used the restroom?" I asked.

"Oh, by all means. You remember where to find it, right?"

I stood with a bob of my head. "I believe so. I'll be right back."

Thankfully, no one offered to join me on my trek into the house. The second I stepped past the door, I darted down the hall to maximize the time I had before they started wondering why I was taking so long.

First I closed the door on the downstairs bathroom so it'd look like someone was inside. Then I slipped up the stairs. I'd already seen all of the rooms on the ground floor, but there were a few upstairs that I hadn't been shown into. My parents' and Carter's bedrooms I wouldn't expect to get a tour of, but what was behind the third?

The door at the front of the house led to the master bedroom, and Carter's had a cheeky DO NOT ENTER sign pasted on it. I'd bet Iris just loved that. But hey, he was a teenager. Pissing off his parents was his job, as far as I'd gathered from my limited TV and movie consumption.

I never really had the option to piss anyone off while I was a teenager living in the household. Not that I'd had parents there anyway.

Two doors down from that was one of dark wood with a knob that jarred at my twisting hand. Locked, as I'd expected.

Because I'd expected it, I'd come prepared. I pulled two small pins from my hair—an excellent hiding place for these basic tools—and stuck both into the lock, using one for leverage. I felt my way around the mechanism in a matter of seconds, jerked one of the pins, and the contraption gave with a click, the bolt sliding over.

I palmed both pins and pushed the door open.

The sharp smell of masculine cologne wafted over me, and I recognized the scent my father often wore. It lingered in this room as if he spent a lot of time in it.

Which I'd guess he did. The space was clearly a home office, with built-in bookshelves along two walls and a sturdy mahogany desk stacked with papers—a little more haphazardly than I'd have imagined my straightlaced father would have stood for. I glanced over them carefully, getting a sense of a personal system of organization that I couldn't decipher immediately.

The wall behind the desk held several framed photos, a few of family, others of important work events, including one where Damien had met a previous president and shaken his hand. I took out my phone and snapped a few pictures as my gaze skimmed over them. My attention settled on a larger frame to the right of the photos.

This frame held a piece of parchment that was yellowed with age, though otherwise in excellent condition. It held a column of writing in brown ink, most of the characters symbols I didn't recognize. Next to those symbols were an ascending sequence of four-digit numbers: *1903, 1904, 1905*… all the way to *1928*.

Were those years? Why did my father have a paper about something from a century ago in his office? Did it have some political or historical significance? Nothing about it made sense to me, and that unnerved me just a little.

I took a picture of that document too, just in case the guys knew what to make of it.

I only spent another few seconds scanning the surfaces in the room before backing into the hallway and relocking it. I was running out of time, and I couldn't risk someone finding me snooping around. I padded back down the stairs quietly and turned toward where my family waited for me outside, taking a brief detour to open the downstairs bathroom again.

The sunlight had just started beaming straight through the bathroom's large, glazed window. It streaked across the hallway on an angle. As I walked through the swath of brighter light, my eyes caught on a detail on the floor that made me pause.

Something about the carpet by the wall just a few feet down from the bathroom was… different from the surface around it. Just a tad flatter than the rest. A slight indent that was a ghost of the more obvious wear in front of the bathroom door I'd just left behind.

As if there was another doorway here that had seen periodic traffic.

All I could see next to that spot was a seamless wall with its striped red-and-gray wallpaper. I frowned, tilting my head to the side as I stepped in to take a closer look—and my mother's voice echoed through the house.

"Rachel, are you all right?"

I jerked back my reaching hand as if I'd been burned. I couldn't delay here any longer. Besides, there might not be anything unusual about the spot I'd noticed at all. Maybe a piece of furniture like a side table had once stood there, and it'd caused the wear.

"I'm coming," I called, forcing my voice to sound friendly. I turned on my heel and strode back toward the lunch my family had prepared for me.

I'd found nothing. Nothing to prove the Hunter's warnings right, and all possible evidence that I had a loving, concerned family.

I couldn't let myself get so paranoid that I wrecked everything good I'd found for myself over the ravings of a stranger.

SEVEN

Blaze

THE COMPUTERS WERE ACTIVELY SCANNING, but it felt wrong not to work alongside them and check for leads as they were split into the backup folders and categorized. If the Maliks posed any kind of threat to Dess, every second could be of the essence.

For every twenty potential leads my searches had turned up so far, I found that only one seemed even semi-relevant, and it led to a dead end that had nothing to do with Damien Malik or his family. I didn't know whether to be frustrated or relieved that I was turning up so little.

Could anyone really be that clean? There wasn't even a speeding ticket on his records, and no more than vague murmurs of overstepping his role or hypocrisy with nothing to back them up—by all appearances the disgruntled rumblings of political opponents.

I was *definitely* frustrated that I'd made no headway into deciphering the symbols on the document Dess had taken a picture of in Damien's home office. They didn't match any language or code I'd encountered before, and apparently the internet had never encountered it either. I scowled at the empty folder still waiting for a real match.

As for the Hunter himself, I'd found nothing tying any government agent or otherwise suspicious personality to the number he'd given Dess or the house his signal had led us to. Unless Belinda Mitchener, 92-year-old grandmother of six and great-grandmother of nine, was simply wearing an old lady suit and faking her severe arthritis, the owner of the house definitely wasn't our man.

Finally, I pushed myself away from the hotel room desk with a restrained growl. I was failing the only job I could do to keep Dess safe —failing miserably, even.

I glanced across the room at where Garrison sat by the large window, tinkering with the miniature-sized telescope that he'd insisted on bringing with us. On the other side of the room, Julius had laid out a few of his army figures on the suite's dining table. I couldn't tell what exactly he was trying to strategize as he moved them back and forth across the top of it. He'd just completed his meditation for the day moments before, and Julius liked to follow his meditation with plan-making.

Talon sat on the other end of the sofa, knitting what was either the sleeve of a sweater or a very puffy scarf with brisk motions of his needles.

"You look pissed off, man," Garrison said, and I realized with a start that he'd abandoned his telescope to join me and peer at the blinking screen of my laptop.

"It's just…" I paused. I didn't normally like to show any weakness around Garrison, since the guy took every opportunity he could to heckle me about stuff, but after seeing him with Dess, I knew better than I ever had how much the snarky persona was for show. I didn't really care if he took a jab at me. Maybe that would even jostle my mind out of this gloom. "From the start, everything around Dess's situation has been nearly impossible to crack."

He leaned against the nearby sofa. "Couldn't that just mean there's nothing *to* crack? I'm not one to trust any politician, but I trust weirdos who give silly code names and lead us on wild goose chases around the city even less."

I took a deep breath, but that didn't stop my knee from starting to bounce of its own accord. "Maybe there's nothing on Malik. Maybe he really is that clean. But I haven't been able to piece together anything all that useful about the organization behind the household. I still have no idea why they kidnapped Dess or what beef they had with the Malik family. Or who hired us to attack *them.* And now I'm coming up empty with this Hunter prick and the crazy secret code too."

"I think the word you're looking for is 'we,' not 'I,'" Julius said from across the room without looking up from his army men. "None of us have been able to come up with any answers. Including Dess. She's not going to blame you."

I'd blame me. I balled my hands to stop them from fidgeting, grappling with the emotions coursing through me.

Garrison shrugged. "From where I'm standing, things are looking pretty good. Maybe we don't have all the answers, but we've made progress. We found her birth family. She's managed to reunite with them. We got all those mercenary groups off our backs. The rest is just a matter of time."

How could he be so confident? But then, that was his constant persona, all cocky assurance. He might have been just as torn up as me underneath and simply choosing not to show it.

Sometimes I might have envied his carefully constructed masks just a little.

"But what if I'm missing something?" I said. "What if the Maliks *are* a threat, and she's walking straight into some kind of trap?"

Garrison arched his eyebrows, and I immediately felt how ridiculous that idea sounded. Dess's birth family had been nothing but welcoming to her. Why would they have an evil agenda against their own daughter? It made no sense.

"I mean, I don't think she should go mentioning the whole criminal career thing to them," Garrison said. "And she probably shouldn't bring us around while publicizing that we make a living offing people. But as things stand, she's been pretty happy with them. She wouldn't keep spending time with them if they were rubbing her the wrong way."

That was true. She was off at her family home right now for

another visit. And something about that fact niggled at me just as much as my lack of progress.

"I know," I said. "I like seeing her happy." When she came back to the hotel after a visit with that new light shining in her eyes, when she talked about her father or mother or brother with that hint of excitement she couldn't totally hide, the thrill of having that family at all… I wasn't sure I'd ever seen her that delighted before. She was usually so serious. "I just don't want her to get hurt."

Garrison cocked his head at me. "Is that all? You're not at all bothered by the whole her-family-would-hate-our-guts thing?"

I scowled at him. Of course he'd pick up on the emotions I was trying not to feel as well as the ones I was talking about. "It's a reasonable concern. If he finds out everything about *her*, he could turn his back on her and break her heart."

"Oh, so it's *her* heart you're worried about?"

"Of course," I grumbled. "Whose are *you* thinking about?"

To my surprise, Garrison's mouth twisted at an angle that looked genuinely conflicted. I rarely saw him drop the confident front. I didn't totally know what to do with a glimpse of vulnerability from him.

"Look," he said. "I'll make it easier for you just this once. I think we're all aware that the more entwined she gets with the Maliks, the harder it'll be for her to stay close to us. I'd love it if you dug up some dirt on these pompous pricks that shows they're not such a model of familial joy after all. But if it's not there, it's not there. Dess isn't the kind of woman who'd let anything get between her and something she's set her mind on. If she wants a family…"

Then she'd stick with that family. Yeah. He'd laid it out more clearly than I'd let myself even in my head.

I swallowed against the tightness in my throat. "I know that too. But there's nothing wrong with making absolutely sure that she knows what she's getting into, right?"

Garrison snickered, back to his usual obnoxious self. "Nothing at all. Just don't blow a circuit trying to make it happen."

Maybe he was right to hassle me about this. How could I say that all I wanted was for Dess to be happy when at the same time some part of me was desperately hoping I'd come across evidence that would destroy the image of the happy family she'd thought she'd found? Just so that we wouldn't lose her.

So that *I* wouldn't lose her. I sure as hell didn't know where I'd find another woman to match her. But I'd let her go if I had to. I just wouldn't like it.

My laptop dinged twice with an alert I hadn't anticipated. It had nothing to do with my searches for information but instead the temporary security systems I'd put in place in the neighborhood of the hotel.

I snapped to attention, leaning close to the screen. My fingers flew across the keyboard as I checked out the movements it'd picked up on nearby streets. A group of men had walked by one of my surveillance cameras, half of them with obvious guns protruding from the backs of their jeans.

They didn't appear to be heading in our direction. Who the hell were they that they'd saunter around so casually while armed? With those tattoos and piercings, they definitely didn't look like cops. Normally regular citizens were a little more discreet.

Furrowing my brow, I dove into the data further to try to trace their path into our neighborhood and figure out where they'd come from while still keeping an eye on their path through the city as they passed us by.

Garrison stepped closer. "Why so serious?"

"Serious gets the job done," I retorted.

"Not for you. You're usually cracking a million jokes a minute while all our lives hang on the line." He folded his arms over his chest. "Seeing you all somber is kind of scary."

I rolled my eyes without meeting his and confirmed that the armed men were still heading in the opposite direction from the hotel. Whatever they were up to, it definitely didn't appear to have anything to do with us.

But we couldn't be too wary. I had to be strong to protect Dess properly, and maybe that did mean I should let go some of my usual carefree approach. Jokes weren't going to deflect bullets aimed her way.

Whether she stayed with us or moved on, I'd never forgive myself if something happened to her that I could have prevented. Even the thought of her taking another wound, physical or emotional, made an ache form around my heart.

The men with the guns had shown up on one street cam outside my private surveillance network. When I tried to trace their path farther back, I didn't spot them. It appeared they'd gotten out of a vehicle hidden somewhere within a gap in coverage.

They'd gotten out just a couple of blocks from the area I was monitoring, and then walked right through the edge of that area with weapons on full display before sauntering on out of that area again.

My instincts twitched with apprehension. That didn't feel right at all. It was almost as if they'd purposefully come through to catch our attention…

And draw it away from what?

Panic flashed through my nerves. My hands leapt across the keyboard. In a matter of seconds, I'd brought up the feeds closest to the hotel building.

Just in time to spot several forms in normal clothes with no overt equipment that would have alerted my systems converging on the building with a purposefulness that had me jumping to my feet. Even as I opened my mouth, all those feeds blinked out into static.

"We're under attack!" I hollered.

The words had barely left my mouth when the windows along the side wall exploded with a hail of glass shards and intruding bodies.

EIGHT

Decima

MY MISSION TO make my brother more comfortable with the surprise sister who'd fallen into his life currently involved a game of 20 Questions while we basked in the backyard in the warmth of the midday sun. The game meant I had to do a fair bit of lying, but I did want to smooth over any awkwardness between us if I could.

And having Carter on my side would make fishing for information about the family much easier.

"Are you a DC or Marvel girl?" he asked for his eighth question, stretching out his lanky legs in the lawn chair. My mom and grandmother sat at the outdoor dining table a few feet away, carrying on with their own conversation about gardening and cooking, which I couldn't say I'd have had much more to contribute to.

I thought back to everything I knew about those specific franchises. Noelle had sometimes included superhero movies in the rotation of media available to me, but I'd only watched a few. She'd cautioned me that they gave an over-the-top impression of the world, and that was exactly why I'd never totally connected with them. I knew how nitty and gritty tackling your opponents actually was. And you definitely didn't get points for flashy costumes.

I didn't think Carter would appreciate that answer, though. I considered the films I had seen and the bits of pop culture I'd managed to absorb over the years. "DC, I guess. I like Batman." At least he had the sense to keep his costume black, even if the cape and the pointed ears were a bit much. And he used training and gadgets rather than superpowers.

My brother crinkled his nose. "Really? More than Iron Man? Or Black Panther? Or Thor and Loki?"

I shrugged. "I'm not much of a superhero fan in general. But maybe I've missed some good ones. What about you?"

He let out a scoffing sound that had Iris glancing over as if worried she might have to defend me from his teenage scorn. "I'm a Marvel fan, obviously," he said as if the question wasn't even worth being asked. "But you know the rules. You have to come up with original questions."

"Do you prefer baseball or football?" I asked, referencing what seemed to be the two most common sports in the country. From what I'd seen, they appealed to very different people with different temperaments—levels of patience, enjoyment of physical aggression.

He opened his mouth to reply at the same moment as my phone released a loud chime in my pocket. "Baseball," he said as I reached for the device. "I played in middle school, but Dad didn't want me to be out in public without bodyguards so much, and it started to feel weird having them tagging along for the games in high school, so I just stopped."

I made a sympathetic face. Even in this family, my life wouldn't have been completely my own. At least Damien hadn't tried to enforce that level of security on me so far.

"That must be really hard," I said. "Does it bother you?"

"Meh. It was just for fun, not anything really important. I had lots of extracurriculars closer to home. Graduated near the top of my class and got a spot at my top pick college, so it all worked out in the end."

I would have asked more about his plans for college, except I looked at my phone then, and my heart stopped. Blaze had texted me a brief message. *Attack at hotel. Stay alert.*

An attack in our hotel? Was it happening *now*? I had to assume that if Blaze had been doing anything other than fighting for his life when he'd composed that message, he'd have explained in more detail —or outright called me. Shit.

"Hold on a second," I said to Carter, and dialed Blaze's number. My heart thumped as the line on the other end rang, but he didn't pick up. When I tried Julius, I got kicked to voicemail too.

My chest was constricting. The Chaos Crew was under attack while I was sitting here making small talk and sipping lemonade. Who the hell had come at them now?

I stood from my chair with the burst of adrenaline and anger, maybe faster than was wise. Grandma Ruby went quiet as I stepped back and away from the table. "My goodness, Rachel."

"I need to leave," I blurted out, and scrambled to compose myself slightly more with an appropriate excuse. "A friend of mine had her boyfriend break up with her suddenly. She's a mess." Personal issues, especially dating ones, seemed to get the most sympathy from the average person.

"Oh, I'm sure she'll be all right," Grandma Ruby said. "At your age, the men come and go."

Iris shot her a look. "At Rachel's age, I was engaged to Damien." She nodded to me. "We've been monopolizing a lot of your time. If your friend needs your support, you should be there for her."

Her understanding response added a pang of guilt to the whirlwind of emotions inside me, but protecting the guys came before anything else. "Thanks. I'll call when I have the chance."

I managed to keep a measured pace as I walked around the house, but as soon as I was out of view of the backyard, I bolted down the street and across it. When I spotted a car in a secluded enough spot that I could break in and hotwire it without being seen, I dashed to it. There wasn't time to wait for an Uber and another driver's law-abiding approach to the rules of the road.

I had the door open in a matter of seconds and the engine running in several more. As I tore out of the driveway, my teeth gritted.

Who would have attacked the crew here? We were so far from home that none of their usual enemies would have been close enough… although I supposed I didn't know how many enemies they might have made during their missions across the country.

Was the organization behind the household making another stab at capturing me? But then, why wouldn't they have come at me here at the Maliks' rather than attacking the guys?

Whoever it was must have had a death wish, because when I found them, they wouldn't stand a chance. If they harmed a single hair on the guys' heads, I would end their lives slowly and painfully.

Nobody messed with my men.

I tore through the city, cutting off other vehicles and racing through red lights until I finally reached the hotel. After slamming to a stop around the corner, I yanked up the parking brake and hurtled inside.

I rushed into the hotel and past the receptionist, who greeted me with a smile, having no idea that an attack was happening in this very building. If it was contained to our suite, it was contained intentionally, either because our enemies were trying to avoid drawing outside attention or because the guys didn't want to put unnecessary people in danger by making it a spectacle.

It could have been either option, I realized. I had no idea who they were facing or what I'd be walking into. I was nearly unarmed and certainly unprotected with no bulletproof vest or padding to speak of. I was about to rush into a potential bloodbath with only the small blade that I always kept at my hip.

There wasn't any question that I would, though. The only weapons I really needed were my bare hands.

I didn't bother waiting for the elevator. Dashing into the stairwell, I stormed up all five flights to the penthouse we'd taken over. The guys had picked this building carefully for discretion, and the soundproofing between the floors was good enough that I didn't pick up the sound of gunshots until I was bursting out into the short hallway that led to the suite entrance.

At least they *were* still shooting. That meant someone was alive.

The damn apartment door was locked. Swearing under my breath,

I fished out my key card, jabbed it into the slot, and barged inside into what could only be described as chaos.

Several bodies already slumped on the floor in the suite's living room, but there were still more attackers grappling with the Chaos Crew around the room.

My gaze caught on Talon first. He was whipping back and forth between three opponents, fending off their weapons. If he'd had a gun to begin with, he'd lost it in the fray. Right now he was fighting with… knitting needles.

I'd have laughed if the situation hadn't looked so dire. His expression was taut with strain. I jumped in, clicking open my small knife as I leapt. I plunged it into the back of the nearest man, jabbing it deep enough to pierce his heart through his ribs. I'd never carry a knife too small to accomplish that.

He crumpled, and the man next to him spun with a gun raised. In the instant before Talon leapt to my defense, the other man… hesitated, staring at my face. He could have taken a shot—and I would have dodged it—but it was almost as if he didn't think he should.

Then Talon was snapping the guy's wrist with a crack of shattering bone.

As I whirled, I spotted Blaze holding his own against two men near the sofa. Another man barreled into view and paused at the sight of me, a lot like the gunman had.

What the heck was up with these guys? Had they never fought a woman before?

Well, they were about to find out that I was an equal opponent.

I whipped the knife I'd withdrawn from my first kill through the air, and it hit the man right in the middle of the forehead. As he slumped over, Blaze managed to get in a shot at one of his attackers, who stumbled backward clutching his gut.

I glanced past Blaze and found Julius fighting three men, Garrison at his back fending off another. Four more men were just clambering through the shattered windows that let in a brisk breeze.

I didn't know who to help first. All of them were getting overwhelmed, and I'd given up my one weapon.

I dropped to the ground and grabbed at the waists of the corpses for anything I could use. My groping hand found a gun. I quickly checked the magazine before pulling back the slide and finding one bullet already in the chamber. Two remained in the magazine. Three bullets total. I'd need to be so careful about how I used them.

A loud groan from across the room caught my attention. I watched as Julius fell to his knees, holding his side as one man circled behind him with a blade and another withdrew a pistol from his hip.

A silent wail of protest filled my head. I didn't think. I reacted.

I lifted the gun I'd pilfered and fired at the man with the pistol. The bullet lodged itself in the side of the man's head. I took down the man with the knife a second later.

Then a body slammed into me from the side. But even as I fell, I saw that Julius had heaved back to his feet. He'd be okay.

I rolled as I toppled and yanked my gun hand around with good enough aim to fire a shot into my attacker's chest before he could do any more damage. He went limp on top of me. I shoved him off, snatching the knife he'd held and swiveling to prepare for another onslaught.

My efforts to thin our enemies' numbers had helped. No new attackers careened through the window, and the men were making short work of the remaining foes. I slashed one man who was raising his gun toward Blaze across the throat and stabbed the knife deep into the back of another's head. A few more shots rang out, and then it was just the five of us, a little bleeding and battered, standing over a heap of corpses.

Garrison caught my eye with a quick nod and a grimace that could have either been acknowledgment of the shitty situation or his disgust at all the gore. He crouched to sift through the men's pockets. "Let's see if we can find out who these assholes are and why they came after us."

"Check fast," Julius demanded. "We're leaving in five minutes. Get your shit so we can get out before the cops get here."

His hand was clamped to the wound on his side. Blood seeped across his shirt. His gaze caught mine, and my heart lurched all over again at the thought of how close he'd come to dying.

"You should bandage that," I said. "No good avoiding arrest if you bleed out."

"I'll be fine," he said with typical unshakeable confidence, but he did march into the bathroom and tear a strip off one of the towels to tie around his waist.

Blaze was grabbing his laptop and assorted other devices off the desk, shoving them into a large satchel. "I texted you so that you could keep an eye out for danger and *avoid* it where you were," he said to me, his tone dry but with a hint of frustration.

"Well, I'm happy I came back," I retorted, "or you all could have been killed."

He made a face, but none of them disputed that fact.

I only had a small bag of belongings that I refused to leave behind, so I rushed to the side of my bed, stepping over corpses as I went. I always kept my things ready to go at a moment's notice anyway, so all I had to do was sling the bag over my shoulder.

"You don't have any idea who these people are?" I asked over my shoulder.

"They're no one I recognize," Talon muttered.

"And they didn't stop to introduce themselves first," Blaze added. "Very impolite."

"I have a hunch." Garrison lifted a phone in the air. "Because there's an interesting text message on this man's home screen."

I hurried over. "What does it say?"

Garrison cleared his throat. "*Don't touch the daughter*. Who do you think that could be?"

I stopped in my tracks. Obviously I was the only person who usually hung out with the crew who could be anyone's daughter. And the way some of the men had shied away from attacking me loomed large in my mind.

Our previous attackers had sometimes gone easier on me, but only because they'd been looking to take me captive rather than murder me. One of the men from the household's organization had outright told me that they had permission to kill me if I proved too difficult to take alive.

This was different.

"Who would have wanted to kill all of you and not hurt me?" I said, and then the thought clicked into place in my head at the same moment as the guys' expressions stiffened with similar realizations.

"Who would think of you foremost as being a 'daughter'?" Julius said. "Does your father know where you've been staying? Has he given any indication that he knows you've been staying *with* other people or that he's concerned about the company you're keeping?"

I shook my head, my pulse kicking up a notch all over again. "No, I haven't gotten any impression of that at all." But Damien Malik did hate criminals, and he was determined to protect his long-lost daughter. Still… "It doesn't totally make sense, though, does it? It's pretty convenient that the guy left that text visible on his screen. Every other time we've been attacked, our enemies have been more careful not to have any identifying info on them."

"That's true," Blaze said, but he was frowning. "Sometimes people make mistakes, though. And if these people came from Malik, they'd be a different breed from the mercenaries who took us on before."

I rubbed my forehead. Adrenaline was still surging through my veins, making my thoughts race back and forth through my head. I didn't know what to make of this when I could barely focus on anything at all.

"It doesn't matter right now," Julius said firmly. "We'll figure this out, but we need to get out of here before someone finds this mess."

"Where are we going to go?" Blaze asked, holding his satchel and suitcase.

Julius took a deep breath before he spoke. "We'll want someplace more secure than a typical hotel. There's a local group that owes us a favor. We'll go to them and see what they can do for us."

NINE

Decima

I DIDN'T KNOW what I found odder—the guys who showed us the house or the house itself.

The house had a… unique security feature, as it had been built into the side of a rocky hill on the outskirts of town—going as far as to use the rock as a structural feature. The back half of the house was embedded in stone and not accessible by intruders, so we only needed to worry about the front.

I ran my fingers down the rocky face on the inside, finding it cool to the touch but polished pleasantly smooth. I wondered how they kept spiders and other insects out of the house when half of the building was built using nature as its guide. Hopefully they'd put a little thought into that. I could handle bugs, but I'd rather not have them crawling on me in my sleep, thank you very much.

The brothers who showed us the place gave off a similarly weird vibe, a mix of warm exuberance that reminded me of Blaze in his typical state and cool competitiveness that came out at unexpected moments.

"We built this place from scratch," the taller, seemingly older brother said, patting the slightly shorter of the two on the back.

His brother scoffed, poking an elbow into his brother's abdomen. "*James and I* built this place from scratch. You supervised when you felt like it."

There were actually three brothers. We'd met James briefly when we'd gone to see about calling in Julius's favor after patching up the guys' injuries from the fight. Warmth had definitely not been in *his* vocabulary. The youngest of the three siblings had simply glowered at us before slouching away.

Now, the older of the two apparently non-identical twins shrugged. "If you'd come out of Mom first, maybe you'd have been given the role of supervisor."

"I'm happy I didn't come out first. I'd probably be as fat as you."

Garrison's snort sent me over the edge where I'd been balancing, and I covered my mouth to silence my laugh. Neither of these men was fat by any means, but the "second" twin was certainly the fittest with lean muscles covered in dark ink down both arms and across his chest.

The younger twin dodged the older one's attempted slap, raising his hands in a feigned defensive maneuver. Was this the kind of relationship I might one day have with Carter? It was difficult to picture.

"Anyway," the older twin said to the rest of us, ruffling his brother's hair in a way that looked more affectionate than hostile, though still aggressive, "you can have the run of the place while you're in town. I think that should make us square, don't you?"

Julius inclined his head. "It'll do very well. We appreciate the hospitality."

"We'll leave you to it then."

As they ambled out the front door, Blaze let out a dramatic sigh and flopped onto the leather sofa. He didn't waste a moment before digging out his laptop.

"Comfortable?" Garrison asked with an amused smirk.

"I'll be more comfortable when I'm sure we're not going to find ourselves under siege again," the hacker muttered. His usual jovial air had dampened quite a bit since the attack. Noticing that sent an uncomfortable pang through me that I didn't know what to do with.

I distracted myself by exploring the rest of the house. I'd want to know all the entry and exit points in case it did come to another battle, after all.

With the wooden walls that expanded out from the stone face at the back, the building looked like a rustic mountain cabin, even though the low hill it was built into was the highest peak around this area. A fireplace stood across from the sofa in the center of the room, constructed of decorative stone that rose all the way to the high, wood-beamed ceiling. A bearskin rug covered the floor.

For all the cabin-like décor, it was all clearly top of the line. To rent this place on the open market I'd guess would have cost at least triple what we'd paid for that already upscale hotel. I was guessing Julius hadn't mentioned the possibility of violent invasion when he'd called in this favor.

Or maybe people in our line of work simply took it for granted as a risk.

"Is trading favors a typical thing in this industry?" I asked. "They're happy to just give us this place for as long as we need it because you helped them somehow in the past?"

"Yep," Garrison said, poking around in the kitchen. "The most successful of us in the underworld have more than enough money, so cash payments are actually less appealing than goods or services we might be able to provide. We've all got different skills, after all." He stepped away from the counter toward the front door. "Speaking of which, I'm going to go and see if I can pick up any word on the street about who might be targeting us locally."

Blaze shot up, wincing slightly at either the old bullet wound that had nearly healed entirely or the bruising he'd gotten from the most recent fight. "Can I get a ride? Some of my equipment was damaged in the fight, and I need to replace it. Plus there are a few new security measures I'd like to put in place, mountainside or no mountainside."

Garrison sighed, but there wasn't much animosity in it. "I suppose I can put up with your company a little longer. Anyone else wanting to hitch a ride? Going once… twice…"

"I'll reach out to the local supplier and stock up on more ammo," Talon said, striding over. "If things keep up like this, we'll need it."

Those words and the sight of the three of them about to step out of view made my pulse stutter. What if our enemies came at them again? Who knew what they might face out there?

It was ridiculous. The Chaos Crew had gone off on all kinds of errands and missions since I'd met them and before then too. They could obviously look after themselves. But in that moment, all I could think of was how close they'd all come to taking a bullet in the brain just a few hours ago.

How empty my life would feel if I lost them.

The words tumbled out before I could catch them. "Can't some of that wait for tomorrow? It'd be nice to get settled in here first."

I cringed inwardly as soon as I heard myself. Garrison would get the best gossip on the day of the attack, and picking up ammo and security equipment weren't optional. We couldn't wait another moment to have all of these things taken care of.

Garrison had raised his eyebrows, his expression turning a bit concerned. Before he could respond, I covered my awkwardness with a laugh. "Never mind. I'm just tired. I think *I* need to get settled in—and maybe take a nap. Go get what you need."

They had each other, after all, and they'd kept each other alive long before I'd been in the picture.

The three guys marched out through the door, and I stayed where I was until the growl of the car's engine faded away outside. Then I took a deep breath and stepped back, sinking onto the sofa. It *was* pretty comfortable, but the buttery leather did nothing to relieve my skittering nerves.

Julius loomed over me, but these days, his commanding form was reassuring rather than intimidating. "Something's wrong," he said. "Were you hurt during the fight? You don't get to brush off your injuries when you insist on us taking care of our own."

"I'm not injured." My gaze dropped to his side, where his shirt now covered a more normal bandage that he'd applied after we'd fled the hotel. The cut he'd gotten had been fairly shallow, nothing remotely life-threatening.

Just enough to throw him off for a few crucial seconds while a gun had whipped toward his head.

My stomach turned. I focused on the man in front of me—the living, breathing man who I had to convince myself was stronger than anything this life could hurl at us. A desperate urge rose up in me to *feel* just how alive he was, to take all that strength into me, to know beyond a doubt that I hadn't even remotely lost him.

A strange heat kindled low in my belly. I pushed myself to my feet and reached up to touch his chest, holding his gaze.

"I'm not totally all right, though. I need you to show me just how okay *you* are. In every possible way." I slid my hand down his solidly muscled chest, more heat spreading up through my abdomen. My voice dropped. "Do you think you can help me with that?"

Lust flared in Julius's eyes. He lowered his head, his breath tickling over my forehead, and set his hands on my shoulders. "I think I could manage that."

"Good," I whispered, pulling my shirt over my head without a moment's hesitation. "There's only one rule. *Don't* be gentle."

Julius's eyes flashed, and his grin turned feral as he slid his hands down to grip my hips. "I don't do gentle."

I pushed myself up on my toes to meet his lips, but Julius had different ideas. He marched me backward and shoved me onto the sofa. It slid back a couple inches as we crashed into it. I barely had a chance to catch my breath before he grabbed my thighs and pulled them toward him.

The smooth leather cradled my back as Julius yanked his shirt over his head and tossed it to the ground beside him. He reached for his pants. I pushed myself up on my elbows, licking my lips as he dropped his jeans, leaving only his boxers behind.

My eyes moved up to the bandage at the side of his abdomen. The recent wound had to hurt. Maybe this was a bad idea.

Julius caught my gaze and must have guessed my thoughts. He braced himself over me, pinning me between his brawny arms and with his dark blue gaze.

"Just a scratch," he said. "It'd take a lot more than that to slow me down." He tapped the edge of my lacy bra. "Take it off."

I peered at him through my eyelashes. "What if I want you to do it?" I teased. I needed him to touch me and surround me. I needed *him.*

"Fine." He knelt over me, grabbing the bra from the front. Before I could open my mouth to speak, he jerked, and the fabric tore from my body.

He reached for my pants and tore them open as well. The button popped right off, flying across the room as he peeled the pants off me. I lifted my hips, and he bent forward, licking a line between my breasts. He moved to the side, and without a moment's hesitation, he tugged my nipple between his teeth and pulled it. A gasp jolted out of me.

His mouth moved down the center of my stomach, straight to my core. He devoured my sex so forcefully that I jerked from the sofa, his hands on my hips the only things that kept me still beneath him. He didn't stop there, utterly wrecking every part of me with his mouth.

"Julius," I moaned, and my voice did something to him. It added a sense of urgency as he tightened his grip on my thighs and plunged his tongue even deeper inside me. Pleasure throbbed through my core, blazing into an inferno.

He nipped my clit and plunged two fingers into me where his tongue had just penetrated, and I came undone. Stars burst behind my eyes as I bucked my hips and panted.

As the afterglow rolled over me, my need was barely sated. I looked down at him and found him eyeing my reaction with an expression of complete satisfaction.

"Fuck me, Julius," I said roughly. "I want you inside of me *now.*"

I reached between his legs to emphasize my point. A second before my fingers closed around his rigid erection, he grasped my hand. Taking charge, exerting control. A giddy quiver ran through me as I let him place my hand against him and show me exactly how he wanted me to stroke him up and down, fast and hard. His cock felt like silk-sheathed steel.

"Condoms are in my suitcase," he said with a rasp.

I didn't want to let go of him. I didn't want anything to break this moment. I tightened my grip behind his guiding hand and studied his face. "I have a birth control implant, and I'm clean. I haven't been with anyone but the four of you, and that was always with protection. If you're clean too…"

A low curse spilled from his lips. His mouth collided with mine, hot and rough. He lifted my hips and lined himself up against me, first letting the head of his cock rub over my clit.

I let out another moan, clutching his shoulder. My sex outright ached now.

"Let me fuck you," I begged, imagining how it would feel to ride him to my orgasm.

Julius's laugh was dark and full of promise. He shoved a decorative pillow under my ass. "I'm the one who does the fucking here," he announced. "Don't think that will ever change."

If I hadn't been ready before, those words sent tingles straight through my body. Then he was plunging into me, and I almost came just like that all over again.

I tipped my head back into the soft leather, reveling in the feeling of him filling me, stretching me, claiming my body in a way I was only too happy to accept. "Please," I murmured, not entirely sure what I was begging for.

Julius was here. He was *right here*, as close as he could possibly be.

He thrust in and out at a pace that soon had us both sweaty and panting. Bliss radiated all through my body as I rocked with his rhythm, and somehow I kept soaring higher and higher. The pressure of my building release was almost as torturous as it was thrilling.

"I promised I wouldn't be gentle, didn't I?" Julius murmured, and bucked into me even harder than before. My body trembled with the waves of pleasure he was sending through me. I rose up to meet him, digging my fingers into his back, and he angled me against him so some part of him brushed my clit.

With a cry, I shattered beneath him. As the flood of ecstasy rolled over me, I opened my eyes, and I found him staring down at me. His own eyes glazed over as he worked to find his own pleasure.

I couldn't help lifting my hand to his face, stroking his cheek. His breath stuttered. He tipped his head back and increased the intensity of his thrusts even more, sending fresh pulses of pleasure through my already giddy body.

"Come for me, Julius," I whispered, my voice hoarse from my orgasm.

He came so hard that a roar left his lips, the single hand on my thigh tightening to a near bruising grip. Then he bowed over me, his chest grazing mine but not crushing me as it could have with his full weight.

I pulled him down over me, wanting to feel all of him. The smell and the press of his body replaced the vision of the gun rising to his head.

Now, all I wanted to do was find the people who thought they could do this to us. I wouldn't be distracted by the thought of what could have happened. I *would* find and kill whoever had attacked my crew.

Julius held me in his powerful embrace for a moment longer and then rolled to the side, withdrawing from me. He brushed a careful hand over the sweaty hair that'd become stuck to my forehead. "Better?" he asked with a gleam in his eyes that told me he'd enjoyed the encounter just as much as I had.

I grinned up at him. "Just what I needed." I pushed myself into a sitting position and reached for my bag so I could retrieve some clothes to replace what he'd ruined. "Now let's get to work figuring out what assholes we need to make pay and how they're connected to me."

A chuckle tumbled out of Julius. He shook his head, but there was nothing but admiration in his gaze. "You're some woman, all right."

"And don't you forget it," I said tartly.

Julius wrapped an arm around my waist and held me in place just for a moment. I couldn't stop myself from gazing down at his nakedness. God, he was an impressive specimen of a man, wasn't he?

"We're going to find out the truth, Dess," he promised. "It doesn't matter what it takes. We're going to dig right to the bottom of this mess so we can fully protect you."

I raised my eyebrows at him. "Since when do I need protection?" I asked, gesturing to the bandage at his side to remind him of exactly *who* had needed protection the last time we'd tangled with these pricks.

"I didn't say you *needed* protection." Julius tugged a lock of my hair and then squeezed my shoulder. "But you have to know by now that we're going to protect you every way we can anyway, because we want to. That's what people do for family."

TEN

Talon

I SHOULD HAVE KNOWN BETTER than to rebandage my wounds with the bathroom door even slightly open. I didn't think the minor scrapes and cuts were anything to fuss about, but after I'd peeled off my shirt and paused to study the marks in the mirror over my shoulder, Dess peeked in.

"Do you need some help with those?" she asked, nodding to the ones on my back. "You'll have trouble reaching them on your own."

Blaze tsked his tongue from the room behind her. "Don't be shy," he teased. "You're just looking for excuses to grope all those muscles."

"Oh, hush," Dess said, rolling her eyes. I had a feeling she'd have had a harsher retort if it'd been Garrison who'd made the comment. Our hacker tended to bring out the softer side in all of us… just like our chameleon tended to do the opposite.

I looked down at myself and decided that patching myself up would go a lot faster with help, even if I didn't like to ask for it. She'd volunteered, after all. And I didn't particularly mind the idea of her hands on my muscles, whether Blaze had only been teasing or not.

"Come on in," I said. "I've already disinfected the ones I can reach."

She slipped into the bathroom with me and positioned herself next to the stone basin that served as a sink, where I'd set out my supplies. I applied fresh bandages to the minor cuts on my shoulder and my chest while she dabbed antiseptic cream on the marks down my back. They stung more now than they had when I'd gotten them yesterday—I'd barely noticed the swipes of the enemy knife in the midst of the surge of adrenaline that'd gotten me through the fight—but Dess kept her fingers light.

"You have almost as many scars as I do," she murmured.

I gave a faint hum. "And you've had about half as much time to build your collection."

"Oh, I don't know about that. When did you start this kind of training?"

The words came out before I'd thought them through. "The earliest ones aren't from any kind of training."

I hadn't meant to bring up my past. It wasn't something I liked to discuss with anyone, and I sure as hell didn't need to drum up sympathy from Dess of all people. But she'd clearly caught my insinuation even from that brief statement.

Her hands paused over my broken flesh. "I'm sorry. I didn't know."

"Of course you didn't," I said. "How could you have? It isn't important now anyway. And even with that, you've still got me beat."

I wasn't any kind of jokester, but I must have managed to work enough dryness into my voice that Dess's mouth twitched with a hint of a smile. To my relief, she laid the subject to rest. Instead, she patted the polished stone of the sink as she reached for the bandages. "This house is… interesting, isn't it?"

"You mean the way it's practically a cave?"

She snorted. "Yeah, that part. It's a little closer to nature than I'd generally prefer to live. I swear I saw a centipede as long as my hand run across my bedroom floor last night."

"Don't tell me you're afraid of bugs?" The thought of Dess, the famous Ghost assassin, being scared of anything that small and weak amused me.

"I wouldn't say *afraid*," Dess said. "More like disgusted. No living creature has any business growing that many legs."

Her fingers brushed against my skin as she fixed the bandages into place, so careful to avoid putting any pressure on the wounds themselves. Even Julius with his medical training didn't offer this light a touch. Maybe the real contradiction was how such a skilled and ruthless killer could be so gentle when the situation called for it.

"I guess I can agree with you on that," I said. If I saw a centipede in my room, it'd be mashed into the floor in two seconds flat.

"There. I knew there was a reason I liked you. We can hate on bugs together."

Dess's tone was playful, but her touch stayed soft and careful. Something about the tenderness of her attentions brought an unfamiliar warmth into my chest. It unfurled further with each graze of her hands. I found myself closing my eyes, wanting to focus on nothing but her soothing presence behind me.

I'd never had a woman look after me like this. Never had a woman who cared enough and understood my kind of life enough to want to. In that moment, I'd have killed anyone who so much as looked at her wrong.

She was *my* woman. The rest of the guys' too, but still mine. I wasn't used to this possessive sensation either, but it felt right somehow.

Some part of me wanted to bundle her up with all the same tenderness she'd shown me and hide her away until all the danger that lurked in this city had passed. Be a shield between her and the rest of the big bad world.

But Dess didn't need that, didn't *want* it—and I wasn't sure I could be tender anyway.

"There. All patched up." Dess stepped back, and I turned to face her. Her brightly affectionate smile provoked a flutter amid the warmth that had filled my chest. A fucking *flutter*.

What the hell was I supposed to do with that or all these other emotions I wasn't used to feeling? My heart had been as much of a cave as this building was before she'd come along—an empty cave.

And suddenly it was buzzing with way too much feeling that I had no idea how to adjust to.

One impulse rang through all the rest—one thing I did know how to do. I *was* going to defend her every way I knew how, every way she'd let me. And that included figuring out how much danger she was in from the man she'd accepted as her father.

"I'd better see if Blaze is ready to head out," I said.

Her smile dimmed a little. I didn't know whether she was more concerned that we'd find something damning about Damien Malik or that we wouldn't and it'd turn out we'd violated her family's trust unnecessarily. I guessed both made sense. Neither were impressions I associated with my own family one bit.

"Right," she said, putting on her determined face. "You're ready to go."

I didn't really have a clue how anything Blaze was planning to do at the Malik home worked. It was all buttons and wires as far as I was concerned. But I didn't need to know. That was his job, and mine was keeping watch and being ready to leap into action if he ran into trouble.

Sneaking around a large house with two people inside wasn't particularly difficult. But the Maliks didn't give us a problem even when they came outside. Iris Malik walked along the porch collecting old beach towels without even glancing toward the garden shed we were using for shelter. Her son—Dess's teenager brother—sauntered around the pool and then back into the house with equal inattention.

I grimaced to myself. One thing was obvious: Dess didn't have a lick of protection from the people living here. No wonder Damien needed professional bodyguards.

When Iris had left for work, leaving just the boy in the house, we slunk across the lawn to the back wall. Blaze stalked along the perimeter, holding a device that beeped faintly, while I peeked through the windows. Dess had told us where her brother's bedroom was, and we were heading in the opposite direction, but we wouldn't want to be spotted from the common rooms.

Blaze paused partway down the east side of the house, where the device had started beeping faster. He spoke under his breath. "The router's around here." He glanced up. "Probably on the second floor."

I cocked my head as he pawed through his satchel for some other electronic box that looked almost the same as the other one to me. "And this is going to let you tap into their internet?" I murmured.

He nodded. "I didn't have the equipment to manage it before—and even now, I need to get this thing very close. Give me a lift?"

I moved without hesitation, bending down and offering my interlaced hands for a boost up. My muscles only strained slightly hefting the slim man's weight. I raised him to the level of the second-floor window above us.

Blaze gripped the ledge for balance. Peering inside, he let out a soft whistle. "Holy cow. They've got a whole games room—this kid has everything. Systems, special controllers, fancy sound system, the works."

A whole room just for playing around? I wondered if the teenager who lived here had ever known a hardship in his entire life. I'd enlisted in the military the second I was old enough, and he had what were likely the most expensive consoles piled recklessly in a room.

It wasn't anger that I felt, and it wasn't jealousy, but when I considered Dess being surrounded by this spoiled family, it just seemed… wrong.

"Bingo," Blaze said. "There's the modem and the router. No wonder I couldn't get into this thing without being closer. It's state of the art."

I held him steady, keeping my ears pricked. Blaze got to work attaching his device, which was about the size of his palm, to the siding next to the window. He'd painted it the same color as the siding ahead of time, and it was so small it'd blend in easily, especially tucked against the protruding frame. I barely noticed it when I looked up, and I knew it was there.

Would we find anything useful from his efforts? I wasn't sure I believed that the Maliks would say anything incriminating even in the privacy of their own internet network. They might not have been great at physical surveillance, but they struck me as awfully cautious about appearances, even with each other.

But this wasn't my wheelhouse anyway. Blaze thought the attempt was worthwhile, and he'd had plenty of brilliant brainstorms to earn the right to experiment.

The hacker was twisting another screw into place when he froze above me. I tensed too.

"Shit," he whispered. "The kid just walked into the room."

He flattened himself against the outer wall. I eased closer too, my pulse speeding up just slightly. I'd have yanked Blaze down, but the thump of his landing seemed like more of a risk for drawing the boy's attention than the chance that he'd crane his neck around looking out the window.

What exactly would we do if he did spot us? Two strange men forming a tower against the side of his house… There was no way it wouldn't be suspicious. I'd been prepared to eliminate any guards who came at us, but Dess's brother himself?

My stomach twisted. The seconds slipped by, both of us waiting in rigid silence. Then Blaze exhaled in a rush.

"He went back out again. I'd better finish this quick. Are you holding up all right down there, Talon?"

"I've carried guns that were harder on my arms than you are," I muttered at the slender man, and he chuckled lightly.

"Just have to get this last screw deep enough in so it stays in place… There." He tapped a few buttons on the outside of the device and nudged my hand with the toe of his sneakers for me to lower him. As he hopped out of my grasp, he aimed one of his broad grins at me, his brown eyes sparkling.

"We're in."

ELEVEN

Decima

"YOU SAID you could stop by for a visit on the weekend?" my mother asked outside the restaurant where we'd just had dinner with most of the extended family.

I dragged in a breath as my Uber pulled up next to the curb. I was getting used to the smaller family get-togethers, but having the attention of ten or more people on me for hours at a time still exhausted me. I guessed that wasn't surprising when for most of my life, I hadn't interacted with anyone other than my trainers. I was used to long stretches with only myself for company, not extended conversations full of small talk and family gossip.

But I did want to be a part of this family. It'd get easier over time, right?

"Bright and early," I replied with a smile I had to force a bit. "See you then."

I ducked into the back of the Uber, and the immediate silence greeted me like a warm blanket. The driver pulled onto the road with a rumble of the engine. As I sank back in my seat, tipping my head against the warm fabric, I caught a motion of the driver's hand. He was setting a phone on the passenger seat next to him and hitting the speaker button.

I sat up straighter, frowning, just as a low voice carried from the phone's speaker. "Hello again, Rachel."

My stance stiffened. I'd recognize that slightly hoarse tone anywhere even after only one previous conversation with the guy. My gaze flicked to the driver, but he stayed focused on the road now. What the hell was going on?

"I know you're there," the Hunter said on the other end of the phone line.

"How did you know I'd be here?" I snapped. "Why are you bothering me again?" I glanced at the doors, wondering if I should make a run for it. I didn't like the idea that I was in a vehicle probably controlled by this strange man with his unknown agenda.

But so far the driver appeared to be taking the correct route back to the house in the hill. And I did want to see if the Hunter would reveal more than he had before. The need for answers warred with my sense of caution.

"That doesn't matter," the Hunter replied. "You're still playing happy family with the bunch of them. I thought you'd have smartened up by now."

I glowered at the phone, not that he could see my reaction. "I've done some investigating of my own, and I haven't seen any reason to think they're doing anything wrong. And since *you* won't give me any specifics, even tell me who you really are, I'm going by my own judgment. If you don't like that, maybe you could give me more to go on."

The Hunter let out a faint scoffing sound. "You have the inside access. You obviously haven't dug very far. Maybe you don't actually want to know the truth. You'd rather live in a happy delusion."

His accusation raised my hackles. "The only one avoiding anything is you. If it's so important to you that I know the 'truth,' you could tell me what you know. The fact that you won't seems like pretty solid proof that you're just trying to stir up problems for the hell of it."

"Oh, the problems in this situation aren't of my making."

"There you go again," I said. "All vague, ominous statements. I don't know you, and I have no reason to trust you. So I'm done with this conversation if that's all you've got to say for yourself. I'm smart enough to realize when someone's just jerking my chain."

I didn't actually move toward the phone. As frustrated as I was, there was a chance that he'd reveal something—at least about his motivations—now that I was turning the conversation around on him.

He chuckled darkly. "Chains. That's a good one. Fine. Listen carefully. There's more digging you should do. There are answers in the soil if you know how to read them. And that family does love its garden."

"What?" I demanded. The remarks sounded like more creepy vagueness. When the Hunter didn't answer, I unclasped my seatbelt and lunged forward in my seat.

"Stop the car!" I shouted at the driver, gripping his shoulder hard enough to hurt. I snatched at the phone with my other hand.

As the driver jerked over to the side of the road, I picked up the phone, scanning the screen for any details about the caller. But it'd gone blank. The Hunter had hung up on me.

I swiveled toward the driver, still clutching his shoulder hard. His face had gone white. "Who was that?" I said. "Why did you set me up like this? Do you work for him?"

"I—I don't know anything about it," the man stammered, looking so terrified I believed him. "I'm sorry. This woman paid me to take the phone and pick you up—she said it was a surprise and that I should stay quiet. I didn't realize—I don't even know who you are! I've got nothing against you."

I eased back my hand, worrying at my lower lip. That did sound like how someone like the Hunter would operate. Missed Connection columns and now this. He liked to put as many layers as possible between me and him. That only made his intentions more suspect.

Or maybe it proved he really did feel he had to be careful because of the danger surrounding the situation.

"The woman," I said. "What did she look like?"

The man rubbed his hand over his face as if trying to produce the memory with the gesture. "Blond hair. A lot of makeup. Honestly, I was more focused on the cash she was offering me."

Blond hair and a lot of makeup. That wouldn't get us very far. The makeup might disguise her true appearance and mess with any chance of Blaze using his facial recognition app against her. But we could still try, if the interaction had been caught on a street cam. Which I had to admit, I didn't think was very likely given the Hunter's usual meticulousness.

"Where did she approach you?" I asked anyway.

"Just around the corner from the place where I picked you up," the guy said. "Outside the shoe store."

"Okay." I shoved the phone into my pocket just in case the tech genius could determine something from it. Sitting back in my seat, I debated my next steps for a moment, but the guy already had the address I'd been going to, which meant the Hunter would have it too. There was no point in trying to hide my current location now. "Take me home. As fast as you can."

The drive passed in what felt like seconds as I stewed in my thoughts. The moment the driver pulled up outside, I leapt out and burst into the house.

All four of my men were in the living room, Blaze alternating between watching his computer's screen and tossing darts at a makeshift board he'd put together. Julius and Garrison were handling the dishes from their own dinner in the open-concept kitchen. Talon looked like he'd just come out of a shower.

They all went still and silent when I barged in. I held up the Hunter's phone and tossed it to Blaze, who caught it easily.

"I had an interesting conversation on my way here," I said. "The Hunter wanted to check in on me."

Julius stepped toward me, his expression darkening. "Are you okay? He obviously upset you."

"Oh, I'm pissed off all right. Mostly he just wanted to needle me about not listening to his vague bullshit as much as he liked." I marched into the kitchen and grabbed the milk and chocolate syrup. I needed a hit of cocoa to finish processing everything that'd just happened. "He's still insisting that there's some dirt on the Maliks that I haven't found. Actually, he mentioned the literal dirt. The soil in their garden. Like I'd find something there if I 'read' it."

Garrison knit his brow. "Like a soil analysis?"

"I guess. Hard to know with him." I paused, stirring the syrup into a glass of milk. The thought of poking around in my birth family's affairs, trying to find some reason to distrust them, brought an ache into my stomach that had nothing to do with hunger.

But what if the Hunter really did know something? He watched them closely enough to know how they felt about their garden. Wouldn't it be better to check and know for sure than have his insinuations hanging over me?

If I could prove to myself that he *didn't* have a case at all, maybe I could let go of that niggling worry completely.

"None of you have found out anything concerning so far, right?" I said.

The men all shook their heads. "Damien Malik runs a tight ship—and a clean one," Julius said. "But that doesn't mean he couldn't have secrets."

Garrison grimaced. "On the other hand, this Hunter prick is shady as fuck."

Talon gazed at me steadily. "What do you want to do, Dess?"

I groaned and flopped onto the sofa, pressing the heel of my hand to my forehead. "I mean, it wouldn't be *hard* to take a little soil from the garden. And it wouldn't hurt anything to check it even if it turns out he's just jerking me around. But if the dirt turns up nothing, then I'm done talking to that weirdo." I opened my eyes to glance at Blaze. "Could you do this soil analysis thing?"

He made an apologetic gesture. "That's outside my domain—all of our domains."

I thought of the way we'd obtained this house, how we'd gotten my DNA sequenced back home to connect me to Malik in the first place. "Then we need to find someone else who can. Someone who won't ask questions about it… I don't have much in the way of money, but maybe I could set up an exchange of favors like you have before?"

Garrison nodded slowly. "I've heard of a woman out in New York who handles a lot of things along that line—chemicals and environmental hazards. I've never dealt with her directly before, but from what the people who've mentioned her have said, she seems to understand discretion and to stick to her word."

I nodded. "Great, reach out to her as soon as you can. And find out what she'd want from me in return."

"From us," Julius put in. "Whatever she wants, between the five of us, I'm sure we can manage it."

A rush of affection filled my chest at his automatic offer of support, not that it should have surprised me after everything else he'd done and said before. But I found myself shaking my head, resolve wrapping around my heart.

"No." I caught Garrison's gaze. "Make sure it's something I can handle on my own. The Maliks are my family, and the Hunter came to me. I should be the one 'paying' to fix that problem."

"We really don't mind," Blaze started.

I cut him off with another jerk of my head. The Hunter's words from our first conversation came back to me, echoing up from my memory. *You still need to be ready in case someone else turns out to be better.*

"I might have been respected as the Ghost, but no one except the four of you knows that the Ghost is me—no one has any reason to respect me as Decima. I need to be able to stand on my own two feet in this world, and that means I have to prove myself on my own. If I want respect, *I* have to earn it."

Garrison gave me a small smile that I thought was approving. It sent a tingle of heat between my legs more intense than anything his usual smirks could have provoked.

"You've got it, sweetheart," he said. "One return favor, catered just to you. It's not like you can't blow them away without any help from us."

TWELVE

Decima

I PAUSED JUST inside the restaurant, taking in the posh surroundings. Crystal glinted everywhere, and the tablecloths shone bleached white. Subdued classical music tinkled through the room. My skin immediately started to itch.

I'd spent time in places like this before to get at various targets, but I'd never enjoyed it. At least I'd known how to dress for the part. I'd selected a modest purple evening gown that hung just below my knees. The neckline wasn't necessarily revealing, though it wasn't prudish either, dipping into a V that just barely accentuated my assets. To top off the look, I'd paired it with a gold necklace and earrings to match a shiny clutch I carried.

From the way the crew's gazes had clung to me as I'd headed out, I knew I'd pulled off the look all right, even if I was way more comfortable in tees and sweatpants.

"There you are." Damien Malik came up beside me, resting his hand briefly on the small of my back to guide me with him. "You look lovely, Rachel."

My father looked taller than usual in his fitted black suit, with an air of authority I hadn't seen him exercise all that much among family. Maybe he was displaying it now because of the company we'd have for this dinner. He'd just gotten back from a longer than usual stint handling political work in DC, and he'd wanted to introduce me to a couple of his close colleagues from the capitol.

I couldn't say I was looking forward to meeting even more strangers, and these ones people I wasn't even related to, but I could tell it meant a lot to my father. And it was part of really becoming Rachel Malik, if I wanted to fully embrace that role.

I just hoped the role of Rachel started to feel more like *me*.

"Just be yourself," Damien assured me with a fatherly smile as we headed toward a table near the back of the room. "They'll go easy on you. I think it'll be good for you to have a deeper understanding of the work that occupies so much of my time. It affects the family in so many ways."

"That makes sense," I said. And it did affect all of the Maliks quite a bit. Like Carter deciding to give up baseball. Like the times when Iris was left to fend for herself when my grandparents visited, because Damien was out of town for the week. But Damien's standing also supported that big house with its expansive property and all the activities that happened in and around it.

We stopped at a table where two men were already sitting, though they got to their feet to greet us. Both were a good match for my father: white, middle-aged, with an air of importance around them as if it never occurred to them that they might not get what they wanted, one way or another. An awful lot of my targets for the household had been people like that.

My skin itched again with that thought. I could only imagine what my father's colleagues would think of *my* line of work.

Damien set his hand on my shoulder. "Clint, Gary, this is my daughter, Rachel. I'm so glad you're finally getting to meet her at last."

Clint, a portly man with bushy eyebrows and a beakish nose, dipped his head to me. "So am I. Such a lot of trouble and trauma on the way to you getting back to your family." He smiled with what looked like genuine sympathy, but I couldn't help feeling there was a patronizing edge to it. Like he thought I'd gotten myself kidnapped as a toddler out of some oversight of my own.

Gary, slim with a short, pointed beard, held out his hand for me to shake it. His grasp was as firm as I'd expect from his confident stance. "It's a pleasure. I can already see the apple didn't fall far from the tree, regardless of how you got there. Nature over nurture!"

"I'd like to think so," Damien said with a chuckle, and we all sat down.

"So, you work with my father in Washington?" I ventured, feeling like I should make some effort to add to the conversation and show an interest in the two men.

"For well over a decade now," Clint said, clapping his hand to my father's back. "Couldn't ask for a better ally among all the goons out there. Hard to find men with real integrity these days."

I thought of the Hunter and all his insinuations, and then mentally kicked myself for giving that stranger's accusations any space in my brain. Garrison hadn't yet confirmed the exchange of favors that'd let me get the Maliks' garden soil analyzed, but at this point, there was no reason to think it'd reveal any horrifying secrets.

"But I'd like to hear more about you," Gary spoke up, tipping his head to me as the waitress went around filling our water glasses. "As much as you're comfortable saying. Have you been able to settle in with your family all right after all this time?"

I would have bristled at the private question if he hadn't spoken so gently. But then, he was a politician, so framing things in the right way to get the answers he wanted must have been second nature to him.

"I think so," I said carefully. "We've only really just gotten started."

My father patted the back of my chair. "I'd say that Rachel has been fitting in exceptionally well, considering the circumstances. She's incredibly resilient."

He didn't even know the half of it, but part of me lit up at the praise despite myself. Noelle had barely acknowledged the strain she'd put me under. She'd taken it for granted that I'd get through everything she threw at me and every assignment I was sent on. But I *had* survived a hell of a lot.

Clint offered a sympathetic grimace. "You'd have to be. You've been through far more than any young lady—than anyone at all—should have to."

"And let's hope we see the perpetrators of that crime duly punished," Gary said. "Thanks to your father's work over the years, they'll face more jail time than they would have when you were first taken. Although some feel even that isn't enough. What are your thoughts on capital punishment?"

I held back a laugh. It hadn't taken long for them to transition from personal condolences to political agendas, had it? I guessed that was probably how things worked in Washington.

I'd never really thought about whether I believed in the death sentence before. Legal forms of murder had been far removed from my existence. I'd have been much more likely to get killed by the people I was intending to do the same to myself than to be caught by law enforcement and sentenced.

But then, what did the Chaos Crew do—what did *I* intend to do from now on with my skills—other than dole out capital punishments of our own?

"I can see some cases where it might be necessary," I said, still picking my words cautiously. I wasn't sure where even my father stood on this subject. "The criminal world is a violent place. Anyone who gets all that involved must know that's a risk they're taking."

Clint nodded. "I couldn't agree more. Although there is some debate about which approach actually puts more strain on the taxpayer."

"And the problems of false convictions," Gary pointed out. "Can't come back from a lethal injection if new evidence comes up later."

"Well, you know that doesn't happen very often."

I cleared my throat, feeling the need to add a little of my own perspective… especially because in their eyes, my men and I were probably among the kind of criminals they'd imagine would get a sentence that severe. "I do think the evidence should be clear. And also the person's motives need to be taken into consideration. Why they did what they did. What the consequences were."

Gary hummed to himself, and I couldn't tell whether it was approving or skeptical. His tone didn't give much away. "You're thinking of those hypothetical 'stealing bread for the starving family' situations."

Well, no, I'd been thinking about the very non-hypothetical "assassins who take out fellow criminals" situation, but I wasn't going to tell him that.

Before I could figure out how to answer, Damien set his hand on the back of my chair again. He'd been watching the whole conversation thoughtfully, and his gaze lingered on my face for a moment before he spoke, as if he was evaluating what he'd seen from me so far. A nervous twitch ran down my back.

But all he said was, "Let's not heap too much shop talk on Rachel all at once. She's here to meet you as friends, not to have her political stances dissected."

"What good are friends if you can't talk politics, huh?" Clint winked at both of us. "I'm sure you must at least share your father's stance on cracking down hard on the criminal element, especially after what you've experienced."

Did Damien's gaze get even more intent as he waited for my answer? My throat constricted just for a second. I did feel put on the spot now, and he wasn't rescuing me this time.

"I'd definitely want to see the people who kidnapped me punished with the full force of the law," I said. My law, delivered by my hands. "No one should steal a child from their home. It's unforgiveable."

Gary chuckled. "Only bread thieves can get off."

I shifted in my chair, trying not to outright squirm. "I don't know. I just think it depends on the crime and the reasons for it. Isn't there a saying about how the punishment should fit the crime? It's hard to make a blanket statement about all of it."

But it did seem like my father believed you could. He wanted every criminal treated more harshly. I wasn't sure he'd ever understand my perspective. Crimes had two sides, and I didn't think Damien Malik had ever been put in the position to see the side opposite his own.

But then, after losing me the way he had for so long, maybe his vehemence was understandable.

"Absolutely," he said now. "The trouble is that the laws have been too lenient across the board. The people who get away with too much vastly outnumber the few who were truly acting with what they thought were good intentions. Take theft—of anything, not specifically bread. Did you know that people don't usually get more than five to ten years in jail for that crime? They're taking away someone's livelihood or rightfully earned belongings, and that's all they face. I'm pushing for double that at *least.*"

I swallowed hard, thinking of the car I'd stolen—and then crashed—as I fled the household that first night. The one I'd grabbed in his own neighborhood to reach the crew in time to help defend them from the surprise attack? Would he have spoken that firmly if he'd known his daughter was a thief too?

Probably. He'd have excused my crime away thinking I'd needed to do it to save my life and those I cared about, that I was one of those rare exceptions. It was everything *else* I'd done in my life that he wouldn't be able to explain away.

Trying to come up with an answer that would satisfy him and hopefully end this line of conversation, I thought of the criminals I'd encountered over the past few weeks. The drug dealers who'd eagerly been packaging their product for the addicts they'd hooked. The movie-making gangsters who'd talked gleefully about murdering some guy for his camera equipment. The attackers who'd tried to kill the crew more than once, as recently as last week…

The man next to me *couldn't* have hired paid killers, could he? Not with attitudes like the ones he was expressing now. It didn't make any sense.

But why would someone else have wanted to murder the men of the Chaos Crew but not "the daughter"?

I shook those thoughts away and focused on my frustration with the underworld we'd come up against. "There are definitely a lot of people getting away with more than they should. I'd like to see a world where fewer innocent people get hurt."

That response seemed to please Damien. His smile grew, and he nodded emphatically. "Exactly. I knew you'd understand."

Just then, the server arrived with the appetizers we'd ordered. I couldn't have been more grateful for the excuse to focus on doing something with my mouth other than hashing out the flaws of the justice system.

Thankfully, my father and his friends veered into other topics during the rest of the meal. Clint and Gary inquired about everything from my sports interests to how much of the city I'd seen, offering tips of landmarks to check out when I admitted I'd barely explored DC. "Don't let them keep you holed up in your father's hometown," Clint said with a wave of his fork. "You've got the chance to see the world now."

If only he knew how many countries I'd already visited. I'd probably been more places before I'd turned eighteen than he had in his entire life.

When all the food had been polished off and the check paid, we waved goodbye to the two men and I summoned an Uber, the nearest one a few minutes away. My father sat on a bench outside in the warm evening air to wait with me for it. He crossed his legs at the ankles and leaned back, looking more relaxed than I'd seen him all evening.

"You did great in there," he said as he gazed at the passing cars. "I know they can be a bit overwhelming. I hope you didn't feel cornered at any point."

I shrugged. If I had, it was for reasons he couldn't have predicted and I couldn't admit. "They weren't that bad."

"Your brother hates things like this. Not that he doesn't agree with the policies we support; he just doesn't see the point in talking about it. More of a doer. Which is important, but you can't get permission to do without knowing how to talk the talk first." Damien shook his head. "Your mother—she has a real knack for playing politics. I can tell you're her daughter." He glanced over at me. "You're becoming an integral part of this family, aren't you?"

Somehow that question felt more momentous than the actual words he'd used. "I'd like to think so," I said. "It's been wonderful *having* a family, a real one."

As soon as I said those words, guilt stabbed through my gut. Julius had referred to me as part of the crew's family. Maybe I wasn't connected to them by genetics, but my bond with them was at least as real as anything I shared with the Maliks.

"I'm glad you feel that way." Damien paused for a moment as if deciding what to say next. "We have a long-established legacy among the Maliks, one that goes back generations. I hope that as we become closer, that's something I can introduce you to. We'd be honored to have you be a part of it."

Something about his tone set my nerves prickling. I was already part of the family, wasn't I? The way he phrased it made it sound almost like a cult or something that I'd be indoctrinated into.

He couldn't mean it like that, though, right? He was just passionate about the family and what they stood for. I'd seen how close-knit and supportive the Maliks were.

"What kind of legacy?" I asked, watching him closely.

"Mostly in standing up for the innocents who need our protection, a lot like you said in there." He smiled at me. "Dedicating ourselves to the public good has been an ongoing tradition that means a lot to us."

Was that what the Hunter wanted to warn me about—that my family was dedicated to doing good? Inwardly, I rolled my eyes at that hoarse voice on the telephone with its ominous warnings. Sure, I'd still take a look at the soil, but there'd been no other indications of any kind of threat around the Maliks. Blaze hadn't even found anything suspicious digging through their internet activity.

"Well, that sounds like the kind of legacy I could get behind," I said, and my mind leapt to one specific crime I'd hoped he'd have more details about after all his time away from home. "I don't suppose the investigation into my kidnappers has turned up any new leads? There's still so much about that situation that I don't understand." And still so many people who needed to pay for the lives they'd upended.

My father sighed. "Unfortunately, the path seems to be very cold. Since you escaped without knowing where they'd been holding you before your trip, I think the investigators are stumped on where to even start. And your kidnappers were very effective in covering their tracks."

His mouth twisted. "The worst menaces in society are getting increasingly difficult to pin down. All the more reason we need to crack down on them more than before. Make it clear that the consequences aren't worth it, to stop others going down the same path.

People who do such horrendous acts should never be allowed out of prison. They should rot and die there."

Even though I wanted to destroy the people who'd wrenched me from my original life and forced me to become their tool, the vehemence in Damien's voice made me tense. I couldn't blame him for being angry, could I? He'd had his daughter ripped away from him, had to think I was dead for all these years. I wanted the people who'd orchestrated that loss dead too.

But there'd been a viciousness that'd crept into his tone that didn't fit with the upstanding politician he usually presented himself as. He might talk as if his policies were for the greater good, but for him, it was clearly very personal as well. And I got the impression he wasn't only talking about the specific criminals who'd taken me but all of them.

Including people like me and the Chaos Crew.

I didn't have time to think of an appropriate response, because my Uber pulled up across from us just then. Damien walked me over and opened the door for me, getting a promise out of me to stop by the house for Sunday brunch. He was the total picture of a reserved gentleman again. His fond wave as he saw me off felt so normal it was hard to believe he'd been wishing death on the entire prison population just minutes ago.

He couldn't realize how close his claims hit to home, and I hoped he never would.

My phone dinged, breaking me from my reverie. I glanced at the screen and found a text from Julius. *Garrison's contact is willing to meet with you. It's time to swap some favors.*

THIRTEEN

Garrison

AS THE TRAIN roared along the tracks toward New York City, Dess kept her usual calm, cool poise in the seat across from me, but I knew her well enough to mark the signs of tension in her shoulders and her jaw. She ran her finger across her lips, drawing my attention to where it really shouldn't be while we prepared for this detour of a mission.

She'd wanted to come alone, but Julius had insisted that I come along, since I was the one who knew the most about our contact and had handled the negotiations as a middleman. *You'll still be delivering the favor and earning hers on your own*, he'd told Dess. *But it's important to us that everyone knows the Chaos Crew has your back.*

Dess must have been a little nervous, because she'd agreed without any further argument.

"Anthea Noble," she said now, adjusting her position as she turned the woman's name over on her tongue. "And she specializes in discreet crimes?"

I nodded. "The word that's gone around is that she's the one to turn to if you need a murder set up to look like an accident or an innocent illness—or if you need to investigate an accident or illness that you think might have actually been murder. Checking the chemical compounds in a soil sample, especially for anything that hints at a crime, fits right in with that. I heard that one time she took down an enemy by lacing his rosebushes with some kind of undetectable poison."

Dess grimaced. "A gun to the head or a knife to the throat is much simpler. Clearer. Are you sure we can trust her?"

I shrugged. "As much as we can trust anyone in this world. She's well-established and connected—the aunt of the head of a major gang in a county called Paradise Bend that's a few hours away from New York. And she seems to care about her reputation, which is that she's cutthroat when she needs to be but fair with those she feels have earned her loyalty. I don't think she'd stab us in the back for no reason. If she does… I'd bet you can deal with her."

A glint of humor lit in Dess's eyes. "I can definitely shoot her before she can slowly poison me."

I let out a laugh. "And good thing, too. But I really don't think it'll come to that. She knows you come with the Chaos Crew's support, and we've got quite a reputation too. The best-connected people don't turn down new connections among the upper echelon. They've gotten where they are by forging solid alliances. She'll see us as just as useful to her as she is to us."

"And this gang she's associated with? Are they going to want a cut?"

"She didn't mention anything about that. It appears that she mainly operates independently, without needing permission or guidance from them."

"All right." Dess leaned her head back in her seat with a sigh. My gaze was drawn to the soft, pale stretch of her neck with the urge to run my mouth across it, but I doubted she'd welcome a PDA.

Was she worried more about the stranger we were going to meet or about what that stranger might tell us about the Maliks?

I didn't know how to ask her that, so I settled for a teasing question instead. "So, here you are about to embark on your first solo mission without the household behind you. No cold feet, I hope?"

Dess let out a dismissive huff. "I was always alone in the household anyway." Her eyes went momentarily distant before refocusing. "They might have funded and backed my missions, but they weren't there to make sure I survived. I relied on no one but myself during those operations just as I'll be doing on this one."

"You're getting to call the shots about what and who you do this time, though. Moving up in the world."

She glowered at me through narrowed eyes. "Are you trying to pump me up or take me down a peg?"

I grinned. "Can't it be both at the same time? We wouldn't want your head to get too big."

She patted her hair. "I think it suits me just fine as it is."

The truth was, I was going easier on her than I might have if I couldn't have told that she wasn't totally confident in this new role. It *was* the first time she'd taken on a solo job as a totally free agent.

And really, she should feel proud of where she'd ended up. She'd endured trainers who only cared about how well she could use the weapons they'd put in her hands, no family to speak of in her entire living memory, and death-defying missions from her childhood. But those trials had only honed her into the strongest woman I'd ever known. Even now, knowing what she did about her past, she hadn't let it shake her all that much.

The sudden urge gripped me to open up a part of myself as deep and painful as the losses I knew she'd faced. My chest constricted at the thought. I *never* let down all my walls, never let the all-too-real agony spill out of me.

But I could give her *something* real. Something I could say honestly without sarcasm or jokes to deflect the impact.

I drew in a breath and steadied myself, forcing my voice to come out with genuine warmth rather than its usual wryness. "I'm looking forward to watching you kick ass on this mission without the pretense of anyone controlling you. I can't wait to see what you'll do on your own."

Dess looked at me, and the softness in her eyes showed that she knew how significant those words had been. She leaned toward me in a burst of motion, taking me by surprise as her lips collided with mine.

Her hand wrapped around the back of my head and tugged the hair at the base of my skull.

She didn't really do gentle, not when it came to physical intimacy. From the hints she'd dropped when we'd hooked up that one evening, I knew the reason was something that'd make me want to tear apart the world to avenge her.

But she hadn't shared the details, so I wasn't going to pry. Not yet, anyway. I just kissed her back with equal passion. My hand fell to her thigh and squeezed, and she let out a muffled moan.

Then she pulled back. The passengers across the aisle from us were watching, not that I minded. Let them see how much I cared about this woman and how much she wanted me.

A playful smile crossed Dess's lips as she ran her fingers through her dark hair. "I'm glad you're here with me," she said. "I *can* do this on my own… but it's better knowing that I don't have to be. Maybe you'll get to find out just how much the Ghost can pull off when she's in her element."

I gave a soft chuckle. "Oh, I think I have a pretty good idea already."

The tension clenching my chest had eased. The world hadn't ended because I'd gone for sap over snark just this once. Dess hadn't shunned me. Everything was still on its proper course. I actually felt a little lighter than I had before. Freer.

Would it be so bad to let my walls down more often? Well, with her, at least. Not with the guys or anyone else…

No, I still needed those inner protections. They were my armor. I couldn't let myself get complacent, or I could screw everything up for both me and the people who stood with me.

It was night by the time we reached the city. We eased through the shadows of the trees in Central Park, veering off the main paths. People were usually warned not to wander around in this place after dark, but I didn't think anyone would bother us. If they did, we could quickly clear up any misconceptions about who the real predators were here.

We stopped amid the brush behind the Civil War Memorial statue, just a few minutes before our arranged meeting time. Dess peered at the branches that loomed overhead. "What are the odds that we have a sniper on us right now?"

I raised an eyebrow. "I don't see anyone close enough to pull off a shot through all this vegetation without the most incredible aim in the universe."

"And why would I want to have someone ready to shoot you anyway, when you're here to give me something *I* want?" a dry voice said.

A woman emerged from the forested terrain to meet us. At the first sight of her, skepticism shot through me.

She was slim and petite, a full head shorter than I was, with her bright red hair coiled elegantly behind her ears and tumbling down to her shoulders. The traditional style matched her subtle flower-print dress, which looked like something a '50s housewife would have worn. But even though she appeared to be no older than her early thirties, she seemed totally at ease with the old-fashioned vibe.

Could this really be the infamous Anthea Noble?

"From what I understand, it's supposed to be a trade," I said. "We're not here to pile gifts at your feet."

A sharp, sly smile crossed the woman's lips, and just like that, I could see the renowned schemer within the domestic homemaker package. "What a shame. I like presents. But I'm not one to expect that kind of generosity from strangers. I'm fully prepared to repay your help with help of my own. Hard to turn down an offer from an associate of the havoc-wreaking Chaos Crew."

"I understand you lean toward a subtle approach," Dess said, folding her arms over her chest. "I promise my methods are less bloody than theirs… unless bloody is what you want."

Anthea's smile grew. "Exactly what I like to hear." She paused for a moment, studying us both, and my skin prickled with the sense that she saw much more than she was commenting on. This definitely wasn't a woman to tangle with—but that meant she could be a very valuable associate if we played our cards right. I was always glad to make a new connection myself.

"We appreciate you taking the time to meet with us and consider our proposal," I said smoothly. "Your reputation precedes you too. And the task we'd like to employ you with shouldn't require any significant risk on your part."

"You have a boring job for me, do you?" She clucked her tongue teasingly and focused on Dess. "I'm afraid I can't say the same, although maybe you'll be happier that way. I've gathered that you specialize in taking down targets that most assassins wouldn't be able to reach—and without leaving any evidence behind."

Dess raised her chin. "That's right. You might have heard of me before. Apparently a lot of my killings have been attributed to 'the Ghost.' That would be me."

I caught the brief flash of surprise that widened Anthea's eyes before she schooled her expression back to its previous unreadable state. "Fascinating. I'd imagine this shouldn't be *too* much trouble for you, then, if you're willing to take the job on."

"What exactly would you like her to do?" I asked evenly. I wasn't going to be pushy about it, but I did want her to get to the point.

Anthea ran her fingers along a branch that dipped low alongside us. "There's a mark I'd like killed. He's tricky to get to—lots of security and very cautious. He's evaded my own resources more than once, and I'd like to simply get the job done once and for all."

"You want me to get to him and kill him," Dess clarified.

Anthea rubbed her fingers together, and her face hardened just for an instant. "I want you to kill him, yes, but not just that. I want him to die in a particularly horrible way. And no one can know that you were involved or that I hired you."

"That shouldn't be a problem," Dess said, but then she hesitated. "Why do you want him dead?"

I understood immediately, with a pang that resonated through my heart. She'd spent too many years blindly killing for someone else's sake. The household had never given her a choice in who she killed, leading her to believe she was eliminating criminals and harmful figures when really she'd been fulfilling their own selfish agenda, whatever that'd been.

But Dess didn't revel in killing for the sake of killing. She wanted to know her targets deserved it, just like we did. She was determined to make her new path a just one as long as she had the choice. Of course that didn't change even when she could gain something from bending her personal ethics.

Anthea's eyes flashed, and her voice came out taut. "This man raped a few teenagers who've since come under my protection. I want to make sure he's never in a position to do the same to any others."

Dess's posture straightened, her mouth pressing flat. Resolve radiated off her as she held out her hand for Anthea to shake. "I look forward to wiping him off the face of the earth. Point me at him, and he's good as dead already."

FOURTEEN

Decima

THE POLYESTER HOUSEKEEPING uniform itched at my arms. I resisted the urge to scratch them as I wiped down the benches at the edge of the hotel lobby. The desk clerk had even made a comment to me about how the one near the door needed a lot of work, so I knew that at least she didn't recognize me as an imposter. The position also made it easy to keep my face at an angle where it'd never be caught on the security cameras.

I didn't normally like to do a lot of playacting for a mission. I'd rather have slunk in unseen, relying on stealth and strength rather than pretense. But Garrison had pointed out to me that while he was here, he might as well help pave the way to completing Anthea Noble's job. My pride had wanted me to say no, but practicality had won out.

Better to do everything possible to ensure the operation went off without a hitch than to insist on doing it totally solo.

Right on cue, Garrison sauntered into the lobby as if he were meant to be there, wearing a dark leather jacket, sunglasses, and a chip on his shoulder larger than the massive hotel. He strode through the lobby and stopped before the farthest elevator—the one labeled PRIVATE. The two guards stationed there stopped him in his tracks.

"This car goes to the penthouse only," one said, placing a hand on Garrison's chest and nudging him a step backward. "There's nothing you need here."

Garrison's dramatic gasp echoed through the lobby. "Do you know who I *am?*" he asked, and I held back from chuckling at the clear change from the voice I was used to. He spoke with a high-pitched, whiny tone that would have had Blaze in hysterics.

"Doesn't matter. Mr. Fitzgerald doesn't have any appointments."

Garrison removed the sunglasses he'd been wearing and placed them atop his head. "He does with me, but what would you know about his schedule? You're just the help."

He made as if to waltz past the men, and one of the guards pushed him backward more forcefully. "I can double check if you're going to make a fuss about it," he grumbled. "But he doesn't like being interrupted unnecessarily."

"Oh, this is absolutely necessary," Garrison insisted.

The guard whipped a phone out of his pocket, but before he could dial, Garrison snatched it out of his hands. "I think *I'd* better do the talking," he said, and dashed for the front doors.

I was already ambling across the lobby with my head low, as if I hadn't noticed the altercation. Garrison ran past me, and the guard hurtled after him. I placed myself in just the right spot that he couldn't help bumping into me at the speed he was going.

"Watch where you're going," he spat at me, staggering, but his attention was still mostly on Garrison. I scrambled out of the way, and the guard hurtled out of the building after the phone thief.

The desk clerk stared at all that wide-eyed. "Should I call the police?" she asked the remaining guard.

He shook his head, looking bored. "Heath can take care of it."

That's what he thought. I meandered on in the general direction of the private elevator, tucking the keycard I'd picked from the first guard's pocket into a pouch sewn on the inside of my sleeve.

It was only a few more seconds before Garrison dashed back in—alone. Somehow he'd made his face go pale as if in a panic. "He's having some kind of fit," he said to the remaining guard. "I don't know—I didn't mean to get him so worked up. Does he have epilepsy or something?"

"What the fuck?" The second guard barged toward the doorway to find out what was going on.

I had no idea how the rest of Garrison's scheme would play out, only that he knew what he was doing. It was time for me to take care of my part.

The instant the second guard had barreled past the lobby doors, I darted to the elevator and swiped my sleeve past the scanner pad. The key card activated through the fabric, and the doors slid open. I slipped into the car and jabbed the button to close the doors before anyone could return and try to stop me.

The elevator car vibrated around me as it ascended. I kept my body turned away from the security camera, my head still tipped down. If anyone checked the footage later, they'd see nothing more of the murderer than the maid uniform and the brown wig I'd pulled over my hair.

Mr. Fitzgerald, the owner of this hotel, lived in the penthouse suite, and he had around-the-clock guards at every potential entrance for his safety. According to Anthea, there were none *inside* the room because he preferred a certain level of privacy. Naturally that also meant that once I got inside, I didn't need to worry about cameras.

He was careful, sure, but I'd dealt with far more difficult targets.

As I neared the top floor, adrenaline began to course through my veins. How long had it been since I'd been out on an assignment, preparing to take down a target as only I knew how? The danger around me and the certainty that I could see this kill through exhilarated me in a way nothing else—not even chocolate—could. I'd forgotten what that feeling was like after the way my discoveries about the household had soured my memories of the work I'd done for them.

The thrill was momentarily dampened by a jab of guilt. Maybe those memories *should* have been soured. The people I'd killed… For a second, I pictured my father's face if he knew, taut with disapproving horror.

But this mission wasn't about Damien Malik or my birth family.

This was about eliminating a man who absolutely deserved it. And there was no one better to fulfill that duty than me.

The elevator opened into a small foyer that led to the main penthouse. Another guard was stationed there.

The instant the doors parted, I sprang into motion. There wasn't a second to waste if I wanted to stop him from raising the alarm.

The guard had inadvertently positioned himself right where I could take full advantage, standing facing the elevator with a gun in his hand and a frown on his face. I sprang at him, jerking sideways to throw him off, kicking the gun from his hand, and swinging out my arm with the knife I'd retrieved from my pocket on the way up.

The blade caught him across the throat before he had a chance to do more than draw in a breath to shout. I sliced through muscle and cartilage, severing his neck all the way down to his spine and shoving him away from me.

Blood spewed out across the floor, only a few flecks catching on the dark fabric of my uniform. As the guard crumpled to the floor, his head lolling on his nearly severed neck, I rubbed the droplets in so they wouldn't show.

Mr. Fitzgerald's closest bodyguards had stood by while he'd raped who knew how many girls, ignoring everything they'd seen and heard. Even if they'd been able to convince themselves there wasn't anything outright violent involved, they'd known their boss was fixating on underage teens. Anthea hadn't asked me to give this man as thorough a punishment as his boss, but I didn't feel any regrets about his death.

The boss was so cautious that no one had the key to the penthouse door other than him. But he also had old-fashioned tastes, preferring to trust actual keys over digitized cards. I couldn't have said he was wrong. If it'd been Blaze coming for him, the hacker probably could have found a way to hack an electronic lock in less than a minute.

Instead, I brought out my picks. The door had a complex mechanism, but I felt my way around the tumblers through the pounding of my heart. A push here and a twist there…

The lock clicked open. I eased the door open an inch, listening at the gap.

No one reacted on the other side. The sound of a TV show—a

news report, from the staccato voice reaching my ears—carried from a more distant room. I caught a faint rustling as if someone had moved on a bed.

Perfect.

I closed the door behind me and slunk through the opulent penthouse to the master bedroom. The trappings of luxury often worked in my favor. The rug was so thick it absorbed my footsteps without much effort on my part.

The door stood halfway open. I peeked inside. A stout, doughy-faced man lounged at the edge of his king-sized bed as he watched the TV. I noted the steel chain of his necklace with a panic button on the central link. I had to work fast before he had a chance to press that.

I judged the distance and the height of the bed. Then I waited until he glanced away from the TV at the wall opposite the door.

The moment there was no chance of him seeing me, I sprang through the doorway. My first few footfalls were so silent he didn't even realize anything was wrong until he turned back and I was nearly on top of him already.

A startled yelp jolted out of him, and his hand flew toward the panic button. But I was prepared for that. My first move was to snatch both his wrists, snapping the narrow bones as I yanked them over his head. When he fell back on the bed, I pinned his forearms under my shin and rammed the side of my hand against his throat.

The louder shout he'd been summoning died with a pained whistle. I'd crushed his windpipe to a sliver of its former self. He could still breathe, so he'd be alive for the vengeance Anthea had asked me to carry out, but he wasn't going to be doing any hollering ever again.

It would have been easier to simply kill him outright, but I found I liked the idea of stretching out his suffering on Anthea's orders. It still wouldn't be anything close to the way his victims must have suffered—must still be suffering.

He started to flail against my hold, making little squeaks of pain when he strained his broken wrists. I put an end to all that struggling with a few plastic zip ties that I'd concealed in my uniform. I hauled him up the bed and attached his arms to the wrought iron headboard. Then I bound his ankles together and ran a rigid line between them and a post at the foot. It stretched him so tightly that he couldn't bend his knees or his waist.

Mr. Fitzgerald stared up at me, wheezing, as I flashed my bloody knife. I jerked open his shirt, letting the buttons pop, and applied the tip of the blade to his flesh like a pen.

"This is for Mika," I said, carving the full name Anthea had given me deep into the skin over his ribs. "And for Carmen, and for Tonya. You're never going to violate anyone like you did them ever again. I'm turning the tables on their behalf."

A whimper worked its way from his battered throat. Blood seeped from the wounds. His muscles twitched as I dug the blade in again and again, drawing every letter that told the story.

I didn't let him bleed enough to lose consciousness. When I finished my etching, I held up the knife again and yanked down his pants.

The man's face was already drenched in sweat and sickly gray. Now he made one last, futile attempt at escape. I shook my head as he jerked this way and that.

"If you lie still, it might hurt a little less," I informed him. Not that I cared how much it hurt.

He didn't heed my advice. He was still wriggling away when I slashed right through the base of his dick. Then a thin wail carried from his throat, only cut off when I finished the last piece of Anthea's request and shoved his member down his throat to cut off his air completely.

It was vicious, but when I sat back and watched his body shudder and sag, there was a certain artistry to the act of justice. I was *proud* to have dealt it out.

My heart kept thumping on with the rush of adrenaline. Mr. Fitzgerald's eyes stared blankly at the ceiling now. A smile crossed my lips. I stripped off the housekeeping costume to reveal the tight black stealth clothes underneath, retrieved the thin but sturdy rope I'd had wrapped around my waist underneath, and went to the balcony.

It only took a minute to rappel down to the ground through the cover of the night. Then I was darting away into the shadows like the ghost the criminal underworld had seen me as for years.

The wig went into a restaurant dumpster around the corner. By the time I reached Garrison where he was waiting outside a bar three blocks away, all my tension had melted away, leaving only the giddiness of the task I'd just fulfilled. I couldn't help smiling again. Garrison took one look at me in the hazy light of the streetlamps and chuckled under his breath.

"Faster than I even expected. And I can tell you got the job done."

"Hell, yes," I replied, falling into step with him as we started walking down the street.

He looped his arm casually around mine. "I could do this every day if there were enough missions to keep us that busy. Such a fucking thrill."

"Yeah," I agreed, with a swell of emotion that had nothing to do with the job itself.

Who else had I ever known who'd really understood that feeling? Even Noelle had been more interested in my results than how I experienced my success.

How lucky was I that I'd found my way into the midst of not one but four men who could relate to the deepest, darkest parts of my heart?

FIFTEEN

Decima

FINALLY, my hands were empty, and all that was left to do was wait for Anthea's results.

I'd dropped off soil samples from a few different sections of the garden—soil that I'd stealthily scooped into little baggies while I'd wandered along the beds of flowers, pretending to be crouching down for a closer look and sniff. Once I'd left the house, I'd packed the samples carefully and sent them off by courier so Anthea would get them later today. She'd said it'd take a day or two for her to produce her results.

When I made it back to the house in the hill, the sun was waning, casting the entire world in a golden light. I found the guys all huddled around the sofa, flipping through channels on the TV and looking like they'd just finished squabbling over who would hold the remote. Unsurprisingly, Julius was the current victor. But the moment they heard me enter, he clicked off the screen and they all turned toward me.

"There she is," Garrison said with a clap of his hands. "Is everything taken care of?"

I nodded and flopped into the space in the center of the sofa that was just big enough for me, right between Julius and Talon. "Anthea promised that when the courier got the samples to her, it would go to the top of her priority list."

"You know, this is how Talon and I tested out new members of the crew," Julius said, letting his fingers brush over my knee in a way that sent sparks right up my leg. "Set them up on a trial mission that they have to handle on their own."

"I wasn't completely by myself," I felt the need to remind him. "Garrison helped with the diversion."

Garrison rolled his eyes. "I hardly did anything. Without me, you would have easily handled the guards. Drawing them away was easy."

"Still, I didn't do it alone."

Blaze cut into the conversation. "Were you alone in the room with the target?" I nodded and opened my mouth to counter, but he stopped me. "And you passed the other guard without a problem?"

"Okay, fine," I said. "But it's not like it's the first operation I've carried out alone anyway."

Julius smiled. "It's the first one you've gone on since you took up with us, and you completed it much to your 'client's' satisfaction and without any blowback. I think that means you're officially part of the crew now."

There was a mildly teasing note in his tone. I elbowed him gently. "Are you saying I wasn't already?"

"I don't know," Garrison said with mock-skepticism. "Should it really count when we weren't the ones who picked the scenario?"

As I debated whether there was something in easy reach that I could throw at him, since I didn't want to leave my cozy spot on the sofa, Blaze tsked his tongue. "Maybe it wasn't our call, but it *was* ten times harder than the trial mission I got sent on. Pretty sure yours didn't involve a nearly unreachable target either."

Garrison leaned back in his chair. "Well, there you go. It's not fair that she got such an exciting scenario for her trial run. I think it's only fair if she does a boring mission like the rest of us before we fully initiate her." His lips twitched with a hint of amusement.

Talon patted my thigh, sending another wash of heat through my body. "I think Dess deserves a promotion for taking on a harder job than the rest of us did," he said in his usual deep, emotionless voice, but when I peered up at him, I caught a glint of humor in his cool eyes.

I stretched out my legs over the bearskin rug. "I guess I'll take Julius's place if you're offering."

Julius snorted and gestured to the rest of the crew. "If you think you can keep them in line better than I can, more power to you."

"Hmm." I tapped my lips. "As my first order as queen of the crew, I demand that you bring me all the chocolate in the city."

Blaze burst out with a laugh, and Garrison's and Julius's guffaws quickly followed. Even Talon let out a chuckle. He stroked my thigh again, and I found myself thinking about things they could do that would be even sweeter than procuring chocolate.

As I looked around at the four of them, basking in the warmth of their admiration and comradery, a surge of affection swelled in my chest. I *had* gotten incredibly lucky to find these four men who complimented me so perfectly. I cared about all of them more than I'd even known I was capable of. If I believed in a higher power, I'd have been thanking it right now for bringing them into my life.

But I didn't believe in that. I was the highest power I believed in. And maybe it was time I showed them all just how much they meant to me.

I reached over and teased my fingers over Talon's thigh in turn. He swallowed audibly, shifting just a tad into my touch. My gaze slid over the other men gathered around me.

I'd been with all of them individually—and Talon and Julius together once—but we'd never come together as a crew, as a *team*, in the most intimate way.

Would they even want to? They did just about everything else together, but Julius and Garrison had gotten pretty uptight at first about the idea that I wanted all four of them in any way at all.

They'd gotten over that hesitation, though. And we should probably find out if we could be a team like this too.

I trailed my hand further up Talon's thigh, skimming just shy of the fly of his jeans. "Actually, I have a better idea. I just want all of you. In every possible way."

The temperature in the room seemed to rise five degrees in an instant. Four gazes burned into me. "*All* of us?" Blaze repeated with an eager light in his face. I should have known he'd be enthusiastic from the start.

"If you think you can handle that," I replied.

Talon answered by gripping my wrist, taking control just how he knew I liked it. He set my hand right on the bulge of his already hardening cock, letting out an approving grunt when I gripped him through the fabric. He showed no sign at all of embarrassment at being fondled like this in front of his friends.

"I'll take you any way you want," he said, his voice gone a little rough.

Garrison got to his feet, an unfamiliar wildness in his eyes. It didn't look like a refusal, at least. He stepped across the rug and grabbed my other hand. "You don't have enough holes for all of us, sweetheart," he said, bringing my knuckles to his lips.

I cocked my head as I held his gaze, swooning silently when he sucked my forefinger right into his mouth and then nipped the tip. "I think I can manage. I've got two hands as well. And hopefully sometime in your lives, you all have learned the basics of taking turns."

Julius led his pack of chaos in this scenario like he always did. He stood and took my hand from Garrison, pulling me to my feet. As his deep blue eyes bored into mine, smoldering with desire, lust pooled between my thighs. Right then, I knew we were really going to do this.

"Which one of us do you want to fuck you first?" he asked in a low voice full of so much promise I soaked my panties. But that wasn't the right question.

"I was hoping you could make a collaboration," I replied. "I thought I made it very clear that I'm not interested in choosing when it comes to the four of you."

I stepped away from him and slid my fingers along the hem of my shirt. The guys all watched me as if I were an exotic animal they couldn't believe they were getting the chance to capture. I raised the hem of my shirt an inch and then another, meeting each pair of eyes that stared at me as I claimed all of their attention with just the faintest lift of my arm.

A smirk crossed my lips as I finally tugged the shirt over my head and tossed it aside. Next I reached for the button on my pants, popping it slowly.

Talon sank back into the sofa's padding, the movement drawing my attention to him. He unzipped his jeans and freed himself, stroking his hand up and down the thick shaft I'd felt through the fabric just moments ago. His eyes stayed fixed on me. Cool and blue, they drilled into me and urged me to continue exposing myself to him. To all of them.

I could hardly look away while I slid my pants down my waist. My breath snagged in my throat as he parted his lips slightly, watching me.

God, I couldn't handle his gaze—not yet. He could finish me with mere glances, and I needed to pace myself if I hoped to satisfy this many men.

My gaze flew to Blaze, standing rigid at the side of the sofa, just as fixated by my movements as anyone. I bit my lip and unclasped my bra, allowing my breasts to fall free.

"Blaze," I ordered, "come here and lie down."

He was the safest, even if the passion in his eyes enflamed me. Talon could finish me with a look, and Garrison could finish me with his cunning words. Julius... God, Julius would unwind me the moment he touched me. But Blaze could take orders. Blaze could take it slow and help me put on a tempting show to get us all on the same page.

Of course, he could give orders too. "Condoms," he demanded as he strode toward me, whipping off his shirt as he came. My mouth watered at the sight of all that lean muscle on display.

Julius tipped his head to one side in a subtle question aimed at me. "I don't think we need them."

I licked my lips, reaching for the waist of Blaze's slacks. "You're the main ladies' man around here," I said, ignoring Garrison's noise of protest. "Are you sure you're clean?"

His pupils dilated, and I'd swear I heard his breath hitch. "Yeah.

It's been a little while—and I've always used protection—test results just a couple weeks ago were clean."

"Anyone else have any reason to think they should wrap it up?" I asked the room at large. "I've got an implant, so I'm covered in that area."

"Fuck," Garrison muttered, but there was nothing but desire in his voice now. "I'm good to go. Whatever you want, sweetheart."

Talon's cock twitched in his grasp. "There hasn't been anyone but you in a long time," he said quietly.

Oh, fuck, now I was even more turned on. My panties, the only piece of clothing still on me, had to be absolutely drenched at this point.

Blaze kicked his pants to the side and tossed his boxers after them. He hooked his fingers into the waistband of my panties and tugged me toward him, eyeing me like I was his next plate of pasta to devour. "Where do you want me?"

"Right there," I instructed, pointing at the thick rug beneath our feet.

He lowered himself to his knees, pulling down my last article of clothing as he went, never once breaking eye contact. Then he eased onto his back, propped up on his elbows. His cock jutted into the air, beckoning me.

I sank down over him, watching the other men's expressions as I did. Blaze gripped my hips, giving me a little of the forcefulness I loved. I ground against him, a shaky breath spilling out of me as his cock slid against my slick folds.

The anticipation of having him ram right inside me was torturous, but somehow that made the pleasure even more exquisite. I tipped my head back and rocked over him, drinking in the stutters of his breath and the way his length hardened even more as he rubbed against me. Then my eyes met Garrison's.

As if the colliding of our gazes was a signal fire, he moved toward me, positioning himself next to Blaze and tangling his fingers in my hair. Then he knelt down and claimed my mouth with all the fiery energy that called to me in him. I fumbled with the buttons on his shirt, wanting to bare his well-toned body as well.

Garrison pulled back just enough to shed it, chuckling under his breath. "Are you going to fuck Blaze or just tease him until he explodes?"

A moan escaped me at the insinuation of those words. Blaze adjusted himself beneath me, and I decided I'd teased *myself* long enough. I fit myself against him and fell down onto him, letting his cock spear right into me with the most delicious friction.

The hacker groaned, bucking his hips to meet me and massaging my hips where he was still clutching me. As I raised and lowered myself over him, taking him deeper with each bob of my body, Garrison straightened up again. He undid his belt and let his pants fall before grasping my hair with one hand.

"Let's see how well you can handle two at once."

He knew how to bring the roughness too. As Garrison tapped the head of his cock against my lips, my pussy clenched around Blaze, the rush of my impending orgasm building inside me. I opened my mouth obediently and flicked my tongue around the other man's shaft. Garrison muttered a curse.

"That's right," he said. "Take me right down like I know you can."

Oh, I'd show him what I could do all right. I sucked him into my mouth, wrapping my lips tightly around his cock and swirling my tongue around him. Then it was Garrison's turn to groan.

I kept bobbing over Blaze, propelling us both toward our release, and Garrison rocked into my mouth at the same time. Just like when I'd taken Julius and Talon at once, there was a special thrill to mastering these two talented men. Making them both come undone at the same time when they rarely made themselves vulnerable to anyone.

I set one hand over Blaze's where he was squeezing my hip and clasped it as if to say we were in this together. I gripped the base of Garrison's shaft with my other hand.

We moved together like some kind of blissful machine. At the pumping of my hand, Garrison's breaths started to fracture. I worked him over faster, sucking harder, and he came with a cry and a flood of salty cum in my mouth.

The taste of him and the urgent pace I'd set with Blaze tipped me over the edge. Bliss crashed over me, and I released Garrison's cock to cling to his thigh as I shuddered with the sensation. Blaze's fingers dug into my flesh, and the hot spurt of his own release filled me.

"So fucking good," the hacker mumbled, stroking me with gentler fingers as I lifted myself off of him. My legs wobbled, but only in the best of ways. We weren't anywhere near done. I still had two other men I hadn't gotten to play with yet.

I glanced down to take in Blaze's sated expression and found that Talon had already made plans of his own. He'd gotten off the sofa, and as Blaze scooted out of the way, the dispassionate killer nudged my shoulders down. "On your hands and knees," he ordered. "You're not done until you've screamed."

A giddy giggle tumbled out of me. "And I suppose you're the man for that job."

"I think we're all going to get you there together. So it'd better be a good scream, or we'll just have to keep working you over."

When he rubbed his palm over my ass with those words, I couldn't say his threat frightened me. What woman in her right mind would say no to that?

"Ass up," Talon demanded. I arched my back, giving him the reins. He gripped my hips with those strong, solid hands and tugged me backward.

In a second, he aligned himself and thrust into my pussy so fast a gasp tumbled out of me. Even with my channel relaxed and slicker than before, Talon's cock stretched me, wider than any of the others.

As Talon pounded into me, making stars spark behind my eyes and propelling more whimpers from my throat, Blaze tugged my face around to capture my mouth. He kissed me long and hard, drinking in my sounds of pleasure, and then gazed at me with heavy-lidded eyes. His attention shifted to the last of the four men who'd just approached.

Julius loomed over me, unfastening his pants. As I swayed back and forth with the force of Talon's thrusts, the leader of the crew crouched down in front of me. I lowered my head even more to lick the tip of his erect cock. Julius growled in approval and tugged me down to take him fully into my mouth.

As I was filled from both ends again, another heady thrill racing through me, Blaze and Garrison refused to be left out. Blaze dappled kisses across my shoulders while he reached beneath me to stroke my breasts, squeezing the slopes and pinching the nipples until I moaned around Julius's shaft. On the other side of me, Garrison had edged down so he could tuck his hand beneath my belly. He teased it even farther down until his fingertips brushed the sensitive spot just above where Talon and I were joined.

The pressure against my clit sent a sharper bolt of pleasure through me than ever before. I bobbed my head over Julius's cock, tightening my lips around him, my moans reverberating through my mouth over his shaft. The crew's commander dug his fingers into my hair and guided my head at an even faster pace.

Talon bucked faster too, and the pleasure building in my core rushed through me like a speeding train. Blaze kept fondling my breasts, ducking his head right under me to lap one nipple into his hot mouth.

With all of us in sync together in this whirlwind of lust, I allowed myself to feel the full extent of my satisfaction. I noted the pulse of my heartbeat between my legs and the steady rhythm of the movement radiating through every part of my body. It was fucking glorious, and I reveled in every second of it.

Talon groaned behind me, and with one mighty thrust, all the pleasure within me built to a breaking point. My back arched further, and my cries became a muffled sound against Julius's skin. My vision whited out with the waves of ecstasy that washed over me one after another in a seemingly endless surge.

As a cry that really was a scream echoed from my throat, Julius jerked out of me and came with a hot splash across my shoulder. Talon gripped my hips with a nearly bruising force and roared his own release into the air. I panted beneath his brutal assault, yet another orgasm reverberating through me on the heels of the second.

We all shuddered to a halt, tangled, sweaty, and flush with carnal delight. Garrison slipped his fingers into his mouth as if savoring the flavor of me. Then he pressed his mouth to mine again.

"You're so fucking hot," he murmured, so much unstated emotion in those words that I trembled with them.

The others stayed close around me, wrapping an arm around my waist, stroking fingers over my hair, surrounding me in the blissful afterglow. A sense of certainty rose up inside me.

Nothing could come between us—not anymore.

SIXTEEN

Decima

THE FUR RUG beneath me was thick enough to insulate my body from the hard floor, and lying pressed into Blaze's body gave me all the warmth I needed to sleep through the night. When I did wake, it was to his fingers running down my back, back up it, around my shoulder, and then taking a similar path downward again. His touch brought shivers to my skin as I burrowed deeper into his natural heat.

The other men stirred around us. I didn't open my eyes to see who had ended up where. In the aftermath of our intense collision last night, we'd all dozed off where we lay.

Blaze's fingers crested my shoulder, tracing a smoothly curved line I knew cut across the skin there. When their motion paused, I opened my eyes to peer blearily at him.

He was studying the scar. "Where did you get this one?" he whispered.

I cleared the sleepiness from my throat before speaking, my voice still rough. "It was a torture attempt. The woman who momentarily restrained me managed to make that cut and break my pinky before I slipped my bindings."

"You've been tortured?" Garrison asked from behind. I peeked over my shoulder and found him sitting on the floor, leaning against the sofa with one leg extended and the other bent upright.

I wanted to laugh at the question. He'd seen the scars across my body, and he knew my history. It would have been more surprising if I *hadn't* been tortured at some point.

"Once or twice," I said with a shrug.

"Who did it?" Talon's deep voice echoed across the room. The ferocity in his tone held a clear threat, maybe one that would have unnerved someone else. But I wasn't that person. It warmed me to realize he'd have wanted to unleash that ferocity on my former tormenter.

"I don't know, but she's long dead now," I reassured him.

Blaze dragged his finger across another scar at the base of my back, a smaller but jagged line. "This one?"

Pursing my lips, I sorted through my memories. "An accident. I jumped through a window and didn't stick the landing. It was from the glass."

I knew the one that he'd eventually ask about—the most prominent of all of them. But he surprised me as he gripped my right hand and opened it, revealing the thin mark that spread across each of my fingers in a straight line. He didn't even need to ask as he ran his thumb across it and met my eyes in a silent question.

I didn't want to delve into that scar. It was more difficult than explaining the ones I'd obtained from missions. The missions didn't matter, and those people and places were a blip on my radar. Scars like the one across my hand—like the one beside my belly button—meant something different. They'd been given to me because of my failures and mistakes.

"Noelle," I admitted, clenching my fist as I thought about her. I broke away from Blaze's eye contact. "I wasn't doing as well using my left side as she'd hoped, so she made sure that my left side *had* to be my strongest one for a while."

"She did this to you?" Blaze asked, and I didn't have to look up to know that he was giving an utterly horrified expression. "She broke your *hand*, on purpose?"

"I hardly remember it. I was so young," I said, as if that made the situation better.

I wasn't lying. I remembered only the crunch when she slammed the edge of a cutting board into my fingers with all the might she could muster, claiming that I'd one day thank her for being a stronger fighter. And it *had* made me a stronger fighter, after all. I'd never had a difficult time using my left side after the weeks when it'd been my only option.

I hadn't realized how consuming the silence was in the room until Julius finally spoke. "And the one on your stomach?"

I hadn't meant to upset them so early in the morning, but I could hear in Julius's voice how angry the thought of Noelle hurting me made him. It wasn't as if there was anything left to avenge now. She was gone, dead at their hands.

But of course, we still didn't know who'd hired her to train me so viciously.

I sighed. "It was another training mishap."

"I wouldn't consider having your fingers intentionally broken as a child to be a training 'mishap,' but please, continue," Garrison said, his usual snarky tone harshened by his own obvious anger—anger I knew wasn't aimed at me but my former captors.

I rolled to my back, tilting my head until I could see all of them. Julius had sprawled across the sofa, and Talon sat half upright at the other end. Garrison was the only other of my men on the floor.

They all watched me intently. Waiting for the story I didn't really want to tell.

I flattened my voice so it'd be as even as possible. "This one really was an accident. Noelle left me alone with a trainer who specialized in weapons, and he was teaching me the basics of the different styles of throwing knives. We got to the part of the lesson where I needed to learn to dodge the knives, and Noelle came barging into the room and distracted me. I didn't dodge one."

I took a deep breath, thinking back to the look of horror on the weapons trainer's face. "They were practice knives, not fully sharpened ones, so it didn't go too far into me, but it lodged itself far enough that I needed stitches. And then I pulled the stitches twice during training in the following weeks, so that's why the scar is still so big."

What I didn't want to say was that I wasn't totally sure any more that it'd been an accident after all. Noelle had liked to surprise me to test my reflexes and instincts. Maybe she'd distracted me on purpose to see how well I'd dodge then. A ten-year-old kid in the middle of having knives thrown at her.

Blaze moved me closer to him and tightened his grip, slipping his other hand between us and stroking the place where the scar marred my skin.

"Do you remember where all of your scars are from?" Julius asked.

I shook my head. "Not all of them. Just the bigger ones. The small scars like this"—I pointed to a tiny scar on the side of my cheek and turned my head so they could all see. From where the other three sat near the sofa, I doubted they could even make out the pale mark—"I have no clue where it came from. I have tons like that."

"I can't remember where most of mine came from either," Garrison said.

Blaze took a deep breath, drinking in the scent of my skin, and I had the urge to kiss his bare chest. "I don't think I know where a single one of my scars came from," he admitted.

"What scars?" Garrison teased. "The ones that you get when you clean out your computer?"

Blaze narrowed his eyes and pushed himself up on an elbow, loosening his grip on me as he scowled at Garrison. "I guess I do remember one. You know, the scar I got when I was shot protecting your ass."

Garrison laughed. "Been there, done that, brother."

Julius spoke up. "I think Talon's the only one of us who *hasn't* been shot at least once," he said, gesturing to his ear with its ravaged lobe. I hadn't realized the injury was from a bullet, but it made sense.

"I think getting blown up is close enough." Talon rubbed at the flare-shaped scar on his thigh—barely exposed beneath his boxers. Looking at it, I guessed it'd been shrapnel from a mine or some other land explosive during his military days. He was lucky he still had his leg.

I cut in before their usual competitive natures could take the conversation on too far of a detour. "Scars don't matter." I sat up and looked over myself. With my nakedness fully on display, all four of them shut up. "What matters now is that we don't add to what we've already got and that we stop dwelling on the past."

I needed to take my own advice, especially when it was my *internal* scars that seemed to drive me forward these days. Although dwelling on my past was really all that I could do when my "past" wasn't completely history yet and seemed to be defining so much of my present.

I glanced at the clock on the rock wall and sat up straighter with a start. It was later than I'd realized. "I'm supposed to meet my dad for brunch at eleven," I said, scrambling to my feet. If I didn't get a move on diving into the shower, I'd either have to show up smelling of sex, nude, or late. I wasn't too keen on any of those options.

"Go do what you need to do," Blaze said with a small smile.

I stopped at the edge of the room just for a second, looking back at all of them as they enjoyed the view of me walking away. It didn't bother me, partly because their mostly naked bodies stirred up plenty of the same lust that I saw in their eyes in me… and partly because I saw just as much admiration and affection there as anything more carnal.

"You know, you're just as much my family as he is," I said firmly. "We've fought together and bled together—you've looked out for me even when you barely knew who I was… You mean a lot to me. I want a relationship with my birth family, but that doesn't mean I'm giving up what I have with any of you."

Julius gave me one of his measured but genuine smiles. "I'm sure we're all glad to hear that. The crew sticks together. Now go get your brunch."

I took the shortest shower in human history, threw on my clothes, and summoned an Uber to make the trip into the city proper. I made it to the café at eleven on the dot and found Damien Malik waiting just outside the wrought-iron fence that surrounded the large patio. He greeted me with a smile and a wave toward the gate.

"It's too nice a day to waste it sitting inside," he said as the hostess guided us to one of the patio tables. With the sun beaming down on us and cheerful music tinkling through the café's open door, I was inclined to agree with him.

"I'm not going to argue with fresh air," I said, taking my seat.

A waitress appeared with a flash of a smile. "Can I start you off with any drinks?"

My father ordered a coffee, but I figured I'd better forgo caffeine, since my nerves were already a bit jittery in his presence with the Hunter's insinuations and Anthea's unknown soil analysis hanging over my head. "Lemonade for me," I said, since I deserved at least a little sugar.

Damien leaned back in his chair, seeming more relaxed than usual. "It's good that you enjoy getting out and about," he said. "Keeps the mind sharp and the body healthy. And it's nice just being out in the sun for its own sake." He chuckled. "Not everything has to be for a purpose, of course."

"Always nice when the enjoyable things are good for you too," I replied with half-hearted amusement.

He tilted his head. "You know, you might enjoy the heat even more if you made use of our swimming pool. Your mother has mentioned that you always leave when most of the activity moves to the pool. We'd love to have you around even more, of course, now that you're getting settled in. There's no reason you shouldn't become a full member of the Malik family."

I curled my scarred fingers toward my palm, thinking of all the other scars I wouldn't be able to hide in a bathing suit. The Chaos Crew had viewed them with the curiosity of men who'd been through similar trials. Their only horror had been at the brutality I'd endured as a child. The Maliks would be horrified by everything about my marked-up skin. I didn't want to have to tell that many more lies.

As I groped for an appropriate answer, I glanced around the open patio. The patrons looked as well off as my father. Pearl necklaces and expensive suits abounded. The only person who stood out from the wealthy crowd was a kid in a T-shirt and jeans who couldn't have been older than fourteen, leaning against the restaurant's siding like he was waiting for someone.

"Chlorine really irritates my skin," I told Damien as I turned back to him. "And I burn too easily to enjoy just tanning." Two small lies to prevent a whole lot of bigger ones. "But if no one minds me hanging around by the side of the pool in regular clothes, I can stay later more often."

The waitress returned with our drinks, and my father sipped his thoughtfully. "I think that would be nice. The more you're around, the easier it'll be for you to find your place in the family legacy."

That word again—*legacy*. He talked about it as if that were the end goal of all these visits, as if there were something more I'd discover about the family once I'd gotten to know them even better. A prickle ran down my spine, the Hunter's insinuations rising up from my memory.

But surely Damien Malik wouldn't talk openly about any kind of legacy that he'd get investigated for.

As I gave some noncommittal answer that I barely paid attention to, the teen by the restaurant adjusted his position, sidling closer to the gate. The furtiveness of his movements put me on the alert. He was doing an okay job of being subtle, but I was trained to recognize when someone had a trick up their sleeve. What was he doing?

I got my answer a moment later when he brushed his hand across the back of a nearby woman's chair—and let his fingers snag on the strap of her purse.

Damien had swiveled in his chair at the same moment to check the board of specials. The kid was being sneaky, but not sneaky enough —he obviously wasn't any hardened criminal. As he jerked the purse off the chair, my father leapt to his feet with a shout.

The young teen looked terrified as my father rushed him and grabbed his arm in a death grip. My pulse stuttered even though I didn't exactly approve of making off with people's purses. It was just— he really *was* just a kid—and the whitening of his face with the tremor that passed through his body showed how ashamed he was at getting caught.

Something had driven him to this point, and I didn't think it was simply callous greed.

"Call the police," Malik shouted out, and turned to the victim of the theft, handing her the purse he'd pried from the boy's fingers. "He almost made off with this."

Someone at a nearby table gasped, and a few others pulled out their phones as if the petty theft required multiple reports. As if this kid really needed to be arrested. He was trembling now, looking seconds from wetting his pants.

I couldn't just sit there. My heart thumping, I pushed myself to my feet and marched over. Damien dragged the boy toward the gate to wait for the police, and as I reached him, I realized his grip on the boy's wrist was even tighter than I'd assumed. He twisted his fingers, and the boy winced in pain. His fingers had balled into a fist.

"What else have you stolen, you little creep?" my father said under his breath in the harshest tone I'd ever heard him use. He jerked his hand down to pry the boy's fingers open, but there was nothing there. With a sharp exhalation, Damien twisted his grip again—and the crack of breaking bone made me flinch.

The boy yelped, tears welling up at the corners of his eyes.

"Garbage like you deserves what you get," Damien hissed. He turned and noticed my presence for the first time. His face reformed into its usual professional mask—he mustn't have thought anyone was close enough to notice.

"First he tries to rob people, then he thinks he can run off without facing the proper punishment," he said, as if the boy had been making a run for it. "He twisted his hand while I was pulling him back. No one to blame but himself. The police will sort it out."

That wasn't what had happened at all, but I had no idea how to challenge the 'facts' he laid out so easily. How would he look at *me* if I sided with the kid? Everyone around us was nodding in agreement, accepting his explanation.

If he'd been anyone else, I'd have torn him a new one right there and then. But this incident only proved that I really *didn't* know the man I was dealing with. And getting into a public altercation with a man with as much political clout as my father blind felt like a very bad idea. What if this was just the tip of an ominous iceberg?

The police roared up with blaring sirens. Malik handed over the kid, getting the woman to tell the story of her nearly stolen purse.

"He broke my finger," the boy said with a sob, cradling his hand to his chest. "He broke my fucking finger."

Malik rolled his eyes, giving the boy a small shove toward the officer who rested a large hand across his shoulder. "He was trying to get away, and it was all I could do to stop him. I didn't mean to break it, of course."

He sounded *so* convincing. Had I not seen it with my own eyes, I would have never believed that he'd fractured the boy's bones with malicious intent. How could he lie so blatantly without an ounce of hesitation in his tone?

The officer looked between them. "I can take it from here, Representative Malik. Your community is indebted to you once again."

The brilliant smile my father gave the officer sickened me. I stepped backward and moved swiftly to my seat. They exchanged a few pleasantries and a handshake as the other officer loaded up the kid in his car.

My father came back over, his mood darker than it had been at the start of our brunch. He looked at me with a grimace, and I wondered if he'd apologize for his actions and admit that he'd been out of line after all.

"I'm sorry that you had to be here for this," he said, dropping into his chair. "If you hadn't realized it before, the crime rates in this neighborhood are rising just like they are everywhere. It's tragic, but that's why it's essential that we crack down on the criminals whenever they pop up. That boy deserves everything that will come to him."

Did that include the cast and recovery for his injury?

I couldn't bring myself to respond. I took a sip of my lemonade and listened as Damien continued his rant about crime, not even considering that lying to the police and breaking a boy's finger was a heinous crime within itself. Did he think he was excluded from the law?

As long as he broke it punishing criminals, it seemed like yes.

As he simmered down and our food arrived, my stomach knotted. It was all I could do to choke down a decent amount of the meal. The truth of the situation was staring me in the face so hard I couldn't deny it anymore.

I was a criminal—one far worse than that kid. There wasn't a chance in a million years that he'd ever accept the true me or the men I considered family too. He wouldn't want to believe it, but when he did, he'd be sending me off to the electric chair. Maybe offering to throw the switch himself.

I'd known that, deep down. I'd been afraid of how he'd see the truth all along. But I'd let myself be lulled into complacency by how welcoming they'd been in general. I'd never had to face just how intense my father's dedication to his policies was until right now.

While the waitress cleared our plates, promising to bring the bill quickly, I debated simply walking away from this brunch and this whole situation. Never speaking to Damien Malik or the rest of my birth family again. All the enjoyment I'd gotten out of having a family around me had soured with this unavoidable revelation.

What did I need them for if they couldn't handle who I really was? I didn't want to have to listen to any more of their rants or watch how they treated anyone they judged as unworthy of compassion.

I'd been foolish to think I could ever have a real relationship with this man at all, given his policies.

The urge to cut my losses and run wound through my limbs as Damien paid the check. It would be so easy. So freeing to put all the stress and pressure of trying to be Rachel Malik behind me. I could almost taste the relief.

But… I still needed answers.

As much as I wanted to leave and never look back, Malik and his investigators were in the best position to find the answers I needed about who had kidnapped me and why. Continuing to act like family with these people might be like playing with fire, but I wasn't done here yet for my own ends.

If my father found out the truth about me and my past before I learned what I needed to, he'd turn on me without hesitation. They all would. I knew that without a doubt. But it was a risk I'd just have to take.

SEVENTEEN

Julius

DESS HAD BEEN WORKING out for the better part of an hour. Even though the house didn't come with our typical exercise equipment, she'd gone through her usual circuit of floor exercises twice, jogged in place as if she had a treadmill whipping away beneath her feet, and worked through several sequences of combat moves.

None of that was particularly out of the ordinary, but the pace she'd set struck me as closer to frantic than focused. Sweat shone on her forehead and arms, but she didn't stop to so much as gulp water before throwing herself into the next set of exercises. Her eyes were glazed, focused on thoughts that had nothing to do with the house around us.

Seeing her like this sent a quiver of apprehension through me. Dess was usually nothing if not controlled. She could rival the best of us with her discipline.

When she started pushing herself this hard, it meant there was something she was trying to escape. Something she couldn't outrun by any normal means. I could take a few guesses at what that might be. The number of catastrophes in her life had been adding up for a while.

I got up from the sofa. "Dess," I said, but her head didn't so much as twitch in my direction. She just kept bobbing up and down in her whirlwind of stomach crunches.

"Dess," I repeated, a little louder, walking over as I spoke.

That time, her name sank in. She spun around and onto her feet in one smooth movement, then stayed crouched there, panting as she stared up at me.

"Is something wrong?" she asked.

I folded my arms over my chest. "That's what I was going to ask you. You look like you're trying to tackle a monster ten times your size."

She bit her lip, the gesture sending a flash of heat through me at the thought of taking that lip between my own teeth. I shook myself out of the memories of last night's epic encounter between the five of us.

She didn't need me lusting over her right now. She needed a confidante.

"It's nothing really new," she said.

I wasn't going to let her dodge the subject this time. "It's bothering you enough that you're going to dehydrate yourself with all that sweat. Why don't you grab a glass of water and then tell me what's bothering you? Even if it can't be fixed right now, there are other ways of letting it out than working yourself into exhaustion."

Dess let out a huff, but she got up and walked over to the kitchen, lifting the bottom of her shirt to wipe her damp face. I couldn't say I *minded* the brief view of her taut stomach. I had plenty of control too, but I wasn't any kind of saint.

She threw back the glass of water in a few long chugs, filled it again, and drank the second one more slowly. Then she set down the glass with a rap against the granite countertop. Her shoulders slouched just slightly.

"You know I had brunch with my dad this morning," she said. "There was a purse thief at the restaurant, just a teenager—I saw how Damien treated the kid, how he talked to him… I know this was obvious all along, but it really drove it home that I can never be who I really am with him."

"You can't tell him about the Decima part of your life," I filled in.

She nodded. "Even though I'm his daughter… I mean, he broke a kid's *bones* for trying to snatch a purse. Even if I switched over to the straight and narrow right now and stayed there from this day forward, if he ever got a whiff of the jobs I carried out before, he'd never look at me the same way again. He'd see me as a monster—the kind of monster he thinks he's fighting."

I hadn't thought that Dess would ever consider going entirely straight, but now that she brought it up, I realized it was an obvious option. It would certainly give her a better chance of integrating into the life she'd been meant to have. But imagining her walking away from us, saying good-bye to not just our company but all the skills that had made her famous among the most hardened of hitmen, wrenched at my gut.

She wasn't ordinary, not at all. She deserved to have that part of herself celebrated, not crushed.

And, damn it, I wanted to be there celebrating it with her.

"Would you *want* to go straight?" I asked, trying to keep my tone even and impartial. As much as I hated the thought of her leaving, it was her decision, and I needed to give her full rein to make the choice herself.

If I pushed her in one direction or another, she might end up resenting me later. After all the ways she'd had her life decided for her in the past, I didn't want to manipulate her now.

She sighed and clenched her jaw. "I don't want to, now. I'm not even sure I could if I decided it was worth trying to so that I could have a more open relationship with my birth family. I'm good at this. It *feels* good, pulling off a job, knowing I took one more prick out of commission who can't do any more harm…" She paused. "Now that I get to pick my jobs, I'm going to stick to the same code as you do—no one who doesn't deserve it. I can't quite believe that's wrong."

"There are a lot of those people," I muttered.

"Yeah. But there are also a lot of people like my father who can't imagine that anyone stepping outside the law could be anything other than a horrible villain."

Something about those words struck a chord in me. Maybe there was something I could say that would help after all—not fix the struggle she was going through, but give her a perspective she hadn't had before.

I'd never talked with Blaze and Garrison about my history. I never even discussed it with Talon—he only knew because he'd been there. But the past existed for a reason: to inform the present. If I could use it to give Dess more tools to figure out the right path for her, then it was worth dredging up those terrible memories.

I motioned her away from the kitchen. "Come with me? There are some things I can tell you that might help you sort through this."

Dess cocked her head curiously and followed me over to the sofa. Talon and Garrison had gone off on a grocery store run, and Blaze was adding a few more surveillance cameras to his network in the neighborhood, so it was just the two of us. Still, my skin tightened before I spoke as if I had an audience of thousands.

The most important part had been my time in the military, but it was better to start right at the beginning, the incident that had set me on this path well before then.

"Dealing out justice was important to me from an early age," I said as Dess settled onto the sofa across from me. "When I was fifteen, I found out that my little sister—she was in middle school—was being abused by a teacher at her school." Even though Christy had gotten through that and no longer showed any lingering scars, just mentioning it brought a fresh wave of anger into my chest. "I didn't trust the authorities to deal with it properly. I was furious, and all I knew was that I had to protect her, so I got rid of him pretty much the same way I would a target now, just without quite as much finesse."

Dess's eyes widened. "You murdered him."

I raised my eyebrows at her. "Don't look so shocked. You were carrying out assassinations when you were, what, eight? By your standards, I was a late bloomer. I'm lucky I managed not to get caught."

She swatted my knee. "I was trained for it. You weren't."

"Don't underestimate the power of protective rage," I said with a small, wry smile. "Dealing out justice that way… It was more satisfying than I'd ever expected. So maybe I was always a little unhinged. I leaned into those impulses the best way I could, by joining the military. I figured I'd get the opportunity to defend our country through violent means, keep my appetite for brutal justice sated and do good at the same time."

Dess studied me. "But it didn't turn out that way," she said.

It wouldn't have been hard to guess that, considering she knew I'd started the crew more than ten years ago, when I still could have had an excellent military career if I'd wanted one.

I shook my head. "It didn't. I gave it a solid shot. Rose through the ranks and was recruited into a special ops team. That's where I met Talon. We were in the same squad, going out and working operations the regular forces couldn't have stomached."

"And then?"

I exhaled slowly. "And then we were sent on what was supposed to be just an information-gathering mission. We were tapped for it because it was in an area with a lot of hostile activity from unfriendlies. It was a small town, people who didn't have much but were willing to work with us because they thought we could get them out from under the thumb of the local insurgents."

I paused to swallow and then went on. "You have to understand that in the military, everyone's expected to know their role and stick with it. And you don't question anyone who ranks higher than you—you just follow orders. So I was focused on carrying out my part of the job, but I couldn't help noticing that the commander seemed to be dropping the ball… not sending out as many sentries as I thought the situation warranted, directing us all into the same part of town instead of having us spread out…"

"So you spoke up, and he told you off?" Dess said.

I grimaced. "No. That's what makes this story so shameful. Well, I made a couple of comments to the commander, but he brushed me off and made it clear that he knew best, and it didn't seem worth arguing about. I thought maybe I was being overly cautious. It was my first year in special ops. He had way more experience than I did."

"But you weren't being too cautious."

"Exactly." The memories rose up, just as horrifying as they'd been fifteen years ago. "A contingent of insurgents swarmed the town. There weren't enough sentries to send out a warning quickly enough for us to be prepared. They shot several of us before we even realized what was happening, and then we spent the rest of the day and night locked in a bloody stand-off… Talon and I barely made it out alive with several of the townspeople we managed to help escape, but it was a near thing." I tapped my earlobe. "That was when this bullet came just a few inches from lodging in my brain."

"Just you and Talon out of the whole squad?" Dess murmured.

I inclined my head. "Everyone else with us, including the commander, died." A couple of cocky nineteen-year-olds who'd just started integrating into the squad. A woman who'd notified the command of her pregnancy earlier that morning. "As well as a hell of a lot of the civilians we should have been protecting." Elderly men and little kids, sprawled bleeding in the streets. I closed my eyes against the barrage of images.

"That's horrible," Dess said, reaching to squeeze my hand.

"It was," I agreed. "And it made me determined not to find myself in that position ever again. But that meant that I had to talk back when I disagreed with higher ranking officers. *Thinking* they knew what was right wasn't good enough. It had to be backed up with a plan where every piece was totally solid."

"I guess they didn't like the criticism very much."

I chuckled darkly. "No, they did not. I got written up a few times and then officially discharged. It wasn't the right fit. But I still had the urge to fight those who needed to be taken down. So I started the Chaos Crew with Talon, where I'd get to operate our missions according to *my* principles. And one of those is to surround myself with other people I trust—other voices who can help me see different perspectives. I don't want to ever start thinking that I always know better than everyone around me."

"That makes sense." Dess squeezed my hand. "I'm not sure I see how it relates to my father, though."

I held her gaze. "When I hear about men like Damien Malik, they remind me of the commander in the field that day. You can mean well and believe you're doing your best—and still be so caught up in doing things your way that you can't see when you need to adjust course. It's never wise to end up on a crusade like your father's where there's no room to pivot or notice the nuances of the situation. He's got tunnel vision… and that leads to people getting hurt who don't deserve it."

Dess nodded, worrying at her lower lip again. For a long moment, she was silent, and I started to worry I'd laid too much on her all at once. Then she rubbed her mouth.

"Thank you," she said, gazing back at me. "I'm sure it's not fun thinking or talking about all that. I hadn't looked at the situation quite that way before, though."

"I'm happy to both listen to other voices and be one when someone else might need it," I said, turning my hand so I could grip her fingers in return.

"You know, it's probably good for me to keep that idea in mind for myself too," Dess went on. "I need to keep an open mind and listen to everything people around me are saying if I'm going to piece together the evidence about my past and my family into a coherent picture. I can't get too stuck on assuming that one thing or another I haven't actually proven is true."

My smile came back. "That's very wise indeed. I'll give you full credit for that part."

She laughed, and her phone pinged with an incoming text. She fished it out of her pocket casually, but the second she glanced at the screen, her brow furrowed.

"What?" I asked.

Dess drew in a breath. "It looks like it's time to get some more of that evidence. Anthea just sent along the results of her soil analysis."

EIGHTEEN

Decima

THE DOCUMENT ANTHEA sent me was a list of minerals and other substances with figures and percentages that didn't have much significance to me. I had no idea whether what I was looking at was normal or concerning. Thankfully Anthea was sharp enough to realize that if I couldn't analyze the soil myself, I also couldn't analyze the analysis, so she gave me a call after I'd had a chance to look over the report.

"First off, there's nothing especially strange here," she said, getting right to the point. "I wouldn't blink twice at this sample if it came from a routine check rather than an analysis prompted by current suspicions."

I only partly relaxed at that remark. "But there's something that would give you pause because of the circumstances?"

"Yes. They don't prove any sort of crime, but they're things I'd keep in mind as I weighed the other evidence." She took a brisk breath. "First, you can see the ash content listed. That's somewhat higher than average, but not bizarrely so. Some people use ash instead of lime to improve the soil, and mostly it appears to be wood ash. Do they have a fireplace in the house or a fire pit?"

I brought up the image of the property in my mind's eye. "They have a fire pit next to the pool."

"Then it's probably from their own fires, not something they had to go out of their way to get. Totally normal, if a tad old-fashioned. But the results suggest it's not *all* from wood."

A prickle ran over my skin. "What do you mean?"

"You see the calcium level? That's again not incredibly high, but unusual for a flower garden. In my line of work, I most commonly see levels in that range when a body's been burned. From the bones."

"A body?" I repeated, unable to hold back my shock. That was the last thing I'd have imagined going into my mother's garden.

"Don't get too panicked," Anthea said with a light laugh. "As I said, it wasn't a tremendous amount. There are totally innocent explanations, like the cremation of a family pet whose ashes were scattered there. Or possibly smaller animals could have died under the ground and decomposed enough that their remains mixed with the ash. It isn't a red flag, more like a yellow one. Something to be aware of if other pieces start to point you in a worrying direction."

"Okay," I said, my stomach sinking. Her report put me basically back in the same place I'd been before, knowing something might be wrong but not being able to prove it one way or the other. I resisted the urge to fidget and had to confirm, "But if you saw these results from a garden no one thought was a problem, you wouldn't assume anything bad had gone down."

"Not at all. It's absolutely possible that there's nothing at all… untoward going on. But I thought you should be aware of the possibilities. Are you satisfied that your favor has been repaid?"

Her tone had gotten brisk again—probably she had plenty of other things to take care of rather than reassuring me.

"Yes," I said quickly. "Thank you for taking the time to explain." I didn't want her to think I was ungrateful. She was clearly good at what she did—who knew if I might need her help again?

Good will and personal opinion were their own kind of currency in both my father's world and the criminal circles I was learning to navigate.

I set down the phone and stared at the stone wall, barely registering the lingering cocoa scent in the air from the mugs Garrison had made before he'd left. How much of a chance was there that anything other than a pet had been cremated and tossed in the Maliks' garden? Even if they'd done *something* wrong, I couldn't wrap my head around them being murderers. They hated petty thieves—how would they have been able to justify stealing people's *lives*?

But the Hunter had known I'd turn up something revealing in the soil. He'd specifically pointed me to the garden. It might not have been terribly unusual, but it'd been unusual all the same.

There could be other explanations that were unnerving but not as far as murder, right? Or, hell, maybe the Hunter had planted that evidence somehow.

I really didn't know, and that fact made me itchy.

Julius had gone off to the other end of the room to consult something on his phone while I'd talked to Anthea. When I got up, he glanced over at me. "Going somewhere?"

I rolled my shoulders, trying to work the restlessness out of me. "I think I'm going to drop in on my family. They're not expecting me. Maybe I'll find out more if they're unprepared." Blaze still hadn't picked up anything from their electronic communications, but a political family would probably be savvy enough not to say anything at all incriminating where it could be digitally recorded. I had no idea what they said to each other when I wasn't around.

Julius inclined his head. "Do you need anything from me?"

I shot him a quick smile. "No, but thank you. I should be back pretty soon."

I summoned an Uber and spent the entire ride stewing over what I'd heard. When we approached the house, I had the driver drop me off a block away so I wouldn't draw my family's notice. My father would be at work now—he'd talked about the meetings he had to get to after our brunch—but there almost always seemed to be at least a couple of Maliks at or around the house. This late in the afternoon, my mother should be back from her work, and Carter didn't have a summer job.

I'd only just set off toward the house, keeping an eye out for any family members who might spot me, when a woman wearing a courier vest sped up next to me on a bike.

"Rachel Malik?" she said, sounding a little breathless.

I stiffened. "Yes."

"This is for you." She thrust a small package into my hands and raced off again before I could ask her a single question.

What the hell? I tore open the package, braced in case it was something dangerous, but all I found inside was a basic headset. I studied it, and sound crackled from it, just loud enough for me to hear a voice. "Put it on, Rachel."

Even as tinny as the voice was through the small speakers, I recognized the Hunter at once. My stomach clenching, I slipped the headset over my ears and stepped back into the shadow of a tree at the front of a nearby lawn.

"What do you want?" I demanded under my breath, abruptly pissed off as well as confused. The only reason I was here at all was because of the garbage he'd stuffed into my head that might not have any truth to it at all. And how had he figured out I'd come to the house right now? Had that woman been hanging around waiting for me to arrive for my next visit—or had he tracked me somehow?

My skin crawled, and I rubbed my arms.

"Ah, Miss Malik," the Hunter said, as if this was a totally normal call. "It's wonderful speaking with you again."

I was done playing his game. "Wonderful for you, maybe," I said. "I've got better things to do than listen to you ramble on about your delusions."

"Oh, you've decided they're delusions, have you? Didn't bother to do your research all that well."

"Or maybe there's just nothing to find."

He guffawed. "There's so much to find when it comes to Damien Malik that I'm starting to think you're willfully blind."

"And yet for some reason you can't tell me any specifics or offer up any proof," I shot back. "I don't work for you. I don't know you, and it's obvious you have your own agenda. If you're using me for whatever goal you have, I'm not interested in being your puppet."

"Then you're just interested in being theirs," the Hunter said.

"I'm nobody's puppet," I spat out.

"Well, the evidence that I told you about should speak for itself, and you can decide what to do with it. Have you dug it up yet?"

I opened my mouth to respond, but I closed it. He didn't need to know what I'd learned. I wasn't working for him, and he claimed to be an investigator. He could do it himself.

"The more you learn, the more you'll see," he went on. "You can't let your desire to have a family close your mind to what's really going on here."

I didn't like having a stranger tell me of my biases, but his remarks echoed what Julius had said to me a couple of hours ago too closely. I did need to listen to people other than myself, because even if I knew I could never have a full relationship with my family, part of me still balked at believing they were awful in ways I hadn't discovered.

But that didn't mean that one of the people I listened to had to be this total creep.

"You don't know anything about what having a family has done to me," I snapped. Then I tore off the headset and tossed it into a set of nearby bushes.

Let the Hunter come and retrieve it if he wanted it. I owed him nothing, and he wouldn't continue using me—not without giving me real information.

But I still had my own mission here.

I walked carefully toward the Maliks' home. A second car was parked in the driveway—not one belonging to either of my parents. It took me a moment to place it as one that belonged to an aunt and uncle. My mom had company.

Well, that meant more people to be having conversations I might want to overhear. If I wanted to get facts, this was the place where I should be able to do it.

I slipped across the lawn and flattened myself to the exterior of the house. The summer day was warm enough that the windows were open to let in the breeze—perfect.

I listened at one window and then another, slinking around the house, prepared to jump away with an excuse if someone happened to step outside and notice me. It didn't take long to determine that most of them were in the family room while my mother puttered around in the kitchen nearby.

When I peeked inside, I saw Aunt Mabel and Uncle Henry were sitting side by side on the loveseat across from my brother, no sign of my cousin Margaret today. But five mugs had been set out around the teapot and the plate of squares on the coffee table. Maybe they were expecting her later—or one of the other relatives might be on their way. I'd have to keep my ears pricked for cars.

Right now, I was more interested in the voices traveling out to me. When I'd first homed in on their voices, they'd been talking about a golf tournament, but it seemed the conversation had shifted. My aunt was saying something about "proper preparations." She tsked her tongue. "I mean, it really isn't the sort of thing you want to spring on someone if they're not ready."

Carter slouched in his armchair, what I could see of his face grim. "Are we *really* going to bring her into all of it? The rituals and everything? She's barely part of the family."

"She's as much family as you are," my mother said firmly from the kitchen, where I couldn't see her at the moment. "But it could be a difficult transition when she didn't have the full upbringing to help her form the right mindset... Your father was able to explain it to me well enough, though. We'll have to see how it goes."

The hairs on the back of my neck stood on end. They were talking about *me,* weren't they? But what "rituals" was Carter talking about? Why would I need a special mindset to understand them?

Uncle Henry cleared his throat. "We have time to sort that out. No need to rush anything. But she's a Malik. She deserves the chance to claim her full birthright if she's up for it."

"As long as it doesn't threaten the rest of us," Aunt Mabel said, twisting her napkin in her hands.

"Right," Carter put in. "I'm just saying we should be careful."

Threaten them? Be careful? They were talking like I was some kind of danger to them.

Did they know more about me than I'd realized? But the second that thought passed through my mind, I shook it away. If they'd realized I was a killer for hire, I'd have expected much harsher words than what I'd just heard. Hell, I'd have expected them to already have called the National Guard on me.

"We'll see," my mother repeated, and then, to my frustration, changed the subject. "Mabel, how was that convention last weekend?"

As Mabel loosened up and started gushing about some event she'd attended about "data retention" or some other concept that related to her job, my gaze drifted through the room from where I was crouched. It snagged on a movement only just visible through the family room doorway.

Margaret had appeared in the hall—next to a door that she nudged back toward the wall with a very deliberate motion. And the second it'd slid back into place… suddenly I couldn't see the edge of it anymore. The striped wallpaper behind her looked as impenetrable as if no one had ever passed through it.

I stared for several seconds before yanking myself down below the window ledge as she headed toward the family room, where she'd have been facing the window. My heart was suddenly beating faster.

That spot in the hall—it was where I'd noticed the faint wear in the carpet when I'd investigated the house before, wasn't it? The signs that I'd thought pointed to furniture that'd once been placed there.

But if my eyes hadn't just deceived me, I'd been correct in my first impressions. The wear *had* been caused by a door, just one that was concealed so well you couldn't find it or open it unless you knew the secret.

What kind of family needed an entirely secret doorway within their own home? And where the hell did it lead? No one had mentioned it during their tours of the house, so it obviously wasn't a fun quirk but something they purposefully kept hidden.

Did it have something to do with the rituals Carter had been talking about?

I rubbed my hands over my face. The more I searched for answers, the more questions I seemed to get instead. How did all the pieces I'd been seeing and hearing fit together? Were the Maliks hiding even more?

Was this what the Hunter had been warning me about?

The second that question crossed my mind, I grimaced. I was all tangled up because of the way he'd been egging me on when I hadn't noticed anything more than mildly awkward before—and that was mostly my *own* awkwardness. There could be totally innocent explanations for all of this. The Maliks were in a position with a lot of scrutiny because of my dad's political standing. Of course they'd keep some things private.

That private, though?

I stifled a groan. Was I getting played by a man I'd never met, or were these secrets just as important and dangerous as the Hunter had claimed?

The one thing I knew for sure was that I needed to see what was in that secret room.

NINETEEN

Decima

"WE WERE NEVER PARTICULARLY CLOSE, but I wouldn't have thought he'd outright screw us over," Julius said as we stalked through the streets with the rest of the crew.

"Are you sure it *is* a trap?" I asked, glancing around. "Maybe he really does have something important to talk to you about."

Garrison let out a huff. "And he really needed to talk to us about it in some random alleyway? If it's a dead end, I say we leave without even sticking around to find out what mess they're trying to pull us into."

Earlier today, Julius had gotten a call from a guy he'd worked with briefly a few years ago, asking for a meet-up with only a vague explanation. Julius had agreed, but he'd suspected from the start that it was some kind of set-up. I guessed it was hard not to be paranoid about that kind of thing when our enemies had already turned several of the mercenary teams he'd once seen as colleagues against the crew.

We were all well-armed with both guns and knives, braced for a confrontation. My senses prickled with alertness as I scanned the buildings around us. We wanted to find out exactly what this was about, but we weren't throwing caution to the wind, that was for sure.

"He sounded nervous," Blaze said. "It could be that he needs help. And either way, we have to get to the bottom of it."

"As long as we don't end up in the bottom of a grave," Garrison muttered.

Talon cast a baleful look over all of us. "Maybe we should shut up and focus if we want to avoid that outcome. We're almost there."

Julius nodded with a self-deprecating smile, and we fell into silence.

At the mouth of the alley, we paused in a defensive formation and peered down it. The passage turned farther in, just as Blaze had expected from the satellite imaging he'd pulled up. No one had blocked it off in any way that was visible from here.

Julius made a brisk motion, and we all followed him, spreading out even more as we strode along the cracked concrete between the looming brick walls. We didn't want to make it easy for anyone to surround all of us at once.

The shadows wrapped around us like a damp sheet, and my nose itched with the sour smell trickling from a nearby dumpster. Julius and Talon rested their hands on their hips over their holsters. Blaze outright withdrew his gun, less confident in his quick draw than the others.

We paused at the bend, looking both ways to where the streets showed at either end. We definitely weren't cut off. But there was no one here yet, and we were right on time. That didn't bode well.

I stayed in the alley we'd entered through next to Garrison. Julius and Talon ambled a few paces down each direction of the longer alleyway. Blaze stopped right in the middle of the T, knitting his brow.

And we waited.

For a long stretch, nobody came—not to speak to us or to descend on us with guns blazing. I stayed tensed, conscious of every sound that came from the quiet warehouse district. Other than the distant grumble of passing traffic and the hiss of a plastic bag caught in the breeze, it was silent.

When it was twenty minutes after the meetup time, Blaze shifted on his feet. "Maybe *he* got ambushed on his way to meet us."

"I don't think we should stick around any longer," Julius said grimly. "If he's got something to say, he can reach out again."

At the same moment, a faint scraping sound reached my ears from behind a door in the side of the building next to me. I stepped closer, my fingers curling around the hilt of one of my knives—

And the door burst right off its hinges into me, slamming into my body and knocking me onto my ass.

Sudden footsteps and gunshots thundered all around me. I shoved at the heavy metal slab that was pinning me down and then squirmed to maneuver myself out from under it.

"Keep her down!" someone shouted, and a figure that I realized was braced on top of the detached door stomped on my hand, making my fingers release my knife before he kicked it away.

Clenching my jaw against the jab of pain, I aimed a punch and managed to clock the guy in the groin—hard. With a strained noise, he swayed on his perch, and I wrenched myself out from under his and the door's weight.

The scene I escaped into was total mayhem. Bullets ricocheted off the walls, bodies heaved this way and that, and voices hollered back and forth. I couldn't tell which were from my men and which from the enemy. Grabbing my gun, I moved to charge into the fray—when yet another opponent charged into me.

I lashed out at him, smacking him in the head with the butt of the gun, kneeing him in the gut. He shoved me backward, barely touching me other than that. Like he was just trying to get me out of the way rather than attack me.

A few more men converged on me. I raised my hand to shoot, and the nearest one knocked my aim off course. Several fists flew at me, but none of them hit me that hard—except the one I couldn't quite manage to dodge amid the barrage, which lost me my pistol too.

For fuck's sake. I whipped out my other knife and fell into a fighting stance, glaring at my four attackers. But they just stood there, equally poised but not closing in. Again, I had the sense that they were trying to keep me *out* of the fighting rather than drag me into it.

Just like the men during the attack at the hotel had hesitated to fight me.

An uncomfortable chill pooled in my gut. I took a few testing swipes at the blockade, and the men simply fended me off with their own blades. A couple of them had guns at their hips that they weren't even trying to use. But there were too many of them together for me to make a full attack on one without leaving myself vulnerable to too many others.

I peered past them at the rest of the battle and spotted Julius ducking to the side as he fired his gun. He hurtled backward toward me, and then stopped, his head jerking to the side and his eyes widening as he stared at someone farther down the alley.

"Petrov?" he said. "What the hell—"

He cut himself off to fire another couple of shots and swing his knife with the other hand as two more men rushed at him. Behind them came a stern, bulky guy with a broad forehead that had a scar angled across it. He was looking at Julius with a strange expression too.

Did Julius know that guy? Petrov wasn't the name of the contact we'd been expecting to talk to. What the hell was going on?

"Someone get to Dess!" Talon's voice hollered from a spot I couldn't see.

I squared my shoulders and prepared to take care of myself. These pricks might *want* to keep me out of the fighting, but we didn't always get what we wanted. A lesson I was happy to teach them after how many times I'd learned it.

I eyed my opponents again and identified a flaw in their formation. My fingers tightened around my knife. Then I sprang into action.

As if I meant to try to stab a guy in the middle, I lunged forward. But just as he moved to deflect me, I swerved in the opposite direction. My slashing blade cut across another man's arm—not enough to take him out of commission, but significantly weakening his stronger hand.

The men shifted to adjust their positions to compensate, and I flung myself at the nearest wall. Using momentum and speed, I rebounded off it and leapt right over the pricks' heads.

They definitely hadn't expected me to end up behind them. Before they could do more than grunt in surprise, I'd punctured two of their hearts from behind. The third guy whirled around, and I slit open his throat. He crumpled into a pool of blood.

That was what they got for thinking they could contain me.

The constraints of the alley had worked against our enemies as much as ourselves. They must have been hoping to take us more by surprise. Bodies littered the concrete around me, and thankfully none of them belonged to the Chaos Crew. I saw Blaze get in a shot that caught one guy in the head, and Talon wrenched his favorite knife through another opponent's belly.

A man sprang at Garrison, the closest of the four to me. I yelped a warning and sprang to help as Garrison leapt out of the way with his gun hand jerking upward. The guy raked a knife across Garrison's forearm, and then ducked and rolled just as Garrison fired at him. Before I could make the attacker pay for the injury, he backed away, panting.

He wasn't the only one retreating. They must have realized they weren't winning this fight. Only three of our attackers were still standing, one of them the bulky guy with the forehead scar. He waved his own knife, smeared crimson, and they took off down the one route open to them without obstacles.

I would have charged after them, but as I raced around the corner, my gaze caught on Blaze, who'd fallen back against the wall with his hand pressed against a cut on his chest. My heart lurched with concern. I dashed to him instead.

"It's okay," he said in a voice that was only slightly strained. "Just a minor flesh wound."

When he lifted his hand, I saw he was right—it was a long cut, but shallow. Maybe not even bad enough to require stitches. When I spun around, our remaining attackers had vanished.

Julius cursed. All four of the men gathered around me, watching the shadows warily in case there'd be another attempt.

"You knew one of them, didn't you?" I asked Julius. "You said his name."

"There's no time to talk about it," he said brusquely. "People will have heard the shots and called the cops. We need to get out of here fast."

With him in the lead, we hustled out of the alley and made it to the rental car we'd arrived in just as sirens pealed in the distance. We dove inside, Garrison behind the wheel, and peeled away from the curb.

Squashed in the back between Blaze and Talon, I kicked the back of Julius's seat. "We're out of there now. Who was that guy you called Petrov?"

To my surprise, it was Talon who answered. "Former special ops. We were on a base with him for a while during our military days."

I stared at him. That was an even bigger coincidence than I'd have imagined. "And he just happened to show up with a bunch of jerks trying to kill you?"

"It obviously wasn't by chance," Julius said, anger thickening his already deep voice. "Whoever's behind these attacks, they know more about us than they should. And they're using every tactic they can against us."

"He won't know much about our current abilities," Talon pointed out, but his tone was somber too.

"Who would know about your connection to him?" I asked. "How do the people who sent him even know that you were in the military?" It wasn't like the Chaos Crew kept a business website with a list of its members and their biographies.

Blaze grimaced. "If these are people who've come at us before, they may have seen enough of us that they could have been able to use their own facial recognition software, or fingerprints, or something like that to make a connection."

Garrison coughed from where he was sitting behind the wheel. "I'm more interested in the fact that they tried to shove Dess off to the side. They didn't do a thing to hurt you once they had you out of the way, did they?"

A flush that was mostly frustration coursed under my skin. "No. Not until I forced their hand, and then they didn't get away with much."

"And who would care so much about keeping you safe while slaughtering us?"

It wasn't hard to see what he was getting at. We'd already discussed this theory the last time.

I rubbed my face. "It could be Damien Malik. I know. But there are other explanations too." Even if I couldn't think of them off the top of my head. The enemies who'd come after us back in the crew's hometown hadn't treated me so gently.

All this had started when I'd reached out to my birth father. Where did it end?

I had no idea, and every passing day brought more questions without answers. The Hunter had told me to dig deeper. I didn't want to follow his instructions—but it was starting to seem like that was the only possible route I could take if I wanted to get through this with my *other* family alive.

An idea twined through my thoughts until it felt solid enough for me to speak out loud. "I need to crack open all the Malik family secrets—and none of us has found any way we can do that on our own. I think it's time I set up another job to exchange a favor."

TWENTY

Blaze

DESS STRODE through the door after her mission looking both exhausted and fulfilled. I studied her as she flopped onto the sofa next to where I'd set myself up with my laptop and a plate of pasta I'd already polished off. She'd refused to tell us exactly what the mission was, handling this one completely on her own.

There were no obvious signs of combat on her clothes or skin. Her leggings and form-fitting top—which showed off some of my favorite assets—suggested work that required precise physical movements, but that covered a lot of areas. All I knew was that she looked content now that it was over.

"How was it?" I asked, setting my laptop on the coffee table in front of me and leaning back into the sofa.

Dess kicked off her shoes and grinned at me. "It couldn't have gone better."

Seeing her like that brought a warm sensation to my chest. Proud and content were two emotions that didn't seem to come naturally to Dess, so I treasured every glimpse of them I got. She deserved to take pride and happiness in what she was capable of.

Seeing her stretch out on the cushions as if she owned the house—as if she belonged with us—only exemplified that warmth.

"Has your search brought up anything?" she asked me, and I jerked my mind back to my own mission.

"I did a deep dive into all the Malik family holdings," I said. "Properties, vehicles, bonds, bank accounts. Everything they own, everything we could delve farther into. Unfortunately, they either don't have much outside of the house we know about and its insured contents, or they're very good at keeping whatever else they own off all the records I can access."

A little of her shine faded. "So there's nothing?"

I wagged a finger at her. "Have a little faith. I said there isn't *much*. I did discover that there's a safety deposit box at a separate bank from where they handle most of their finances in your grandmother's—Damien's mother's—name."

"Grandma Ruby," Dess said, sitting up straighter. She used the name with a familiarity that sent a weird twinge through me. She was suspicious of these people and she knew they'd never accept her, but she'd become a part of their collective all the same. "What do you think is in it?"

I shook my head. "There's no way to know. But the fact that it's at a separate bank suggests that it might be something more secret than your typical safety deposit contents. It's the best lead I turned up."

"And you're the best at turning up leads," Dess said, with a softly sly smile that heated me up in very different ways. She rubbed her mouth, her expression turning pensive. "Getting into a bank would be pretty difficult, but I think the guy who owes me can handle it. Garrison said he's an expert robber and safe cracker, known for getting at just about anything you could need that's locked away… I wanted to keep my options open since I didn't know what you'd find."

She picked up her phone and dialed the guy up. The conversation didn't last long—maybe two minutes of exchanging information and setting a time to do it—before she ended the call and gave me a mischievous look.

"Good news," she said. "We can go tonight. He said a tech expert would be an asset, so it'll be you, me, and Echo. I hope you're ready."

While Dess and I showed up a half-hour early in the still of the night, the man who called himself Echo was already waiting at the meeting spot down the street from the bank building, smoking a cigarette where he stood in the shadows between the beams of two streetlamps.

"Isn't the first rule of robbery *not* to leave DNA behind?" I murmured to Dess. I hoped Garrison had done his due diligence on this guy.

She shrugged. "Not our DNA, not our problem. Anyway, what are the chances the police would make anything of ash on the sidewalk a block away from the place. If this goes well, no one will even know the bank was broken into."

I had to admit she had a point.

The guy was certainly a character. He stood taller than both of us, but his height seemed to be all he had going for him. His arms and legs were skinny enough that I wondered if he'd been through a food shortage—and whether he couldn't have stolen himself some meals if he needed them so badly. His tortoiseshell framed glasses looked like they were meant to be a fashion statement, but they slid down his nose as he lifted his head to look at us. Even his clothes hung loosely on him.

Should I buy this guy a cheeseburger when we finished here?

Dess nodded to him. "Echo."

He grinned awkwardly down at her, showing a mouth of nicotine-stained teeth, and tossed his cigarette butt into the gutter. "You're early."

"So are you. Are we ready to go?"

He clucked his tongue. "I need to explain first."

Dess held up her hands. "Of course. We're ready to listen."

"Good." He gave a little twitch of his shoulders that made me wonder if he had a few screws loose in some literal sense as well as being half-starved. "Security guard, cameras, silent burglar alarms at every door, window, and room entrance, control panels at the vault and each secure door. That is this bank's security. We can't get into the vault without setting off an alarm, so no money. You can't steal money from this bank. You *can't*."

I was starting to get a bit annoyed. Did this guy think *we* were amateurs? "It's a good thing none of us is looking to steal any money, then, isn't it?"

Dess nudged me gently with her elbow. "Echo has broken into hundreds of secure buildings. Without setting off any alarms like we did the last time we did a major break and entry. He's never been caught."

I shut my mouth at the mention of the near-debacle we'd faced at the genetics storage center, an embarrassed flush crossing my cheeks—I still didn't know where my instructions had gone wrong to trigger that alarm—and tipped my head to the other guy.

"You're just looking to get at the safety deposit boxes," he said. "I know. That is doable. But I highly recommend against taking anything out of them too. We can get to them and get out again, but as soon as you remove contents, you alert your target that they have an enemy."

That consideration at least made sense. "Got it," I said.

"Can you walk us through the steps for getting to the boxes?" Dess asked.

Echo started flicking off points on his fingers. "We need to take out the security guard, but you can't kill him. Fred is a good man. The cameras need to be diverted from the outside. Your tech man can help with that. The motion-detecting alarms are at knee level, so we can avoid those. The control systems are turned off with a key swipe, and the guard has the key card for most rooms. We lift it from him. I can handle the inner doors and the box itself by my own means which I prefer not to share." He looked between us. "Shall we get started?"

"Absolutely." I pulled out my tablet. "I may be able to handle the outside cameras from right here."

It turned out that I needed to walk a little closer for the signal to be strong enough, but then I hacked into the feed quickly enough that this dude *had* to be at least a little impressed—not that it should matter to me whether he was. Examining the setup, I winced. "I'll have to 'adjust' them one at a time as we pass them. Mess with them all at once, and the guard in the camera room's bound to notice something."

Echo shrugged. "Do what you have to do. Just make sure no one sees us."

He strode ahead of us and went straight to the back door. It opened easily in his grasp, and he glanced back at us with a twinkle in his eyes. "I took care of this one earlier."

Okay, maybe the guy did know what he was doing.

I continued looping and resetting the feeds as we slipped into the building and made our way through the narrow, darkened halls at the back of the building. Echo pointed to four small panes low down on the wall. "Sensors."

We stepped over them no problem, swinging our knees high, although I couldn't see the lasers that we were avoiding. Tension wriggled down my spine. I'd never been the most coordinated of the crew. It would *really* suck if I somehow broke Echo's perfect record my first time on a mission with him. I'd never live the infamy down.

"How do we know if we activate a sensor?" I asked, switching the cameras again as we hurried onward.

"We'll hear sirens," Echo claimed nonchalantly, continuing forward with quiet footfalls. When we reached a door, he bent next to it with some gestures I couldn't make out and disabled the lock on that one with a faint click. He closed it behind us after we'd darted past it.

He paused before we turned a corner, and the thump of footsteps reached my ears. "Fred's doing his patrol. You want to take care of that?" He glanced at Dess with a confidence that made me wonder again what favor she'd done for him to earn this one in return.

Dess slipped around the corner without hesitation. We waited in silence. The footsteps halted with the briefest rustling of a scuffle, and then there was nothing. Whatever Dess had done, it'd taken her only a matter of seconds.

She returned from hiding the unconscious body in less than a minute, brushing her hands together like she did this every day. Which I guessed was almost true, at least in her previous career under the household's control. She flashed the key card she'd grabbed. "He's fine," she reassured Echo. "He'll wake up in a few hours."

Echo didn't bother speaking again as we approached the room that we most needed to enter—the one that held the safety deposit boxes. He stopped us in our tracks and pointed to the invisible sensors that would have sent us straight to prison. Lifting his scrawny legs high, he walked through them without much effort, and I went second this time, trying to move with extra caution.

Part of me expected it not to work when Dess used the guard's keycard to swipe into the room, but the lights flashed green. She glanced over a shoulder, giving me a look of absolute confidence. We'd made it to the room with her grandmother's deposit box, just moments from figuring out what lay inside.

I hoped it made all this trouble worthwhile.

Echo stepped into the room first. "Which one?" he asked under his breath.

"476," I said automatically, reciting the number I'd ingrained in my memory.

He turned to the smallest set of lockboxes on the wall and pulled a tool from his pocket. Apparently he was truly worried about someone stealing his techniques and, I don't know, making a fortune by showing them off on TikTok or something, because he placed himself very deliberately between us and his hands so I couldn't see what he was doing with the thing. But he jammed it into the compartment somehow or other, and the next thing I knew, it was popping open.

Echo motioned Dess over to open the drawer behind the door he'd opened. I followed her, pulling out my camera. We might not be able to take the contents with us physically if we wanted to keep our intrusion here a secret, but we could steal away any evidence we found in other ways.

Dess shone the beam of her small flashlight into the open drawer. The first couple pieces of paper at the top of the pile were nothing all that exciting: something to do with stocks or bonds, very official looking and nothing salacious. Dess nudged those aside and froze, staring.

The Polaroid photograph beneath the papers showed a little boy, no older than seven or eight, lying naked on his side. His staring eyes and the bluish pallor of his skin made it clear he was dead.

But it hadn't been an easy death by any means. His body was mottled with vicious wounds. I'd seen a lot of gore in my life, but nothing quite like this. My stomach heaved.

Who would do something like that? Who would keep a *record* of it?

Damien Malik's mother, it appeared. At least as the answer to the second question.

Dess had closed her eyes, her lips pressed tight as if she was resisting the urge to vomit. I wouldn't have blamed her if she'd given in to that urge, even though it would have made our exit a lot trickier. She drew in a few shaky breaths and forced her eyes open again.

Together, we sorted through the photos. There were five of them in total, each of a different child. The youngest I'd estimate was four and the oldest maybe ten. All of them were dead; all bore similar wounds that spoke of horrifying torture.

By the end of it, I didn't want to steal the contents of the box. I wanted to burn it out of existence. And preferably out of my mind too, if that'd been possible.

Dess was still staring at the last photo, which showed a girl who looked to be about six years old. Her blond hair was streaked with her own blood, two of her delicate fingers chopped right off her hand where it'd stiffened against the floor in death. Dess drew her forefinger over one of the wounds on the corpse's side, a jagged one that gaped open.

"The knife they'd have had to use to do that kind of damage," she said in a strained voice. "And the way they must have dragged it through her body to make that kind of mark… It would have been excruciatingly painful. I'm not sure I'd do it to my worst enemy, let alone a kid. And they all have cuts like that, more than one. How could anyone be *that* cruel to someone so helpless?"

A memory flickered up in the back of my mind of a different broken body, and I swallowed thickly. "Some people are just horrible."

"And why does my *grandmother* have them?" she added, that additionally horrible layer to this situation sinking in.

Echo glanced at the photos and shuddered. "That is fucking sick," he muttered, and pulled back toward the door as if he couldn't stand to even be near the images. I gave him a few points for having some sense of morality.

With my jaw clenched against my nausea, I snapped my own photos of each of the Polaroids. The thought of having those images on my phone made me want to set *it* on fire too, but we needed to be able to examine them later. There might be clues we didn't have time to pore over right now… and I'd like to be able to have a bucket at the ready when I did, in case my stomach finally heaved itself up my throat.

None of this made any sense. Yes, we'd had our suspicions that there was something fishy going on with the Maliks, but never in a million years would I have thought it'd involve torturing children.

Of course, the torture and the deaths themselves might not have anything to do with any of them. Maybe these were images from crimes they'd discovered that they were trying to fight back against.

If that were the case, though, I didn't know why they'd have kept the evidence in a safety deposit box instead of giving it to the police.

As soon as I'd gotten my photos, Dess shoved the box shut. Echo scurried over for just long enough to lock the door that hid it. Then he ushered us out of the room with as much urgency as if it were filling with poisoned air, which I hoped wasn't actually the case. The mission had gotten noxious enough as it was.

We dodged the same security measures on the way out, Echo moving with ruthless efficiency. As soon as we were back out in the night air, which tasted unbelievably fresh washing into my lungs, he shot a glance at Dess. "I want nothing more to do with this," he said, and marched away without another word.

I couldn't say I blamed him.

Dess was silent all the way to the car. When we reached it, she got into the back instead of the front and dropped her head into her hands. I slid in next to her, not sure whether she'd want to be touched. Not sure whether I could manage to touch her in a way that'd be comforting when I was so twisted up inside myself.

"Why did she have those pictures?" she whispered. "Where did they come from? What's this supposed to mean?"

"We'll figure it out," I said, my voice sounding distant to my own ears. "We'll get to the bottom of it."

"Five of them." Her head jerked up, her eyes widening with panic. "What if it's still happening? What if whoever hurt those kids is still doing it?"

I knew the right answer to that question. Resolve hardened inside me, pushing down my queasiness. "Then we'll stop them," I said firmly.

Dess's forehead furrowed. "How can you be so sure?"

"I just know we'll find a way. *I'll* find a way." I paused, and then let the story spill out, as much of it as I was willing to say. "You know what I'm like—how hyperactive I am. I was even worse as a kid. I got on people's nerves, and a bunch of kids in the neighborhood bullied the hell out of me for it. The worst of it was—"

The words stuck in my throat despite my intentions. Dess frowned, gripping my hand. "What happened?" she asked softly.

The obvious concern in her tone unlocked my voice. "I had a dog. A mutt, no special breed—fox terrier mix or something. He was the only thing I had back then that didn't mind how I was. And one day the bullies—they grabbed him out of my yard—I found him in the back alley, all battered and bloody. Dead. It looked like they'd kicked him back and forth until his bones broke, and then they smashed his skull with a rock."

Fury flared in Dess's gaze. "That's more than bullying. They were psychopaths."

I shrugged. "They were vicious kids. I don't know how much they even understood what they were doing. Maybe they thought of it like a stuffed animal. Whatever. It doesn't help anything for me to rage about it now. But when it happened—I was so mad at myself that I hadn't managed to protect him. That he'd gotten hurt like that because of me. That was when I swore to myself that I'd never be so powerless I couldn't save the things and people that matter to me again."

"You don't even know those kids in the photos," she pointed out.

"I do know that I've seen them," I insisted. "And I sure as hell care that it doesn't happen to anyone else. So you'd better believe I'm going to fight until we destroy whoever's responsible."

And it wasn't just the kids. Did Dess even realize that she now topped my list of people who mattered to me?

If uncovering the story behind those children would help her, I'd walk through Hell itself to figure out what happened and how it was connected to the Malik family. I wouldn't let her meet a similarly horrific fate.

I *would* protect her, no matter what I had to give to do it.

TWENTY-ONE

Decima

I'D TRIED to sit a few times while Blaze worked silently on his laptop, but the lack of movement unsettled me. If I wasn't in motion, my mind could only dwell on the tormented childish figures that I'd seen in the photographs.

I couldn't walk away from them, but at least staying on my feet kept the most crippling sense of horror at bay.

Blaze stirred with his usual restlessness and shot me an apologetic glance. "With kids, there are a lot fewer images available, and those photos didn't give the clearest view of their faces. I'm doing my best to find at least partial matches."

I nodded. "It's okay."

But it wasn't, not at all. If Grandma Ruby had those photos in a safety deposit box, they must have been important, and she must have wanted them hidden. But for her to have them at all…

What if the Hunter was disgustingly right about the Malik family, beyond any crime that'd ever occurred to me?

I stalked toward the kitchen, where Talon was drinking from a bottle of kombucha while he sharpened his favorite knife, and then strode back across the living room again. My hands clenched at my sides. I really wanted to punch someone, but I didn't have anyone to punch.

Who were the villains here? Could this have been some kind of setup? Maybe the Maliks were being framed.

Blaze let out a pleased sound, and I hurried over to join him. "You've got something?"

He waved at his screen. "These are partial matches, like I said, but I think I've identified a couple of the kids. A boy, aged five, and a girl, aged eight. Both of them had missing child reports filed with their local police departments."

"Local departments," I repeated. "You mean they weren't from here in DC?"

Blaze shook his head. "The boy was from Jersey City and the girl… Detroit. Not *too* far away, but whatever was going on, it wasn't restricted to this state."

"Whatever *is* going on," I corrected. "For all we know, this is still happening. When did they go missing?"

"The boy… three years ago. The girl, twelve." He grimaced. "Whether it's still happening or not, the murderer has been at it for a while."

I frowned, my stomach twisting even tighter. "You said there are just the missing child reports. No documentation of a definite crime? Did no one ever find the bodies?"

"It doesn't look like it. I haven't turned up any articles or records of unidentified bodies discovered in that condition. Although there are always remains turning up here and there that've deteriorated beyond recognition and were never identified."

"Or the killer disposed of them in a way that wasn't discovered." After taking those pictures as the sickest of mementoes. My fingers flexed and clenched again. "What about the other three?"

"I haven't located them at all so far. Maybe they were from farther abroad or longer ago, and they'll pop up eventually. Or maybe they weren't even reported missing, at least not with a photograph to go with the report."

A sour taste entered the back of my mouth. The kids had been so alone that nobody had even realized they were taken, tortured, and killed? How could anyone let a child remain missing without reporting them? Didn't their schools or neighbors notice when they disappeared without a trace? More importantly, shouldn't their parents have known?

But if they'd been that neglected, maybe that'd made them ideal targets.

I let out a frustrated sound and buried my head in my hands. "How could the Maliks have anything to do with this? It would ruin all of them—everything they're so committed to working toward. It doesn't make any sense."

"I agree," Blaze said gently. "It's a lot to swallow."

"But the evidence is right there. Maybe I'm too biased—of course I don't want to be related to people who'd do something that horrific." I groaned. "How can I trust my judgment about them? The actual evidence points right to them. No one could have known I'd find that safety deposit box. What would be the point of planting evidence where it wouldn't be used?"

Blaze got up and rubbed my shoulder. "There are so many factors we can't account for. I don't think we can draw any definite conclusions yet. Other than there's at least one very sick murderer out there, and they're connected to your family in one way or another."

"I didn't get more answers. I only have more questions—worse ones. Where do we go from here?"

I wasn't aware of Talon crossing the room until he came up on my other side. He gripped my elbow firmly, grounding me with his solid presence. "We'll keep looking and keep digging until we have the answers," he said. "No one's beaten us yet."

"And you're not being biased," Blaze put in. "It *is* a bizarre idea that your family would be responsible for crimes like these. If I come across any indication that they're being set up, I won't be remotely surprised."

"But you haven't come across anything like that so far," I said.

"No, but I haven't come across anything that gives further proof that they committed the crimes either."

"Other than the photos being in a box in my grandmother's name."

"That's just one piece of proof without any context," Blaze said.

I let out a growl of frustration and raised my head. "I feel like there's nothing I can do. If I knew who'd done it, I could go destroy them and make sure they never hurt anyone again. But I have no idea and no way to figure it out. And more kids could be dying right now because I can't."

"You're doing your best," Blaze said, but his reassurance bounced right off me.

Talon turned me toward him. He tugged my hands away from my face and fixed me with his impenetrable gaze. "You're stronger than this, Dess," he said. "Stronger than those fears. Stronger than the asshole who killed those children. If you need help remembering that, come at me. I know you could take me if you really tried."

I stared at him. "Hurting *you* isn't going to prove anything."

The corner of his mouth curled up with a hint of a smile. "You won't hurt me. I'm made of pretty tough stuff. But I think you need a reminder of just how much you can tackle. Now come on. Don't tell me you're afraid of a little sparring all of a sudden."

I made a face at him, and he pinned me with those cool blue eyes that would have sent anyone else running. Instead, they brought a warmth flaring up inside me. "Let's see all that power you've got in you," he taunted.

A surge of defiance raced through me, and I swung a fist at his shoulder. Talon dodged and tapped my side with his knuckles. He didn't hit hard—it was a dare to fully commit to the fight.

My competitive nature rushed to the surface. It felt *good* to focus on this, to feel the power he'd talked about. I sank into that sensation and came at Talon with twice as much determination as before.

We bobbed and circled each other, exchanging blows, our breaths roughening as our movements sped up trying to catch the other off-guard. I almost forgot about Blaze until another fist rapped against my shoulder blade.

I spun around and shoved the hacker down on the sofa, pinning him there before I'd fully processed what had happened. He just grinned up at me, not a hint of worry in his bright eyes.

"What are you doing?" I demanded. Talon loomed behind me.

Blaze tipped his head to the side with a slyly innocent expression. "I figured if you feel better beating up on one of us, two would be even better. Although…" He shifted his position beneath me where I'd straddled him with one hand to his throat and the other on his chest, and I was abruptly aware of his erection brushing my sex. Heat had pooled there without my realizing it. "Now I can think of other ways you can dominate us that might be even more fun."

A tingle of desire passed through me, but at the same time something in me balked. "I don't think I should be having *fun* right now."

Blaze reached up to place his hand over mine where it still loosely held his throat. "Don't think of it as fun, then. Think of it as showing your strength and remembering who you are. You're having trouble even thinking clearly—you need a break. More than that, you need to believe in yourself, and I know that you do when we're together."

I raised my eyebrows "You're awfully confident that you can make me feel that way."

Blaze chuckled. "I don't think anyone can make you feel that way. But I know that you can make yourself feel strong if you're in control of both of us."

In control of both of them. The thought provoked an eager quiver despite my initial doubts.

I glanced back at Talon still braced behind me. Handling all the guys the other night had been a rush, one that sent a heady flush through me just at the memory.

Maybe this *was* what I needed—a reminder that I wasn't as weak and powerless as I felt. I'd ordered Blaze around before, but with Talon I'd only encouraged his own aggression. What would it be like to take control over a man that domineering? To have both of them totally under my sway?

The thrill that came with the idea made up my mind for me. Before I could second-guess the impulse, I leaned back to grab Talon's bicep. With a heave, I yanked him down on the sofa next to Blaze.

Then I adjusted my position so I straddled one of each of their thighs, my knees sinking between their legs.

"Stay still," I ordered both of them, with a push of their chests toward the back of the sofa. Then I gripped the front of Blaze's shirt and captured his mouth.

He kept his hands to himself, but he kissed me back with all the passion I knew he was capable of. I finished with a flick of my tongue over his and turned straight to Talon, who was watching me with smoldering eyes.

First I buried my face against his neck, taking in the masculine scent of him and grazing my teeth against his skin in a way that made his hips jerk toward me. "I said 'stay still,'" I murmured, and raised my head to nip his earlobe. "You've done a good job at fucking me in the past. But this time, I'm going to show you what it's like to be fucked by me."

A flicker of emotion passed through Talon's normally impassive face, lust and admiration and more that I couldn't identify. It definitely wasn't true that the man didn't feel, no matter how emotionless he tended to present himself as.

I ran my fingers over his smooth scalp and dug them into the back of his neck as I pressed my lips greedily into his. He met me with just as much fervor. The unrelenting passion in the kiss had my toes curling. My hand worked its way between us and began pulling down the joggers that he wore.

He managed to pivot his hips and allowed his pants to slide down his legs at my coaxing. His boxers followed, and I traced my finger up his thigh with an intensity that felt immoral. I moved it so, so slowly that I saw his attention split between me and the finger that I trailed up his leg.

It must have been a noise from beside us that drew my attention back to Blaze. His name had never fit him more with the hunger that shone from his face. I couldn't neglect my other lover.

"I want both of you," I said in a voice that came out huskier than I expected. He reached for his jeans, managing only to unclasp the button before I stopped him with a hand on his wrist. "That's my job."

I pulled myself up and allowed my one finger to trail down Talon's still clothed chest, all the way to the base of his impressive length. As I stood, I twirled my finger around it slowly and meticulously before releasing him.

The heat that roiled through my body had my limbs trembling. I pulled Blaze up so we stood chest to chest with each other and reached a hand into his pants—surpassing the fabric entirely as I gripped him beneath the belt. He dipped his head backward and groaned toward the ceiling as I stroked him just as slowly. Despite being the one theoretically in control, I couldn't help but still feel completely out of control at that moment.

I hooked my other hand through his pants and tugged them downward, but he didn't seem to notice in the slightest as I continued my teasing motions. Fuck, at this moment, Blaze was one of the most attractive men I'd ever seen. The way his light red hair hung back as his breathing increased in tempo—as I increased the rhythm of my motions—was almost godlike. His fists, balled at his side, showed the restraint that he was exercising.

I wanted more than that. But I could make that kind of command too, couldn't I?

"Don't hold back on me," I said. I might be in charge of this encounter, but I didn't want them to treat me like I was fragile and incapable. "I want everything you can give me. Show me just what you want to do to me—no holds barred."

Blaze's eyes flung open, and I saw the restraint there too. I knew he was doing whatever he thought would make me feel the most in control, but more than anything, I wanted to know how *he* wanted this moment between us to unravel.

Blaze's eyes flashed with uncertainty before he placed his hands on my hips. "Are you sure?"

I smirked. "Positive."

He didn't waste any time considering his options. One of his arms dipped around my back, and the weight of his body forced me to fall backward. I clutched the fabric of his shirt as he slowed my fall and draped me across the coffee table. Blaze immediately went for my pants, tugging them down my legs and trailing kisses in the wake of the fabric.

The tender treatment might have raised my hackles in another context, but I knew Blaze so well now that it stirred no memories of the villain who'd violated me before. And after all, this man was doing exactly what *I'd* told him to do.

And oh, was I pleased with the result. The hacker hooked his arms under my legs and tossed my feet over his shoulders. In an instant, his tongue had slipped inside of me, devouring my core.

I thrashed, my cry of both surprise and pleasure reverberating through the room as Blaze feasted. He seemed to know intuitively where it would be best to devote his tongue and lips. Then he inserted a finger into the mix and pumped it inside of me with the same tempo as his tongue had offered a second before.

I panted beneath him as the waves of my pleasure grew and eddied. With each swell, the bliss intensified until I was near my breaking point. But Blaze wasn't finished with me yet. He sent me right up to that edge before letting me drift back down just shy of release.

"Blaze," I growled. He only looked down at me through lowered lashes as he inserted a second finger into me and went back to work. I tightened my thighs around his head and gave a direct command. "Make me come."

The second I'd spoken, he started working me over even more relentlessly. He put every ounce of knowledge and experience into his fingers and his tongue to bring me to that edge once again—before tossing me even higher and allowing me to plummet over it.

With a cry, I released everything I'd been holding back—all the pain and uncertainty, all the sadness and frustration. I replaced it all with the feeling of this man wreaking blissful havoc on every inch of me.

I didn't even have a moment to wind myself down before Blaze moved to the side and Talon bent over me. "Do you still want to be the one to fuck me, or can I have the honor of fucking you instead?" he asked in a tone that practically made me come just like that.

"Why not both at the same time?" I said, still breathless and dazed from Blaze's claiming. "Give me everything you've got. I'll meet you there."

"I know you will," he rumbled, and tugged my legs toward him to wrap around his hips. I pushed myself upright to yank him to me, and his cock slid into me so perfectly we both groaned.

We rocked together, both of us bucking into each other's bodies. Talon glanced down at the place where our bodies met, and his voice turned even more heated. "There's nothing like fucking you. Watching you go almost cross-eyed when I push inside of you. And then all the ways you move, all the sounds you make."

He demonstrated, pulling himself out and then thrusting back into me. I couldn't help but gasp as that complete feeling of fullness took over my senses—as the lingering satisfaction from Blaze pulsed inside of me, enhanced each time Talon moved.

I glanced over at where Blaze watched, his breathing just as fast as ours. I didn't speak, instead gesturing for him to come to me in an unspoken command. As he came up beside me, I reached to clasp his cock in my hands. "You're mine too," I informed him, and opened my mouth, licking the head.

With a groan of his own, Blaze braced himself against the coffee table—which I hoped was *very* sturdy given all the action it was seeing today—and aligned himself in front of my mouth. I drew him in between my lips, still rocking against Talon at the same time.

He tasted delicious, warm and musky, exactly the flavor I'd imagine desire would be. Giddiness swelled in my chest as he moved with the motions of my mouth, as more pleasure raced through me with each crash of my and Talon's bodies against each other.

I *was* strong—strong enough to master both of these men. Strong enough to handle four lovers who were the most powerful men I'd ever known. And I'd have them with me every step of the way, supporting me with their own power.

Together, it was hard to believe anything could stop us. We'd do whatever needed to be done.

Blaze's hand gripped my hair as I sucked on him. Talon's rough palms on my hips held me with him, and I found myself on the verge of another climax. Unlike before, it didn't come in waves. It hit me at once, taking me mercilessly as my body pulsed around both of them.

I moaned against Blaze's erection. "Oh, fuck," he muttered, and pulled back just in time to let loose his own release across my chest and neck. He gazed at me with total adoration, panting but beaming.

I could feel Talon getting closer and closer with each thrust that I met. He bucked into me faster and harder until he gave one final slam of his hips and clutched onto me like a lifeline. I sagged into his embrace for the long moment before he finally pulled out.

It'd been good. It'd been *fantastic*. But even as the sense of power continued to resonate through me as I smiled at my lovers and swiped the sweat from my face, a tendril of uneasiness crept up inside me.

No matter how strong I was, we still had a horrible villain to bring to justice. One more enemy on top of the others we'd already accumulated. And I couldn't help wondering if this was even the end of it, or if there was even worse to come.

TWENTY-TWO

Decima

FOR THE FIRST TIME, I'd been conscripted into helping with the serving of dinner in the Malik household. As Grandma Ruby, Grandpa Bo, Aunt Mabel, and Uncle Henry chattered in the dining room, I grabbed serving spoons and potholders in the kitchen on my mother's instructions.

Carter dumped a small pan of green beans into a serving dish, and a few drops of melted butter spilled across the marble countertop. Iris had her back to him, but she seemed to innately sense the mess, turning with raised eyebrows.

"I know, I know," he said, grabbing a paper towel.

She tsked her tongue. "Try to be more careful to begin with. Rachel, dear, would you scoop the potatoes into a dish?"

It was still weird being called by my birth name. I wondered if I'd ever get used to it. It was even harder now that I had all these suspicions about the family crowding my head.

I moved past Carter to deal with the potatoes, glancing briefly out the window in the direction I knew Garrison and Talon were waiting just out of sight. My brother glanced over at me. "You're roped into the chores now too," he teased.

"I'm going to eat, so it's only fair that I help dish it out," I said with forced cheer. I picked up the tongs and started moving the crisped potatoes from the baking sheet to a decorative white bowl.

"I thought you worked in a restaurant," Carter remarked. "You kind of suck at that."

I wrinkled my nose at him with what I hoped was suitably sibling-style annoyance as my heart stuttered briefly hearing my cover story questioned. "I'm a hostess. I lead people to their tables and take reservations, no food handling. But if you think you can do a better job…" I waved toward the tray in offering.

Carter snorted and took the beans over to the dining table. But by the time we'd all joined our relatives in the dining room, me seated next to my brother as usual, he turned to me with a bit of an arrogant air. "You know, now that you're part of the family, you don't have to keep a menial job. You can start working toward whatever career you want. Mom and Dad would obviously be happy to help you financially to get you on the right course."

Before Iris could jump in and agree, I gave a little laugh. "I'm sure they would, but I like paving my own way. Anyway, the job I have suits me just fine for now."

Carter frowned. "Don't you want a career that *matters*? I'm going into law enforcement, and I'll make a difference there. I know I will. It's a lot more important than pointing people to the right restaurant table."

I forced a casual shrug. "Sounds a little too dangerous to me. I've had plenty of that in my life already."

A bit of a hush fell over the rest of the table at that remark. I'd thought the reference to my kidnapping would stop Carter in his tracks too, but he seemed determined to push my buttons, even though I doubted he'd ever find himself facing anything as dangerous as I'd done in my real job a hundred times over.

"But you'll never accomplish anything with a life working at some restaurant," he blurted out. "You'll never get to do anything meaningful. That would be such a sad life."

"Carter," our mother chastised. "Your sister is allowed to do whatever she wants with her life. As long as she's happy, that's all that matters. Plus, you don't have to have a career in law enforcement to support your father and advocate for putting away criminals."

"As long as she supports the family legacy, that's really all that matters," Aunt Mabel said as she dabbed at her mouth with her napkin.

Grandma Ruby chimed in. "Protecting the country from evil-doers is our curse and blessing, and it may be yours one day, too. If you decide to stick around with this crazy crew, that is."

Right. Because the only possible meaningful work had to be throwing criminals behind bars—or breaking their hands, or whatever, I supposed.

My mother smiled in agreement. "We don't expect you to fully commit to all of this right away, dear. It's something that we'll introduce you to over time."

I bit into one of the potatoes I'd dished out, trying not to show how uneasy the conversation was making me. The tone the conversation had taken sounded even more cultishly obsessive than when my father had brought up the family legacy the other day.

But if the Maliks were this dedicated to the cause and so willing to do everything to defeat crime, I couldn't imagine how they'd ever be involved in what we found in the safety deposit box. It didn't make sense. Maybe they'd gotten those photographs to remember just how horrible criminals could get?

But there wasn't any record of the murderer being caught or the bodies being found. Where had they gotten the pictures *from*? Why keep them locked away like that?

My head was spinning again. My gaze instinctively followed Uncle Henry as he straightened up over the baked chicken and lifted the butcher knife to carve off some more meat. He plunged the blade into the breast, twisting his wrist in a circular sawing motion that made my breath catch in my throat with a jolt of horror.

The motion looked just like the kind that could have marked those jagged wounds that'd gouged the children's flesh.

I blinked, and then he was cutting through the meat in totally normal slices, as if he always had been. I watched, looking for any indication of that same twisting cut, but he didn't do it again.

For fuck's sake. Had I imagined that because I was so horrified by the pictures, so desperate for answers? This quest was turning me paranoid.

Grandma Ruby must have caught something in my expression that I hadn't quite been able to hide. "Are you all right, Rachel?"

The words brought me back to the moment, and I nodded, plastering a fake smile on my face instinctively. I knew from experience that they wouldn't be able to see through it.

"I'm great. I just got a little lightheaded for a second. I probably haven't drunk enough water today." I set down my fork and took a gulp from my glass. "Do you mind if I excuse myself for a moment and go use the restroom?"

A worried expression crossed my mother's face. "All this talk about legacy and crime would be enough to overwhelm anyone. I'm sorry. You go take care of yourself, and let us know if you need anything."

I dipped my head graciously and hurried out of the room. As soon as I'd passed out of view into the hall, I tapped a quick message into my phone—the message the men were waiting for. They were going to buy me more time than a simple bathroom excuse could manage.

I strode toward the bathroom and slipped inside, my ears pricked. It only took a matter of seconds. Then a bizarre squawking sound pierced through the walls, like there was a flock of rapid chickens congregating right outside the house.

What the heck had the guys orchestrated? As my relatives' voices faltered and then their footsteps hustled over to the back door to see what was going on outside, I had to resist the urge to join them. The crew could tell me all about it later. I could just imagine how much Garrison would enjoy conveying the story.

Instead, I darted out of the bathroom and over to the spot opposite the family room doorway where I'd seen Margaret emerge seemingly through the bare wall. My fingers slid over the striped wallpaper, testing it with years of honed experience. I couldn't expect the crew to keep my family distracted forever. If I took too long, my relatives might return and catch me in my stealthy investigation.

My fingertips caught on the faintest of grooves and traced it up and down, confirming that it was straight and tall enough to mark the edge of a door. My pulse kicked up a notch. There.

But there was no knob, no obvious way of opening it. How had Margaret done it? I hadn't seen her go in.

There were a few basic mechanisms to concealed doors, so I just had to figure out which one this operated by. Trying not to let the voices filtering in from outside distract me, I gave the door a general shove with my shoulder. Nothing. Then I ran my fingers along the edge of the seam again, pressing every couple of inches.

At hip height, the surface depressed just a fraction. Something in the wall gave a small click, and the door swung open.

My breath caught in my throat. I peeked through the doorway and found a plain flight of stairs leading down into the darkness of a basement room.

Without hesitation, I slipped inside and found a handle that let me pull the door shut. At least no one would be able to figure out where I'd gone, even if they noticed I'd been gone for a while.

I pawed at the walls on either side of the stairwell until my palm hit a light switch. When I flicked it upward, brilliant light spilled into the space at the bottom of the stairs. All I could see was polished wood flooring and the edge of a maroon rug that looked as thick as the ones in the main rooms upstairs.

As I eased down the stairs, a crisp scent—smoky and herbal—tickled my nose. It reminded me of the incense in churches and temples I'd occasionally had to carry out missions in or around. I couldn't place the exact scent—it might not have been quite the same as any I'd encountered before.

There was no sign of its source when I reached the bottom of the stairs. I came to a halt and stared at the room that opened up beyond the steps.

It looked like a large den. Bookshelves lined two of the walls, stuffed full with thick volumes and antique-looking decorations. In the center of the room, on top of the rug I'd seen the corner of, squatted a large desk piled high with more books and various other documents. A large leather office chair sat behind it, with a few more traditional wingchairs scattered through the rest of the space.

Damien already had a home office space upstairs. Did my mother work down here? I hadn't gotten the impression that her job would require anything so elaborate. And why would she have kept it hidden?

I slunk closer to the bookshelves and scanned the spines. Most of them appeared to be volumes on law, politics, and criminology. I found one row with stranger titles, things like *Channeling the Inner Spirit* and *The Energy of the Great Beyond*. No one in the family had mentioned any kind of spiritual interests, but I guessed they could have those books more out of an academic interest rather than because they believed in the contents.

I snapped pictures of all of the shelves and then studied the items placed here and there in front of the books more closely. Some of them were antiques as I'd thought, a fancy old candlestick here, an intricately carved trinket box there. Others I had a lot more trouble making sense of.

Knitting my brow, I paused over a small shoe that must have belonged to a child. It was a dress shoe, but not particularly fancy or pretty, just a glossy black shell that looked like it was made out of plastic and a narrow strap with a tiny flower over the snap. The toes were lightly scuffed.

Normally when people kept mementos from their children, they bronzed them, didn't they? And I didn't see how this could have belonged to me or Carter. It was too large to have belonged to the toddler I'd been when I was kidnapped, and too girly for me to imagine a five- or six-year-old Carter donning it. But the style was fairly modern, so I couldn't picture it belonging to my parents' generation either.

Maybe it'd been Margaret's? But then why would it be here in my parents' house and not at Aunt Mabel and Uncle Henry's?

The shoe wasn't the only oddity. There was a little figure with a face roughly carved into the wood and a scrap of fabric as clothing. What appeared to be a hair clip in cheap metal shaped like a butterfly. A thin, folded cloth that might have been a napkin or a handkerchief.

Why would my parents have used things like that as part of the décor? It didn't match the rest of the room at all.

By the time I turned to take in the far wall, my skin was already creeping. What I found myself staring at didn't exactly comfort me. It held a few more framed parchments like the one I'd found in Damien's office, but these looked progressively newer and less worn, which fit with the numbers I was now more convinced were years. They continued on in a steady progression until they reached the 2000s, at which point they started to double up, two of the same before going on to the next.

The rest of the notations next to them looked like the same unfamiliar code as on the matching document upstairs. As far as I knew, Blaze had never managed to crack it.

Maybe he'd be able to with more examples to work with. I took pictures of those parchments too, holding my hands as steady as I could.

I'd seen a lot of horrible things in my time. I hadn't actually uncovered anything specifically horrible *here*. But the whole vibe of the secret room—and the fact that it was secret at all—was making my skin crawl in a way I'd never experienced before. I couldn't shake the sense that *something* was very, very wrong.

At the end of the row of parchments, there was one more framed picture. This one was a faded photograph of a house with a broad front porch and vines crawling up one side. It sat on a wide, open property with no near neighbors, like it was out in the countryside. I didn't recognize anything about it either, and my parents hadn't mentioned owning a country home. Blaze hadn't found a deed or other record for it in all his searching.

So what was so special about it that they'd framed this photograph and hung it here?

I frowned at it and added it to my phone along with the rest. Then I turned my attention to the desk.

The papers I could see were printouts of news articles marked up with a few notes in what I could recognize as my father's handwriting. There was nothing particularly odd about them—they were reports on recent crimes here in DC, with things like the police response time circled. He was analyzing the performance of local law enforcement, which seemed like a totally Damien Malik thing to do.

I would have dug deeper, but just then a floorboard creaked somewhere above me. My nerves jumped, and I froze in place.

The family had come back inside. If I went back up now, they might spot me using the hidden entrance. They might already be wondering where I was.

My hand darted to my phone. I tapped out another quick text to Garrison that an additional distraction was needed ASAP.

I'll take care of it, sweetheart, he shot back with a blowing kiss emoji I couldn't help seeing as sarcastic. A moment later, whatever he'd done, the footsteps above creaked away in the opposite direction.

There was no time to examine anything else right now. I dashed up the stairs, placing my feet as quietly as I could, and pressed my ear to the door. When I heard nothing on the other side, I nudged it open and squeezed out.

I shoved it back into place and was just starting down the hall toward the dining room when Grandma Ruby appeared from the back of the house. I swiped my hand over my hair, hoping I didn't look too rattled.

"Well, you certainly know how to miss a party," she said with an eye roll that didn't seem particularly hostile. I relaxed just a tad. If I'd been even a few seconds slower…

"What happened?" I asked in as casual a tone as I could summon.

She shook her head. "I'm still not even sure. We heard the strangest sounds, like there was a whole farmyard out there, and then some shouts for help, but we couldn't figure out where they were coming from. Then just as I'd come back inside, because really, it's dinner time, your mother shrieked like they were being murdered." She let out a huff. "It was only a rock that landed in the garden and crushed a few flowers. Nothing worth fretting about."

Somehow I thought she'd have taken a different tune if it'd been her own garden assaulted. "How strange," I said innocently.

I joined her back at the table. In less than a minute, the rest of the family poured back in, exclaiming to each other with their theories about what had been going on—neighbors acting out, poultry escaped from a delivery truck, a prank from a political opponent.

They were all so engrossed in their speculation that I didn't have to say anything at all, just eat the rest of my dinner in silent reverie. My body might have been at the table, but my mind was stuck in the room downstairs, trying to make sense of its strange contents alongside the photographs we'd found in the bank.

Noelle and Anna had always claimed that they were protecting me, that they'd taken me in to shelter me from the cruelty of the world. I knew that was at least partly a lie… but what if there was some truth to it too?

My parents hadn't died, obviously, but maybe the household really had seen kidnapping me as a way to protect me. Because I was starting to think that whatever my birth family was up to was way worse than anything my former captors had done.

TWENTY-THREE

Decima

"A SHOE?" Garrison said, leaning into the counter with an expression that told me he was thinking just as hard about the situation as I was. He looked down at the printed-out photos I'd set between us, shaking his head. "That is pretty weird. And the papers and symbols are just as bad."

I grimaced. "I just wish I understood what all of this means—if it means anything, you know?"

"Did you snap any pictures of the desk before you left?" Julius asked, scanning the photos of the bookshelves.

I shook my head. "I ran out of time. Maybe I can go back down there the next time I visit."

Talon's eyes shot up and captured mine. "You're not going back."

I frowned at him. "I have to."

He gestured to the photos. "Not until we know what all of this means. It's definitely disturbing, especially after what you found in the lock box. We're not sending you into a potentially deadly situation for information. You're not a spy."

I narrowed my eyes in challenge. "No, but they *are* my family. It's not like any of you could waltz in there and get access anywhere near as easily."

"Talon's right," Julius said. "It would be reckless to go back without more information. We won't tell you where you're allowed to go, but please, give us a chance to see what we can make of this first."

"I wasn't planning on heading right back there today," I said. "But even if I did, I can take care of myself."

Garrison nudged me with his elbow, his tone wryly affectionate. "Sweetheart, nobody claimed that you couldn't. But you do have a bit of a blind spot for your family, and we won't let them exploit that—exploit *you*."

I wanted to argue that I didn't have a blind spot, but it would be a lie, and all of them knew it. No matter how much evidence arose against the Maliks, a part of me still wanted to believe it wasn't possible. I couldn't help searching for ways to deny the facts that had been laid out before me.

Blaze pulled the photo of one of the coded documents toward him, running his finger below each of the numbers that looked like years. "If these are dates, as the numbers suggest, it's possible they'll match up with some factor to do with the missing kids that I've found… Now that I have this, I might be able to break the rest of the code. I'll see what I can do."

He switched back and forth between the photos and his laptop, so immersed that he didn't even glance at the rest of us. A weird tremor formed in my stomach, both anticipating the answers I'd worked so hard to get and dreading them at the same time.

"Was there anything else strange about the basement room outside of these pictures?" Julius asked.

"I took pictures of everything that seemed at all significant." I lifted the photo that showed the image of the country home. "Any idea what this could be about when there's no record of them owning another home? Why would they keep a picture hanging on the wall of some random house?"

"It could be one that used to belong to them and passed out of the family," Talon suggested.

I hummed to myself. "I guess it could be that. Something they lost somehow and want to remember. No one's ever mentioned an old house that they miss to me, but obviously there's a lot they haven't revealed so far."

"They're definitely keeping a lot of secrets," Garrison muttered.

But what did it all mean? We didn't know what the dates meant, just like we didn't know anything about the house or the odd items on the bookshelves. There wasn't nearly enough proof to draw any kind of conclusion. The only hope we had of finding evidence was Blaze, and he was currently frowning at his laptop with no sign of cracking the code yet.

"Where do we go from here?" I asked when nobody else offered any insight. "We have all of these clues, but we have nothing to connect them to. We don't even have a working theory."

Julius leaned into the countertop and swiped his hand across his face. He didn't know either. Whatever the Maliks were hiding, they kept it hidden too well. What if Blaze couldn't figure out what the parchments meant? We still wouldn't have gotten anywhere.

Garrison straightened up and took on a brisk tone. "It's no good standing around here brooding while the tech head does his work. Staring at the pictures isn't going to make them speak to us." He tapped my arm. "Why don't you and I go scope out the place where Malik's wife works? You said she takes Fridays off, right? So she won't be there to notice. I can chat up her colleagues and see what they'll let slip about her, and you can pickpocket a few phones we can scan for texts and emails exchanged with her."

My legs itched to move, to have something more to do, but I hesitated, biting my lip. "I don't know. Iris hardly talks about her job. It doesn't seem like she's that invested." All I knew about it was that she worked in insurance.

Garrison shrugged. "What's more likely to turn up something—standing here doing nothing or trying out a little more scouting?"

I had to admit he had a point. And now that he'd proposed the idea, the thought of sitting around in the house made me want to explode.

I glanced at Julius, and he gave me a nod. "You'll want to be careful about it, but you already know that. As does Garrison." He shot the younger man a pointed look. "Be quick. We don't want anyone realizing why you were nosing around."

I bounced on my feet, restless energy coursing through me. "All right. Let's see what we can find."

"We won't do anything that you wouldn't do," Garrison said to Julius with a wink, and headed with me to the doorway. Once it'd firmly closed behind us, he smiled wickedly down at me. "Now, Julius has done a lot of reckless things, so if you want to jump into something crazy before we go to the office, the option is still on the table."

I let out a genuine laugh for the first time in what felt like forever and bumped shoulders with him. "I think we should wait until after if we want to do anything too wild."

Garrison looked down at me as we started our walk, and when I met his eyes, I found unrestrained joy there. It was almost as if coming out here with me had cleared his mind, and now he gazed at me as if I were the most valuable thing he'd ever seen.

"Are we thinking skydiving, bungee jumping, maybe stealing a police car for a joyride?" he asked.

I threw a mock punch into his arm. "I don't think that Julius has ever stolen a cop car."

Garrison shrugged. "I wouldn't put it past him under the right circumstances."

"I don't think we have the right circumstances going for us right now," I teased, and glanced toward the driveway. "Do you want to take the rental car? Or we could get an Uber if we don't want the license plate caught on street cams in the area. It'd be a long walk." I imagined it'd take at least an hour, although in my current state of frustration, I wasn't sure I'd mind that much exercise.

Apparently, Garrison felt the same way. "I'm okay with walking a few miles if you are," he said. "I've barely gotten much chance to stretch my legs in the past few days."

"Other than arranging phantom farmyards and fighting for your life."

He shrugged and smirked at me. "Yeah, other than those minor adventures."

We turned the corner to walk past a couple of old industrial buildings, and the screech of tires made my head jerk around.

A van roared into view and skidded to a stop right next to the sidewalk. In the space of a heartbeat, three men in ski masks had leapt out, clamped their hands around Garrison, and hauled him into the back.

I leapt after him, my hand snagging on one guy's shirt. The guy kicked back at me at the same time, and in my startled panic I didn't dodge quite well enough. The heel to my gut sent me staggering to the side.

As I threw myself forward again, the van was already peeling away from the curb and racing away, the back doors clanging shut with Garrison behind them.

My body reacted on pure instinct. Some part of me believed that if I just pushed my legs fast enough, I'd be able to catch the van, even as the engine roared.

I sprinted after it faster than I'd ever run in my life, my feet pounding on the asphalt. A yell of rage lodged in my throat, but I couldn't spare enough breath to let it out. My gaze darted over the few cars parked along the road, but if I stopped for long enough to break into one of them and hotwire it, I'd lose sight of the van and have no way of chasing after it. The license plate was covered, so I couldn't even use that to believe I'd be able to track it down later.

So I kept running, propelling my body forward with all the strength I had in me. My hands darted to my hips. I hadn't brought my gun for this excursion, but I did have my usual concealed knives. I'd started carrying two in light of recent events.

I drew out one and then the other and hurled them at the tires of the van, praying that I could hit one well enough to deflate a tire and force the vehicle to slow. But the driver must have noticed in the rearview mirror that I was up to something. The van swerved left and right on the wide road, and my knives clattered uselessly against the pavement.

Swallowing a curse, I raced onward, searching the ground for anything else I could use to try to stall the van in its tracks. As I passed the places where my knives had fallen, I scooped them up without breaking my stride. Then I veered toward the curb and grabbed a chunk of concrete that'd tumbled there.

In one last-ditch effort, I heaved the chunk at the van's window. The vehicle swerved again at the last second, and the concrete only dinged the bumper. The van roared around the corner.

I dashed after it, sweat trickling down my back from the exertion. My legs were starting to feel numb from how hard I was pushing my muscles. I sped around the buildings onto the cross-street—

And found the van was gone. The engine sounded somewhere beyond my view, but it was dwindling too fast for me to catch up.

"Fuck!" I shouted at the sky, coasting to a stop.

I couldn't do this on my own. I needed the rest of the crew—Blaze would be able to check traffic cams—Julius had contacts in the city. We'd figure this out.

Wouldn't we?

As I hurried back to the house, my stomach knotted. What had the men in the van wanted with Garrison? Who had they even been? I had no idea if they were related to the attackers we'd faced in the city before, or our various earlier opponents in the crew's hometown, or maybe they were some totally new force we hadn't known about.

The look he'd given me a minute before the car pulled up—full of happiness and pride—reverberated through my mind. I swiped my hand across my face, but the gesture couldn't shake my anguish.

They might be torturing him, even killing him, right now. While I loped along here unable to do anything about it. If I'd grabbed at him just a little sooner, reacted just a little faster—

I pushed my legs harder again. Any extra second could help Blaze find the van before it disappeared forever. I didn't allow myself to consider the breathlessness or the exhaustion that wreaked havoc on my limbs. I just sprinted until the house came into sight.

I burst through the doorway, my breath so ragged it took me a few moments to gather myself enough to form words. "Garrison," I gasped. "Some men grabbed him. Black van. Took a left on Meridian Street."

"Hey, hey," Julius said, striding over with his arms reaching for me.

I shook my head and pushed him away. "They took him! Don't worry about me. We have to find him."

Blaze stared at me with wide eyes. Why wasn't he already pounding away at his laptop's keyboard?

"We know," Talon said, his tone chilly with anger. "We just got a text message from his phone."

"What?" I sputtered. "What did it say?"

The men exchanged a look. They were calm—too calm. I'd seen that measured stillness on their faces before missions. This was the calm before the storm. I braced myself for what they were about to tell me.

Julius cleared his throat. "It said that unless we track him down in the next twenty-four hours, there's no chance we'll find him alive."

TWENTY-FOUR

Decima

"THAT'S IT?" I demanded as Julius's last words rang in my ears. "What do they want? Did they even say for sure that he *will* be alive for twenty-four hours?"

Blaze got up from his chair. "No. They didn't say anything else. But it's obvious they want us to try to find him."

"And if we don't soon enough, they'll definitely kill him," Talon said flatly.

Nausea curdled in my stomach. "It's a trap," I said. "Obviously, right? They wouldn't be sending us on a manhunt just for fun. They want to get us someplace vulnerable and take out the rest of us."

Julius tipped his head in acknowledgment. "It looks that way. Whoever's responsible, they must have realized we're too strong all together for them to tackle us that way. So they've picked off one of us and are hoping it'll set the rest of us off-balance."

I rubbed my face, the images of what Garrison might be facing at the hands of his attackers rising up again. "We can't just abandon him. We have to find a way around their stupid trap and get him back."

"Of course," Julius said, so firmly a tiny bit of my distress subsided. "We're a family. We don't leave each other behind, no matter the consequences. But we have to do this carefully, or we're all dead meat. They've given us a timeline. We'll figure out as much as we can so we can go into this trap prepared to destroy it."

"The first part is who's behind the operation in the first place," Talon said, and paused.

My stomach sank. I already knew where that line of thinking was leading.

"The Maliks," I said. "That's where the evidence we found before pointed, even if it wasn't much. And now this happens right after I broke into their secret room? Maybe it's a coincidence, or maybe they realized someone had gotten in there, and they're striking back."

Blaze made a face. "Unfortunately, I have to agree. If I could just get this code worked out… I'll see if I can track the van's route too." He gave a small growl under his breath and went back to his computer.

Julius folded his arms over his chest. "All right. Assuming Damien Malik is responsible, where can we think of that he might have taken Garrison to?"

"He could just keep him in the van," Talon said.

"Possible, but risky. If they keep driving around, they'll need gas soon, potentially exposing them to bystanders. And they must suspect Blaze will be able to search for matching vehicles. I think they'd want to stash him away somewhere more secure." Julius glanced at me. "How about that secret room? That seems like a reasonable place to hide away someone you don't want found."

I thought back to the study-like space I'd crept into and balked at the suggestion. "It wasn't like a dungeon. It was too cozy—like it's used for family meetings and sitting around reading rather than their dirty business. I can't imagine them bringing him there. Besides, it'd be awfully risky having him right there in the known family home. They've got to have other properties somewhere."

Blaze shook his head without looking up from the computer. "I didn't find anything under any of the Maliks' names except the houses they're currently living in. I guess they might have brought him to your grandparents' house or one of the aunts and uncles'?"

I frowned. "That still has the problem of being too easily tied to the family—and I don't know if the other houses have secret rooms too." That seemed like a bit much, although I couldn't dismiss the possibility entirely. But there was another option. "What about the house in the basement photograph? Have you run an image recognition search for it?"

Blaze sighed. "Yes, but nothing's popped up based on that picture. It obviously isn't in a high trafficked or photographed location. But that secluded location could be anywhere in the world for all we know right now."

"Damn it," Julius muttered, pacing the room in a rage that I'd never have thought I'd see from the controlled commander. Witnessing his unrestrained frustration made the situation feel more real. More terrifying.

Garrison was counting on us, but we had no solutions. No way to find him. No leads. I could tell from Blaze's increasingly despondent expression that following the van wasn't getting him very far either.

But I had to do *something*.

Just as I thought that, my phone vibrated in my pocket. The guys went still and silent as I pulled it out, other than the clacking of Blaze's fingers on the keyboard. I studied the text message that had appeared on the screen, gritting my teeth as I processed it.

"It's from the Hunter," I said, glaring at the phone.

"What does he want?" Talon loomed next to me, and I knew that if he faced any opponent right now, he'd come out victorious. He'd kill anyone with his bare hands if it meant finding Garrison alive, and I couldn't say I didn't share the sentiment.

"He wants to meet," I said. "He's mentioned a place nearby that he wants me to go to."

"Give me the spot, and I'll give him a piece of my mind about how he's put you through the wringer," Julius grumbled, striding toward the door. I leapt forward and caught his arm, holding him back.

"He said he only wants to speak to me. That he'll leave if anyone's with me." My chest constricted.

"Like hell," Blaze said. "We can't send you out there alone to meet a guy who's essentially a stranger, especially not this Hunter who has been leading you in circles for weeks. We lost Garrison today, and we're not losing you, too."

"I'm going with you," Talon insisted, walking to join Julius and me by the door.

I pushed both men back a step. "None of you are thinking straight. Get off your high horses and consider what this means. Of all the times the Hunter could have sought me out, he chose the moment when I needed answers the most—the day that Garrison was taken. If I don't follow his demands, do you think he'll tell me anything? I can't risk losing whatever information he's willing to share. It could make the difference between whether we find Garrison or not."

Julius's muscles flexed, but his mouth pressed into a flat line rather than arguing. He understood the stakes just as well as I did. "What if he's the one who took Garrison?" he said finally.

"Then he'll definitely know where to find him, won't he?" I shot back, and let out a huff of frustration. "But most likely, he noticed something about the Maliks with his surveillance that tipped him off to what they've done. Look, so far every time we've been attacked here in DC, I've been ignored and even shoved out of the fray while they focus on you guys. I'm the one who's the *most* safe out there. If I see anything remotely suspicious, I'll leave. I won't take any risks I don't have to."

Talon's jaw worked. He marched away and returned seconds later with a pistol in his hand. "You're not going out there unarmed," he said, and I knew he'd accepted my plan.

I accepted the gun with a nod of thanks and tucked it into the back of my sweatpants. "I wouldn't dream of it."

Julius exhaled roughly. "For the record, I don't like this at all. But you're right. Just—don't get too close to him and keep an eye out for anyone else suspicious nearby. And if you're not back in ten minutes—or if we hear shots fired—we're coming after you."

I let out a humorless chuckle. "If he doesn't manage to say anything useful in ten minutes, then I'll already be leaving. Maybe after shooting him for wasting my time all over again."

Confident that my self-appointed bodyguards wouldn't stand in my way any longer, I tucked my knives back into their usual places and quickly donned a second gun in an under-shoulder holster that I hid beneath a lightweight hoodie. Plenty of options was always a good thing. And my bare hands were weapons all on their own. I couldn't get much better armed than this.

Looking at the men around me, I gathered my resolve. The message said to come alone, but I wasn't completely alone. They were with me in every way they could be.

The Hunter had probably known where I was staying from the moment I'd given the address to the Uber driver he'd conscripted. He'd asked me to come a few blocks down the street from the house to a parking lot beyond an old office building that was now boarded up.

As I approached, I heard the rumble of a motorcycle's engine before I saw anything. Coming around the building, I found a tall, broad-shouldered man sitting on a thrumming chopper. A helmet covered his head, the visor reflecting the mid-morning sunlight back at me rather than revealing his face. I could only make out the vaguest shapes of his eyes and nose when a tuft of cloud briefly passed over the sun.

I walked closer, keeping my hands in easy reach of my weapons. There was no sign of any other figure around. It was just me and him.

When I was about ten feet away, he held up his hand. "That's close enough," he said, and his voice confirmed my suspicions. Even slightly muffled by the helmet and the drone of the engine, I knew it immediately.

This was the Hunter himself.

I stopped, setting my hands on my hips. "You called me out here, and now you're acting like I'm a threat?"

A hint of amusement came into his tone as he pitched his words over the engine's rumbling. "I have to be careful, you understand. I don't know where your loyalties lie. You are a Malik, after all."

I grimaced at him. "Just because I was born a Malik doesn't mean I am one."

If I'd expected him to lead with information about Garrison, he was just as disappointing as usual. "Have you done any more investigating to substantiate what I told you about them?" he asked.

Was that all this was again? Another excuse to badger me, at the worst possible time?

My teeth set on edge. "Are you here in person because that way I can't just hang up on your shit?" I demanded. "I'm done with this game."

As I spun on my heel, his voice stopped me in my tracks. "Then you haven't found any concerning photographs?"

I froze, unable to decide whether I wanted to entertain this conversation after all. Whether I wanted to give away what I *had* found to this man.

But he must have already been able to guess. "You did, didn't you? You're sharp enough to have gotten that far. Then you saw a little blond girl along with the others."

The memory of the photo smacked me with enough horror to make me glance back at him. "What about her?" I said, the question coming out raspy.

Even though I could barely make out his face, I felt his stare boring into me through the helmet's visor.

"That was my daughter," he said. He kept his voice even, but rage reverberated through it all the same. "The Maliks stole her from me and killed her as brutally as you saw. I've never been able to prove it definitively, but I know it was them. That's why I've been investigating them, and it's why I was worried about you coming into the fold."

My stomach roiled with the urge to puke. He was confirming my worst nightmares about my family—but I still didn't know for sure if I could trust him. It still didn't make any sense. But then, how could he have known about the photographs if his story wasn't true?

How could I focus on that right now when Garrison's life hung in the balance this very second?

My back straightened as I realized that there was one answer that would help me solve both problems. "Do you know where the killings might have been carried out? Where they took the kids?" It'd have to be someplace they felt was secure. Someplace that'd work just as well to hide a kidnapped hitman.

The Hunter paused. "I think the family must have a property

nearby—one under the radar and isolated. I've been searching, but I haven't found it yet."

Before he could say anything else, his phone chimed loudly in his pocket. He glanced at it and revved the engine on his motorcycle. "I've got to go," he said, and tore out of the parking lot without giving me a chance to respond.

"Wait!" I hollered after him. "I have more questions." But he was already roaring down the street. I couldn't tell if he'd even heard me.

He'd told me nothing at all about Garrison. He didn't have any more idea about where the Maliks might be hiding him than I did.

Actually, that wasn't totally true. I pushed down my hopelessness as everything he'd said sank in. We hadn't found any other properties the family owned, but the Hunter was sure they had another one—one in the area. All I had to do was figure out where.

But the only people who'd know were my birth family, and they hadn't mentioned anything about it so far. If it *was* where they murdered children and stashed kidnapping victims, it wasn't likely that they'd tell me in a casual conversation.

They were my family, though. They'd been talking about bringing me into the legacy, about me being one of them. Was there some way I could use that?

As I hurried back to the house in the hill, my mind whirled, and my thoughts centered on Garrison in a different way. He was the one in the group who got information out of people rather than computers. I didn't have him to guide me, so I had to figure this out myself. How would he have convinced someone to cough up an address? I'd watched him in action before.

He'd get people talking. He'd catch them off-guard and set them up to reveal more than they meant to before they even realized how much they were spilling. He might act like he knew all about what he was fishing for already to put them at ease with confirming or correcting his suggestions.

What if I could do the same? If I wanted to save Garrison, I'd have to become him for one phone call.

I took out my phone and scanned through the limited numbers. Who would be the most likely to fall for this kind of gambit? Someone who didn't already have decades of experience pretending *not* to be a mass murderer, presumably. But someone who was familiar with the family's "rituals."

After a moment's debate, I tapped my brother's number and raised the phone to my ear.

Carter answered after just a couple of rings, nothing in his tone giving any indication that he knew I had a reason to be upset. "Hey, Rachel. I wasn't expecting to hear from you." He sounded mildly surprised but not concerned or shifty. Maybe he wasn't in on this particular part of our parents' plans. Or maybe he was a very good actor.

I'd just have to be better.

"Hey," I said in a brisk but warm tone. "Dad wanted me to meet him out at the country house so he could show me around. I'm excited to find out more about everything the family's involved in, but I seem to have misplaced the address. Can you remind me where I'm going?"

Calling Malik "dad" sent shivers down my spine, but I held up the ruse through my whole spiel.

Carter answered automatically, just as I hoped. "It's just off Eckleberry Lane, if you've made it that—" He caught himself, and his tone turned abruptly wary. "Dad wanted you to *meet* him there? What did he say he wanted to show you?"

"Don't worry about that," I said. "You've told me enough."

I hung up the phone and dashed back to the crew with the street name on my lips.

TWENTY-FIVE

Talon

THE RENTAL CAR sped down the country road, frequent potholes jarring Dess and me in the backseat. It was obvious not many people drove down this way, which made sense if the Maliks had set up some kind of torture home out here.

As soon as Dess had come rushing back to report on her conversations with the Hunter and her brother, Blaze had identified the only Eckleberry Lane remotely in the vicinity. From there, it'd taken a matter of minutes for him to skim through satellite footage and identify a house just off it with a footprint and roof that appeared to match the Maliks' photograph.

With the threat to Garrison in mind and the knowledge that Dess's brother could alert the rest of the family to her likely arrival, we'd jumped into the car without much preamble—though of course we'd paused long enough to grab some necessary equipment. Dess and I were quickly and efficiently loading up the assortment of guns we might need to bring to bear. I had my usual knife strapped to my hip, and I knew Dess had at least a couple of blades concealed on her body.

If our brother-at-arms was hidden away on that property, there was no way in hell we weren't bringing him back, no matter how many bodies we had to drop along the way.

Julius jerked on the wheel and swerved around a turn, and Dess swayed with the movement. My hand instinctively rose to her back, but she continued loading one of the semi-automatics, hardly even seeming to notice the movements of the car or her own body. She was so far in her own head that I wondered if any of us could really get through to her.

Garrison was usually the one who could break her hard exterior, even if sometimes he did it by heckling her until he got a rise. I had no idea what to say. Out of all of us, I was the worst choice as an emotional support guide. I barely knew how to feel my own emotions, as few of them as I noticed having at all.

"I'm going to kill all of them," she murmured as she set the last gun atop the pile between our seats. She paused for a second, her hands flexing, and reached for one of the earlier ones to give it a brisk cleaning.

"We'll kill them together," I replied firmly. It shouldn't need to be said that I'd have her back—that all three of us would. These people were worth nothing to me after what they'd done to our crew and to her. Seeing them dead would bring me a shitload of satisfaction.

That emotion I'd definitely feel when it came.

Blaze let out a triumphant sound in the front passenger seat where he'd still been hammering away on his laptop. Both of our heads jerked in his direction.

"I've got it. Fucking finally!" he crowed, and swiveled for a second to catch our eyes. "It was the parents, not the kids. That's what threw me for so long."

"The parents what?" Julius said gruffly. "Why don't you back up a bit for those of us who weren't code-breaking alongside you."

Blaze blinked at him as if it hadn't occurred to him that we couldn't read what was going on in that restless brain of his and then launched into an energetic explanation. "The code in the documents the Maliks have in Damien's office and their secret basement room. I suspected they had something to do with the murdered kids, and I was right. But I was expecting the symbols to match up with the kids' names, and that was a dead end. I finally realized there's a parent named for each date instead."

Dess leaned forward in her seat, the weapons momentarily forgotten. "What do you mean?"

Blaze held out his laptop so we could see it from the backseat. He zoomed in on part of one of the parchments and ran his finger along a line of data that still looked like scribbles to me. "The part on the right is a full date. This one is May 27th, 2019. The name next to it is Harvey Little. He's the father of one of the kids in those pictures that I found a police report on."

I frowned. "Why would they have listed one of the *parents* when it's the kids who were murdered?"

"I'm not sure," Blaze said. "I have the computer automatically translating the rest of the entries now. I'll look up the other names and see what I can make of them."

We waited in tense silence while he tapped away, the rumble of the car's engine filling the cramped space. Dess didn't tear her eyes away from the back of Blaze's head. He sucked a breath slowly through his teeth, tapped some more, and then let out a thoughtful noise.

"What?" Julius prodded.

"I'm finding a bit of a common theme," Blaze said. "Some of these people appear to be ordinary citizens, but at least half of them so far have had criminal records. Significant ones. Armed robbery, extortion, multiple counts of assault, that kind of thing."

"Oh," Dess said, that single syllable so pained that my gaze shot straight to her. She'd turned to stare out the window now, her face pinched with tension, her jaw tight.

I wished I could peek past her guarded expression into her head, but she made it so difficult to see anything that she didn't want to show us. It'd been obvious before that she was unsettled by all the information we'd been uncovering related to the Maliks, though. The fact that she was withdrawing even more meant she was under increasing strain.

The only way she knew to survive was by hiding herself.

Finally, she glanced at the rest of us again. "That's the missing piece. The motive. They're killing the children of criminals. I'd be willing to bet that even the ones you didn't turn up a record for, the Maliks found out they were involved in some illegal stuff. I guess, in their eyes, murdering their kids must be some kind of punishment or revenge, or balancing the scales—an eye for an eye..." She shuddered. "Or maybe they think the kids will turn out the same as their parents and that it's better to cut it off at the root. I could believe it from the way they've talked."

Blaze let out a low whistle. "That's fucking psychotic."

"It's *sick*," Dess spat out. She rubbed her eyes with the heels of her hands. "*They're* sick."

And they were her family by blood. The more we learned about them, the more this had to hurt her. The cuts from this revelation, I realized, would go deep and never completely fade. She'd witnessed and dealt out a lot of violence in her time, but clearly nothing on this level.

Maybe the household had done her a disservice in more ways than one by sending her after businessmen and politicians rather than criminals. She wasn't totally prepared for how depraved the worst of society could get.

I wouldn't deny that the Malik family was a rare breed, but it was one that I recognized. I'd met plenty of psychopaths who justified beating up on the most fragile members of society. Hell, I'd been raised by two of them.

Had my life gone a little differently, I could have become one of them.

Julius continued the drive without a comment, but I knew he was silently processing the information, marking it to his memory as he drove. Blaze was occupied with tracking down the other entries on the coded lists. I was the only one who could see how off-balance Dess looked. It didn't fit the woman I knew at all.

How could I get her back on track?

"It's awful, but we'll put an end to it," I told her in the most reassuring tone I could offer. "We'll end *them*, and not one more kid will die at their hands."

Dess completely buried her face in her hands and gave a shaky sigh. "It's not just that. If it was just that, I wouldn't feel like this."

I hesitated and then forced myself to ask, "How are you feeling?"

Her shoulders drooped, but the muscles in her arms flexed at the same time. "It's just—" She took a deep breath. "I hate them with everything in me. I hate that the Malik family has apparently been killing innocent children for a century, and I hate that they've gotten away with it. I hate that they're sick and demented, and I want to kill them for taking Garrison from us."

She stopped again, almost as if she was done speaking. I could tell she wasn't really finished, though.

"But?" I prompted.

She cleared her throat and lowered her voice. I didn't know if it was because she didn't want to be heard or if it was because she felt guilty saying whatever was about to leave her lips. I leaned forward, intent on hearing every word of it.

"I just found them," she whispered. "I thought I'd get a chance at having an actual family, the way I was supposed to if the household hadn't kidnapped me, and it almost happened. They welcomed me, they were so happy to have me back… and the whole time they were *monsters*. It'd give anyone whiplash, wouldn't it?"

"Of course it would," Julius said in an even voice.

I studied Dess's face, sensing that she hadn't quite finished spilling her guts. She looked too agonized still.

She dropped her hands into her lap and looked down at them. "They're not *that* different from me. I go out and kill criminals, and say it's fine because those people were hurting innocents. They're killing in order to hurt criminals."

"It isn't the same," I said with a rare surge of anger. "We attack the people who are the actual problem. Those kids couldn't have done anything wrong. They torture and murder the innocents *we* would be protecting. It's the opposite."

"I know. It's just… a lot to take in. And I have to deal with them as soon as possible, I have to look at them after everything…" She growled to herself.

If it'd been anyone else responsible for those deaths, I was sure she'd have been ready to mow them down without any hesitation. But she'd been drawn in by the dream of having a loving family, and it had to be hard not to want to try to put the pieces back together even after that dream was shattered. She'd finally found her relatives after more than twenty years, and now she had to kill them to stop something even more horrible from continuing.

For her not to feel conflicted about that, she'd have to be made of steel and stone. Like me.

I'd been out of my depth for this entire conversation, but suddenly it occurred to me that I might be the best person to tackle her current dilemma. It meant dredging up memories I preferred not to dwell on, let alone talk about, but for her, I could ignore the minor discomfort.

It was just the past. Julius already knew the basics. I didn't mind if Blaze did too. They were my family now—the truest family I could ever want.

"I'm going to tell you a story," I said.

Dess peered at me, knitting her brow, and waited.

I leaned back in my seat, holding her gaze. "My parents died when I was a toddler—not much older than you were when the household took you. I was sent to live with my maternal grandfather and his new wife. They were… not happy about being saddled with me. Or maybe they weren't happy about much of anything."

"They didn't treat you well," Dess filled in, and stiffened. "Your scars."

A humorless chuckle fell from my lips. "Yes. I don't think a day went by without them yelling at me and beating on me in some way—smacks and kicks from my grandfather, pinches and cigarette burns from his wife. Occasionally they went off in a wild enough rage that I ended up bleeding or with a broken bone. I'm probably lucky they didn't kill me."

Dess winced. "I'm so sorry."

I shrugged. "It was a long time ago. But it's shaped a lot of who I am today. They were most often set off by any sign of emotion—if I laughed at a funny TV show. If I cried over a bee sting. Shit like that would definitely mean a beat-down. So I learned not to show what I was feeling." And after a while I'd stopped feeling much of anything in the first place.

But that wasn't what I was telling Dess this story for. I pushed onward. "No matter what I did, they used me as a punching bag. The most I could control was just how bad it got. It took me a long time to realize that kind of treatment wasn't normal. I couldn't remember being 'parented' any other way. But even before I realized just how awful they were, I knew I hated it. As I got older, I threw myself into training—muscle-building, fighting techniques, weapons—anything I could find through videos on the internet or other means that gave me back a sense of power."

"That makes sense," Dess said quietly. The compassion shining in her eyes woke up a strange ache inside me that I didn't know what to make of.

"But it wasn't just to get a sense of control," I said. "I wanted to know I was *stronger* than them, so that—when I was old enough that I didn't need their support anymore, I paid them back for all the pain they'd inflicted on me for all those years, all at once. They got what they deserved, and that was the end of it."

I didn't have to spell out what I'd done any clearer than that. I could tell Dess caught my meaning.

I braced myself for shock or horror. I'd chosen to remove the bastards from my life—carefully enough that I'd never been pinned with the crime—and nothing would convince me that I hadn't made the right decision. But that wouldn't make it easy to see her recoil from me.

All she did was shake her head and reach out to squeeze my forearm. "I don't blame you."

Those four words cracked open a wall I hadn't even known I had inside me. My breath came out in a rush. For a second, I was so overwhelmed by the unfamiliar sensations sweeping through me that I couldn't even speak.

I groped for a steadier sense of calm so that I could finish what I'd meant to say to her. I hadn't been looking for her sympathy. I wanted her to understand that I wouldn't blame *her* either. No one in their right mind would.

"The point is," I said, "family means nothing. You don't choose who gives birth to you or who raises you, and sometimes they're awful people. Sometimes they need to be taken down, just like any other random person might. You didn't ask to have these pricks as your family, and you'll be doing the whole world a service by taking them out of it. So feel whatever you feel, but don't for one second think there's anything wrong with you for doing what has to be done."

Dess squared her shoulders. Her mouth still slanted at an uneasy angle, but her eyes held a resolve that hadn't been there before. "Thank you. It helps knowing you've been there before in your own way."

My lips formed a smile that didn't often come naturally to them, warmth spreading through my chest despite the lingering awkwardness of my confession. I didn't know what it meant, but I didn't care. All that mattered was that I'd given everything I could to make sure this incredible woman made it through the next few hours unscathed.

TWENTY-SIX

Decima

MY SPINE STIFFENED when Blaze gestured to a dirt lane up ahead. "That's the turn-off," he said. "Another half a mile and we'll reach the house."

Julius took the turn with ease, and a white-walled building immediately came into view in the distance, expanding gradually as we zoomed toward it. I couldn't see it perfectly yet, but I could already tell it was the house from the basement photograph.

And that wasn't the only thing we could see. At least six cars were parked outside the building. I recognized Damien's, Aunt Mabel and Uncle Henry's, and my grandparents'. The other three might have belonged to other relatives I'd spent less time with.

"Looks like we have plenty of company," Julius said, taking them in.

Talon handed one of the pistols we'd cleaned and loaded to Blaze and brandished another himself. "Nothing we can't handle."

Were all of those family members in on Garrison's kidnapping? My stomach knotted as we reached the end of the lane.

How had they justified *that* crime to themselves? Saving me from bad influences? Did they know what the crew did but somehow didn't realize that I was in the same line of work? Or did they just figure they could bring me over to the "right" side once they'd gotten rid of my men?

My jaw clenched. It didn't matter what they wanted. They were sick, child-murdering psychopaths, and every kindness they'd ever offered me was tainted by that fact. I knew I wouldn't feel at peace until every one of the Maliks who'd had a hand in the murders was six feet under themselves.

Talon was right about one thing: some people needed to be taken out of this world before they could do more damage. Who better than me to deliver that sentence?

Julius parked at the side of the lane a short distance from the official parking area where the other cars stood. So far there'd been no signs of movement. No one stirred in or around the vehicles. The house's windows were dark. A small barn stood beyond it across about twenty feet of scruffy grass, its tall double doors shut and latched.

"Everyone ready?" Julius asked.

I slung a holster over my arm, tucked another gun into one at my hip, and wrapped my fingers around a third. We couldn't go into this too prepared, as much as a small part of me, the part that'd craved a real family, still balked at the idea of firing the weapons at the people I'd thought of as that family. "I am."

We got out onto the dusty earth, the guys similarly armed. The wind swept over us, carrying a dry scent that itched in my nose, like stale hay.

We'd only just walked past the cars, starting to cross the stretch of patchy grass between the parking area and the covered porch, when the front door swung open. The four of us halted, guns at the ready.

Nearly every person I'd met at that first reunion spilled onto the porch before my eyes. Aunts, uncles, and cousins, my grandfather, and of course, my father. The only people missing were Carter, Grandma Ruby, and my mother. Had my brother spilled the beans about my call, or had the rest of the family been waiting here already in case we figured out where they'd taken Garrison by some other means?

I stepped a little ahead of my men, my finger curled around the trigger of my gun. If any of the men and women before me were armed, I could blow them away before they so much as set their hand on their weapon.

"Where is he?" I demanded.

My father pushed to the front of the crowd, resting his hands on the porch railing. I couldn't read his expression, it was so stern and yet haunted at the same time. His gaze slid from me to the men around me, and his forehead furrowed. Had he expected me to come alone? As if the crew wouldn't stand by their lost member.

"Who the hell are these people?" he demanded.

As if he didn't already know. "The closest thing to a family I actually have," I said. "Now answer the question. Where is he?"

Damien's attention jerked back to me. "Your brother? I told him and your mother to stay home after he told me you'd found out about this place. I don't know what led you to it, but I promise you, I can explain."

Fury seared through me so fast it burned away everything but my horror at everything else I'd discovered. "Explain what?" I spat. "Why you torture and murder little kids for your own enjoyment?"

If I'd still had any doubts about whether the Maliks were responsible, Damien's flinch was enough to dismiss them. The rest of the family stirred around him with restless murmurs. Aunt Mabel made an uncomfortable grimace. Margaret's eyes flashed as if she was eager to have this secret out in the open. Grandpa Bo shook his head as if he was disappointed in *me*.

"That's a vast simplification of a complex and honored process," the older man said.

"An *honored* process?" I said. "Are you kidding me? I've seen pictures. What you did to them is nothing but sick."

Damien raised his chin. "It's the opposite of sick. The Maliks have a divine mandate going back over a century to *stop* the spread of the criminal sickness through this country. We offer up the pain and lives of the tainted children to a higher power to prevent more pain and lives lost at the hands of those who'd turn to unlawfulness and sin."

I stared at him. It took all my willpower to stop my jaw from gaping open. "You seriously think that some sort of god wants you to torment innocent kids as a way of stopping crime? You're fucking insane."

"Insanity is in the eye of the beholder," Margaret muttered, as if that was helpful.

"We don't enjoy the process," Uncle Henry insisted, though from the look on Margaret's face, that wasn't true of everyone. "Only the outcome we're working toward."

My father nodded. "It has to be done for the good of everyone in this country. Sacrifices must be made to set the energies among us on the right course."

Suddenly the supernatural-sounding books in the library made a lot more sense. Where had the generations of Maliks before them first gotten these crazy ideas? What had convinced them to keep acting on them?

It didn't matter. The people in front of me had been carrying out their horrific legacy their whole lives. I could see from the flash of determination in my father's eyes that they had no intention of stopping even with my discovery of it.

But I had to try anyway.

Bile had risen in the back of my throat. I swallowed it down and fixed him with my firmest stare. "You're an educated man. Can't you hear how ridiculous this sounds? How could killing children possibly have any impact on whether other random people commit more crimes?"

"You'll understand," Damien said. "I promise you, once we bring you into the rituals, you'll see how it all connects. It *is* an honor, being chosen to carry out this divine calling—"

I couldn't stand to listen to him anymore. I took another step forward, and Aunt Mabel flinched. "I'm *never* going to understand, and I'm sure as hell never going to be a part of this psychotic cult of yours. I'm going to ask you again. Where. Is. Garrison?"

My father's brow furrowed, and I expected him to dodge the question again, continuing this stupid game of not knowing what I meant. But at the same moment, a clanging sound reverberated from the direction of the barn. My gaze shot straight to the other building.

From this angle, I couldn't help noticing another, smaller structure tucked next to the barn. A big brick chimney with a wrought-iron belly… A furnace.

The nausea gripping my stomach expanded up through my chest. Ash. Calcium levels in the soil. Signs of bodily remains.

Just like that, I knew that furnace was where they burned the results of their "offerings." That was why no murders had been reported—no bodies had ever been found.

And then the Maliks took a little of the ash and scattered it in their garden back home to fertilize their precious flowers of justice. My gut lurched, and I thought I might actually vomit.

But the sound had come from the barn itself. Was that where they'd locked Garrison away? What state had they left him in?

The urgency of my worry drowned out my queasiness. Turning away from the house, I set off toward the barn with the rest of the crew at my heels.

It seemed the Maliks didn't like that. They all poured down the steps, hustling to get between us and the barn.

"You've gone far enough," Grandpa Bo said in a growl.

My father's gaze flicked over the men with me again. "We can't have strangers poking around in our most private and sacred business. We can't have them *knowing* what we do here."

Margaret snickered. "You gave them a death sentence."

Who did she think she was? I ignored her, glowering at Damien. This confrontation was going to end in death, but I wanted to make sure that Garrison's life was no longer on the line before blood got spilled… if I could.

"You don't want to start this fight," I warned him.

A tremor ran through him, but then his expression set with determination. "There are only two options now that you've come this far, Rachel. Either you accept your role as part of the family—or we can't let you leave here alive."

"I think she's already made her position perfectly clear," Uncle Henry said with a flash of dark metal as his hand leapt up.

Julius saw it too. Before my uncle even took aim, the crew's commander blasted him away, a clean shot through the center of his forehead. And then the scene erupted into total chaos worthy of the crew's name.

The rest of the family charged us, whipping out guns and knives, from little paring blades to blocky cleavers. Most of them threw themselves at the men, aiming to close the distance before the crew could take any easy shots.

My father lunged at me.

Shots boomed and grunts and groans filled the air all around me. I didn't have time to look and see who was responsible for which sounds. Damien snatched at my hair, and I had to dodge faster than I expected to escape his grasp—which sent me colliding with one of my uncles. I whirled around, and a boot slammed into my calves. My legs buckled.

I landed on my hands and knees and immediately rolled to the side. As I sprang back onto my feet, my father barreled into me, knocking me back to the ground.

When he loomed over me, there was a moment when I could have shot him. I still had a pistol clutched in my hand. But my damn heart stuttered, I hesitated for a split-second, and the next instant he was kicking the gun from my fingers.

He shoved me down with a knee on my abdomen and the muzzle of his own gun pressed to my forehead. My pulse lurched for a totally different reason. But it seemed Damien Malik wasn't all that keen to kill the daughter he'd only just discovered was still alive.

"This could have been so different," he said in a ragged voice. "I didn't want it to come to this. If you'd given me time to ease you into it, to show you everything..."

As if there was anything he could have shown me that would have convinced me that killing kids out of a delusional sense of divine justice was a-okay. But I kept my mouth shut, knowing that one twitch of his finger would add me to his list of murders.

One of my knives was just inches from where my hand lay. If I could just get him distracted enough to give me the space to make a move—if I could get him to withdraw his gun just a tad...

"I don't want to do this," he went on. "It was a miracle to have you returned to us."

"You don't have to do anything," I dared to say, shifting my fingers a smidge to the left at the same time.

Damien gave no indication that he'd noticed. He leaned more weight onto my chest with his knee, the pressure turning my breath shallow and sending an ache through my previously-broken ribs. His hand trembled, but he kept the gun pressed right against my skin.

"We wanted you to join us, but we've been doing this for too long to let you destroy our legacy now," he said. "Blood doesn't matter if you can't fulfill our calling."

"I thought blood was everything to this family," I said. "Is it so different with me just because I was gone for so long?"

"It has nothing to do with you being gone," he shouted. "You've desecrated everything we stand for with your dismissive words and the violence you've brought here. If I have to kill my only daughter to keep our legacy alive, I will do it."

He clearly meant it. I relaxed my body as well as I could to give me a wider range of motion, but I let my voice come out taut with hurt. "You kept me in the dark for so long. What was I supposed to think when I stumbled on the evidence? You have to know how it looks. To believe in some kind of higher power guiding all this… You never really gave me a *chance* to understand."

His gun-hand shifted just slightly. "I'm trying to now," he rasped. "If you'll join us, if you'll open yourself to the energies and the mysteries we celebrate and the mission we're fulfilling, it'll be even better than when you didn't know. All you have to do is show you'll give it a chance."

I latched on to that opening with everything I had in me. "Of course. I didn't see at first how devoted you all are. There must be something more to it." Damien's hand wavered while I spoke and then dipped to the side, away from my head. I kept talking, my words covering the faint rustle of my clothes as I slid out the knife. "I'll do whatever I can to make up for the things I said, to show you—"

Relief spread across his face as my fingers tightened around the hilt, and in that moment, I didn't feel the faintest trace of regret. I slammed the blade upward, raising my voice into a yell. "—to show you there's no fucking way I'll ever buy into that insanity!"

The knife dug into my father's throat before I'd finished my defiant exclamation. I wasn't sure he even heard all of it.

Blood gushed down over me from the artery I'd severed, and Damien sputtered, his body already going slack with the life rushing out of it. As his body sagged, I shoved him off me. He lolled on his back, his eyes hazing as even more blood pooled beneath him. Then he was totally still.

There was silence all around me. More bodies littered the ground —every member of the Malik family who'd joined this confrontation. Julius, Talon, and Blaze stood among them, breathing hard and with a few small scrapes here and there, but nothing concerning.

Of course not. My birth family hadn't known how to fight a crew of highly trained hitmen. Their typical opponents had been literal *children.*

I stared down at my father's corpse, the blood that'd soaked my shirt and hair cooling against my skin with the breeze. Somehow I wanted to feel at least a tiny stirring of guilt, a reminder that I was still human. But all I could think of was those pictures of the children, mutilated far beyond anything I'd done to him.

The only thing that mattered now was finding Garrison. Making sure they hadn't given him the same treatment.

My gaze jerked toward the barn, where that sudden sound had come from. The building the family had tried to cut us off from.

I motioned to the crew, praying all the while that my instincts were leading me right. "Come on. Let's get our man back."

TWENTY-SEVEN

Garrison

FUCKING PATHETIC.

I twisted and jerked at my hands, trying to find any way to maneuver myself out of my bonds in the barn where my captors had left me, but I was getting nowhere. My arms had been extended too far above my head, and the ties were too tight to slip through them. I could lift my legs if I tried hard enough, but the only thing that stood below me was a wobbly barrel. If I knocked it over, I'd be left dangling by my arms, gagged, and unable to yell for help. That'd be even less fun than this.

I paused to take a breather—as well as I could breathe with the sour-tasting rag stuffed in my mouth. The men who'd brought me here had disappeared what felt like ages ago. As far as I knew, I was completely alone in the building.

An ache was spreading through my wrists and down my arms. It brought an awful sense of resignation over me. I had to wait for the crew to find me. I'd always been the most reluctant fighter of the bunch, and now I was the weakest link in another way.

If I'd been better able to fend off the pricks who'd grabbed me—make some kind of break for it—

But no matter how I'd thrashed and struggled, I hadn't been able to stop them from trussing me up like a fucking pig. And now I was being used as bait in what was obviously a trap. I didn't even know what Dess and the guys would be walking into when they came after me.

Part of me almost hoped they wouldn't. Better that I faced the consequences for my incompetence alone than that they all suffered for it too. I was the newest member of the crew—unless you counted Dess—along with being the weakest link. They didn't have to be as loyal to me as they were to each other.

I had the feeling they'd come anyway, though. Dess would insist on trying to rescue me. Julius would see it as a point of honor. Talon went wherever Julius led, and Blaze probably jizzed himself at the thought of solving whatever puzzle our enemies had laid out.

I tested my arms again, but I already knew that situation was hopeless. I was stuck in this position until someone cut me down. The best I could do was take stock of as much of my surroundings as I could in case something about them would prove useful later.

Only a few streaks of muted sunlight drifted through a high window somewhere behind me. I studied the walls of the barn in the dimness. Symbols I didn't recognize but that looked arcane enough to unnerve me marked the wood all around the space.

Was this some kind of cult thing? I thought of the symbol tattooed on the back of Dess's neck that connected her to the organization that had kidnapped her, but none of the carvings looked anything like that teardrop with its diagonal line.

The Maliks had their weird code that Blaze had been trying to decipher. Maybe these connected to their bizarre "legacy" somehow?

I had no idea which of our enemies might have kidnapped me. The men had all worn ski masks to conceal their faces. None of them had said so much as a word to me.

The smell of the musty hay that scattered the floor around me filled my nose. No sounds reached me except the creaking of the rafters. Then several car engines rumbled outside.

I stiffened. The engines cut out somewhere nearby, and it sounded like around a dozen people tramped across the ground in the near distance. But they didn't come my way, and their urgently muttering voices were too quiet or too far away for me to make out any words. Hinges squeaked, and a door thumped shut. Then it was quiet again.

I couldn't tell how long it was before another engine growled up. The car doors slammed, and more feet rasped across the ground. The door hinges squeaked again. A voice pealed out loud enough to reach my ears, instantly recognizable.

"Where is he?"

Dess. And if she was here, the rest of the crew was too.

I closed my eyes against the wave of relief that rushed through me. I shouldn't be *happy*. It was a fucking trap, and they'd walked right into it for me. The thought of Dess getting injured, even killed, because she'd been determined to find me constricted my innards from my throat all the way down to my gut.

Specifically Dess. I didn't want anything to happen to the guys either, but with her—with her it was a sharper pain than I could remember feeling in ages. Maybe not even since the aftermath of my family's car accident, fifteen years ago.

It had been my fault that they'd died, and if I lost Dess because she came for me…

I couldn't think like that. Dess could kick just about anyone's ass, and it wasn't as if the guys were any slouches either. But the fear kept wrenching through my body, and a startling realization dawned on me.

I cared about that woman more than I'd cared about anyone or anything since I'd lost my parents and my brother as a kid. More than I'd thought I was capable of caring for anyone with all the walls I'd put up. I'd been so sure that really connecting with anyone would be dangerous somehow—for me, for them—but it'd happened anyway…

And I was okay with it. It fucking hurt, but I'd take all the agony in the world just to see her walking past the barn door with that little smile of hers and the triumphant gleam in her eyes that'd say she'd kicked even more asses today.

A clattering sound jerked me out of my thoughts. It'd come from somewhere behind me, but when I twisted my head, I couldn't make out the source. The barn held at least one side room. Were some of the men who'd kidnapped me still lurking around, planning a surprise attack to turn the tide?

I grunted against my gag, but I was hardly in a position to shout out a warning. It sounded like the people outside had caught on as it was. The voices rose, sounding closer than before—Dess arguing with her father, other voices I didn't recognize tossing out ridiculous comments.

Then a gunshot reverberated through the air. I flinched, and the next second dozens more shots thundered outside, along with thumps, wordless shouts, and pained noises that set my heart thudding faster.

The crew had better know what they were doing.

Even though I could tell it was hopeless, I strained at my bindings again, trying with all my might to break free. Then the gunfire stopped. I inhaled shakily through my nose, fear clamping chilly hands around my lungs.

The footsteps pounded toward the barn now. My heart leapt to my throat, but an instant later the door flew open to reveal the exact four figures I'd wanted to see on the other side, none of them looking all that worse for wear. Well, other than the fact that Dess appeared to have poured a bucket of blood over herself. From the steadiness of her gaze and her posture, it wasn't hers.

At the sight of me, she let out a little yelp and ran over, the guys rushing with her. Dess hugged my legs while Talon hauled a crate over to stand on so he could slice the ropes that bound my arms. The next thing I knew, I was tumbling fully into Dess's damp embrace.

Someone yanked the gag from my mouth, and the meaty stink of fresh blood flooded my throat as well as my nose. Normally it'd have turned my stomach, but right then it was the perfume of victory. I hugged Dess back, reveling in the strength still radiating from her body and the little noise of relief she made at having me in her arms.

"Are you okay?" she murmured. "They didn't—"

"All they did was tie me up," I said quickly. "Nothing's damaged but my ego."

"And we know you had more than enough of that anyway," Blaze teased, and a ripple of startled but joyful laughter rippled through our group.

"I heard a noise in one of the back rooms," I added with a jolt of memory. "If there's anyone else lurking around…"

Talon strode over to check the rest of the building with his usual ruthless calm. He returned in a moment with a grim expression. "There's no sign of anyone around. I think we got them all."

"Good. We don't want to stick around here too long," Julius said in his typically commanding way. "I don't think there are any neighbors near enough to have heard the shots, but I'd rather not tempt fate by thumbing our noses at it. Let's get cleaned up so we don't *look* like we've just carried out a massacre and then get out of here."

Dess nodded, drawing back enough that I realized the blood was smeared all across her neck and the ends of her hair as well as drenching her shirt. What the hell had *she* been through to get to me?

The set of her mouth told me she didn't want to talk about it—and I got a clear enough story when we marched outside, her arm still wrapped tightly around mine.

The bodies of several people I recognized from the Malik family—and a few I couldn't recognize at all because of bullets they'd taken to their faces—scattered the stretch of grass between the barn and a house I recognized from the photograph Dess had shown us. Right in the middle of them sprawled Dess's father, his throat slit, a puddle of blood seeping into the soil around him. I had no doubt at all who had delivered that killing strike.

I reached down and grasped Dess's hand in a show of solidarity, not minding the prickles of receding numbness that bit into my nerves at the motion. Dess swallowed audibly and squeezed my fingers in return.

"It had to be done," was all she said, and that was all I needed to know.

The door of the house was unlocked. We pushed inside, and Julius motioned Dess upstairs. "You need a whole shower," he told her. "I'll see if I can find some clothes around for you to change into." He and the other guys had a few splatters of gore on them, but nothing compared to her drenching.

Dess glanced at me and made a face. "I made you a mess too. I'm sorry. Come on." Her fingers curled even more firmly around mine as she tugged me toward the bathroom. "Look for something new for Garrison!" she called over her shoulder.

She didn't let go of me until we'd reached the large bathroom with its pearly gray walls, as if she was afraid she'd lose me again along the way. There, she pulled back the shower curtain and sighed happily. "There's plenty of soap." She turned on the shower hot enough for steam to immediately start fogging the air.

When she turned back to me, I still barely noticed the blood coating her skin and shirt. All I could see was *her.* This strong, stunning woman who'd destroyed her own family to save me.

An impulse gripped me that thrilled and frightened me at the same time. My hand moved of its own accord, my thumb swiping a scarlet drop off her temple while my palm lingered against her cheek. Dess's gray eyes turned a bit puzzled as she gazed back at me, maybe wondering if I'd suffered a hidden brain injury.

I needed to say it. She needed to know. If today had proven anything, it was how quickly our circumstances could turn sideways.

Next time I might not be bait. Next time I might be dead. The thought of leaving this life without her knowing how much she meant to me scared me more than being so whole-heartedly genuine.

"I love you," I said, not giving myself another moment to think about the words. I forced my masks to drop in the hopes that she could see all the emotions that ran through me as I spoke the words. That she'd know how true I was being in this moment.

Dess's eyes widened. She placed her hand over mine against her face and leaned into my touch, but her expression was as uncertain as it was appreciative. My gut started to twist with apprehension as she opened her mouth and closed it again, no sound in the room but the hiss of the water.

"I—" she started, and swallowed audibly with a little shake of her head. "I don't know if I can say that back. I feel like I'm still learning how to be a normal person overall. I hardly even know what love is supposed to mean."

My throat tightened, and I had the urge to yank my walls back into place. To toss out a snarky remark that would turn the situation around and make it seem like I'd only been joking. But I held myself firm against it. I felt what I felt, and I would own it no matter how she responded.

"That's okay," I said. "I didn't say it because I expected anything from you. I just wanted you to know how much you matter to me. How much I'd have hated to lose you if something had gone wrong today." A self-deprecating laugh slipped from my lips. "From the moment those pricks grabbed me, that was pretty much all I thought about."

A soft smile curved Dess's mouth. "I can talk about *that*. Maybe I don't know what love will be for me, but you and the rest of the crew are more important to me than anyone else in the world. I'd kill for you. I'd die if I had to go that far to protect you. I wouldn't hesitate for a second."

The honesty of those words rang through her voice and washed away any trepidation I'd felt about my confession. How many people offered that level of devotion when they did say, "I love you"? Her declaration meant more than those three little words would have.

"That's more than enough for me," I said, my voice getting rough, and pulled her into a kiss.

I didn't care that a hint of metallic flavor lingered on her lips or that my fingers slid through still-damp blood as I tucked my hand around her neck. She was *my* woman even if she was the other guys' too, and in that moment I needed to confirm that fact in every possible way.

Our mouths crashed together with a ferocity that grew more heated by the second. Dess gripped my shirt and arched into me with another groan. She was making me even more of a mess than before, but I didn't give a shit about that either. I had her, and that was all that mattered.

I hefted her onto the sink counter and pushed between her legs without breaking the kiss. As I kicked off my shoes, I yanked off hers.

Then, ignoring the rest of our clothing, I whipped her around and stepped over the edge of the bathtub.

Dess growled eagerly as I pinned her up against the tiled wall, nothing supporting her but one of my hands and the pressure of my hips. The steam billowed around us, the warm water pelting us, and our mouths grew slick as we kissed again and again. I couldn't get enough of her.

The blood that had smeared her skin and mine streamed off us into pink trails that wound through the bottom of the bathtub toward the drain. As a path cleared, I moved my lips to the crook of her neck and left nipping kisses down its length.

"We're still dressed," Dess murmured around an amused gasp.

"We weren't getting back into these clothes anyway," I reminded her, my mouth brushing her shoulder as I spoke. "But believe me, I am planning on taking care of that."

Keeping one hand on her thigh, I used the other to tug up her shirt. It took mere seconds to unclasp her bra. Then I was massaging her breasts skin to skin, running my calloused fingers over each of her tender nipples. Dess's head dipped backward as she gasped out her pleasure.

When I'd had my fill—for now—of her gorgeous breasts, I trailed my hand downward and dipped it beneath her waistband. She ground into my finger the moment it brushed her clit, and I smirked against her lips. I curled that finger right inside her and groaned at the slickness waiting for me there.

"So fucking wet for me," I muttered.

A giddy giggle fell from her mouth. "In more than one way."

True. I lowered her for just long enough to strip her soaking shirt right off her and then tug off her pants. She yanked at the buttons on my shirt in turn. As she delved into my jeans next, she ran her hands up and down my rigid erection until I practically went blind with pleasure.

Then she grabbed the bottle of body wash and held it up. "We're still kind of messy. Are you going to wash me?"

Holy fuck, could she have gotten any sexier? The slyly seductive question made me want to shove her back against the wall and thrust into her there and then. But taking her up on her offer would be even more enjoyable in the long run.

I poured a generous amount of soap into my palms and rubbed them together, eyeing the canvas of her body before me. Then I got started, lathering the soap meticulously across the front of her, paying extra close attention to the most important areas. She dipped her head back beneath the water as I massaged all her curves with the floral-scented soap, her breath quickening at my attentions.

"Turn around," I demanded, and she did exactly as I asked, exposing her entire back and ass to me. I gripped her hips and moved her toward the back of the shower until she placed her hands against the wall. Dropping to my knees, I began washing her just as I'd been doing before, running my hands over each calf, and then her thighs. I reached her ass in no time and rubbed the soap into it with rough palms before standing and starting on her back.

She swayed toward me in anticipation, but I continued washing her back as if I didn't notice. My own motions went jerky from lust as she brushed her ass against my jutting cock. I slapped it, and she whimpered encouragingly.

"Put your arms up," I demanded, and she did as I instructed, resting both of her forearms against the wall above her head. "Bend over."

She bent, pushing her ass up toward me. I rinsed the suds from my hands and pressed one between her thighs. She ground into my touch. I couldn't wait any longer.

I lined myself up and plunged into her slick cunt as far as I could go. Dess's welcoming cry pealed through the air, and if the other guys hadn't figured out that we were doing more than washing up in here, they had to know now. The thought only drove me faster.

God, she felt so good around me. I thrust again, placing a hand on one of her hips and using the other to press her into the wall with the force I knew she liked, maybe even needed to fully surrender to the moment. The feeling of her skin against me and her heat around my cock sent me so close to the edge that I feared I'd barrel over it before she could find her own satisfaction.

I slowed my pumping, bringing myself deeper into her rather than rocking faster against her. Dess let out another moan. She was close—almost as close as I was to finishing.

I pulled myself out and gripped her hips, turning her toward me. Then I pushed her back into the shower wall facing me and thrust so deep into her that her eyes went out of focus, her mouth falling open.

Planting my forearms over her head, I trapped her body with mine and pressed my lips against hers. A tremor ran through her, her channel clenching around me. I could feel every inch of her when she came for me, and I pounded into her harder, drawing her release out with each motion.

I couldn't hold on for long. She ran one hand into my hair and scratched her fingernails down my back, and I stiffened with my own release.

My lips remained cemented to hers as we both came down from the frantic fucking. I kissed her again, more gently this time, and took in the emotions whirling in her stormy eyes.

I'd swear I could see my whole life in that pensive, passionate gaze, and I wouldn't have wanted it any other way.

TWENTY-EIGHT

Decima

"RIGHT," Julius said into his phone as Talon drove us back into the city. "Take care of all the bodies and wipe down the house and barn. Leave everything else as is."

I sank into the back seat between Blaze and Garrison, grappling with mixed feelings about our leader's instructions to the local clean-up crew he'd gotten in touch with. On one hand, we didn't want to risk leaving any evidence at all of our involvement once the murders of my family were discovered. But on the other, there was probably evidence of all the murders *they'd* committed on the country property, and the cleaners might erase that too.

Well, they were dead. I wasn't sure their crimes needed to come to light now that their legacy could end here. Surely the few remaining Maliks couldn't keep up such a horrific conspiracy on their own?

We'd just passed the city limits when Blaze's phone pinged. He fished it out and glanced at the screen.

"Huh," he said, and glanced over at us like he had something he wanted to say but wasn't sure the news would be welcome.

I elbowed him. "What is it?"

"Well, not to send us off on another chase after all of today's excitement, but… I did get a partial license plate for the Hunter's bike when he met you this morning. I had it running through the system, and I've just gotten a match from some street-cam footage in downtown DC."

I jerked over to peer at his phone. "Really?" I might have been exhausted from everything we'd been through, but the news set my nerves on high alert all over again.

Blaze motioned to the screen, which showed a man getting off a motorcycle outside what looked like a nightclub from the exterior décor.

I frowned at the image. "That's not the guy I talked to." He was too thin, and when he pulled off his helmet, he was clearly too young as well, not much older than I was.

Talon had tuned into our conversation. "It's not uncommon for an organization to have a pool of vehicles if they don't want any individual member to be easily tracked."

"Or he could have stolen it and returned it," Garrison suggested.

"He's supposed to be law enforcement," I reminded him, but my need to say "supposed" reminded me of how little we still knew about the man who'd reached out to me with his ominous warnings.

"It doesn't make much sense to me," Julius said, his forehead furrowing as he turned in his seat to join the conversation. "How a man with the kind of resources he obviously had and a clear enough idea of what the Maliks were doing couldn't manage to prove it."

Blaze nodded slowly. "You're right. Not to downplay how brilliant we all are, but we put the pieces together in just a few weeks, partly because of the tips he gave us. Sure, Dess had more access to their house, but anyone could have broken in. I haven't matched an entry to the girl he said was his daughter yet, but I've IDed the kids from the last five years, so it's farther back than that. He must have been investigating this for a while."

I rubbed my arms, abruptly chilled. "It's a loose end. I don't like not knowing how he really fits into the whole situation. Why don't we go over to the club and just see what we see? Even if he's not there, maybe we'll find something out about the people he works with if that guy with the bike is a colleague of his. And if not, it wouldn't be a bad thing to have a drink and unwind, right?"

"Here, here," Garrison said in a mildly sardonic voice, and knocked his knuckles against my hand as if offering a toast. I grinned at him, the gleam of his eyes sparking renewed heat in me after the interlude we'd just shared and the emotional declarations made on both sides.

Whatever we found, whatever we faced, the five of us had each other's backs. That was a hell of a lot more than I could say for the "real" family that'd kidnapped Garrison and tried to murder the rest of us today.

By the time we reached the club, the sky had darkened with the setting of the sun. We parked a block away and walked over, scanning the street as we went.

Garrison stopped us a few storefronts shy of the club itself. A few patrons were standing outside, being waved in one by one.

"It doesn't look like a public event," he said. "The bouncers are checking something—looks like some kind of invitation."

Julius took in the club-goers and then us. "I think we can blend in if we find an alternate entrance. They're dressed a little fancier than we are, but nothing that should make us stand out too much."

I nodded. I'd ended up decked out in linen pants and a silky blouse since there hadn't been anything *less* fancy on offer in the Maliks' country home. "We'll just take a quick look around then?" I suggested. "In and out?"

"In and out," he agreed.

Being five mercenaries with plenty of experience penetrating buildings without being noticed, we found a moment to slip through a back door with barely any trouble at all. Inside, we slunk through a hall and out into the main room of the club.

It was a pretty upscale place with a sleek steel bar counter, mahogany tables in the booths, and marble tiles covering the floor. Amber lights fixed along the middle of the ceiling gave the room an atmospheric glow. Servers circulated the room with flutes of champagne, weaving between the crowd of party-goers who were laughing and chattering with each other energetically. The whole event had a celebratory vibe.

It was mostly men, I realized as I studied the crowd. There were women here and there, hanging off the guys' arms in skimpy dresses, but they appeared to be there for the men's entertainment rather than their own. The back of my neck prickled.

"I wonder what they're celebrating," I said.

Garrison tipped his head toward the crowd and snatched a champagne flute off a passing tray. "Let's see if we can find out. Nudge us if you see the Hunter."

I wasn't sure I'd recognize him at a glance. Maybe if I heard him talking. I'd only seen him with his motorcycle helmet on.

I took a glass of my own and held it in front of me as I made my way into the festivities. I tapped the arm of one younger guy I passed and gave him my best innocent smile.

"Hey," I said, pitching my voice over the bass of the music. "What's the big celebration? My date didn't tell me what's up, and now he's gone off somewhere."

The guy chuckled. "Beats me! I'm just here for the babes and the booze."

I forced a laugh and moved on. Maybe one of my fellow women would be more helpful.

I fixed my attention on a redhead who moved from one man to another as confidently as if she owned the place and eased over beside her. When she glanced over at me, I motioned to the room around us. "Crazy party, isn't it? What are we celebrating anyway?"

She shrugged but grinned. "All I know is the boss is very happy about something. That's good for all of us." She flicked her hand toward the bar.

There were several men gathered there, but as soon as my gaze settled on them, I could tell which one had to be in charge. There was a guy with his back to me who stood a few inches taller than the others, the artificial light gleaming off his silver-and-blond hair. All the men around him were facing him, jostling like puppies eager to catch their master's attention.

He pushed himself a little away from the bar, grasping the beer bottle the bartender had passed to him, and my heart skipped a beat.

Those broad shoulders, that posture, and that height—the way he moved… And the blond parts of his hair were the same color as the little girl in the photo, weren't they?

I was abruptly sure that I was looking at the Hunter, fully revealed. He was "boss" over all these people, not just an investigator in a larger organization?

And he was hosting this celebration *now*, right after the family he'd been working against for years had fallen… Could he already know what we'd done? How? Or was it just a coincidence and there was some other special occasion?

I glanced over my shoulder toward the guys, who'd followed me from a discrete distance. At my look, they drew in closer around me.

"The older blond guy by the bar," I said, tilting my head in his direction without looking right at him. "I swear that's the Hunter. And someone just referred to him as the 'boss'—that he set up this party."

Garrison knit his brow, taking in the room again. "If he's got all these people working under him, it makes even less sense that he couldn't tackle the Maliks without getting you involved."

"There's only one person who can explain that," I said. "Let's see if he'll talk to me properly for once. Or maybe we'll overhear something useful."

We moved through the crowd toward the Hunter, who'd turned so that I could make out his profile. He had a craggy face like it was sculpted out of rough granite, with a high forehead and a strong jaw. I etched it into my memory as I pushed my way closer.

Our intentions must have been obvious, because we were only five feet away when another man broke from the Hunter's side and intercepted us. He held up his narrow hand, his close-set eyes flashing. "Now isn't the time to petition the boss with your problems. You can wait until tomorrow, whatever it is."

He spoke with an air of authority—he must have been a close associate of the Hunter's. But he didn't seem inclined to answer any questions himself.

I raised my chin, putting on my best appearance of assurance myself. "We're not petitioning him. He specially invited us, and it'd be rude if we didn't at least say hello."

The man snorted. "I know everyone he'd have 'specially' invited, and I have no idea who you are. Now scurry along and stop with the bullshit. This isn't a game of Candyland."

Behind me, Garrison sucked in a sharp breath. I might not have backed down if his obvious reaction hadn't worried me. I stepped back from the man who'd interrupted us and turned to face the crew.

Garrison grabbed my wrist before I could say anything and dragged me several steps farther away. The other men followed, looking confused. "What's going on?" Julius asked in a low voice.

"That Candyland line," Garrison muttered, his expression tense. "You remember our contact for the household job? He went by the code name Viper? I talked to him a few times after because of their supposedly missing "property," and I'd swear he used almost the exact same phrase a couple of times. It's not the kind of thing you hear all the time, either."

A chill condensed in my gut as a vague memory rose up of the voicemail message he'd played for us one time. I'd been too upset to commit the exact words to memory, but the "Candyland" part did send a tremor of recognition through me.

"The household job," I repeated. "You think that guy is the same one who hired you to slaughter everyone in the household?"

Garrison inclined his head, his mouth flattening. I glanced back toward the man in question, who was now standing right by the Hunter's side, his eyes narrowed as he fended off another possible petitioner.

What were the chances of that? The man who'd approached me about investigating my family was also the boss of the man who'd destroyed my captors' home? And not just that. Like Garrison had said, 'Viper' and his people had wanted to get their hands on me too. We'd had every reason to believe they were behind the attacks on us back in the crew's hometown.

Nausea coiled through my abdomen. This all felt way too wrong.

And then, as my gaze darted through the room, my eyes caught on one of the skimpily dressed women, a young brunette who was perched on an older man's lap. He caught up her hair in his hand and tugged her head toward him, and a dark blotch showed just above her hairline at the back of her neck.

My pulse hiccupped. Unable to think, barely able to *breathe*, I stalked through the room straight to her and lifted her hair higher.

The woman squawked and jerked away from me, and the man started to sputter, but I'd seen enough in that brief glimpse. She had a tattoo imprinted at the back of her skull—a tattoo of a droplet with a line slicing through it diagonally, just like the one on my own neck.

The mark of the organization behind the household. What the hell was going on?

The thumping of my heartbeat had drowned out most of the noise around me, but the commotion I'd caused had drawn other patrons' attention—including the boss's. I glanced up, locked in my daze of shock, to find the Hunter striding toward me.

The crew pulled close around me in a protective formation. The Hunter didn't look remotely fazed. He walked in a straight line, trusting that those around him would dart out of his path if they were in his way—and they did. It was only a matter of seconds before he came to a stop just a couple of feet from where I stood, his expression impenetrable.

Had he stolen that woman from another location like the household, the same way he'd tried to steal me? Or was something even bigger going on here? I was too off-balance to sort through everything I'd just discovered.

The accusation tumbled out of me. "You had them killed. The people who kidnapped me. You were behind the massacre at the household."

He cocked his head slightly to the side as if trying to feign confusion, but his voice came out too steady for me to believe he didn't understand. "I believe you'll find that Damien Malik was responsible for that incident."

What? I might have been bewildered, but I knew that one statement was impossible. My birth father had clearly had no idea whatsoever that I was alive when I'd first approached him. He'd still believed that I'd died in a car crash as a toddler.

As the Hunter stared me down, the understanding sank in that I might be in the middle of a game much vaster than I'd ever suspected. I had no idea where I stood or what the rules were.

And the man in front of me, standing tall amid his crowd of underlings without any sign of concern that I'd found him, could be an even bigger monster than the one I'd just killed.

KILLER REIGN

THE CHAOS CREW #4

EVA CHANCE

ONE

Decima

IF THERE WAS one thing I'd learned in the past few weeks, it was that monsters rarely looked like horrific creatures of the night. No, they could lurk right in front of you within a politician's glossy smile or a mother's desperate hug.

They could stare down at you from an impervious height, all craggy, chiseled face and sleek silver-blond hair, like the man who called himself the Hunter was doing to me right now.

The party carried on around us, music echoing through the nightclub alongside laughter and the clinking of champagne glasses. This celebration was for *him*, the guy who apparently was "boss" to all these people. And the sick sensation in my gut came from my growing suspicion about exactly what they were celebrating.

Just a couple of hours ago, the men of the Chaos Crew and I had murdered most of my birth family. It'd been for a good reason. The Maliks had been torturing and making bloody sacrifices of innocent children for generations. But the man in front of me had wanted to bring about the Maliks' downfall. He'd given me clues and nudged me toward the discoveries I'd made. He somehow seemed to already know it'd happened.

How large a hand had he really had in pushing me toward this end?

But that wasn't even the biggest question looming in my mind. At least one woman in the club had the same bisected teardrop tattoo that I bore on the back of my neck, the one that connected me to the household where I'd been held captive and trained as a deadly assassin for more than twenty years. The Hunter's right-hand man appeared to be the same person who'd hired the Chaos Crew to slaughter everyone else in the household—who'd demanded they return me to him when I hadn't turned up in the mansion.

Too many pieces were colliding all at once, but I couldn't make them fit together into a picture I understood. My mind was spinning so fast it was dizzying me. What the hell was going on?

Moments ago, when I'd accused the Hunter of arranging the massacre at the household, he'd acted as if it was Damien Malik's fault instead. I knew that was bullshit, and I wasn't letting him get away with his non-answer.

I pushed a little closer, my muscles flexing with all the strength my combat training had given me, and glared up at him. His cool stare wasn't going to intimidate me.

"I know you're behind the killings at the household," I said. "How were you connected to them? What did you have against them?"

Why did you want me*?* I thought but couldn't quite bring myself to say.

The Hunter simply shrugged his broad shoulders and started to turn away, as if my questions didn't even warrant his verbal acknowledgment. My teeth gritted. I snatched at his arm before he could dismiss me completely.

"Why were you after the Maliks too? Did they even really kill your daughter, or did you make that up like everything else you've apparently lied about?"

The Hunter's attention snapped back to me with a brief flash of anger in his eyes. He wasn't totally impervious.

That fact lent truth to the words he said next. "I'd never lie about my daughter. We should both be happy with the outcome we got. Go have a drink and enjoy yourself now that you're here. Tonight I intend to celebrate, not submit myself to an interrogation."

He turned his back and strode to the bar. A few toughs who I guessed were bodyguards fell in to flank him in tight formation. They stopped when he did and turned to watch me as if sensing this clash wasn't finished yet.

It definitely wasn't. The Hunter hadn't bothered giving me a single answer. Typical.

I whirled around to face my men, frustration thrumming through me so violently they could probably see it in my stance. "This isn't over," I said to Julius, the leader of the crew.

His jaw was tight, his deep blue eyes coolly fierce. Having *his* substantial frame, which was even taller and brawnier than the Hunter's, standing over me settled my nerves a little rather than rattling them, because I knew this man would do whatever he could for me with his power. He didn't argue, simply nodded and motioned for all of us to pull back to the far end of the bar.

We tucked ourselves into a booth in the back corner, away from the noisiest parts of the party. I kicked at the table legs, my fingers curling toward my palms. "That fucking jackass," I growled.

"Definitely not the most pleasant guy I've met in my life," Garrison remarked with typical snarkiness, swiping his hand through his rumpled blond hair. "We're not bowing out that easy, are we? This prick's got to have every answer you've been looking for since the day we found you."

Julius snorted. "She's not planning on leaving." He lifted his chin toward me. "What do you need us to do?"

The loyalty and dedication he showed in those seven words could have torn my heart into shreds. He didn't ask to hash out my strategy first or for me to explain my reasons. He didn't need to. He knew that this was my mission, and I'd call the right shots. And he intended to be right there with me when I did.

All four of my men did. A sharp-edged smile crossed Garrison's lips, and Blaze shifted in his seat with typical restless eagerness. The hacker's brown eyes gleamed bright beneath his shaggy red hair. Talon sat next to him as a still and solid presence, the amber lights gleaming off his shaved scalp, but I felt the weight of all his attention on me.

The Chaos Crew was ready for action, and right now I was the one directing them.

I was too tangled up about the situation to take much enjoyment out of my newfound authority. "We've got to get the Hunter away from his security," I said. "As long as he can use them as a shield, we're not getting anything from him. If we can drag him out of here, we can interrogate him properly. That's clearly the only way he's going to open his mouth."

Even then, I wasn't betting on cracking him open being an easy process.

Garrison glanced at the crowded room. "With the atmosphere and the amount of drinking going on, we've got more leeway than we might otherwise. It'll still be tough to shake the muscle from their boss."

Blaze grinned. "Sounds like we need a distraction."

I smiled back at him. "That's exactly what I'm thinking. We need to get the Hunter out the back door"—I tipped my head toward the hallway we'd entered through—"and knock him out so we can haul him away without him making a fuss. It'll probably take three of us to manage that. The other two will create a little chaos to catch the bodyguards' attention right when we want to strike. We'll need him near the back hall to begin with so we don't have to drag him far, but if we can manage that… I think we can pull the rest off."

"I know we can," Julius said firmly. "But let's do this right. He might be getting on in years, but he can clearly pack a punch. Talon and I should stay with you for the hauling part. Distractions are more Garrison's area anyway, and I'm sure Blaze can find his own special ways to be useful."

Blaze had pulled out his phone and was tapping away on it. "Already two steps ahead of you."

While he made periodic interjections, the rest of us spent several more minutes going over the finer details of the plan. Then we got up. Garrison and Blaze melded into the crowd in opposite directions, off to handle a few separate tasks before their paths converged. Julius,

Talon, and I slipped into the short hall that led past the restrooms to the back door.

We stood with our backs against the wall, just far enough into the shadows there that we could only see the figures who passed right by the entrance to the hall. We'd know it was time to move when the Hunter entered our sphere of vision.

Talon rested his hand briefly on my shoulder. The man was rarely outright gentle, but there was a tenderness to his touch that brought a lump into my throat. He was saying without needing any words at all how much he supported me.

I'd had to put down the family that should have been mine, but my real family, the one I'd chosen, was right here all around me.

We knew something was happening because of the gradual shift in the sounds of the party. A particularly raucous round of laughter carried through the room. Then there was a chorus of little shrieks as if in dismay. Someone hollered at someone else, angry words that were mostly lost in the music. The celebratory air was starting to fragment.

My men did know how to sow their chaos well.

Right around now, Blaze would be dropping the digital bait and Garrison setting up the real-life evidence to draw the Hunter's curiosity and then his actual self over to this end of the room. I could imagine him weaving through the crowd now, taking measured steps and skimming his gaze over his subjects.

His bodyguards would form a semi-circle around him, but their job was to protect him, after all. If they saw something that made them think there was a threat coming from a different direction, they'd have to divert their focus to deal with that.

My heart thumped in my chest, counting out the seconds. A grunt and a thump reached my ears from closer by than the earlier sounds. "Now, now," the Hunter's voice said. "You'd better get this all sorted out."

"What about *that*?" someone demanded, and the man we were waiting for stepped into view.

Another shriek reverberated through the room at the same moment as someone shouted, "Yahtzee!" That was our cue, our signal that the Hunter's guards were temporarily diverted.

The three of us sprang forward together. I ducked low to sweep my leg against the Hunter's ankles and knock him off his feet. Julius and Talon charged in on either side to yank him back into the hall the second he was off balance. One of them would hit him across the head hard enough to daze him, and then—

But we never got that far.

I swung out my leg, sure, and Julius and Talon lunged—but just as my shin smacked into the Hunter's calf, unexpected figures hurtled at us from both sides. Guns jammed against the men's temples. Another guy tackled me to the floor.

The Hunter had even more bodyguards than we'd realized. This bunch must have been blending with the crowd, watching him from more of a distance so discreetly we hadn't realized they weren't merely more revelers. They were dressed in similar dressy but more relaxed clothes like the other partygoers rather than suits like the official guards.

I lashed out, catching my attacker with an elbow to the throat and a knee to the gut, but even as he flinched with a loosening of his grip, I knew our chance was gone. The Hunter had pulled away from us, the bodyguards we'd identified rushed back to his side. We'd lost all element of surprise.

My attacker tried to pin me again, and I jabbed my fingers into his eyes. While he groaned, I managed to scramble up. Julius was just shoving his opponent backward into the crowd, Talon knocking the gun from the other guy's hand, but the other bodyguards were pressing toward us now.

Shit. We'd have to make a run for it.

My gut sinking, I reached for my men, about to tug them toward the hallway with me when the Hunter let out a low, rolling chuckle. The sound was dark enough to send a cold shiver down my spine.

My gaze jerked to meet his, and instead of the rage I'd expected, I saw only amusement in his expression. And maybe even a gleam of… appreciation?

"Leave them," he said in a commanding tone. His men backed up a step, braced for further orders. I paused, torn between wanting to run to relative safety and my need to see this confrontation out to the end, wherever that might lead me.

The Hunter considered me with his head cocked at a predatory angle that unnerved me even more than his chuckle. He shook his head, still with a small smile playing across his lips.

"Interesting," he said. "You got closer than I'd have expected. Maybe even I underestimated your skills and determination—and your choice in allies."

"I wasn't looking for compliments," I informed him. "I want answers, and I'm going to get them one way or another."

"Hmm." He looked me up and down and rubbed his jaw. "You know, I think I can spare a few minutes to talk after all."

Seriously? My spirits leapt. I motioned to Julius and Talon, not wanting to draw attention to the other two crew members wherever they'd ended up in the crowd. "We're ready when you are."

"Oh, no," the Hunter said. "There's no 'we' in this game. This is between you and me, Decima. I'll talk to you and only you. That's your offer—take it or leave it."

TWO

Decima

HE KNEW MY NAME.

In the first instant after the Hunter had spoken, that thought blotted out everything else in my mind. No one knew the name I currently went by, the name the household had given me, except the members of the household, who were all dead, and the Chaos Crew. And this man.

My questions were multiplying by the second.

I knew this was his one and only offer to talk. The Hunter wouldn't reconsider, and if I turned it down, I had a feeling he'd simply kick us out of the club and call it a day.

But the thought of going off with him alone on his own turf made my skin itch with apprehension.

"You're not taking her alone," Julius said, who'd flanked me. "What makes you think we'll trust you not to kill her the moment you two are alone?"

The Hunter gave him a blandly bored look. "What makes you think I couldn't have had her killed a dozen times over before now if that's what I really wanted?" He shifted his attention back to me. "Unless you don't actually want answers as badly as it appeared. Make your decision. I'd rather not waste more of my time waiting on you."

I felt Talon tense beside me, but I spoke up before either of my men could argue further. In the end, it was my call. "I'll do it. Where do you want to talk?"

Julius adjusted his weight restlessly but kept his opinions to himself. I knew he and the rest of the crew would be watching over me as well as they could from a distance. I didn't think I had to worry about my life in this situation, though. The Hunter had invested a lot of time and energy in developing a connection with me. I might have hated how much he'd manipulated me, but I didn't think he'd have bothered with all that just to off me on a whim.

A small smile crossed the Hunter's lips, chilly rather than warm. "I knew you'd make the right choice. Step into my office."

He made a casual motion with his hand and led me around the bar to a discreet door. Two of his bodyguards followed us into the room on the other side, which did appear to be a pretty typical office. A big wooden desk took up a substantial portion of the space, with a heavy leather chair behind it, a bookcase on one wall and a liquor cabinet with a small private bar area on the other.

The bodyguards stopped by the door as it closed behind us. I couldn't tell whether they were watching to make sure that I didn't escape through it or that no one barged in after us. Maybe both.

The Hunter moved to the bar with the assured air that seemed to come naturally to him. He flicked his hand over his slicked-back hair and started pouring himself a glass of scotch.

"Can I get you anything to drink?" he asked smoothly, as if we were about to broker some high-class business deal rather than discuss his dirty underworld dealings. "You look like you need a shot or two."

I folded my arms over my chest. "I don't drink when I'm working." I sure as hell wasn't going to give him even more of an opportunity to mess with my head.

"Is that what we're doing?" He carried his glass over to his desk and sat behind it. "I thought we were simply going to have a quick chat. The ability to unwind can be just as useful as any other skill."

"The only thing I want to unwind is your role in my life," I said, fighting to keep an impatient edge out of my voice as I stood across from him. "Why were you pushing me to look into the Maliks' history? What's your connection to the group that called themselves 'the household'? How do you know my name?"

The Hunter tsked at me. "Patience, patience. Another important skill." He took a slow sip and smiled with evident satisfaction. Then he set the glass on the desk by his left hand and retrieved a pistol from a drawer at his right. He laid that on the desk too, pointed off to the side but in easy reach. "Just so we're clear that I'm quite capable of defending myself even without my guards, if you had any aspirations."

"I just want answers," I snapped. "Did you plan on giving me any or not? It seems like you're the one wasting *my* time, yet again."

"Oh, I don't think any of the time I've spent on you has been a waste," the Hunter said with an amused glint in his eyes that made me want to poke them right through his skull.

"Then you shouldn't have any trouble explaining it to me."

He leaned back in his chair with a subtle sigh, folding his hands in his lap. I noticed he didn't have any other seating in the room—I guessed that for whatever meetings he normally conducted in here, he purposefully kept the other parties standing to stop them from feeling fully comfortable in his presence. An interesting tactic for a man teasing me about not being able to relax.

Taking another sip, he studied me over the glass of scotch. "You want to know how I'm involved in your life. And whether I've lied to you."

"That'd be a good start."

"Well, as I've already told you, my daughter *was* killed by the Maliks, almost thirty years ago. That's what started us down the path we're essentially at the end of. *They* set those events in motion. I merely paid back what they deserved."

The Hunter had kept up his disinterested cool through the entire conversation so far, but with those words, I caught a ripple of grief and rage in his voice. I didn't think he was lying. He had one sore spot in the death of his child, one small point of weakness, as awful as it'd be to make use of that kind of loss for my own ends.

"She was the blond girl in the picture," I said, and paused. "Did you leave those photos for me to find? You set up that box in my grandmother's name figuring I'd find it?"

He lifted his shoulder in the slightest of shrugs. "Everything I showed you about your family was true. I didn't need to invent any horrors when they'd already committed plenty of perfectly real ones. Yes, I put some of the pieces together for you and pointed you in the right direction to get you to the truth sooner, but I won't apologize for that."

I wasn't sure I could demand that he did. I *was* glad that I'd found out the truth about my birth family before I'd gotten any more enmeshed in their lives. Before I'd cared even more about my place with them and losing what I'd only just regained. I couldn't challenge the Hunter's claims—the Maliks had admitted to their child-torturing cult when I'd confronted them. My dad had been so delusional he honestly believed that killing kids would somehow create supernatural energies to stop other crimes…

It made me queasy just remembering his determined expression. The way he'd talked to me about bringing me into the fold. So convinced of his righteousness despite the horrible things he'd done.

But there were other answers I needed.

"Why wait so long?" I asked. "You said your daughter was killed almost thirty years ago. You've obviously got resources. Why were you only trying to get vengeance now—why did you have me do it? Wouldn't it have been more satisfying to take your revenge with your own hands?"

A different sort of gleam came into the Hunter's eyes, this one predatory enough to make the hairs on the back of my neck stand on end. "Oh, no, there couldn't have been a more perfect vengeance than the one I crafted so carefully. He stole my daughter from me, so I stole his from him. I sculpted her—you—into the perfect killing machine to cut him down, so he'd not only know what it's like to lose a child but to meet his end at her hands."

The nausea in my gut coiled tighter. He'd just added one more piece to the puzzle I was still struggling to fit together. "*You* stole me from him? But—it was the household that took me and trained me. You had them slaughtered."

Another of those barely perceptible shrugs. "They were mine to do with as I pleased. They carried out the task I gave them—to raise you so that you could deliver the most poetic justice possible—and then they sacrificed themselves to point you in the right direction." His gaze hardened for a second. "It was unfortunate that a break in protocol meant you were left to your own devices for some time. But all's well that ends well."

I stared at him. They "sacrificed" themselves? It definitely hadn't looked to me like the people of the household had given themselves up to the slaughter willingly. Anna clearly hadn't had any idea that the attack was part of some master plan in which I'd be spared. She'd let me out of my rooms in an attempt to protect me.

That was the break in protocol he was talking about so coldly, wasn't it? The only act of real caring I'd gotten in my entire time under their—or his?—rule.

I reached to the back of my neck, to the spot I'd seen using a mirror where I'd been tattooed with a shape like a teardrop with a line slicing diagonally through it. "The mark on my neck—there was a woman out there in the club with the same one. She belonged to the household too?"

The Hunter chuckled. "You all belong to me. I sometimes mark my property to ensure it can't be stolen from me."

I bristled automatically. "I don't *belong* to anyone."

"I made you who you are, Decima. If it wasn't for me, you'd have been one of those duplicitous Maliks, spoiled and rotten to the core. You should thank me for making you mine."

My teeth gritted, but I held back any cutting remarks about gratitude while there was so much I still didn't understand.

"So you're saying that the household worked for you. You ordered them to kidnap me and train me. And then you hired hitmen to murder all of them—well, almost all of them." Noelle had survived, who knew for what purpose other than possibly to control me as she'd tried to in vain. "Why would you kill your own people?"

The Hunter spread his hands in front of him. "There were a lot of factors that went into that decision."

I glowered at him. "How about you lay them out for me?"

"My reasons are hardly relevant to our current situation."

"Then why are you hiding them from me?" I demanded. "Or are you ashamed of the choices you made? I thought you were so pleased with your whole plan, and now you don't want to tell me about it?"

One of the guards stirred on his feet at the jab, but the Hunter made a brief gesture that stilled the other man. My pointed remarks seemed to have gotten through to him.

"Your path toward your father and the rest of your family was meant to be much straighter and smoother," he said evenly. "Your main handler was to have released you from your rooms later that night after we were sure the mercenaries were no longer observing, and with her, you'd have discovered evidence pointing to Malik as the instigator of the massacre. You'd have gone after him and destroyed him simply for that."

At the matter-of-factness of his tone, my stomach flipped right over. "You killed dozens of your employees so that I'd believe a lie?"

"You needed the right motivation," the Hunter said. "It'd have been easier if you'd come to it directly. All of my people are willing to die for me if required. I choose my employees carefully. They rarely know when that moment might come."

But I doubted they ever expected it to come from their boss's hand, not while they were seeing through his orders with all the loyalty they could offer. My fingernails dug into my palms. All those people had died—Anna had died—so this monster could play his little game.

"It didn't work," I had to point out. "They all died, and you never got to put on your little charade of framing my father."

The Hunter rubbed his jaw. "A miscalculation, I'll admit. Your escape threw everything out of order, and I had to think on my feet to reach my goals. But we got there in the end, and I think in an even more satisfying way than I originally conceived."

Killing dozens of people—people who'd devoted their lives to carrying out his work—was nothing more than a miscalculation to him? I restrained a shudder.

“None of that matters now,” the Hunter went on, as if oblivious to my revulsion. “Revenge has been served, and we can get down to other business.”

I arched my eyebrows at him. “Other business?” What made him think I’d want anything else to do with him after this?

He inclined his head. “Thanks to me and my resources, you’ve been trained exceptionally well. I don’t think I’d be overstretching to say you may be the best solo assassin in the world. I’ll give you as much credit for that as I give myself.”

Oh, he would, would he? Somehow he got half the credit when I’d done all the training? “Thank you so very much,” I said with a heap of sarcasm.

The Hunter ignored my tone. “Now that I’ve seen the results of my efforts in action, I’m quite pleased with what you’ve become. I’d like you to come onto my payroll officially.”

My jaw nearly dropped right off my face. “You… want me to come work for you?”

“Was some part of my wording unclear? I can offer you anything you could possibly want or need so long as you contract yourself to me and only me. I’m powerful—more powerful than you may realize, Decima. Nothing is beyond my reach. I have extensive connections all around the world. You would never want for another thing again as long as you carry out your work as well as you always have.”

I closed my mouth, but my thoughts kept spinning. Even if the Hunter could offer everything he said, I’d just heard straight from his lips how little consideration he had for his employees. He saw no issue with having them killed if it happened to serve his purposes at any given moment. I doubted he’d see me as any less expendable. One wrong word, one wrong move—or even just happening to make a convenient scapegoat—and I’d be at the wrong end of his gun.

Besides, there was nothing he could give me that I wanted. I *had* everything I wanted: the family I’d made with the men of the Chaos Crew, my freedom, the knowledge of who I was and how I’d come to be that person.

It didn’t seem wise to throw the offer back in this man’s face so blatantly, though, especially when he had a pistol a few inches from his hand right now and two armed men between me and my escape route.

"I don't even know who you really are," I said, hedging. "Obviously your real name isn't 'the Hunter.'"

"It's close enough," the Hunter said. "People at my level don't give out their real names to anyone but family. To everyone else that matters, I'm known as the Blood Hunter."

He flicked a business card across the desk at me, and I found myself staring down at a symbol that was far too familiar. A blood-red droplet sliced through diagonally by an arrow.

The back of my neck itched. *That* was the image tattooed on me. Not a teardrop but a drop of blood; not simply a line but an arrow. The Blood Hunter.

He'd all but written his name onto my body. I wanted to scratch the ink right off my flesh.

"That's my mark," he said, as if I hadn't figured that out. "There are only twelve others as powerful as me in the world, and together we form the Devil's Dozen. We control more than you could imagine—every significant criminal endeavor on this planet. Take me up on my offer, and you'll be an essential player in manipulating global events. You'll be more than you ever thought possible."

This game wasn't about making me happy or giving me what I wanted, though. He wanted to control *me*. But I'd already decided I was never going to be a pawn in anyone's game ever again.

I raised my eyes to meet his gaze steadily. "I appreciate the offer, but I'm not interested. I like the freedom I've gained since I left the household, and I plan to keep it."

It was a polite enough refusal to his offer, but I could see the frustration in his eyes. "I don't know if you understand what you're turning down here."

"I'm perfectly capable of making my own decisions. Even if you haven't generally given me much of a chance to."

The Blood Hunter stood up, shaking his head. "You're going to regret that decision." He flipped over the card to show a phone number printed on the back and pushed it the rest of the way to my end of the desk. “I’ll give you two days to fully think it over. If you change your mind, use that number to contact me. And Decima?”

“Yes?” I said with trepidation, knowing I’d already done all the thinking I needed to.

His cool gaze pierced into me. His voice came out as smooth as ever, but somehow it sounded like a threat all the same.

“Make your final decision wisely.”

THREE

Talon

"I MEAN, in a way this is a good thing," Blaze said, bracing his elbows on the dining table as he tried his best to put a positive spin on the situation. "You found the root of all your problems, and it all comes down to the same guy."

Dess grimaced as she stalked restlessly through the open concept room. She poked at the rocky wall at one end of the living area that served as a reminder that the house we'd borrowed was literally built into the side of a hill. "It's not good at all. I got answers, and the main answer is that this Blood Hunter guy has been controlling me from behind the scenes practically my entire life. How many of my decisions have really been my own? He's had his fingers in everything."

"He hasn't managed to get his hands on you, not since you got free," I felt the need to remind her. I'd seen the tension building in her from the moment we returned here, while she laid out everything the man we'd known as the Hunter had told her.

Some of that tension burst out now with the slam of her first against the top of the sofa. "Small victories. You know what pisses me off the most? He obviously thinks there's no way *we* could ever touch him—that we haven't got a chance at taking him on if we wanted to. He thinks he can get away with everything because of all his power."

I didn't want to think it, but for all we knew, he was right. That thought was clearly weighing on Dess too. I'd never been affected by other people's emotions much before, but my God, I would have done anything in that moment to lift some of the stress and frustration radiating off her.

She'd finally found out the whole truth about her life, and it'd been more horrible than any of us could have guessed.

Julius shook his head, his jaw tight. "All this secret organization bullshit. We'll find out exactly what this asshole is up to and work from there. No one's invincible, fancy aliases or not."

His voice came out as gruffly commanding as usual, but I knew him well enough to recognize that he was nearly as tense as Dess was. The bulky muscles in his arms flexed, and his hands kept shifting in little increments where they were resting on the top of a chair, like they were feeling for something to hold on to.

Just this once, our leader didn't have the situation already in hand. He'd found out that we'd *all* been played by the Blood Hunter. The man had been manipulating our actions at every turn, even when Julius had thought he'd been strategic. It had to be eating at him that he hadn't realized and that he didn't know exactly how to throw off that yoke immediately.

"We don't have to change our plans," he went on. "We were talking about flying home tomorrow. That would give us some distance to regroup—and it'd send him a very clear message about your disinterest in working for him."

Garrison rubbed his finger over his narrow chin. "It'll definitely send a message, but I'm not sure that's the message we *want* to send. It could look to him like we're running scared. And we'll have a harder time investigating his operations from afar."

Dess leaned against the sofa and groaned. "I'd like to go home," she groused, and despite the problem in front of us, something in me lit up at hearing her refer to the crew's apartment as *her* home too.

Blaze lifted his eyebrows. "What, you're not in love with the unique architecture we've been blessed with here?" he teased.

Dess wrinkled her nose at him. It was true that the house's unusual features, being half embedded in rock, gave it natural air conditioning and built-in defenses against attack. But Dess had at least a few reasons beyond homesickness not to appreciate it.

"There are a lot fewer bugs in the apartment." She gave a little shudder of disgust.

"He said he'd give Dess two days to decide," Garrison put in. "What's he going to do after that? Is he really going to accept a 'no,' or will he try to force the issue?"

Blaze frowned. "He obviously doesn't have any issues with using force. All the attacks we've faced since we arrived in the DC area must have been orchestrated by him, right? One more way to cast suspicion on the Maliks while accomplishing his own ends."

Julius's eyes darkened. "He was targeting us rather than Dess. Probably hoping he could take as many of us out of commission as possible so we couldn't influence her decisions away from what *he* wanted."

Dess let out a huff that was almost a growl and pushed herself away from the sofa. "Fucking prick. There's no way in hell I want to work for him, period, but if he hurt any of you… He already has." She glanced around at us, her gray gaze turned stormy. "I don't care if he's the king of the universe. He's been a threat to me since I was a kid and to all of us for the past few months, and that means we need to take him down."

"Hey." Garrison leaned across the table, his normally nonchalant expression turning intent as he tipped his head toward Julius and me. "During one of the attacks, we ran into a guy you two knew. There's our in. He got dragged into this mess by the Blood Hunter somehow. You've got ties to him. We should tug on those and find out what he knows."

It'd been strange, spotting that familiar face in the middle of the fray, aged by fifteen years since we'd last encountered him. I'd almost thought I was wrong until I'd seen Julius's momentarily startled reaction. How a guy we'd trained with back in our military days had ended up on the other side of this conflict would definitely be some kind of crazy story.

"I'm not sure we'll get anywhere with Petrov," Julius said. "I haven't spoken to him in over a decade. His loyalties are clearly elsewhere now."

Garrison rolled his eyes. "You obviously have a history you can lean on. Or we can literally lean on him until he bows under pressure. There are five of us and only one of him. He's the only person with a connection to the Blood Hunter that we know of."

I could tell Julius wasn't happy about this idea either, but I couldn't think of a better option. We did have a little leverage, and we had nowhere else to start.

Julius balked for a few seconds longer and then nodded. "You're right. It's by far our best lead. I'll reach out to him and see what kind of approach we'll need to take."

"When you question him, I want to be there with you," Dess chimed in. "There's plenty I'd like to know about the Blood Hunter's whole set-up, and I've seen and heard more about it than the rest of you, so I'll know the right things to ask."

That point made sense too, but the thought of her in the same room as a known enemy sent an unexpected jolt of ice through my veins. My chest constricted, and suddenly I was back in the nightclub a couple of hours ago, watching her walk away with the Blood Hunter into his office without any way of following, any way of protecting her. My hands clenched at my sides.

Dess was the strongest person I knew. There was no reason for me to worry, let alone panic, about her taking part in a simple interrogation. So why was this emotion clamping around my lungs when I barely ever felt anything at all?

Because of her. Because the more time I spent in her presence, the more I cared, beyond anything I'd thought I was capable of. More than I'd ever cared about anyone, even my brothers-in-arms.

Was this… love? This desperate need to stand by her and watch over her in every way I could? I hadn't ever expected to feel anything that intense, but I couldn't deny that something powerful gripped me whenever I thought about her, whenever I looked at her.

I wasn't sure I liked it. She deserved that much feeling—she more than deserved whatever loyalty and admiration I could offer her. But the pang of emotion that resonated through my heart seemed like a weakness. Was I going to be able to fight to my full ability when I needed to if I couldn't shut away all those impulses and give myself over to cold, unshakeable focus?

But if that was the trade-off, I couldn't think of anyone worthy of making it for other than her.

Dess's hand jerked to her pocket. She pulled out her phone, which I guessed had given a vibrating alert. As she peered at the screen, her expression stiffened. I stepped forward, automatically going into protective mode from that reaction alone.

"What's the matter?" Julius demanded with equally fierce concern.

"It's my mother," Dess said quietly. "She texted me—she knows Damien and the others are dead. She says… she says she knows what we did. Turn on the TV. Channel 6."

Garrison was closest to the TV. He leapt for the remote and switched it on before the rest of us could do more than turn around. Then we all stood there staring at the footage playing on the screen.

Blaze managed to speak first, with a weak sort-of chuckle. "Looks like the clean-up crew didn't get there in time."

"There" was the Maliks' country home. We'd only spent an hour on the property at most, but I instantly recognized the pale building with its broad porch and the barn in the background, where Garrison had been tied up. In front of those structures, police officers milled around while figures carried black-bagged bodies to a coroner's van.

A news reporter came into frame, blatant horror etched across her carefully made-up face. She cleared her throat and launched back into what must have been a continuing spiel.

"The police haven't yet released a definitive statement about the official number of victims or their identities, but there's evidence of a much more devastating crime at play here. We have reason to believe that a group targeting children for horrific ends was operating out of this property. There is speculation that Damien Malik is among the deceased, and that perhaps this was a revenge killing for his role in that group. Clearly, we still need more answers. Tune back in at the top of the hour for the latest information on this case."

Dess's lips had parted with shock. "There wasn't any evidence about the child killings when we were there," she said. "Nothing that was obvious enough that it should have come to light this quickly."

Julius's expression darkened. "The Blood Hunter is playing more games. He wanted his revenge on the Maliks for his daughter, right? Having Damien's daughter murder them wasn't enough. He wanted to ruin their entire legacy. He must have sent people in right after we left to plant the evidence."

Garrison sucked a breath through his teeth. "Or maybe they were already there. *Someone* grabbed me and left me there as bait, and I think we can assume now that it wasn't anyone operating under the Maliks' orders. The Blood Hunter used me to lure you out there for the final showdown."

My eyebrows shot up, but the moment he said it, I could see how much sense that made.

"You're right," Julius said, his voice even tauter than before. "And he must have called in the cops too, to make sure they found everything he wanted them to before our clean-up guys got there."

"Fuck." Dess's fingers tightened around her phone. She stared down at the message for several seconds longer and then shoved the phone into her pocket without replying. I certainly couldn't have offered any suggestions about how to tackle this subject with her sparse remaining family.

"There's nothing I can tell them that would make any difference," she said stiffly, and wandered down the hall to the stairs.

That might have been true, but the fact obviously unnerved her. I didn't like seeing her shaken. How could she not be when her life had been ripped apart and then the pieces shredded into even smaller pieces?

As I moved to follow her, Blaze straightened up too. Seeing me, he held himself back and offered me a respectful nod. Maybe he figured that I spoke little enough that he should give me room to when I was going out of my way to talk.

I found Dess in the bedroom she'd claimed as her own, sprawled on top of the covers, her hands folded over her abdomen. She was staring at the ceiling as if deep in thought, not stirring when I entered, though it was hard to believe she'd missed my entrance. That suspicion was confirmed when I reached the edge of the bed and she spoke, still gazing upward.

"Is this what people mean when they say that life sucks?"

I couldn't stop the corner of my mouth from twitching into a smile. Sinking down onto the bed next to her, I rested my hand on her shin in what I hoped was at least a vaguely comforting gesture. "You're still upset about what you had to do."

"No—yes—I don't know." She scowled at the ceiling. "I don't feel like I had a whole lot of choice. And they were *sick*. Child-murdering psychopaths, any way you slice it. How can I feel bad about ridding the world of them?"

The hint of roughness in her voice suggested that some small part of her did anyway.

I rubbed my fingers gently up to her knee and down to her ankle. "You know I've been there. Killing my parental figures. And they'd actually raised me—and they weren't going around torturing kids."

"But they'd tortured *you*," Dess muttered, her eyes flashing as she must have remembered the story I'd told her during the drive to the country house.

"One is less than many," I said. "But… After I did it, I felt a little guilty. Maybe for a day or two. And then that faded away beneath the knowledge that it'd been for the best, and… that might be the last moment I really felt anything in a long time."

Finally, Dess tipped her head to the side to look at me. "It sounds like not feeling anything would be easier."

I shrugged. "It might be. But given what I know about normal human behavior, somehow I think it's better for you to have your feelings and work through them rather than losing them like I did. It just means you're a better person than your family was, because you do care. You didn't want to hurt them. You did what you had to do, and you should know that you didn't do a single thing wrong, but it makes sense that it was hard."

"Well, I guess if even you think that…" she grumbled, but she sat up and scooted closer to me. When she leaned into me, accepting the slide of my arm around her waist and tucking her head against my shoulder, so much emotion swelled in my chest that it was difficult to imagine I'd really spent years feeling nothing at all.

"Thank you," she murmured. "We'll get through this. Because none of us are alone."

My arm tightened around her as if I could imprint into her body how true that statement was. No matter the cost—no matter the consequences—I'd protect her from the forces working to control her life all over again. I'd see that she got all the justice she deserved for the crimes committed against her.

FOUR

Decima

I HELD myself still and calm in the back of the car as Julius parked by the diner where we'd arranged to meet his old military colleague. Blaze had managed to dig up Petrov's contact information with his usual skill, and he'd agreed to speak with us. Well, with Julius and Talon, but I'd insisted on coming along for additional back-up as well as to help with the questioning.

This guy had been part of one attack on us. He and whatever pricks he was working with wouldn't hurt my men—not again.

Blaze was watching the streets around the café from afar, ready to alert us if he saw any signs that the former soldier had brought company. We'd chosen this spot partly because of the extensive street cam coverage in the area.

The diner was kind of dingy, not unusual for this neighborhood on the fringes of the city. Only one of the rickety patio tables was occupied—by an elderly couple who didn't look like much of a threat. We scanned the nearby buildings cautiously through the car windows.

Julius frowned. "This could be another trap. We reached out to him, but who knows what he did after that. The fact that he was involved in that first ambush means he's not the same man I once knew."

I touched the gun concealed at my side. "If he makes one wrong move, he'll regret it."

Talon gave me a grim look, but I thought I caught a hint of amusement behind his pale eyes. "I think we should try to avoid shooting anyone unless it's definitely necessary. We've got to give him the benefit of the doubt. Why are we here otherwise?"

Julius nodded. "Wary but open to listening. We're ready for whatever he's got in store." He sat up a little straighter. "Here he is."

I recognized the man immediately as he came into view. He was nearly as tall and brawny as Julius, with tattoos that stretched up his neck and over his forearms. The shadows under his sunken eyes suggested he'd been dealing with stress, health issues, or drugs—or all three, for all I knew.

His gaze swept over the street just as ours had a moment ago. He looked as apprehensive as I felt. That reassured me a little. He wasn't trying to put on a show and lull us into a false sense of security. It seemed like he was worried about what *we* might do to him.

Julius checked his phone. "Blaze says the area is still clear. No sign that anyone else has come with him. Let's go."

As we got out of the car, Petrov was just sitting down at one of the larger tables at the opposite end of the patio from the elderly couple. He spotted us immediately, his posture tensing. I kept my own senses on the alert while we approached, watching for any indication that I needed to go on the attack.

The guy stayed rigid in his seat when we sat down across from him. He considered each of us in turn, his gaze settling on Julius. "It's been a long time," he said.

"It has," Julius agreed. "And our initial reunion didn't exactly go how I'd have preferred."

Petrov's mouth curved into a grimace. "That's why you wanted to speak to me. I figured."

Julius folded his arms over his chest. "Someone's been working against us for a while now. It seems you've gotten caught up in their agenda. I'm hoping you have enough respect for me and the work we once did together to tell me what you can about your employer and what the hell is going on. Unless you went into this knowing you'd be trying to take me down."

Petrov shook his head in a jerky motion. "I had no idea I'd be seeing you until I was, well, seeing you. And it wasn't a happy sight. That's why I'm here. But I'm not sure I can tell you anything all that useful. I don't know shit about the man who gave us that mission."

"Tell us everything you do know," I said firmly.

Petrov blinked at me but turned back to Julius at the other man's nod. "Technically I'm still working for the army. A bunch of us got assigned to this special squad, and every now and then we get sent on missions that aren't what we'd typically do. I don't think those orders are coming from within the military. My best guess is that someone's been buying off or otherwise getting some of the higher-ups under their sway."

"What makes you sure it's not internal?" Julius asked.

"Well, we never get any indication of the reason for the missions from the commanding officer who passes on the orders. I don't think he knows either. And like I said, they're not things we'd typically be doing—not within the army's purview."

"Like what?"

"Like what happened the other day," Petrov said. "We've had two other missions like that—we're sent in locally to attack small groups of what appear to be skilled criminals. With you, we were told to go in for the kill if possible, but with the others, they only wanted us to draw blood and then retreat. We were supposed to do that with your crew as well if we couldn't manage to take you down completely."

Julius's deep blue eyes hardened. "And you did. Your guys cut up a couple of ours pretty badly. Why would they want that? Why would they want *only* that when it came to the other groups?"

Good question. I studied Petrov as he formed his answer. His forehead creased with what looked like honest confusion. I wished Garrison had joined us for this meeting too—he was the expert at reading people.

"I don't know that either," Petrov said. "We were instructed to keep all the blood on our blades and turn them in to our command for processing. They put the weapons in lab bags, but I have no idea where they took things from there."

A prickle of apprehension ran down my spine. I rubbed my arm, remembering the scientist we'd had take a sample of *my* blood. That'd been for our own purposes, at least. She'd sequenced my DNA, and we'd then been able to match it to Damien Malik's so I could find my birth family.

"Could they be testing it for something?" I said. "Or—if they planted it at crime scenes, they could frame people for things they didn't do."

"Either of those is possible," Julius agreed, his frown deepening. "I don't like the sounds of it."

Neither did I. We knew the Blood Hunter was behind most of the attacks on the Chaos Crew. Probably he was the figure behind this one too, manipulating the army by whatever means he had at his disposal, which were clearly a lot. It would fit his name to be collecting criminals' blood, wouldn't it? And he always managed to stay several steps ahead of us. It didn't seem like this situation was any different.

What did he have in store for us next now that I'd officially refused his invitation? His two-day deadline had passed last night.

I cleared my throat and focused my attention on Petrov again. "From the missions you've been given with this special group, have you gotten any idea what the person behind them might want other than blood? What their larger agenda could be?" Surely the Blood Hunter hadn't bought or blackmailed his way into control over part of the army just so he could do a little DNA sampling. There had to be easier ways if that was his only goal.

"All I can tell you is that he's got to be someone with a lot of power," Petrov said. "Not anyone I'd want to go head-to-head with, so I wish you luck there."

"Are there other squads like yours that might have been given different missions?" Talon asked.

Petrov splayed his hands in a helpless gesture. "I don't know about that either. They keep us mostly in the dark."

"Why the hell do you go along with all this, then?" I demanded.

"Strange secret missions, attacking people you used to work with now… Why don't you walk away? Or expose them?"

Julius shot me a cautioning glance, but Petrov simply hung his head. "It's a reasonable question," he said, and ran his fingers over his thinning hair. "It's been made clear to me by various methods that my family would be 'punished' if I go against my orders. If it was just me, I'd say fuck it. But when I have no idea how much they'd hurt my wife or my son…"

My stomach twisted with sudden understanding. Of course he wouldn't want to provoke a threat to his family. I should know better than anyone here how hard it was to face the possibility of losing your family—it'd been hell for me even when that family had been made up of psychotic child-torturing lunatics.

I relaxed a little in my chair, letting my hand drift farther from my gun. This guy wasn't the enemy, not really. He was only protecting the people he cared about from an impossible situation. He hadn't wanted to attack us. It said a lot that he'd come here to talk to us at all with the threat to his family hanging over his head.

"I'm sorry for coming at you the other day," Petrov went on, looking at Julius. "I don't think any of us on the squad really likes the position we're in. If we saw a way to get out of it safely, we would."

Julius inclined his head and stretched his arm across the table to shake his former colleague's hand. "I understand. The powers we're up against have put us all in difficult situations. I appreciate you coming to share what you do know with us—I know even that was a risk."

"It was." Petrov shook his hand quickly and stood up. "Which is why I'd better get going. I hope the little I could tell you helps you figure this out. We'd all be grateful to be out from under this asshole's thumb, whoever it is."

He strode off down the street, and I walked with Julius and Talon back to our car. I stayed silent until I'd dropped into my seat.

"Do you believe what he said?" I asked Julius. He'd known the man the longest, so I trusted his judgment over my own.

Julius started the engine and pulled away from the curb. "Considering we didn't have anyone shooting at us, I'd say his story was pretty believable. It wasn't a trap—he really did want to talk to us.

He wouldn't have come to meet us if he didn't want to help us, especially when his family's safety is on the line."

"He sounded like he was being honest to me," Talon put in. "But he didn't know a hell of a lot."

"True." I rubbed my hand over my mouth. "Collecting blood from criminals. Manipulating army commanders. It's got to be the Blood Hunter behind all that, right? Everything else we've been dealing with has come back to him."

"From what we've seen, he definitely has the resources to pull off something like that," Julius said. "The real question is, what's his master plan? Where is he going with this?"

Silence filled the car, undeniably ominous. Whatever the Blood Hunter was up to, it now felt way bigger than just a complicated revenge scheme against a single family. And knowing about his other activities and the global influence he'd claimed to wield, I had trouble imagining it could be anything good.

The ring of Julius's phone broke the quiet. He quickly tapped it, putting it on speaker phone. "What's up?"

Blaze's voice filled the car, and I knew something was wrong the second I heard his tone.

"You need to get back. You won't believe what's on the news now."

FIVE

Decima

WE'D BEEN SITTING on the sofa staring at the TV for a full minute after getting back to the house before any of us spoke.

"You've got to be shitting me," Julius said, staring at the photos of Garrison and Blaze that were showing on the screen while the reporter announced that they were wanted in connection with multiple murders over the past five years thanks to new DNA evidence.

Blaze was pacing back and forth in the room behind us. "This shouldn't even be possible. None of us has DNA on file with any law enforcement agency. I made sure of that. And we've been so careful during our jobs."

"We were careful specifically *because* we knew how easy it is to leave behind a speck of blood or a hair accidentally," Julius pointed out grimly. "We've carried out hundreds of jobs. It's not surprising that we could have missed a trace or two in the chaos somewhere. Those would have been kept on file, and now the Blood Hunter has added profiles for you to the databases."

Garrison's head jerked around from where he'd been glowering at the TV. "What? How the fuck could he do that?"

The three of us who'd gone to meet Petrov exchanged a glance. We hadn't had the opportunity to tell the other men what we'd learned from Julius's former colleague yet.

Julius sighed. "In the ambush in the alleyway, the Blood Hunter instructed the attackers to keep any blood they drew during the attack. Now we know why."

"He wanted DNA he was sure was yours so he could tie you to those murders," I filled in, my stomach twisting. We were lucky he hadn't gotten his hands on samples of all the guys' blood. "But it's not like it matters when they don't even know where you are, right?"

"It matters enough for this to be an effective move on his part," Talon said. "Blaze and Garrison won't be able to go out in public without risking being recognized and having the cops called on them."

"Half of the crew taken out of commission," Garrison muttered. "I can't do my job properly if I can't talk to anyone face to face."

Anger rippled through me on their behalf. "It's because of me. The two-day deadline he gave me has passed—he knows I'm not taking him up on his offer. He told me I'd regret it if I didn't. So now he's punishing you to get to me."

Garrison caught my gaze, his eyes flashing. "It isn't your fault, sweetheart. This shit came directly from that one big asshole."

"Do you think that's why he's done it with the other groups of criminals he had Petrov's squad attack?" I asked. "So he could get them out of the way?"

"Or so he has blackmail material to hold over their heads if he wants something from them," Julius suggested. "Knowing that he *can* set them up for a fall if he decides to."

I didn't particularly like that possibility either. The Blood Hunter was obviously used to getting whatever he wanted, and he was way too fucking good at it.

"They still don't know our names," Talon said with sober satisfaction. "Or our aliases. They can't tie this to your pasts."

Even the pictures were photos that must have been taken from security footage—from the vague bits of background around the guys' faces, it looked like the images were from the Blood Hunter's night club. But they were still way too recognizable.

It took a moment before Talon's comment fully sunk in. I glanced at him. "Aliases?"

Garrison flopped back in his chair. "Really more like our real names now. Who's used the name their parents gave them in the last five years? Anyone?"

My gaze leapt to him and then to the other two men. "The names I know aren't your birth names?"

Julius tipped his head forward in acknowledgment. "We didn't want anyone having access to our birth names that are tied to our public records. And we wanted names that we'd chosen for ourselves, since none of us has fond memories of our formative years. I went with Julius after Julius Caesar. You've got to admire his brilliant military strategy, even if he wasn't so popular with the masses."

Talon shrugged. "I wasn't worried about anything that complicated. I liked the sound of Talon, and it's something brutal that can cut straight to the point."

I could admit it was very fitting for his ruthless killer instincts. I looked to Blaze next. "And I guess yours is because of your hair?"

Blaze managed to laugh, a bit of a sparkle coming into his bright eyes as he winked at me. "And because it reflects my blazing speed zipping through the internet—and the heat I can bring into the bedroom."

Garrison snorted at that proclamation and rubbed his jaw, looking a bit awkward. "I'm a garrison of my own making," he said. "No one gets inside this fortress. All you see is the walls and how I decide to decorate them." He paused, his voice softening just a tad. "Unless I decide to let someone in."

His name was even more fitting than Talon's. I shot him a little smile, hoping he knew how privileged I considered myself to be one of the few people—possibly the only person—he'd ever let those walls down for.

Blaze took a deep breath and went back to his laptop where he'd left it on the dining table. "Do you trust the brothers to let us keep staying here without any problems?" he asked Julius over his shoulder. "Or is this going to be too much heat for them?"

Julius frowned in thought. "I think we're good for now. It doesn't affect them as long as we haven't been connected to the building. But, Garrison, you should put out feelers for alternate accommodations in case we need to move quickly."

Garrison nodded and got on his phone. The news report had switched to another story, so I turned off the TV and stood up. Anger was still churning inside me. "We can't let the Blood Hunter get away with this."

"We won't," Julius said firmly. "He isn't going to win."

But he didn't know that. None of them did. That menace had orchestrated every bad thing that had ever happened to me, and I had a feeling that I didn't even know the half of it.

I turned my attention to Blaze. "Have you found out anything about him? Even something small could make all the difference right now."

Blaze's knee stopped bouncing for a moment as he looked up at me and shook his head sadly. "He's kept a low profile. Such a low profile that there's no talk of him on any forums or dark websites. He's so far underground that it's hard to believe he exists."

"Have you tried tracking the security cameras after the celebration the other night?" I proposed.

"Nothing. There's no sign of him on any cameras across the city. Not a single one has shown his face. To make matters worse, I don't have an image to feed into my recognition app for a quick scan. I snapped some photos with my phone in the club, but I had to be careful about it so his security didn't notice and confiscate the phone, and the best I got was the back of his head. So I've spent hours trying to manually find even a partial face. But there's nothing. If I hadn't seen him with my own eyes, I'd swear he was a ghost."

Garrison kicked the wall beside the TV, and I startled at the loud noise. He stretched his arms over his head as he took a deep breath to calm himself.

"I'm going out to see if I can hear anything on the street. We're not having any luck with any other strategies, and I can't just be a sitting duck," he said.

My pulse stuttered. I gestured to the blank TV screen. "But the news—someone will recognize you—"

He rolled his eyes at me. "I'll put on a disguise. I know how to change how I appear to people—that's one of my main specialties. As is gathering information."

"I'll keep looking in all the ways I know how, but it's hard to find answers when I don't know anything about him other than an alias that doesn't turn up results." Blaze's fingers drummed restlessly on the table beside him.

Julius motioned to Talon. "We'll start packing the weapons and our other supplies just in case we have to make a hasty exit. We need to be ready."

They headed toward the bedrooms where I knew they'd stashed a bunch of the crew's equipment. Blaze was fully immersed in his computer, and Garrison…

Garrison was over by the front door, getting ready to leave.

My heart skittered all over again. I tried to tamp down my nerves, but we'd only just gotten him back a few days ago after the Blood Hunter had kidnapped him to use him as bait in a larger plan. The thought of him being taken again—hurt again—made me want to throw up.

But Garrison needed to feel he was contributing. I knew how much he hated acting like a weak link. How could I prevent him from doing his job—doing everything he could to protect the crew, just like I planned to do?

I went to join him by the door. "Please, just be careful."

He arched an eyebrow at me. "So concerned for my well-being?"

I gave him a light sock to the shoulder. "You know I care about you. Don't be a jerk about it."

Some of his usual cockiness faded from his face. "I'm not trying to be. I'm really not." He touched the side of my face, holding my gaze, his hazel eyes turned green in the shadows. "I'm still not used to this whole 'showing my real emotions' thing. But I'm trying my best, as much as I can. If I revert back to my old snarky self at a bad moment, feel free to give me a good wallop."

That last remark got a brief laugh out of me. I set my hand over his and leaned in to give him a quick peck on the lips. "It's okay. You have no idea how much I appreciate the effort."

The corners of his mouth quirked upward in response. "You have no idea how lucky we are that we found you."

He bent down and reclaimed my lips, his mouth soft but determined as it molded to mine. I hooked my hand around his neck and pressed myself further into him, pouring all my desire for his well-being and safe return to me into the kiss.

He pulled back just slightly, his forehead resting against mine. "You know," he whispered, "it's all going to be all right. Right now it might seem like everything's crazy, but we'll figure this out. We always do."

I nodded, but I couldn't bring myself to verbally respond. I knew he was trying to comfort me, but nobody knew how this mess would end up.

"You're getting bad about hiding *your* emotions, sweetheart," he murmured, tapping the tip of my nose. "It *will* be okay. Imagine all the other things we've survived together. It wouldn't make sense for it all to end here. We've made it this far, and we'll finish this together."

But life wasn't a movie, and there weren't always happy endings.

I forced myself to hide the uncertainty in my eyes as I looked at the utter kindness in his. "I think I like this side of you," I teased.

Garrison moved his hand down my chin and pinched it between his fingers, meeting my lips again. "Well, don't get used to it. I can't be chivalrous and nice forever. I have a reputation to uphold over here."

I tipped back my head with a grin. "Oh, you do?"

"I do indeed. And that includes my reputation for going incognito." He fished in the pockets of the satchel he'd left by the door. In a matter of seconds, he'd transformed his face with a pair of sunglasses, a fake moustache and goatee, and a spiky black wig that hid his blond hair. He spread his arms. "Who's going to think of that guy on the news now?"

"No one," I had to admit, and swatted him. "All right, go out there and do your work."

He pressed one last kiss to my forehead. "I'll be back in no time. Don't waste your time worrying about me."

The old Garrison would have heckled me more about my worries, but I could tell he understood how much I'd been affected by almost losing him so recently. The gentleness of his tone brought a warmth into my chest that was the first real comfort I'd felt today.

As he left the house with a smile on his face, I knew he shouldn't be identified, but what did it matter as long as the Blood Hunter was still out for his head? I'd gotten the entire crew tangled up in this crazy revenge plot, and I needed to find a way to fix it. Things were only getting worse the longer he persisted, and I simply *wouldn't* let the Blood Hunter get to Garrison or any of the others again.

We had to shut him down, and we had to do it quickly… somehow.

SIX

Blaze

I'D USED ALL the possible methods I had trying to track down the Blood Hunter's vulnerabilities. Just one would have been enough. I'd searched government databases, news articles, and archived reports on both the normal and dark web. I even spent hours searching the cameras around the city and the club for any sighting of the Blood Hunter's face, but the man was too fucking careful.

So I was left pacing the rug, hoping that the constant movement would give me an inkling of another idea. That was all I needed: one idea that would bring results.

This was now all-out war against the Blood Hunter. I couldn't leave the *house* without being recognized as a criminal, and that was all because of him. The man knew what he was doing by tearing us apart one piece at a time, and I was the only hope at finding some weak spot we could use to give him a taste of his own medicine.

I had to figure this out for all of our sakes, but most importantly for Dess's.

I looked across the room to where she sat on the sofa, her legs crossed in one of Julius's meditative poses. I could tell that it wasn't working for her as her closed eyelids twitched every few seconds from the thoughts that likely whirled through her mind. After a moment, she readjusted her position… again.

She might act strong, and she could certainly put up a fight whenever one was required, but she needed help tackling this monster. Help I hadn't been able to give her. I'd never cared about anyone as much as I did about her, and yet I couldn't figure out a way to keep her safe. Wasn't that the most important part of caring about someone? Keeping them *alive*?

A heaviness settled in my chest at the thought. It was a pretty familiar sensation these days, no matter how much I tried to suppress the feeling. Even as I walked around the room, I couldn't summon any of my usual light spirits—my ability to get through all the challenges and keep going forward as if nothing could drag me down. Now, I felt like my feet were sticking to the floor, unable to guide me through even half of the upcoming obstacles.

If I couldn't protect Dess from those obstacles, I'd lose her. There would be nothing any of us could do to stop it.

No new inspirations were jostling loose in my head. I was probably thinking *too* hard now, jamming up my creativity with the stress I was putting on myself. I forced my feet to stop and rubbed my forehead, my gaze settling on Dess again.

Even struggling to quiet her own thoughts, she was gorgeous. And not just because of the lovely lines of her face and the dark waves of her hair. So much strength and ferocity emanated off her. She really was the perfect woman for this crew.

For me.

A different feeling swept through me—an unexpected one that made my heart flip over. I wasn't coming up with any new plans. She didn't have any missions to put in motion. Why shouldn't we milk the moment for all the enjoyment we could get out of it? There was no way of knowing when we'd have another chance… *whether* we'd have another chance. I didn't want to spend what might be my last moments in her presence pacing and gritting my teeth.

I didn't have to be miserable, and neither did Dess. Hell, maybe enjoying our time together would be the best way to clear both of our heads and spark an idea that would get us through this disaster.

"I can feel you staring at me," Dess murmured, straightening her shoulders beneath her tank top.

I smiled at her. "That's probably because I am."

"Is there a reason for that?"

She didn't sound irritated, only amused. I cocked my head. "I'm not allowed to stare at a beautiful woman?"

"Someone is laying it on thick."

But finally she opened her eyes and looked over at me. She uncrossed her legs and planted her feet on the floor before her, stretching her arms to the ceiling and twisting her back with a small groan. I couldn't bring myself to look away from the locks of dark hair that tumbled over her shoulders and across her breasts, a few small pieces getting caught down the front of her tank top.

I had no doubt that we could squeeze quite a lot of enjoyment out of whatever time we could get together.

I walked over, holding out my hand. "Come with me?"

My heart had a minor palpitation when she clasped my fingers without a single moment's hesitation, using my weight to pull herself from the sofa. "Sure. What's up?"

I let my lips curl into a slyer smile. "You'll see."

What had I ever done to deserve someone like Dess? She followed me willingly as I led her into the bedroom I'd been using here on the first floor. I'd made the bed, but not particularly well—I always got too impatient to tug all the wrinkles out of the covers. Not that it mattered right now.

I kicked the door shut behind us and didn't give myself one moment to second-guess my decision. Gripping her hips, I shoved her backward into the nearest wall.

Dess's gasp cut off with the force of the impact. Then I was pressing my lips against hers with an intensity that I had never used with her before.

I typically preferred a gentler seduction, gradually drawing out every possible pleasure from an interlude. But I knew that wasn't Dess's style. She liked a little brutality in her foreplay—in the act itself. It might not be my go-to approach, but I could deliver what would excite her the most. Knowing how much she'd appreciate it already had my dick hardening.

Dess's lips moved against mine, a soft sound escaping her throat. I deepened the kiss, prodding her tongue with my own and molding my body to hers. Every hard and soft part of her reacted beneath me, responding to my forcefulness. I knew this was what she liked most, and I'd give it to her. I'd give her everything I could.

When she rocked against me, my cock stiffened even more. I let it press between her legs through our clothes, and a groan spilled out of her. But I hadn't managed to totally turn off that sharp mind of hers.

"What—" she said, her voice cut off between my kisses. "—are you doing?"

The answer was so obvious I could have laughed if I hadn't had better things to do with my mouth. Somehow I'd never let myself speak it out loud before, but I shouldn't let the moment for that slip past me either.

This wasn't just random fucking. It mattered because of how much we both needed it—needed each other. It mattered because of the way I felt about her.

"I love you, Decima," I told her, yanking up her shirt to palm her breast and pressing determined kisses down her neck. "I'm not going to waste any more time leaving that unsaid. I'm going to show you how much I mean it, and then I'll keep proving it in every way I can for as long as we're together."

I felt her tense briefly against me. She tucked her arm around my neck. "Blaze, I—"

"It's okay," I said. "You don't have to say it back. I just want you to know how I feel. And I want to make *you* feel all kinds of other delicious things." I leaned in to whisper into her ear, allowing my breath to trickle down her neck. "I'm going to fuck you so hard you're shaking for more, Dess." My tongue darted out, gathering the lobe of her ear and nibbling it just hard enough that her gasp showed her surprise. "Do you want to know all the things I'm going to do to you?"

I peeled her tank top over her head, and when both her arms lifted, I gripped her delicate wrists and pinned them above her head with one hand, the other lingering between her breasts. Her heart beat viciously against my palm, and I knew that mine was matching it.

"What?" she gasped, struggling to find her words, her pupils dilating with desire just as I'd hoped.

I brought my other hand lower, unfastening the button of her pants with a flick of my fingers. "First," I said, taking control of the encounter in the way that Dess had always done before. I slid her pants low enough that I could mold my hand around her pussy, using my thumb to roll teasing circles at the apex of her thigh. Her hips bucked involuntarily as I drew a short moan from her. "I'm going to finger-fuck you until you come on my hand. Then, I get to taste you."

She quivered at my words, and I proceeded to work my hand between her panties and the skin there—the warm skin that had turned slick with her arousal. I swirled a finger in that proof of her pleasure as I watched her gray eyes roll toward the ceiling in the ecstasy my touch provoked.

As she bucked into my hold, straining to touch me in turn, I tightened my grip on her wrists. "Not yet," I murmured. "This time I'm calling the shots."

No doubt she could have jerked free if she'd really wanted to. I had plenty of physical conditioning under my belt, but nothing compared to her training. Instead, she panted and moaned as I plunged one finger into her, working slow circles around her channel. With the way I was holding her, my grip on her wrists might actually have been a little painful now.

And she liked it.

As I worked her over with one finger and then two, she basked in the sensations, her muscles tensing and loosening with the waves of the pleasure. Had she not reacted with so much blatant interest, I might have been uncomfortable with this pose, but there was no denying the eagerness of her moans.

I listened to the way her gasps intensified as she swayed into my hand and then inserted a third finger, filling her. God, she felt so incredible against my body. I wanted nothing more than to bury myself deep inside of her.

It only took a few more swivels of my hand before she writhed with the impact of her climax. I pressed my lips into hers and devoured all of the cries of pleasure that I wrung from her. Only when they dwindled did I pull back for the next stage of our love-making.

My cock throbbed beneath my pants. I released her hands, eying her with an intensity that drove my fingers to my mouth. I sucked on the dampness there, taking in the sweet taste of her as she watched. Then, when I withdrew them, I pointed to the bed.

"Lie on your stomach," I demanded.

Even after the reactions I'd just witnessed, it surprised me a little that she did exactly as I asked. She walked over to the bed, peeling off her pants and undergarments as she walked. She sprawled out on the covers, revealing the entire expanse of her naked body.

If it was possible, I throbbed even more beneath my pants. I stripped them off in record time as I took slow steps toward her, surveying the gorgeous terrain I had to work with. I gripped the bottom of my shirt and pulled it off in a fluid motion, leaving me standing just as bare behind her as she was before me.

Maybe one day, we would do this again, and we would be able to stay in bed all day long, just the two of us.

I climbed atop the bed—atop her—and began rubbing the heels of my hands against her back.

"What are you going to do next, Blaze?" she asked in a voice that was sweetly sultry. Just like that I was twice as hard all over again.

Ideas sprang into my mind with brutal intensity as I considered what she seemed to like the most. I restrained a groan, deepening the massage on her back. "I'm going to fuck you with my cock this time."

She turned her head and looked up at me with teasing narrowed eyes, biting her bottom lip. "Oh, that's all?"

I reached forward and placed a hand beneath her chin, lifting her head more. I knew the gesture would momentarily take her breath away, and she writhed beneath me as I did it. "Among other things."

I dropped her chin and sat up, lifting her ass in the air and pressing the small of her back down in a delicate arch. Then I ran a finger down her crack to her still pooling arousal. She jerked, and I smiled before rearing back a hand and lightly slapping her ass.

I expected her to gasp, but the moan that escaped her as she bent back into me sent need throbbing through my dick. As I lifted a hand and smacked it down on her ass once more, I aligned myself with her pussy. Her sounds intensified with the greater force I used. She leaned back into me, urging my cock to drive into her, and her gasp turned breathy. "I understand what you meant by 'among other things' now."

I laughed as I did it again, and this time I thrust in time with the slap, gripping her hip with my other hand as I rocked into her. The sweet satisfaction of plunging into her without a barrier—without anything separating us—was unlike anything I'd ever experienced. We'd all gotten tested, and she was on birth control, so protection was no longer necessary, thank all that was holy.

"Harder," she muttered, and I shuddered, spanking her ass just as firmly as before. I wouldn't hurt her, not really. If she wanted me to push this farther, I wasn't sure I could. Instead, I leaned in and gripped a handful of her hair, tugging her head back as I pounded into her heat.

"God," she rasped, her cries of satisfaction filling the room.

I slowed my thrusting, holding myself together as I tightened my grip on her hair. I was too close to the edge, and she deserved everything I could give her. Dropping my head, I trailed my tongue up her spine.

"Fucking harder, Blaze," she cried, and what could I do but oblige? She asked, and so she received. I bucked into her faster again, and just like that she clenched so perfectly around my cock. A ragged noise escaped my lips as I felt her reach her second release, quaking beneath me.

I sped up the tempo of my thrusting even more. With each slam of my hips, her breasts swayed, her mouth slightly agape as she panted through her release. She glanced over her shoulder at me, and the sated expression on her face sent me toppling over. Her eyes brought me more release than thrusting into her ever could.

I spilled myself inside her, tingles racing through every inch of my body. My world exploded around me, and her moans grounded me. I caught my breath above her, breaking eye contact and looking to the ceiling. "Shit," I whispered as I withdrew myself from her and collapsed to the bed beside her.

She lay there, sucking in deep breaths as she stared at the same ceiling. I wondered if we looked at the same spot as we collected ourselves in one another's presence. When I tucked my arm behind her head, she tipped her face toward me, pressing the gentlest of kisses to my shoulder.

My heart swelled, but I couldn't remember another time when my mind had felt so clear—so ready to tackle the problems that surrounded us.

All of the problems.

Something clicked into place. I'd been searching all the usual places I knew—his associates and colleagues, the club's ownership records, and his possible appearances around the city—but there was an entirely different angle that I hadn't even considered. My eyes widened. "I think I know what to do."

Dess looked up at me, but I was already springing to my feet. If this worked, I could find him. This *would* work. It had to.

"You know what to do about what?" Dess asked.

"The Blood Hunter," I said, louder than I'd expected. I tugged on my boxers and hustled for the door in just those. On the threshold, I paused and glanced back at her, the thought of leaving her so soon after having my way with her tugging me in the other direction. I turned back toward her. "It can wait a few minutes."

She laughed without any hint of offense. Of course not. Dess knew to take me at face value. "No," she said, waving me toward the hall. "Go and do your magic."

She didn't have to tell me twice. I rushed to my laptop. I could finally solve our biggest problem if I played this right.

SEVEN

Decima

I'D NEVER THOUGHT I'd come back to my birth family's home. I'd never *wanted* to come back to this horrible place where so many awful acts had been planned and celebrated. But I was running low on options, and if the new thread Blaze was pursuing didn't pan out as well as he hoped, we'd need all the information we could get.

The Maliks had targeted the Blood Hunter years ago, stolen and murdered his daughter. They'd obviously investigated his dealings enough to know about his criminal activities. Now I needed to know what they knew.

I'd left Blaze back at the house where we were staying, working away with the same fervor he'd shown yesterday after our intense bedroom interlude. He exuded excitement, but he hadn't wanted to tell any of us what he was working on until he was sure it'd bear fruit.

The rest of the Chaos Crew had wanted to join me on my expedition, worried about my protection—and in Garrison's case eager to make more progress than his efforts yesterday had accomplished. But I'd insisted that he stay home and Julius and Talon follow only at a very discreet distance. There'd been a lot of reporters circling the Malik home recently, wanting to nab whatever juicy details they could get from the surviving family members. The last thing we needed was even more of the crew exposed.

The only relatives I had left were my grandmother, my mother, and my brother, Carter. None of them were particularly physically fit. They were used to attacking weak opponents—children—not fully trained adults. I'd come armed just in case, and I didn't plan on getting into any compromising situations. If I couldn't handle my own against the three of them, I didn't deserve to survive.

At the other end of the block I got out of the Uber I'd hailed and walked the rest of the way on foot, scanning for news crews. It seemed their interest had dwindled with the shifting news cycle. This early in the morning, before my mother would have been heading off to work, no one was staked out near the house.

Relief rushed through me. *I* wasn't wanted for anything, but I could only imagine what questions they'd have for me as Damien Malik's recently discovered long-lost daughter.

As I walked up to the porch, I took one of my pistols into my hand, holding it at my side where no one would be able to see it from the street. I'd just reached the top of the steps when the front door opened. I froze in place.

My grandmother stepped out, her eyes red-rimmed but as flinty as ever. My mother, Iris, followed her, her wan face tensed and her arms folded tightly over her chest. As they stopped in front of the doorway like a tiny brigade, Carter peered out from behind them. His tawny hair was even messier than usual, his gray gaze as dark as a thunderstorm.

"What are you doing here?" Grandma Ruby demanded.

The chill in her voice made it sound like I was an outsider rather than part of the family. Someone who didn't belong and never would. A week ago, that might have bothered me. Now I knew I didn't want any part in the Maliks' legacy.

I shifted my arm to draw their attention to the weapon I was holding so they knew not to risk making any aggressive moves. "I need answers."

She sputtered. "*You* need answers? We're the ones who've been left bereft. Or have you come to finish the job you started, to slaughter the rest of us too, just as shamelessly as you did your own father."

Despite her words, her voice was less steady than usual, without its typical sass. The loss of her husband, children, and most of her grandchildren had cracked her impervious façade.

"We know it was you," Carter spat out. "You called me and asked about the house on Eckleberry Lane. Dad and everyone else went out there to find out what you wanted, he let us know you showed up with a bunch of strange men, and now they're dead."

Iris drew her chin up. "Was this your plan all along? Are you working with the criminals who kidnapped you—leading us into a trap so they could ruin our lives even more? I thought—I thought my daughter had come back to us, but really you're the same sick scum we've been trying to eradicate."

I didn't see any point in trying to deny my part in the murders, but I wasn't going to confirm my exact role or what I'd become under my former captors' guidance either. Especially not when the accusation set off a flare of fury deep in my chest. "And what do you call people who torture and murder *children*?"

Grandma Ruby glowered at me. "We don't murder anyone. We create a better world."

"Through murder. You massacre innocent children who would have lived long, happy lives, and you torment them before you do it. So don't act like you've got some moral high ground."

Iris's voice came out in a hiss. "Of course we do. We make sacrifices to improve the world, and you—I have no idea why you turned on us like this. We are saviors who make sacrifices to reduce the crime in the world, and you're despicable."

And how much had crime been reduced by their actions? They probably gave themselves credit for any small improvement in the crime rates and assumed any increase was in spite of their efforts, totally wrapped up in their spiritual delusion. I couldn't argue with them when their minds were that warped. It was hopeless.

I wasn't here to argue sense into them anyway. I needed answers, and then I'd leave and pray that I'd never need to speak to them again. They wouldn't be able to get away with hunting down more children now that it was just the three of them and they'd be facing so much more scrutiny.

And I'd be keeping an eye on them from afar for the rest of their lives to ensure that was true.

I shifted my stance, studying each of them in turn. "Believe whatever you want. I'm here to learn about the Blood Hunter."

I wasn't sure what reaction I expected, but I got nothing at all. The three remaining Maliks stared at me blankly.

"The *what*?" Carter said.

I glared right back at them. "The Blood Hunter. The very powerful criminal whose daughter you murdered nearly thirty years ago. I guess you go through so many of them you might not remember well. She was blond, around six years old. I've seen a picture of what you did to her—and so has he. And he's your real enemy in this scenario."

Iris had stiffened. "What are you talking about?"

"He's the one who's the most responsible for what happened out at your country house," I said. "He's been plotting his vengeance for a long, long time. I'm not sure he'll stop until he's taken care of the rest of you too. But I intend to bring *him* to justice, and to do that, I need to know everything you found out about him before you took his daughter."

Ruby's eyes flashed. "You're a thieving, lying murderer, and we have nothing to tell you."

I snorted, unable to stop the laugh that erupted from me. "When did you decide that I was a thief and a liar? What have I stolen or lied about?"

My mother was quick to answer. "All you sinners are the same. I'm sure you lie and steal just as much as you murder. Once one sin is committed, the rest are just as likely."

And what makes you not murderers? You may be murdering with a purpose—a psychotic one—but you're still just as much a killer as I am. I held my tongue, knowing the accusation would bounce right off them.

I chose my words carefully. "Whether I'm a sinner or not, the Blood Hunter is a man with a mission. He's carried out most of it, and you've seen the results plastered all over the news. Do you really want him to go free, or do you want me to do what I can to make sure he's no longer a threat to this city?" And who knew how many others besides.

Carter nudged his mother. "We can't help her after what she did."

Iris simply looked at me. "What will you do if we answer your questions?" she asked. "Are you going to use the answers to kill someone else? Is that the kind of justice you're talking about?"

Oh, for fuck's sake. Wasn't that how they dealt out their twisted version of justice too? At least killing the Blood Hunter would end his reign of terror. What they'd done to his daughter had only made things worse.

"Does it matter?" I asked through gritted teeth.

"We're not going to facilitate you killing someone."

I held myself back from rolling my eyes. "My main goal is to make sure *he* doesn't kill anyone else. I'm going to be preventing murders. Isn't that what your holy mission is all about? Wouldn't you be defying your legacy if you *don't* help me stop him?"

All three of them remained silent other than Carter grumbling wordlessly under his breath. My jaw clenched. "Fine. If you'd rather 'facilitate' him organizing all kinds of crimes across the country…"

I turned on my heel and started walking down the steps. Silence followed me long enough that I wondered if they'd stop me, but just as I reached the bottom step, Iris's voice stopped me.

"I think I remember the girl you're talking about," she said. "She was the sacrifice in one of the first of the rituals I was involved with after I came into the family."

"Iris," Ruby said in exasperation, but Iris held up her hand to quiet her mother-in-law.

"Okay," I said, peering up at her. "What did you see him doing? Who was he associating with? I need to know everything you do about his past crimes."

Her mouth slanted at a pained angle. "Unfortunately, there isn't much I can tell you. I had no idea he was powerful enough to arrange anything like what you're talking about. We'd simply seen him interacting with a few of the gangs in DC, smaller operations, and we found out he had a young daughter… He seemed like an ideal target."

I blinked at her. "You thought he was just a petty criminal.

Someone who didn't have much clout." A wave of queasiness washed over me.

That approach made their legacy even worse. They didn't try to take on the biggest, baddest criminals. They purposefully targeted low-level perps, no doubt because it was easier to attack their families without any backlash. But they had no idea why those criminals had gotten into that kind of life. Someone at that level might simply be desperate and see no other choice, not like the real overlords of the underground who reveled in hurting those who got in their way.

Maybe I could still get something useful out of this conversation. "Which gangs was he working with?" I demanded.

"I don't remember," Iris admitted weakly. "It was so long ago, and I wasn't involved in gathering the information. We don't keep records, of course, because there can't be a trail..."

"Damien suspected," Ruby said abruptly.

All our gazes shot to her. "Suspected what?" I asked. "That the Blood Hunter was more important than he looked?"

My grandmother pursed her lips. "I don't know if he connected his concerns to that particular ritual, but—I think he was worried that your supposed death had something to do with our mission. And after you came back, he spent some time mulling over our past targets. He must have realized your kidnapping could have been revenge."

"Did he say anything else about that? Had he done any more investigating?"

She shook her head. "He didn't share his thoughts with me. A mother can simply tell. And now he can't share anything, because you wrenched him from us and this world." Her eyes burned with anger again.

My hopes deflated. This visit had been a total waste of my time. The Maliks had set this whole horrible situation in motion, and they'd had no clue the whole time.

"All right," I said. "Then we're done here."

"That's it?" Ruby sputtered before I could turn to go. "You killed our family and then came to ask questions about some lowlife. You're not even decent enough to apologize for what you've done?"

Apologize?

A laugh built in my throat—a vicious one that I knew would cause more trouble than it was worth if I released it. So I held it in and gave them my darkest smile—a smile that showed exactly who they dealt with and what I thought of them. I was entirely Dess with this smile, not the sweet Rachel they'd believed me to be.

"Let me make myself clear," I said, quietly but firmly. "I don't want to kill you any more than I wanted to the others. But you need to understand one thing. I will put a total end to what's left of your family and your legacy if you try to hurt me or any more children ever again. This is your second chance. Keep your hands clean, or you'll be the ones I'm bringing to justice next."

I didn't give them a chance to respond, just spun around and stalked away. My job was done, and I wouldn't be back unless they gave me no choice.

As I headed down the street, a reporter leapt out of a van that'd just pulled up to the curb. "Rachel Malik," she said breathlessly, waving a microphone in my face as her cameraman fumbled with his equipment. "Do you have a moment to speak? What are your thoughts on the recent discoveries about your father and the rest of your birth family?"

Oh, I had some thoughts. I swallowed most of them down as I met her eyes, but I couldn't force myself to stay totally silent.

"What the Maliks have done is horrifying. That man will never be my father."

I strode away at a quicker pace, ignoring the reporter's shout after me. I'd said all I needed to.

The crew was the only real family I'd ever had, and I was okay with that. But I needed to get us out of this mess before the Blood Hunter destroyed them too.

EIGHT

Decima

THE RENTAL CAR rumbled as we drove deeper into the town a couple of hours from our usual home base near DC. Only a few lights still beamed into the night from windows on the buildings we passed.

Blaze pointed to a street up ahead. "Turn left there. Then three streets down, take another left on Elm."

Julius followed his directions without complaint, like he had since Blaze had first started us on this quest. Garrison stretched out his legs where he was sitting next to me in the back seat.

"Are you planning on finally telling us exactly where we're going?" he asked in his usual snarky tone.

"We're almost there," Blaze said.

Garrison took a deep breath in a rare show of self-control. I'd seen how frequently he and the hacker fell into squabbling, especially during extended trips like this one. "And where is *there*? What are we looking at in this place?"

Blaze tore his gaze away from the map on his phone, looking first at Julius. "You'll see an old theatre in about a mile. Park across the street." Then he glanced back at Garrison. "A theatre," he repeated slowly, as if Garrison wouldn't have understood him when he said it to Julius.

Garrison narrowed his eyes. "No shit, Sherlock. Why are we going to a theatre? I'm assuming it's not to watch a show."

Blaze smirked at Garrison. "Finally, you figured out the important question."

"Finally, you're getting your head out of your ass long enough to tell your *crew* what you've been working on for four days straight."

Julius let out a huff and laid down the law in a firm tone. "What did you find, Blaze? We should know what we're getting into."

"Of course," Blaze said, a little chagrinned now that the boss had stepped in. "I just figured it'd be easier to explain when we can see the place." He motioned vaguely to the windshield. "This theater is the site of a top-secret event tonight, one I'm convinced is connected to the Blood Hunter's shady business activities. He might even be there."

I sat up straighter between Garrison and Talon, who'd been sitting silently, taking the conversation in. "How did you find it? I thought you hadn't been able to dig up any leads."

Blaze grinned. "I realized I was looking at the problem from the wrong angle. I was focused on the Blood Hunter himself and the people he works with, but that's exactly what he'd expect—where he'll have taken the most steps to cover up any evidence. He doesn't give his victims quite the same consideration."

Talon frowned. "What victims?"

"Well, I don't know for sure. I was just guessing based on Dess's experience. The Blood Hunter tattooed her with his emblem to claim her as his property when he had her kidnapped. There were other women at the party who had the same tattoo. So I'm assuming at least most of them didn't come into his clutches by choice."

My eyebrows jumped up. "You were able to trace some of them?"

"Yep." He waggled his phone. "I told you I managed to take some pictures of the party while we were there. I ran my image recognition search on several of the women. Most of them didn't turn up anything, which is suspicious in itself because regular people would be out on social media and so on. But it doesn't help us. What does help is the two I did find matches for, both of them on the dark web. Both appearing in connection to an event I determined takes place at this theater once a month."

"They work at the event?" I asked, puzzled.

Blaze rubbed his mouth. "I don't think it's quite like that. I couldn't dig up much in the way of details, but I got the impression they were more like… incentives. I don't know exactly what goes on at these get-togethers, but it doesn't seem good. The event's definitely not listed anywhere official. As far as the general public knows, that theater has been shut down for years."

Incentives. My stomach turned. The Blood Hunter obviously had no qualms about stealing people away and using them as he saw fit—look what he'd done to me. But the women at the party hadn't looked like they'd been trained to fight.

No, their purpose had appeared to be much more risqué than that.

Julius parked down the street from the theater, and I peered through the window at the dark building that loomed on the corner ahead of us. No lights at all gleamed in its windows, and only a few cars were parked on the street closer by. But as we watched, a sleek sedan cruised by and stopped just long enough for a thin man in a fitted suit to step out and disappear around back. Then the car drove on. I supposed it'd circle back around to pick him up when the event was over.

I wet my lips. "When we first met, when I was trying to figure out what happened at the household, you told me that they were involved in human trafficking. Was that a way to get under my skin, or did you actually have evidence?"

"That was legit," Julius said. "I also told you we always research our targets before we agree to go through with a job."

Blaze nodded. "The Blood Hunter's people working out of that mansion had been up to a lot of scummy stuff."

A shudder ran down my spine. I wasn't sure I wanted to find out what this building had in store for us, but we couldn't ignore the situation either. I dragged in a breath. "Okay. How are we getting in there to spy on this meeting?"

Blaze pointed toward the roof. "I looked up the blueprints. There's an attic where they used to stash old equipment, enough room for a person to move around up there but not spacious enough that it'd be used to host a gathering. You should be able to get access from there without anyone seeing you. Of course, first you have to get *up* there…"

I gave a heave to pull myself up to the attic's small window, which Talon had already reached and unlocked. As he helped me in, Julius hefted himself after me. I stretched my arms, working the aches of the climb out of them.

"Maybe we shouldn't let Blaze come up with plans like 'scale a three-story building with nothing but your bare hands' when he gets to sit around in the car in the meantime," I muttered.

"He had a point that grappling hooks might have made enough noise to draw attention," Talon said.

Julius grunted as he eased into the room, setting his feet carefully on the floor so as not to make a sound. "Not the most fun I've ever had in my life, necessary as it might be." He tapped his headset. "We're in."

Blaze and Garrison had stayed behind to stand guard in their various ways, Blaze monitoring nearby street cams with his computer and Garrison keeping watch with his eyes, ready to create a diversion if need be. The hacker also hoped to tap into the internet and cellular networks in the area to grab data from the devices of the events' participants. Who knew what he might be able to find out from these people?

Still, I couldn't help envying his cushy seat in the car while we crept through the dark, dusty attic that smelled like mothballs.

Faint music and periodic warbles of a voice filtered through the floor, too muted for me to make out any words. At least it'd have drowned out any small noises we'd made during our climb.

"Let's see," Julius murmured. He prowled through the space, avoiding the stacks of film reels and projection equipment. When he reached a trap door in the floor, he knelt and cautiously eased it up.

The voice got louder. "I hear thirty thousand. Can I get a thirty-five? Thirty-five K, anyone? There, thirty-five thousand. How about forty?"

It was an auction, I realized. But what were they auctioning?

Julius motioned Talon and me over. We slunk down the worn ladder beneath the trap door onto the theater's small balcony.

No one was seated up here. It didn't look like anyone had made use of the three rows of seats around us in ages. The velvet cushions were covered with a thick coat of dust.

Below us, maybe two dozen figures were clustered in the seats at the front of the theater, right by the screen. An image was projected there, smaller than a typical movie, only taking up about a quarter of the space. But I could still make it out just fine from here, and what I saw made my gut knot.

The video playing showed a young woman sitting on a chair, surrounded by concrete walls. She looked uninjured, but her eyes were wide with terror, her limbs posed stiffly around her lingerie-clad frame. Her gaze darted over her surroundings, only occasionally glancing at the camera.

And if we'd had any doubts about the Blood Hunter's involvement in this production, his emblem showed like a logo in one corner of the recording.

Someone in the crowd raised a small sign. "We have forty thousand!" the voice said with a slight crackle of static. It was being projected over speakers—I couldn't see the man who was talking. He must be staying out of view while he carried out this auction.

This auction for the woman in the video. The figures below us were bidding for the right to *own* her. The Blood Hunter was offering her up as merchandise.

I swallowed thickly, more nausea bubbling up inside me. The bidding ended at forty thousand, and the projector screen went briefly blank as someone cued up the next offering. I peered over the railing, but I couldn't see any sign that the women were actually here.

There was nothing we could do to save them, not right now. My hands itched to strangle every rich asshole in the gathering below, but that wouldn't help their victims. We needed to find out more so we could protect the women from their intended fates.

Was the Blood Hunter here? In the darkness, I couldn't see anything other than the vague shapes of the people below. The voice didn't sound like his. It'd probably make more sense if he kept his distance from the most horrendous crimes he orchestrated. Just like he had when he'd sent me after the Maliks.

Julius gripped the railing next to me. His voice came out raw. "This is sick. Fucking disgusting."

And it got even more horrifying. Another video flashed onto the screen, and this one brought bile to the back of my throat.

It was a child. A literal child, no more than thirteen, her immature curves clothed in lingerie just like the woman before her. Her face was frozen in a rigid mask of fright. She clutched the edges of the stool she was perched on, looking ready to faint.

"The bidding on this fine specimen, guaranteed virginal and fully obedient, starts at twenty thousand," the announcer said. "Do I have twenty?"

Oh, God. My jaw clenched so tight my cheeks started to ache. If I got my hands on the prick listing off her selling qualities and price, I'd tear him to pieces. Julius looked as if he was considering the same thing.

"We can't let this happen," I hissed under my breath.

Talon grasped my shoulder. "We can't do anything yet."

Julius nodded, though his expression was taut with anger. "If we charge in there, all we'll do is temporarily break up the show. The Blood Hunter will find other buyers, and he'll know we're on to him. We find out everything we can and let Blaze do his thing too, and then we crush the bastards like the roaches they are."

My fingers curled into my palms, but I knew he was right. Still, as the bidding raced up to seventy-five thousand before the auction finished, the need to take action quivered through every muscle.

The people seated below me were the worst, most vile parts of humanity. Lord only knew what horrible things they'd put these girls and women through. And the Blood Hunter held these "events" every *month*. How many victims had he sold over the years?

The Maliks had done sickening things. I would never think of them as anything other than monsters. But watching this show, a sense of certainty gripped me like never before.

What I'd thought when I'd confronted the Blood Hunter face to face for the first time was true. He was an even bigger monster than those I'd already taken down, and we still didn't know how to topple him.

NINE

Julius

WHEN DESS and I had finished explaining what we'd seen in the theater to Blaze and Garrison while Talon sat in quiet grimness, the following silence reverberated with fury. I couldn't tell whether it was coming from all of us or just me, my own rage was so vast.

I wanted to go back inside and kill every single person in that audience. I wanted to burn down the theatre for ever allowing such a showing to take place.

When I blinked, I saw my sister's fifteen-year-old face, streaked with tears when she'd told me how her teacher had been abusing her. The way she'd flinched when I'd reached to hug her, as if she'd thought I meant to punish her for what'd been done to her instead of offer whatever comfort I could.

I still wished I could tell her what I'd done to the man who'd violated her. How much he'd suffered before I'd let him meet his end.

And then there was Steffie. My first memories of our long-time housekeeper and general assistant had risen up in my mind as well.

When Talon and I had stormed into the gang den where she'd been working, we'd found her scrubbing the bathroom floor in a maid uniform that barely covered anything, bruised and battered by the men who pushed her around as much as exploited her sexually now that she'd gotten older. Her whole life for decades had been acting as a punching bag and sex doll for men she'd then had to clean up after.

The girls and women we'd seen in the auction videos would meet a similar fate. I'd have wondered if Steffie's buyers had purchased her from the Blood Hunter if I hadn't known she didn't have his tattoo on her. It wasn't as if he was the only crime lord out there in the business of human trafficking. But that didn't make what we'd seen any less nauseating.

The Blood Hunter had no doubt put hundreds of women through the same sort of horrors my sister and Steffie had experienced. He was about to send several more to the same fate. Unless we stopped him.

But how the fuck did we do that?

We'd driven half an hour from the theater before parking to have this discussion. Every particle of my body clanged to grab the wheel and tear right back to the building, to paint the faded walls with the blood of the men who'd bid on those women.

I knew what I'd said to Dess was right, though. Slaughtering those perverted assholes wouldn't help anything in the long run. It'd only serve as a warning to the Blood Hunter. When we came for him, we needed the element of surprise. He'd gotten the upper hand on us too many times already.

I had to admit that fact added an almost frantic edge to my anger, an off-balance sensation I'd rarely experienced before. For most of the Chaos Crew's existence, I'd handled every problem thrown at us with careful planning and meticulous strategy. But this man had blown through all my attempts at regaining control of the situation. *He* was in control here, staying multiple steps ahead of us at every turn, taking us by surprise, luring us into traps.

When had I ever felt this over my head before? Not since that day when insurgents had torn up the village I was meant to be protecting during my time in special ops. And then, I'd had a commanding officer who was partly to blame.

I was the commanding officer here. If the crew fell, it'd be on me.

And I didn't have a clue how I was going to ensure their safety, let alone save all those women we'd seen tonight.

"Human trafficking must be a significant part of the Blood Hunter's business dealings," Garrison said, finally breaking the silence. "If he's holding these auctions every month and selling several girls at a time."

Dess rubbed her arms. "And that's just what he's doing near DC. He told me that he has influence all around the world. He could have an auction going someplace or another every *day* for all we know."

My hands clenched in my lap at the thought. "He uses them for himself too," I said, my voice rougher than I liked. "We saw at least a few women with his mark at the night club during his party. He could have dozens of them just on his own staff—if you can call it that when they're essentially slaves."

Dess's hand leapt to the back of her neck, and my heart wrenched. She'd almost been one of those girls. If the Blood Hunter hadn't wanted her for his revenge, if he hadn't decided to mold her into a killer rather than a sex toy, the woman I knew—and adored—today would never have existed. And he'd stolen so much from her even so.

Another surge of anger made my teeth grit.

"Any idea where they were from?" Blaze asked, his eyes glued to his laptop.

I shook my head. "The backgrounds in the videos gave no indication of their location, and their clothes had obviously been picked for show, not what they'd typically have worn. They were a mix of ethnicities: half of the ones we saw were white, a couple Asian, one who looked Latina."

He hummed to himself and tapped away on his keyboard.

"So we have no idea of where they're being kept either?" Garrison asked. "Are they even in the area yet?"

"No way of knowing," Dess said. "The auctioneer said something about the buyers collecting their purchases tomorrow night, so they weren't right there, but otherwise…"

"Okay. If we don't know where they are, is there any way to know where they're going? Could we track any of the buyers?"

"They were very careful entering and leaving the building," Blaze said without looking up. "I wasn't able to find any identifying information via the street cams. I'm still working on the bits and pieces of data transfer I was able to pick up in the area."

Talon shifted in his seat and glanced at me, his expression solemn but otherwise unreadable. "Our main goal was to ensure the Blood Hunter doesn't compromise us or hurt Dess any more than he already has. Is this the best area of focus for that?"

He didn't sound as if he were saying it wasn't, only that he wanted me to clarify my position. Which made sense, since I was still the crew's leader, as much as I felt like going batshit crazy in a lone wolf sort of way right now.

Those emotions gave me my answer, even though I still felt unsteady. I was sure of this one thing.

"This isn't just about protecting the crew anymore," I said. "We want to do that, yes, but at this point, I think we need to consider this a job we're hiring ourselves for. It doesn't matter if no one is paying us to destroy this asshole. We're among the few who know what he's doing. We have a responsibility to take him down. And that'll solve our problems with him too."

To my relief, the rest of my crew nodded in agreement. "I'm all for crushing him into a pulp," Dess said tightly. "But where do we start?"

"We have an entry point now." I motioned in the direction of the town we'd just left. "We might not be in a position to outright crush him yet, so we'll interfere with his business interests as much as possible. We need to identify key associates we can eliminate, ways we can intercept the delivery of these girls, anything that'll threaten his reputation and his support network."

Garrison clapped his hands together. "Sounds good to me. But we still need a name or a place if we're going to do that."

"I'm working on it," Blaze mumbled, typing even faster. Then he let out a little whoop. "And I've got it! Thank fuck." He shot a triumphant look at Garrison. "Oh ye of little faith."

As Garrison snorted, I snapped my fingers to bring their attention back to the matter at hand. "What have you got, Blaze? What do we have to work with?"

His gaze shifted to me, a grin stretching across his face. "I can't help you with the names of the people—everything's encoded with aliases, just like we work. But I can give you a place. I caught a transmission that includes the address of a private airfield not too far from here with instructions for a 'pick-up' tomorrow night."

Dess inhaled sharply. "That's where they're handing off the girls."

Blaze nodded. "I think so, probably after bringing them in on a private cargo flight. I haven't been able to find an exact time or flight number, but knowing the airfield is enough for me to narrow it down. I'll keep monitoring activity there, and we can get in place tomorrow night to be ready to dive in and raise hell as soon as they arrive."

"It doesn't seem likely that the Blood Hunter himself would show up for the hand-off, does it?" Dess said.

Garrison shook his head. "No, he's trying not to get too mired in his own shit. But we can take down a few of his trusted associates and draw police attention to his trafficking operations. It'll definitely be a blow."

"It will," I said, but my heart still felt heavy. It *was* a start, and it was the first concrete trail we'd found that could lead us to striking down the Blood Hunter in the end. But with the images of the women he'd sold lingering in the back of my mind and the four people who meant more than anything to me around me, I couldn't help feeling that it wasn't even close to good enough.

TEN

Decima

AN HOUR before Blaze had determined the flight we were targeting was due to arrive, we were already staked out in the darkness around the private airfield. Blaze was still in the car we'd parked on a side road, out of view of the staff parking lot where a couple of small vehicles stood off in the corner under the beams of the sole security lamp. The rest of us had concealed ourselves around the perimeter, weapons ready, senses on the alert.

Like most private landing strips, this one didn't have a whole lot of security, relying on its isolated location to ensure there'd be no witnesses. We'd easily scaled the chain-link fence that surrounded fields around the property, dispatching the one patrolling security guard with a few blows and a syringe full of a sedative. The people who handled the "merchandise" obviously knew what they were a part of, but we had no idea how complicit that man was.

That would be for the police to investigate once we got everything ready for them to storm the place.

One of the two cars in the staff lot must have belonged to him. The other I assumed belonged to the guy who'd been stationed in the airfield's one building, a little cabin near one end of the rectangular runway. Talon had made short work of him and was now lurking in the cabin along with Garrison.

So far there'd been no sign of anyone waiting to pick up the shipment. I knew better than to question Blaze's information, though. In a situation like this, no doubt the people involved would want to linger here for as little time as possible.

It was nearly midnight now, the sky totally black above us other than a speckling of stars. The only substantial light for miles around was the security lamp by the lot. A line of glinting markers outlined the runway, but their glow only reached about a foot around them, barely penetrating the shadows on the ground.

The night had brought a cool edge to the breeze, but if anything I felt overwarm inside my black long-sleeved tee and leggings. My heart was thumping faster than usual, my nerves buzzing. I had the weird sense that I was somehow both here on the ground and up there in that plane, captured and bound and awaiting my terrible fate.

This was the first job I'd ever taken on that involved women like me. Women the Blood Hunter had stolen and used for his own ends. It *could* have been me, if he'd decided to take a very different sort of revenge on the Maliks.

And by freeing the women who'd arrive here tonight, I might be taking a significant step toward fully freeing myself from the Blood Hunter's control. It seemed fitting.

I just hoped we were getting to the girls before he damaged them beyond repair.

Julius stepped closer to me where we were poised by a shed at the opposite end of the parking lot. He had his treasured Beretta in his hand, finger off the trigger but ready for action.

"How are you doing?" he asked quietly, his low voice perfectly clear in the night's stillness.

My pulse hitched just for a second as the thought of the girl I could have been washed over me again. I swallowed thickly, willing my mind calm and focused the way Noelle had taught me.

How awful was it that I still relied on her lessons even after I knew how horribly she'd manipulated me, molding me into her little killer?

Into the Blood Hunter's little killer. But they hadn't been *bad* lessons in terms of survival and doing the job that now felt like a part of me regardless of how I'd come to it.

"This mission is hitting me a little harder than they usually do," I admitted. "I'll be better when all the victims are safe."

Julius nodded. "That makes two of us. And you know, it's okay to be affected by the things we encounter. Some of the crimes we find out about *are* horrifying. I don't want to ever stop recognizing that."

"Yeah," I said, not knowing what else to add, but his words sent a deeper calm through my nerves.

Of course it was okay for me to be angry. Okay for me to be sickened by the man who'd shaped so much of my life. I'd let those emotions fuel me rather than distract me.

Blaze's voice carried through our headsets. "There's a small transport truck heading this way—looks like military issue. I can't one hundred percent confirm that its destination is the airfield, but there isn't much else out here. Get ready. If it continues this way, it should reach us in about five minutes."

My muscles coiled, prepared for action. I tapped the knives strapped to my waist and thighs and adjusted my grip on the pistol I was holding. Talon slipped out of the cabin, Garrison remaining behind in case he needed to intercept communications from the Blood Hunter's people on the ground or in the air.

We heard the rumble of the truck's engine before we saw it. It pulled into the lot and drove to where it'd be closest to the end of the runway, making a three-point turn so it backed into the spot just ten feet from the shed where Julius and I waited.

A couple of men got out of the cab and two more hopped out of the cargo area after raising the back door. They gathered together by the back of the van, exchanging some remarks that had them all chuckling. I heard one say something about the "pretty pieces of ass," and my hackles rose.

Oh, this bunch knew exactly what they were doing here. And soon they'd regret it.

Julius spoke into his headset under his breath. "It's a small group, but we want them all down at the same time so there's no one to sound the alarm to the people on the plane. Talon, can you get in a shot or two from where you are without them seeing you get in position?"

"Roger," Talon replied, his voice sounding distant in my ear. "I've got one of them in my sights right now and I can get another right after."

"Perfect. You take the ones on the south side, and Dess and I will handle the north." Julius glanced at me, and I nodded. "On my command. Three, two, one—*now*."

We sprang around the side of the shed, guns already raised, keeping ourselves angled slightly to the side of the truck so that we wouldn't end up in Talon's line of fire or him in ours. The men were only just starting to turn at the sound of our footsteps when shots rang out through the night.

The Chaos Crew *could* be neat when they weren't purposefully maximizing the gore on a client's request. Julius took down his target with a single bullet to the temple while I caught mine in the back of the head. Talon's gun boomed twice, the other two men crumpling with similar head wounds. Just like that, we'd cleared the slate.

"Get their phones and any other electronic devices they have on them," Blaze said over the headset with evident glee. "I'll have lots of data mining to do tonight!"

"And we're looking forward to hearing the results of it," Julius said dryly.

Talon hustled over, and together the three of us heaved the bodies into the back of the truck where they wouldn't be visible to any incoming vehicles, including the soon-expected plane. Then we patted the men down, pulling phones out of pockets and a small tablet out of one guy's vest. Blaze would have a field day with this.

We were just clambering back out with the devices in a bag when one of the phones started to ring. I froze up, but Julius immediately jerked his arm toward the cabin.

Garrison sprinted over, holding out his hand for the phone. Working with the people we couldn't kill yet was his specialty, after all. I fished the phone out and thrust it into his fingers. He yanked it to his ear, managing to smooth the slight rasp of the exertion out of his voice with impressive control.

"What?" he said, putting on a gruff tone that barely sounded like him at all. Even his stance changed to mimic the new tough-guy persona he was putting on for this performance. He paused and then let out a huff. "That's five minutes later than expected. What's the hold up?"

I raised my eyebrows at Julius, wondering if we should really be hassling the people we were waiting for, but apparently it fit a strategy our commander agreed with. He shot me a flash of a smile.

"Fine, fine," Garrison grumbled. "Yes, it's all clear down here. You're good to land. Just try not to dawdle anymore. We've got places to be."

He hung up, his aggressive façade falling away with the gesture, and grinned at us. "No problem. They'll be here in ten minutes."

Julius motioned to the cabin. "Why don't you take the rest of the phones in there so you've got access to all the communications equipment at once. We don't want to be caught in the lurch if anyone else checks in."

Garrison gave him a jaunty salute and then glanced at me with a wicked gleam in his eyes. Without warning, he swooped in and gave me a quick but firm kiss. Then he was jogging back to the cabin. I could feel his smirk even with his back to me, but I couldn't say the gesture hadn't sent a flare of heat through me that'd melted even more of my uneasiness.

We were halfway through the job. The Blood Hunter had obviously been running this operation for so long without interference that it hadn't occurred to his employees that anything could go quite this wrong. But we didn't know exactly what to expect from the plane's passengers or crew.

"We're going to need to approach the plane with more caution," Julius said as if his thoughts had headed in a similar direction. "We don't want to harm any of the girls while we're dealing with the men who are holding them, and they'll probably come out in a group, making sure the captives are under control."

"And we don't know how many men there'll be," I said.

"We don't." He frowned, considering the situation. "I'll get in position to shoot the pilot and anyone else in the front. Talon, you and Dess switch to blades. Let them start walking the women out, and when you have eyes on all of the targets and know you can reach them, dive in there. Cut them off from the vehicle and take them down as quickly as you can. I'll get in as many shots as I'm able to safely."

His gaze slid to me. "They might try to take one of the girls as a hostage if we can't get to all of the men fast enough. Are you good to maneuver in a situation like that?"

Would I be able to act with a clear enough head to land a killing strike even when a woman's life was on the line in front of me, he meant. I nodded with a jerk of my head. "It'd be my pleasure to show anyone who tries it that they can't get away with using their victims as human shields." I knew every vulnerable spot on the human body, and no person could cover all of them.

"Good." He spoke into the headset again. "Blaze, as soon as you see that the plane's arriving, I want you over here by the truck. We need them to see someone waiting for them so they don't get suspicious as they're disembarking."

"Aye, aye, captain," Blaze said. "That means I'm on my way right now. There's a small cargo plane just getting in position to come in for a landing."

Julius motioned to me and Talon. We darted across the runway to the swath of grass in the middle of its rectangular formation and flattened ourselves in a dip approximately where the back of the plane should end up. Julius ducked back into the thicker shadows behind the shed.

The roar of the plane's engine reached my ears. I spotted its light like a shooting star against the darkened sky, growing as the plane descended. Bracing myself, I tucked away my pistol and pulled out a knife in each hand. Talon already brandished his usual curved blade.

"We've got this," he said abruptly. "They're all going to fall, and we won't let one hair on those girls' heads get hurt."

"Right," I said, a twinge of affection filling my heart. Talon wasn't much for emotions, but he could obviously tell *I* had a lot of feelings about this situation. It meant a lot that he wanted to reassure me.

The plane soared out of the sky. Its wheels thumped against the asphalt with a couple of bumps before it totally connected with the runway. There was a whirring sound as the pilot hit the brakes. Just before the vehicle blocked off our view of the parking lot, I saw Blaze standing in position next to the back of the truck.

Talon and I stayed low as the plane rasped to a halt. "The hatch where they'll come out is on the other side," he murmured to me as our eyes focused on the vehicle in the dim light. "We've got to move."

As we scuttled across the grass and then dashed to the side of the plane, using it for cover, the hatch opened with a creak. We slipped around the tail in time to see three men ushering out a stream of girls and women ranging in age from preteen to twenty-something. The captives' wrists were bound, their mouths gagged. Their postures were slumped and defeated. Several were trembling.

Another man followed in the middle of the pack. We couldn't be sure that was all of them, though. Chances were that at least one would be bringing up the rear.

With my heart thumping louder than their footsteps, I held myself still until two men emerged with no more women behind them. As one reached to close the hatch, Talon and I sprang forward as one being.

Julius fired at the same time, the cracking of glass telling us that he'd hit his mark at the front of the plane. I launched myself at the man by the hatch, slamming one knife into his neck and shoving the doorway the rest of the way closed with my shoulder. We didn't want them having any avenues for escape.

Talon had already ripped his knife through one of the other guards' chests. I flung a smaller blade at a man who charged at me, and it sank straight into his heart. He keeled over.

The women were pressing close together, frightened sounds seeping past their gags. When another shot split the night, a couple of them jerked with shock. One of the remaining guards lunged at a girl who couldn't have been more than twelve, and I hurled myself forward. He'd barely gotten his hand around her neck before I was stabbing my blade into the side of his. His arms went limp, releasing her.

I pushed her out of the way as gently as I could and whipped toward the last of the guards still standing. Talon got there first. He plunged his blade into the man's gut and heaved it upward, carving right through the center of his torso. With a gurgled groan, the man collapsed.

Julius loped over to join us, scanning the runway and the girls huddled together on it. They looked as terrified of us as they had of their captors. My heart sank. I quickly sheathed my knives.

"You're safe now," I said, letting my voice ring out for the first time since we'd arrived here. "You'll never have to deal with men like this again. We're going to get you help. Get you home, if that's where you want to go. Okay?"

I got cautious nods in response. The first woman I reached for still flinched when my hands grazed her face, but when I untied her gag, she sighed, her shoulders sagging in relief. As Talon, Julius, and Blaze helped me free the others, Garrison came into the cabin doorway.

"Let me know when I should make the calls."

As much as I hated the thought of leaving these women alone in the dark, we couldn't take them with us. They'd be in far more danger hanging out with the Chaos Crew than with the proper authorities looking after them and figuring out where they belonged and what could be done for them. I glanced at Julius, who checked the time on his phone.

"Contact the cops now," he said. "The local police, the FBI, the CIA, and the DC task force for trafficking victims, as discussed." The more separate departments we had involved, the less chance there was that anyone could manipulate the investigation or the victims into disappearing.

He turned back to the women. "We have to go, but we'll be keeping an eye on things from a distance. The people who come for you next will want to help you too. We won't let anyone else who'd use you get to you."

"Here." Blaze had brought out the sack of water bottles and prepackaged sandwiches we'd stashed in the car, not knowing how long it'd have been since the trafficked women had gotten anything to eat or drink. They ended up sitting in a cluster on the pavement, gulping water and tearing into the cellophane packages, their stances starting to relax just a little.

Garrison signaled that he'd made the calls. We hurried back to our car, a pang shooting through me at leaving the women behind. But we were still watching over them. We drove a short distance along the lane and then parked there with our lights off, Blaze scanning the radio frequencies and whatever video footage he could access, the rest of us watching the main road to the airfield.

When the first vehicles to arrive were cop cars with lights flashing, I exhaled in a rush. "Everything sounds legit," Blaze reported.

The Blood Hunter hadn't found out that we'd meddled with his operations in time to launch a counterattack. The women were in the hands of the proper authorities now. We'd done everything we could for them.

But we were far from done with the Blood Hunter… and as soon as he found out about this, I had no doubt that he'd be gunning for us even harder.

ELEVEN

Decima

AS LATE AS it was when we made it back to the house, the exhilaration of our victory thrummed through the air too thickly for any of us to think about sleeping just yet. Blaze grabbed a plate of leftover pasta from the fridge and dug in while he started sifting through the data on the devices we'd grabbed from the Blood Hunter's men. Garrison cracked open a beer and joked with Talon.

"They were so utterly unprepared to deal with anyone who isn't already tied up and beaten into submission," he said with a roll of his eyes. "Some henchmen."

Even Talon offered a rare smile. "I'm glad we got the chance to show them what real opposition looks like."

Only Julius remained a solemn presence in the midst of our minor celebration. He stood by the sofa, still and watchful in a way that stopped my spirits from lifting too much.

"Let's not get too proud of ourselves," he said. "We've made one step forward after a lot of setbacks, and we have no idea how the Blood Hunter is going to respond."

"Well, I'm responding right now by enjoying the fact that we screwed him over majorly," Garrison retorted, and took another swig of his beer.

Julius shifted on his feet, and I noticed how his hand had clenched at his side. My stomach twisted. As the man in charge, the risks of any given operation always weighed on him the most, and I'd seen how frustrated he was getting in our quest against the Blood Hunter. But I didn't think it'd do the other guys any good if he took out that frustration on them.

He'd lost a lot of his control over the situation we'd found ourselves in. Would he lose control over his own actions too?

It seemed better to head off that possibility, just in case. Anyway, my own nerves were still jangling as much from worry over the consequences of tonight's raid as from excitement. I could probably use a breather too.

I sidled over to him and brushed my fingers over his arm. "Hey, can we talk for a minute?"

The crew's commander glanced down at me from his substantial height, and I felt a little of the tension come out of his stance just at the thought that I might need his help—that I trusted him to deliver it. "Of course," he said.

I led him over to the bedrooms, choosing my own since I didn't want to impinge on his privacy without an invitation. I pushed the door shut behind us, and Julius peered down at me.

"Is something the matter?" he asked. "I know seeing those girls, relating them to what you went through yourself—it must be uncomfortable."

I let out a huff of breath. "It was, but I'm working through those feelings. That's not what I wanted to talk to you about."

He raised his eyebrows in question, but even that motion didn't disguise the sober shadows that darkened his eyes from their usual deep blue to almost black. "What did you want to talk about then, Dess?"

I prodded his chest lightly with my forefinger. "I was wondering if something's bothering *you*."

Julius's mouth pulled into a grimace. "What makes you think that?"

I arched my eyebrows right back at him. "I've gotten to know you pretty well. You seem to be having trouble appreciating the fact that we finally scored a win against the Blood Hunter tonight. Sure, we've got a long way to go before he's no longer a threat, but don't you deserve to take a little satisfaction in our victories when we have them?"

Julius sighed. Then he sank down on the end of my bed, swiping his hand over his face. Seeing the hint of vulnerability come into his expression when he was so often solidly impervious brought an ache into my heart.

We'd all been through a lot in the past several weeks, and it appeared to be weighing on Julius more than anyone except maybe me.

I sat down next to him, leaning against his well-built form. "You're still the same great leader you always were, you know. None of us were prepared for what we'd find here. I sure as hell wasn't."

He let out a raw chuckle. "I guess the Blood Hunter has done a bit of a number on my head. I keep thinking that no matter what happened tonight, it could all have been part of *his* plans somehow. We could be right under his thumb, doing exactly what he expects of us, and there's nothing we can do to get out."

"I don't really see how that's possible," I said. "I mean, even when he manipulated me into turning on my family, he approached me, he was feeding me information. Blaze had to pull out all the stops to follow the threads to that shipment of girls. It didn't feel like information that'd been planted for us. How could he have known we'd find those small pieces and put them together or respond the way we did? This is the first time we've attacked any of his operations."

"You're right." Julius sighed. "I'll admit it isn't a rational thought. I'm just not used to having the ground I'm standing on feel so shaky. I operate based on certainties and carefully weighed probabilities, and I don't even have the latter now. How am I supposed to see this mission through and make sure all of you get through it alive when I can't see even two steps ahead?"

Oh. Of course he felt responsible for all of us, given his position. But he really shouldn't, not like this.

I nudged him with my shoulder. "We're all in the same position. None of us expects you to be a human shield for the rest of us. I'm sure I can speak for the guys when I say we all know you're doing the best you can to see us through this situation with what we have."

"I should have *more*," he said, his voice roughening.

"But you don't," I said gently, gazing up at him. This massive, powerful man who cared so deeply underneath the menacing exterior. The hard bulges in his arm pressed against mine, warming the most fundamental parts of me. "Sometimes you have to make a gamble with safety and outcomes when it's really important, when you have no other choice. I'd bet the most important things are almost always a gamble."

"I know that. But I built everything I am around controlling situations. My life. My career. My entire personality. It's the way I make sure the right people survive and the people who deserve it suffer. Without that ability…"

I swiveled around to plant myself firmly on his lap so I could meet his gaze more fully. "Without that ability, you're still just as skilled and smart as you've always been," I insisted, resting my hands on the planes of his chest.

Julius's gaze held mine, his hands moving to circle my waist instinctively. Heat tickled through my body with a sharper awareness of the position I'd put myself in, of how closely our bodies were aligned now.

He'd taught me a lot since I'd crossed paths with the Chaos Crew. Maybe there were a few things I could teach him too. Like how to relax into the idea of not being fully in control.

I shoved him backward, abruptly enough that he fell back onto the bed at my push. "What are you doing, Dess?" he asked, but his gaze had flared with desire. His fingers curled into my shirt, no doubt ready to tug me after him, but that wasn't what I had planned here.

I braced my hands against his abdomen and smirked down at him. "I'm going to show you just how fun it can be when you let go of that obsessive need for control. For now, I'm the one giving the orders, and you're going to follow them."

Julius's grasp on my shirt tightened. His internal struggle, the desire to claim me with his usual authority warring with his willingness to accept my declaration, played out on his face. Before he seemed to quite resolve it, I put my hands over his and took charge.

"Take my shirt off," I demanded.

He was only too happy to oblige *that* command. Julius tipped forward to yank my shirt over my head and immediately reached to palm my breasts through my bra. I swatted his hands away.

"Oh, no. I'm calling the shots, remember. Next I want *your* shirt off."

Julius glowered at me, but a lustful light had come into his eyes at the same time. The air of defeat that'd hung over him was fading, replaced by a growing enthusiasm.

He undid the top buttons on his Henley and all but tore it off. In its wake, I smoothed my hands over his bare chest and ground my hips against his groin. My sex pressed into the hardening erection beneath the fly of his jeans, and a gasp escaped my lips in time with his half-swallowed groan.

I pinched one of his nipples and grinned at the sound he made in response. "*Now* you can remove my bra," I instructed him, rocking against him again. My own arousal was building between my thighs at the thrill of having this powerful man responding to my bidding. A flush warmed my cheeks.

Julius must have noticed it. He stroked quick fingers over the side of my face before unclasping my bra and tossing it aside. "What can I do for you now, seductress?" he asked, his voice even lower than usual with unspoken hunger. Maybe it turned him on seeing how much this switch in roles turned *me* on.

I dipped lower, letting my swaying breasts graze his chest. My nipples pebbled at the contact. "You stay right there," I murmured. My lips brushed the side of his neck, the crook of his shoulder, marking increasingly emphatic kisses over his scorching skin.

Julius let out another groan, gripping the bed covers on either side of us as if he needed to hold on to them to stop himself from grabbing me and taking over. "Fuck, Dess," he muttered when I flicked my tongue across his throat.

"Yes, that's the general idea." I eased up and lifted myself enough to tug down my leggings. The muscles in Julius's arms flexed as he held himself back from caressing my thighs. I stroked my fingers along the path I suspected he wished he could follow and traced the line of my panties. "Do you think you can handle helping me remove these without doing anything else until I say so?"

"Whatever you wish," he said in a tone so wry and heated that it sent the flush straight down to my core.

I edged closer, and he dragged the panties down my legs, his gaze fixed on the aching place he'd uncovered. I sank down over him again, opening the fly of his jeans. Julius let his hands come to rest on my hips. When he started to pull me closer against him, I shook my head with a tsking sound and pushed them back onto the covers.

"I'm in charge here," I reminded him, and rubbed my sex against his cock where it strained against the fabric of his boxers.

"God, Dess, let me touch you," Julius said, his composure unraveling.

"I think I can handle that for both of us to start with," I teased, and dipped my hand between my legs. Julius's eyes grew heavy-lidded as he watched me curl a finger right inside my molten core. His breath came out ragged.

Feeling his eyes on me while I stroked my own hand over the most sensitive parts of me where I'd let him go soon enough, I was ready to spontaneously combust. A whimper spilled out of my lungs. Every time I ground into Julius's rigid cock, pumping my hand in time, he bucked upward to meet me. I couldn't help but imagine how it would feel when I finally allowed him to thrust inside me. The utter pleasure of being filled completely…

At the thump of my bedroom door opening, I withdrew my hand and jerked around.

"I got a text from Steffie," Garrison was saying. "It's not urgent, but she wanted to check—"

When he looked up from his phone, he froze on the threshold, taking in our pose, my bare body poised atop Julius. His throat worked.

"Fuck," he whispered with a rasp. "I didn't realize—I can—"

"Stay," I said before he could retreat. His gaze had set off a fresh flare of heat through my body. And why shouldn't he join in? "The more the merrier."

His gaze darted from me to Julius as if he needed the other man's permission as well. I guessed that wasn't surprising. I knew Garrison had insecurities about being the youngest and least established member of the crew, as deep as he liked to bury any vulnerability. He might talk a good game, but he wasn't going to intrude on his boss if he thought it was a situation where he might cause real offense.

To my relief, Julius just smiled. "Get in here and close the door. She's been driving me crazy. Maybe you can pay her back for me."

Garrison's expression relaxed, and he let out a chuckle as he shut the door firmly in his wake. "I'd be more than happy to take on that mission."

I looked at Julius with narrowed eyes. "You're taking control back in whatever way you can," I scoffed. "I should have known."

But Julius's laugh sounded genuine enough that I didn't really mind his minor mutiny. He *had* gotten to let go a little while I'd played with him. And now we could all have our fun.

Garrison had stripped off his clothes to match our state of undress. He stepped closer and rested his hands on my hips. Instinctively, I lifted my ass and pressed myself toward him. One of his hands slid up my waist and around my chest until his fingers gripped my chin, one pressing between my lips. I nipped it, sucking it into my mouth and releasing an intentional moan around it.

I hardly noticed when Julius's hands came up, pulling me atop him with little effort. I ground into his erection and tugged his cock free from his boxers.

Garrison's arm wound around my waist as I sucked his finger. He pulled me up slightly, allowing me to position Julius beneath me before dropping down, taking him into me in a fluid motion. Both of our shuddered breaths filled the room as I absorbed the sensation of the commander's hard shaft filling me. Garrison's lips came down on the side of my neck.

I sucked his finger harder, moving my hips back and forth over Julius. The older man clasped my hips again, but this time I grabbed his wrists and pinned them to his chest, giving him a scolding look.

"Garrison," Julius said in a growl. "Finger her clit."

The arm around my waist tightened, and Garrison trailed his other hand down without hesitation. He teased his fingertips over the spot most essential for my release. I leaned my head back on his shoulder, moving my hips in circles with Julius within me and Garrison drawing every additional bit of pleasure he could from my body.

I'd been planning on showing Julius how it felt to be out of control, but now all I wanted was to lose control myself. I bent my neck until my breath fanned across Garrison's ear, reaching behind me at the same time to grasp his hardened cock.

"I want you in my mouth," I whispered to him.

The arm around my waist rose and tightened, pressing lightly into my lungs as his arousal became obvious in every part of his body. He fingered me faster, and I matched his pace on Julius's cock, bobbing my hips up and down in a flurry of motion. "I want to suck you off until you cum on my chest." My voice was hoarse from the way he held me so tightly and the way that I unraveled at his touch.

I didn't want to wait any longer to taste him. I lifted myself from Julius. Garrison's arm fell away as I turned to face him, I planted myself back in position over Julius in reverse cowgirl style. As Julius thrust into me again, I opened my mouth with a gasp of pleasure.

"Fuck my mouth, Garrison," I begged, dipping low, and he did. He planted himself against my lips, holding my chin as his shaft slid inside. The power I felt in that moment only grew as my release built and eddied, a roiling creature that could only be contained for so long.

I swiveled my tongue around him, and Garrison groaned his pleasure to the ceiling, his grip on my jaw tightening.

Julius's hoarse voice carried through the room. "Pull her hair. She likes that."

Oh, I certainly did. Garrison released my chin and took my hair in an iron grip, tighter than Julius had ever held it. He didn't hold back as he bucked into my mouth, bringing a plethora of eager sounds from my throat.

It was then that Julius finally shuddered beneath my assault, thrusting himself deeper one last time. My release was so close—so damn close that I whimpered when he stopped. But Garrison, bless him, looked at Julius and yanked on my hair even harder. "It's your turn to finger fuck her," he demanded.

Julius did just that, the pulse of his fingertips bringing me right back to the cliff where I'd been hovering. When Garrison thrust into my throat again, I fell over that edge. Tumbled over it with no hope of escape.

I fell and cried my pleasure across his skin. I all but melted as Garrison, too, found his release against my chest.

I sagged over Julius, who rolled us onto our sides. Garrison clambered onto the bed to sandwich me between them. I nestled between their bodies, finally ready to give myself over to sleep with the afterglow reverberating through me.

There was definitely something to be said for giving yourself over to the moment and finding out where it could take you. If only all our endeavors along that line could be as enjoyable as this one.

TWELVE

Garrison

AS IT TURNED OUT, military bases were the furthest thing from impenetrable, especially with the right props. Blaze had tracked the points outside of the usual guard gates to find me a practical entrance, and it was as easy as cruising through it on my borrowed motorcycle and turning off one of the tracked vehicle trails and onto the main road. With a helmet, a set of cammies, and an ID badge our computer guru had doctored for me, I fit right in.

Talon and Julius had explained that though it was technically a marine base, many army guys were stationed here for jobs, and the general's office was in one of the administration buildings, likely tucked behind the offices of a few other higher-ups. I'd impersonated military staff before, but they'd given me plenty of tips to ensure I was prepared to breach the upper echelon.

Blaze had found a variety of interesting information about the Blood Hunter's military corruption in the files he'd found during our airfield takedown. Most interesting was the fact that a general stationed on this base appeared to be one of the crime lord's main contacts. It looked like the prick might be responsible for organizing squads like the one Julius's former colleague was part of.

And now we were going to undermine that connection just as we had the Blood Hunter's slave trade. I was going to get into that office, grab whatever classified files I could put my hands on that we could use as leverage, and get out. Then we'd see whether Mr. Top Brass cared more about the financial benefits the Blood Hunter had offered him or the country he'd sworn to serve.

For the first time in weeks, I felt totally confident about the job ahead. I knew that I could do this. I wasn't the weak link. I'd let down my walls with the people who meant the most to me, and the world hadn't crashed down on my head. With the security generated by my new sense of inner peace, I could tackle anyone. Be anything.

All because I could be myself with Dess.

I rode through the on-base streets that didn't look so different from regular streets in the city I'd left behind a hundred miles distant. The traffic was just as bad as the traffic off-base, and the drivers all seemed normal other than the uniforms. The rank insignia on my own, chosen with care, placed me just a couple of levels below the general himself in authority. No regular soldier was going to question me.

Keeping up my persona of domineering authority, I pulled into one of the admissions lots next to the two-story building that should have housed the general's office. I removed my helmet carefully so as not to dislodge my wig of military-short ruddy hair, nudged my prescription-less glasses up my nose, and ran my hand over the fake beard I'd applied before I'd left.

No one was going to connect me to the pictures of blond, beardless, glasses-less Garrison that had been plastered all over the news.

It was early enough that many people were en route to work, but I was just in time for the six-thirty PT accountability, which was what I'd been hoping for. Fewer people to run into while inhabiting my fake identity.

I approached the first door, gathering myself with a deep breath. For the next hour, I was Colonel Daniel Firth, I reminded myself. I was confident and wouldn't bow to anyone lower than me. I wouldn't accept questions from anyone either. I couldn't use the device on the door that would prompt it to open, but that didn't matter. All I needed to do was time my entrance just right.

Ah ha. Through the polished windows, I spotted a young man just approaching on the other side of the door and picked up my pace on my way up the ramp. Just as I reached it, making a motion as if reaching for a key card in my pocket, the door flew open.

The soldier looked at me, his eyes catching on my insignia. "Colonel," he said with a bob of his head, holding the door open for me.

I offered him a brisk nod in return, no smile, barely any eye contact. Important business to attend to, no time to bother with lowly cannon fodder.

The lobby to the area was nearly empty, though I knew it would fill quickly when accountability had been taken. I nodded at the receptionist as well, and she gave me a quick lift of her hand, allowing me to continue on my way. It was all in the confidence of my walk. I acted like I knew where I was going, so she allowed me to pass without question, though Julius had warned me that some of the receptionists were more rigid about asking everyone for their IDs and proposed location.

This woman didn't seem to care, especially when it appeared that I outranked her substantially.

It was amusing to see how much weight these people gave to rankings and how easy it made it for an imposter to slip by each of them. Appearances were everything. That was how I'd gotten by in my work for so long.

I made my way toward the stairwell. Marching up one step at a time, I passed another woman with a slicked-back bun—one that looked incredibly tight and professional. I almost missed her rank, which mercifully was a step down from mine, so I gave her a nod and a good morning as she breezed past me without a second glance.

Maybe these people weren't observant because it was so damn early. I'd left the house before the sun had even risen, a sacrifice I only made when I absolutely had to. It'd gotten me here at what seemed like the perfect time, though, so I didn't linger on that frustration as I opened the door to the second story and marched inside.

I glanced both ways and went with the flow of the numbers until I reached the end of the hallway, where a secondary secretary was sitting at her computer. She glanced up and held my gaze as I strode over. This one seemed much more intrigued by my arrival than the last, and I internally cursed. I couldn't continue getting lucky forever, I supposed.

I gave her nametag a quick, discreet scan from a distance and sauntered over with all the confidence in the world, acting as if I belonged there.

"Leto," I said with a smile as if we'd spoken at least a few times before. "You weren't here the last time I came by. How have you been?"

She did an immaculate job at hiding her surprise, her gaze flicking to my prominently displayed ID. "It's nice seeing you again, Colonel Firth."

She was good, I realized, playing along with me as if she'd done this a million times. Quite possibly she had. There must be so many people coming and going that she regularly couldn't remember who she'd met before and who was a total newcomer.

I leaned against her desk and took on a conversational tone. "Is the general here? He was supposed to be here for a meeting during accountability today. I hope he's not late coming in again."

She made a sound that seemed to be part acknowledgment and part confusion. "It doesn't look like he has any appointment on the books this morning," she commented, tilting her head and double-checking. "It wouldn't be the first time he forgot to inform me of a meeting if it was arranged at the last minute, but usually if it's not in my books, he'll have forgotten about it too."

"Ah, that explains it," I said with a snap of my fingers. "We just set up the meeting yesterday over beer and burgers. He must have gotten distracted on the way back and it slipped his mind."

Her eyes widened. "Oh, really? That's interesting. I thought he had a fundraiser yesterday evening."

Was that suspicion in her eyes? I barreled right past it. "Oh, no, this was a quick bite and drink before he headed over there. He said they'd only have appetizers, and he didn't want to starve. There is a limited budget in some of his departments that he is hoping to improve."

I lowered my voice and shot her a sly smile. "Between us, I think he's going to propose that I share a little of my recent inheritance. We'll see how sweet he makes the offer—and what my wife thinks about it, since she'll have my head if I don't let her have her say too."

The secretary laughed. Mentioning a wife seemed to loosen women's suspicions, especially when I'd started out the encounter with a friendly vibe. Now I'd seem like a generous, easy-going man who valued his wife's input, and that was what I needed to get her to trust me.

"I could wait in his office," I proposed. "It's much more comfortable than sitting out here in one of these flimsy plastic chairs. He mentioned making myself comfortable if I arrived before him. Could you do that for me?"

She was butter in my hands now. "Usually we wouldn't allow this, but since you two are friends, I don't see why not."

She stood and made her way toward the door, using a set of keys and unlocking it before turning on the light and gesturing me inside. "I'll let him know you're here when he comes back. If he's not quick, I'll give him a call."

I waved my hand, taking a seat on a small leather chair across from his desk. "Don't worry about it." I withdrew my phone. "I'll give him a call and let him know I'm waiting."

She smiled and closed the door behind me.

I stayed put for several seconds in case she popped back in immediately. From the chair, I gave the contents of the room a quick scan. One entire wall was smothered with medals and certificates with the general's name on them. All those honors, and he was going behind his employer's back to manipulate their resources for his own greedy ends. Shame on him.

He was just one more person putting on a mask to the world while a totally different man lurked underneath. We'd get at whatever weaknesses he was trying to hide.

I was stronger than him because I'd accepted who I was under the mask instead of being terrified of discovery. If you could own who you were, then you could be whoever you wanted. It really was a fantastic sort of freedom.

When the secretary didn't return, I leapt to my feet, pulled on a thin pair of gloves, and stalked quietly through the office. Stacks of documents sat on the desk with no sense of organization that I could decipher. I flicked through them swiftly and grabbed a couple of folders with a classified stamp on the top paper. A quick glance didn't reveal anything particularly momentous contained within, but it was a start.

I eased open the drawers one by one. The third was locked. Jackpot. That was where the real goods would be.

Desk locks were easy pickings. With a tool from my pocket and some jiggling, I had the drawer open in less than a minute. I pawed through the contents, my skin prickling with the awareness of how much time had already passed.

There was a flash drive, which I pocketed, and also a small folder with some schematics of what looked like a new model of military vehicle. Highly classified. Perfect. I tucked those into the briefcase I'd brought along with the other files. Then I set the note we'd prepared ahead of time on top of the drawer's remaining contents.

If you don't want a public outcry over the files you lost, you'll cut your ties to the man from outside. We know you've been betraying your country and the soldiers serving under you.

There. That might be enough to scare him off all on its own, but Blaze would place a phone call to follow up later today.

Now it was time to make my exit. If the general arrived and caught me here, I'd be screwed. Manipulating *him* into believing I was his good friend who he'd had burgers with yesterday was going to be a hell of a lot harder than pulling one over on the secretary.

I removed my gloves, kept one over my fingers as I turned the door handle before dropping it into my pocket, and held my phone to my ear with my other hand. "One second, sir," I said to the dead air in the speaker as I stepped outside the office, and flashed a smile at the secretary. "Ms. Leto, it was a pleasure seeing you again. It seems I'm going to meet the general at the armory, so I'll be on my way."

She beamed back at me and waved me off without a hint of concern.

I carried on the charade as I walked away. "Alright, sir, I'm back. What were you saying?"

I didn't lower my phone from my ear until I'd reached the stairwell. I passed a few more people as I strode through the administration building, and by the time I reached my bike, tucking the briefcase beneath the seat, I knew I was home free.

THIRTEEN

Decima

THE COOL MORNING air whipped across my cheeks as I loped along the sidewalk. I sucked it into my lungs, letting the freshness of the breeze wash through me.

Now that we'd spent a while in the house where we'd shacked up during our extended visit to the DC area, I had a regular routine—when I didn't get diverted by any other responsibilities, at least. I'd always loved running to clear my mind, and the freedom of being able to stretch my legs in the open air rather than staying in place on a treadmill was exhilarating. I had a three-mile circuit I'd established along quiet residential roads where I could almost always count on having an open path.

Even though the route was familiar and I'd never encountered any trouble on it before, I stayed cautious. My gaze skimmed over my surroundings, watching for any threat. The Blood Hunter had to be angry—let's be real, most likely furious—about the ways my crew had interfered with his operations in the past week. It was only a matter of time before he retaliated one way or another.

But this early in the morning, most people were still in bed or, at best, puttering around putting their breakfasts together. Only a few cars rumbled past me, early birds heading to work. A woman weeding her front garden tipped her head to me, and I nodded back as if I were just another regular neighbor out for a jog. It was kind of freeing to pretend I was one of those regular people, even if I couldn't imagine enjoying such a mundane life.

My heart thumped in a fast but steady rhythm. My thoughts flowed through my mind in time with the pounding of my feet on the pavement. For this brief span of time, nothing really mattered except—

A shout broke the peaceful atmosphere. Then another, a pained cry for help.

My head jerked around. The sound was coming from around the bend where I usually turned the corner. I pushed my legs to a sprint, all my senses on high alert.

Rounding the corner, I spotted the problem immediately. Gangly legs with bright sneakers that immediately made me think *teenager* squirmed where the rest of the figure was trapped under a ride-on lawn mower. Somehow the guy had ended up wedged between the two sets of wheels. The machine didn't sound as if it were on, thank God, or he'd have been sliced to bits.

I should have wondered how anyone could have ended up in that situation. Maybe if I'd looked closer before rushing in, I'd have noticed some telling detail that would have tipped me off that this wasn't a simple accident. But as much as I was a killer, I also had a strong instinct to protect those who needed it. I raced over at top speed, worried that the blades might switch on at any moment. The mower must have been moving when the kid had gotten stuck under it, right?

I dropped down next to the machine and heaved it upward so the kid could pull himself out if he wasn't too injured. "Are you hurt?" I asked, just as my gaze jerked to the face of a teenage boy… who was definitely not hurt at all. He was shoving upright as if he'd never really been trapped in the first place. And his defiantly triumphant face was one I knew.

"Carter?" I sputtered, yanking myself backward, away from my brother—but it was a split-second too late. Carter had already jabbed a syringe into my thigh, the needle piercing right through my sweatpants and into the muscle.

I still tried to scramble away, but a rush of dizziness swept over me, followed by a prickling darkness that closed around my mind. My last thought before I slumped over and the whole world went black was that I might have just discovered one way that the Maliks had captured their many victims.

And now *I* was one of those victims.

The first sensation I noticed upon waking was the painful crick in my neck and shoulders. I dragged in a deep breath and moved to stretch, and a bite at my wrists stopped my movement. They were trapped behind my back—bound tightly.

My eyes popped open despite the heaviness weighing down my head. My last memory flooded my mind—Carter, the setup with the lawn mower, the syringe.

I was lying on my side on a rug, the smell of leather and old paper filling my nose. Whatever drug Carter had injected me with was still hazing my senses, making it difficult for me to concentrate, but recognition sparked in my mind.

The secret basement study in the Malik family home—that's where I was. Surrounded by the evidence of the murders they'd carried out: the records of dates and deaths, the photo of the country house where they carried out their rituals… and all the strange objects I'd noticed during my first exploration here. A child's shoe, a toy, a hairclip—it made a sick kind of sense now.

Those had to be mementos from their victims.

They weren't getting anything like that from me.

As I flexed the muscles in my arms to test my restraints, a voice reached me from behind. "She's awake."

It was Grandma Ruby. I guessed that was no surprise. Carter wouldn't have been acting of his own accord. He'd simply been the family member left who'd been most able to carry out a plan that relied on quick physical action.

I kept my ears perked, trying to get a sense of my grandmother's position in the room as I subtly tugged at the cord wrapped around my wrists. It was tight, but I'd gotten out of jams worse than this before. These people were used to tying up children who didn't have a fraction of my strength or skill. If I could just focus better, I'd be able to work the bindings loose with little twitches and minute movements right under my captors' noses.

If they didn't murder *me* before I had the chance to complete my escape, that was.

Footsteps rasped across the floor. Three figures came into view in front of me, making me crane my neck to see their looming faces. Ruby, Carter, and my mother.

"Is this your way of proving that you're not criminals?" I asked, my voice coming out with a bit of a croak. "Because I'm pretty sure kidnapping is against the law."

"You've been corrupted by evil-doers," Iris said, her face as sallow as it'd been when I'd come by to ask about the Blood Hunter. "Brainwashed into something as evil as they are. We have to help you."

Ruby snorted. "If she can be helped. She was in their hands for more than twenty years. I think she's rot all the way through by now."

Iris turned to look at her mother-in-law. "It isn't her fault. She was all sweetness when she was born."

"That was a long time ago. She's made her choices since then. She's old enough to own them and the awful allegiances she's made."

The understanding seeped into my gradually sharpening mind that they still didn't know exactly what the Blood Hunter had shaped me into. They had no idea that I was just as brutal a killer as the men who'd come with me to the country home—they probably thought I'd simply instigated the slaughter and stood back to watch.

Which worked in my favor. I could already feel the bindings around my wrists starting to give way. And they hadn't bothered to tie up my legs. Filled with hubris until the end.

"We have to give her the chance to throw off their influence and be who's she's meant to be," my mother insisted, and peered down at me again. "You can break through it and become a real Malik. We'll welcome you."

"Or else my granddaughter really did die in that crash two decades ago in every way that matters, and only a monster is left," Ruby muttered.

Irritation flared in my chest. I was so sick of the expectations these people put on me, the way I'd had to pretend to be someone I wasn't around them, when they were the biggest hypocrites I'd ever met.

"The only monsters in this room are the three of you," I spat out. "I've never harmed a *kid* in my life."

"Don't you dare dishonor the sacrifices we make by referring to us that way," Ruby hissed and leaned down to slap me across the face. The blow jarred me enough that my senses sharpened even more, but the sting was short-lived.

I'd spent my entire life being punched and kicked by trained professionals, and she thought a slap would cow me? I laughed, working on the knots at my back. It was only a matter of time before I'd slip past the bindings.

And then…

I didn't want to think about what it'd come to.

"You could have just left well enough alone," I said, seeking out my mother's gaze since my grandmother had obviously already condemned me. "You didn't have to grab me and tie me up. I made it clear that I'd leave *you* alone as long as you stopped your own crimes."

Before my eyes, Iris's face hardened into a rigid mask. My heart sank before she even started speaking. "We can't *stop* our divine calling, Rachel. The world needs the work we do."

"It's not work," I shot back. "It's *murder.* Stop pretending it's anything glorious and face up to what you're actually doing. Those kids never hurt anyone. They can't help who their parents are. And you didn't just kill them, you tormented them first."

Carter stirred restlessly behind the family matriarchs, and I thought I caught a flicker of uncertainty pass through his expression. For a second, he looked almost queasy at my words. Maybe there was some hope for this family after all.

"We let loose the brutality of their genetic line to disperse that energy into the universe, away from the innocent people it was harming," Iris insisted. "You haven't even tried to understand."

Then her voice softened again. She blinked, a watery glint coming into her eyes. "I don't want it to be like this. Maybe you think the ways you've been taught are the only way you can survive, but if you would just let us show you that there are different ways, you can break free of their influence and become a real Malik. Please. I want my daughter back."

I'd loosened the cord just enough that I could feel the give that would let me slip my hands free when I was ready. I held them in place as I glared at Iris. "The last thing I'll ever be is a Malik while that name means slaughtering children. You can't even admit the truth of what you're doing, and you talk about *me* not understanding?"

"She's too far gone, Iris," Ruby said in a disgruntled tone. "Your little girl doesn't exist anymore, only this fiend someone else created in her place. And you know what that means."

Iris's mouth twisted, but she inclined her head in acknowledgment as if she agreed with Ruby's assessment. My gaze darted between them. "What does it mean?"

"We can't allow a menace like you to continue wreaking havoc in this world," Ruby declared. "We brought you into it, so it's our responsibility to take you out of it."

"You're going to *kill* me? Because I won't join you in torturing kids?" I'd have laughed again at the absurdity of this conversation if it hadn't been so horrible at the same time.

Iris folded her arms over her chest, her entire body stiffening now. I could see her accepting this new sacrifice she'd decided she had to make. "We'll be putting you out of the misery it seems you're unable to shake. It'll prevent so many more horrors in the long run."

Maybe it was a stupid remark, but I couldn't stop the words from tumbling past my lips. "Funny, that's the exact same thing I thought when I sliced through your husband's throat."

A wounded little cry spilled from Iris's lips, and her hands clenched at her sides. She reached and took a long, thin knife from the shelf next to her. "You're not my daughter. You can't be. The people who took her created a monster, and we can't let the abomination they've created continue."

Every inch of her body and every note in her voice told me how committed she was to this course. She was never going to accept anything other than my obedience or my death—and possibly even the former wouldn't have swayed her now. To her delusional mind, killing me was somehow an act of heroism.

My grandmother watched with avidly gleaming eyes. Only Carter showed any hint of hesitation, his eyes going wide as he stared at his mother. His throat worked with a thick swallow.

A sense of resolve settled over me. I didn't like it, but I knew how this would have to end. Monsters *would* meet their deaths today, but none of them would be me.

Iris bent down over me, holding the blade poised as if preparing to stab it into my heart. She pushed my shoulder to force me onto my back—and at that moment I jerked free.

As I flung the cord that'd bound my wrists aside, I swung around so my leg collided with her calves. My mother tumbled onto her ass, the knife slipping from her grasp. She threw herself after it, her fingers grasping frantically for the handle.

I leapt for it at the same moment. She caught hold of the handle and jabbed the blade toward me, but I wrenched her hand around. Any lingering guilt I might have felt over ending her life fled at the vicious snarl she aimed at me in the instant before the knife plunged into her own chest.

Ruby shrieked. I whipped around in time to meet her onward charge, a small machete I hadn't known she had within reach clutched in her hands. I dodged to the side and slammed my elbow into her back, sending her stumbling into the desk.

She shoved herself back toward me with a wild swing of the blade. I snatched the knife from my mother's chest and parried the desperate blow. She heaved it through the air again, and before I could duck, a fist pummeled my shoulder from behind.

My brother had joined the skirmish. I kicked back at him, sending him crashing to the floor, and spun out of the way in time to escape with just a shallow cut across my arm. Ruby hurtled toward me, and I caught her wrist in my hand. A flash of panic showed in her eyes in the instant before I flipped the machete around and let her fall on it throat first.

As my grandmother slumped with a gurgle and a splatter of blood across the floor, I whirled around. Carter was hauling himself to his feet, his movements shaky. He groped around him, probably searching for anything he could use as a weapon. Before he had the chance to catch hold of anything, I knocked him to the ground.

He started to wriggle away, but I knelt over him, pinning him down with Iris's knife still clenched in my hand. My brother stared up at me, horror and fury and fear all rippling through his expression.

I could have cut him down too, right now, and ended every part of the Malik family line except me. But as I scowled down at Carter, taking in the twitch of his jaw and the pallor of his face, I remembered the hesitation I'd seen in him earlier. The momentary nausea I thought I'd caught when I'd talked about the family's crimes.

He was only eighteen. Just out of high school, basically a kid himself. He'd been brought up his whole life hearing the Maliks' delusional garbage spewed at him from all sides, never knowing anything else.

I knew another kid who'd grown up similarly. Who'd had her mind and her morals warped by the people who'd wanted to use her for their own ends. But I'd carved my own path when I'd gotten the freedom to break from their grasp.

Didn't my brother deserve the same chance?

"Think about the 'sacrifices' you watched or maybe even joined in with," I said, low and steady. "Think about the kids you all cut up and beat and burned before you killed them. Think about the way they must have cried and whimpered in pain. Do you really believe that was okay? That it was something *good*? That it was right for them to die that way?"

Carter opened his mouth and closed it again. His jaw hardened, but at the same time, he stared at me like he was one of those kids himself, frightened and confused.

He wasn't completely committed to the party line. Some part of him still had doubts. I had to give that part the opportunity to turn his life around.

He sucked in a breath, his eyes narrowing as if he was going to make some snappy remark as his previous anger returned. I didn't want to hear it. I rammed my fist into his temple in just the right spot to knock him out, sending his head snapping to the side.

His body slackened. I hefted him up into a fireman's hold and turned toward the secret staircase.

I'd made *my* choice. Now we'd have to figure out what to do with him from here on.

FOURTEEN

Decima

I SPENT most of the conversation staring at my brother as he lay on the sofa, a bruise developing on the side of his forehead from where I'd knocked him unconscious in the basement. He'd woken up again after I'd first gotten back to the house and made such a fuss that we'd sedated him by more peaceful means. Now he lay limp as a noodle.

Julius stared down at him with a frown. "I understand that you wanted to give him a second chance, but we're having enough trouble keeping ahead of the Blood Hunter on our own. He's an unneeded complication."

"I couldn't leave him at the house," I reminded him. "He'd have been calling the cops on me, and then my mug would be all over the news too. It was either bring him here or kill him, and… he's just a kid, really. My family messed with his head, but maybe we can un-mess it."

"He's a kid who's taken part in killing other kids," Garrison put in with an edge in his tone. "I say that we let him suffer the consequences. Even after you gave him a second chance, he jumped up and tried to attack us. Poor Blaze nearly kicked the bucket yet again."

I glanced over to where Blaze sat in an armchair with his laptop. He raised his eyebrows. "Poor me?" He pointed at Talon. "He was the one who caught a fist."

I could tell from Garrison's sly expression where this was about to go, and I didn't have the time to stop it. "Talon can handle a hit from a teenage boy. He elbowed you trying to get out. Are you *okay*?" He dragged out the last word with faux concern.

Talon looked as emotionless as he'd been the day I met him, but I'd swear he was restraining himself from rolling his eyes at the bickering. Garrison was right about him catching one of Carter's fists, but it hadn't seemed to faze him any more than Blaze had appeared injured by what had really been just a graze of an elbow.

I stepped between them before they could take the heckling any further. "This is on me. He's my responsibility, and I'll make sure he doesn't become too much of a liability. Okay?"

Julius inclined his head. "As long as you understand that if the situation gets rough, my priority is going to be getting the rest of you through it, not him."

"Understood." I looked at Garrison. "And you? Stop picking fights. We have a lot of shit to worry about, and you causing unnecessary drama isn't going to be on that list. Understood?"

"I'd consider it unnecessary *fun*, but—"

"Garrison."

He let out a huff and smirked at me. "Fine. Serious matters only. Got it."

I looked back down at Carter. He'd be out for hours if the sedative worked as expected, but I couldn't keep him unconscious forever. He was going to need to eat and relieve himself… and I could hardly make a case to him about changing his sense of morality while he was dead to the world.

"Julius is right," I said. "We'll keep him with us if we can, but we're not protecting him above ourselves. Hopefully, he can figure out that what he and his family did was wrong so we can let him go and start his life sooner rather than later. I know we don't really have time to deal with this, but thank you all for trusting me."

Garrison folded his arms over his chest. "Now are we going to talk about the fact that your family kidnapped and drugged you?"

I shook my head. "There's nothing to talk about. They tried to kill me, and it didn't take. Now they're all dead except my brother, and I'm still here. End of story."

"Dess took care of herself like she always does," Talon said in a voice that dared anyone to continue pursuing the subject.

"Indeed she did." Julius sighed and pressed his hands together. "Let's get down to business. We were going to hash out a strategy after Dess got back from her run. We have information on a few more of the Blood Hunter's associates. Who's our best next target? Has there been any sign of retaliation from the Blood Hunter in response to our efforts so far?"

Blaze was quick to answer. "Nothing that I've seen. We can't even be sure that the general has pulled his support. He sounded upset when I prodded him yesterday, but you never know—"

With a bang that echoed through the floor, the front door flew open. One of the side windows shattered at the same instant. Heavy boots thumped onto the wooden floor all around us, crunching the fresh shards of glass beneath them. Just like that, we were facing off against men dressed all in black and armed to the teeth.

We'd been prepared that we might need to leave the house, but we'd expected more warning than this. Most of our weapons were stashed in the closet near the front door. Our attackers stood between us and it. And the hillside that guarded the house's rear now blocked us in. There was no back door to flee through, and they'd cut us off from the windows too.

As the men opened fire, Talon launched into motion, yanking me down behind the sofa and firing off a few shots from the one pistol he'd kept on him over the top. Garrison leapt over beside us. As far as I could tell, he was unarmed.

Blaze ducked behind the armchair, hugging his laptop to him and jerking out a pistol of his own with his other hand. Julius flipped the dining table for additional cover, dropping behind it and taking a few shots around its side.

How much ammo did any of them have on them? I didn't have a

gun at all, only my usual knives that the Maliks had taken off me in their basement room that I'd retrieved before I left. I tugged one into my hand, ready to throw or stab when a good moment presented itself.

Stabbing was better. Stabbing meant I could use it again.

The men who'd come for us obviously didn't have any concerns about their ammunition supply. They flooded the living room with bullets that thudded into the furniture and walls. I didn't think the gangster brothers who'd lent us this place were going to be happy about the violent renovation.

And through it all, Carter lay still and slack on the sofa, protected by its back but utterly unaware of what was going on around him. Shit. How was I going to protect him too?

The thought popped into my head that the squad attacking us now might not be so different from Petrov's. The Blood Hunter obviously made a habit of getting any skilled people he could under his thumb. Was he blackmailing these men? Threatening their families?

"We don't want to fight you," I hollered over the sofa. "We know how the man you work for operates. You don't have to do what he says. We're trying to take him down so you don't have to follow his orders anymore. Let us go, make it look like you did your best, and we'll both win."

One of them snorted and let off another few shots. "As if we can trust you to have our best interests at heart."

"We both want the same thing," Julius said, adding his appeal to mine. "To live without the Blood Hunter lording it over us. Why shouldn't we work together instead of letting him divide us."

"We don't have any choice," someone snapped back. "Someone's got to die here, and it's going to be you, not us."

Well, if that was how they were going to be about it, we didn't have a whole lot of choice either. Just like when faced with the remainders of my family, I intended to see *my* crew survive, no matter who I had to go through to ensure that.

"Come out and fight like men," a third man growled.

I sputtered a laugh. "You're in for a cruel surprise if you think a man is the worst threat you're going to face."

I bobbed around the side of the sofa and whipped one of my

knives across the room. It sank straight into one of our attackers' throats, and he crumpled. The crew fired into the crowd again, and one of the men near the back yanked something out of a bag he was carrying.

"We can do things another way then," he barked, and tossed the canister into the middle of the room.

The attackers immediately surged out the door. A faint shrieking sound carried from the container, and the hairs on the back of my neck rose.

"It's a bomb!" I hollered. "Get out of the house!"

Julius and Talon barreled forward first, Talon taking a few precious seconds to yank open the closet door and heave a backpack full of weapons and ammo over his back. I scooped Carter off the sofa as quickly as I could and slung him over my shoulder like before. Garrison darted ahead, snatching my knife from the fallen man's neck and tossing it back to me. As Blaze hurried after us, I snatched the handle out of the air and shot Garrison a grateful smile.

Of course, we were fleeing the bomb into the street where our attackers were waiting. Julius and Talon started shooting as they burst out the door, forcing the black-clad men to fall back. The rest of us dodged to the side, ducking behind our rental car. Julius managed to pick off two of the men who were closest to the vehicle just before a furious *boom* reverberated through the house behind us.

The ground rocked beneath my feet, and fire shot out the windows. I ducked my head even lower, feeling my hair singe, covering Carter with my body. The brothers were *really* not going to be happy about the new state of their guest house.

The blast had thrown a few of our attackers off their feet. The Chaos Crew recovered first, Talon digging a fresh gun out of the backpack and tossing another to Julius. But as they took their next shots, an even less welcome sound reached my ears.

The wail of a police siren started up, way too close for comfort. It sounded like it was only a block or two away.

Blaze swore. "There's no way they could have responded to the fight that quickly without advance warning."

I glanced at him. "You mean the Blood Hunter tipped them off?"

Even as I said it, the sense that strategy made clicked in my head. The Blood Hunter wanted us disposed of by any means necessary. He hadn't trusted the squad he'd sent after us to get the job done after we'd escaped similar attacks in the past, so he was counting on the cops to finish the job, just like we'd let the police wrap up our assault on his business at the airfield the other night. All he'd need to do was call in an anonymous tip, just like we had.

There definitely wouldn't be any reasoning with cops. And I didn't like the idea of being arrested any more than I wanted a bullet in my skull.

"Get in the car!" Julius bellowed. "Talon and I will cover you."

They pulled their triggers, and the rest of us hauled open the passenger side doors. Garrison dove over the gear shift into the driver's seat, fumbling with the keys. Blaze leapt in next to him. I dragged Carter into the back, bracing him on my lap like I was a mother cradling an immense baby. It wasn't the most comfortable position I'd ever been in, but I didn't have time to find a better place for him.

As Garrison gunned the engine, Julius flung open the door on the other side of the back seat. Flashing lights were just racing into view in the rearview mirror. Julius and Talon hurled themselves into the back, cramming in with me and Carter, and Garrison hit the gas before they'd even slammed the door closed.

We tore down the street. I couldn't tell what had become of our original attackers, only that the bangs of gunfire had cut out. Had they taken off too to avoid their own arrests?

"The cops are following us," Julius announced, craning his neck to peer out the back. I followed his gaze and spotted two police cars roaring after us, their sirens blaring away.

Garrison whipped around a turn.

"Can you lose them?" I asked.

"I don't know," he admitted, taking a second sharp turn. "But I have an idea."

"They're gaining on us fast," Blaze said. "This car doesn't have the horsepower to outrun them."

"That's fine, if this works." Garrison's hands clenched around the wheel. "Hold on."

I gripped the handle above the window with one hand, unable to stop Carter from slumping over the other two men's laps. There hadn't been time for seatbelts.

As Julius and Talon braced themselves, Garrison wrenched the wheel in a last-second turn into a parking garage. He blew through the security gate and zoomed up the ramp to the second floor. One of the cop cars hadn't been able to turn in time, but the other swerved after us, hot on our trail.

Garrison simply hit the gas. When I saw where he was heading, my eyes widened. "Garrison…"

There was a boarded-up section of wall at the far end of the garage where it looked like there'd once been some kind of exit, maybe only for pedestrians onto a second-floor passage between buildings that'd been taken down. Garrison must have noticed it from the outside in his explorations of the neighborhood. He sent the car hurtling toward it at top speed. I gulped and squeezed the handle tight.

The hood screamed as we rammed into the plywood, but the boards smashed apart with the impact. For a few seconds, we were soaring through the air, nothing at all beneath the wheels.

The car hit a road below, the tires squeaking with the impact. Then they screeched as Garrison hit the gas again.

My heart was still beating so fast I half expected it to burst through my chest. I could hear the faint whistling of one of the tires starting to deflate, but Garrison didn't let that slow him down. He sped through the streets, no cops behind us now since none of them were crazy enough to follow us in that crazy jump. Just as the flattening tire started to bump against the asphalt, he pulled off onto a side street where a few other cars were parked nearby and drove into an alley.

"Now we steal another," he said with a rasp of ragged breath.

We all scrambled out, Julius helping me haul Carter. Talon shook his head at Garrison. "You're one crazy son of a bitch."

Garrison flashed him a wide smirk. "Only when I need to be. It got the cops off our tail, didn't it?"

A hoarse laugh escaped me, but I couldn't hold on to that humor for long. Julius glanced around with a grim expression.

"For now."

FIFTEEN

Decima

"WHERE CAN we go that he won't find us now?" I asked, glancing around at the guys in the cramped space of our new vehicle.

Knowing the car we'd nabbed after our mad escape would be reported stolen at any moment, Julius had managed to rent something else under one of his many aliases so that we could ditch the sedan we'd taken. He'd gone with a minivan, kind of dumpy-looking on the outside but at least a little more space than we'd enjoyed before. But between the five of us and Carter sprawled in the third row of seats, in the grips of the sedative but maybe not for much longer, it was still a tight squeeze.

We were parked in a suburban neighborhood on the outskirts of town, a stretch of trees on one side of the road and a sprawl of identical brick houses on the other. But I had no idea how safe we were even with the various stealth measures we'd taken. The Blood Hunter clearly had extensive resources at his disposal. He'd tracked us down more than once before, and now he was more motivated than ever.

Blaze could hack into any camera in the city, so it made sense that the Blood Hunter could do the same and who knew how much more. With squads of soldiers and untold numbers of criminals in his back pocket, did we really stand a chance?

"He could already know where we are," Garrison muttered, echoing my thoughts. "We don't know what he's using to track us."

"Could he be tapping into our phone signals?" Talon asked.

Blaze shook his head. "We've been constantly swapping out burners for a reason. I have a proxy set up that's been redirecting our numbers every time we make a call or send a text—no one we've contacted has any idea what the real numbers are to trace them."

And who would we be calling anyway? I had no family left to contact, and the men weren't exactly friendly with anyone in the city. I didn't have anyone's phone number except theirs, the Maliks', and…

My thoughts stilled around the idea that had suddenly occurred to me. "So if we call someone, they shouldn't be able to track our location from the call in any way?" I clarified.

Blaze shook his head. "The phones are safe. But there are all kinds of other methods. Street cams, satellite footage, even random sightings can help narrow things down. He must have a lot of people out on the streets. One of them gets a glimpse of us, and it's that much easier for him to connect the dots."

"We need to stay on the move," Julius said. "We can't afford to stay in any place for very long—no more than one night, leaving the next morning."

Garrison hummed to himself. "Do you think we *should* go back home to the apartment now? As far as we know, he still isn't aware of our home base."

His question caught me off guard. "We can't go home until we find out how to take him down. If we run away now, he'll either follow us or screw things up for us there too, or he'll have the chance to solidify his position here. We've only just gotten him on the defensive."

Garrison gave me a baleful look. "I'm not sure how much that was defensive vs. aggressive, sweetheart. I'm just saying it might be worth taking the time to regroup after all."

He might have had a point, but I couldn't stop picturing a mass of armed men bursting into the penthouse apartment I'd started to think of as *my* home too. My stomach twisted. "He's out to destroy us now, and the only way to stop him is by destroying him first. We have to be close so we can take advantage of any opportunities we get."

"Dess is right," Julius said. "We entered a war, and now we need to finish it. Running off with our tails between our legs isn't going to help us."

They'd entered a war because of me. The guilt twined through my gut didn't release even with his agreement.

The Blood Hunter had only been interested in me at first. My association with the Chaos Crew had pulled them into this mess, made them his targets too.

If he succeeded in killing them, it'd be my fault. I could have suggested we walk away as soon as I'd taken care of the Maliks, but instead I'd insisted on pursuing the other mysteries we'd encountered, and look where that had gotten us.

Maybe I'd never have been free of the Blood Hunter regardless, but that didn't change the fact that I was responsible.

His interest in me also gave me a little bit of an edge, though, didn't it? My fingers itched to grasp my phone. But I knew what the guys would say if I told them what I was thinking of doing.

I had to try. He'd never been willing to speak to anyone but me.

I wiggled my legs and reached for the door. "I need to go for a walk."

Garrison sat up straighter. "I don't think you should go anywhere alone right now."

I cut a glance at him. "I need some space to think properly. I know how to look after myself."

He grimaced, and I half expected him to argue. But then he simply reached behind him and offered me the pistol he'd grabbed from our reduced stash. "At least make sure you're properly armed."

I recognized the peace offering for what it was and accepted it, ensuring the safety was flipped on before tucking the gun into my waistband. Then I stepped out of the car and headed through the trees beside the road. No street cams or passersby where there weren't any streets. I should be safe enough from prying eyes there.

What could I say to the Blood Hunter that might convince him to back off? How could I stop him from continuing to attack us when we had no intention of letting up on him? It might be an impossible problem, but I wouldn't know what might come up until I tried. Maybe he'd let something slip that we could use.

I tramped through the woods for several minutes, putting plenty of distance between me and my men, until the trees gave way to a stretch of fields full of patchy grass and wildflowers. Insect life thrummed in the vegetation around me. I couldn't see any buildings or vehicles from my current position. It felt secure enough.

I pulled out my phone and looked up the number on the card I'd photographed in case I lost the actual item. My finger hovered over the keypad for several heartbeats before I finally tapped it in and brought the phone to my ear.

He answered on the second ring, the low dark voice I recognized at once spilling through the speaker. "Hello?"

"It's Dess," I forced myself to say. "Decima."

The Blood Hunter made a scoffing sound. "If you've decided to take me up on my offer after all, you're too late. We're well past the deadline I gave you. I don't take on people who can't follow simple instructions."

I resisted the urge to grit my teeth. "That's not why I'm calling."

"What is it, then?"

"I'm calling to suggest that it's in your best interests to back off on me and my crew."

A startled chuckle carried through the line. "You want *me* to back off? After what your team has done to undermine my business?"

"We only went on the offensive after you blacklisted two of my men with the police," I retorted.

The Blood Hunter didn't speak for a moment, and I thought I heard the growl of an engine in the background. He inhaled slowly. "I told you that if you made the wrong choice, you'd regret it, didn't I?"

I grimaced. "All you've done so far is make me even more convinced I made the *right* choice. You aren't entitled to ruin my life more than you already have, and you aren't in control of the crew or what we do. You don't own us. And we're going to hit back every time you try."

"Correction," he said with a small laugh. "I don't own *them*—not yet. That tattoo on the back of your neck shows that I do own you, and there's nothing you can do about that."

I reached automatically to the back of my neck and rubbed my fingers where I knew the mark was branded into my skin. When I had enough breathing room to consider it, I'd need to shave the hair there and have the tattoo removed.

"Sticking your mark on a kid doesn't make them belong to you," I said. "I don't belong to the people who brought me into this world or the person who stole me from them. I only belong to myself."

"We'll see about that, won't we?" The Blood Hunter paused again, for long enough that my skin started to prickle with apprehension. "And what exactly are you going to do if I continue taking whatever steps I can to crush your little band of mercenaries?"

As if I'd reveal our plans to him. Hell, I didn't even know what our next plans would be. We were basically flying by the seat of our pants here.

"All you need to know is that they'll hurt as much as what we've already done—or worse."

The Blood Hunter let out a soft but menacing laugh. "Do you really think you've done that much damage? A couple of minor irritations, like a mosquito taking little bites. Soon enough I'll swat you, and *my* life will continue as usual."

"Funny," I said. "You're awfully determined to crack down on us if we're nothing more than mosquitos to you. I think we've hit you harder than you want to let on."

"Do you now? You underestimate me, but then, you have all along, in so many ways."

In the silence that followed, the engine's thrum seemed to get… louder. But that didn't make sense if I was hearing it through the phone while the Blood Hunter drove. Unless—

My gaze darted over the landscape around me. I picked out a figure on a motorcycle that'd just zoomed into view on a country road

I hadn't noticed, a few hundred feet distant across the field. My heart lurched.

It couldn't be. How could he have located me so quickly? Blaze had said the phone wouldn't be enough... But maybe the Blood Hunter had methods our hacker didn't know about. How else could he have eyes on me?

Before I could wonder if it was just a coincidence, the motorcycle pulled onto the shoulder and the man riding it swung off it. He walked into the field straight toward me, leaving his helmet on. It looked fitting atop his broad frame. His hands appeared to be empty, but it seemed unlikely that he didn't have some kind of weapon on him within easy reach.

I pulled out my gun, flicking off the safety, and walked sideways until I was close to the trees again. When the Blood Hunter was only fifty feet away, I raised it, hanging up the phone call. "Stop right there," I shouted across the remaining distance.

He halted, cocking his head to one side. I didn't need to be able to see his face to recognize the smirk that carried through his tone. "I thought you were so eager for a proper conversation, Decima. And now it bothers you that I've come at your beckoning?"

I didn't want to show him how unnerved I was by his sudden arrival. "What do you want?" I demanded, holding the gun steady.

"I want you to realize who you're dealing with and that you can't win," he said, with a snarl in his voice that he couldn't quite disguise. Oh, we'd hurt his operations all right. He was absolutely enraged, as much as he was trying to hide it. "Your life is mine, and for your interference, I'm going to take the lives of your friends as well. It's only balancing the scales."

"Fuck you," I spat. "You don't own me, and you don't stand a chance against us."

I hoped that was right. His vehemence proved that we'd been doing exactly as we'd meant to do. We were weakening him.

I felt the Blood Hunter's glower through his visor. "For what you've done, they won't just be killed quickly. Your crew will be tortured for *days.* I will wipe them off the map when I find them, and it's all because you tried to defy me."

Maybe if I provoked a little more anger, I could get something out of him he didn't mean to reveal. I pushed my mouth into a smirk of my own. "What's wrong? Are you pissed that you can't control your *property* as thoroughly as you thought?"

This time, the Blood Hunter's laugh was chilling enough to send a shiver down my spine. "You don't think I have full control over you? From the time you were a child, I've manipulated every part of your life. I gave orders to your handlers for years, sending you on missions to advance my agenda. I had you kill remorselessly, and I created that killing power inside of you whether you acknowledge it or not. And when I finished turning you into the killer I knew you'd become, I slaughtered everyone but your handler to spark your rage. Even your outside sources—the girl in the tech shop and the guy in the bakery. Everyone. *I* did that."

I'd wondered what had happened to Jay and Scarlett. Now I had my answer. Even though I'd barely known them, my throat constricted at the thought that they too had been caught up fatally in this war that I hadn't even realized I was fighting back then.

I jabbed a finger at him. "You failed. I'm still walking free. Your plans went to shit because you can't control everything. Because nobody is that powerful."

"I can't?" he asked, and I could hear the smile on his face. "Maybe I didn't account for the Chaos Crew taking you, but I sent out a call for their deaths, not because I thought it would work, but because I knew it would bring you closer. And when you finally trusted them, I let you come here where I knew they'd help you kill your family. I set up a failed bombing at Malik's office to focus your attention on him. I've been guiding you for your entire life, and you never even noticed, did you?"

How could he possibly have known we'd come here when we had? It hadn't been the bombing that had brought us here, and we'd nearly died getting the genetics information that'd allowed Blaze to match me with Damien Malik. The Hunter had to be bluffing. But he spoke with such confidence it sent the shivers deeper into my gut.

"From start to finish, I orchestrated your birth family's destruction," he went on. "You never suspected I was the one attacking your allies. You bought into the clues I left that pointed to your father as the culprit. I sent you running out to that home they kept hidden by kidnapping that man of yours, and you didn't hesitate for a second. You thought you were protecting him from them when it was me all along."

We'd put those pieces together, but it was still unsettling hearing the man gloat about it. I groped for something that would shatter his ideas of grandeur.

"I would have taken out the Maliks anyway," I said. "I didn't kill them because of anything you did but because of what *they'd* done. They really murdered those kids. They believed in torturing children. That's why they died. You only gave me the clues I needed to figure it out and deliver justice. So really you were serving my agenda."

Just as much as I'd served his, but I didn't see the need to mention that part when he was emphasizing it so much already.

My reframing obviously pissed him off even more. He exhaled roughly. "And is your agenda also seeing the men you've allied yourself with dead? Killing them has always been a part of the plan—every second since the moment I found you with them. Their deaths will be your final punishment before you follow them."

"Is that why you haven't tried to kill me right now?" I taunted, my heart pounding faster as I all but dared him to try. "Because you want me to suffer through their deaths first? Or maybe you're afraid you can't match me after all. You told me that I'm the finest assassin you've ever known."

The Blood Hunter guffawed. "You're a fine soldier, but I'm your commanding officer. No single soldier is going to eliminate me, Decima. You can be sure of that."

After everything, he was still confident enough to look me in the face while I held a gun on him and speak so arrogantly. My nerves wobbled. What if he could make good on his threat after all? Look at how easily he'd found me here. If he destroyed the crew…

He'd said he wouldn't accept me as an employee now, but he might have been speaking out of anger rather than the full truth. If I offered to set down my weapon and go over to his side, was it possible he'd spare them after all?

But every piece of my body screamed against the idea of giving myself over to his manipulations. I couldn't allow myself to become a puppet ever again. I had to trust that my men and I would find a way to defeat this monster.

I was just drawing in my breath to answer when his voice rolled out through his helmet again with a strange but far too familiar phrase. "Garlic milkshake."

A prickling sensation rushed through my mind, my muscles starting to seize. A flare of panic followed, but in the same moment, I heard Julius's voice, guiding me. *Imagine a wave that washes over you without catching hold.*

The conditioned command didn't have to control me. I hadn't let Noelle use it, and I wouldn't let this psycho force my obedience either.

I pictured the wave sweeping all the phrase's influence away, and my limbs loosened.

"You can be sure that I'm never going to stop fighting," I snapped at the Blood Hunter, and pulled the trigger.

I should have known he was prepared for his gambit not to work. The Blood Hunter's head jerked back, but only a few inches before he righted himself. The bullet had dented his helmet without coming close to penetrating the material. His hand whipped to his side, to a weapon he must have had concealed there, and all I could feel was how very vulnerable my body was in comparison.

Not knowing what other protective gear he might be wearing, I didn't risk taking another shot while I left myself open. A sense of urgency was creeping over me that I needed to get back to my men anyway—we all needed to get out of here in case the Blood Hunter had called in others to join him.

I threw myself into the shelter of the forest and ran back toward the road. No sounds of pursuit came from behind me, only a cool, rolling laugh that made me sick to my stomach.

I could run away now, and we could keep running, but how long would it be before he hunted us down exactly as his name and his words promised?

SIXTEEN

Decima

I LOOKED AROUND THE DANK, dim interior of the abandoned warehouse and stopped myself from making a face.

It didn't matter how gloomy and rundown this place was. We just needed an isolated, sheltered spot to crash for the night where Blaze felt there was the least chance of us being traced. I'd told the crew about my encounter with the Blood Hunter as soon as I'd raced back to the car, and we'd taken off with an hour's worth of evasive maneuverings, but I couldn't shake the sense of being watched, even with walls all around me.

I turned back toward my men, who were setting up makeshift beds of the blankets and sleeping bags we'd been able to scrounge up in the factory's main room, within easy reach of both the front and back exits. A different sort of apprehension crept over my skin as I watched them from that short distance.

The Blood Hunter's words had squirmed deeper under my skin all through the day. I couldn't stop his voice from ringing in my ears. His claims that he owned me, that I belonged to him.

I knew that wasn't true, no matter how much he believed it. But it was hard not to consider that I'd *never* been truly on my own in a situation where I wasn't being influenced by someone else. I'd run straight from the household into the Chaos Crew's grasp.

They treated me as an equal now. They cared about me. More than one of them had even said they loved me. But how could I know if *this* was right for me any more than staying under the Blood Hunter's thumb would have been when I'd never had the chance to experience anything else?

I didn't like those doubts, but they kept creeping through my mind anyway. I couldn't shake the need to step apart from them, to center myself so that I could figure out what *I* was really doing here. How could I be a real part of this war if part of me was starting to question every decision I'd ever made?

I had to get my head on straight, one way or another.

Blaze pulled out a deck of cards he must have grabbed during our forays for supplies. He shook out the cards and shuffled them with swift movements of his hands. "Who's up for a game of rummy? Dess?"

I shook my head, keeping my voice as gentle and even as I could. "Not right now. I think—I should try to talk to my brother again."

Julius nodded, but I felt four pairs of eyes follow me as I picked up one of the bags of food we'd bought and walked over to the smaller side room—where we'd shut Carter away so there was even less chance of him being heard if he managed to shout for help. How much had the men noticed my apprehensive mood?

I owed it to my brother too—to figure out who I was and how I wanted to be that woman. I'd dragged him into the new life I was leading. Would he be any more open to considering becoming a part of it now that he'd had ample time for reflection?

I unlatched the door and peeked inside, not that I thought there was much chance of Carter having escaped his bonds as I had when he'd captured me. He didn't have the same extensive training, and Talon was much more skilled at tying knots than anyone in my family had been.

I found my brother sitting against the wall where we'd left him, one of the sleeping bags spread open beneath him, his wrists tied in front of him and his ankles bound together. We'd left a thin gag in his mouth.

When he'd woken up from the sedative, I'd made it clear that I didn't want to knock him out again, but that I would if he put up a fight. He'd seemed to decide he was better off keeping his consciousness this time. Maybe he could tell that even if I'd opted to spare him, my men wouldn't hesitate to kill him if he gave them much more reason.

"We're going to be staying here for a little while," I told him. "I've brought you some food, and I thought maybe we could talk. Will you stay quiet if I take out the gag? No one's going to hear you except my crew, and they'll just be pissed off."

Carter tipped his head to indicate agreement and then raised his chin. I released the gag and quickly stepped back, out of range if he tried to heave himself at me. Reaching into the bag, I retrieved a bottle of juice that I opened for him and placed in his hands before backing away again.

As he gulped from the bottle, relief washing over his face, I unwrapped a grocery store burrito for him. He set down the juice and accepted that, but he dug into it with less enthusiasm than he'd brought to the drink.

"What exactly do you want to talk about?" he asked, his voice rough from disuse. "You're holding me here like a prisoner."

"Not because I want to," I said. "Only because it's the only way I can be sure you won't turn on us. For our own safety, it's either this or…"

"Or what you did to Mom and Dad," he shot back, his eyes darkening.

I swallowed thickly. "Yes. I'm sorry about that. I didn't want to hurt them either. But the things they were doing… I couldn't let them keep carving up little kids for their crazy rituals either. And both times, when I actually did it, they were trying to kill *me*."

"They were our *parents*," he said, but he didn't seem to know how to follow that up. He took a small bite and took a while chewing it. A look of concentration took over his face. "You should let me go. I can make it worth your while. I have access to most of the family accounts."

I wrinkled my nose. "I don't want your money. Anyway, if I did, I could get it myself as one of—possibly the only—remaining Malik."

"Fine. Then—you and your 'crew' are on some kind of mission. Maybe lots of them. I have skills that could help with that if you'll release me."

I raised my eyebrows. I didn't trust for a second that he'd come back to fulfill any favors if I set him loose, but I couldn't help being curious. "What kind of skills?"

"I'm good at forgery. I've used it dozens of times with the family, covering up disappearances and getting us access where we need it. I can sign off on things and pretend to be someone important. No one's ever seen through them."

I could imagine that talent coming in handy, but that didn't change the rest of our situation. My breath came out in a sigh. "Frankly, Carter, I don't trust you out there on your own. Just this morning you helped arrange my kidnapping and near-murder. You're obviously upset with me about what happened to the family. I'm not sure you believe yet that what they—and you—were doing to those kids was wrong."

His mouth twisted. "I can't earn trust sitting here tied up, Rachel."

I caught his gaze and held it firmly. "Rachel is the name that family gave me. I don't want any part of it. I go by Dess now."

He blinked. "Dess," he said, as if trying out the sound of it. His shoulders tensed. "Is that what the people who stole you away called you? You're keeping their—"

"It's the name I grew up with, the only name I remember having," I said, cutting him off before he could go on any kind of rant. "It's mine now, and I've decided to keep it. Believe me, I have no love for the people who held me all those years either. The men out there, my crew, they're not connected to those people at all. They helped me get away from the real villains."

Carter snorted as if the idea that anyone could be worse villains than my men was absurd. My jaw clenched despite my best intentions.

"Look," I said, my voice hardening. "You know that our family were villains too, don't you? They tortured and killed innocent children simply because of who their parents were. The idea that doing it somehow reduced crime has no basis in reality. Rates have gone up and down over the decades with no influence from those bloody rituals. Killing all those kids did nothing but cause unnecessary tragedy and make them feel good about themselves. So that the Maliks could believe in their own importance, they tore apart so many other families."

Carter shook his head. "You don't understand," he said, but his voice wavered.

"I think I do," I replied. "I've heard every explanation our parents and the rest of the family offered, and none of it sounded anything short of batshit crazy. Maybe it can start to seem like it makes sense when you grow up surrounded by people who believe it, who constantly reinforce those ideas, but you've been out in the real world too. You know how delusional anyone else would think it is. Have you *ever* seen any evidence that those rituals helped anyone or anything other than your egos?"

Carter's jaw worked. After a moment of silence in which he didn't appear to have an answer, I went on with a flicker of hope.

"I want to stop criminals too, you know. The worst of them. I've already been working on that. But I don't slaughter innocent people to make it happen, because that won't *make* it happen. I go straight at the source, the people doing the harm, and take them down. Shouldn't you applaud me for doing that instead of seeing *me* as a villain? I'm accomplishing exactly what the Maliks claimed to want, only much more effectively."

My brother seemed to need a moment to take this all in. At least he was listening. Thinking about what I'd said.

Then he exhaled sharply. "There were a lot of reasons that we couldn't go after the criminals. The effects—we wanted something broader and not focused on the individual level…"

"And did you see any broad effects?" I demanded.

I caught a slight wince that seemed to unwillingly acknowledge my point.

"My way makes a hell of a lot more sense than going after

innocent kids," I said. "We're tackling the problems right at the source. And you could help us with that. Or you could go off and live your own life and let us keep at it without either of us getting in each other's way. Either would be fine with me."

I knew Carter was stubborn, but I also knew he wasn't stupid. It was just hard to sway him after our family had spent years conditioning him to believe the opposite. I hoped that I'd be able to get through to him, especially since the Maliks' goals and mine were so similar. The way we went about doing it was different, but the morality of it all was the same, in essence.

"We followed the rules," he said finally. "Our rules, but they were still rules. We didn't just go around murdering people left and right."

"And neither do we." I let out my breath and stood up. "I don't think there's anything else I can say right now. This is a lot to take in. Please just think about it. Remember everything our family did—not just what you thought was good, but the parts that were obviously bad. I'll let you finish your dinner, and then I'll have to come back and put the gag in again."

He sat in silence as I stepped out. Garrison came over while I pushed the latch back into place.

"I can try talking some sense into him," he offered, tipping his head toward the room. "Give it my best shot."

The idea sent a jolt of resistance through me. What could Garrison say that I hadn't? He didn't know Carter at all. If my brother was going to come to his senses, I couldn't imagine him believing anyone but me. At least I was family too, if in a detached sort of way.

"I think we should keep it between family for now," I said. "But if I need your help, I'll let you know."

He cracked a smile. "Please do. Chatting people up is my main job here, after all."

I glanced past him to the other guys, who'd paused their card game to watch our conversation. My skin seemed to tighten around my body. The uneasiness the Blood Hunter's words had stirred up hadn't left me.

"I know," I said. "I'm going to explore the rest of the building. I'll stay inside and not make any phone calls—don't worry." We'd all gotten new phones and ditched our old ones after my encounter with the Blood Hunter anyway, and we were only going to use them to contact each other unless there was an absolute emergency.

Garrison waved me off, but again I felt his gaze and the others' trailing after me. Probably wondering why I suddenly wanted all this time to myself.

I wished I could have given them a real answer.

SEVENTEEN

Talon

I WOKE first as I often did, my muscles stiff from a night on the hard floor with only a sleeping bag for padding. I couldn't say I'd slept *well*, having jolted awake a few times at distant sounds that sent a peal of warning through me but had proven to be nothing of concern, but I was used to operating on minimal rest from my time in the military. What we'd faced so far had nothing on my most intense special ops missions overseas.

But that didn't mean the stress couldn't weigh on us all the same. I sat up quietly, glancing across the sprawled bodies of my sleeping comrades—Julius's spot empty while he took the current watch by the front of the building—to where Dess lay.

She looked almost peaceful in sleep, but there was still a tension to the way one of her arms was drawn up to her chest, her hand balled against her collarbone. A slight furrow marked her brow.

She'd set her sleeping bag a little apart from the rest of us, halfway between our cluster and the door that led to the room where we'd imprisoned her brother. For most of the evening, I'd sensed her pulling away from us, withdrawing into her own head.

The situation was obviously getting to her, stirring up more uncertainty than ever before. She'd had to kill almost her entire family, for fuck's sake. She'd found out that even more of her life had been manipulated by outside forces than she'd already known. How could it not be bothering her?

I didn't like the idea that she might feel she couldn't turn to us for support, though. We were hard men, yes—and I was the hardest of us all—but I'd thought we'd shown her how much she mattered to us. Imagining her leaving set off a burning sensation all through my chest.

My instinct was to suppress the emotion and push it aside. This once, I didn't let myself. I absorbed the full impact of the discomfort, feeling out what it meant to me. As I gazed at Dess, the sensation gradually transformed into something softer.

I knew this emotion. That was the feeling that had driven me closer to Dess over the months—the feeling that had convinced me to allow myself to feel anything at all again.

And if I was honest with myself, I didn't hate it. It seemed *right* for Dess to hold this special place in my heart, to have opened it up in a way no one ever had before. *She* was special, after all.

Did she understand how much?

An unexpected impulse rose up inside me, but I didn't hold myself back. I eased out of the sleeping bag and padded across the floor to where Dess was nestled. She'd opted to use her entire sleeping bag as a mattress and pulled a blanket over her. It'd slipped partway down her torso as she dozed.

For a second, I grappled with how to handle the moment. Then I sank down behind her, stretched out on the edge of the sleeping bag, and tugged the blanket up to her shoulders and over my own in the same gentle motion. I tucked my arm around her waist and lowered my head against the soft waves of her hair.

This was some kind of bliss right here, feeling her body aligned with mine, soft with sleep. Other urges woke up inside me along with a surge of heat to my dick, which was positioned against her ass. I forced myself to ignore those desires for now, simply breathing in the delicately sweet scent in her hair. She needed her rest, as much as she could manage to get.

I dozed a little more myself, only snapping awake when Dess stirred against me. Her ass brushed my groin in a way that had me rising to attention in an instant, which obviously didn't go unnoticed.

"Someone is having naughty thoughts," she murmured in a voice raspy with sleep.

I couldn't resist stroking my hand over her stomach. "I plead the fifth."

She snorted and rolled over to face me, meeting my eyes with her still drowsy ones. The flush of her cheeks with her increasing alertness and the softness of her gaze had my heart racing in an instant. I reached out and smoothed a few stray strands of hair behind her ear.

"Did you have trouble sleeping?" she asked in a lightly teasing tone. "I don't mind being used as a teddy bear, but I wouldn't have figured you needed one."

I opened and closed my mouth, grappling with the best way to put my thoughts into words. Finally, I simply said, "I wanted to talk to you."

Her eyebrows shot up. "You want to *talk*?" She sounded both amused and a little concerned.

"Yes," I said firmly, holding her gaze. "I know that you're dealing with some difficult crap right now. And obviously you're going to deal with it in your own way. But I want you to remember that I'm ready to support you with whatever you need."

"Talon," she said, shaking her head as if to tell me that I didn't need to say that.

I kept going anyway. "The crew and I will be here for you no matter what, Dess—if you need help or just a person to talk to. We want to see you make it through this mess as the powerful woman you are. *I* want to see that." I paused, my chest clenching up for a second before I said the final part, maybe the most important part. "I love you."

Dess stared at me, startled into silence. I wasn't sure what response I'd have wanted, but a second later, she wrapped her arm around my shoulders and pulled me into a kiss. There was so much eager passion in it that I couldn't have asked for anything more.

My erection was straining against my pants now. I pressed into her, and she ground against my hips in return, making me ache with hunger. As I swallowed a groan, she let out a light laugh. Then I pushed into her harder, rocking against her clit through our clothes, and she muffled a whimper of her own against my mouth.

I flicked my tongue between her lips where it tangled with her own. My hand slipped under her shirt and rose to cup her breast. As I swiveled her nipple beneath my thumb, I brought my mouth to the side of her neck. Her breath was already breaking into those little gasps I loved to hear.

"God, Talon," she muttered. "You're—"

The front door banged open so loudly we jerked apart. As we both scrambled up out of the blankets, the other guys heaving to their feet nearby, Julius strode into the room. His expression was so tense that all lingering heat from my encounter with Dess fled my body.

"We've got company," he announced.

I leapt for the guns I'd kept at the ready next to my sleeping bag. I had a feeling we'd be abandoning nearly everything else we'd brought into the factory with us. Garrison and Blaze kicked aside their own blankets, pistols in hand. Blaze's gaze darted around the room. "How many? What are we dealing with?"

"Several cars just pulled around back. If we're fast enough—"

Dess was already racing to the room where we'd stashed her brother. But we wouldn't have made it out in time regardless. It seemed more men had shown up in the few seconds it'd taken Julius to rouse us. Engines roared near the front door as well.

They were surrounding us.

"How the hell did they find us?" Garrison grumbled.

"It doesn't matter," Julius said. "You, handle Carter. We need Dess able to fight. And let's get out of here before even more of these assholes show up."

For once, Garrison didn't make any snarky remarks about the indication that he was the least skilled fighter out of the five of us. He knew his talents lay elsewhere, and I doubted he wanted Dess hindered in combat any more than Julius did. He dashed over to catch the boy's elbow where Dess was just urging him upright and hustled him toward the rest of us. Dess snatched up a gun in one hand and a knife in the other, her eyes gleaming with nervous anticipation.

Julius swept his arm, urging us toward the window closest to where we'd parked the car. We'd left the pane propped open specifically in case we needed to make a hasty exit while the doorways were more of a danger. We all hurtled toward it, leaving sleeping bags and blankets behind without a care.

Julius shoved the window higher up and sprang onto the ledge—just as a multitude of bodies slammed through the doors at either end of the main room. Our commander opened fire outside as the rest of us blasted away at the men coming at us from the inside now.

"Don't kill them unless you have to," Dess said, taking one shot and another that simply incapacitated the attackers she'd aimed at—one bullet smashing through a man's gun hand, another toppling one with a wound through the thigh. "The Blood Hunter is probably forcing these people to come after us like the others. They're just trying to survive."

"*Us* surviving is my first priority," I said, even as my awareness sharpened with my sniper instincts homing in on my targets. "If anyone hurts you, they're dead."

She didn't bother to argue, picking off more men with her impressively honed aim. I followed her example, disarming and crippling with my shots rather than outright killing.

But there were too many of them to follow that ethical stance all the way to its limit. When several of the men pointed their guns at us at the same time, I had to add a few kill shots to the mix to ensure I hit all of them hard enough to stop them in time.

"All clear outside," Julius hollered, leaping through the window. I automatically bent to give Dess a leg up, still firing with my other hand. My bullets caught more wrists and calves and thighs, toppling men left and right—and occasionally slamming right into their skulls when I saw no other option. Not one of them managed to get a good shot in at my crew.

As I hefted Carter and then Garrison after Dess through the window, a sense of cool exhilaration spread through my mind, only intensifying my focus. I did love this woman, with every particle of my being, but that emotion wasn't a distraction from my work. Quite the opposite. The knowledge that I had her fighting alongside me and the determination to protect her bolstered my motivation and energy for the battle like nothing else ever had.

These unfamiliar feelings that'd been emerging inside me were making me *stronger*, not weaker.

Blaze vaulted over the window ledge next. More shots rang out on the other side of the wall—some of our attackers had dashed around to confront us once they'd realized our gambit. I took down a few more before heaving myself over the ledge after the others.

Garrison had jumped into the driver's seat of the minivan, Carter staring out the back window with a bewildered, near terrified expression. Dess blasted the kneecap of a man charging toward us and caught another in the forearm, forcing him to drop his weapon, but a third attacker loomed, hefting a rifle, none of him visible to me other than the top of his head showing beyond hers.

I didn't have a choice. My next bullet shattered apart his skull.

Dess let out a rough breath, but she didn't criticize my methods. She knew as well as I did that this war was an imprecise situation at best. Staying alive mattered above all else, as much as I'd rather not destroy the lives of men who'd been forced into coming at us.

This was the Blood Hunter's doing like so much else. Fuck that prick and all his influence over this city—and who knew how much of the rest of the world too. We needed to destroy *him* before he ruined even more lives.

The van's engine growled. "Get in!" Garrison hollered.

Everyone dove into the vehicle, Julius and I providing cover for Blaze and Dess before leaping in ourselves. We fired off a few more shots through the open windows as Garrison hit the gas. The van groaned and lurched forward, speeding away from the factory and the men who'd done their best to end us.

"He found us again," Dess said, her voice tight. "Where the hell do we go now?"

Blaze had already flipped open his laptop, because of course he had. His fingers clattered across the keys. "I was working on something last night," he said. "It might only take another hour or two to get all the information we'll need…"

"Need to do *what*?" Garrison demanded with typical impatience.

Blaze glanced around at us with the nearly manic grin I'd learned to be wary of. "To make it a lot harder for the Blood Hunter to manipulate *anyone* into doing his bidding."

Julius nodded. "Sounds good to me." He slapped the back of Garrison's seat. "Keep driving while our computer guru does his work. And let's keep the tires on the road this time?"

Garrison let out a rough chuckle. "I'll do my best."

EIGHTEEN

Decima

SOMEHOW I'D BEEN EXPECTING an ominous, super high-tech structure like the government facility we'd broken into to sequence my DNA. Instead, the place we were approaching in the thin early-morning light looked like an ordinary office building. It could have passed for an accounting firm or a call center.

I guessed I should have known better when it came to the Blood Hunter. He made a living out of keeping his illicit activities unnoticed. But Blaze thought that this place, which on paper was merely the offices of a company that dealt in industrial chemicals, was where the Blood Hunter was storing his main archive of stolen DNA samples.

I couldn't help glancing at the hacker, who was checking something on his phone. "Are you sure this is the right spot?"

He nodded without looking up. "I traced information from one of the phones we nabbed through a few different contacts to someone working here. Strangely for an industrial chemical business, they have an expert in DNA sequencing on staff. The Blood Hunter would have to process the samples he gets *somewhere*."

Julius, the only other crew member joining us in the hands-on assault, grunted. "Wouldn't he have it all backed up on the 'cloud' or whatever?"

Blaze shrugged. "I'm sure he has more than one copy. But he's got to balance the risks of losing the data with the risks of it being discovered by the wrong person. He won't have spread it around very much. And if I'm right that this is the center of that part of his operations, I should be able to connect to any other networks he's shared the information to from inside and wipe them as well."

And then hopefully fewer mercenaries would be compelled to come after us.

Julius contemplated the parking lot. "It looks like quite a few employees are in already. How did you want us to handle them?"

A grimace twisted Blaze's lips. "I think that's unavoidable. There are staff here 24-7, but this is the time of day when the fewest are on hand. These are people who willingly choose to work for the Blood Hunter's business, though. I've seen signs of various other illegal operations that are being concealed by this front. I don't think we should have any sympathy for the people who've sided with that prick."

He looked at me, probably thinking of the way I'd hesitated to kill any of the mercenaries attacking us if we could find another way. I set my jaw. "These people are all helping the Blood Hunter terrorize the world for their own gain. We can't give them the chance to alert him or get in our way. That means we take them out."

Julius nodded in somber agreement. He raised his phone to his ear. "We're going in," he informed Talon, who was watching the building from a farther distance with Garrison, ready to provide whatever backup we might need from the outside—and babysitting Carter.

"There's not going to be any question that the Chaos Crew was here," Blaze said with a wicked smile. "And while the first priority is destroying the DNA files, maybe I'll be able to steal a bunch more data on the Blood Hunter's operations that'll allow us to create even more havoc later."

I smiled grimly. "Sounds good to me."

Julius slung the duffel bag he was carrying over his shoulder, gas canisters clanking together inside. We didn't want to leave any possibility of the Blood Hunter retrieving data from the computer terminals inside—so that meant that when Blaze had done all he could, the whole building was coming down. Or rather, going up in flames.

Our commander raised his chin toward the building. "Let's go."

We marched toward the front door together. A security guard was visible just inside beyond the glass pane of its window. I drew one of my knives into my hand, holding it close at my side as we reached the entrance.

When we pulled the door open, the security guard frowned. "I don't know you. If you have business with—"

I didn't let him finish that sentence. With a swift swing of my arm, I'd severed his throat and the arteries that bordered it. Blood spurted out as he crumpled to the floor.

The reception desk was empty this early in the morning. We stormed through the first floor, taking down another guard and a couple of men in lab coats so quickly none of them had a chance to raise the alarm. Blaze pointed us to the second floor.

We paused at the door on the landing, peering through the narrow window into an open-concept room filled with cubicles, several of them inhabited. There was also a row of office rooms along the far wall. Blaze pointed toward them. "One of the computers in those rooms should have the access I need. I'll head straight there. Assuming you two can take care of the rest?"

Julius's eyes glinted. "That's what we're here for."

We burst through the doorway together, Julius and I firing our silenced pistols the moment we set foot on the linoleum tiles. One after another employee dropped, some of them in the process of scrambling for their phones or reaching to their waists where they might have had weapons of their own. Too late. In a matter of seconds, they were all slumped by their desks, blood pooling beneath them.

Destroying them was so easy that a twinge of guilt passed through me, but then I thought about Petrov talking about the threats to his family. About the girls and women who'd been stolen from their homes to be used by sick men. Everyone in this building had helped the Blood Hunter make those things happen. They deserved their fate.

Blaze had pushed into one of the smaller offices. There was a bang as he must have dispatched the owner of said office. Julius and I hustled across the room and kicked in the doors of the others, confirming they were empty.

We were just turning around when a pair of security guards barreled into the room. "What the hell—" one was in the process of saying. He was only just raising his gun when Julius planted a bullet in his skull. I caught the other in the chest and then the neck with my own.

We strode through the rest of the building, checking the breakroom with its stale coffee smell lacing the air, the restrooms, and a storage area where we found one more security guard, grooving to tunes on his headphones while he peered through the window, blissfully unaware that the building had been compromised until I blasted his brains across the wall.

Julius prodded a couple of the boxes on one of the shelves. "Looks like they've got a drugs operation, or at least part of one, funneled through here. These are the kinds of supplies you'd need in a meth lab."

"Lovely," I said. "Well, they're all going up in smoke too."

He opened up the duffel bag and handed me one of the canisters. We took opposite ends of the room, splashing gasoline across the shelves and leaving a trail leading to the door. We created a stream down the hall and then liberally sloshed it across every desk and piece of computer equipment except the station Blaze was working at.

One of the screens I soaked showed an image of a woman much like the videos we'd seen at the auction—the worker lying dead beneath his chair had been editing it. To make her look like a more appealing purchase? To conceal any evidence of who her seller was? My stomach turned, and I kicked the asshole in the ribs, even though he was already gone from this world.

"Blaze," I hollered. "There are files here on the trafficked women. Grab those if you can!"

"I'll do my best," he called from the office where he'd set up shop. I could hear his fingers racing across the keyboard from all the way across the large room. "Unsurprisingly, he's got some tricky security systems protecting the most vital data. I haven't quite gotten to the DNA files yet. If you're done prepping the place, keep watch on the parking lot. We need to be out of here before the regular daytime shift shows up. There's no way we'll be able to handle all of them without someone getting away and tipping off the Blood Hunter."

"Dess, you watch the windows," Julius ordered. "Blaze, you've got to have a dozen flash drives on you. Toss me a couple and I'll back up whatever I can from the computers out here."

He hustled over to Blaze's office and snatched what Blaze threw to him out of the air. As he hurried back to the nearest computers, I stalked to the row of windows that looked over the parking lot.

It was still early, but traffic was starting to pick up with morning commuters. Blaze had said we should be fine until eight-thirty or so, but he'd also cautioned us that we couldn't be sure no one would turn up before then. If they did, we'd need to take them out before they saw the carnage downstairs and raised the alarm.

Somewhere behind me, Julius made a disgusted sound that told me he'd found more unpleasant material. The gasoline fumes in the air were making me a little dizzy, but they also fueled the anger inside me. I couldn't wait to see this stronghold of the Blood Hunter's burn.

Blaze let out a little whoop, so I knew he was at least partway to his goal. I shifted my weight, feeling the seconds slip by us with thuds of my pulse. The sun slowly crept up behind the rooftops across the street, streaking their eavestroughs with a golden glow. More cars zipped by along the nearest street.

My eye caught on movement near the parking lot. A light gray sedan was pulling in. My hand dropped to my gun. I drew in a breath to give the guys a heads up before I headed downstairs to take care of the problem, and then I noticed that the woman behind the wheel wasn't alone.

A small figure sat in the backseat, leaning close to the window. My heart flipped over. It was a little girl, fine blond hair framing her pale face.

Why would anyone be bringing a *kid* to this building? They wouldn't march one of their slaves around in broad daylight, would they? And anyway, she looked significantly younger than the other girls we'd seen trafficked, who'd all been at least on the verge of adolescence. I'd place this kid at seven or eight tops.

Maybe they weren't coming to this building at all? The woman might have preferred to park here when heading to another office or store down the street.

I unlocked my voice just in case. "Someone's in the parking lot. A woman, looks like a professional, nice suit, and a little girl. They're just getting out of the car."

"A little girl?" Julius said, his head jerking toward me in surprise.

"Yes. I don't understand— Shit." The woman had opened the back door for the girl, who'd scampered out, and they'd both turned toward the office where I was standing. The girl was wearing a school uniform that only emphasized her youth, a pale blue shirt with a plaid skirt that hung to her knees, stripes of blue, green, and yellow woven together.

A second later, they were heading across the lot to the front door. My stomach lurched.

"They're coming here. We can't—I'm not going to shoot a kid."

Julius swore. "As soon as they see the guard in the lobby, we're screwed."

I whipped my phone to my ear, tapping it to dial Garrison's number. He picked it up on the first ring. My heart pounded so loud I could barely hear my voice.

"We need a diversion in the parking lot, *now*," I said. "There's a woman bringing a kid to the building—we need to stop them from coming in."

My stomach continued to list as I imagined the little girl walking in and seeing the bloodshed. The nightmares and daytime terrors that might follow. I'd been brought up on violence, but no child really should be. She wouldn't understand.

Thankfully, Garrison understood without my having to say

anything else. "On it," he said without hesitation. "What car did she come in?"

"It's a silver sedan," I said. There was only one of those in the lot right now, thank God.

I heard a squeak of hinges just before Garrison hung up. I didn't have to wait long to find out how he was going to handle the problem.

Tires screeched down the street. A sports car came zooming into the parking lot and crashed straight into the woman's sedan. A hoodie-clad figure I knew was Garrison leapt out and immediately dashed off.

At the noise of the crash, the woman had spun around, just ten feet from the door. She clapped her hand to her mouth and then hurried back toward her car, waving for the girl to stay with her. Relief trickled through me, but not enough to settle my nerves completely.

"They won't be distracted for too long," I said to the others. "We've got to set this place burning and take off before they come back to the building." I didn't want to hurt the girl, and that included protecting her from the horrifying sights inside.

Julius sighed. "I was able to transfer a few things that look useful."

"I'm done," Blaze announced breathlessly. "All digital files are destroyed, and the triple backups are wiped, too. As far as I can tell, I got it all. I wish I could have grabbed more for our own use..." He paused in the doorway, gazing longingly at the machine. "It's all on the network, no point in taking the computer itself."

"There's no time," Julius said grimly. He nudged Blaze aside to heave the last of his gasoline over the equipment in there.

We hustled to the back stairwell. On the threshold, Julius held a lighter to a ball of paper he'd stuffed into a mug from someone's desk. When the paper went up in flames, he hurled it into the middle of the room.

The ceramic sides smashed. The fire licked out across the trails of gasoline, flaring brighter as it crawled across the room with increasing speed. I took in the welcome sight of the Blood Hunter's hard work turning into ash for a couple of beats of my heart. Then Blaze tugged at my arm.

"We've got to get out of here," he reminded me.

Of course. I turned on my heel, and we rushed down the stairs together. Just as we burst into the back alley, the sound of shattering windows reached my ears. The fire was roaring all through the second floor now.

The woman would see it—she'd know not to bring the kid anywhere near the place now. My work here was done, in more ways than I'd expected.

NINETEEN

Blaze

I STARED at my computer screen for a few seconds, processing what I'd found, before I lifted my voice. "I think I know who that little girl was."

Dess immediately stood up and came over from where she'd been all but inhaling a chocolate bar from our stash of food. My setup in the foreclosed retail building where we were hiding out while we regrouped wasn't anything to brag about, but I did have a chair, if wobbly, and a built-in counter, which was more than I'd had at my disposal in the warehouse before. I'd set my laptop where the cash register probably used to sit as I worked away.

"What?" Dess said, setting her hand on the back of my chair. "I didn't even know you were looking for her."

I savored the faint brush of her fingertips more than was probably healthy, but then, I'd never claimed I was a model of mental stability. "I wasn't actually trying to, but it wasn't even that hard once I started poking around in the right direction." I grimaced as I mentally compiled everything I had to share.

Dess was peering at the photo on my screen which showed a girl in profile, her blond hair tucked behind her visible ear, her slim frame clothed in a private school uniform. "That's her," she said, sucking in her breath. "Or at least it looks a hell of a lot like her, and the uniform looks the same too. How did you find her? What do you mean about looking in the right direction?"

I motioned to my computer. "Well, what I was *trying* to find was the Blood Hunter's true identity. You seeing that girl made me think about the other girl, the one that was so important to him."

"His daughter," Dess filled in, her eyebrows rising. "But she's dead —and that was almost thirty years ago."

"Yes," I said. "But thanks to the records the Maliks kept with their creepy parchment posters, we know the year and month the Blood Hunter's daughter went missing. We know that she was going to school in or near DC, or they wouldn't have had easy access to her. Once I put those pieces together, it wasn't hard to scan the databases of attendance records and see when a girl of the right age had suddenly stopped coming to school."

Julius came over from where he'd been reloading all our guns so they'd be ready if it came down to another shootout. Talon and Garrison looked over too.

"Did you get the Blood Hunter's real name?" our commander asked.

I shook my head with an apologetic twist of my mouth. "He kept that under wraps. The name for parental contact was a woman who I managed to link to a shell corporation that's also turned up in other threads of my investigation, but I haven't been able to follow that chain any further to its source. I'm sure she was an employee, just a placeholder to keep his own identity secret. There are no other records about her either. But that did confirm to me that the girl I found was his daughter. Her name was listed as Brittany Banks."

"Brittany," Dess repeated quietly, as if honoring the tortured blond girl we'd seen in one of the photographs the Blood Hunter had arranged for us to find.

"But is that *her* real name?" Garrison demanded.

"I'm guessing it was a fake last name," I said. "But I think the first name was correct. It'd be hard for a little kid to adjust to being called one name at home and another at school, and he wouldn't have wanted to raise suspicions if she got confused. At the time, it was an incredibly popular girls name so it wouldn't have seemed very identifiable."

Garrison huffed. "So basically you got nothing."

"That's not what I'm saying." My stomach knotted a little as I thought about how much else I had to reveal. "I got something I didn't expect at all. When I was running all possible searches to try to find out any other information out about the Blood Hunter's family, I stumbled on a girl named Brittany—different last name—who's going to a private school in DC. A private school with a uniform just like the one you described. A girl who matched your description too. And Brittany *isn't* a very common name anymore."

Dess's brow knit. "What are you saying?"

I dragged in a breath. "Well, I didn't know what to think at first, but it was a lead I had to chase. I dug into her records as much as I could, and just like the first Brittany, the woman listed as her guardian is essentially a ghost, the bare minimum of records under that name, one of them linking her to another shell corporation. Probably another of the Blood Hunter's employees, providing a front for him like the first woman did."

"A front because… the Blood Hunter has another daughter?"

"Sort of." I waved toward the photograph. "I compared facial structure and other factors between their photographs as well as I could. They look superficially similar, but they're too different in the ways that indicate genetics to share a parent. I think he obtained her by the same methods he uses to gather all the women he sells. It'd be easier than waiting out an entire pregnancy, and he wouldn't have known for sure how a kid he fathered naturally would look or even that it'd be a girl."

"So he stole her," Talon said solemnly.

I nodded. "He found a girl who reminded him of his former daughter in looks and either kidnapped her or bought her from desperate birth parents. She's been registered at the school for four years, so he's had her at least that long. I'm not sure why he'd have taken that step recently instead of decades ago. Maybe once he saw that you were fully grown, Dess, and he knew it wouldn't be much longer before he sent you after your father, he felt at peace enough to want to start over. But it looks like that's what he's doing. He picked out a kid with similar looks, gave her the same name… She's his replacement kid."

Dess winced. "And he's already involving her in his businesses somehow. That woman was going to bring her to the office. I don't know how much they've told her, but she's being exposed to it, with everything going on around her…"

"He's grooming his heir," Julius put in. "That's another reason he might have decided to go for it now. He isn't getting any younger—if he had a six-year-old almost thirty years ago, he's got to be in his late fifties at least. He'd have realized that he needed to start raising another kid ASAP if he wanted to hand over the reins to someone he'd sculpted from that young an age."

"Just like he had me molded to be what he wanted," Dess said, hugging herself. Her eyes looked tormented as she took in the girl's picture again. "Is there anything we can do for her?"

I shook my head. "Not right now. There's no way to prove any wrongdoing to get Child Services or anyone else involved."

She exhaled through her teeth. I stood from my chair, touching her arm, about to pull her into my arms. I wanted to be closer—close enough to soothe the rage that only seemed to grow the longer it went unchecked in her eyes. I wanted to hold her and show her that she wasn't alone in her fury.

But I couldn't do more than offer that brief touch before Talon's head snapped around. He'd been standing closest to the shop's grimy windows, and he eased closer now, peering past the smudges.

"A couple of police cruisers just pulled up a couple of stores down. The cops are getting out. It looks like they're checking all the buildings in the area."

Shit. My pulse stuttered, and I leapt back to my computer. "Are they coming straight here?"

"No. The Blood Hunter mustn't have been able to tip them off to exactly where we are. Maybe he figured out the neighborhood, or maybe they're patrolling for other reasons."

"But either way it isn't good," Garrison added, snatching up as many bags of supplies as he could lift into his arms. "Let's get the fuck out of here."

"Hold on," I said quickly. "I think I can divert them, and then we won't risk a chase. Let me just…"

My hands whipped over the keyboard. There. I sent a falsified signal to all the police scanners nearby—an alert of gunshots fired reported at a location several blocks away. A second later, the thump of footsteps reached my ears.

"They're running back to their cars," Talon reported, and tipped his head to me. "You pulled it off."

"For now." I rubbed my hand over my face. We kept getting found, kept having to flee at a moment's notice, and I could only use that trick one or two more times before calling wolf stopped being effective. Next time I might not be fast enough, or close enough to my computer—next time they might barge right into the building we were hiding out in, no chance to deflect them.

I glanced at Dess again as she went to grab her brother from the back room where we'd left him. A pang ran through my chest. That short interlude we'd had together back at the guest house felt centuries ago. When would we finally be able to relax again and enjoy the closeness we both got so much out of?

I might have managed to get at least some of the mercenaries off our backs with our attack on the office building yesterday. Interfering with the general could have put a wrench in the Blood Hunter's military efforts as well. If only I could find a longer-term solution to keeping the police at a distance too…

An idea clicked into place in my head, so brilliant and also bonkers that I could already imagine what the others' reaction would be. I said it anyway.

"I think I have a way to make sure the cops won't be on our tail for at least a day or two so we can properly regroup. But I'm not sure you're going to like it."

"Why do I feel like I am so dead?" Dess whispered through the headset that I'd given her.

"There's no need for theatrics," I teased. "We're just... diverting all the resources of the police department."

Okay, that was a bit of an overstatement... but only a bit. I intended that when we were done here, no amount of anonymous tips would be able to convince the police to look for us anywhere other than where I'd pointed them.

But I needed help on the ground to accomplish that, and Dess had been the ideal accomplice. She could move faster than Julius or Talon, she was highly skilled at stealthy maneuvers, and she was smaller, so she could hide in more places than either of them. It was a no-brainer.

I wasn't sure she'd be thanking me for giving her the honor, though.

"All you have to do is plant three more bombs, and we're home free," I reminded her.

"Right. Three more bombs on top of the dozen or so I've already placed, positioned perfectly so they won't actually hurt anyone but will make a commotion to draw attention, *and* leave traces of the blood you ever so helpfully donated. Piece of cake. I should do this every day."

The corners of my mouth quirked up. I loved a lot of things about Dess, and right now I was particularly loving the sarcastic side of her that'd come out.

"And I trust that you'd pull it off perfectly every time," I assured her with a grin.

She sighed, and then the connection went quiet as she must have come up on her next target location. I'd plotted out a map of key spots all in the same general neighborhood where it'd look as if the terrible criminals the police had been tracking based on their new DNA results were attempting to wreak havoc on a rival gang that operated there. Both the investigation and the clashes with that gang should keep a whole lot of officers *very* busy for at least a little while.

The tips the Blood Hunter had been giving them hadn't gotten them anywhere. They had to be wondering how many of those were calling wolf too. There wouldn't be the manpower to follow up on anything unverified while they had so much obvious evidence to sort through and leads to pursue.

I hunkered down in the middle seat of the van, monitoring police activity on my laptop. A minute later, Dess tuned back in. "Okay, it's done."

"Only two more now!" I told her cheerfully.

She snorted, sounding not even a little out of breath as she loped through the back alleys to the next target. "Lucky me. When I get back, you are going to owe me *so* much chocolate."

"I can think of other ways of repaying you," I said slyly, and her laugh electrified me.

"I'm sure you can," she said. "Here we go. Give me a second."

It took more like thirty, but I wasn't going to complain when that was plenty speedy all on its own. A buoyant warmth filled my chest, and it occurred to me that despite the stress of the past few days and our current predicament—not to mention the crazy stunt we were about to pull—I felt *happy*.

Even when our lives were going to hell, I was delighted to be working with this woman, fighting alongside her, making up plans and carrying them out. It was just as much of a thrill as making love to her. Even if we were on the run forever, it would be worth it as long as Dess was here with me.

Dess's voice carried to me again. "One more to go. You're going to pick me up, right? Or do I have to run back through this entire hellhole?"

I chuckled. "We'll come get you." I thumped the back of the driver's seat, and Talon started the engine. "Berkley and King Street," I said to both him and Dess.

Ten minutes later, the woman I loved was scrambling into the van next to me. She slammed the door and flopped back in the seat with a sound that was half exhilaration, half exasperation.

"Wasn't that fun?" I said, and she whacked my arm in protest. But a smile curled her lips as we drove away from the scene of our soon-to-be crime.

I checked my laptop once more, confirmed we were well away

from the routes the police would take, and gave the command to detonate.

The bombs went off in the distance like the crackle of popping corn. Sirens split the air moments later. I glanced across at Dess, and she grinned back at me, her eyes gleaming despite her earlier grumbling. "We did it," she said.

"Hell, yes, we did." And Hell itself would have been a worthwhile trip with her at my side.

I did hope it didn't come to that, though.

TWENTY

Decima

I DIDN'T KNOW how we'd gone from a luxury home built into the side of a rocky hill to a garage in an abandoned house, but here we were, squatting in the dingy space like a group of drug addicts waiting for our next fix. Our efforts at undermining the Blood Hunter hadn't given us the freedom to settle into proper accommodations yet. I wished I had some idea of what it would take.

But we had another mission ahead of us that might get us closer to the goal of taking him down for good. Blaze was working out the final details on his computer, and the other men were clustered around him in the far corner near the door to the rest of the house, going through our equipment. I'd brought a sandwich and a bottle of water over to Carter, who I'd set up on a blanket we'd scrounged up.

One of the reasons we'd picked this garage was that it appeared that some previous inhabitants had used it for band practice. The walls were heavily soundproofed. I couldn't hear a thing from outside, which meant that even if my brother decided to holler, no one out there would hear him. We still had his ankles bound together and one of his wrists now handcuffed to a heavy steel bar that protruded from the concrete wall. He wasn't going anywhere.

Which was a good thing, because this mission required all hands on deck. We were going to leave him here on his own for a few hours, because I didn't trust him alone in the van out where we were going. There was too much chance of him drawing attention one way or another, or of someone noticing him in the vehicle and getting concerned if we drugged him.

If only we could have trusted him to be on our side in this, to fight with us instead of against us… but I knew that was unlikely. All the same, I sat down across from him while he dug into the sandwich.

He ate in silence for a few minutes. Then he glanced toward the men. "Are you guys going somewhere?"

I inclined my head. "We've got another job to do."

"Looking for more Maliks to kill?"

The snark in his tone didn't quite land. He mostly sounded tired, like he thought he should be a brat about it but couldn't put his heart into it. I studied him carefully.

"It's a job that we're hoping will get us closer to destroying the Blood Hunter," I said. "The man who's *really* responsible for most of those deaths."

"You're responsible," he retorted. "The person who wields the weapon is the one who made the final choice."

I gazed back at him. "By that logic, you and the rest of our family are the only ones responsible for the deaths of all those innocent kids. In which case all I did was eliminate a bunch of child murderers from the world."

"That's not what they were," he protested, but that response sounded weak too. He was getting fed up with this debate, and maybe a little worn down, realizing how hard it was for him to justify what our parents and the rest of the family had done. I *hoped* he was realizing it. I didn't know how I could be kinder to him without putting the rest of us more at risk.

"I know they were more than that to you," I said quietly. "I can't imagine what it's like to have your family torn away from you, no matter what else they were doing or how cruel they could be. I'm sorry for how you're hurting. I didn't *do* it to hurt you. It was the only way I could save myself and the people I care about. And it's what the Blood Hunter intended to happen all along. He set everything up so that I'd be in that position."

"I don't know why you're bothering harping on about that."

I folded my arms in front of me. "I'm reminding you about it because if you're really interested in stopping bad people, you've got the perfect opportunity if you cooperate with us. I'd be happy to give you a part in what we're doing to crack down on the Blood Hunter's crimes. If we succeed, we'll take down the man responsible for your family's deaths. Hell, I'd say you have the right to be involved in getting justice. I just have to be sure you're on our side."

Carter glowered at me. "Why do you care anyway? You might as well just kill me like the others."

My heart sank. I hadn't thought it was all going to be okay just like that, but I obviously wasn't making any more headway right now.

I stood up. "It's not about caring, Carter. It's about doing what's right. There's a part of you, even if it's still small, that knows what you all did to those kids isn't okay. That realizes you bought into a delusion that was about power rather than justice. As long as that part is there, you deserve the chance to shake off the sick ideas the rest of the family indoctrinated you with. I know you're not a monster. I just hope you get to the point where you can admit I'm not one either."

I checked him over quickly to make sure he was both as comfortable and secure as we could make him. "There's no point in yelling after we leave. The building is soundproofed. You might as well save your throat. I'm not going to gag you if I don't have to."

"How nice of you," Carter muttered. He slumped back against the wall, clutching his bottle of water. I walked over to the men.

"Are we ready to get going?" I asked. "Because I'd really like to shoot some perverted assholes now."

The corner of Julius's mouth twitched upward. "I think that can be arranged."

"This should be a good time," Garrison muttered with obvious sarcasm as we stared down the mansion that was our target from a partly sheltered perch along the top of the stone wall that surrounded the sprawling property. The house was pretty sprawling too, a three-story neoclassical monstrosity that could have swallowed the building I'd grown up in whole, as big as the household had been.

The place belonged to one of the Blood Hunter's biggest clients in the human trafficking business. We'd determined with the data we'd gathered during our previous missions that Mr. Gordell had bought more than a dozen girls over the years, most of them underage or not much over eighteen. Lord only knew what he'd done with them since then.

Armed guards stood at the main gate into the property, but we'd circumnavigated them completely. If this went well, they'd never know we'd been here until after we'd already left—with the women their employer had purchased.

"No one posted at the back door," Talon observed.

"No one *outside* it," Blaze clarified. "We know Gordell has a contract with a private security firm—one known for not minding getting involved in dirty business. I'd bet he has ten or more men on the inside patrolling and ensuring the women don't make a run for it. It could be as many as twenty."

"We can handle them," Julius said grimly. "We just have to make sure none of the women get hurt in the crossfire. Use blades as much as you safely can; be careful with your aim."

I nodded, fully agreeing with his sentiment. The last thing I wanted was to accidentally wound or even kill one of the women I was trying to save.

I pointed to the stand of cherry trees just to the right beyond the back of the mansion. "We can get within twenty feet of the back door without being seen by using the trees for cover. After that, it's going to get trickier."

Julius slipped off the wall, his boots thumping softly on the grassy ground. "Let's take a closer look and figure out our best approach from there. Once we're inside the house, we spread out, take down everyone in league with our target on the first floor. Talon and I will head upstairs and tackle anyone up there as well as sending any of the women we find downstairs. Garrison, you go up too and stand watch by the front windows over the foyer in case they manage to call in back-up before we're out. Blaze and Dess will get the women ready to run by the back door." He glanced at me. "You're probably going to need to do a lot of the talking. We have no idea how much they'll trust any man after what they'll have been through."

"That's no problem." I just hoped they believed me when I told them we were here to help.

And not just them but other women like them. Once the Blood Hunter's clients realized that they were vulnerable too, they should start pulling away from him. Maybe someone would even turn against him to preemptively save their own skin.

We set off across the expansive lawn, keeping the cherry trees between us and the windows of the house. As we stepped between the trunks, my feet trod over fallen blossoms turned brown and rotten. A faint, sickly sweet scent lingered in the air. It turned my stomach, which was already churning.

Stopping in the shadows at the edge of the trees, we studied the back of the house from closer up. I thought I made out a form through the frosted window of the back door, but it didn't move, so it was hard to tell whether it was a guard or something else. *Someone* would probably see us if we just marched across the open ground to the door and spent the multiple minutes it would take to break through the lock. Shattering windows would announce our presence more loudly than we'd prefer too.

An idea wriggled out through my mind. My first impulse was to dismiss it, but it wasn't so different from tactics I'd implemented in the household's service before. Why shouldn't I use every bit of training the Blood Hunter had arranged for me to receive against him?

"I've got this," I said, unbuckling the holster at my waist and handing it to Blaze for safekeeping. "Wait until I've cleared the doorway, and then run for it as fast as you can."

"What are you going to—" Blaze started, looking confused, and snapped his mouth shut when I pulled off my black tee as well, leaving me in only my bra from the waist up. Julius had raised his eyebrows.

Garrison let out a soft whistle. Only Talon gave little reaction, but I could feel his gaze burning into my skin.

"I know what I'm doing," I said, glowering at them all, and tossed my shirt to Blaze too. My other gun was concealed at my calf under the loose leg of my sweatpants, my favorite knives in hidden sheaths in my hip pockets. At a glance, I'd appear unarmed. I shoved my fingers through my hair to tousle it as if I'd been wandering in the wind for hours and then stumbled out onto the open grass.

I drifted this way and that, wandering toward the house in a vague zigzag, swaying a little on my feet. For effect, I swiped at my eyes as if I'd been crying.

It took less than a minute before the back door swung open and two men in suits stepped out, both with guns at their hips. They hadn't even unholstered them. Ha.

"Who are you?" one of them demanded.

I froze, staring at them with widened eyes. "I—I need help. Please…" I let my voice rasp and shake. Then I wobbled closer to them, holding out a hand.

The first guard glanced at the other. "How the hell did she get out?"

The second shook his head. "Fuck if I know. Hey, what's your name?"

I pretended to swallow a sob. "Delia."

"All right, Delia. Let's get you back inside where you belong."

I hunched my shoulders, which conveniently brought my hands closer to my knives. One man put his hand between my shoulder blades to guide me into the house, the other turning next to me to scan the grounds, and I whipped into action.

I grabbed both knives at the same time. One I jabbed backward at the man partly behind me, carving open his throat. The other I thrust sideways into the second guard's jugular. Neither of them stood a chance. After a few twitches and spastic gropes toward their guns, they slumped over onto the grass.

Footsteps were already pounding toward me across the lawn. I wiped my knives on the grass quickly before hauling one man over to lie him close against the side of the house where the shadows would partly conceal him, and Julius and Talon joined me to heave the other out of view. Blaze caught up with us on the threshold and tossed me my shirt and holster.

As I yanked them back into place, Garrison leaned close to murmur in my ear. "Has anyone ever told you how hot you are in action?"

I tsked my tongue at him. "Keep your mind on the mission."

"That's right," Julius said in a low voice. "Fan out and take them all down. The faster we work, the less chance a call for backup goes out."

We marched into the house as if we belonged there. Julius went left and Talon went right, so I strode on straight ahead, my pistol in one hand and my knife in the other.

At a movement by a nearby room, I pressed close to the wall and darted forward. I caught a guard just as he stepped through the doorway. He got out half a shout before I clapped my forearm over his mouth and drove my knife into the side of his neck. He sagged in my arms. Similar thuds from around me told me the men were keeping equally busy.

I glanced into the room the guard had come out of and found myself staring at two young women in dresses that covered little more than their breasts, bellies, and hips. One of them was biting her lip, her stance rigid. The other was trembling, sucking in a breath as if she were about to scream.

"No!" I protested as loudly as I dared. "We're here to get you out of this place. No one's going to own you again. No one's going to use you again. We want to help."

She blinked at me, looking bewildered, but her mouth closed. I pointed down the hall the way I'd come. "Gather by the back door. If you see any of the other girls who were brought here against their will, get them to come too. We're going to escort you away from here as soon as it's safe."

They clutched each other's hands without a word, but they scurried past me the way I'd indicated. I ducked back out, picking up my pace as I approached the front of the house.

I paused at the end of the hallway, peering out into a vast foyer with a ceiling that loomed two stories high, a second-floor mezzanine wrapping around the space over the front door. A crystal chandelier glittered overhead. I gritted my teeth against the urge to shoot at it and shatter all the vicious wealth it represented.

Two more security guards were standing by the front door. It was too much distance to cross to hit them by stealth—at least, not both of them. Things were about to get a bit noisy.

I leapt forward, hurling my knife and pulling the trigger on my pistol at the same moment. The blade and the bullet both lodged in their target's heads, and the men toppled over. Even with the silencer, the bang of the shot reverberated off the high ceiling. I winced as I darted across the room, scanning it.

Another shot rang out elsewhere in the house. Garrison jogged into view, a streak of blood marking his shirt. "All clear that way," he said. "I'll take my position upstairs."

He hustled up to the mezzanine overlooking the front of the house, and Talon and Julius followed moments later. Blaze hadn't appeared yet. I wondered how many more girls had been on the first floor—were they all waiting by the back door, ready to flee?

A motion near the edge of the room caught my eye. I stepped closer and spotted a girl who couldn't have been more than fifteen crouched in an alcove, shivering. I walked over, holstering my gun.

"It's okay," I said. "We're going to get you out of here."

She simply stared at me blankly. I crouched down, a lump rising in my throat. "Can you manage to walk to the back door? I'll take you if you need me to."

Her lips parted, but no sound came out. Then her gaze flicked upward with an expression of panic just as a faint creak reached my ears. I leapt up and spun around to find a knife slashing straight toward me.

TWENTY-ONE

Garrison

I PEERED out the windows over the vast lawn at the front of the house, scanning the front drive and the little I could see of the road beyond for approaching cars. For the moment, there was no sign of reinforcements coming to the aid of the men we'd taken down here.

It felt strange to be standing in the warmth of the mid day sun for an operation. Normally we relied on darkness to make stealth easier. But with a mission at a residential home, we'd known we'd find *less* resistance during the day, when the owner of this house and any of the regular people who lived here with him would be off at work.

What a sight Gordell was going to come home to.

A smirk tugged at my lips. I glanced down at the foyer below—just as Dess whirled around from where she'd been crouched off to the side to parry a blow from a knife-wielding man who'd managed to sneak up on her.

My pulse stuttered, but I held myself in place. Dess was more than capable of fending off one attacker, even taken by surprise—more capable than I was at physical combat, that was for sure.

But as she grappled with the man, who looked like he must have been regular staff rather than official security from his more casual clothes and wiry frame, another figure emerged into view from beneath the mezzanine, just raising his gun.

Dess hadn't seen him—she had her back to him, only just managing to smack the knife from her attacker's hand. It would take no more than a split-second for the gunman to put a bullet in her brain.

I reacted on pure adrenaline—okay, and maybe a little panic. Before I'd even thought about what I was going to do, I leapt over the railing and plummeted down toward the gunman, trusting his bulky body to break my fall.

It wasn't an enjoyable landing. I slammed into the gunman, and we both went sprawling, a grunt bursting from his lungs. My hip jarred against the floor as I toppled off him. I wrenched around as quickly as I could, grabbing for his weapon, which had slid a few inches from his fingertips.

I wasn't fast enough. The man snatched up the gun and rammed it into my face so hard pain splintered through my skull. My thoughts felt as if they were rattling around in my brain. I groped for my own gun at my side, and then Dess was there, firing her pistol.

Blood splattered across the floor. The gunman crumpled to the ground. I glanced past him to see Dess's other attacker lying in a ruddy pool, just as limp.

We didn't get any time to celebrate. Footsteps thundered from down one of the halls, and Blaze's voice echoed through the space. "Incoming!"

Two more men burst into the foyer, already firing at us. More shots boomed somewhere farther away, I guessed wherever Blaze had stirred up a hidden nest of hornets. I'd have to remember to thank him later—maybe with a fist to the head.

There wasn't time for more than a flicker of annoyance. Then there was nothing to think about other than survival. Dess hauled me to my feet and yanked me toward a side hall. "I have to reload," she said in a strained voice.

We dashed into what appeared to be a dining room. As the men charged after us, we lunged behind the table for cover. Dess shoved a fresh clip into her gun, and I managed to get my own pistol out to join the party.

The men barreled around opposite sides of the table, spewing bullets from their semi-automatic rifles as they came. Motherfuckers. I rolled under the table, kicked a chair into the closer guy's legs, and fired a couple of shots, managing to catch him in the calf. But as he dropped to his knees, he pulled the trigger again, his bullet smacking into the floor just inches shy of Dess.

I kicked out again, slamming my heel into his hand. His gun dropped from his fingers. I whipped mine around, but he was already tackling me, wrenching at my wrist.

The man tried to twist my arm so he could fire my own gun at me, but I weakened his grasp with a knee to his gut. I couldn't manage to dislodge his weight, though. No matter how I twisted, he remained on top of me, attempting to wrestle me into submission. I was barely holding him at bay, shaking with all the force he used to press down on me.

If I didn't do something fast, he'd win. And I would die.

I wasn't the strongest member of the team in combat, and my real skill sets wouldn't help me here. That didn't mean I was going to give up. I couldn't—not with Dess fighting another man mere feet away. As long as his attention was focused on me, he couldn't hurt her.

In a moment of adamant rebellion, I shifted my weight to one side quickly and finally threw my attacker off balance just enough that when I shoved back onto my other hip, he all but fell off me. I used the rest of my strength to jerk my arm from his grasp and pull the trigger.

I hit him square in the forehead. As he collapsed in a heap next to me, I resisted the urge to imitate his slumped pose while I caught my breath. Instead, I squirmed out from under the table, intent on protecting Dess any way I could. But I emerged to find Dess poised over the other man, one of her knives protruding from his throat.

She spun around and stared at me on the floor. "Are you okay?" she asked, breathless.

"Just peachy," I replied, groaning as I pulled myself upright.

She offered her hand to help me stand. "Thank you. The other guard in the foyer—I hadn't even noticed him. If you hadn't tackled him…" She shook her head with a tightening of her jaw.

I didn't like seeing her doubting herself. I offered my best cocky grin in an attempt to lighten the mood. "I'm always here for you, sweetheart."

It set off a rush of pride in me to realize that I *had* saved her. If I hadn't leapt off the mezzanine to tackle that prick, she might not be with me right now. She was standing in front of me like death incarnate, but she'd needed me.

A grin that was probably a little too goofy to be totally appropriate stretched across my face. Dess knuckled my arm, nudging me out of the dining room. "Let's see if the others need any help. And if the building's clear now, we need to get the girls out of here."

We strode back to the foyer just as Julius and Talon came into view at the top of the stairs at the far end. They were herding several more young women down, and Blaze was standing by the hallway, urging them down it toward the back door.

"I think we got everyone," Julius said as he and Talon reached the bottom of the stairs, and then frowned at me. "What are you doing down here? You were supposed to—"

He was interrupted by the crash of the front door bursting open. A squad of armed men burst into the room, pelting us with semi-automatic fire in an instant.

We flung ourselves to the floor instinctively, but some of us more purposefully than others. My gut lurched as I watched Talon jerk backward and fall on his ass, blood blooming from a shot to his chest. He clutched at the wound but managed to fire into the sudden crowd of attackers as well.

I squeezed my own trigger, aiming into the horde as well as I could. Dess was shooting frantically, as was Blaze where he'd crouched at the edge of the hall. As my pulse pounded in my ears, one thought pealed through the thrum of frantic adrenaline.

This was my fault. I'd been assigned to watch the front drive—if I hadn't left my post, I'd have seen the reinforcements approaching and been able to warn everyone. We'd been taken by surprise because of my negligence. *Fuck.*

Another grunt of pain reached my ears. My gaze darted to where Julius had dropped. He was gripping the side of his abdomen with one hand while he kept shooting with the other.

"Julius!" Dess cried out, and whipped her remaining knives at the incoming attackers alongside our hail of bullets.

The last of the men in the room toppled over. Dess didn't waste any time dashing to the front door. She fired several more times, and thumps carried from outside. Some of the newcomers had thought to hang back and assess the situation, but they'd met the same fate as their colleagues.

"That's all of them," Dess said, her voice tight, as she sprinted back to where Julius and Talon had fallen. "Oh my god. Are you all right? I—what can I do?"

Practical thoughts started racing through my head alongside the blare of guilt. "We have to get them out of here," I said. "Medical attention. Fast."

"Keep pressure on the wounds," Blaze added, rushing in to help Julius to his feet as Dess did the same for Talon. A large red welt marked Julius's lower abdomen. He held as firmly as his paling fingers could manage. Talon had two wounds—one in his side and another through his thigh—both bleeding just as profusely as Julius's. I leapt in, wrenching off my shirt so I could wrap it around Talon's leg as a makeshift bandage.

"What the hell happened?" Blaze said in disbelief as we hustled down the hall toward the nervously waiting girls as fast as we could.

I swallowed thickly. "I left my post. I wasn't watching—I didn't see them coming."

Dess gave me a sharp look. "You left to protect me."

But maybe I should have gone back after I'd taken the first guy down. Maybe I should have assumed she could handle the other arrivals by herself. Had I gotten so caught up in playing hero for her that I was now going to have the deaths of not one but two of the men I respected most on my conscience?

"There's no point in assigning blame," Julius said, his voice rough with pain. "We need to get out of here before more guards come. Small change in strategy. Dess, you and Blaze take the truck we set up for the girls to the place already discussed. Garrison, you drive us in the van. I assume you've got a contact or two in the area who's medically inclined?"

His voice was already faltering by the end of that set of commands. His steps were wavering. I nodded with a jerk, my mind scrambling. I *was* to blame, and so I'd better fucking fix this. Who was the best person to turn to? Who could we trust that the Blood Hunter hadn't compromised?

As we reached the girls, Dess shepherded them out the back door ahead of her, still supporting Talon. She glanced back at Julius, her mouth set in a pale line. I knew she didn't want to leave them, but she'd feel a duty to the girls we'd just broken out of this prison too. She wouldn't let herself fail them.

Thankfully we'd already identified a door in the wall at the back of the property that we'd intended to use to bring the girls out through rather than over the wall anyway. It'd been deadbolted and padlocked from the inside, but Dess made short work of the lock now that we had direct access to it. We hurried through, Julius and Talon's steps stumbling even more than before, their heads drooping. Guilt burned a hole right through my stomach.

Dess motioned the girls toward the truck we'd parked out of sight around a treed bend. "Head over there. We'll be with you in a minute." The girls looked at us like deer in headlights but managed to wander in the right direction. I ran ahead to the van, unlocking it and diving into the driver's seat as soon as I reached the door. While Blaze and Dess helped the other guys into the back, I started the engine and strained my brain.

Where could I take them? Hospitals were obviously out. This was the job I *was* supposed to be good at—gathering resources, maintaining contacts. There had to be—

Fucking hell, how had I almost forgotten? I'd done some cautionary research when we'd first arrived in the DC area and identified a doctor who took private clients of the questionable sort under the table. He was independent, not under any gang's thumb, and it was a small-time practice. If the Blood Hunter even knew about him, it was doubtful he'd bothered to harass him.

As soon as the doors slammed shut, I hit the gas and roared away from Gordell's home. Keeping one hand on the wheel, tuning out the pained breaths carrying from behind me, I whipped out my phone and flicked through it for the contact.

The doctor answered on the third ring with a faded but audibly irritated Irish accent. "Who's this?"

"Someone who had reasons to get this number," I said. He used a separate line for our kind of clients. "I've got two patients for you, urgent—but we can pay very well."

"Well, look here, I've got appointments this afternoon—"

"Bump them," I snapped, and reined my temper in. I had to play this right. Had to use the skills of social manipulation that'd made me part of the Chaos Crew to begin with. "With the kind of money we can offer you, you'll be able to buy every bit of equipment you've dreamed of to cure those patients faster the next time they see you."

"Who says money's the deciding factor?" he asked, but I could hear the interest in his voice. It hadn't been quite enough to convince him, though. I took a gamble, assuming he cared about bumping those patients at the last minute because he actually cared about *them* and not because he felt like being a dick.

"How about this as a bonus: you'll also be helping the crew who took down a child-torturing cult and who will be ending a human trafficking ring if you patch us up all right."

The man sucked in a breath. For a second, in my desperate state, I was afraid I'd miscalculated his concern for the rest of humanity. But my instincts had obviously kicked in even through the haze of guilt and terror in my head.

"Fine," he said. "Bloody hell. Fine. How soon will you get here?"

"If you're still working out of your usual address on Painter Avenue, I'll be aiming for under half an hour," I said. "Be ready."

When I reached the building where the doctor carried out his less legit work, I swerved around back and braked with a squeal of the tires. As I wrenched open the back doors, the doctor came out of the building. He took one look at Julius and Talon and dashed back inside for a couple of stretchers.

I helped him load one man and then the other onto the rolling beds. Julius had nearly passed out from blood loss, mumbling incoherently. Talon was entirely unconscious. I didn't like the look of the bloody stains they'd left behind on the seats.

"Wait out there," the doctor barked at me after I'd helped him wheel the stretchers over to the building. The door closed, and all I could do was slump against the side of the van and wonder whether I'd gotten them here in time.

Julius and Talon were the strongest men I'd ever known. This *couldn't* be what beat them. No fucking way.

But even if they survived, their injuries were severe enough that they'd be laid up for several days if not weeks. Without the strength of our full crew, how could we ever take out the biggest threat we'd ever faced? The Blood Hunter wouldn't wait for us to heal, and we couldn't take him on like this. We might not even be able to defend ourselves from his next attack.

By leaving my post, I could have screwed over the crew more completely than I'd ever imagined was possible.

TWENTY-TWO

Decima

CARTER DIDN'T EVEN LOOK at me when I set down the hamburger and fresh water bottle I'd brought for him. We'd locked him up in the basement bathroom of the current house we'd broken into, a windowless underground space from which no shouts would be overheard. But he didn't seem inclined to make any noise at all. He just glowered at the wall.

I couldn't bring myself to care all that much about his reaction. I had bigger concerns on my mind.

"Don't starve yourself," I told him briskly, and shut the door on my way out.

On the first floor, behind boarded up windows that ensured no one would notice our presence, Julius and Talon were sprawled at one end of the small living room, their makeshift beds just a couple of feet from each other. The doctor Garrison had reached out to had offered us a couple of padded mats that normally adorned stretchers, and we'd laid sleeping bags on top of those to make the two men as comfortable as possible, but it didn't feel like enough.

At the same time, how lucky were we that they'd survived this long at all? It'd been two days since the doctor had done his emergency surgery, stitching up the organs that had been torn by the bullets of Mr. Gordell's security guards. By some small mercy, neither of them had faced heart or lung damage.

After Blaze and I had dropped the women we'd rescued off at a local shelter where they could get help, not sticking around long enough for anyone to ID us or ask questions, we'd retreated to a city a few hours away from DC to give Julius and Talon time to recover. We were hoping that the Blood Hunter wouldn't be extending his search for us this far abroad, and for the time being our luck had held there too.

But for how much longer? The doctor had said that moving around after the first few days of bedrest would help speed their healing, but that they shouldn't attempt anything more than brief, careful walks for the first couple of weeks. They weren't likely to be ready for normal physical activity for at least a month. There was no way they'd be able to make a run for it or fight off attackers if anyone stormed this house.

We'd decided to stay here one more night to give them as much undisturbed rest as possible to begin with, and then to move to another hideout tomorrow morning. Then we'd be back to switching locations every day. Maybe we'd pull back even farther from the territory the Blood Hunter had been scouring for us, but my gut twisted at the thought.

As long as our greatest enemy was out there, we weren't really safe no matter where we went. And the longer he continued to operate unchecked, the more time he'd have to recover from whatever damage we'd already done to his business endeavors and allegiances.

Julius and Talon had been awake on and off over the past day, though a bit hazy with the painkillers they were taking. They'd managed to eat and drink but not much. Right now, both men were dozing, their bodies unsettlingly slack under the light blankets pulled over their well-muscled forms.

I stood over them for a moment, confirming that their chests were rising and falling in a regular rhythm of breaths, that the sound of those breaths was soft and not strained. Then I glanced toward my other men.

Blaze was sitting cross-legged in the far corner of the room near a thin beam of sunlight that seeped past the plywood boards that covered the window there. He'd set up several alerts on his laptop that would sound the alarm if any concerning activity popped up on nearby traffic cams and the like, but he couldn't seem to stop checking it manually too, maybe simply because he didn't have much else to do. His genius didn't extend to hacking the human body and programming it back into better working order.

He'd spent all yesterday digging through the files he'd stolen from various Blood Hunter operations and still hadn't been able to come up with a definite solution that would destroy our enemy.

And Garrison… Garrison was pacing from one end of the room to the other, as he had been for most of the day. Guilt and frustration radiated off him so palpably it hung in the air like a cloud. My gut tightened even more, watching him.

I walked over, catching his hand just as he turned at the back of the room. He halted, blinking at me as if he'd forgotten I was here—that there was anyone in the room except him and his self-recriminations.

"Hey," I murmured, keeping my tone light. "You're going to wear a hole in the floor at this rate."

He let out a quiet snort. "Like it'd matter if I did."

I frowned, squeezing his hand and tugging him around to fully face me. "This isn't your fault. You need to stop beating yourself up over what happened."

His gaze darted up to meet mine, sharp with derision. "Are you kidding me? It's *all* my fault. I left my post, and that was the only reason those guards managed to come up on the house and surprise us. If I'd been there—"

"If you'd been there instead of helping me, there's a good chance I'd have been killed by the other guard," I broke in. "How would that have been better?"

"Obviously it wouldn't have been," he muttered. "But I just assumed you *needed* my help. Why would you? You're ten times the fighter I am. I got caught up in going to your rescue instead of sticking to the plan…"

I held his gaze firmly. "Garrison, I've been trained in combat since I was two years old, and I *know* I needed you there. I didn't even realize that man was in the room until I heard you tackle him. In another second, he'd have shot me. And I didn't have an easy time with the other guards who came at us, even with your help."

He swiped his hand over his face. His expression still looked haggard. "It always happens," he said in a voice so quiet I barely made out the words. "I get people hurt. That's what I do. It's always better if I just play the part I need to and forget what I really want or any ideas about who I actually am… At least then I can be sure I'm doing something useful."

The words brought an ache into my chest. He'd told me about his family—how he blamed himself for the car accident that'd killed his parents and brother when he was just a kid. So many masks he'd worn to try to escape that old guilt, and this situation had obviously brought it blaring back to the surface.

I didn't know what to say to him. I hardly knew how to argue against my own lingering emotional hang-ups. So I just wrapped my arms around him and hugged him with all the compassion I had in me.

Garrison hesitated and then let his arms rise to embrace me in return. His head bowed over mine, but there was still something despondent in his pose.

I had to say *something*. I groped for the right words. "It's a dangerous job. We've all gotten hurt in the line of fire before. *You've* gotten hurt. That's just how it goes, and it has nothing to do with who you are or how real you're letting yourself be. The Blood Hunter put us in this awful situation, and you had to choose between two evils. There wasn't any winning or any way to protect everyone. At least the way you chose, we all survived in the end."

Garrison sucked in a breath, but he didn't answer. I didn't think I'd quite convinced him. As I struggled to think of how I could ease his pain, a rustling behind me drew my attention.

Julius and Talon were stirring on their makeshift mattresses. Talon rubbed his eyes and grimaced at the ceiling before reaching for the bottle of water we'd left next to him. Julius sat up gingerly and checked the bandage on his side, which was mercifully free of blood.

Inspiration sparked in my mind. I dragged Garrison over to the two wounded men. Blaze set down his laptop and meandered over too, bringing a bag from our stash of food in case they were hungry.

Julius eyed us contemplatively. He could probably sense the tension in the room as well as I could. I nudged Garrison. "Ask them if *they* think you did anything wrong?"

Garrison's mouth flattened. Julius arched his eyebrows slightly. "Wrong when?" he asked in a voice that was only a little rough now. "Have you been getting into trouble while we've been napping?"

"No," Garrison said tersely. "You know what she's talking about. You saw that I left my post as lookout at Gordell's house. If I'd been where I was supposed to be—where you ordered me to be—then I'd have seen the new squad coming. You wouldn't have gotten shot, because we'd have been prepared."

Talon propped himself up on his elbows, watching the proceedings in silence.

Julius looked at Garrison steadily. "Why did you have to leave your post?"

Have to. I noticed that even in the words he chose, Julius was indicating that he knew Garrison would never break from the plan without a damn good reason.

"It doesn't matter," Garrison said. "I—"

"Like hell, it doesn't matter," Julius interrupted. "Did you leave because you needed to piss? Did you get bored and decide to go elsewhere to join in on the action?"

"Of course, not—"

"Exactly. So why did you?"

Garrison's jaw clenched before he answered. "Dess was being attacked. I wasn't sure she could handle it on her own, so I jumped in."

"Literally," I piped up, unable to stay quiet any longer, especially when he was still using a tone as if he'd done something abominable. "And he almost definitely saved my life."

"While almost getting them killed," Garrison insisted.

"But we're still here, and so is Dess, it sounds like thanks to your quick reaction." Julius shifted his position with a wince he couldn't totally hide. "Sometimes missions go sideways, and we need to think on our feet. You should know that better than anyone—you're our main improviser, aren't you?"

Garrison grimaced at him. "When I'm working people, sure. This was different."

"Not as far as I can see. I've never expected any of you to follow my orders to the letter if you realize some other action needs to be taken to meet our main goal. And our most primary goal above all others is that we make it through to the other side. What you did accomplished that. We're all still here. Do you really think I'd rather have come out of that mission uninjured but without Dess?"

"Of course not," Garrison said without the slightest hesitation.

Julius's mouth curled into a small smile. "There you go. You did good. I'm perfectly comfortable putting the full blame for this damned gunshot on the Blood Hunter, Gordell, and their minions. What do you think, Talon?"

The other man grunted. "I think the kid has delusions of grandeur if he figures he could have somehow played that scenario better."

His voice was gruff, but the teasing wryness of the remark and his calling Garrison a kid seemed to relax the younger man more than anything anyone else had said. Garrison's shoulders came down a smidge.

"Not that I expect you care all that much about my opinion, but I think you made the right call too," Blaze put in in a typically cheeky tone. "Maybe the execution could have been a little smoother—"

"Blaze," I said, narrowing my eyes at him, and he just grinned.

But Garrison seemed to lighten even more with Blaze's jab. It was the way they communicated—the way the team worked in sync. I couldn't really imagine Blaze responding any differently.

Looking at the four of them, my heart swelled with more emotion than I could ever remember feeling before. These men shared so much respect and loyalty, with bonds that only death could sever. They were a true family, and they'd let me join them so easily and with so much trust.

I didn't think I'd ever stop being thankful for all of them.

I didn't think I'd ever stop *loving* all of them.

I hadn't been sure before that I was capable of love at all. I'd never experienced it, not really, so how could I know how it even felt? But in this moment, with the giddy warmth expanding through my chest, it seemed impossible that I could *not* love them—these gorgeous, supportive, dedicated men, brutal as they also were. I loved them all for different reasons, but I couldn't deny the fact that I felt more for each of them than I'd felt for anyone else in my entire life.

They'd all expressed their commitment to me in their own ways. Why hadn't I offered the same to them?

"Is something wrong, Dess?" Julius asked, studying my face.

"No," I said, with a rush of exhilaration. "It's very, very right." The words spilled out of me faster than I could control them. "I love you. All of you. I've never felt the way I feel when I'm with you. I'd give up anything to keep you safe and happy, and I'm so proud to be a part of this crew. You're all so strong and brilliant on your own, but when you come together, you're unstoppable. It's the most impressive thing I've ever seen."

For a second, there was silence around me, but I felt no doubt about the reception to my admission. Blaze was beaming at me, Garrison flushed with what looked like pleased embarrassment. A hint of a smile touched Talon's lips. Only Julius had sobered, but the gravity in his voice when he finally spoke only made his own confession sweeter.

"I love you too. God knows how much I'd be kicking myself if I'd died before I got to say it. I should have said it sooner." He chuckled, some of his seriousness falling away. "Somehow I'm guessing I'm last to the party on that one. But I suspect we all started falling for you back in the very first moment you just about kicked our asses trying to escape us. There's certainly no other woman in the world like you."

To hear the man who ruled us all owning up to that passionate sentiment sent a thrill through me that propelled me to his side. I knelt down in the space between his mat and Talon's and touched the side of his face.

"I admire your strength and the way you get yourself and the rest of us through everything the world throws at us. You give me the room to let go of my own need to be strong and in control so I can be part of a team instead of a lone wolf. I can always trust that you have a plan that'll get us through whatever we're facing. I feel *safe* when I'm with you."

I leaned in and pressed my lips to his with a firm intensity. Julius kissed me back, resting his hand on my waist as if to draw me closer, but he released me when I eased back.

I turned to Talon, letting the subtle adoration in his icy blue eyes wash over me before teasing my fingers over his cheek in turn. "I've found you sexy from the first time I saw you pummeling a punching bag with all that honed strength and power. I've always been able to be my whole self around you without facing judgment. I love learning how to *feel* with someone who won't judge me for trying, and I love seeing you doing the same."

When I closed the distance to kiss him, the melding of our mouths was gentler than anyone other than me could have imagined this man was capable of, full of the emotion that flowed between us without restraint.

I straightened up and walked to Blaze next. His eyes sparkled as he gazed back at me. He opened his mouth as if to make his own proclamation, but I touched my finger to his lips to stop him. It was my turn.

"You never pushed me away, even though I lashed out at you when we were first getting to know each other. That optimism and the way you enjoy life, no matter what's happening around you, is the reason I love you most. You've never tried to hide who you are or what matters to you, and you've helped me find things I'd lost that were hidden away inside me."

Blaze wrapped his arms around my waist and pulled me to him before pressing his forehead against mine. We held that position for a few beats of our hearts before I tipped my face to meet his lips. The moment was so sweet I had trouble pulling myself away.

But I had one more man to address. I turned from Blaze toward Garrison and curled my fingers into the front of his shirt.

"Now why on earth would I love you?" I teased, getting the smirk I was aiming for in return. When I pulled him to me so I could murmur the words right into his ear, his smile only widened.

"I love the way you can make me laugh even when I want to punch you," I said. "And every glimpse I've gotten of the man behind the masks you wear has only made me love you more. I see so much of myself in you—in your anger and pain over losing out on a normal, happy life, in your determination to protect everyone in every way you can, even from yourself."

Garrison drew my mouth to his and planted a kiss on me so electrifying that an eager quiver ran straight through me and heat pooled between my thighs. "I'd like to see myself in *you*," he said slyly as he drew back just a few inches, and my desire seared even hotter.

"Sounds good to me," I said, grinning back at him. "But I want the real Garrison. Show me all the affection and passion I know you've got in you. Your true emotions aren't going to hurt anyone. They'll only make me happier."

His breath stuttered, and I felt the tension return to his body where it was aligned with mine. But only for a moment. Then he slammed his lips down on mine with a hunger I recognized and reveled in.

He devoured me, pulling up my shirt at the same time, only breaking the kiss for long enough to yank the fabric over my head. "I fucking love you," he growled against my mouth, biting my bottom lip hard enough to provoke a gasp. "I'd fucking die for you, Dess. I'd do anything to hear that pretty little moan come from your lips."

"Yes," I said, kissing him back just as hard.

His hands dropped to my pants. When he flicked open my fly, I couldn't help arching an eyebrow at him. "You don't want to take your time?" I teased.

He only gave me a smug smile and yanked the jeans down my hips, allowing his fingers to trail down the outside of my legs. Blaze took a step closer to us and then paused, and I glanced over my shoulder at him.

"Don't be shy," I said, and then glanced at both Julius and Talon. "None of you need to be shy. We're all in this together."

"I guess I can handle sharing with this one," Garrison groused playfully as the hacker set his hands on my bare waist. When Garrison reclaimed my mouth, Blaze stroked his fingers up over my sides. He unclasped my bra and cupped my breasts from behind, stroking my nipples until they pebbled against his touch. An encouraging whimper spilled out of me.

The gazes of the other two men blazed over my skin, but Julius had no inclination toward shyness, even if he couldn't get all that physically involved in his current state. "You know she likes it rough," he ordered. "I'd pinch those nipples until she can't stand still."

Blaze grinned against my shoulder. "Happy to oblige," he said, and squeezed the tips of my breasts with increasing pressure. Imagining Julius standing with us, joining the encounter, had me squirming between Blaze and Garrison in no time flat.

Blaze applied his teeth as well, nipping the crook of my neck. As I gasped, Garrison trailed his hand down to my panties. His fingers dipped beneath the waistband and slicked over my core.

"Fuck, you're already so wet," he muttered, his breath washing hot over my skin. I shivered with pleasure and rocked into his touch, and he curled two fingers right inside me. Heady tingles flooded my body, and a needy growl escaped my throat.

Blaze looped one arm around my torso, still working over my breast with the other hand and nibbling along my neck with lips, tongue, and teeth. Garrison's fingers plunged in and out of me in an escalating rhythm, his thumb flicking over my clit. I could already feel myself soaring toward release.

"Pull her hair, hard," Julius ordered, his voice thickening with his own desire. Without missing a beat, Garrison brushed his other hand over the side of my head and grasped my hair with a sharp tug that had me moaning. He and Blaze were everywhere, and I could no longer differentiate the sensations—not as they both worked together to send pleasure rushing through me in waves.

But I didn't want this moment to be only them. Even if Julius and

Talon couldn't join us on their feet, I wanted to bring them into the team effort as much as I could.

"Take me to Julius," I murmured, and the two men who'd pinned me between them complied. Garrison eased down onto the floor between the two mats and drew me down with him while Blaze helpfully tugged off the younger man's jeans. As I straddled Garrison and swayed against his erection, I bent sideways toward Julius's lap.

The crew's commander raised a hand to caress my hair. I shot him a warning glance. "Relax and let me do the work. This won't be fun anymore if you open up that wound."

"I'm in this too," he insisted, but he didn't push himself any farther. He just twisted his fingers into the dark strands as I unzipped his slacks. I freed his cock from his boxers, sliding my hand up and down the rigid shaft so he groaned.

At the same time, I sank down onto his cock with my mouth and Garrison's with my sex. Garrison mumbled a curse and gripped my hips. Julius's grasp on my hair tightened. His musky, masculine flavor filled my mouth. Garrison's shaft hit the perfect spot inside me, and I was almost a goner just like that.

Blaze had stepped away for a moment, but he hadn't abandoned the team. His warm frame leaned over me from behind, and his fingers dipped between my ass cheeks with a slickness I hadn't expected. "I might have picked up a few… special supplies while we were grabbing everything else," he said. "Just in case."

I hummed my approval as he worked the lubrication over my other entrance, kneeling braced over Garrison's legs. When Blaze's dick aligned with my ass, I was more than ready. He slid into me gradually, adding to the pressure alongside Garrison's cock. I moaned around Julius's erection and then sucked so hard that his hand jerked in my hair.

The sweet pleasure of being utterly filled hit me as Garrison and Blaze thrust their hips in unison, Garrison's hand slipping between us to fondle my clit as well. It was overwhelming all on its own, but Julius knew how to deepen my bliss even more.

"Fuck her harder," he demanded in a rasp.

Garrison and Blaze bucked into me faster, deeper, and as the delight of their roughness rushed through me, I applied the same advice to my attentions to Julius. I wrapped my tongue around his shaft with increasing force, bobbing my head just as quickly as the other two men were pounding into me.

Julius's hips jerked beneath me. Before I could feel more than a flash of concern at his movement, his fingertips twitched against my scalp and his cum gushed into my mouth. I swallowed it down, nearly delirious with the taste of his release while I careened toward my own.

But I wasn't done yet. I gave Julius's cock one last swipe of my tongue and swiveled toward Talon.

The other man had pushed himself more upright, bracing himself with one hand. He'd already pushed down his sweatpants, his other hand curled around his cock as he stroked himself while he watched the rest of us.

When I reached toward him, he grasped my hand and placed it over his erection, shaking his head when I started to dip lower.

"I want to see your whole face when you come," he said raggedly. "I want to come with you while I see it."

Oh, fuck, yes. I wrapped my fingers around his rigid length and stroked him hard and fast as Garrison and Blaze bucked into me with the same fervor. I had to hold on long enough to bring this fearsome fighter to the brink—but I was already spiraling so high on the swell of ecstasy that was building like a tsunami within.

Garrison flicked his fingers faster against my clit, slamming his hips up to meet mine. I glanced at his face, and the avid adoration etched across it tipped me over the edge.

I cried out, tipping forward and tightening my grasp on Talon. As the final wave of bliss crashed over me, a spurt of heated liquid flowed over my hand. Blaze's chest hitched where he was bowed over me, and his heat flooded me as well.

Garrison groaned, his other hand digging into my thigh. With one last thrust, he came inside me. My mind shattered with one more burst of pleasure.

Blaze, Garrison, and I slumped together in a sweaty tangle of limbs and naked skin. Julius reached over to caress my shoulder, and Talon brushed his fingers down my side. A poignant sense of certainty settled over me.

I didn't have a clue how we were going to survive our war with the Blood Hunter, but I knew beyond a doubt that despite the physical injuries we'd been dealt, we were stronger as a crew than we'd ever been before.

We *couldn't* let him tear us apart. I simply wouldn't let him.

TWENTY-THREE

Julius

I COULDN'T SAY I'd ever felt more pathetic in my life. I could barely walk to the bathroom to take a fucking piss, my body so shaky I had to trail a hand along the wall for support. Even with a fresh dose of painkillers in my system, the wound on my side throbbed as I sat with the others eating dinner. I couldn't even enjoy the food, focusing on forcing down the most nutrient-packed morsels I could since my stomach wasn't up to a large meal.

I was supposed to be leading the crew. How the hell could I do that when I was a bed-bound invalid?

But as much as my current state of health niggled at my nerves, a sense of peace settled over me as I looked at my brothers-in-arms and my woman. We were still together, still alive, still ready to fight.

The Blood Hunter hadn't conquered us yet. He *wouldn't* beat us, no matter what state I was in. Being a leader was about a hell of a lot more than running around tackling people. I could holler orders just fine without moving an inch.

I just had to figure out the right orders to give. And my crew would help me find them. That was why I'd surrounded myself with these talented people.

I glanced around the rough circle we'd formed in the barn that was our current hideout. My sleeping bag was cushioned by straw now—I'd slept on worse beds. The dry scent tickled my nose.

"Our team has taken a major blow, but we're not beaten," I said. "But we might only get one more chance to make a solid strike, and we need to make it soon, before he regains more of his balance. We have to be smart about this."

Blaze glanced toward his laptop. "I've been following every trail I can, but I don't know what would make for a definitive move. There are a couple more clients whose homes we could raid, but that doesn't affect the Blood Hunter directly at all. There won't be another local shipment of girls for a few weeks, and I haven't been able to identify any of his other auctions around the country." He paused. "Not that you or Talon is in much condition for an extended road trip."

I grimaced at the truth in his words.

"What about the military angle?" Dess asked, tapping her knee against Garrison's where he sat next to her. "Has the general Garrison targeted pulled his support?"

"I think so," Blaze said. "But I don't know who else in the military the Blood Hunter might have influence over."

"And that doesn't get us right to him either." I paused, the facets of the conversation sinking in. An unexpected revelation rose up in my mind in their wake. "We've been coming at this wrong."

Talon glanced over at me from where he reclined against a bale of hay. "What do you mean?"

"Listen to us," I said. "We've gotten distracted from the goal of destroying the Blood Hunter completely, focusing instead on the parts of his business that *we* find most personally offensive: the human trafficking and his manipulations of fellow soldiers and mercenaries. But those avenues aren't necessarily where *he's* the most vulnerable. We need to figure out what angle we can come at him from that gives us the best access to him, the best chance to end him once and for all."

Garrison nodded slowly. "We've undermined him in a few areas, but a man like that must have dozens of income streams. Hurting him financially isn't going to crush him. And the DNA gathering missions seem to be a pretty new thing, not something his dealings rely on."

"Exactly." I rubbed my jaw. "But we can't eliminate him by our usual methods, going straight at him and taking him down with violent chaos. We've already seen that he's too carefully protected for that."

"He has to have some weaknesses," Dess put in. "Everyone does." Her gaze drifted away from us through the wooden structure, her expression going distant with thought. Then her eyes snapped back to me. "You said that we got distracted—that's been our weakness. But distraction isn't good for anyone. Is there a way we could distract the Blood Hunter—enough that he'd make a fatal mistake and give us the opening we need?"

Garrison snapped his fingers. "I like the way you're thinking, sweetheart. To distract someone, you need to dangle something they care about. Anything that matters to him is a potential weakness, a way to get access. What do we know that this prick has a hard-on for?"

Blaze wrinkled his nose. "I wouldn't put it *that* way, but he obviously cares a lot about his daughter. Or daughters. The one who died, and presumably the one he's replaced her with too."

"And Dess," Talon said.

Dess blinked at him. "He's trying to *kill* me. That seems to indicate he doesn't care all that much."

"No, Talon's right," I said. "He might not care about keeping you alive, but he cared a hell of a lot about what you represent, about the plans he had for you."

"About his revenge against the Maliks," Garrison filled in.

"How can we use that?" Dess knit her brow. "Everyone in my birth family is dead—except my brother, but he wasn't even born when the Maliks killed the Blood Hunter's daughter. I doubt he cares about Carter."

"Just add it to the list," Garrison said. "He also cares about his businesses, even if they're not essential. You said he sounded pretty pissed off about how we've interfered that time you talked to him."

"It matters to him to stay in control," I said, understanding rushing through me as the words came out.

I might have more in common with the Blood Hunter than I'd ever have wanted to believe. I'd told Dess that I'd built my life around maintaining near-perfect control, and wasn't our enemy the exact same way? Possibly even more so. He'd manipulated every detail of Dess's life, orchestrated her clash with her family beat by beat. I wouldn't be surprised if he was as furious that we'd managed to shake up his plans *at all* as he was about the specific businesses we'd messed with.

"What we've been doing should only be minor harassment to a man with as vast a criminal empire as he claims," I went on. "He said so himself to Dess. But he's incredibly angry. He's been pulling out all the stops to squash us, expending far more resources than really makes sense relative to the minor damage we've done. He's too used to everything going his way, to being able to ensure it does. Having anyone slip through his fingers—that's definitely a distraction."

Blaze hummed to himself. "Then in a way, we're already partway there."

"His need for control is a strength and a weakness, then," Talon said. "Being pissed off at us hasn't toppled him on its own. How are we going to use his control-freak tendencies to stop him?"

Garrison—always the schemer—stood and began marching across the room as he contemplated. "We can't go straight at him because of his protections… so we have to lure him to us, into a scenario where he's vulnerable. We need bait that matters so much to him that he'd keep chasing it even while we're stripping him of his guards along the way. What would compel him like that?"

"His daughter," Dess said quietly. "We take her. He'd do anything to get her back."

"I'm not sure that'd be quite enough," Garrison said, but a glint had lit in his eyes that told me his own manipulative skills were coming out in full force. When Garrison really understood a person, they'd better fucking believe they were in trouble. A smirk played across his lips. "We might need a little help, but I think I know exactly what'll make this chase totally irresistible to him. He'll come running, all right."

"You figure out how to make it happen," I said, a greater calm filling me alongside my sense of resolve. I *could* lead my crew from here in this barn if I needed to. I could lay out the pieces and figure out how we'd take them down without needing to be charging into the field alongside them, as much as I wished I could.

Looking at each member of my crew, I could feel the loyalty and determination that emanated from every one of them. They trusted me, and that meant more than they'd ever know. It didn't matter how many bullets I took. I could lead them, and I could do it well.

And that was why the Blood Hunter wouldn't stand a fucking chance against us.

"You're still going to have to deal with his bodyguards and whoever else he brings with him," Talon pointed out. "There's no chance he'll set out on a quest alone just because we ask him to."

Garrison snorted. "We're not even going to ask. That would be showing too much of our hand. But if we make a sort of treasure hunt out of it, have him racing from one clue to the next, we should get opportunities to pick off his protections bit by bit. Dess can handle a lot of that, and we'll set things up so Blaze and I can manage the rest. You two can keep sitting on your asses."

I couldn't hold back a guffaw at that remark. "Be glad we are stuck on our asses while you're making comments like that."

"He'll need to be really invested to keep going even after we start eliminating his guards," Blaze said. "Or he'll just wait until he can call in more."

Garrison's smirk stretched wider. "Oh, this'll do that. He'll be slavering at the bit to get to the bottom of it, distracted beyond all rational thought. It's going to be *fun*."

Dess prodded him. "Are you going to tell us what this magic ticket you've figured out is?"

He aimed his grin at her. "Magic is right. We're going to bring a man back from the dead."

TWENTY-FOUR

Decima

I UNLATCHED the door to the storage room in the barn where we'd set Carter up with his usual restraints and efforts toward making him comfortable. I didn't know if he'd be any more receptive to my overtures this time than before, but with our final attempt to take down the Blood Hunter on the horizon, I couldn't resist the urge to give him one more chance. Especially when his skills could get us closer to our goal.

Maybe if he contributed, if he played a role in taking down a real monster directly, he'd understand how much better it was than the sick, convoluted ceremonies our family had carried out. But I couldn't force him to comply. He could just as easily screw us over.

I needed to see if I could trust him enough to give him this small but important responsibility.

My brother was lying on his sleeping bag when I came in, the food I'd brought earlier eaten and his water bottle half empty. He wasn't sleeping, though. At the squeak of the hinges, he pushed himself upright. We'd taken off his gag again as soon as we'd gotten here, since the vacant farm was too far from any other habitation for calls for help to reach anyone's ears, but I doubted he was happy about the handcuffs or the tie around his ankles.

"What do you want now?" he muttered, sounding exhausted.

My heart wrenched despite myself. For all the horrible things he'd been party to, he wasn't much more than a kid himself, only a few months into adulthood at eighteen. I didn't *like* that I'd had to treat him this way, but trying to justify it again seemed pointless. My reasons didn't matter to him.

I sat down on the hard, straw-scattered ground across from him, just out of reach if he made a move to attack. "You said before that you might be able to help us with our missions. It turns out we have a plan where your forgery skill could come in handy. It might allow us to take down the Blood Hunter for good."

Carter's eyes narrowed at me. "If I do you a favor, are you going to let me go?"

I sucked my lower lip under my teeth and just barely managed not to worry at it. I had to be honest with him.

"No. Not just like that. But it'd be a step in the right direction. I still need to be sure that you're not going to turn on us, and what we're about to do is too important to leave any loose ends. Once the Blood Hunter is gone, we'll at least be able to figure out where to go from here without being constantly on the run. We can bring you someplace where you'll be more comfortable—we'll have more time to talk."

"Great. So I'll be a more comfortable prisoner. I'm not seeing why I should bother."

I inhaled slowly to settle my temper, which started to flare at his stubbornness. "Your entire life has been about stopping crime and injustice, and the Blood Hunter is the root of a hell of a lot of both of those things. He sells people like they're animals, he slaughters his own employees on a whim, he manipulates the people who should be serving our country into doing his bidding, and that's only the start of it. If we stop him, his crimes and all the harm he's doing will end with him. Shouldn't you want that?"

He shrugged. "All I've got is your word that he's doing those things. Why should I believe you when you lied about so much else?"

I couldn't hold back a snort. "*I* lied? The only thing I lied about was what job I currently do. With everything else, I just left out the details that I knew our family wouldn't accept. You and the rest of the family hid at least as much from me as I did from you. If you can understand why *you* didn't spill the beans to me upfront, you should be able to understand my perspective."

"That still doesn't mean I should side with you."

"Well, then, how about this? You're still here, still alive. Because I don't kill people I don't think deserve it. I know you didn't come up with the idea to hurt those kids on your own, and you didn't attack me the same way Iris and Ruby did. Both they and the Blood Hunter have treated so many innocent kids so horribly. So from where I'm standing, I don't see how I could look like the worse choice here. And I'm giving you the chance to be part of exactly what you always thought you were doing."

Carter simply hung his head without a response. Had I actually *lost* ground with him? What would it take for him to accept what I was offering? I didn't see how I could lay this situation out in any clearer terms. For all practical purposes…

I paused over that thought. Giving him all the logical reasons why he should support my cause hadn't gotten us anywhere in all this time. But he'd asked me for something else before. He'd asked why I cared. At the time I'd dismissed the question because I hadn't seen how it mattered—but maybe it did, more than anything else.

What the Maliks had been doing hadn't been based on any concrete evidence, after all. It'd been all about *feeling* they were making a difference.

I scooted forward a few inches, watching his face until he lifted his head just enough to meet my gaze.

"You asked me before why I care," I said, "and I told you this situation wasn't about that. But it is. I'm sure we could find another forgery expert if we wanted to. I didn't need to spare your life. I did because I care about *you*, about keeping some part of my family if I possibly can."

"You *killed* the rest of our family," Carter spat out.

I swallowed thickly. "I did. But…"

The words stuck in my throat. Did I really want to open up to him this much—to admit how hard it'd been? How much I'd cared about *all* of this?

How could I expect him to trust me if I didn't?

"I hated having to do that," I went on. "You have no idea how much I wanted to be part of a happy family, to belong and be accepted. I never had that in my entire life. I had trainers, but otherwise I was basically alone. I was willing to suppress so much of who I am to try to fit in with all of you. I'd have given just about anything to shake Mom and Dad and everyone else out of their delusion. But not only were they tormenting and murdering children, they made it clear that they wouldn't let me live my life unless I was willing to join them. That was a price I wasn't willing to pay. Because I *don't* want to cause unnecessary pain."

"Then why don't you kill me too?"

"You're the only family I have left. And even if I hate what you were a part of, I can't help holding on to that bond when I think there's still a chance we could be *real* family, the kind of family that supports and relies on each other. No matter what you've done, you're my brother."

Carter stared back at me, and in that moment I saw a flicker of the uncertainty that'd made me take a chance on him in the first place. His defiance had faltered. When he spoke, his voice quavered. "What makes you think I'm any better than the rest of them?"

Was that part of the problem? Did *he* think he was too far gone to come back from the crimes he'd been a part of? Maybe that was why he was clinging to the family legacy even after the rest of them were gone—because he was afraid of what it'd mean about him if he admitted what they'd done had been wrong.

I could relate to that fear more than he could have imagined.

"Do you want to know how I really grew up, Carter?" I said softly. "The Blood Hunter sent me to be raised by a criminal organization. They trained me from when I was a toddler to be a killer, someone he could send to assassinate whoever he had a beef with. I thought the people who looked after me were the good guys and that I was taking down threats to our safety. But I was wrong. When I realized how many innocent people I must have murdered, I was horrified. I hated who I'd been and what I'd done."

Carter's forehead furrowed. "How did you stop hating yourself?"

I gave him a small smile. "It took some help, but I recognized that I hadn't been given a choice. I'd been brainwashed into believing what I was doing was right for as long as I could remember. But as soon as I found out that I'd been wrong, I made a promise to myself not to hurt anyone who didn't deserve it. To make sure my actions really did stop others from getting hurt. Now that I know, I can make an actual choice, and *that* choice defines who I really am."

I paused and motioned to him. "You're in the same situation in so many ways. You were brainwashed by our family into believing that the rituals were for the greater good. You didn't have anyone pointing out the flaws in their stories. But I've seen that some part of you can tell that it wasn't right. You aren't set in their ways like the rest of them were. You could make different choices now that you're free from them, and I want to give you the chance to make those choices. To be who you'd really want to be, not who they expected you to be."

"You and I aren't the same," Carter said, but his protest sounded weak. There was something hungry in his expression at the same time, as if he *wanted* me to convince him.

"I know we're not," I said. "I just understand your situation in a way most other people couldn't. I can't force any decisions on you. It has to be your own choice for it to mean anything anyway. And you don't have to agree with me. I just hope you'll find it in you to break away from what our parents taught you and make up your own mind with everything else you've learned. You're smart enough to recognize that their claims don't hold water. What you do from there is up to you."

He lifted his free hand and ran it through his hair. His gaze had slid away from me, his expression tensing in a way I couldn't read. Then his jaw wobbled. He swallowed audibly, like he was trying to hold back his emotions. Like he was adrift with no idea where to turn and terrified about the road ahead.

Like a lost kid who had no idea how to find home again and no one he thought he could count on to really care.

I'd told him that I did care, but words weren't necessarily enough. An impulse ran through my body that I balked against, wary that this might be another trick like his stunt with the lawn mower. But everything from the slumping of his shoulders to the hitch that'd come into his breath felt genuine to me. His questions had gone from accusing to confused.

How could I expect him to believe that he wasn't a monster if I acted too scared of him to really reach out?

I shifted forward to kneel beside him, sliding my arm around his back tentatively in case he jerked away. But after a momentary tensing, he leaned his face into my shoulder. A tremor ran through his body. I let myself wrap my other arm around him, squeezing him in a gentle but emphatic hug.

"I'm here with you," I said. "I'll help you get through this and find your way as much as I can, if you want me to. That's what true family does."

He gulped, and then his arms rose to return my embrace. He clung to me for a few minutes, just struggling to smooth the rasp out of his breathing. When he finally eased back, he was blinking hard. His voice came out rough.

"That's the first time— Since I was twelve— When I got old enough, Mom and Dad stopped offering any kind of gestures like that, physical affection or whatever. They said I was becoming a man, and I should be strong enough to stand on my own. But sometimes I felt so alone…"

A lump rose in my own throat. I squeezed his arm, still sitting close. "You're not alone now. We're in this together. As long as you're willing to try."

"I'm really confused," he admitted. "So much has happened. I miss them, but I also— I only ever wanted to make sure there'd be less pain in the world." He lifted his head to look me in the eyes. "You really think that taking out this Blood Hunter guy will do that?"

"I'm sure of it," I said, my certainty ringing through my voice.

Carter sucked in a breath. "Okay. Okay. I don't know about everything else, but we can figure that out later. For now… I'll help you stop him. Just tell me what you need me to do."

TWENTY-FIVE

Decima

I WATCHED the entrance to the school from the driver's seat of the sedan we'd commandeered for the first stage of our plan, my heart thumping at a brisk rhythm. Garrison had disappeared through the doorway a few minutes ago, wearing business casual clothes, a wig, fake facial hair, and an air of total belonging. If he couldn't pull off this maneuver, no one could.

If he couldn't, our plan was finished before it'd even really gotten started.

I drummed my fingers on the steering wheel, willing my nerves to stay calm. There was a long road ahead of us after this. I had to stay cool and focused—not buckle under the pressure like we aimed to make the Blood Hunter do.

My latest burner phone rang. I yanked it to my ear. "Hello, this is Carolyn Markle speaking."

"Oh, hello, Ms. Markle," the woman on the other end said. "I just wanted to confirm—we have a Mr. Beverly here with a note from you requesting an early pick-up for Brittany?"

"Yes, that's correct," I said, keeping my voice as smooth as possible. "She has a doctor's appointment, and I wasn't able to get out of work."

Blaze had hacked into the school network and changed the parental contact number for the girl's supposed mother so we'd be set if they double-checked. Garrison had gone in with a note Carter had forged for us, imitating the signature on file on a note of business paper that Blaze had created using an exact copy of the logo from the Blood Hunter's business card.

That was more than I'd imagine the Maliks had access to when they'd kidnapped the first Brittany, but we still hadn't been sure if that would be enough. The Blood Hunter had almost definitely requested extra caution—but he probably hadn't considered that we'd find his adoptive daughter at all. And it was the first week of school after summer vacation, with all the chaos that must come with that, so the staff had to be more distracted than usual.

"Good to know. Sorry for bothering you," the school secretary said, and I sank back in my seat.

Less than a minute later, the school door opened again and Garrison came striding out with a little blonde girl bounding along beside him. She peered up at him, looking a bit puzzled but chattering away all the same. He smiled and nodded as if he found her comments the most fascinating thing he'd ever heard, and she looked like she was eating up the attention. It was kind of sweet, seeing how well he set her at ease.

When this was all over, she'd have a better life. A safer one, not ruled by a controlling, vicious man who'd dragged her into his life as a stand-in for another daughter.

Garrison would have told Brittany that he was a colleague of her father's and that her father had arranged a little trip for her. I found out the details he was offering about that trip when I stepped out to meet them.

"…and I bet she'll bake her famous cinnamon snap cookies for you—there's nothing like them fresh out of the oven."

The girl let out a little gasp. "I *love* homemade cookies. Will she let me help? Our cook never likes me in the kitchen."

"I'm sure she will," Garrison said, his voice dipping as if he was as affected by that statement as I was. A pang formed around my heart. How much did the Blood Hunter and his staff control his adoptive daughter's life? How much *was* she allowed to do?

As I opened the back door for her, Brittany paused and stared up at me. Her eyes narrowed with a wariness that didn't fit her young age—a sense of caution the Blood Hunter must have drilled into her. "I don't know you either." She took a step back, knitting her brow. "I don't like this. I want to talk to Father."

My pulse stuttered. We couldn't give her that. The secretary's approval of Garrison had been enough to reassure Brittany about him, but seeing another stranger had set off more alarm than we'd anticipated in the girl herself.

With a jolt of inspiration, I grasped the ponytail I'd gathered my hair into and yanked it upward, ducking down and turning so the back of my neck was level with the girl's line of sight.

"I work with your dad," I said, motioning to my tattoo with my other hand. Who would have thought that the mark I hated, the ink he'd used to brand me as his, might end up being the key to carrying out our plan for his destruction?

Brittany let out a huff of breath with a little giggle. "Oh. I'm sorry! He just—he didn't tell me we were doing anything different today, and he always says I should never go anywhere with people I'm not sure he's approved of. But you're with him, so it's okay."

I turned, giving her a smile I couldn't stop from being a little sad around the edges. "We are. And you're going to have a wonderful time with Steffie."

Brittany climbed into the car with no further hesitation. Garrison checked that she'd buckled her seatbelt and sat in the back with her, encouraging her to tell him about the math test she'd had today. As she started reciting her multiplication tables, I pulled away from the curb.

The first part of my route Blaze had deliberately mapped out so that we'd pass several street cams. We were counting on the Blood Hunter seeing this vehicle—and its license plate, which we'd registered to Damien Malik.

Next I zipped into a shabby residential neighborhood where cams were few and far between. I drove halfway down a back laneway between two rows of houses and parked next to the SUV Steffie had rented under a fake name when she'd arrived in DC this morning.

The Chaos Crew's housekeeper shot me a warm smile in greeting before fawning over the girl who'd come out to meet her. Garrison made the introductions, and Steffie cooed over Brittany's outfit before telling her how much fun her father had arranged.

"Why don't you let me hang on to your school things while you go have a great time?" Garrison said amicably.

The girl handed over the crest-emblazoned jacket she'd been carrying rather than wearing due to the late summer heat and then her backpack. I suppressed a twinge of nervous dread as she and Steffie got into the new car, a sunshade pulled down over the window next to Brittany to hide her from prying eyes and cameras.

We'd picked out a perfect hiding spot far from the city for them to stay busy while we carried out the rest of this mission. And besides, the Blood Hunter would be diverted onto a totally different trail. While I'd been driving over here, Blaze had sent another forged note by courier to the night club we knew the Blood Hunter owned, the place where I'd first truly met him. This note Carter had written in our father's handwriting, full of taunts and malicious glee, with details and phrasing only someone in the family would know.

Damien Malik had stolen one daughter from the Blood Hunter, and we were doing everything in our power to lead him to believe that the politician had stolen another as well. I couldn't think of anything more guaranteed to throw the Blood Hunter into a frenzy.

A frenzy big enough to forget himself and his sense of security, if we got our way.

When Steffie's SUV had disappeared out the end of the alley, I turned to Garrison. "Time for part two."

"That it is." He reached over and touched my cheek, staring intently into my eyes as if it was the last time he'd see me. "We want *him* getting in over his head, not you. Don't push it too far. Wait until you're sure he's vulnerable enough. We've got plenty of time to whittle away his defenses. None of this matters if we lose you."

My throat tightened. "Same to you," I said. "I know what I'm doing. We've got this."

Please, let that be true.

Garrison nodded and then tugged me to him, meeting my lips in a motion of pure passion and desperation. It was a goodbye kiss if I'd ever felt one. He moved his hands, gripping my jaw and wrapping his long fingers around the back of my head, holding me in place in a way that told me he never wanted to let go.

I didn't either. I didn't want to leave him to an unknown fate, but we had to do this. With only three of us fully mobile, we couldn't afford to stick together. And as the one with the most combat training, I could handle myself better on my own than he or Blaze could.

I slowly pulled away, giving Garrison's hand a quick squeeze. "This isn't good-bye," I insisted. "I expect an even better kiss than that when we meet up again afterward."

My comment provoked a chuckle, a little of the somberness in Garrison's hazel eyes fading. "Oh, I'll do a hell of a lot more than kiss you then, sweetheart. That's a promise."

We exchanged one last look and then split up, Garrison jogging toward the third car he was going to put in place for a later part of the plan, me heading off on foot. After getting a few blocks of distance from the scene of the hand-off, I summoned an Uber using a new account Blaze had set up with no links to my real identity.

The next stage of the plan relied on me alone. We knew exactly where the Blood Hunter would go first.

When I got to the Malik family home, it was still and silent. I'd half expected police tape, but it occurred to me that the bodies of Iris and Ruby probably hadn't been found yet. I'd left them down in their secret basement room. I wouldn't be surprised if anyone who'd wondered about their disappearance assumed they were running from a potential trial after the evidence that'd been discovered about their murderous activities.

That was no problem. It made it even easier for me to waltz into the house as if I belonged.

I went upstairs to the master bedroom with its bay window overlooking the front lawn, pulling over the wing chair from the corner to sit and wait. The room's smell, crisp and slightly acrid, made me think of my father. He'd have applied cologne in here while he got ready to face the world in his role as defender of justice. What did his political supporters think of his ideals now?

We hadn't been sure how long it would take for the Blood Hunter to realize what had happened, but he must have gotten the message quickly. I'd been waiting at the house for less than an hour when four cars pulled up outside, flanking the motorcycle the man himself rode on.

Of course he'd come, but he'd brought a small army with him. Fifteen men spilled out of the cars, all of them armed and slightly bulky beneath their crisp shirts in a way that suggested bulletproof vests. The Blood Hunter himself kept his helmet on, his own chest clearly protected. He wasn't panicked to the point of foolhardiness—not yet, anyway.

Four of the men marched up to the front door in formation around their boss, shielding him from potential shots. The Blood Hunter's strides were hasty, his hand jerking at his side as he snapped out orders. I could see the tension reverberating through him. He wasn't his usual cool, collected self. We'd rattled him at least that much.

He had to be both raging at this violation of his family and unsettled by the possibility that he'd made an even greater mistake.

"If Malik's in there, find him," he spat out, sounding as if he was practically frothing at the mouth.

He didn't know whether he'd failed in his revenge, whether he was going to lose another daughter. The plot he'd spent nearly thirty years planning might have gone off the rails without him even realizing it, and now he was teetering on the brink too.

A few more guards hustled up to the front door behind the Blood Hunter's cluster, and the rest fanned out around the building to check the back and possibly enter through windows as well. I darted downstairs and slipped into my chosen hiding place just in time. I'd locked the front door to give the appearance that no one wanted them to enter, but the man at the head of the pack smashed it open without missing a beat.

That was just fine by me. I wanted them inside where I could do my real work too. There was no way I could hope to strike at the

Blood Hunter directly right now, but the fewer guards he left this house with, the easier the rest of our task would be.

"Malik!" the Blood Hunter bellowed as he charged inside. "Face me for once, you fucking coward!"

He and his core group of guards hurtled upstairs. As more busted open the back door, a few men came toward me down the hall. I watched them from the top of the secret basement staircase, where I'd left the hidden doorway open a crack.

One of the guards noticed the gap in the wall, just as I'd intended. I crouched down as he hurried toward me. "Over here!" he shouted to his colleagues.

Three of them burst past the door. The second they stepped into the darkness, I swept out my leg and slammed out my hands.

The guy at the back heaved forward into the others, and they all tumbled partway down the steps. I leapt out and hurled a knife into each of their heads before they could recover. As they slumped on the stairs, I slipped out and closed the door firmly behind me.

A guard was just emerging from the dining room. His gun arm whipped up, his mouth opening to raise the alarm, but I sprang at him and snapped his neck before he could get out more than a grunt.

More footsteps were thumping toward me from various directions. The Blood Hunter would have seen that the second floor was empty. I darted the short distance to the back door and braced myself there in the mud room, using the narrow wall for cover.

"Man down!" someone shouted as the body by the dining room was discovered.

The Blood Hunter stormed into view. "Where the hell is he? Where is that prick?"

I stepped into view, ready to leap out of range in an instant if need be. "He's not here. He's taking your daughter somewhere you'll never find her again."

"*You*," the Blood Hunter said in a voice that was pure rage. The men flanking him raised their guns, but he held out his hand to stop them.

He wouldn't want to kill me when I might have information that would bring his daughter back to him. But he couldn't stop himself from spewing more fury at me. "I should have slaughtered you like your family did to Brittany when I first got my hands on you, you bitch. Where is she?"

I snorted. "Like I'm going to tell you. And it seems to me that you're *my* little bitch. I've run circles around you. Did you really think I'd choose you over my family—over the people you stole me from? You raised me to be a killer, and you assumed I'd have a problem with their little side business? You didn't think that through too well, did you?"

"There were bodies," he snarled, his composure disintegrating by the second. "Autopsy reports. There—"

"You should know better than anyone how easily records can be faked and bodies can be misidentified," I interrupted with a grim smile that hid my apprehension. I was taunting a very powerful man who still had more than ten armed guards backing him up. "Of course I made sure they didn't really die. I just gave you what you wanted to see, and you ate it up."

A tremor ran up his arms from where his hands were clenched at his sides. His knuckles had paled to pure white.

"I'm running out of patience," he said, and I heard the promise of death in his tone. "Where is he? Where did he take her?"

"I told you," I replied. "Someplace you'll never find her."

The flick of his fingers was so swift I almost missed it. I dove for the back door just as two of his men opened fire, aiming for my lower legs. They wanted to slow me down so he could question me at his leisure, but I wasn't giving him the opportunity.

I crashed through the door and sprang out of range, positioning myself deliberately so that the side of my sweatpants scraped against the sharp edge of a metal lawn ornament I'd positioned there for that purpose. The pocket at my hip that I'd already frayed tore completely open, and a phone I'd placed there tumbled to the ground.

I whipped around as if to try to snatch it up, but the Blood Hunter and his guards were already barreling out the door after me. "Shit!" I spat out. It was all I could do to dodge out of range around the house, leaving the phone behind.

One of the men raced into my line of sight just as I ducked behind the compost bin, and I shot him between the eyes, not worried about the noise now that the Blood Hunter's men had made enough of a racket. But only that one guard came near me. I heard a hitch of breath as the Blood Hunter must have checked the phone I'd "lost" and seen the most recent text thread that we'd set up for him to find.

"Forget the bitch," he hollered to the others. "We've got somewhere else to be. Move it, move it, *now*!"

Their footsteps thundered back through the house. Tires screeched as the cars they'd arrived in tore away from the curb, the thrum of the Blood Hunter's motorcycle mingling with their engines. They roared away, the sound quickly fading into the distance.

The faint wail of a siren told me I needed to get moving too. The neighbors in this peaceful part of town wouldn't have hesitated to report gunshots in the area.

I hopped the hedge at the back of the yard and sprinted through the streets until I reached the park where I'd meant to regroup. Hunkering down in a small glade of trees, I pulled out the phone I'd been using for my actual business and dialed Blaze's number.

It didn't even finish a full ring before he picked up. "Dess?"

"They're on their way to you."

Blaze released a deep, relieved breath. "Everything went according to plan?"

"As much as we were able to plan it," I said. "He had fifteen men with him; I took care of five of them. They've got four cars between them, and he's on his motorcycle. He kept his helmet on the whole time, and I believe they're all in bulletproof gear."

Blaze must have put me on speaker phone, because Garrison's whistle carried from a little farther away. "Are you sure the phone did the trick?" he asked.

"He gave every indication that he was sure he'd figured out where to look next, and there was nothing else on there that should have given him a clue. I think he's smart enough to put the pieces together quickly from those texts. I'd bet you'll be seeing him in twenty minutes or less."

"Fun times," Blaze said cheerfully. "We're ready for them."

We'd set up the Blood Hunter to follow the trail to a storage facility on the edge of the city. It wasn't a place we'd ever been before, but it'd seemed fitting when I remembered the trap he'd set for us at a similar compound of storage lockers back in the Chaos Crew's home town. He probably wouldn't even make the connection in his current state of agitation.

Why would he anyway? He thought he was chasing Damien Malik now, not the Chaos Crew.

"I'd better get to the next location," I said. "Keep me updated."

"Will do."

I connected the phone to a headset, hearing the clatter of Blaze's laptop keyboard as I did. As I loped through the park to the car Garrison had left waiting for me, the guys rustled around, setting up their own traps. Blaze made periodic sounds of approval, which occasionally Garrison responded to with a snort. I shook my head at them silently as I turned the car toward my final destination.

The place where, if all this worked out, our war with the Blood Hunter would end.

As I wove through the streets to the highway, a sudden *boom* reverberated through the phone line. Blaze chuckled darkly. "There goes one of those cars, and at least three men with it. Oh, he does look pissed. You can tell even with that stupid helmet on."

He'd switched out of speaker phone, so I couldn't hear much more other than his slightly heightened breath as he must have moved through the facility to a different perch. Garrison would be off taking care of things from a different vantage point. The storage units offered plenty of opportunities to get the jump on the men.

"Garrison just tripped up another of the guards," Blaze reported. "And now I'm going to…" A metallic clang loud enough to reach the speaker reverberated into my ear, followed by another chuckle. "So long, suckers."

"Don't get too cocky," I warned him, even though I was smiling.

"No such thing," Blaze retorted. "I'll have you know—"

The blast of a gunshot blared in my ear, cutting off whatever he meant to say. My heart flipped over, and the line went dead.

TWENTY-SIX

Decima

THE SILENCE on the other end of my connection to Blaze blared in my ears. Nothing broke it, no sound reaching me other than the rumble of my own car. My heart thumped faster, my hands tightening on the steering wheel.

I had the urge to jerk the wheel around, pull the tightest U-turn in human history, and race to the storage facility to defend my men. To make sure there was something left of them *to* defend. What had happened to Blaze? Was he injured—was Garrison okay?

The frantic thoughts whipped through my mind, but my arms stayed braced in their previous position. Despite the turmoil inside me, one fact stood out clearly.

The guys wouldn't want me to come rushing to their aid. If I could talk to them right now, even if they *were* bleeding out over the storage lockers, they'd tell me that seeing our plan through was the most important thing. That they could handle themselves, and I had to focus on doing my part.

If I ruined everything we'd orchestrated so carefully, we'd never get another chance like this. We might not live long enough to even consider another attempt once the Blood Hunter was through with us.

Blaze and Garrison knew what they were doing. They wouldn't be taken down easily. Lord knew they must have been worried about me while I was off on my own, without even a partner to call on. And how must Julius and Talon feel as they waited for the rest of us to complete the mission they'd been too injured to take part in beyond the planning stages?

If they could be strong and hold steady, then I could too. I owed it to them.

I gritted my teeth and drove onward.

When I reached my destination, I stopped at the end of the drive and looked up at the Maliks' country house. We couldn't have picked any place more fitting for our grand finale, since the Blood Hunter had used it for the finale in his own scheme to have me murder my family. While Blaze and Garrison had been taking down as many guards as they could, they'd also have been surreptitiously leading the Blood Hunter toward one final clue that would convince him his daughter was here.

The white walls looked somehow drearier than before even in the beaming late-afternoon sunlight. The yard's grass was far more trampled thanks to all the investigators who must have come and gone after my family's bodies had been discovered.

It'd been a few weeks, and the rainfall since then had washed away any lingering traces of blood. Nothing remained to indicate that this had been a crime scene except a few stray strands of caution tape that'd caught on a fence post near the barn. The property was still and silent. The Blood Hunter and I would have it to ourselves once I'd dispatched however many guards he managed to retain after my men were through with them.

I got out, bringing a rifle Talon had picked out for me and the bait Garrison had left in the passenger seat. Striding up the steps to the creaky porch, I draped Brittany's school jacket over the railing at the top, arranging it so the tell-tale crest would be clearly visible.

The lock on the front door had been busted. I pushed inside and set Brittany's backpack at the base of the stairs. Just a couple more jabs to send the Blood Hunter into an even deeper rage.

On the second floor, I slung the rifle over my shoulder and climbed out one of the bedroom windows, leaving it open so I could quickly slip back inside. I hauled myself onto the slate-tiled roof and crawled along until I found a good vantage point over the front yard while staying concealed behind the chimney.

Before he'd been cut off, Blaze had already reported taking down enough of the Blood Hunter's remaining guards that I should be able to pick the rest off with one clip as long as I was quick enough. The more of them there were, the faster I'd have to be.

No call came to let me know the Blood Hunter was on his way, but I kept my position anyway. *Something* had clearly happened to part Blaze from his phone, but that didn't mean anything else was lost. I swallowed down my jittering nerves and ignored the queasiness roiling in my gut.

Finally, a faint thrum reached my ears. A motorcycle zoomed into view along the country road that led to the house, just two cars with it now. I couldn't tell how many figures lurked behind the reflections gleaming off the windows.

They parked farther back from my car, the Blood Hunter still wary enough to realize someone might be staked out in or around it. As he swung off his bike, the car doors opened—and only two men got out. Whatever had happened with Blaze and Garrison, they'd managed to whittle down his protections to just those two guards.

Even with his helmet on, I could identify the moment the Blood Hunter spotted and recognized his daughter's jacket. His shoulders stiffened, and he marched forward twice as swiftly as before, a pistol clutched in his hand. His guards jogged to catch up, their heads swiveling in an attempt to maintain the caution their boss had nearly thrown to the wind.

They didn't see me. They never had a chance. The second they slowed, flanking the Blood Hunter, I pulled the trigger in quick succession. The bullets burst out the back of their skulls.

The Blood Hunter didn't even flinch as his guards crumpled on either side of him. A second later, he was out of view of my current perch, but I couldn't have easily taken him down like this anyway, not with his helmet and bulletproof vest. Shooting at his hurrying legs from above would have required sniper skills that would have challenged even me.

I was better at close quarters combat anyway. I'd taken down his remaining back-up. If he'd paused to call in more, they hadn't reached him yet.

I had to end him before they had the chance to.

His voice bellowed from inside the house. "Where are you, Malik? What have you done with her? I'm going to tear you apart with my bare fucking hands the way I should have to begin with."

I dropped the rifle on the roof, knowing it'd be more of a hindrance than a help indoors, and dropped back down to the window. I lowered myself to the ledge with the faintest rasp of my feet and eased silently inside.

As I slunk to the bedroom doorway, I took my pistol in one hand and a knife in the other. The bangs and crashes from below told me that the Blood Hunter was still on the first floor, and he was furious enough to take out his frustrations on the furniture.

"You're not going to get away with this!" he hollered, his breath hissing through his teeth.

If I could sneak up on him and get a good enough opening before he noticed me, I might be able to shoot him in the leg before I went in for the kill. That'd weaken him, slow him down, even if all his vital areas were covered.

Then I'd just have to get that damn helmet off him and sink my knife into his throat… The thought of him gazing up at me as the life drained from his arrogant face gave me a shivery thrill.

He'd made me what I was, and now I'd be his downfall just as much as I'd been to the man who'd genetically fathered me.

Before I could reach the stairs, the Blood Hunter stomped toward them. I ducked back into the bedroom, knowing he'd come to me soon enough. Hiding behind the open door, gun at the ready, I tracked his footsteps through the upper rooms.

"Are you still skulking around on the roof like some kind of vermin? What the fuck have you done with her? Get out here and face me!"

He burst into the room I was hiding in. The second he stepped into sight, I fired at his thighs.

The bullets slammed into him… and rebounded, falling to the floor. The impact made the Blood Hunter stumble, but not even enough to bring him to his knees. As he whirled toward me, I realized with a chill that he must have been wearing Kevlar pants too. Fuck.

There wasn't anything to do but throw the pistol aside and reach to snatch up another of my knives as I lunged to meet him. Bullets might bounce off the material he was wearing, but a sharp blade could stab right through it.

The Blood Hunter threw himself at me with more speed and force than I'd been prepared for. He smashed me into the wall so hard my fingers jerked away from the second knife's hilt and the first trembled in my hand. I lashed out, heaving at him, focusing on his gun hand.

I managed to send his pistol spinning away across the floor, but he battered my wrist at the same time, forcing me to drop the knife. Then he butted me right in the face with his shatterproof helmet. The blow radiated pain through my entire skull and left my thoughts scrambled.

"Where is he?" the Blood Hunter roared. "What did he do with her?"

He rammed me against the wall again hard enough that I felt one of my weaker ribs crack. More pain splintered through my side. I'd expected him to be strong, but not like this, like a fucking train bearing down on me.

But then, I'd never fought an opponent who was anywhere near this angry before. Had that been my fatal miscalculation?

I wrenched myself downward and managed to dodge his next pummeling blow, but as I grabbed for my fallen knife, the Blood Hunter kicked me in the gut. I rolled to the side and pushed myself toward the weapon, and he pounced on me, slamming me into the floor like a tiger pinning its prey. The whack of his fist against my temple had me seeing stars, and not the good kind.

The Blood Hunter's voice, no longer smooth and confident but desperately harsh, reached me as if from far off down a tunnel. That wasn't good either.

"Did you think I'd go easy on you because you were my tool?" he snarled. "That's all you are. A piece of equipment that's outlived its usefulness. I don't need you, and I don't need your fucking skills. I can take any number of kids and train them in the same way as I trained you. Only this time, they'll be better. I won't let them experience the slightest shred of affection. I won't let them escape. And if they fuck me over, I'll kill them too and start again. They're all expendable, just like you are."

I couldn't see anything but the vague impression of his eyes through the glass of his helmet, but the hatred in his tone spoke of how much he meant those words. He meant to kill me now, that was for sure. Aches were spreading all through my body where his limbs pressed into me. He wrenched one of my arms to the side so he had a hand free to reach for my throat, and I couldn't resist him.

A different kind of resistance was building inside me, though. His threat woke up something feral within me. The thought of another child—any child—ever enduring the upbringing I'd gone through sickened me.

No. I couldn't let it happen. Never again.

"You're a monster," I spat at him in a rough voice.

He paused with his hand resting against but not yet clenching around my throat. "You think so, do you?" he sneered. "You helped your father steal my daughter away from me, set him up to carry out his bloody rituals. You're just as bad as *he* is. So don't lay your judgment on me."

My gaze darted around me and focused on the knife—my knife, lying just a foot away from my shoulder. If I could just shake him up enough that he'd loosen his grip and I could get my arm free...

I gazed up at him, letting my lips curl into a smirk. Even if my last gambit didn't work, even if he beat me here, I'd still beaten him in ways he'd never forget. I'd turned the Hunter into the prey.

"Your daughter has been perfectly safe this whole time," I informed him, holding my taunting smile in place. "She's probably making cookies right now with the woman who's looking after her with more care than *you* would have ever given her."

He sputtered a laugh. "As if I'm going to believe you and show you mercy if you spew some absurd lies." But his fingers twitched around mine minutely.

I let out a chuckle of my own. "You've already bought into my lies. You really believed that my father was still alive? Fuck, no. I killed him myself weeks ago. But my crew and I wrapped you up in our little charade, we led you on this wild goose chase, we stripped you of every man you brought to protect you while you let us… Now you know what it's like to be played like a puppet the way you did to so many other people. The way you did to me."

The Blood Hunter stiffened as the shock hit him. It was only for a second, but that second was all I needed.

I yanked my wrists out of his hold. As one hand wrenched his helmet upward, the other closed around the handle of the knife. I shoved his head up and plunged the blade into his throat in one swift movement, so deep the tip scraped his spine.

Blood gushed down over me. The Blood Hunter gagged and spluttered. His weight sagged over me, and I heaved him to the side, tugging his helmet the rest of the way off at the same time. I stared down into his craggy face with a smile I totally felt now.

"Truth won," I told him as his eyes started to glaze. "Love won. You made me into your tool, but I've become so much more than that, so much you could *never* take away from me. And now I'm your hunter. Enjoy your time in Hell."

His hand jerked against the floor, but that was his last jolt of life. A wet gasp spilled from his lips alongside the blood pooling under him, and then his expression went totally slack.

I watched him for a few more minutes, confirming that he was really gone. His lungs had stilled. His heart had stopped. Even if his lackeys came charging to his rescue, there'd be no saving this man.

The reign of the Blood Hunter was at an end.

I stood up, swaying a little with a rush of dizziness. Triumph wrapped around my chest, but I couldn't immerse myself in it yet, not when another concern was gnawing at the back of my mind. I needed one more thing before I could be sure we'd totally won.

Well, two more things. Two more *people*: Blaze and Garrison, standing in front of me, alive.

I walked out to my car, stepping past the fallen guards without a second glance. My head still throbbed from the beating my skull had taken, and my side ached with my broken rib, but those physical discomforts fell away in the wake of my new goal. I started the engine and turned the car toward the city—toward the storage facility where my men had last spoken to me.

I tried to adhere to the speed limit as I drove, but the numbers blurred, and the speedometer on the dash seemed to jump of its own accord. It still took too long to get there.

The gate of the facility was hanging open. I parked down the street and darted over on foot. The second I walked in, I spotted the two men I'd wanted to see crouched next to one of the storage units.

Garrison was leaning over Blaze, wrapping a bandage around his hand. "I'm going to spit on the gauze if you don't stop bitching," he was saying. "See how you like an infection."

"Don't threaten a man wounded in the thick of a battle," Blaze retorted. "Next time it's your turn to get shot."

A grin sprang to my face even as tears burned in my eyes. I raced over, and both men's heads jerked around at the sound of my feet.

"Dess!"

I wasn't sure I'd ever heard a sound more joyful than my name on Blaze's lips like that, all the pain that'd been in his voice before swept away by it. He started to leap toward me.

Garrison hauled the hacker back, clutching his hand. "I'm not finished, you idiot." Then he caught my gaze, a smile brighter than anything he'd offered before lighting up his face. "You did it. He's done?"

"Dead as a doorknob," I said.

A guffaw tumbled out of him. "Nice work, sweetheart."

"We're going to need the whole story," Blaze said, his leg bouncing as he waited for Garrison to finish tying the bandage. "And I'm about to hug you to Kingdom Come."

"I'm looking forward to that," I said, choked up. "What happened to you? When the call dropped…"

Blaze shook his head in apparent exasperation. "The bastards shot the phone right out of my fingers." He held up the hand Garrison had just relinquished. "I'll be typing a little slower for the next few weeks, but I'm okay."

He wrapped me in his arms, and Garrison joined us, tucking me into a joint embrace. A deeper sense of relief than I'd ever known welled up inside me.

I was free. Free of the Blood Hunter's influence and attacks, cut loose from his puppet strings. The Chaos Crew had survived together. A few tears spilled out, maybe the first I'd ever released in the presence of my men, but neither of them commented on it. Garrison just kissed my cheek.

"We'd better get out of here," he said. "The cops don't care much about this part of town, but eventually they'll come to investigate the ruckus we made."

"Yes," I said. Back to Julius and Talon, who were keeping watch over my brother while they healed. Back to Steffie. Back to the rest of my life now that it was fully mine.

I started grinning at them all over again. "It's time to go home."

TWENTY-SEVEN

Decima

IT DIDN'T SEEM to matter how many times I woke up in the Chaos Crew's apartment—each morning, I felt refreshed, rejuvenated, and ready to tackle any challenge that came to our doorstep.

Part of my vigor might have been the realization that we *had* no more substantial challenges at our door. The mess I'd gotten the guys into when I'd first crossed paths with them had ended with the Blood Hunter's life. They'd gone for years before now without any significant threats from other criminals, and we could continue our business for years more with his manipulative designs behind us.

I walked out of my room, stretching my back, and found Steffie in the kitchen with Brittany. The housekeeper was standing at one side of the stove, the girl at the other on a stool, Steffie giving strict instructions for our breakfast.

"Whisk the eggs, don't stir them, lyuba," Steffie said with her stern, lightly accented tone. "You want them fluffy, do you not?"

Brittany only nodded and tried to mimic Steffie's gesture slowly. She didn't quite get it, but it seemed to be close enough for Steffie's approval, so she smiled down at the girl.

"Looks delicious," I said with an awkward smile. I never knew quite how to behave around the little girl we'd unwittingly found ourselves in custody of. When Brittany looked up at me with a hopeful glance, I added, "Steffie will teach you how to make eggs better than any you've ever tasted."

The girl brightened, and she continued whisking the way Steffie had instructed. Her other hand drifted to the worn stuffed tiger sitting on the counter next to the stove. She'd kept it close to her side since I'd offered it to her when we'd arrived here.

I'd assume the Blood Hunter had given her much fancier playthings than my ratty old toy. But it was the best we'd had, and maybe she could sense how much love had been poured into it. How much comfort it'd provided to another little girl who'd found herself far from home among strangers.

She could keep it, wherever she ended up after this. She needed it more than I did now.

I turned toward the table where Blaze and Garrison sat. They'd been hard at work since getting home, trying to find a living situation for Brittany, because it wasn't as if she could live with us forever. I was just getting used to the idea of being a free human being—I had no clue how to be a parent on top of that.

The Blood Hunter had adopted Brittany at a young enough age that she had no idea who her birth parents were, and Blaze hadn't been able to find any record tying her to another family. So we were looking for new adoptive parents, vetted much more carefully than the Blood Hunter had evaluated his own aptitude for fatherhood. Blaze was doing extensive background checks on every couple we considered, and Garrison would go out and maneuver himself into an assessing conversation with those who made it to our shortlist.

It was a complicated process, but we didn't want to risk putting Brittany into another bad situation.

When she'd asked about what had happened to "Father," as she referred to him, we'd told her that he'd had an accident and couldn't take care of her anymore. I didn't have the heart to explain the full truth, and probably it was too much for a kid to handle anyway. She'd withdrawn since hearing the news, but Steffie's presence always cheered her up at least a bit, so the housekeeper had been a constant presence in the apartment over the past few days.

I ran a hand across the back of Blaze's shoulder as I approached, and he leaned back into my touch, slowing his impressively swift one-handed typing. "So many dark secrets to unearth," he said with a laugh. "I'd lose my faith in humanity if I still had any. Maybe we should just hang on to her."

I rolled my eyes at him. "Right, because we're model parental figures here."

Garrison tapped a pen to his lips. "I don't know. Julius gives off definite dad vibes from time to time."

Blaze snorted. "I never thought I'd hear you call Julius 'Daddy,' Garrison."

Garrison glowered at the hacker, who grinned cheekily in response. Some things never changed, and I could tell their constant heckling was one of those.

Then Garrison shrugged, pitching his voice low so Brittany wouldn't overhear. "Hell, it's not as if we could be worse parents than the Blood Hunter."

"Not exactly a high bar to meet," I said dryly. "Keep at it. Even I know that it's a bad idea to raise a kid in a home full of deadly weaponry."

Garrison didn't look as if he was disappointed by my refusal. He cocked his head as he considered the latest file Blaze had passed on to him. "I think these people could actually have real potential. We'll just have to see if they let any red flags slip when I chat them up in person."

Right then, Talon's door swung open, but it was Carter who walked out. We'd brought him back to the apartment with us too, of course, but ever since I'd told him how his forgery efforts had helped us take down the Blood Hunter, something in him had relaxed. Maybe it was Steffie working her mother hen vibe on him too, or maybe it was him seeing how gently we were treating Brittany. Maybe he'd simply needed proof that he really could contribute toward his quest for justice in a different way, one that didn't require hurting innocents.

In any case, after our first day back, we'd felt comfortable removing his restraints. We'd set up a cot in Talon's room mainly because he was the one who'd grumbled the least about having to share. Julius was already talking about arranging a new home base—somewhere we could all have our own bedrooms and I wasn't stashed away in the workout room anymore on a cot of my own.

The thought of a home designed with me in mind made me a little giddy.

We were still keeping a close eye on Carter, but he hadn't shown any signs of regretting his new allegiance with us so far. The contrary, really. As he bustled over to us, Talon stepping out behind him with a baleful look in Carter's direction, I could tell my brother was on another of his crusades.

He came up to the table and caught my gaze, keeping his voice quiet with obvious awareness of the little girl nearby. "I've got a whole list now."

"A list?" Garrison muttered. "What are we, a grocery store?"

Carter made a face at him and then turned his attention back to me. He seemed to have decided that I was the ultimate authority in the crew even though that honor technically still belonged to Julius, but I didn't mind him relying on me. That was exactly what I'd been hoping to offer as a big sister.

"A list of the worst crimes that've been reported in this city in the past few weeks," he said. "We should figure out who committed those crimes and take them out. It'll keep us busy for a while."

As much as his use of "we" warmed me, I almost choked on my saliva at his declaration. Before, he'd only pointed out a couple of news stories that he thought we could apply our "justice delivery" skills to. Now he was scheduling the rest of our year?

"That's… not really how we usually do things, remember?" I said carefully.

Carter waved off my objection. "Right, right, you wait until someone hires you. But no one hired you to destroy the Blood Hunter. Why shouldn't we tackle other criminals in our free time?"

"Because we enjoy *having* some free time?" Garrison said with an arch of his eyebrows. "Why should we do the cops' jobs for them? They should get paid for something too."

My brother ignored him. "Don't we have the resources to go after these people?" he demanded, still focused on me.

"Of course we do," Blaze answered for me. "But we're not superheroes. We wouldn't have those resources if we focused on pro bono cases." He paused and then motioned to Carter. "Send me your list. I'll have a look. We might be able to fit in one or two if the trail is warm enough and they're a real menace to society."

My brother beamed despite Blaze's use of "might" and tapped on his phone. "I'll shoot it over right now. I included links to the news articles and everything."

"Excellent data gathering and organizational skills," the hacker told him while Garrison hid a smirk behind his hand. "I'm sure that'll come in handy no matter what path you end up taking from here."

Pride lit my brother's face even more. I nodded, smiling back at him. "You can always tell us about your ideas, even if we're not necessarily going to go along with them."

Carter let out a huff. "I guess that's fair," he allowed.

"Breakfast is ready!" Steffie called out, prompting Julius to emerge from his bedroom too. Before I could settle into a chair at the table, my phone vibrated in my pocket.

Frowning, I stepped off to the side. As far as I'd known, the only people who had this number were here in the room with me.

"Hello?" I said warily.

"This is Decima of the Chaos Crew, I trust?" said the woman on the other end of the line. She spoke in a crisp professional tone that I didn't recognize at all, with a mild accent that sounded like a blend of English and German.

My posture tensed. "Who is this, and how did you get this number?"

"Oh, we have our ways. I'm a representative from the Devil's Dozen, and I'm calling in regards to your inheritance."

The Devil's Dozen. That was the group the Blood Hunter had said he was a part of—the thirteen crime lords who controlled the entire world's illicit underground activities, if he was to be believed.

What kind of "inheritance" would they have in store for me after I'd murdered one of their number?

"I'm not interested in any inheritance," I said, "and if this is supposed to be a threat, you'll be asking for just as much trouble as the Blood Hunter faced."

The woman laughed, a cool tinkling sound. "I'm sorry, you must misunderstand. We've gathered that you're the one who conquered the previous Blood Hunter fair and square. He left no heirs who can take over. That means the position at our table and all his holdings pass on to you. You've earned them fair and square."

I blinked in surprise, momentarily lost for words. Was she serious? "I—I don't know anything about that. I wasn't looking to take over his job."

"Well, it's all yours if you want it. Before you decide, why don't you join a couple of us for a little chat so we can go over the details face to face? I'm quite intrigued to meet the woman who brought about his end. You can choose the time and place and bring whatever defenses you like, but I promise, we simply want to talk."

I wavered on my feet, part of me wanting to reject anything to do with the Blood Hunter and his colleagues outright, part of me tangled up with curiosity. If this elusive, exclusive organization really did rule over all crime in the world, wouldn't it be to our benefit to at least find out more about it? Her terms would make it easy to keep myself safe during the meeting.

I wet my lips and decided. "All right. Let me talk about it with my crew, and I'll get back to you with the details."

The two figures who waited for me at the picnic table in the park—the very spot where I'd first told the Chaos Crew the truth about my upbringing—looked more like business professionals than master criminals. But then, the same could have been said for the Blood Hunter. Maybe that *was* what master criminals looked like. After all, they wouldn't get very far wearing flashing signs proclaiming themselves mafia bosses on their foreheads.

The woman sat with rigid poise, her gaunt face topped by a swirl of silver hair. Her thin body was clothed in a sleek indigo dress suit that made her dark eyes shine starker over her hollowed cheeks. The man next to her looked maybe a decade younger, his hair still dark other than its speckling of gray, though he was already developing heavy jowls to go with his thickset frame. He wore a suit as well, fitted and pinstriped.

I approached them with caution but no real fear. We'd scoped out the entire park ahead of time and watched these two arrive. They hadn't brought any backup with them that we'd been able to identify. If they intended me any harm, they'd have to contend with all four of my guys stationed in concealed positions around this glade, guns already trained on them. I had a pistol of my own in a holster under my arm and knives hidden by my hips.

I sat down at the table across from them, keeping my posture loose and ready to react. The woman's lips curled into a subtle smile. "I'm glad you agreed to come, Decima."

It was the voice from the phone, but I'd figured as much. I gazed straight back at her and her colleague. "Here I am. Maybe you can start explaining why the hell you'd give the Blood Hunter's entire estate to some stranger who's not only a total unknown to you, but also his killer."

The man chuckled. "We're offering it to you precisely *because* you're his killer. We have a code of honor, and we recognize when strength beats strength. Anyone who can topple one of us deserves a place in our ranks."

"So you're Devil's Dozen members too?" I clarified. I hadn't been completely sure whether they were the Blood Hunter's equals or simply high-ranking lackeys of his fellow overlords.

The woman nodded. "We want to see our membership filled with those fully capable of handling the pressures and responsibilities that come with it. You've proven yourself adept at both strategy and stamina. And you're hardly an unknown. We know about your kidnapping and your training under the Blood Hunter's watch. It's a pretty irony that he orchestrated his own destruction."

"I don't know anything about ruling a criminal empire," I said.

She shrugged. "Few do. I believe you can step up to the challenge. If not, you can always choose an inheritor and step away. But it's generally easiest in a squabble like this for the winner to take the spoils. You'd get control over all his business assets and personal property."

"And what's in it for you? Why don't you all divide it up amongst the rest of you?"

The man shook his head. "That's not how we work. The Devil's Dozen maintains a balance of power between the thirteen of us. If we started consolidating, it'd ruin us in the long run. No one can hold on to too much without their empire imploding. You'll be helping us by stepping in to fill that power vacuum as a force to be reckoned with before less deserving parties start making a grab for it."

I was still grappling with the idea of all this being possible. "You just arrange to have everything transferred to my control? Simple as that?"

The woman's smile came back. "The process will take some time, but yes, it is relatively simple in the long run. We can provide you with a little guidance, and I'm sure the men who have us in their sights right now will help you settle into your rule. All you have to do is say you'll take the inheritance, and we can get started."

I swallowed thickly. This seemed too incredible to be true and too intimidating at the same time. I didn't *want* to be associating with criminals who were on the same level as the Blood Hunter. I'd be stepping farther into the fire instead of pulling back from it. I was never going to run things the way he had…

But maybe that was exactly why I should take this chance. I didn't have to do things his way. If everything belonged to me, I could make my own decisions about what happened to his empire. I could disband the operations and income streams I disagreed with. I'd have access to all his records, the data I needed to help the other girls he'd sold and whoever else he'd victimized.

If I walked away, my life would be easier, sure. But whoever stepped up to fill the void instead might revel in the human trafficking trade. They might expand the Blood Hunter's pursuits into even more horrifying areas.

This was my chance to make a difference on a global scale, to end so much of the kind of horrors I'd endured as a child, from right inside the den of corruption.

Part of me still balked, but I lifted my chin high. I couldn't pass up this opportunity—I couldn't abandon all the people I now had the ability to save.

"All right," I said, the words falling heavy from my mouth. "I accept."

TWENTY-EIGHT

Several months later

Decima

I STEPPED out of my car, palming the keys as I looked over the estate that the guys and I had gradually been making our own. Renovating the Blood Hunter's primary residence had been one of our first orders of business once we'd realized that we suddenly had a perfect replacement for the old apartment, one with plenty of space for us to sprawl out in.

The property stood alone on a small hill on the outskirts of DC, a perfect vantage point for the many security guards we now had patrolling the outer walls on a regular basis. The house itself looked oddly modest on the outside, flat stucco with plain windows and trim. But inside it was an immense modern oasis. Light poured through those windows, and air circulated through the space when they were open to the breeze like they were on this warm spring afternoon.

And there were so many rooms. We each had our own bedroom

alongside a few extra guest rooms, even though I often ended up sharing with one or more of the men any given night. Garrison had claimed a small study with bay windows for his telescope and all the "souvenirs" he liked to collect from his jobs. We had a room just for weapons storage, and to Talon's contentment, we'd knocked down a wall to transform two rooms into a single, large workout room. Naturally, Blaze had his own office, stuffed with all the technology he could ever hope to use.

It felt strange being able to drive up and walk straight to the front door after weeks of sneaking in and out of the penthouse, but we had a reputation that protected us from minor players now and the resources to ensure no major player could get close.

I stepped inside onto the hardwood floor we'd put down in place of the tiles that had once covered every inch of flooring. Now ceramics were restricted to the basement, the kitchen, and the bathrooms—all five of them, which I appreciated quite a bit when it meant I never had to wait for any of my men to get a move on. We'd repainted too, taking this broad entryway from dark red to a welcoming yellow. We didn't want the hue of blood reminding us of who had owned this house before us.

Technically, *I* was the Blood Hunter now. That was the name the members of the Devil's Dozen called me by when I attended their monthly meetings, though I suspected most if not all of them were aware of my real name. The new employees called me "boss," which I found much more comfortable.

One of my first orders of business once I'd taken on that role was to remove the last trace of the former Blood Hunter's ownership over me. The hair at the nape of my neck was still growing back from where I'd had to shave a chunk to allow the laser technicians access. Nothing was left of the tattoo except a faint smudge of a scar which you couldn't see at all through my hair.

I could tell Steffie had been by the house this morning from the fresh flowers in the vase on the hall's side table. We'd set her up with a new residence of her own, a townhouse she'd picked out in the city proper where she could continue being an extra pair of eyes and ears for the Chaos Crew, as well as her periodic cleaning and cooking duties.

I drank in the softly sweet scent of the flowers and smiled. The place was finally starting to feel like *home*.

Cocking my head, I made out voices from the kitchen, so I strode toward the noise. It sounded like Blaze and Garrison were bickering in their usual way, debating the merits of fresh vs. dry pasta, of all things.

"If you keep going on about it, I'll stuff a bunch of that pasta down your throats so you can analyze it up close and personal," Julius said dryly as I stepped into the gleaming space, which was all mottled gray-and-white surfaces and stainless steel. The crew's commander glanced over at my entrance and stepped to my side to slip an arm around me and steal an emphatic kiss. "There's our woman. How's Brittany?"

The other three guys—Blaze and Garrison braced by the kitchen island, Talon sitting at the table in the side nook cleaning a gun—looked over at me to hear my answer. I'd been making regular visits to check on the former Blood Hunter's adoptive daughter in her new home ever since we'd placed her there, to make sure everything was going well with her new family.

"She still seems happy," I said. "She was chattering away even more than before—no sign that anything's weighing on her now. And it's obvious how supportive Linnaeus and Carla are. They've been keeping up the family therapy sessions to help her adjust. I don't think we could have found better parents for her."

"Good," Julius said, and Blaze and Garrison shared a grin of matching relief. Finding her new home had mostly been their responsibility, after all.

One of the many bedrooms here had once been Brittany's. I'd debated what to do with the surprisingly sparse selection of clothes and toys it'd held, and in the end we'd donated them to a women's shelter. I hadn't wanted her bringing anything into her new life that would remind her of the Blood Hunter's influence. I'd set up a trust fund with some of the money so she'd be set for college and plenty more when she turned eighteen, but she wouldn't find out about it until it was necessary.

I wandered over to Talon and slung my arm across his shoulders, drawing a small smile to his lips. The feel of his well-muscled frame and his musky scent gave me a familiar zing right to my core.

"Need any help?" I asked playfully, reaching for a piece of the rifle he'd already taken apart.

"Have at it." He handed me the small bottle of CLP, and I poured a liberal amount onto the exterior of the weapon. I scanned for any rust, but Talon took good care of his weapons. A microfiber cloth was sufficient for coating the exterior. I wiped it down and handed it to Talon. He began reassembling the parts.

Seeing him back in his element—cleaning guns and preparing for future jobs—sent a different sort of electricity through me. A lot might have changed, but these were still the men I'd fallen for. And you wouldn't have known it to look at him or Julius that they'd been on death's door less than a year ago. Each time I saw them going about their usual routines, I couldn't help but feel a sense of utter gratitude for how our situation had turned out. It could have been so much worse.

"Is Carter coming for dinner tonight?" Blaze asked, looking down at his phone. "Steffie popped out to do some grocery shopping before she gets down to cooking, and she wants to know how much food to bring back."

I shook my head. "He's extra busy studying for exams this week. He said he was looking forward to taking a break and stopping by on the weekend."

Julius chuckled. "After the way he was talking when he first bought into the Chaos Crew way, I'm surprised he went back to the legal methods of obtaining justice."

I grinned. "He is bringing a unique perspective to those methods now. And I think he's still hoping he can convince us to take on some side cases with him as a sort of hobby."

Carter had entered the criminology program he'd already been accepted into before our lives had collided, studying the legal strategies for identifying and cracking down on criminal behavior. He'd lived in the house with us for a couple of months, but it'd become more obvious with each passing day that he was shedding the

Malik family legacy completely and becoming his own man. He'd ended up finding an apartment closer to the school so he didn't have to make the long commute every day, but he came by to visit regularly.

"As long as the kid doesn't turn on us, he can do whatever he wants," Talon remarked.

"I'm still not sure he isn't going to turn *into* one of us," I said.

Garrison set the kettle on the stove and turned on the burner. "What flavor today, boss?" he said in a teasing tone. After hearing the security staff refer to me that way, he'd taken to using it jokingly when he wanted to rib me.

I was still "sweetheart" too, though, as soon as a spark of passion lit in those hazel eyes.

I considered the offerings in his vast cupboard of hot cocoa. "The cinnamon one. I feel like I need a little spice."

He clicked his tongue against his teeth as he pulled down the box and took out two mugs. "In the mood for some heat, are you? I think we can take care of that urge." His tone had turned suggestive, and he smirked over his shoulder at me.

Oh, I bet they would. We'd had plenty of nights to remember, christening the various rooms of this place in my favorite way.

"Your brother is definitely still thinking outside the law enforcement box," Blaze said, his foot swinging back and forth as he skimmed through emails on his phone. "He's just sent me another of his wish lists of targets. *Hey Tech Guy*," he read out loud, and rolled his eyes. "When is he going to learn my name?"

"You've got to admit he has a knack for compiling key articles," Garrison said.

Blaze raised his eyebrows at the other man. "I never *have* to admit anything."

Garrison handed me a mug, and I breathed in the chocolatey steam with a sigh that brought all the men's gazes snapping to me with looks as heated as the liquid I was holding. Garrison leaned back against the counter, taking a sip of his own drink. "Speaking of vigilante justice, I managed to direct the cops to another of the old Blood Hunter's sex slave buyers today. That's three more girls free."

"That's wonderful!" I said, my spirits lifting as much from the news as the sweet beverage I was savoring.

One of my first orders of business after I'd taken over the former Blood Hunter's accounts had been to figure out how much of that business I wanted to dismantle. We'd scrapped the DNA collection program, destroying a few remaining files that Blaze hadn't been able to catch in our assault on the office building, cut all connections to military figures, and ended the shipments of trafficked women. Now we were working through the slow process of exposing those who'd purchased from those shipments before.

As I'd pared down the former Blood Hunter's income streams, naturally less money had been coming in. But we didn't need money. The Chaos Crew had already held substantial savings, and the old Blood Hunter had been downright miserly, judging by the size of his accounts.

"Even though we've been subtle about it, people have got to be realizing that there's a pattern to the takedowns," Blaze commented. "We might be making some enemies. And I don't know how the rest of the Devil's Dozen will feel about it."

I let out a dismissive huff. "They're my assets now. My contacts and my connections. I can use them however I like—and destroy them however I like."

The hacker grinned at the assurance in my voice. "Has anyone ever told you how badass you are, Dess?"

I leaned in and nudged my shoulder against his. "Only my four favorite men."

I believed it, too. I believed with every ounce of my being that I was just as badass as they told me I was. I'd taken down the former Blood Hunter, and I was singlehandedly dismantling every rotten thing he'd ever built. More than that, though, I knew that nobody would dare to stop me—not when I had one of the fiercest crews supporting me and my decisions.

Not when I myself was a force to be reckoned with.

The other twelve members of the Devil's Dozen were watching us with interest and skepticism, sure. They might not like what they saw. But they'd offered the position to me, and if they ever decided to come for me—to challenge what I was doing here—I'd respond just as mercilessly as I'd been trained to do.

I finally had the life I wanted, and *nobody* would take it from me. I'd never be controlled again. And I had more family standing with me than I'd ever imagined was possible a year ago. A family built on strength, respect, passion, and a healthy dose of chaos.

Just let anyone try to tear us apart, and I'd be happy to prove to them that love could win all over again.

LOST TIME

A CHAOS CREW BONUS EPILOGUE

Dess

I'D ENJOY WATCHING these men cower on the asphalt at my feet more if their poses didn't remind me of the women I just finished rescuing from the assholes. The way the dozen skinny, bruised figures cringed and quivered when I first burst into the truck.

"We didn't know," one of the pricks crouched in front of me whines. "We always used to be able to bring our shipments through this—"

I interrupt in a voice as blunt as the pistol in my hand. "They're not shipments. They're people. This has been my turf for five years now, and I made it clear to *everyone* who does any kind of illegal business around here that I don't tolerate treating women like merchandise."

"It sounded like a temporary thing," one of the other traffickers sputtered. "You can't take away such a huge part of—"

"Yes, I fucking well can." I glanced through the darkness of the vast parking lot toward Julius, who was striding over from one of the vans we'd arrived in. "They're all secure?"

The massive leader of the Chaos Crew dipped his head in a nod.

His expression was cool and collected as always, but I caught a feral gleam in his eyes that would have thrilled me under better circumstances. "Need any help?"

"I can handle this myself." I just didn't want the women who've been victimized so much to have to witness even more violence.

I flicked off the safety on my pistol and aimed it at the man in the middle of the trio—the one I'd heard barking orders at both the other two and the women as we'd approached. "You didn't really think you were allowed. You just figured you could get away with it. This is the proof that you were wrong."

With one squeeze of the trigger, a *bang* thundered through the night. The jerk slumped with blood pooling beneath his head.

I waved my pistol at the two lackeys, and they scrambled to their feet.

"Go back to whoever *his* boss is. Deliver my message for me. And if I see your faces around here again with any other 'shipments' like this, you'll be kissing the pavement too."

I didn't need to tell them twice. The two gangsters dashed for the emptied truck like their feet were on fire.

As the engine roared and they tore out of the parking lot, Julius stopped beside me with a low chuckle. "You put them in their place."

"You'd think so." I grimaced at the corpse on the ground. "We'll have to deal with that."

Talon approached at my other side, the same ominously quiet presence as usual. "I'll take care of it."

Blaze leaned in from behind me and slung a lean arm around my shoulders. "Why do you sound upset, Dess? We won—you caught them before they got very far."

"It was still too far." I sighed and turned back toward our vans. "I shouldn't *still* be having to put assholes like this in their places. I'm the Blood Hunter. My word is supposed to be the law—that's the whole reason I accepted the job."

"Old habits die hard," Julius said, running his hand over his short dark hair. "We're seeing a lot less of the human trafficking crap than there was under the old Blood Hunter."

"Any amount is too much," I muttered.

The bloodthirsty psychopath whose place I'd taken had left quite the mess in his wake. Even after ending all the trafficking deals he'd personally had a hand in, other operations who'd carried out their business within his territory kept popping up, thinking they could still get away with it.

As we reached the main van, Garrison was just hopping out through the back doors. He leaned inside to offer one final reassuring comment to the women we'd freed and eased the doors shut before turning to the rest of us.

"They're about as comfortable as they can be," he said with one of his wry smiles. "I told them we'd get everything sorted out, whether they want to stay here or go back home."

"Good." I exhaled in a rush, not really feeling like there was much good about the situation.

How ironic was it that the former Blood Hunter's people had raised me to believe I was meant to stamp out the evil in the world... and it'd turned out an awful lot of that evil had been orchestrated or at least approved of by the man himself?

Garrison gave me an evaluating look and tipped his blond head toward the other van. "You should get back to the hotel. You deserve some rest." A sly glint came into his eyes. "We have big things planned for tomorrow."

I frowned. "Big things? We haven't talked about—"

Blaze tugged me toward the vehicle with a flash of a grin. "You might be the boss most of the time, but we're taking charge for a day. It's time for a little change of pace. You trust us, don't you?" He leaned in to peck a kiss to the side of my head.

It was hard not to melt a little when the hacker took on that sweet tone. And there really wasn't anything for me to do *right* now that would help anyone. The employees I'd brought on since becoming the Blood Hunter knew how to set up new lives for these women better than I did.

I bumped my elbow against Blaze's. "You know I do. Fine. To the hotel it is."

I woke up the next morning to a flurry of hushed but urgent conversation from the living room of the big suite we'd booked while we investigated the latest trafficking ring.

"Don't we have an umbrella? It was on the list!"

"I think we can rent one there. Nothing worth worrying about."

"Did you seriously get me a *Speedo*?"

"Hey, if you leave all the shopping to me, you get what you get."

Hearing the Chaos Crew guys squabble in their usual companionable way was nothing new. But normally they were bickering about things like guns and entrance strategies, not... whatever it was they were talking about right now.

I squirmed out from under the covers and pushed open the door. "What are you four up to now?"

The men all paused with vaguely guilty expressions over an assortment of bulging canvas tote bags. Blaze broke from the tableau first.

"We're going to the beach!" he announced, bounding over to me with typical irrepressible energy and shoving a bundle of fabric into my hands. "Get dressed, and we'll head right over."

The beach? I hadn't realized any of my men were hankering for fun in the sun, but I could humor them until I figured out what this "change of pace" was really about.

The bundle turned out to include a sporty maroon two-piece bathing suit and a gauzy cover-up that I imagined my pale skin would appreciate. I tucked my feet into the flip flops Blaze had also handed over and gamely followed the men out to the car.

While I'd been getting changed, so had they—into tropical print polo shirts and matching shorts. Talon looked down at himself with an inscrutable expression as if he was considering burning the stuff right off his body, and Garrison kept fiddling with his collar, but Julius wore his comfortably enough. And Blaze had never looked happier.

"We're just a half hour from one of the best beaches in the country," he informed me as he hopped into the driver's seat. "So it made sense to start with this little outing."

"Start?" I repeated.

Garrison cracked a grin. "We're all getting our turns choosing today's activities." He kicked the back of Blaze's seat. "I think Blazey here just wanted to ogle women in bikinis."

"Hey, there's only one woman I'm interested in looking at. And plenty of other things to enjoy at the beach."

"We look forward to you proving that," Julius said dryly.

Blaze parked amid a crowd of cars, and we tramped over the sand through the other beach-goers under the mid-morning sun. A light breeze wisped over me, carrying a pleasant summer warmth, and the ocean lapped at the shore in low waves.

It turned out we *could* rent beach umbrellas. The men acquired two and set them up side by side before stretching out our towels underneath. Then Blaze started digging through the rest of the bags.

"We've got a frisbee, a beach ball, snorkeling gear… Everyone should put on sunscreen. I packed a cooler with cold drinks, but obviously we need to get a hot dog from the stand over there for lunch. I think it's hot dogs that people usually eat at the beach?"

Talon raised an eyebrow. "Aren't you supposed to know that already?"

Blaze clapped his hands together. "Hot dogs. Definitely hot dogs. But it's not time for that yet. What do you want to do first, Dess?"

I glanced around at the clusters of people around us. There were couples lounging together and groups of friends and families with kids of various ages dashing across the sand. It all felt weirdly normal… Weird because it wasn't at all where *we* would normally be.

But there was something both soothing and exhilarating about the hiss of the waves and the sprawl of the ocean. I pulled off my cover-up. "I think I'd like to go in the water."

"Sounds good. Swim time!" Blaze tugged off his own shirt.

Talon hunkered down on one of the towels in a position that made me suspect he had a pistol tucked in the back of his shorts. "I'll keep an eye on our stuff."

I quickly confirmed who had been grousing about the Speedo. Garrison chucked off both his shirt and his shorts and glanced down at the tiny, tight swim suit with an incredulous expression.

I laughed and tapped his chest lightly. "I like it. It gives me an excellent view."

His lips curved into a smirk as he met my eyes. "I guess I like it too, then."

Julius strode ahead of us down to the ocean, seeming to clear a path with his brawny form without making a single gesture or glower. As I plunged into the cool water, a gasp slipped from my throat. Then I was bobbing with the surf and paddling around between waves, grinning with the tang of salt in my mouth.

I'd been down near more than one ocean plenty of times on missions, but I'd never actually gone for a swim. It was both refreshing and soothing… Maybe we should add this to our regular habits.

Garrison and Blaze got into a minor battle of splashes, and Julius swept in to claim a kiss from me while they were otherwise occupied. When I'd had enough of the water, we padded back over the sand, where I tossed the beach ball back and forth with Talon and Julius before accepting a game of frisbee with Blaze.

The hot dogs, when we finally grabbed them from the stand, were greasy and slathered in ketchup and relish, but I had to admit I couldn't think of a more fitting meal for our current environment.

"All right," Garrison said as I licked the lingering ketchup off my fingers. "We did Blaze's beach thing. Now it's my turn. Come on. We can get changed on the jet."

"Changed for what?" I asked.

He moved to start rolling up one of the towels, shooting me his smirk over his shoulder. "You'll see."

Two hours later, we were back in DC, stepping into a lobby that smelled like butter and salt.

I took a curious peek at Garrison. "You had a craving to see a movie?"

"Not just any movie," he insisted. "One of the best movies ever made, in our own private theater—so no annoying people talking through the good parts. You're about to experience Casablanca as most people currently alive never have."

He glanced around, his gaze landing on the concessions counter. "We should get popcorn, right? Regular people get popcorn."

Was that the point of all this? To pretend we were regular people? I still hadn't quite figured out what was going on with my men today, but I was enjoying the ride enough not to complain.

A couple with two young kids in tow walked up to the counter as we watched and left it with four overflowing bags of popcorn. Talon nodded. "It does look like popcorn is the thing to do."

We gathered our own bags of buttery goodness, and Garrison led the way into the small screening room he'd booked just for us. We set ourselves up right in the middle of the rows of chairs, Julius stretching out with his feet resting against the seat ahead of him.

Garrison gave a little wave to whoever was in the projection booth, and the screen flickered to life. I tossed a handful of popcorn into my mouth and let the kernels melt on my tongue as the story began to play out before me.

By the end of the film, my heart was squeezed tight. A man who tried to convince himself he didn't care about the world around him but realized he did so very much? No wonder Garrison loved this movie.

I glanced over at him in the darkness as the credits started to roll and grasped his hand. "Lucky you. You don't have to choose between saving the world and getting the girl."

A flush spread across his cheeks. "I'm not sure what I do is on quite the same level."

"Speak for yourself," Blaze declared, tossing a piece of popcorn at the other man.

Garrison rolled his eyes, but when his gaze came back to me, it hold mine intently. "You enjoyed the show? You mentioned one time that you've never really watched a movie in the theater. I figured it might be a good one after seeing how much you love that silly spy show."

I hadn't ever sat down to watch a movie at a public venue, although I had once assassinated a target in a theater. It hadn't seemed wise to stick around after the fact.

"It was great," I said. "Other than obviously Ilsa should have figured out she could have *both* of them and then everyone could have been totally happy."

Julius laughed and tugged me to my feet. "That would make everyone's lives a lot easier, huh? I think Talon has something else in store for you not far from here."

When I raised my eyebrows at the taciturn man, he offered one of his quiet smiles. "I came up with something a little different from the others."

As we stepped into the squat gray building, a chorus of barks and grunts reached my ears. I hesitated, instinctively looking toward Talon again.

He nodded and gently rested his hand on the small of my back to usher me up to the reception room's front desk, where a harried-looking woman with a frizzy ponytail was tapping at a computer keyboard. The other men followed behind us.

The woman gave us a quick smile. "How can I help you?"

Talon's hand rose to squeeze my shoulder. "My wife is going to adopt a pet. We'd like to look at the animals you have available."

The men referred to me as their "wife" from time to time when we felt the need to label our relationship to each other in public, even though we'd never formally gotten married. It still gave me a tingle to hear the word while my mind started spinning.

I didn't want to act confused in front of the animal shelter worker. So I kept my mouth shut as she ushered us into one of the rooms off the lobby. There, rows of cages stood along both walls, all the way down the narrow space and around a corner.

"Dogs in this section, cats and other smaller animals around the corner," the woman said. "Don't reach inside the cages. If you have any questions or want to take one out, I'll be right here."

She stayed by the door to give us space to consider the animals. My heart skipped a beat meeting all the dark, hopeful eyes behind the cage bars.

I waited until we'd walked halfway down the room before leaning closer to Talon to murmur to him. "You figured I needed more company?"

"I thought…" He paused, gathering those thoughts, which I knew he didn't always feel confident expressing. "It'd be your first pet, wouldn't it? I get the impression it's nice to have an animal to come home to. And Steffi would like the company when we're away."

"A first pet is a rite of passage, for sure," Blaze said, with a laugh rough enough that I turned to check his expression. My stomach twisted as I took in his tensed features, his gaze fixed on the dogs in the cages next to us.

He'd had a pet of his own once. A dog his childhood bullies had killed. I didn't think he'd gotten another one since.

My throat tightened. None of the snuffling or yipping creatures around me felt quite right anyway.

I tucked my fingers around his elbow. "You know, I think I'm more of a cat person. It seems like they'd get along better with our kind of lifestyle anyway."

Garrison chuckled under his breath. "Headstrong, independent, quick to defend itself. That does sound like someone we all know."

I narrowed my eyes at him in a mock-glower and continued around the corner into the other section of the room.

Several mews rose up as the cats caught sight of us. There had to be at least thirty of them, a few scruffy kittens and others fully grown.

I walked along the rows, studying each in turn. Some cowered, and some rubbed their sides up against the bars. Some pretended not to care, giving themselves a tongue bath and acting as if they hadn't even noticed us.

I'd always reached the end of the row when a slim orange tabby flung itself at the bars of its cage and clung there, peering out at me. It bobbed its head with a questioning meow.

When I stopped, it tilted its head the other way, like it was evaluating me as much as I was it. Then it reached its paw through the bars as if trying to invite me to play.

A smile I couldn't contain sprang to my lips. "That one."

Julius shook his head. "It looks like trouble—but it also looks like it's already taken to you."

Talon gave my hair a light tug. "We're fans of trouble, aren't we?"

When the woman unlocked the cage, the cat leapt right out into my arms. It stared up at me and tapped its paw to my chin, its claws retracted.

Tentatively, I stroked my hand down its back. It blinked and then started purring like a motor.

"Yes," I said, beaming down at it with a heart suddenly full in a way I'd never experienced before. "This one."

It was only after we arrived at the Blood Hunter's main mansion in the dimming evening light that I realized something was missing. I set down my new furry friend, who I'd decided on the drive home I'd call Jack—short for Jack-o-lantern—in the foyer and turned to Julius.

Before I needed to ask, he lifted his chin toward the staircase. "Change into one of the dresses you'll find on your bed and then come right back down. We'll set up everything for Jack and get ready ourselves. The day's not over yet."

Dresses? Intrigued, I dashed up the stairs to see what else my men could possibly have in store for me.

Steffi must have brought the new purchases over while we were away. Four dresses lay across my bed—but not the sleek evening gowns I typically wore for the kinds of missions we ended up on. These all had wide skirts, one twinkling with sparkles embedded in the fabric, another embroidered with a gold lace pattern along the neckline. Princess dresses, I'd have called them.

I stared at them for a few minutes before stirring into action. Two I immediately dismissed as too poofy and cumbersome. I wavered between a strapless indigo gown with a skirt more flowy than billowy and a deep green gown with spaghetti straps and the sparkles, and decided I'd rather look like a shadow than stars.

When I descended the stairs in the gown and a pair of black pumps that worked well with it, I found all four of my men waiting for me in the foyer, each in suits so smart I practically drooled. Julius stepped forward with a blue flower in his hand that he pinned to the bodice of my gown. "I thought you might pick this one. Come on out —our limo awaits."

He wasn't kidding about the limo—a stretched black one was parked outside the gate. We all piled into the smooth leather seats at the back.

"Are you going to tell me where we're going?" I asked, and Julius only offered a secretive smile.

The limo pulled up at a grand event hall, the old stone face glowing with amber light. Julius ushered me inside and into a reception room decorated with streamers and sparkly banners and even—

"A balloon arch?" Garrison asked, shooting a skeptical glance at Blaze.

The hacker raised his hands. "It came up in a bunch of photos. I was going by my research."

Music started to pipe through speakers through the room—an energetic pop song. Julius grasped my hand.

"Let's dance."

I laughed and let him sweep me around the room, which apparently was just for the five of us. Blaze and Garrison and Talon all claimed my hand in turn, although Talon didn't do much more than bob with the rhythm. I didn't mind—I didn't know how to do much more than a two-step myself.

It was a crazy end to a crazy night, but I still couldn't totally make sense of it. Other than with every glance around the room, similar images from the movies and TV shows I'd seen wavered up from my memory.

"Is this supposed to be a school dance?" I asked Julius when we all stopped at a table that held various snacks and a punch bowl to get a drink.

He dipped his head. "I guess we got some of the details right. I was thinking prom—the biggest school dance there is."

I sipped the sweet punch and scanned the room again. "And why did you feel the need to set up a prom just for us? Why any of the things today? Not that I didn't enjoy myself—I just don't understand."

Blaze's smile softened. "We were thinking... You never had a normal childhood. Or teenage-hood. It seemed like it was about time you got to have some of those normal experiences from growing up."

Garrison snorted. "Except none of us exactly had normal childhoods either, so you'll have to forgive us if we messed it up a bit. We didn't have much direct experience to draw from."

Julius motioned to the room around us. "When she was still her bubbly self, my sister always went on about how she couldn't wait for her first prom. It seems like it's a big deal to a lot of people."

And going to the beach and to the movies—those were things normal families did, like the ones I'd seen. Having a pet—so many kids who weren't raised by psychopaths had that opportunity.

My throat closed up. "Thank you. It's been wonderful. And some of those things, I'd like to do again. But… why *today*?"

The men exchanged a look.

"She really doesn't remember," Garrison said.

I frowned. "Remember what?"

"She will." Talon nudged Julius. "Once she sees the last part."

Julius nodded and raised his hand in a signal.

All at once the music fell away. A banner dropped from the ceiling with the words *Happy birthday!* as a mass of figures burst through a set of double doors at the far end of the room, shouting, "Happy birthday!" at the same time.

My jaw dropped. Oh, God. I hadn't even been paying attention to the dates. I'd never known exactly what day I got to celebrate my birthday in a minor way in the household, and since leaving, I'd never seen the point in bothering.

But I knew what day Rachel Malik had been born on. A day twenty-nine years ago as of today.

"I did forget," I mumbled.

Blaze laughed and grabbed me in a sideways hug. "That's why we're here to remember for you. Consider all of today our birthday present to you, to make up for all the proper birthdays you missed. And all these people wanted to celebrate with you."

I recognized a few of the faces in the small crowd rushing over to join us. My younger brother Carter reached us first, and I grabbed him in a quick hug.

"Happy birthday, Dess," he said. "I'd have done something before, but I didn't know the exact date, and you didn't seem to want—"

"It's okay," I interrupted. "This is great. This is perfect."

I turned to greet Lou, the petite woman who'd almost become the next Deadly Rose but now only killed it on the ice in her figure skating routines. Her eyes glinted happily as she gave my hand a quick squeeze. "I'm glad I could help do something good for you after all the ways you helped me."

"It was nothing," I said. "I did what anyone should have."

"But most people wouldn't." She waved her hand toward the refreshments table, where all of my surprise guests are setting down gift bags. An auburn-haired man I recognized as her skating partner raised his hand in return as he set their offering down. "We all pitched in with our present—and if you ever want great seats at a skating event, just let me know."

"I'll keep that in mind."

I glanced around in a bit of a daze and locked eyes with the one other member of the Deadly Dozen who'd been willing to help Lou. The current Storm ambled over with a blond woman by his side, who I was willing to bet by the affectionate arm he had around her waist was the girlfriend I'd helped *him* locate when one of our rival crime bosses had arranged her kidnapping.

"Blood Hunter," the Storm said with a warm grin I'd come to know he offered naturally. "Happy birthday. It's nice to get to see you outside of stuffy meetings and tense stand-offs. I'd like you to meet Madelyn. If it wasn't for her, I'm not sure I'd have made it this far."

Madelyn guffawed in disbelief and offered me a shy smile. "It's good to meet you. Logan's here too—he still tells the story about how you and Blaze tracked me down when things were… bad."

I found myself smiling in return. "It's great to see they've gotten better. I'm glad you could make it."

I really was. When had I ever had an actual *party*, rather than simply sneaking into one as an uninvited guest looking to murder someone or at best screw them over?

"Here's an old friend," Garrison said, coming up at my side. He gave a jaunty little wave to the redhead who was sauntering over.

Anthea Noble, the poisons expert who I'd exchanged favors with back when I'd first met my men, gave us a mock curtsey, but her smile was nearly as warm as the Storm's. "Quite the gathering you have here. I feel like I'm rubbing shoulders with the elite."

I motioned awkwardly to my men around me. "They set it up. I didn't even know this was happening."

"An actually surprising surprise party. That's impressive in itself." Anthea peered over her shoulder. "With permission from your partners, I brought along my nephew and a couple of friends… They didn't have the easiest dealings with the Devil's Dozen when a couple of your colleagues barged into our county, but I've only had good things to say about you."

An athletic woman with her dark brown hair pulled back in a ponytail hustled over, flanked by two men, one well-built with ruddy brown hair close to Anthea's scarlet shade and the other leaner and sandy-blond.

"Hey," the woman said, holding out her hand. "I'm Mercy Katz, from Paradise Bend, not that you've probably ever heard of it. I hope you don't mind us crashing your party. Anthea said the more of us, the bigger the surprise."

"Blame Blaze for that," Julius muttered in a low but amused tone.

I laughed as I shook Mercy's hand. "There's nothing to apologize for. If you're a friend of Anthea's, then you're welcome here. And it is an awfully big room for all of us to fill."

"We're not quite done yet," Garrison said. "Ah, Talon's bringing them in now."

I hadn't noticed the larger man leaving our little cluster. The lights glanced off his shaved head by a side door he'd just pushed open. He held it wide so one after another and another slightly awkward-looking woman could ease out into the decorated space.

My eyes widened. I recognize one of their faces—and another. And there was one of the girls I'd gotten away from the former Blood Hunter's operations years ago…

"We arranged to bring as many of them as we felt it was safe to ask and who were comfortable coming," Blaze announced from behind me. "They wouldn't have much of a life at all if it wasn't for you, you know. So they sure as hell want to celebrate your existence. More than forty of them showed up, but you've gotten more than two hundred women free over the past five years, you know."

I hadn't realized it was quite that many. And seeing the once-trafficked women under the colorful lights, shy but healthy and happy, my spirits lifted.

Yes, there were more women out there I needed to save. More wrongs I could still put right.

But I'd done an awful lot right already.

I walked over to welcome the women who'd once been slaves—or on the verge of it. "Thank you so much for coming. I couldn't have asked for a better present than seeing you doing so well."

One of the women at the front of the group hesitated and then flung her arms around me. I tensed in her embrace, but only for an instant before I returned the hug. My heart felt as if it'd swelled to twice its normal size.

As she stepped back, I raised my hand over my head and lifted my voice. "Let's make this a night to remember!"

A cheer went up through the room, buoying my spirits even more.

One thing was for sure—I was never going to forget my birthday again.

ABOUT THE AUTHORS

Eva Chance is a pen name for contemporary romance written by Amazon top 100 bestselling author Eva Chase. If you love gritty romance, dominant men, and fierce women who never have to choose, look no further.

Eva lives in Canada with her family. She loves stories both swoony and supernatural, and strong women and the men who appreciate them.

Connect with Eva online:
www.evachase.com
eva@evachase.com

Harlow King is a long-time fan of all things dark, edgy, and steamy. She can't wait to share her contemporary reverse harem stories.

Printed by BoD™in Norderstedt, Germany